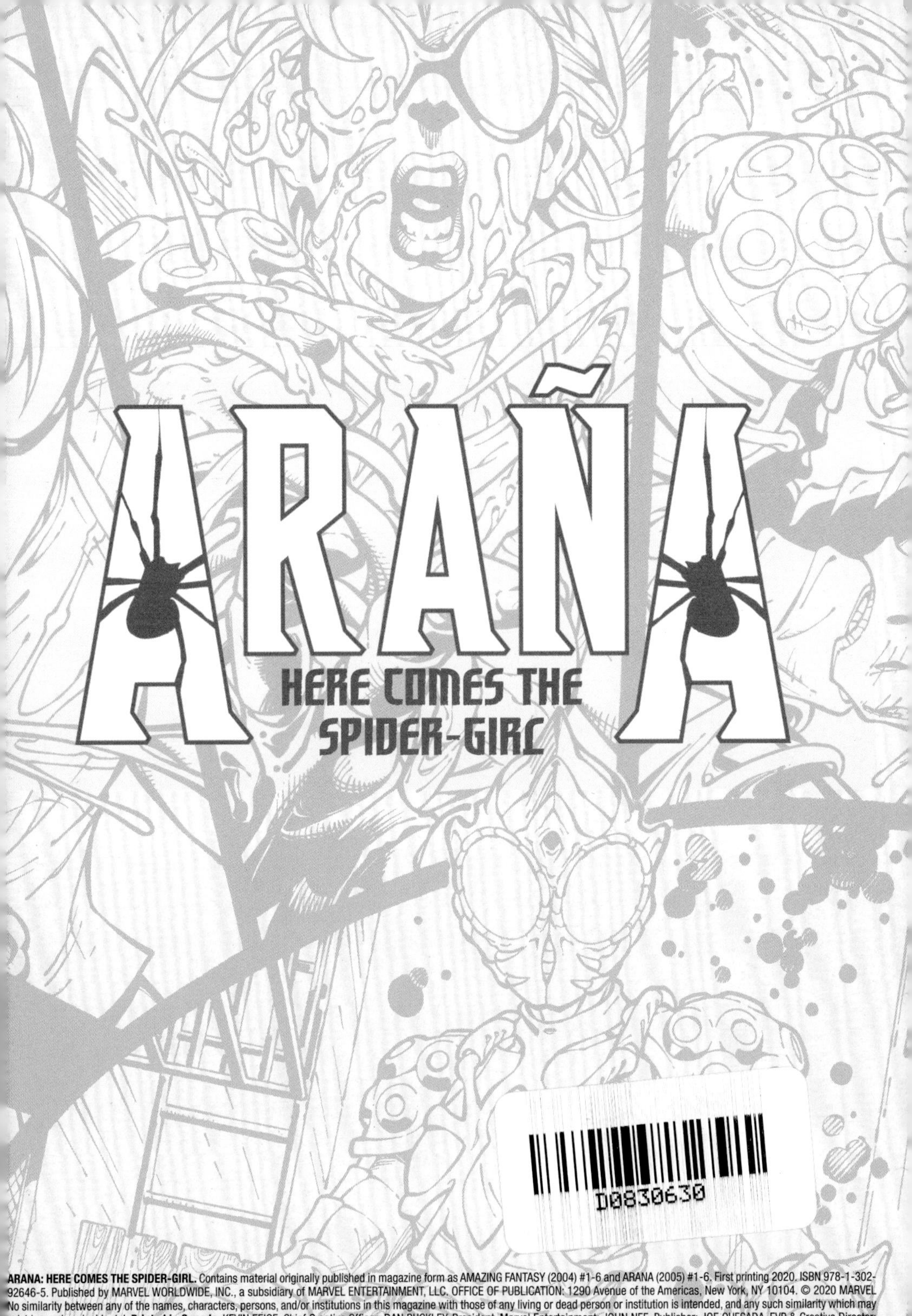
ARAÑA
HERE COMES THE SPIDER-GIRL
D0830630

ARANA: HERE COMES THE SPIDER-GIRL. Contains material originally published in magazine form as AMAZING FANTASY (2004) #1-6 and ARANA (2005) #1-6. First printing 2020. ISBN 978-1-302-92646-5. Published by MARVEL WORLDWIDE, INC., a subsidiary of MARVEL ENTERTAINMENT, LLC. OFFICE OF PUBLICATION: 1290 Avenue of the Americas, New York, NY 10104. **Printed in Canada.** KEVIN FEIGE, Chief Creative Officer; DAN BUCKLEY, President, Marvel Entertainment; JOHN NEE, Publisher; JOE QUESADA, EVP & Creative Director; TOM BREVOORT, SVP of Publishing; DAVID BOGART, Associate Publisher & SVP of Talent Affairs; Publishing & Partnership; DAVID GABRIEL, VP of Print & Digital Publishing; JEFF YOUNGQUIST, VP of Production & Special Projects; DAN CARR, Executive Director of Publishing Technology; ALEX MORALES, Director of Publishing Operations; DAN EDINGTON, Managing Editor; RICKEY PURDIN, Director of Talent Relations; SUSAN CRESPI, Production Manager; STAN LEE, Chairman Emeritus. For information regarding advertising in Marvel Comics or on Marvel.com, please contact Vit DeBellis, Custom Solutions & Integrated Advertising Manager, at vdebellis@marvel.com. For Marvel subscription inquiries, please call 888-511-5480. **Manufactured between 10/23/2020 and 11/24/2020 by SOLISCO PRINTERS, SCOTT, QC, CANADA.**

10 9 8 7 6 5 4 3 2 1

ARAÑA

HERE COMES THE SPIDER-GIRL

WRITER
FIONA AVERY

AMAZING FANTASY #1-6
PENCILERS
MARK BROOKS (#1-2, #5-6) & ROGER CRUZ (#3-4)
INKERS
JAIME MENDOZA (#1-2, #5-6)
& VICTOR OLAZABA (#1-6)
COLOR ARTISTS
UDON'S LARRY MOLINAR (#1-2, #5-6)
& JEANNIE LEE (#3-4)
LETTERERS
VC's CLAYTON COWLES (#1-4, #6) & CHRIS ELIOPOULOS (#5)

ARAÑA #1-6
PENCILER
ROGER CRUZ
INKER
VICTOR OLAZABA
COLOR ARTISTS
JEANNIE LEE & UDON STUDIOS
LETTERERS
VC's RUS WOOTON (#1, #3-6)
& CHRIS ELIOPOULOS (#2)

COVER ART
MARK BROOKS, JAIME MENDOZA & UDON STUDIOS

ASSISTANT EDITORS
CORY SEDLMEIER &
NATHAN COSBY

EDITORS
JENNIFER LEE
& MARK PANICCIA

EXECUTIVE EDITOR
AXEL ALONSO

CREATIVE CONSULTANT
J. MICHAEL STRACZYNSKI

collection editor JENNIFER GRÜNWALD
assistant managing editor MAIA LOY • assistant managing editor LISA MONTALBANO
vp production & special projects JEFF YOUNGQUIST • research JEPH YORK • director, licensed publishing SVEN LARSEN
svp print, sales & marketing DAVID GABRIEL • editor in chief C.B. CEBULSKI

CONTENTS

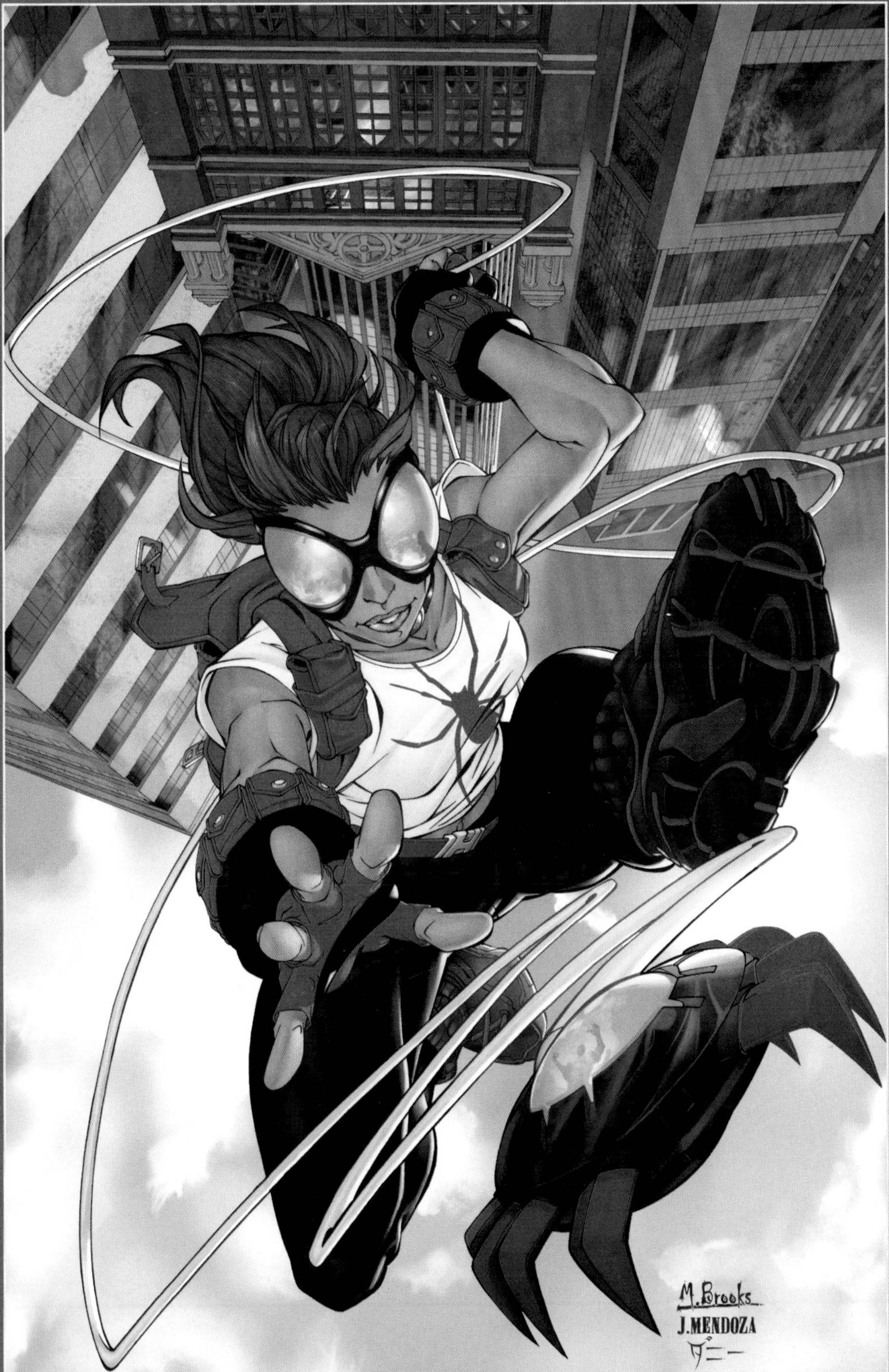
M. Brooks
J.MENDOZA

AMAZING FANTASY #1

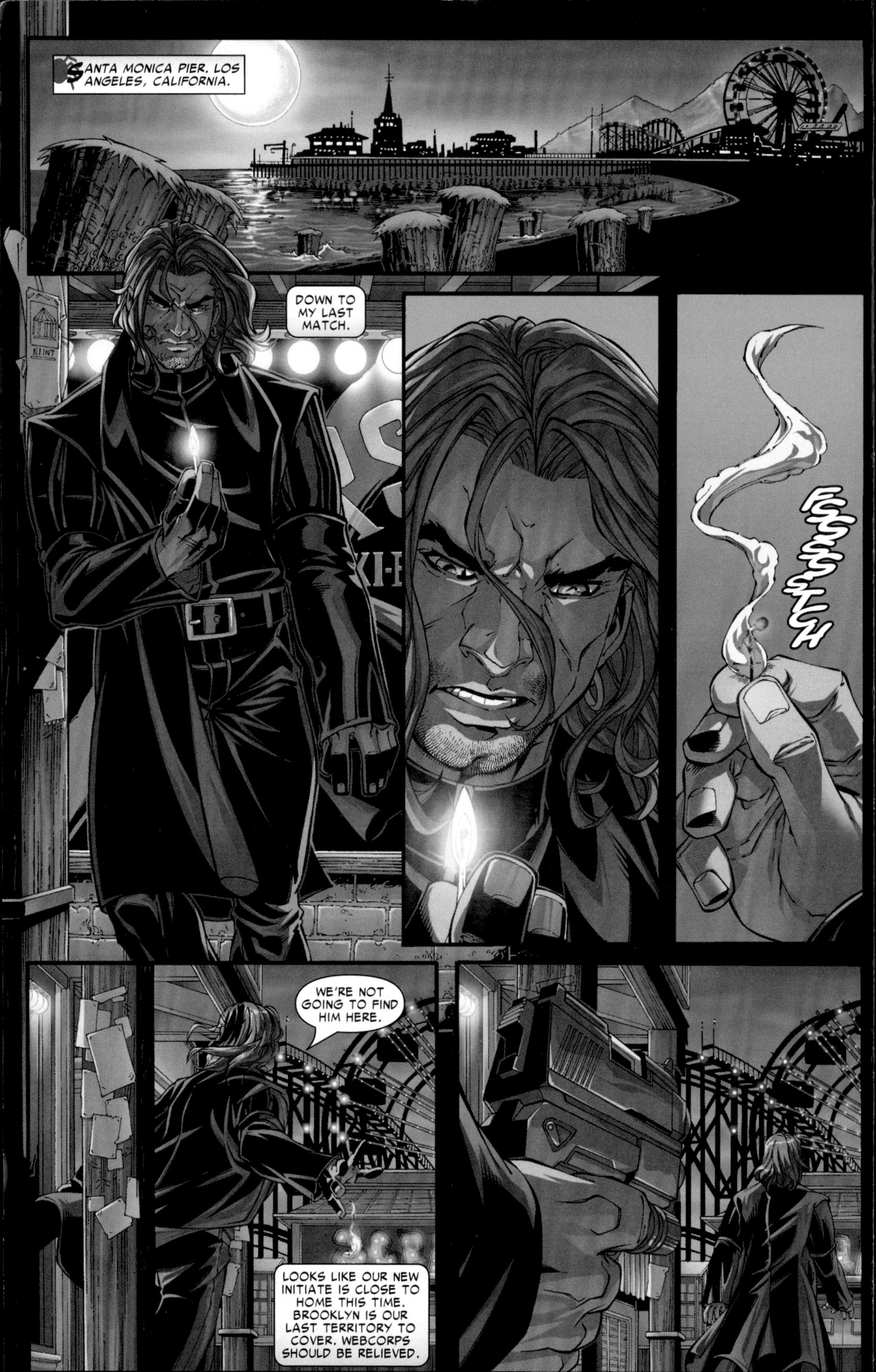
SANTA MONICA PIER. LOS ANGELES, CALIFORNIA.
DOWN TO MY LAST MATCH.
FSSSSTCH
WE'RE NOT GOING TO FIND HIM HERE.
LOOKS LIKE OUR NEW INITIATE IS CLOSE TO HOME THIS TIME. BROOKLYN IS OUR LAST TERRITORY TO COVER. WEBCORPS SHOULD BE RELIEVED.

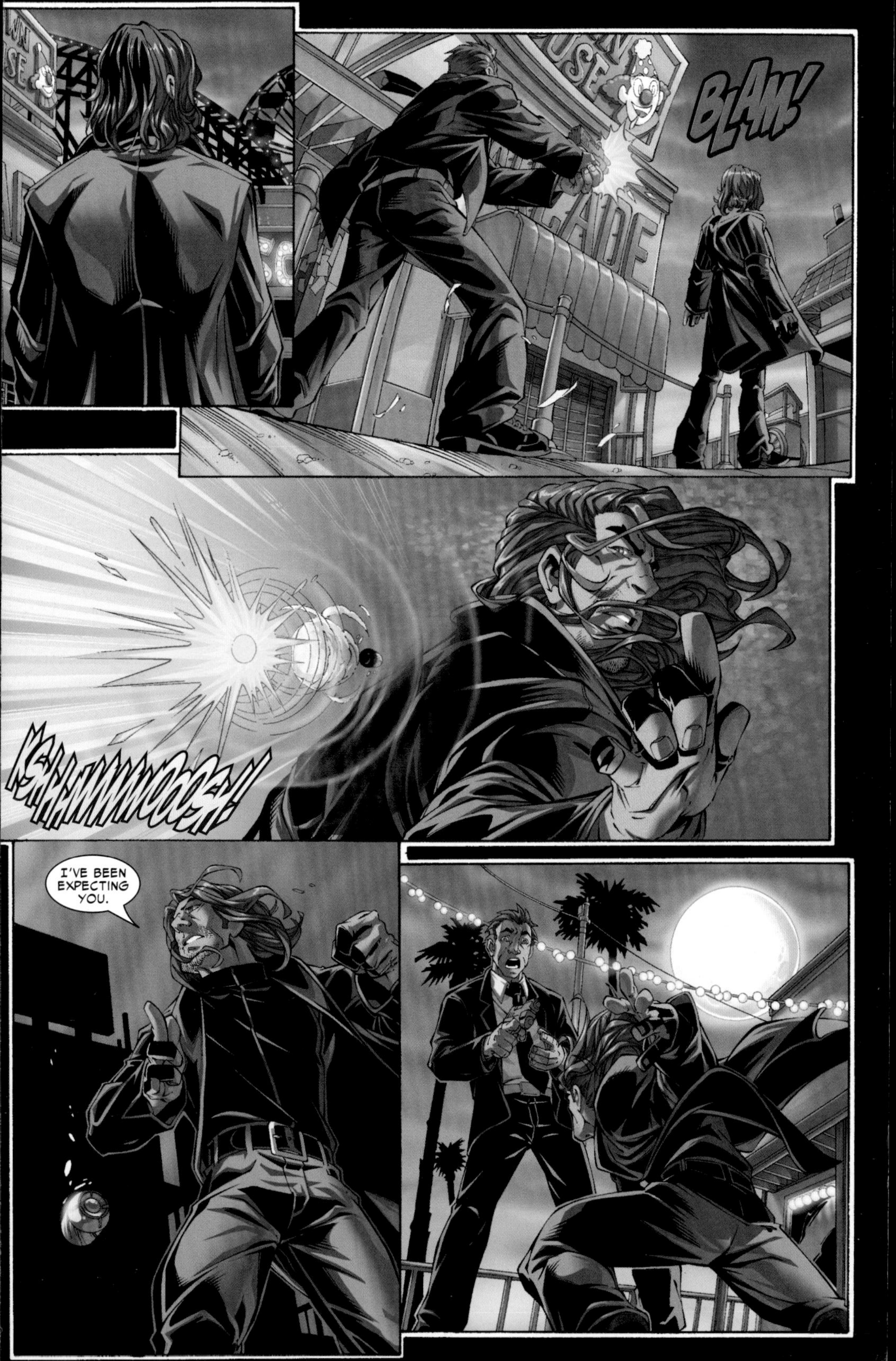
BLAM!
KSHHWWWOOSH!
I'VE BEEN EXPECTING YOU.

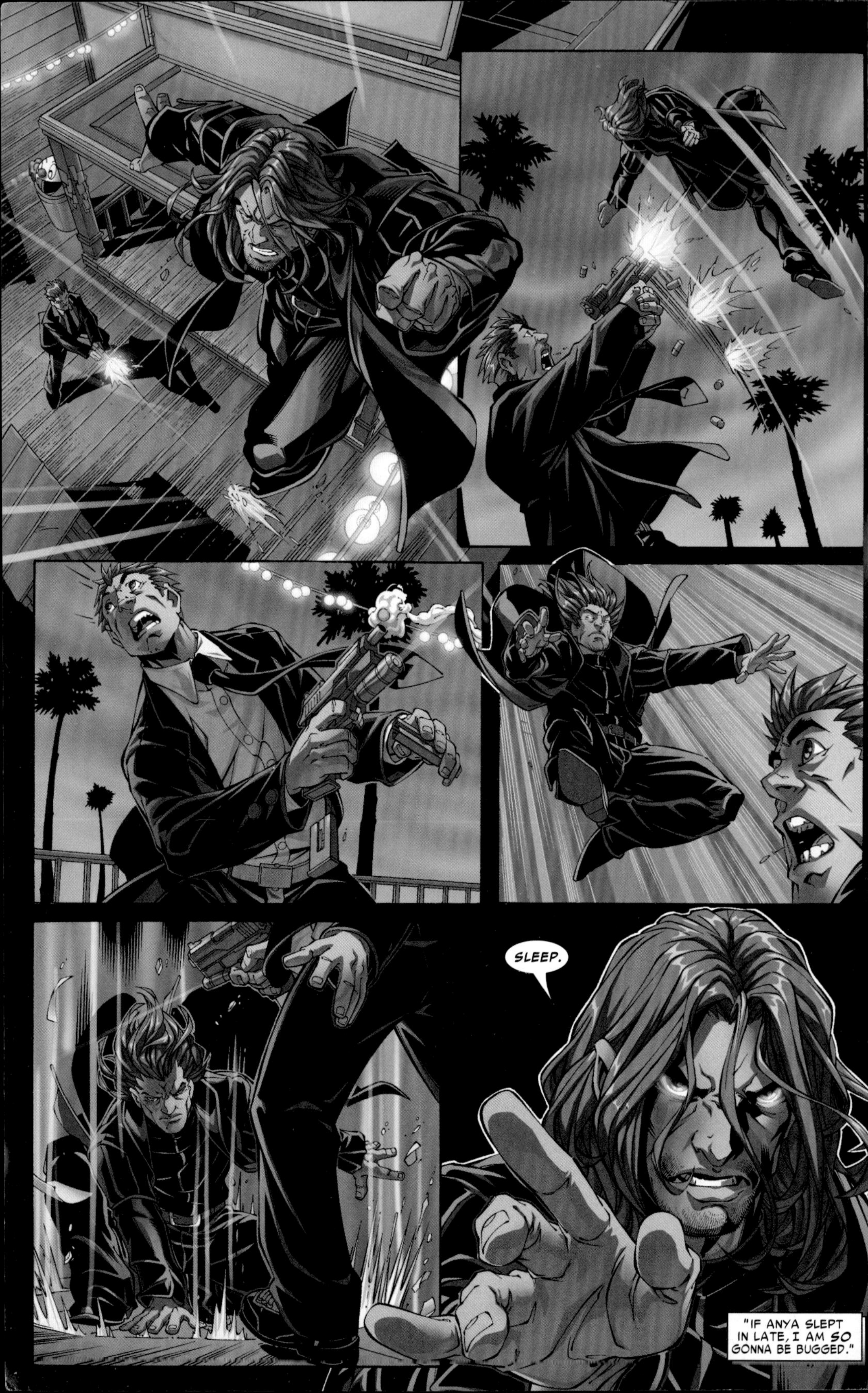
SLEEP.
"IF ANYA SLEPT IN LATE, I AM SO GONNA BE BUGGED."

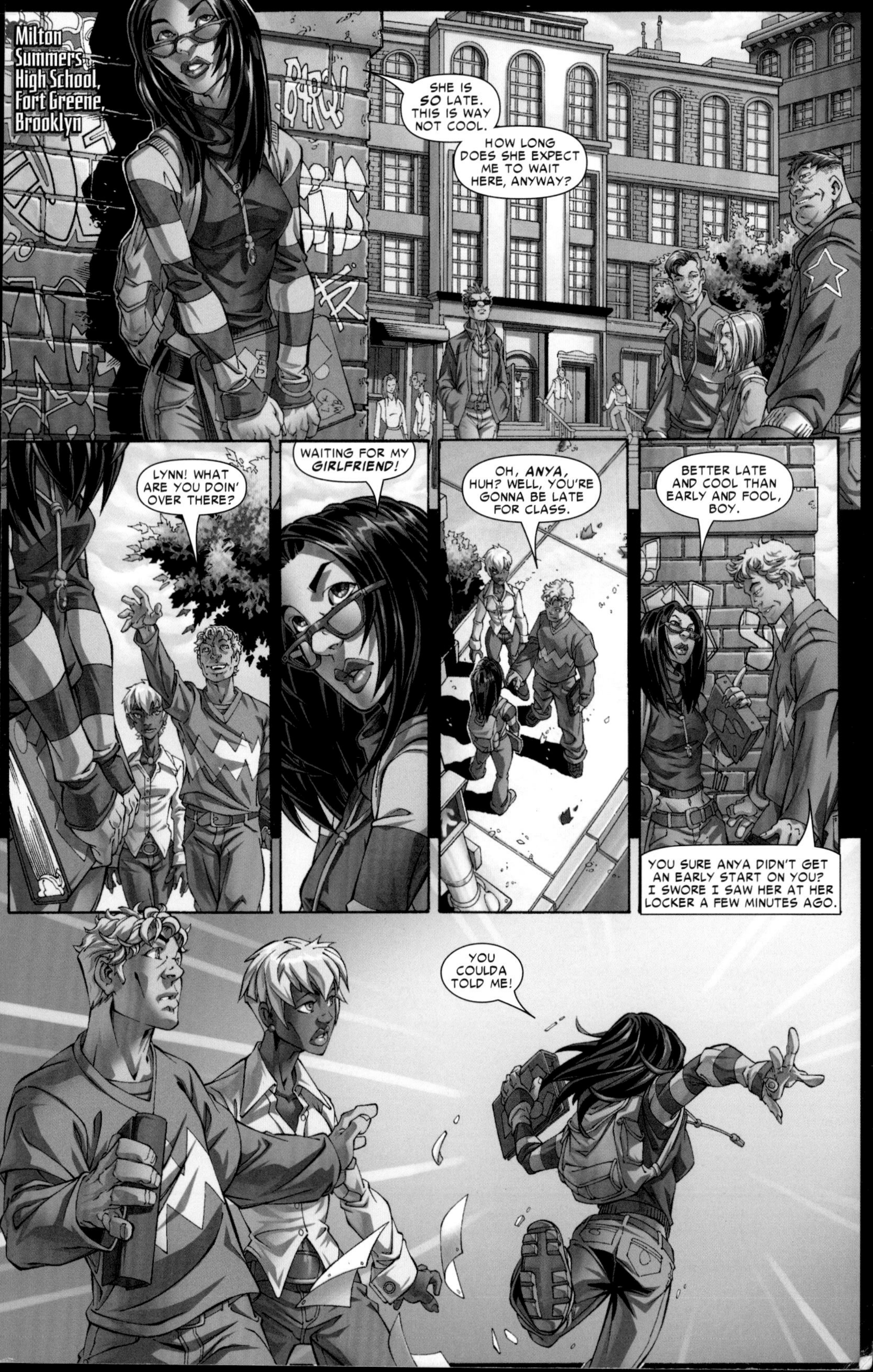
Milton Summers High School, Fort Greene, Brooklyn
SHE IS SO LATE. THIS IS WAY NOT COOL.
HOW LONG DOES SHE EXPECT ME TO WAIT HERE, ANYWAY?
LYNN! WHAT ARE YOU DOIN' OVER THERE?
WAITING FOR MY GIRLFRIEND!
OH, ANYA, HUH? WELL, YOU'RE GONNA BE LATE FOR CLASS.
BETTER LATE AND COOL THAN EARLY AND FOOL, BOY.
YOU SURE ANYA DIDN'T GET AN EARLY START ON YOU? I SWORE I SAW HER AT HER LOCKER A FEW MINUTES AGO.
YOU COULDA TOLD ME!

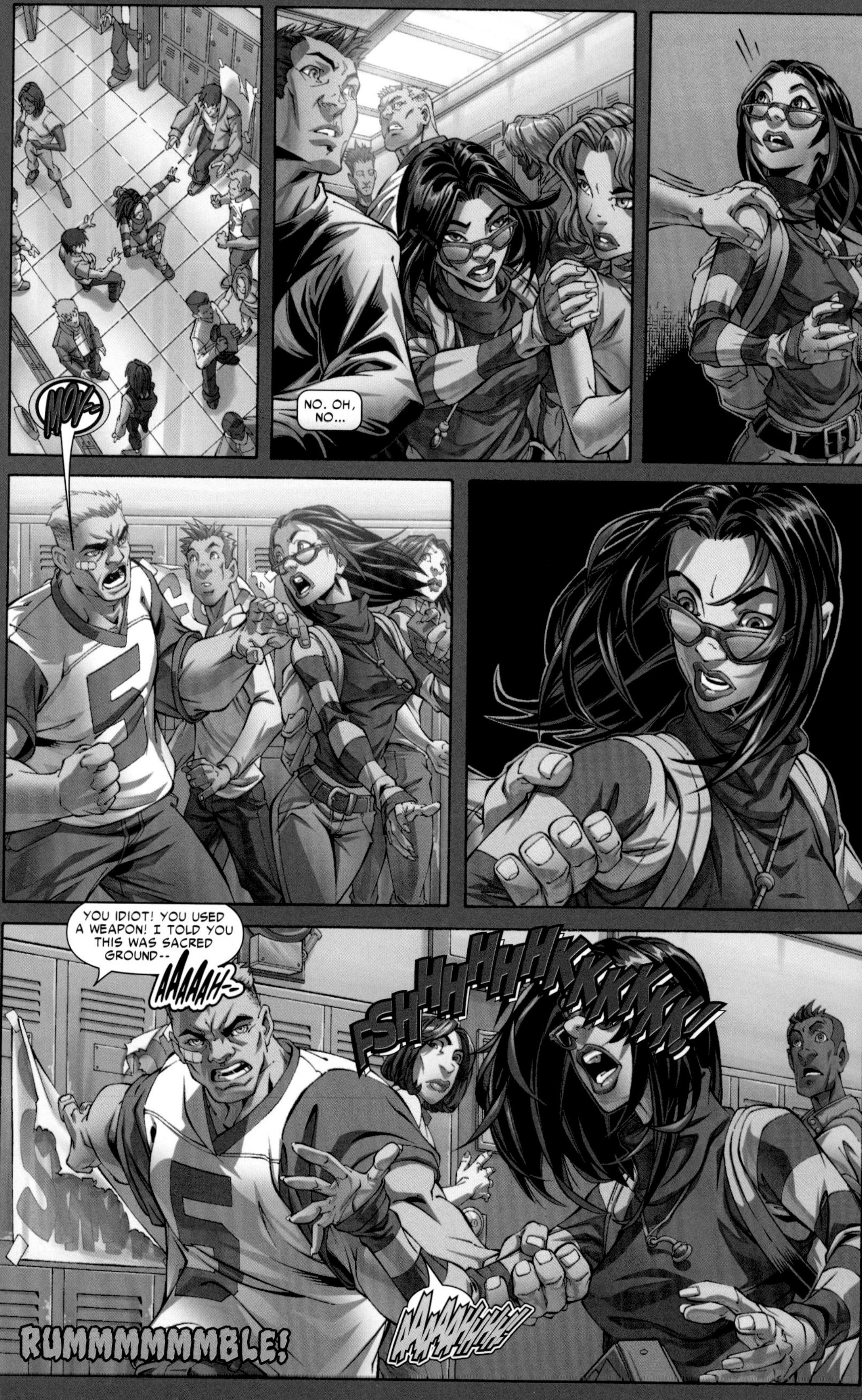
MOVE
NO. OH, NO...
YOU IDIOT! YOU USED A WEAPON! I TOLD YOU THIS WAS SACRED GROUND--
AAAAAH--
FSHHHHHHKKKKKK!!
AAAAHHHH!!
RUMMMMMMMBLE!

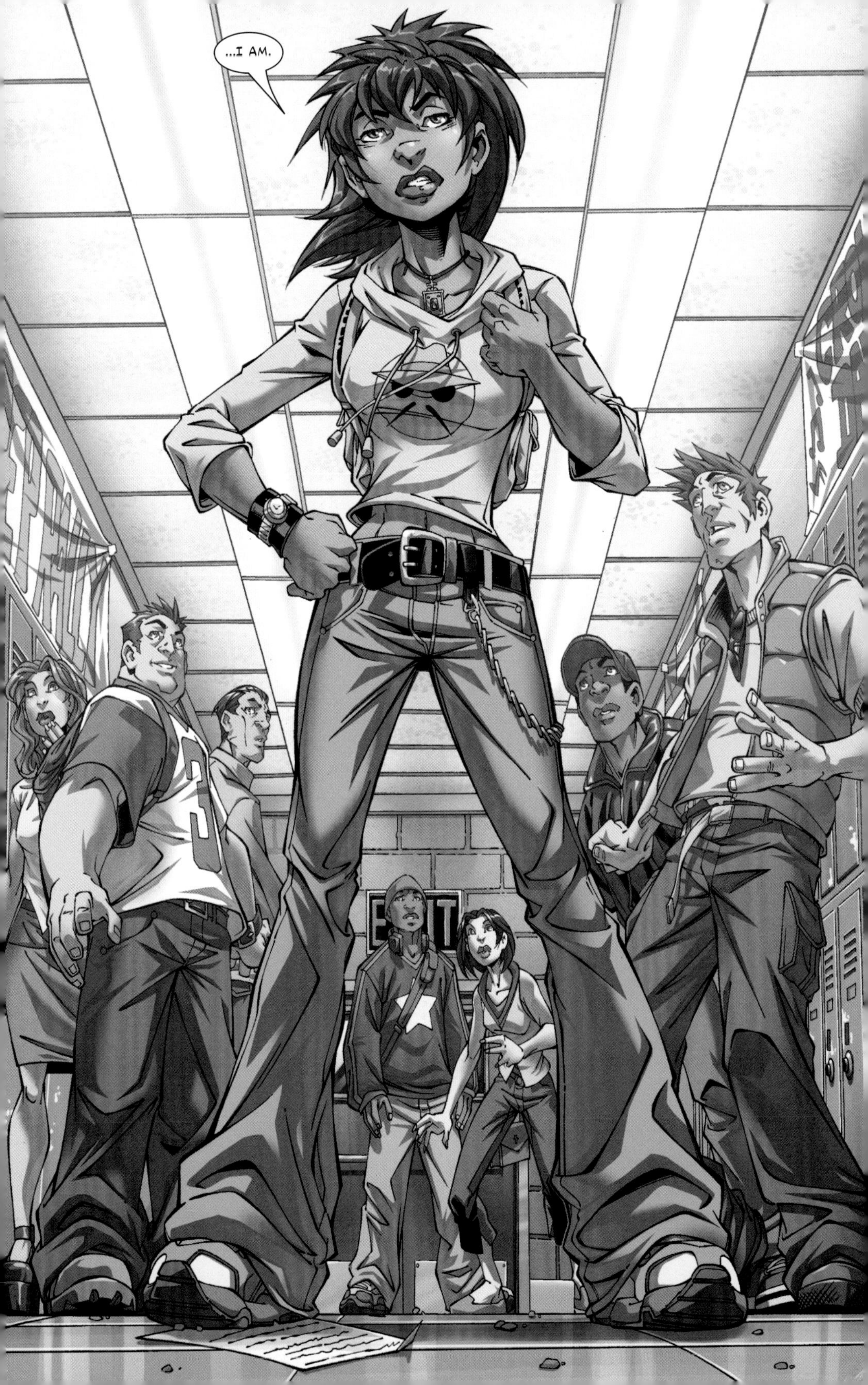
...I AM.

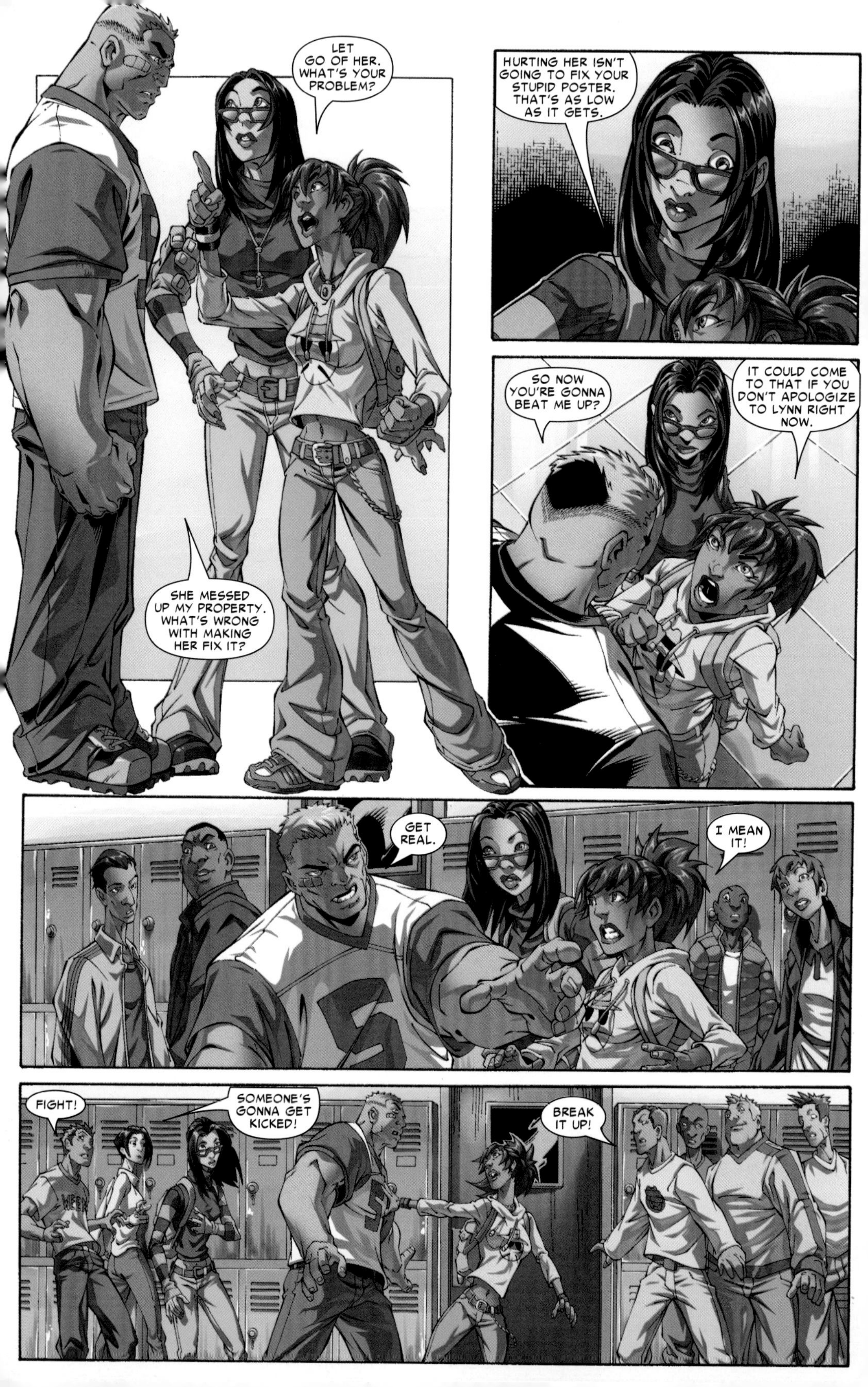
LET GO OF HER. WHAT'S YOUR PROBLEM?
SHE MESSED UP MY PROPERTY. WHAT'S WRONG WITH MAKING HER FIX IT?
HURTING HER ISN'T GOING TO FIX YOUR STUPID POSTER. THAT'S AS LOW AS IT GETS.
SO NOW YOU'RE GONNA BEAT ME UP?
IT COULD COME TO THAT IF YOU DON'T APOLOGIZE TO LYNN RIGHT NOW.
GET REAL.
I MEAN IT!
FIGHT!
SOMEONE'S GONNA GET KICKED!
BREAK IT UP!

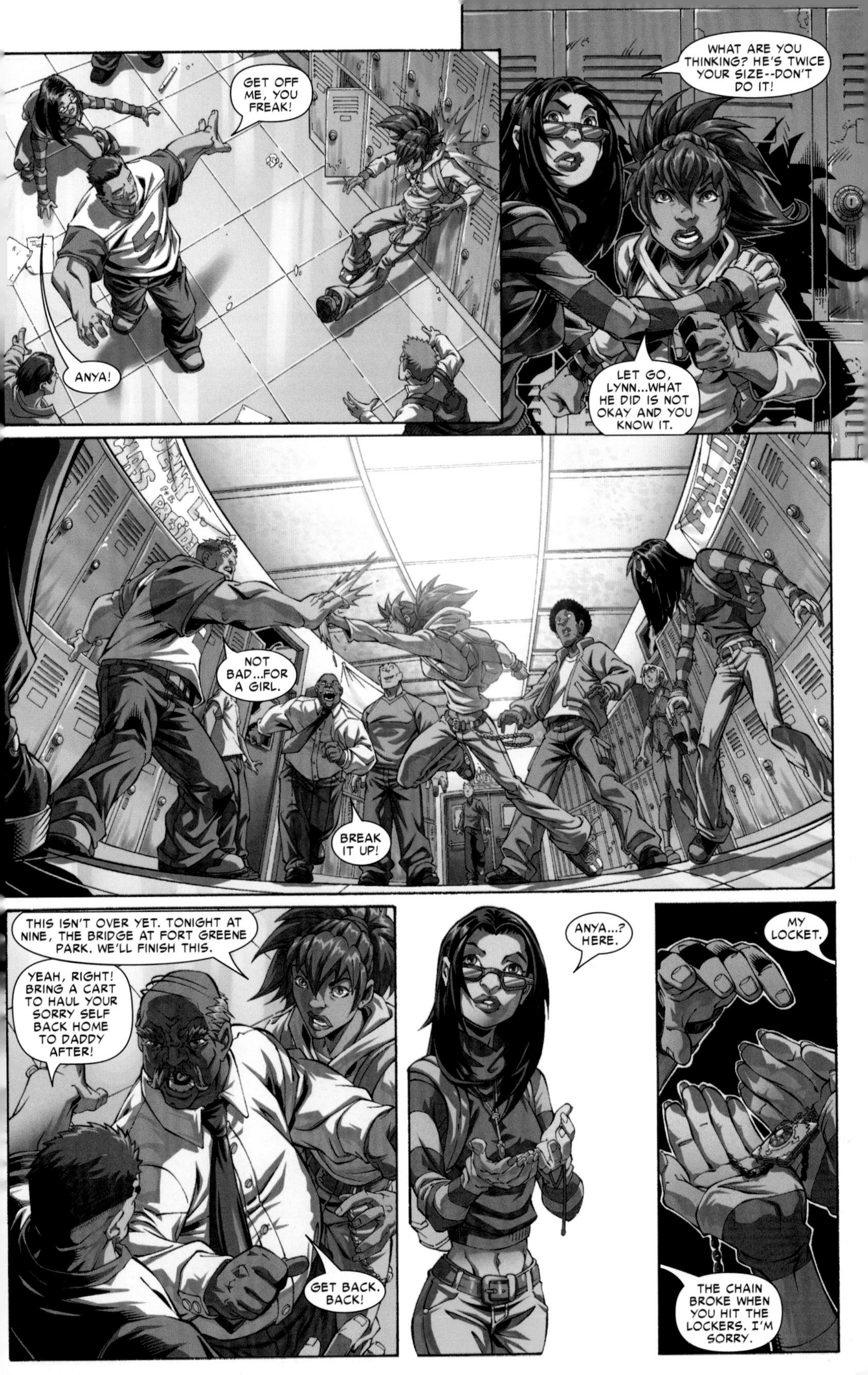
GET OFF ME, YOU FREAK!
ANYA!
WHAT ARE YOU THINKING? HE'S TWICE YOUR SIZE--DON'T DO IT!
LET GO, LYNN...WHAT HE DID IS NOT OKAY AND YOU KNOW IT.
NOT BAD...FOR A GIRL.
BREAK IT UP!
THIS ISN'T OVER YET. TONIGHT AT NINE, THE BRIDGE AT FORT GREENE PARK. WE'LL FINISH THIS.
YEAH, RIGHT! BRING A CART TO HAUL YOUR SORRY SELF BACK HOME TO DADDY AFTER!
GET BACK. BACK!
ANYA...? HERE.
MY LOCKET.
THE CHAIN BROKE WHEN YOU HIT THE LOCKERS. I'M SORRY.

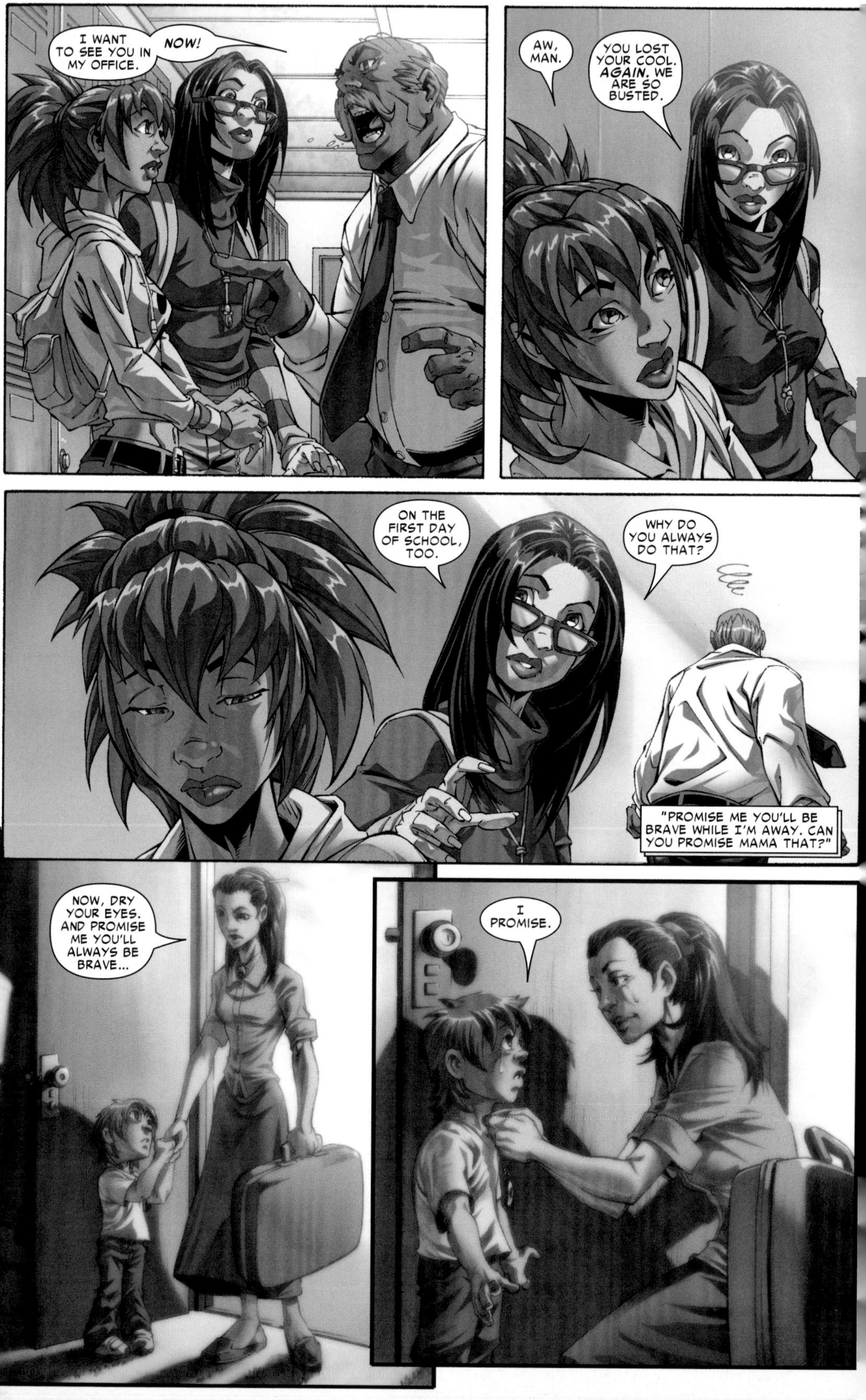
I WANT TO SEE YOU IN MY OFFICE.
NOW!
AW, MAN.
YOU LOST YOUR COOL. AGAIN. WE ARE SO BUSTED.
ON THE FIRST DAY OF SCHOOL, TOO.
WHY DO YOU ALWAYS DO THAT?
"PROMISE ME YOU'LL BE BRAVE WHILE I'M AWAY. CAN YOU PROMISE MAMA THAT?"
NOW, DRY YOUR EYES. AND PROMISE ME YOU'LL ALWAYS BE BRAVE...
I PROMISE.

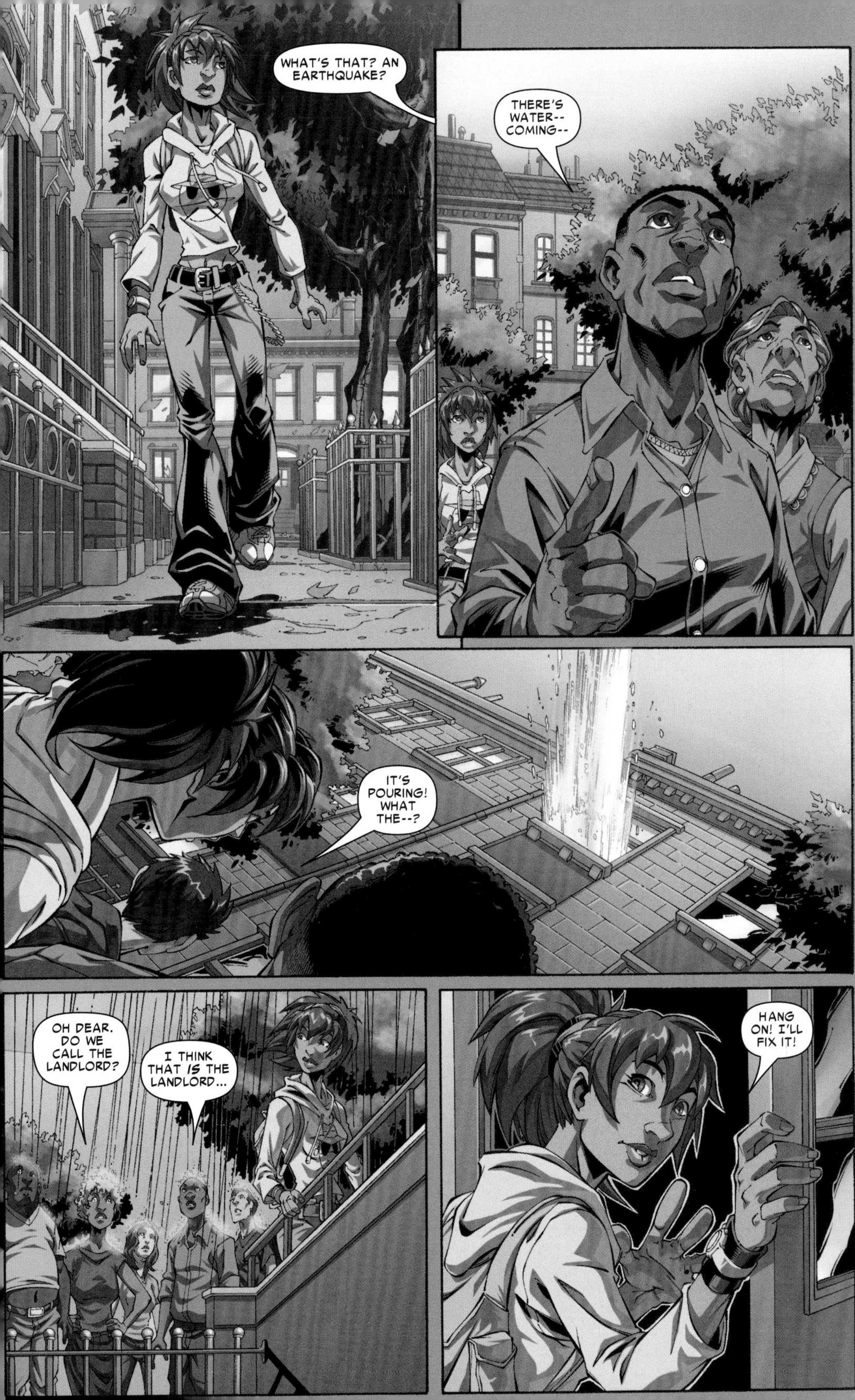
WHAT'S THAT? AN EARTHQUAKE?
THERE'S WATER-- COMING--
IT'S POURING! WHAT THE--?
OH DEAR. DO WE CALL THE LANDLORD?
I THINK THAT *IS* THE LANDLORD...
HANG ON! I'LL FIX IT!

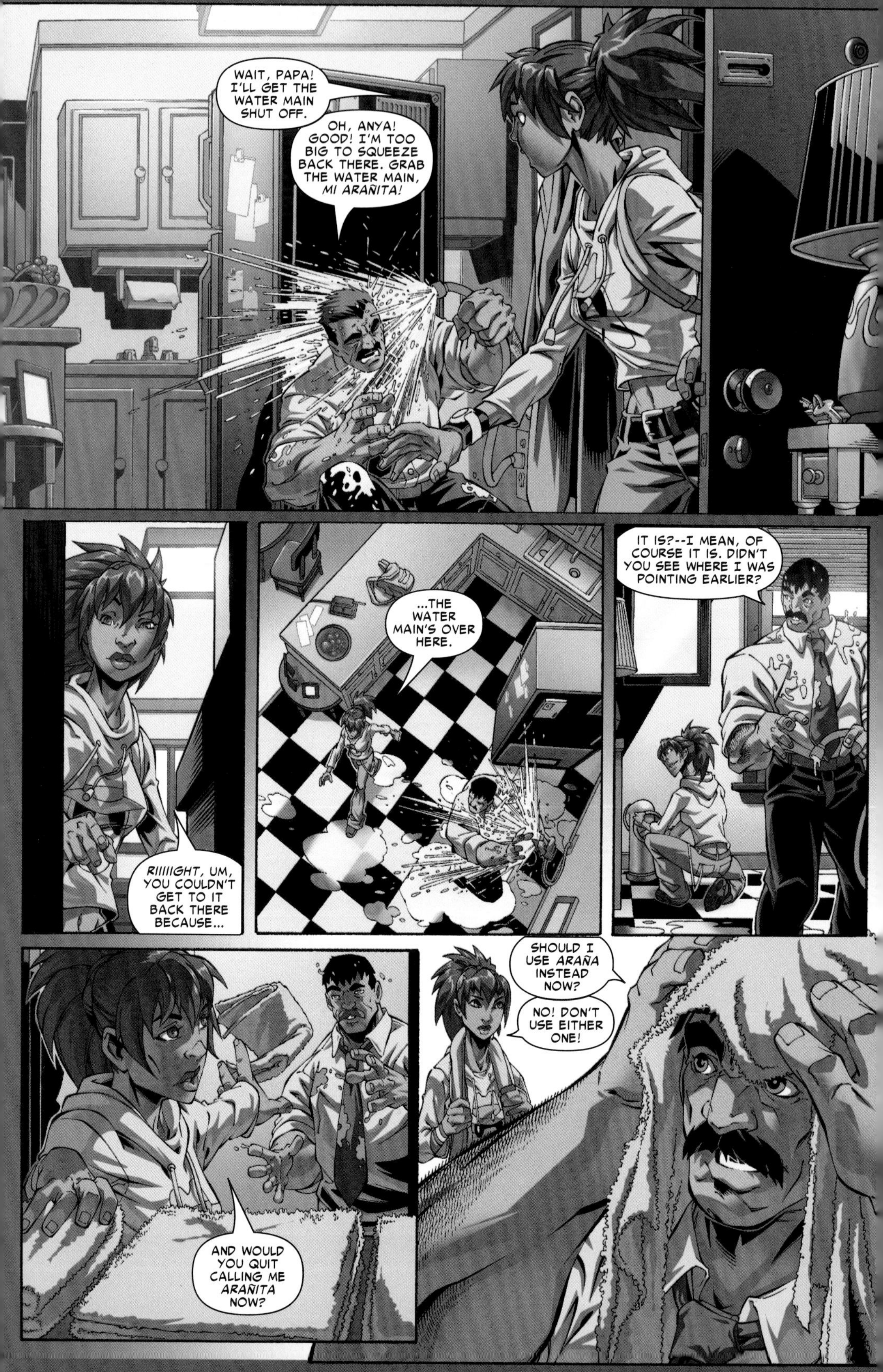
WAIT, PAPA! I'LL GET THE WATER MAIN SHUT OFF.
OH, ANYA! GOOD! I'M TOO BIG TO SQUEEZE BACK THERE. GRAB THE WATER MAIN, *MI ARAÑITA!*
RIIIIIGHT, UM, YOU COULDN'T GET TO IT BACK THERE BECAUSE...
...THE WATER MAIN'S OVER HERE.
IT IS?--I MEAN, OF COURSE IT IS. DIDN'T YOU SEE WHERE I WAS POINTING EARLIER?
AND WOULD YOU QUIT CALLING ME *ARAÑITA* NOW?
SHOULD I USE *ARAÑA* INSTEAD NOW?
NO! DON'T USE EITHER ONE!

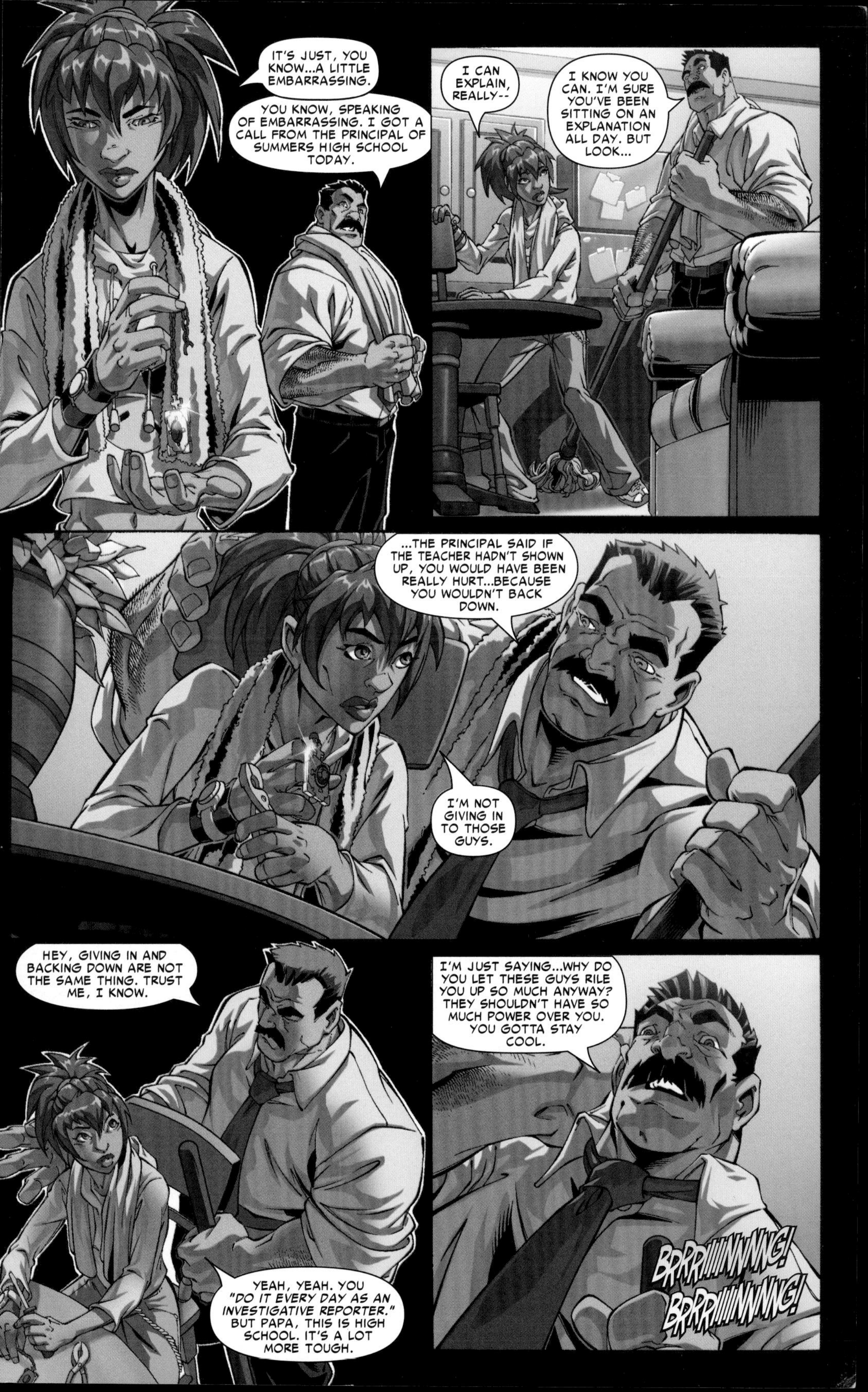
IT'S JUST, YOU KNOW...A LITTLE EMBARRASSING.
YOU KNOW, SPEAKING OF EMBARRASSING. I GOT A CALL FROM THE PRINCIPAL OF SUMMERS HIGH SCHOOL TODAY.
I CAN EXPLAIN, REALLY--
I KNOW YOU CAN. I'M SURE YOU'VE BEEN SITTING ON AN EXPLANATION ALL DAY. BUT LOOK...
...THE PRINCIPAL SAID IF THE TEACHER HADN'T SHOWN UP, YOU WOULD HAVE BEEN REALLY HURT...BECAUSE YOU WOULDN'T BACK DOWN.
I'M NOT GIVING IN TO THOSE GUYS.
HEY, GIVING IN AND BACKING DOWN ARE NOT THE SAME THING. TRUST ME, I KNOW.
YEAH, YEAH. YOU "DO IT EVERY DAY AS AN INVESTIGATIVE REPORTER." BUT PAPA, THIS IS HIGH SCHOOL. IT'S A LOT MORE TOUGH.
I'M JUST SAYING...WHY DO YOU LET THESE GUYS RILE YOU UP SO MUCH ANYWAY? THEY SHOULDN'T HAVE SO MUCH POWER OVER YOU. YOU GOTTA STAY COOL.
BRRRIIIIINNNNG!
BRRRIIIIINNNNG!

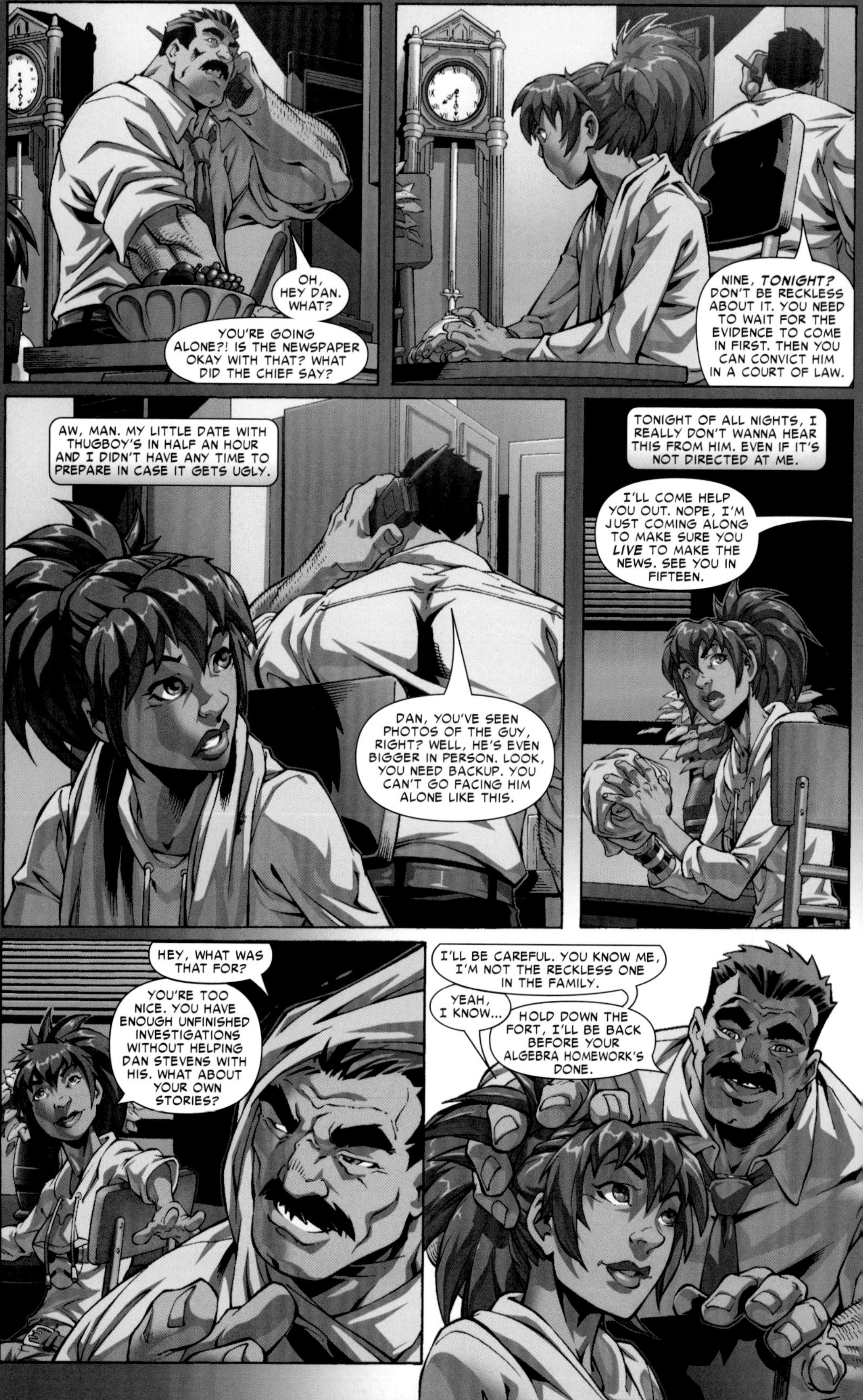
OH, HEY DAN. WHAT?
YOU'RE GOING ALONE?! IS THE NEWSPAPER OKAY WITH THAT? WHAT DID THE CHIEF SAY?
NINE, TONIGHT? DON'T BE RECKLESS ABOUT IT. YOU NEED TO WAIT FOR THE EVIDENCE TO COME IN FIRST. THEN YOU CAN CONVICT HIM IN A COURT OF LAW.
AW, MAN. MY LITTLE DATE WITH THUGBOY'S IN HALF AN HOUR AND I DIDN'T HAVE ANY TIME TO PREPARE IN CASE IT GETS UGLY.
DAN, YOU'VE SEEN PHOTOS OF THE GUY, RIGHT? WELL, HE'S EVEN BIGGER IN PERSON. LOOK, YOU NEED BACKUP. YOU CAN'T GO FACING HIM ALONE LIKE THIS.
TONIGHT OF ALL NIGHTS, I REALLY DON'T WANNA HEAR THIS FROM HIM. EVEN IF IT'S NOT DIRECTED AT ME.
I'LL COME HELP YOU OUT. NOPE, I'M JUST COMING ALONG TO MAKE SURE YOU LIVE TO MAKE THE NEWS. SEE YOU IN FIFTEEN.
HEY, WHAT WAS THAT FOR?
YOU'RE TOO NICE. YOU HAVE ENOUGH UNFINISHED INVESTIGATIONS WITHOUT HELPING DAN STEVENS WITH HIS. WHAT ABOUT YOUR OWN STORIES?
I'LL BE CAREFUL. YOU KNOW ME, I'M NOT THE RECKLESS ONE IN THE FAMILY.
YEAH, I KNOW...
HOLD DOWN THE FORT, I'LL BE BACK BEFORE YOUR ALGEBRA HOMEWORK'S DONE.

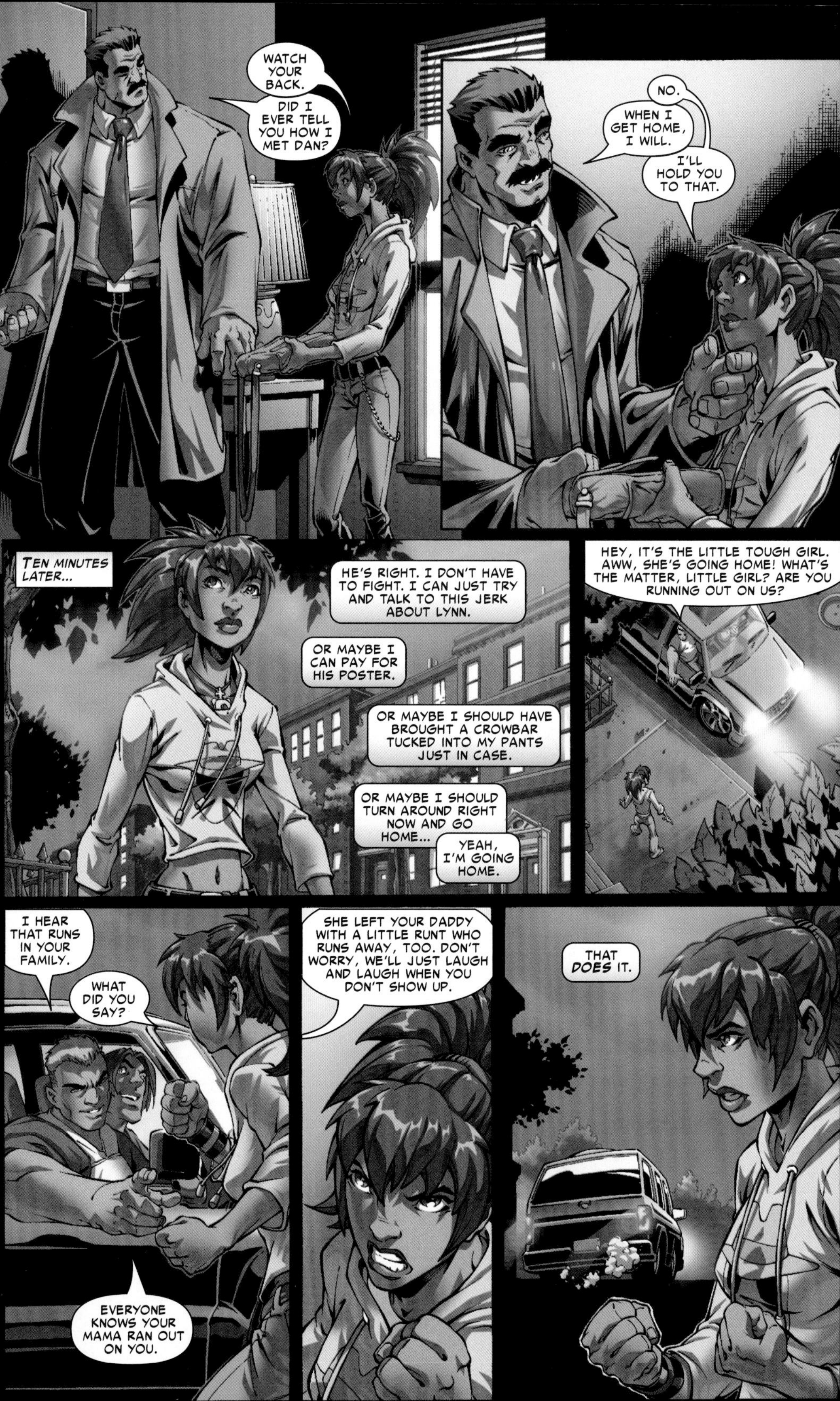
WATCH YOUR BACK.
DID I EVER TELL YOU HOW I MET DAN?
NO.
WHEN I GET HOME, I WILL.
I'LL HOLD YOU TO THAT.
TEN MINUTES LATER...
HE'S RIGHT. I DON'T HAVE TO FIGHT. I CAN JUST TRY AND TALK TO THIS JERK ABOUT LYNN.
OR MAYBE I CAN PAY FOR HIS POSTER.
OR MAYBE I SHOULD HAVE BROUGHT A CROWBAR TUCKED INTO MY PANTS JUST IN CASE.
OR MAYBE I SHOULD TURN AROUND RIGHT NOW AND GO HOME...
YEAH, I'M GOING HOME.
HEY, IT'S THE LITTLE TOUGH GIRL. AWW, SHE'S GOING HOME! WHAT'S THE MATTER, LITTLE GIRL? ARE YOU RUNNING OUT ON US?
I HEAR THAT RUNS IN YOUR FAMILY.
WHAT DID YOU SAY?
EVERYONE KNOWS YOUR MAMA RAN OUT ON YOU.
SHE LEFT YOUR DADDY WITH A LITTLE RUNT WHO RUNS AWAY, TOO. DON'T WORRY, WE'LL JUST LAUGH AND LAUGH WHEN YOU DON'T SHOW UP.
THAT *DOES* IT.

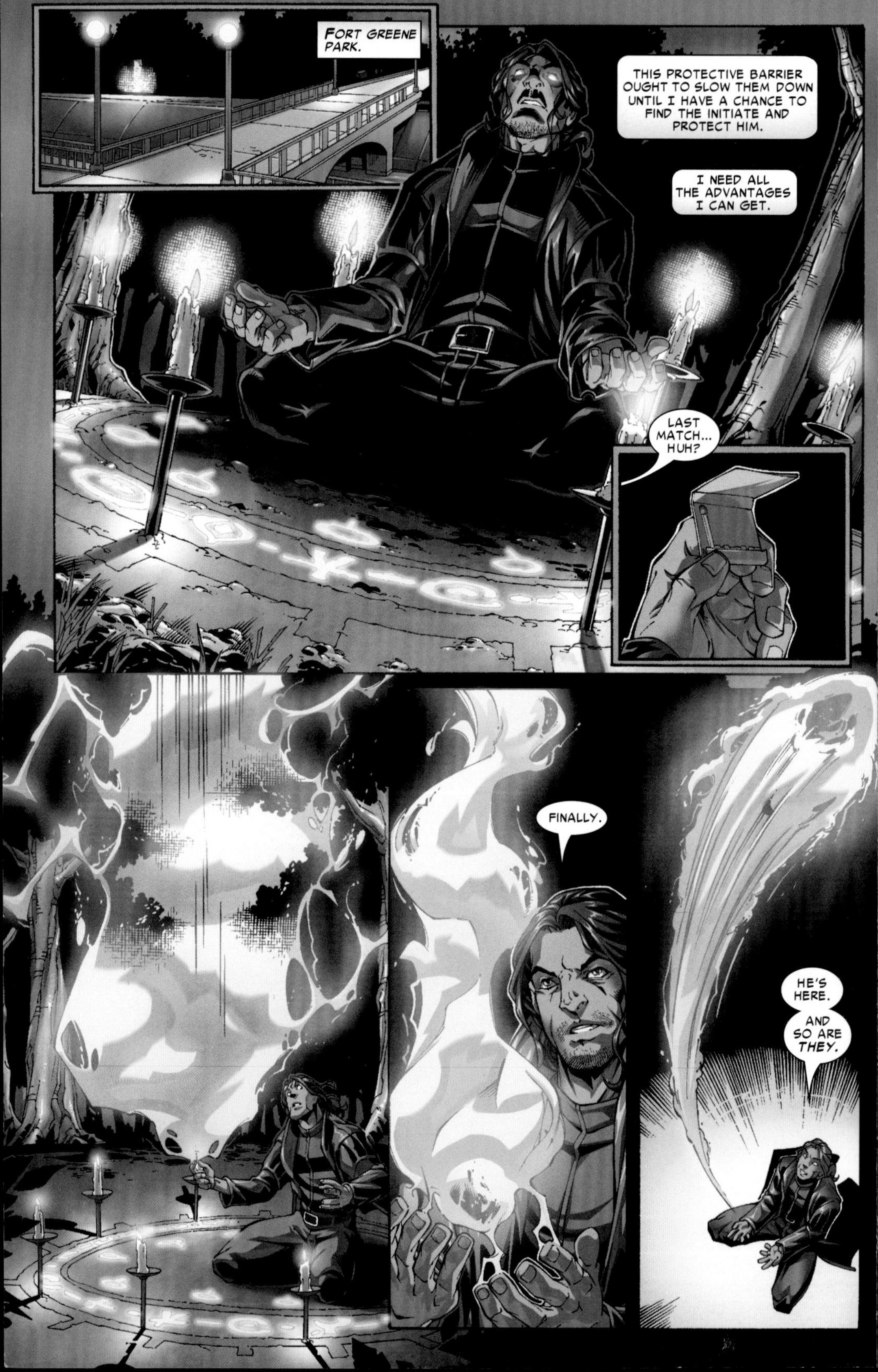
FORT GREENE PARK.
THIS PROTECTIVE BARRIER OUGHT TO SLOW THEM DOWN UNTIL I HAVE A CHANCE TO FIND THE INITIATE AND PROTECT HIM.
I NEED ALL THE ADVANTAGES I CAN GET.
LAST MATCH... HUH?
FINALLY.
HE'S HERE.
AND SO ARE THEY.

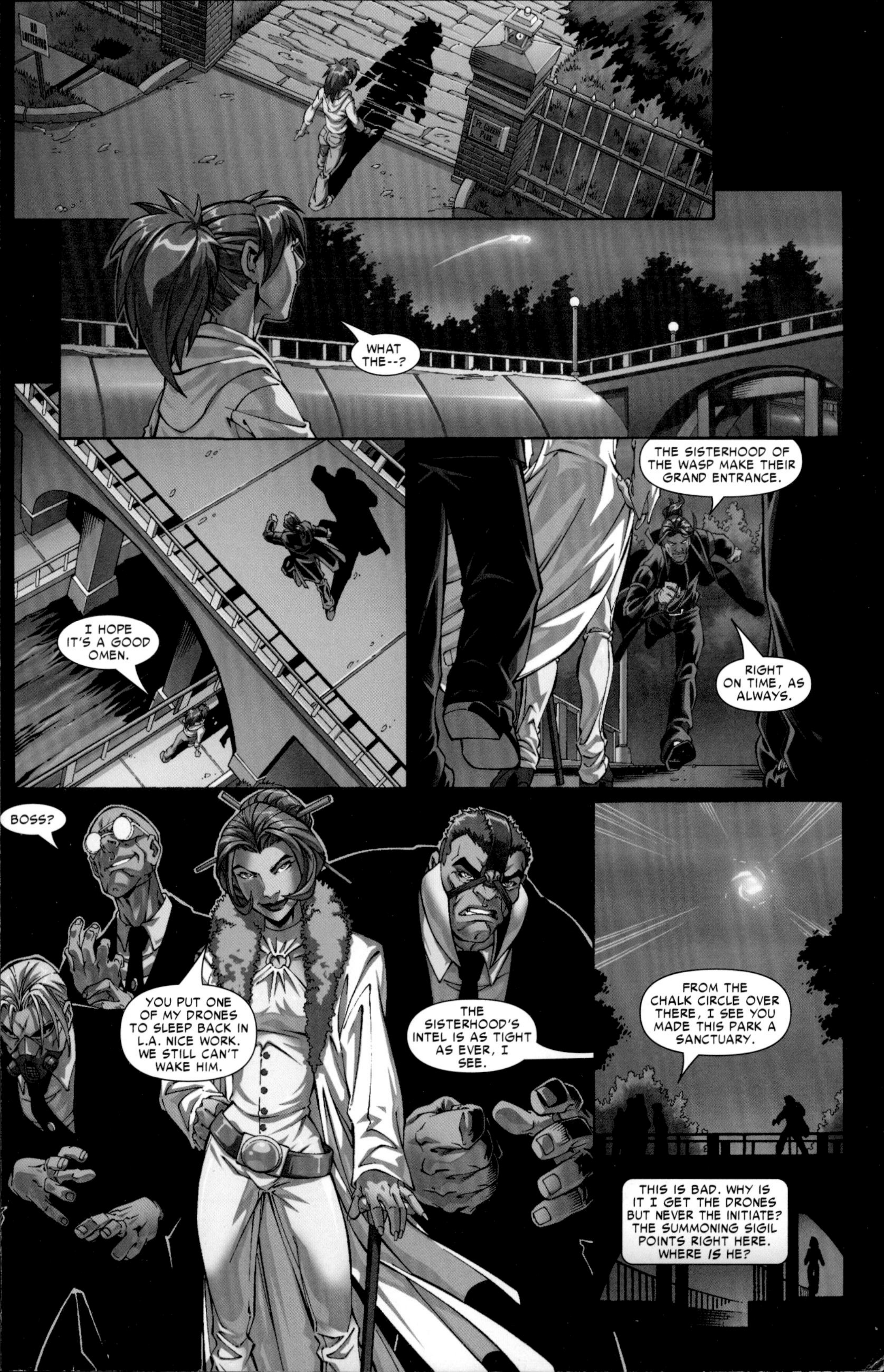
NO LOITERING
FT. GREENE PARK
WHAT THE--?
I HOPE IT'S A GOOD OMEN.
THE SISTERHOOD OF THE WASP MAKE THEIR GRAND ENTRANCE.
RIGHT ON TIME, AS ALWAYS.
BOSS?
YOU PUT ONE OF MY DRONES TO SLEEP BACK IN L.A. NICE WORK. WE STILL CAN'T WAKE HIM.
THE SISTERHOOD'S INTEL IS AS TIGHT AS EVER, I SEE.
FROM THE CHALK CIRCLE OVER THERE, I SEE YOU MADE THIS PARK A SANCTUARY.
THIS IS BAD. WHY IS IT I GET THE DRONES BUT NEVER THE INITIATE? THE SUMMONING SIGIL POINTS RIGHT HERE. WHERE *IS* HE?

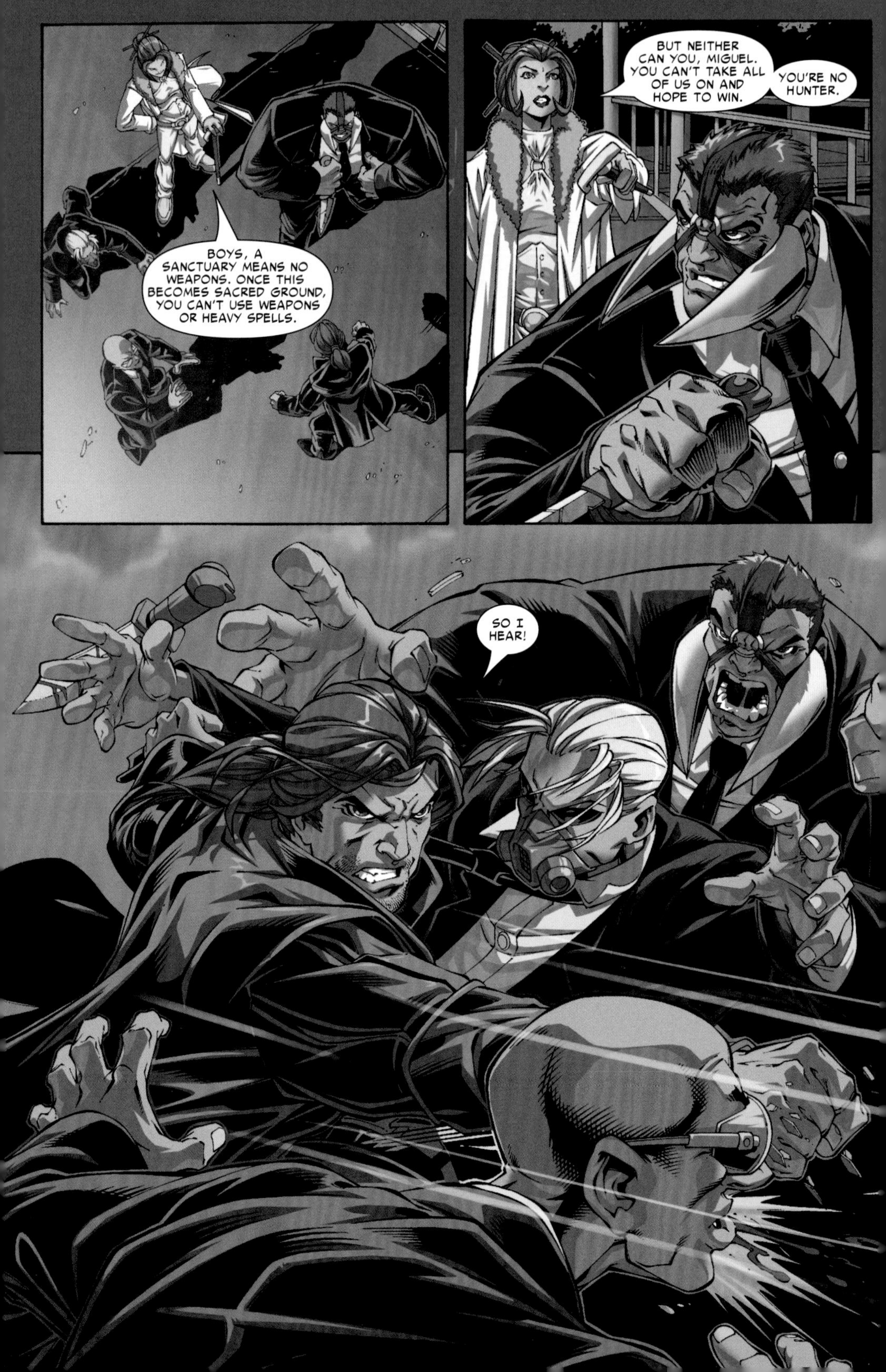
BOYS, A SANCTUARY MEANS NO WEAPONS. ONCE THIS BECOMES SACRED GROUND, YOU CAN'T USE WEAPONS OR HEAVY SPELLS.
BUT NEITHER CAN YOU, MIGUEL. YOU CAN'T TAKE ALL OF US ON AND HOPE TO WIN.
YOU'RE NO HUNTER.
SO I HEAR!

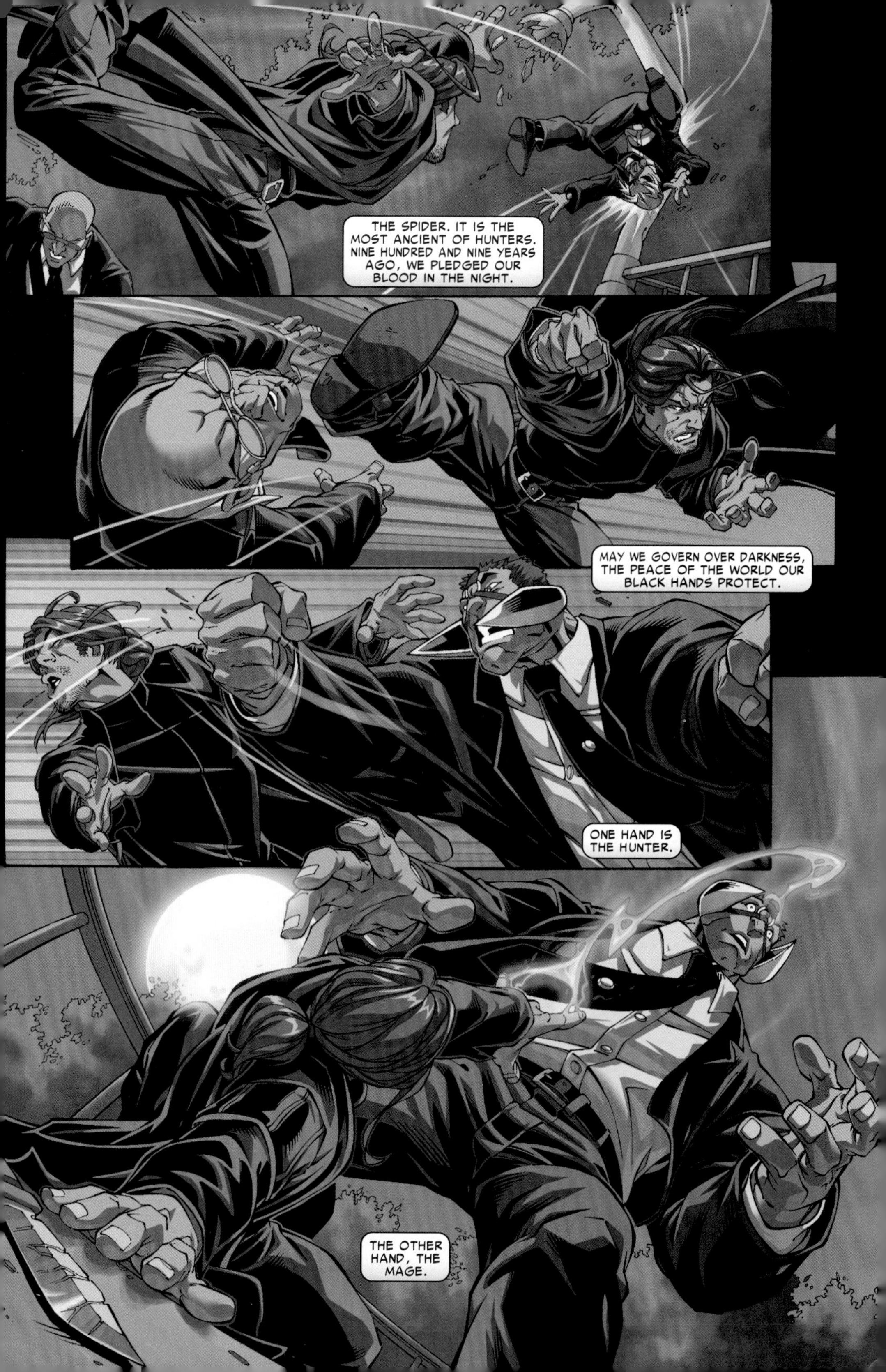
THE SPIDER. IT IS THE MOST ANCIENT OF HUNTERS. NINE HUNDRED AND NINE YEARS AGO, WE PLEDGED OUR BLOOD IN THE NIGHT.
MAY WE GOVERN OVER DARKNESS, THE PEACE OF THE WORLD OUR BLACK HANDS PROTECT.
ONE HAND IS THE HUNTER.
THE OTHER HAND, THE MAGE.

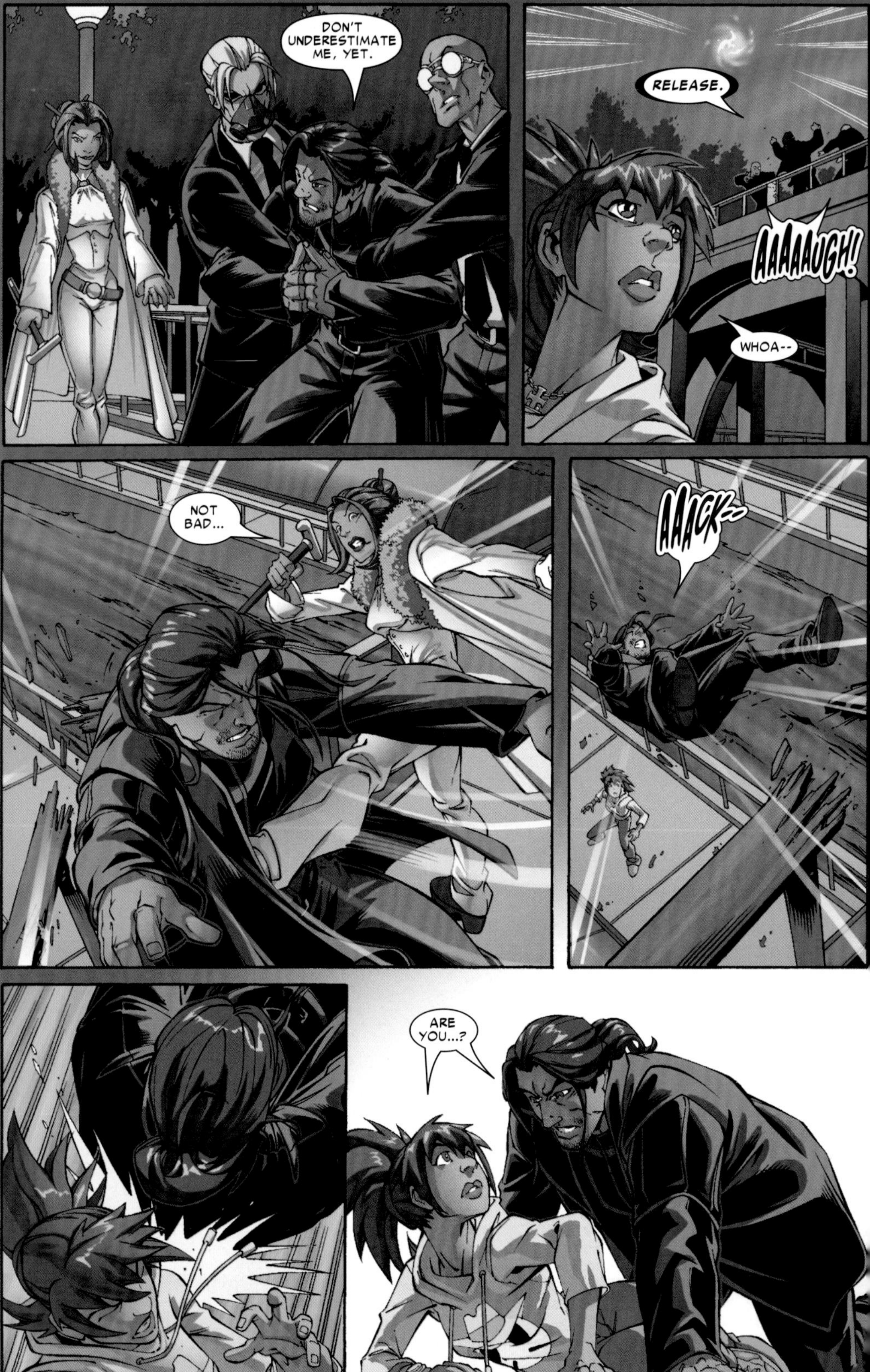
DON'T UNDERESTIMATE ME, YET.
RELEASE.
AAAAAUGH!
WHOA--
NOT BAD...
AAACK--
ARE YOU...?

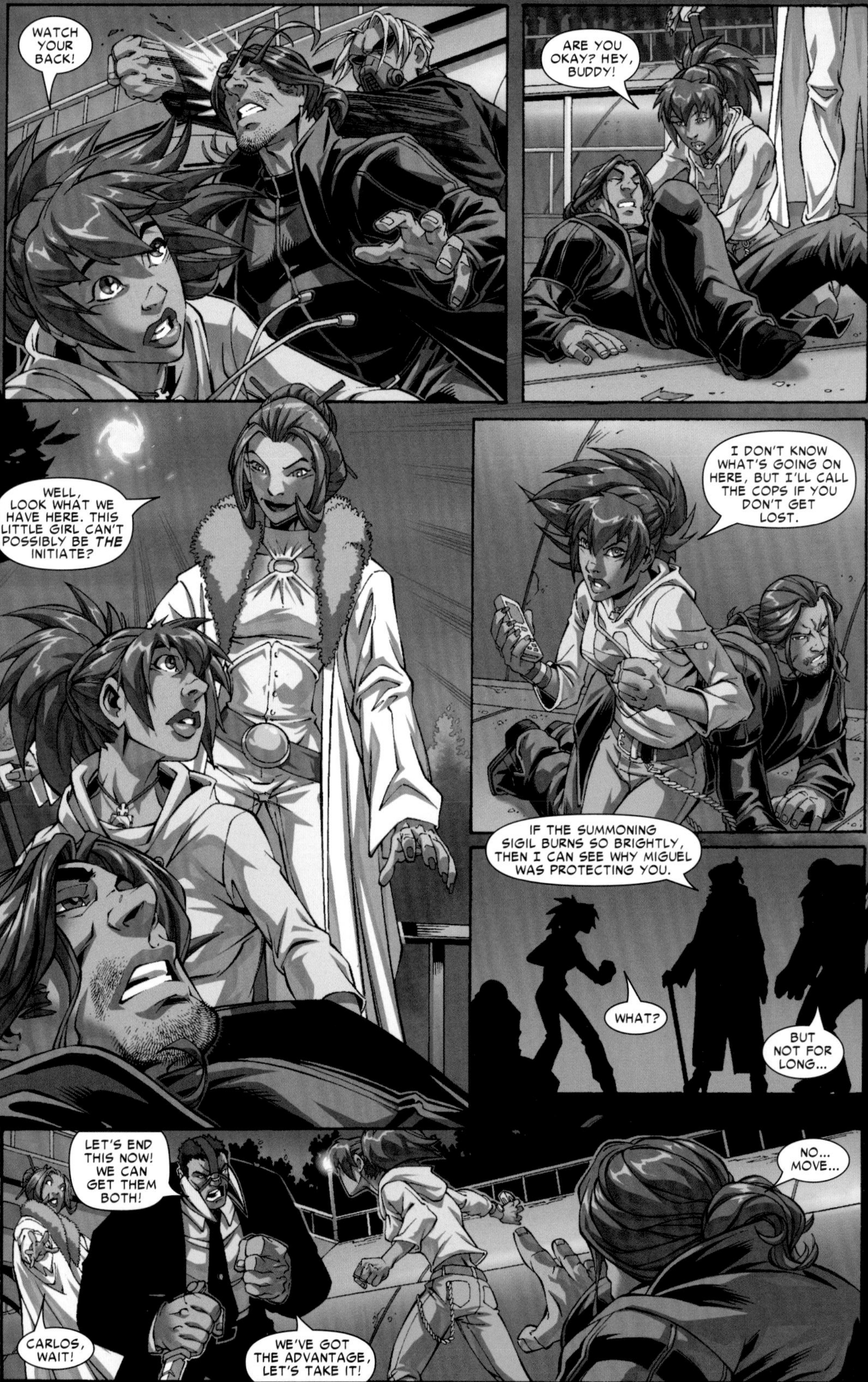
WATCH YOUR BACK!
ARE YOU OKAY? HEY, BUDDY!
WELL, LOOK WHAT WE HAVE HERE. THIS LITTLE GIRL CAN'T POSSIBLY BE *THE* INITIATE?
I DON'T KNOW WHAT'S GOING ON HERE, BUT I'LL CALL THE COPS IF YOU DON'T GET LOST.
IF THE SUMMONING SIGIL BURNS SO BRIGHTLY, THEN I CAN SEE WHY MIGUEL WAS PROTECTING YOU.
WHAT?
BUT NOT FOR LONG...
LET'S END THIS NOW! WE CAN GET THEM BOTH!
NO... MOVE...
CARLOS, WAIT!
WE'VE GOT THE ADVANTAGE, LET'S TAKE IT!

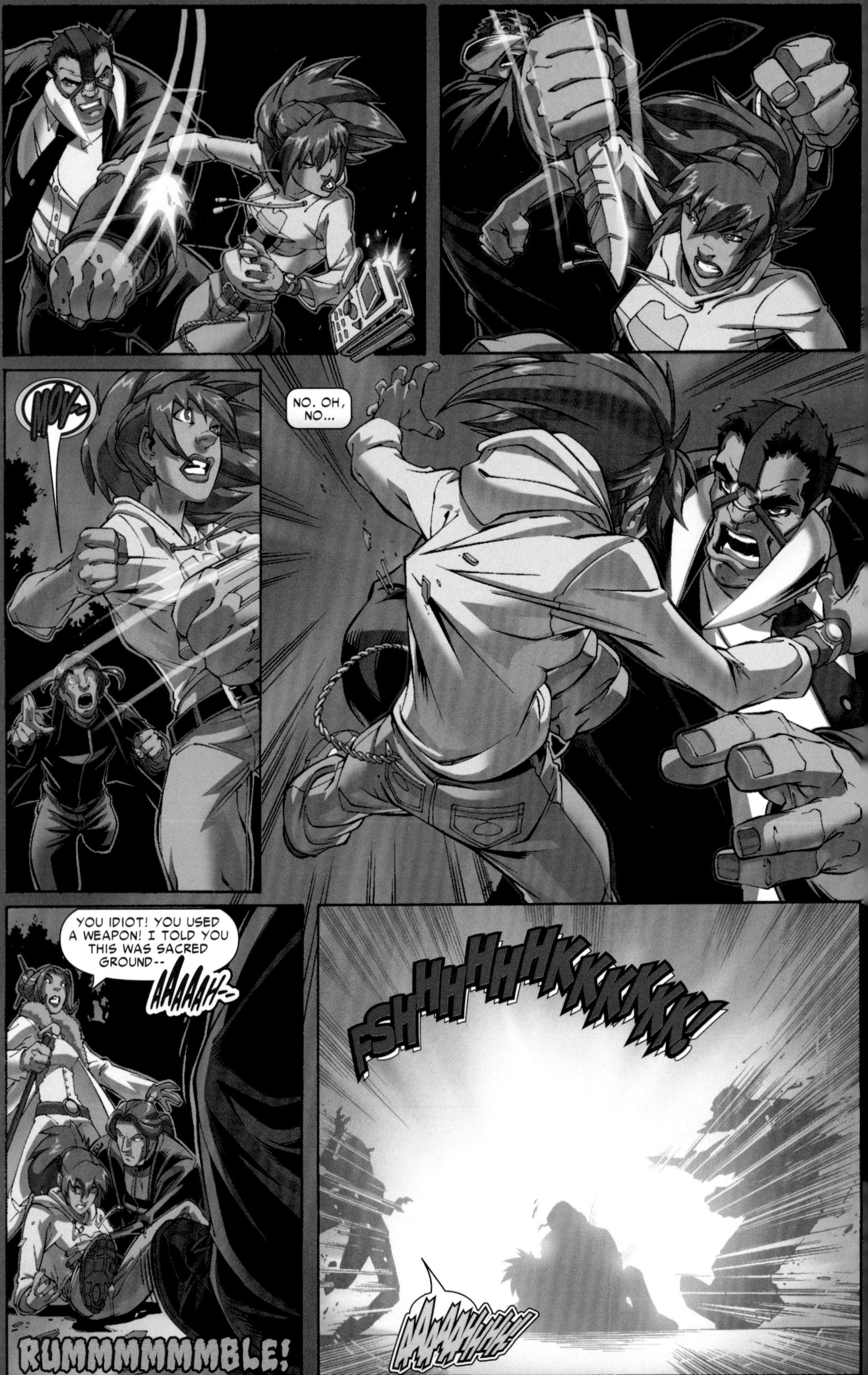

MOV-
NO. OH, NO...
YOU IDIOT! YOU USED A WEAPON! I TOLD YOU THIS WAS SACRED GROUND--
AAAAAH--
RUMMMMMMMBLE!
FSHHHHHHHKKKKKK!
AAAAAHHHH!

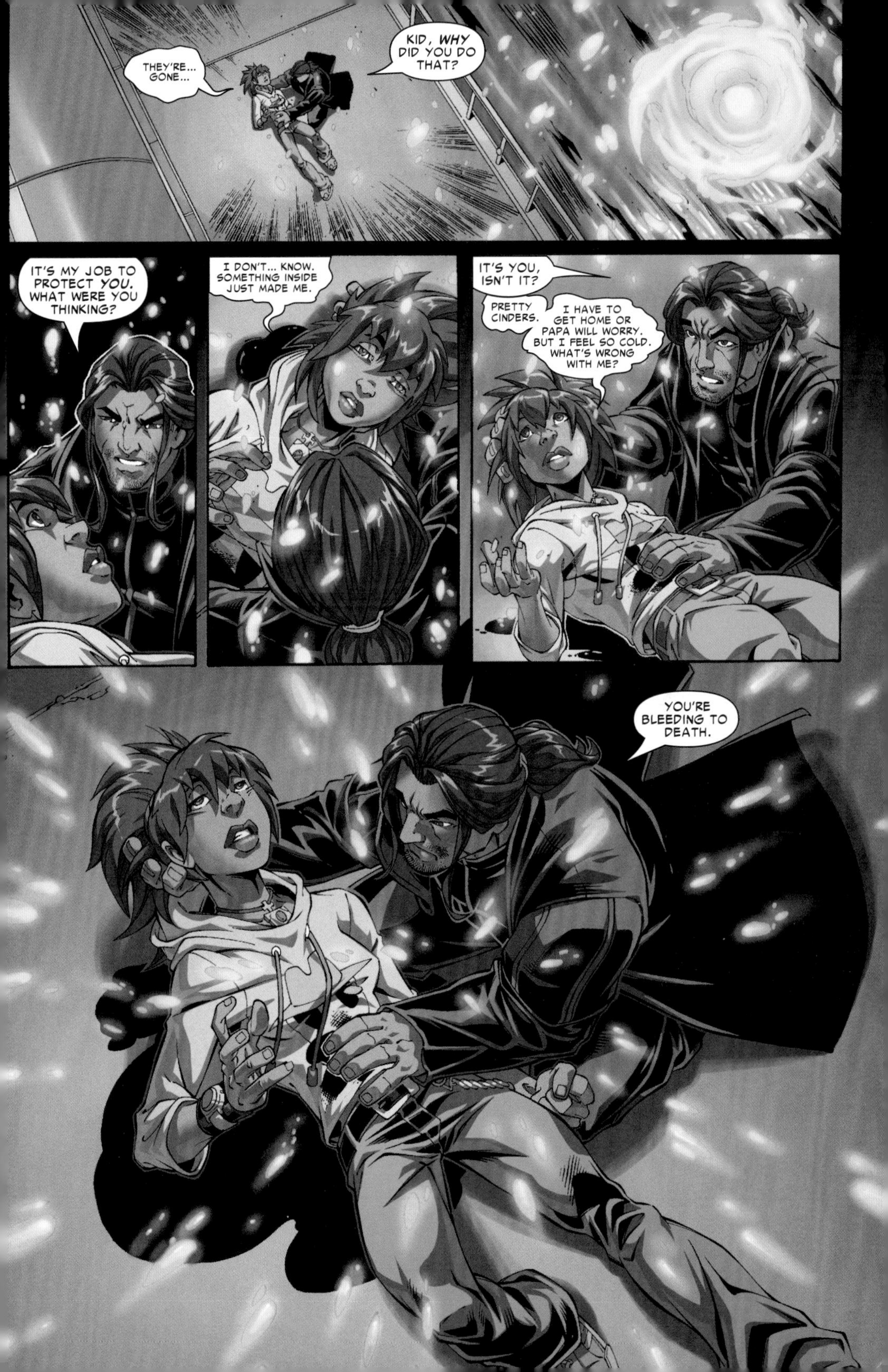
THEY'RE... GONE...
KID, WHY DID YOU DO THAT?
IT'S MY JOB TO PROTECT YOU. WHAT WERE YOU THINKING?
I DON'T... KNOW. SOMETHING INSIDE JUST MADE ME.
IT'S YOU, ISN'T IT?
PRETTY CINDERS.
I HAVE TO GET HOME OR PAPA WILL WORRY. BUT I FEEL SO COLD. WHAT'S WRONG WITH ME?
YOU'RE BLEEDING TO DEATH.

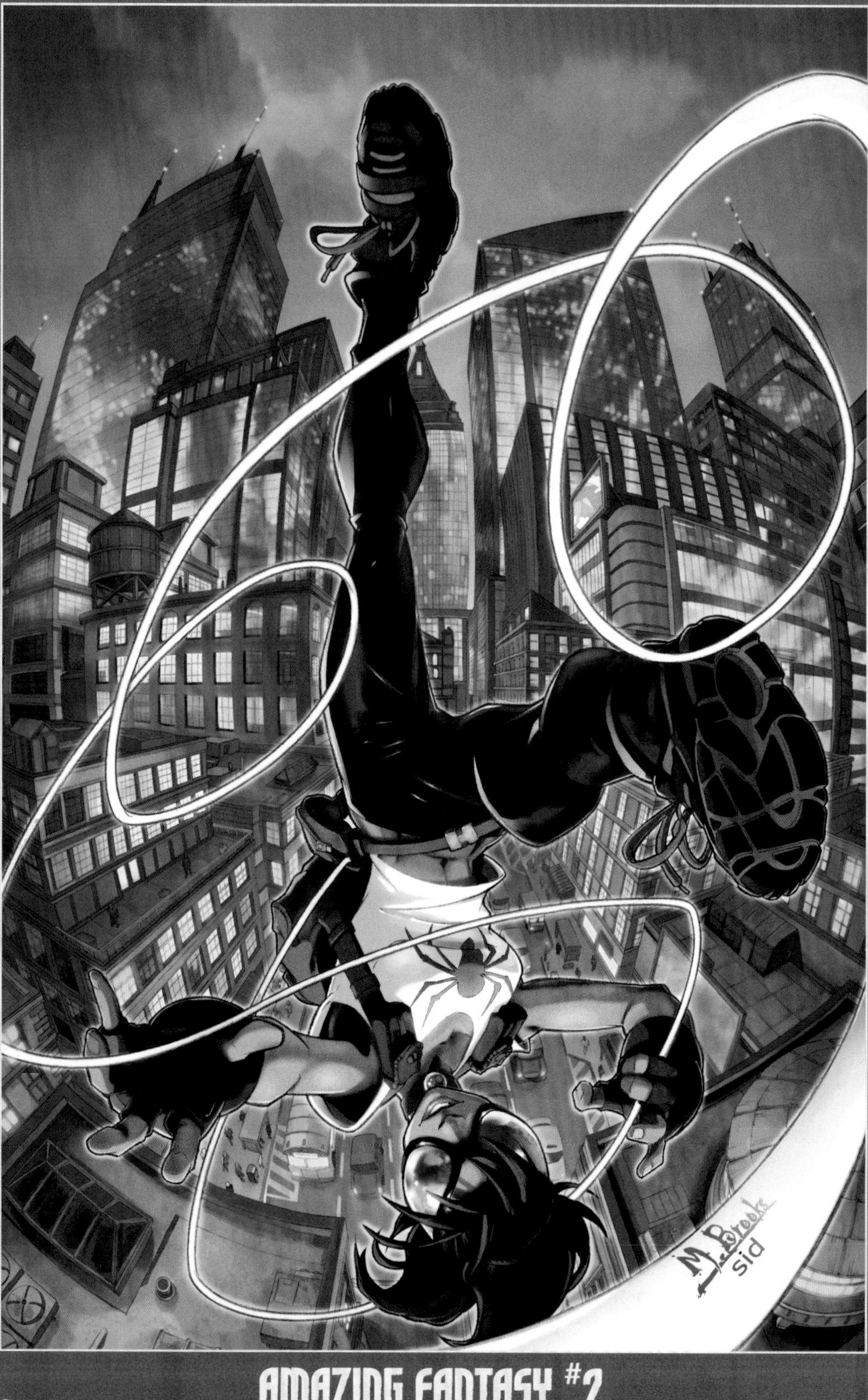
M. Brooks
sid

AMAZING FANTASY #2

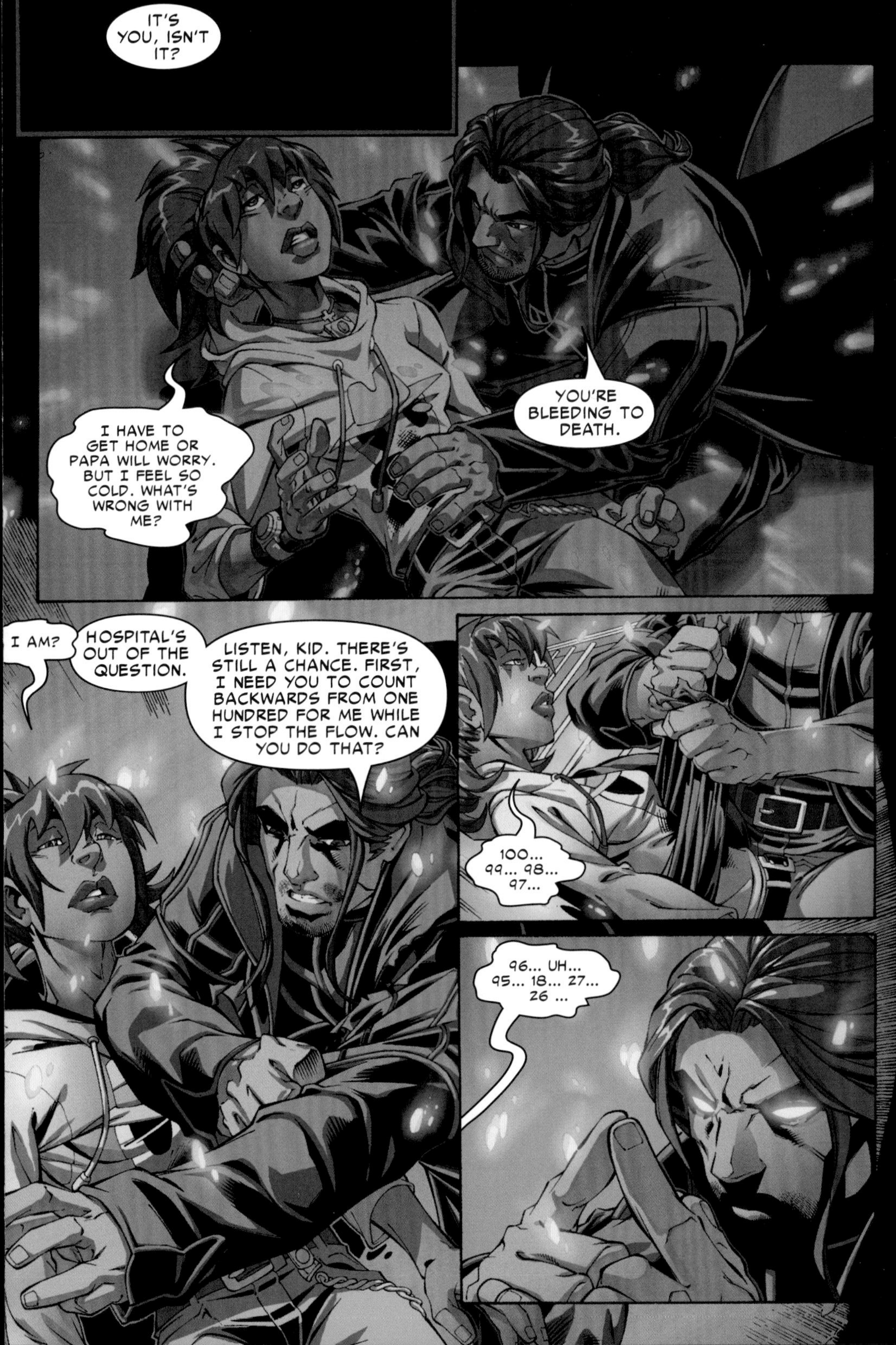
IT'S YOU, ISN'T IT?
I HAVE TO GET HOME OR PAPA WILL WORRY. BUT I FEEL SO COLD. WHAT'S WRONG WITH ME?
YOU'RE BLEEDING TO DEATH.
I AM?
HOSPITAL'S OUT OF THE QUESTION.
LISTEN, KID. THERE'S STILL A CHANCE. FIRST, I NEED YOU TO COUNT BACKWARDS FROM ONE HUNDRED FOR ME WHILE I STOP THE FLOW. CAN YOU DO THAT?
100... 99... 98... 97...
96... UH... 95... 18... 27... 26 ...

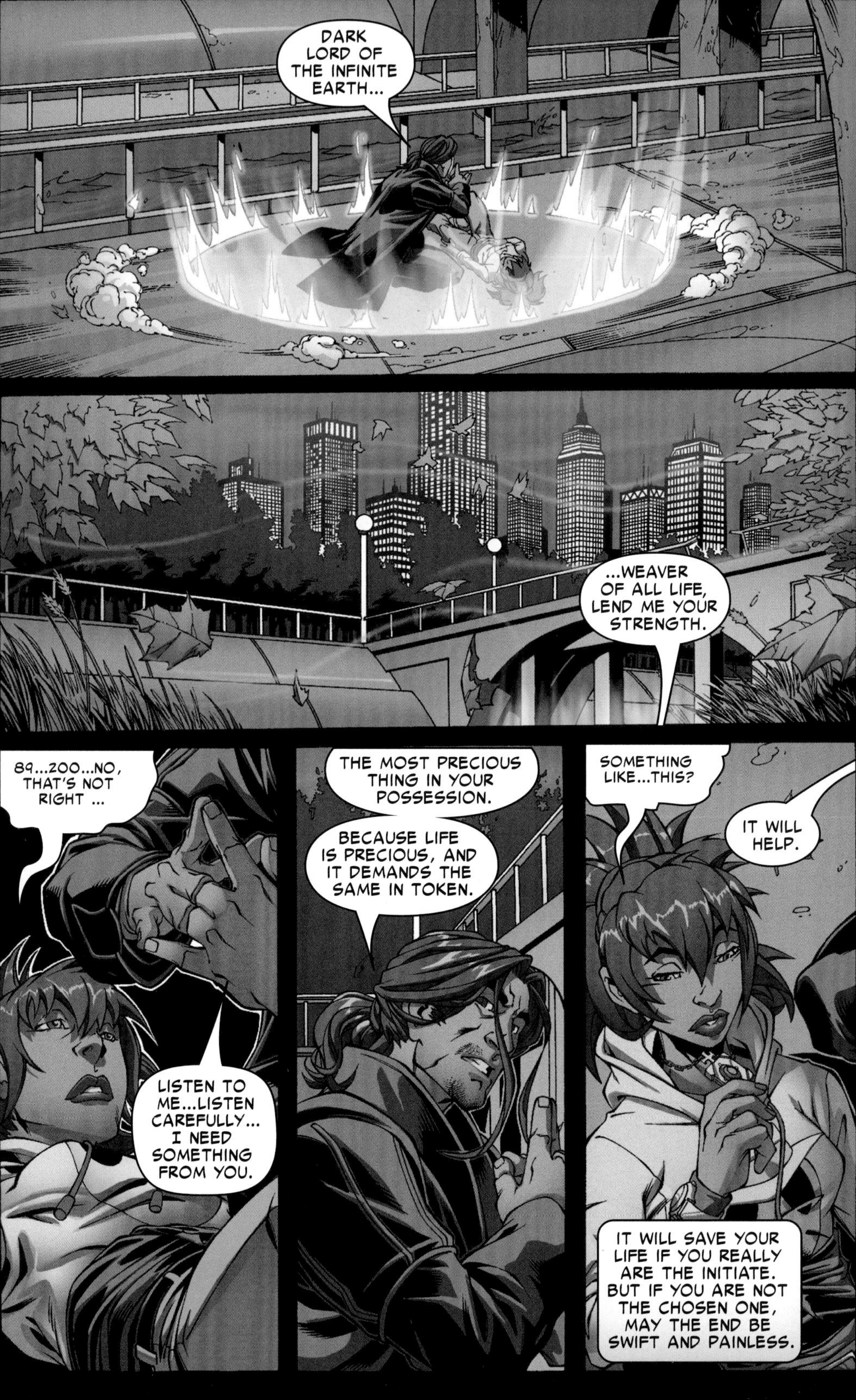
DARK LORD OF THE INFINITE EARTH...
...WEAVER OF ALL LIFE, LEND ME YOUR STRENGTH.
89...200...NO, THAT'S NOT RIGHT ...
LISTEN TO ME...LISTEN CAREFULLY... I NEED SOMETHING FROM YOU.
THE MOST PRECIOUS THING IN YOUR POSSESSION.
BECAUSE LIFE IS PRECIOUS, AND IT DEMANDS THE SAME IN TOKEN.
SOMETHING LIKE...THIS?
IT WILL HELP.
IT WILL SAVE YOUR LIFE IF YOU REALLY ARE THE INITIATE. BUT IF YOU ARE NOT THE CHOSEN ONE, MAY THE END BE SWIFT AND PAINLESS.

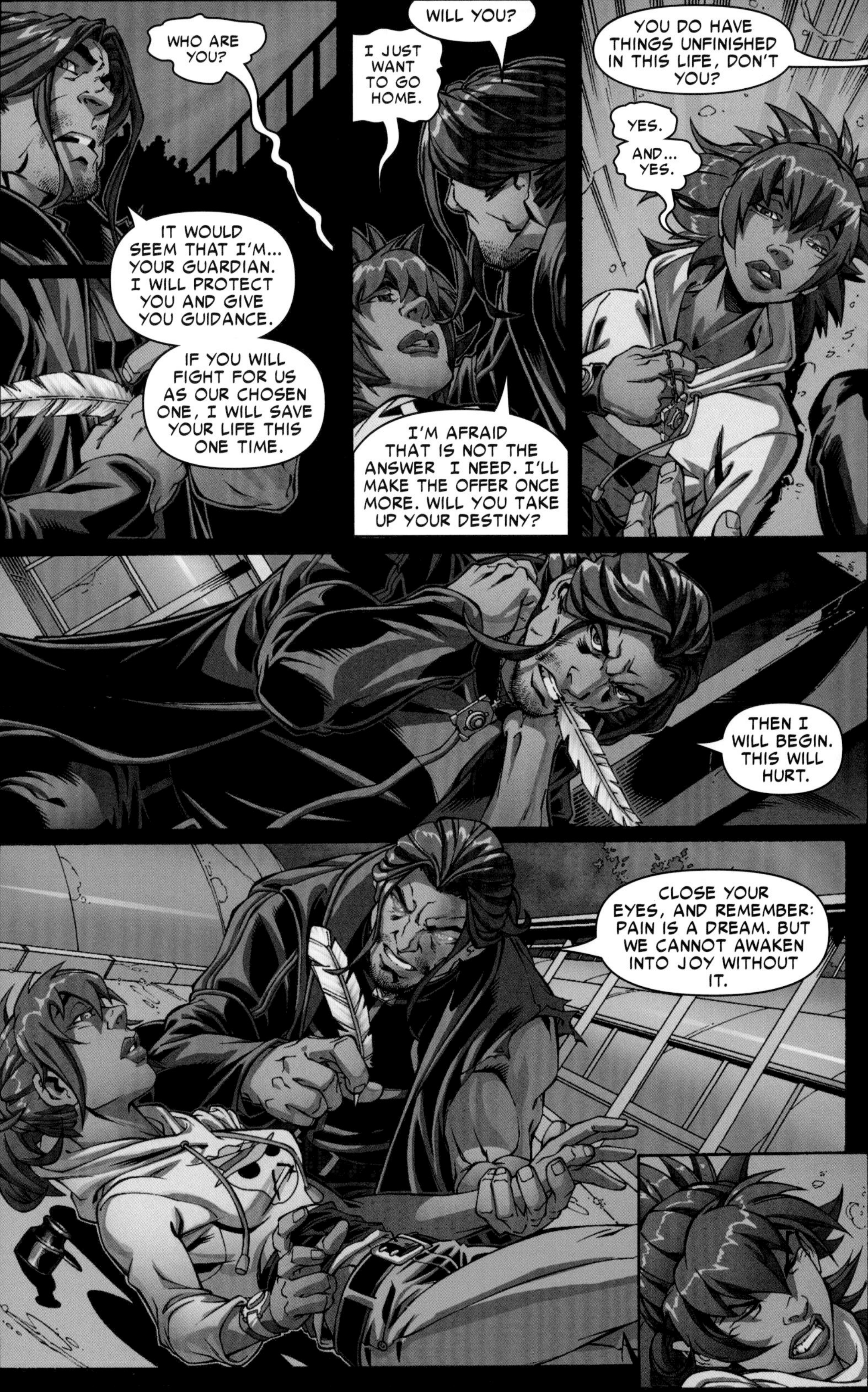
WHO ARE YOU?
IT WOULD SEEM THAT I'M... YOUR GUARDIAN. I WILL PROTECT YOU AND GIVE YOU GUIDANCE.
IF YOU WILL FIGHT FOR US AS OUR CHOSEN ONE, I WILL SAVE YOUR LIFE THIS ONE TIME.
WILL YOU?
I JUST WANT TO GO HOME.
I'M AFRAID THAT IS NOT THE ANSWER I NEED. I'LL MAKE THE OFFER ONCE MORE. WILL YOU TAKE UP YOUR DESTINY?
YOU DO HAVE THINGS UNFINISHED IN THIS LIFE, DON'T YOU?
YES.
AND... YES.
THEN I WILL BEGIN. THIS WILL HURT.
CLOSE YOUR EYES, AND REMEMBER: PAIN IS A DREAM. BUT WE CANNOT AWAKEN INTO JOY WITHOUT IT.

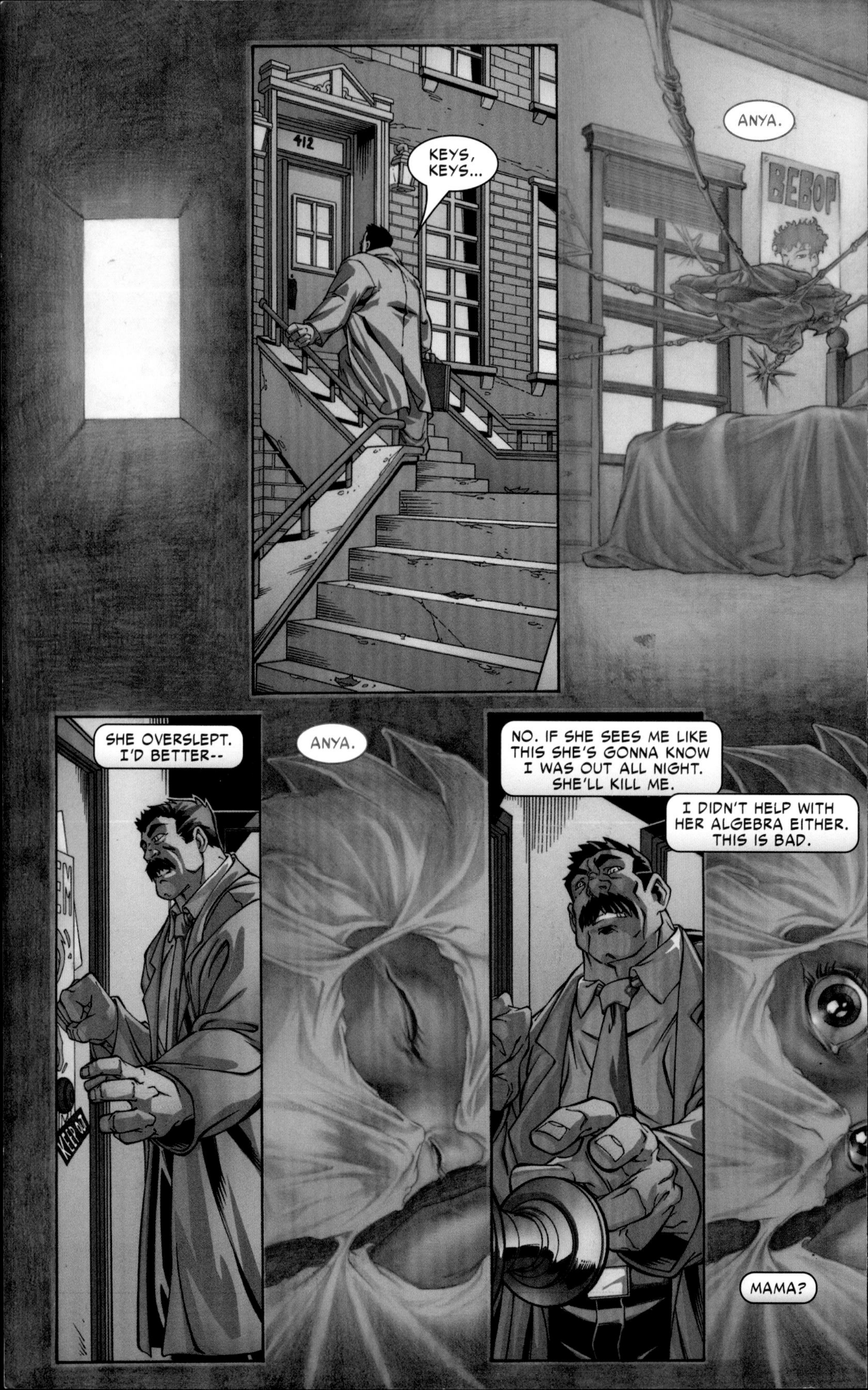
KEYS, KEYS...
ANYA.
SHE OVERSLEPT. I'D BETTER--
ANYA.
NO. IF SHE SEES ME LIKE THIS SHE'S GONNA KNOW I WAS OUT ALL NIGHT. SHE'LL KILL ME.
I DIDN'T HELP WITH HER ALGEBRA EITHER. THIS IS BAD.
MAMA?

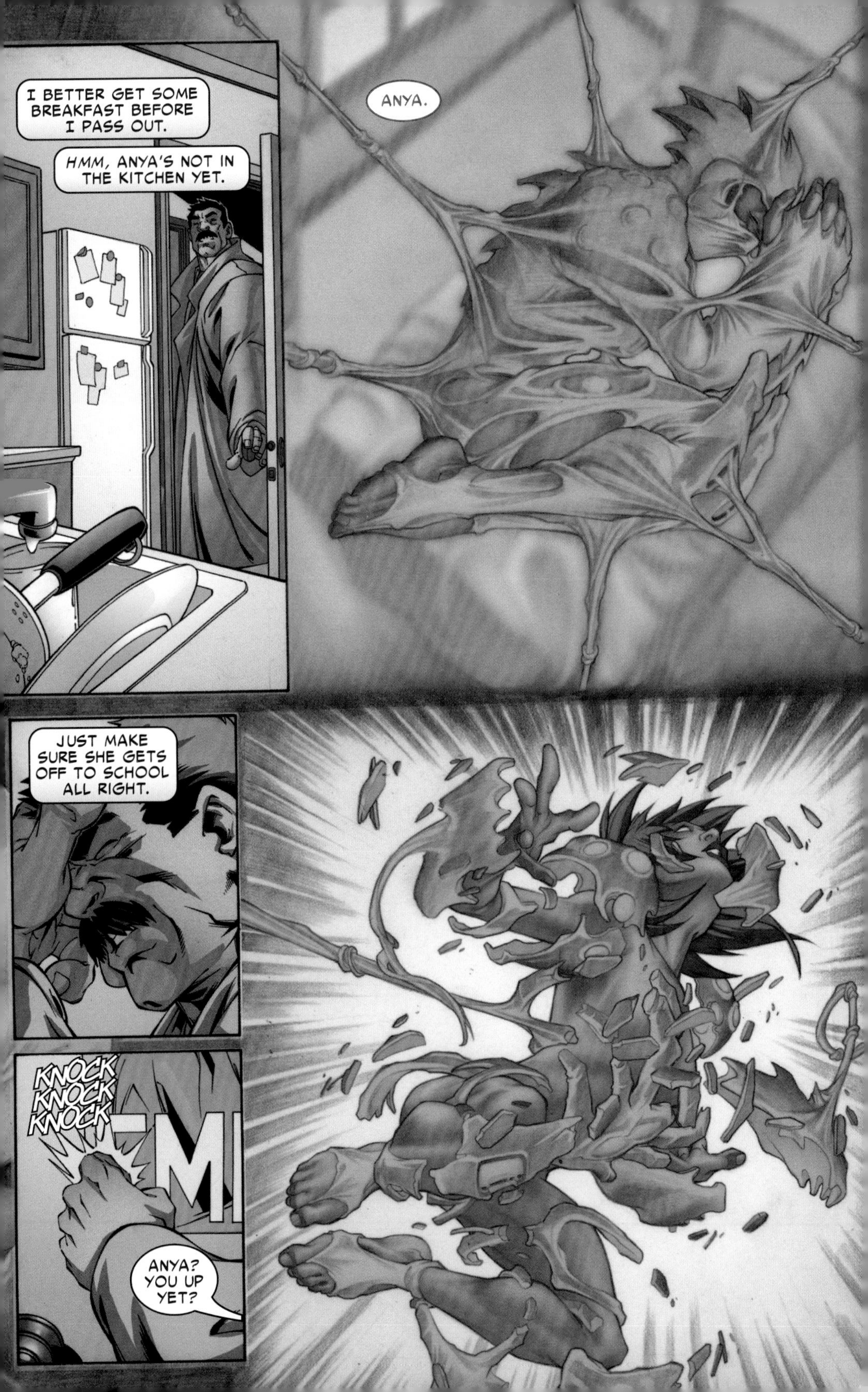
I BETTER GET SOME BREAKFAST BEFORE I PASS OUT.
HMM, ANYA'S NOT IN THE KITCHEN YET.
ANYA.
JUST MAKE SURE SHE GETS OFF TO SCHOOL ALL RIGHT.
KNOCK KNOCK KNOCK
ANYA? YOU UP YET?

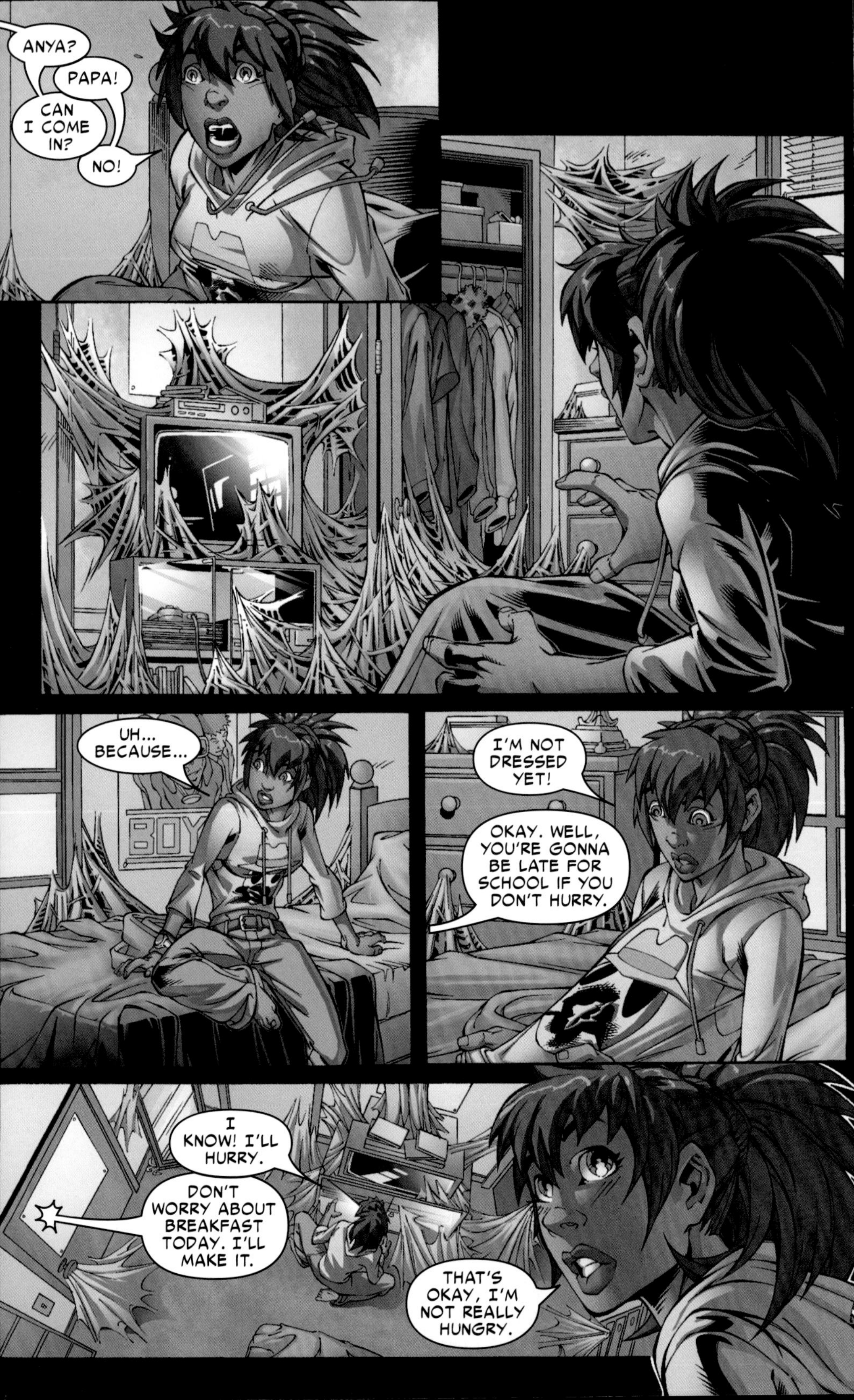
ANYA?
PAPA!
CAN I COME IN?
NO!
UH... BECAUSE...
I'M NOT DRESSED YET!
OKAY. WELL, YOU'RE GONNA BE LATE FOR SCHOOL IF YOU DON'T HURRY.
I KNOW! I'LL HURRY.
DON'T WORRY ABOUT BREAKFAST TODAY. I'LL MAKE IT.
THAT'S OKAY, I'M NOT REALLY HUNGRY.
BOY

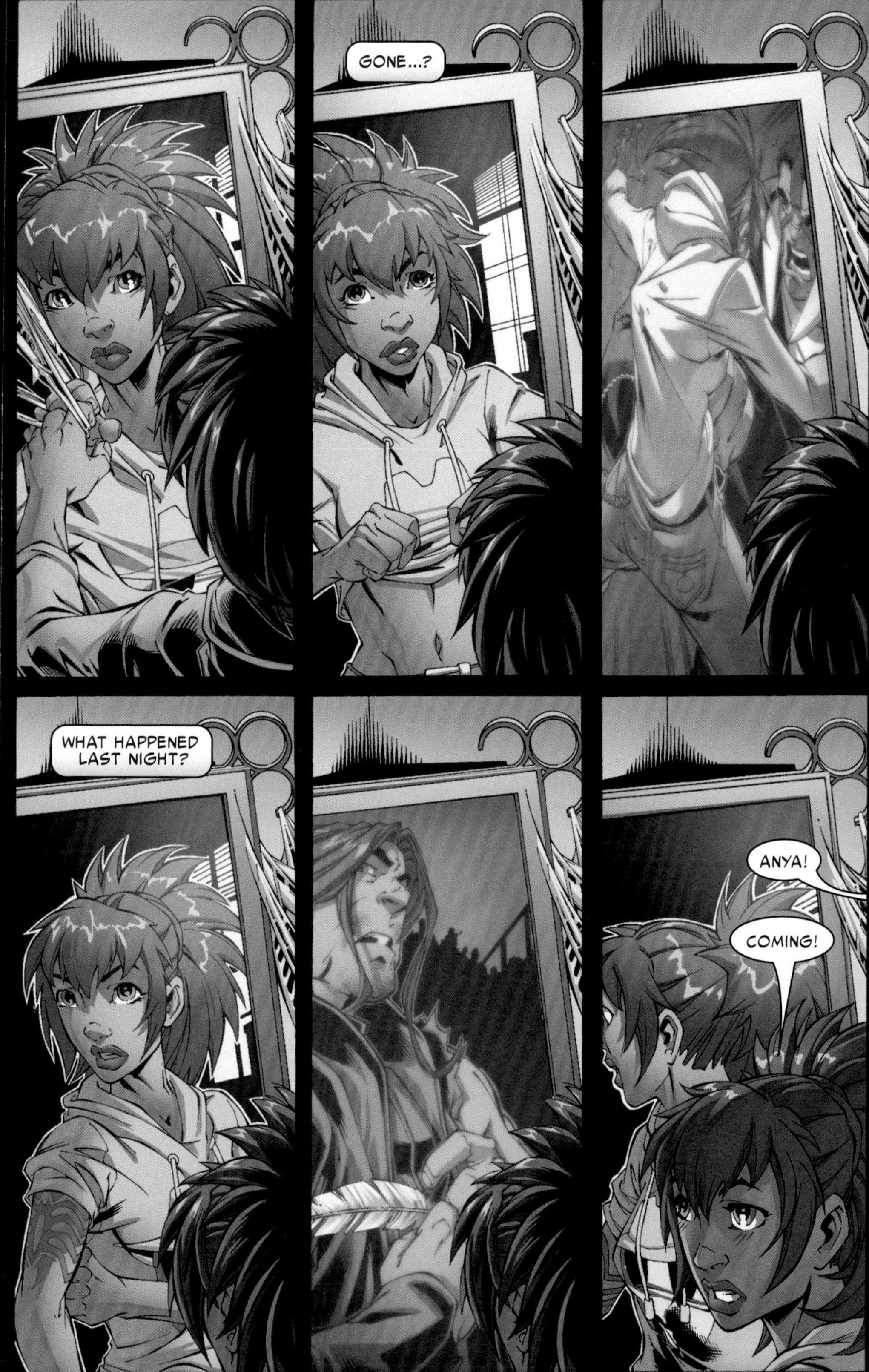
GONE...?
WHAT HAPPENED LAST NIGHT?
ANYA!
COMING!

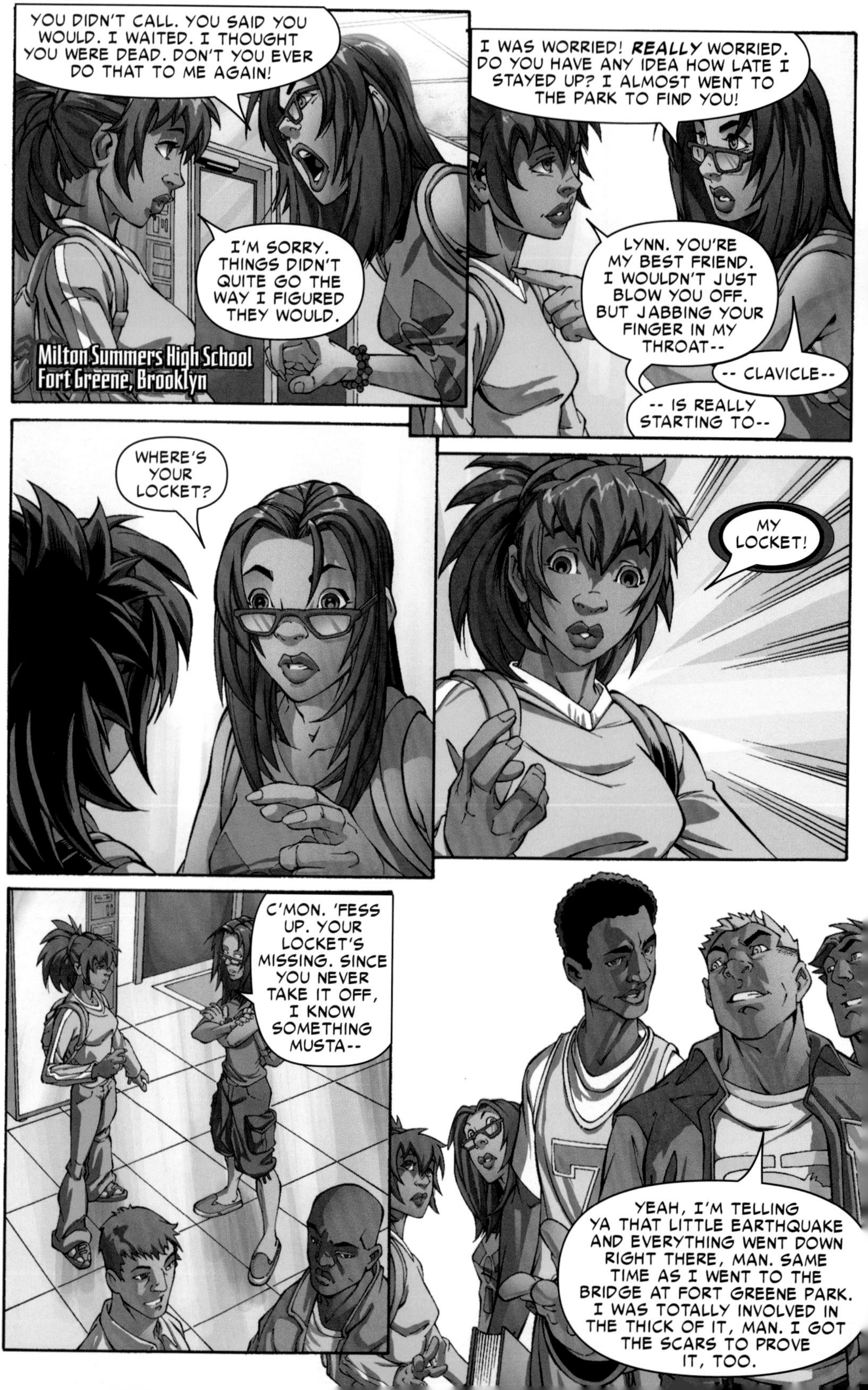
YOU DIDN'T CALL. YOU SAID YOU WOULD. I WAITED. I THOUGHT YOU WERE DEAD. DON'T YOU EVER DO THAT TO ME AGAIN!
I'M SORRY. THINGS DIDN'T QUITE GO THE WAY I FIGURED THEY WOULD.
Milton Summers High School
Fort Greene, Brooklyn
I WAS WORRIED! REALLY WORRIED. DO YOU HAVE ANY IDEA HOW LATE I STAYED UP? I ALMOST WENT TO THE PARK TO FIND YOU!
LYNN. YOU'RE MY BEST FRIEND. I WOULDN'T JUST BLOW YOU OFF. BUT JABBING YOUR FINGER IN MY THROAT--
-- CLAVICLE--
-- IS REALLY STARTING TO--
WHERE'S YOUR LOCKET?
MY LOCKET!
C'MON. 'FESS UP. YOUR LOCKET'S MISSING. SINCE YOU NEVER TAKE IT OFF, I KNOW SOMETHING MUSTA--
YEAH, I'M TELLING YA THAT LITTLE EARTHQUAKE AND EVERYTHING WENT DOWN RIGHT THERE, MAN. SAME TIME AS I WENT TO THE BRIDGE AT FORT GREENE PARK. I WAS TOTALLY INVOLVED IN THE THICK OF IT, MAN. I GOT THE SCARS TO PROVE IT, TOO.

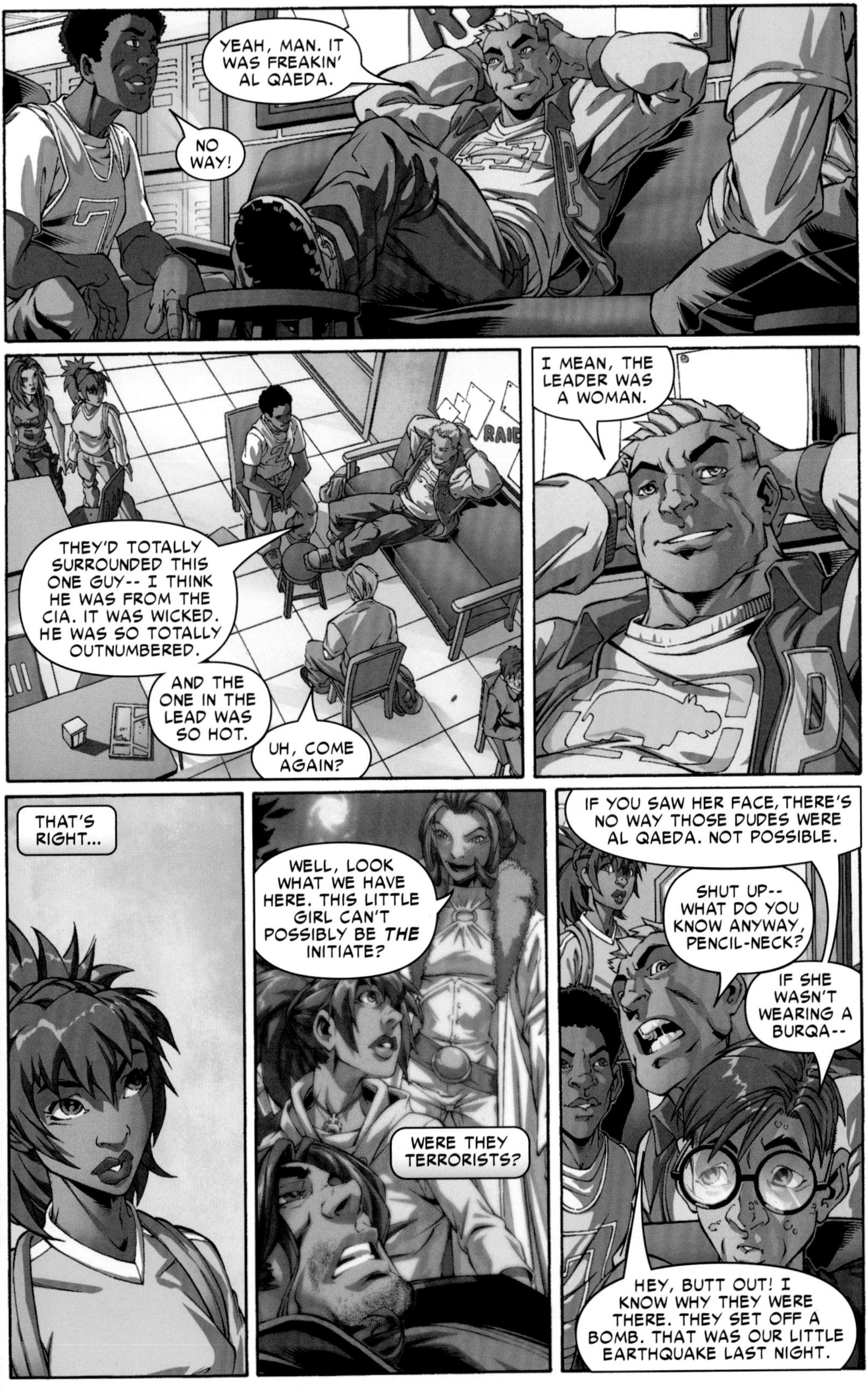
YEAH, MAN. IT WAS FREAKIN' AL QAEDA.
NO WAY!
I MEAN, THE LEADER WAS A WOMAN.
THEY'D TOTALLY SURROUNDED THIS ONE GUY-- I THINK HE WAS FROM THE CIA. IT WAS WICKED. HE WAS SO TOTALLY OUTNUMBERED.
AND THE ONE IN THE LEAD WAS SO HOT.
UH, COME AGAIN?
RAID
THAT'S RIGHT...
WELL, LOOK WHAT WE HAVE HERE. THIS LITTLE GIRL CAN'T POSSIBLY BE *THE* INITIATE?
WERE THEY TERRORISTS?
IF YOU SAW HER FACE, THERE'S NO WAY THOSE DUDES WERE AL QAEDA. NOT POSSIBLE.
SHUT UP-- WHAT DO YOU KNOW ANYWAY, PENCIL-NECK?
IF SHE WASN'T WEARING A BURQA--
HEY, BUTT OUT! I KNOW WHY THEY WERE THERE. THEY SET OFF A BOMB. THAT WAS OUR LITTLE EARTHQUAKE LAST NIGHT.

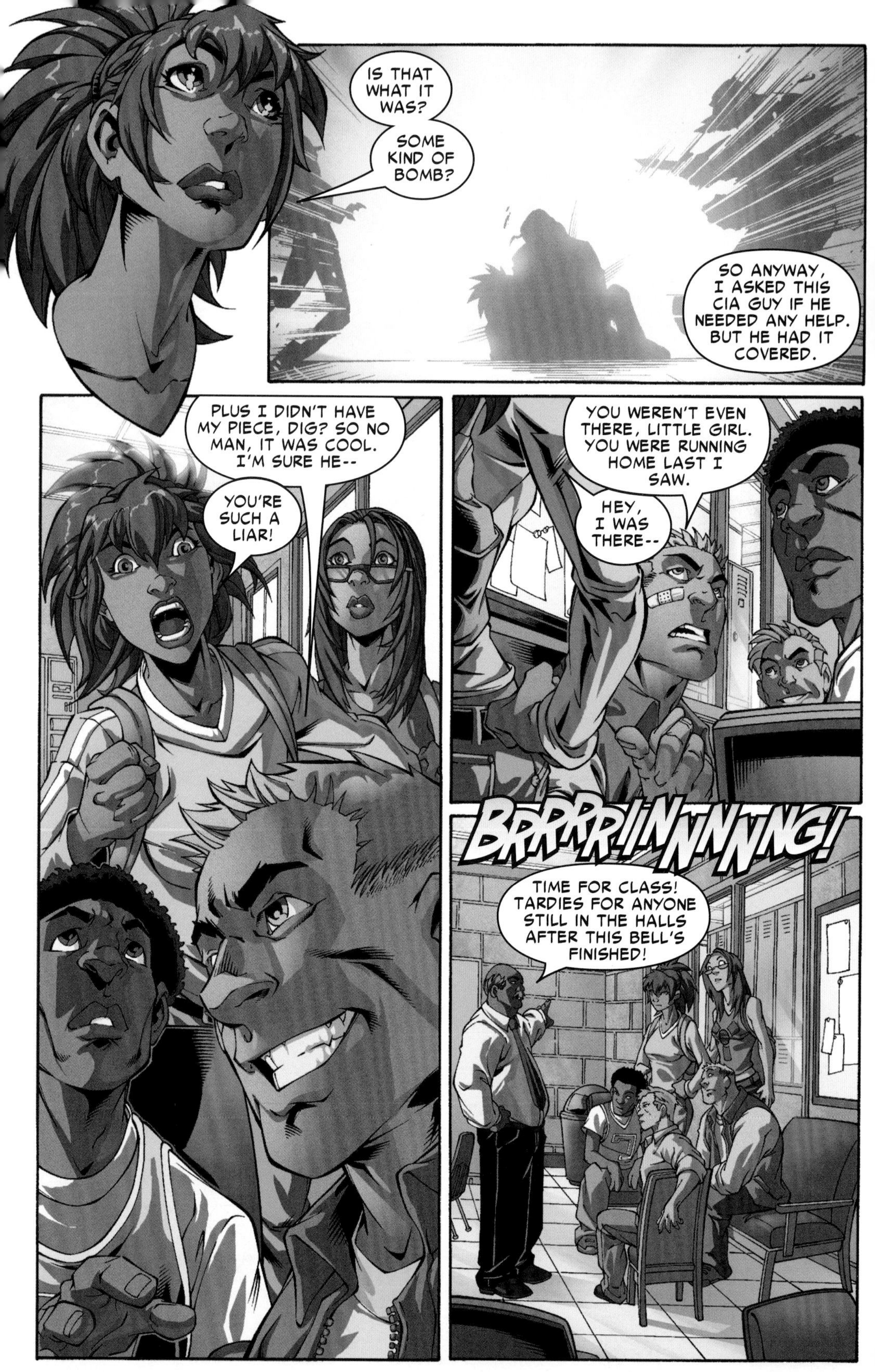
IS THAT WHAT IT WAS?
SOME KIND OF BOMB?
SO ANYWAY, I ASKED THIS CIA GUY IF HE NEEDED ANY HELP. BUT HE HAD IT COVERED.
PLUS I DIDN'T HAVE MY PIECE, DIG? SO NO MAN, IT WAS COOL. I'M SURE HE--
YOU'RE SUCH A LIAR!
YOU WEREN'T EVEN THERE, LITTLE GIRL. YOU WERE RUNNING HOME LAST I SAW.
HEY, I WAS THERE--
BRRRRIINNNNNG!
TIME FOR CLASS! TARDIES FOR ANYONE STILL IN THE HALLS AFTER THIS BELL'S FINISHED!

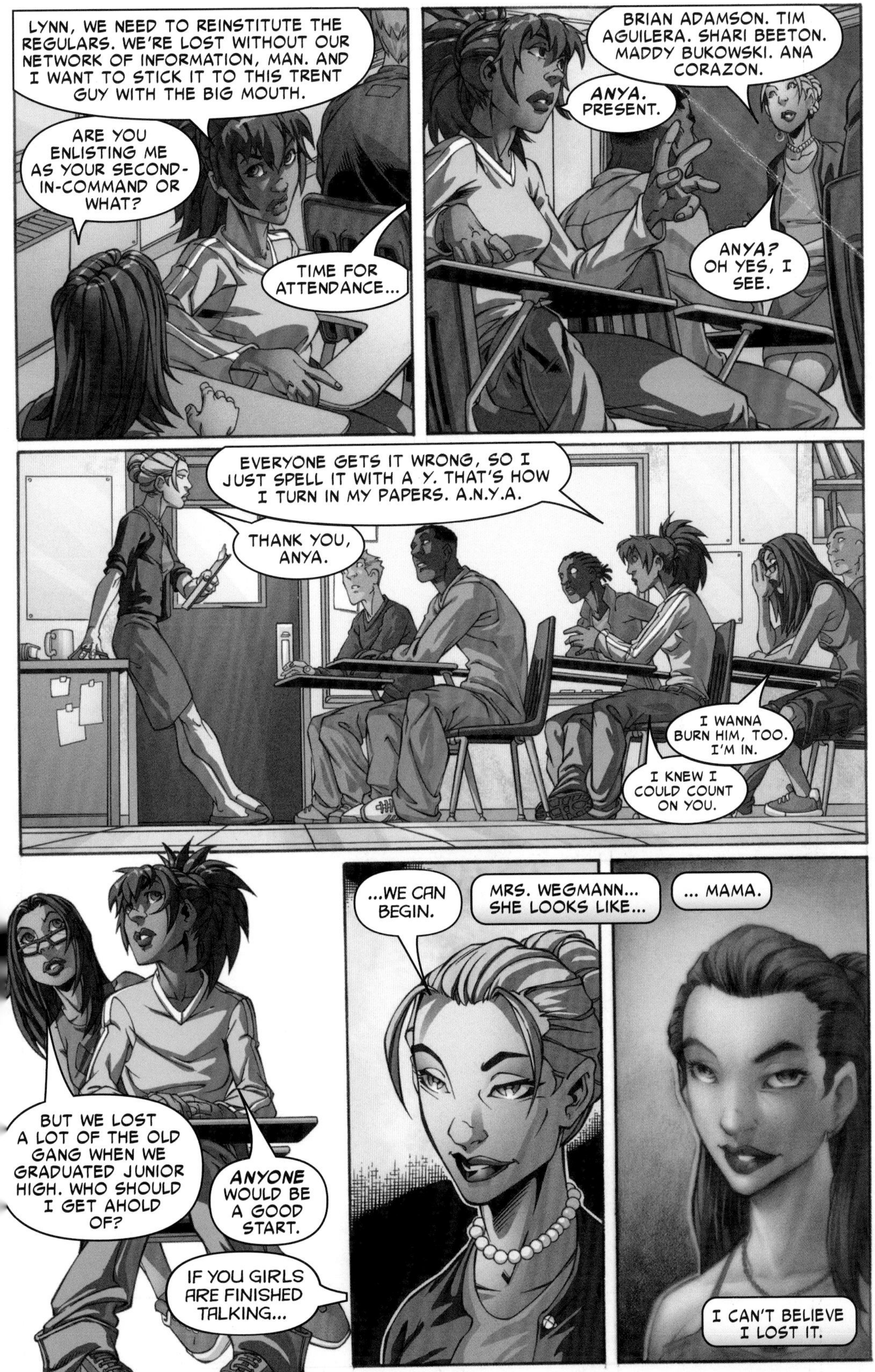
LYNN, WE NEED TO REINSTITUTE THE REGULARS. WE'RE LOST WITHOUT OUR NETWORK OF INFORMATION, MAN. AND I WANT TO STICK IT TO THIS TRENT GUY WITH THE BIG MOUTH.
ARE YOU ENLISTING ME AS YOUR SECOND-IN-COMMAND OR WHAT?
TIME FOR ATTENDANCE...
BRIAN ADAMSON. TIM AGUILERA. SHARI BEETON. MADDY BUKOWSKI. ANA CORAZON.
ANYA. PRESENT.
ANYA? OH YES, I SEE.
EVERYONE GETS IT WRONG, SO I JUST SPELL IT WITH A Y. THAT'S HOW I TURN IN MY PAPERS. A.N.Y.A.
THANK YOU, ANYA.
I WANNA BURN HIM, TOO. I'M IN.
I KNEW I COULD COUNT ON YOU.
BUT WE LOST A LOT OF THE OLD GANG WHEN WE GRADUATED JUNIOR HIGH. WHO SHOULD I GET AHOLD OF?
ANYONE WOULD BE A GOOD START.
IF YOU GIRLS ARE FINISHED TALKING...
...WE CAN BEGIN.
MRS. WEGMANN... SHE LOOKS LIKE...
... MAMA.
I CAN'T BELIEVE I LOST IT.

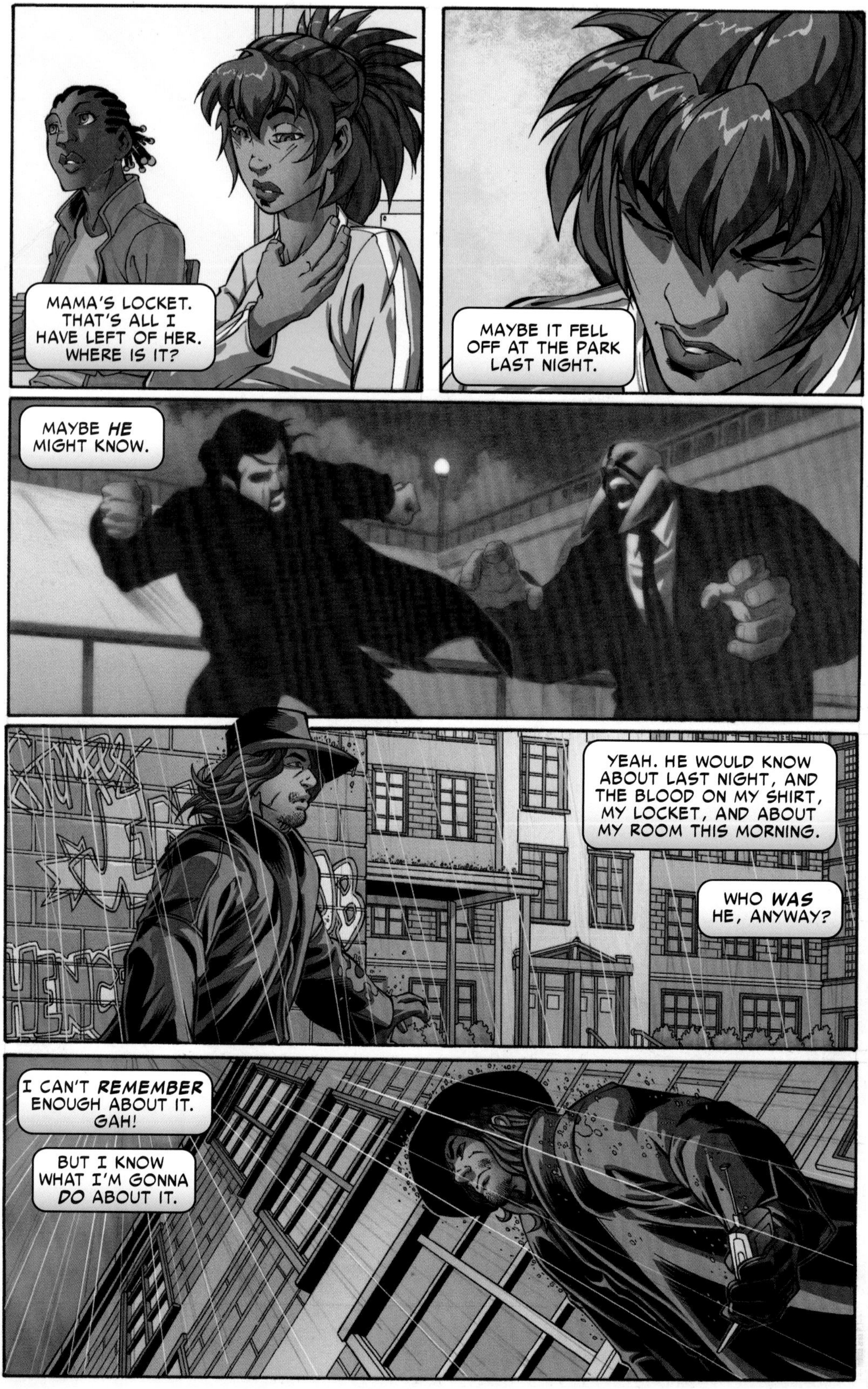
MAMA'S LOCKET. THAT'S ALL I HAVE LEFT OF HER. WHERE IS IT?
MAYBE IT FELL OFF AT THE PARK LAST NIGHT.
MAYBE *HE* MIGHT KNOW.
YEAH. HE WOULD KNOW ABOUT LAST NIGHT, AND THE BLOOD ON MY SHIRT, MY LOCKET, AND ABOUT MY ROOM THIS MORNING.
WHO *WAS* HE, ANYWAY?
I CAN'T *REMEMBER* ENOUGH ABOUT IT. GAH!
BUT I KNOW WHAT I'M GONNA *DO* ABOUT IT.

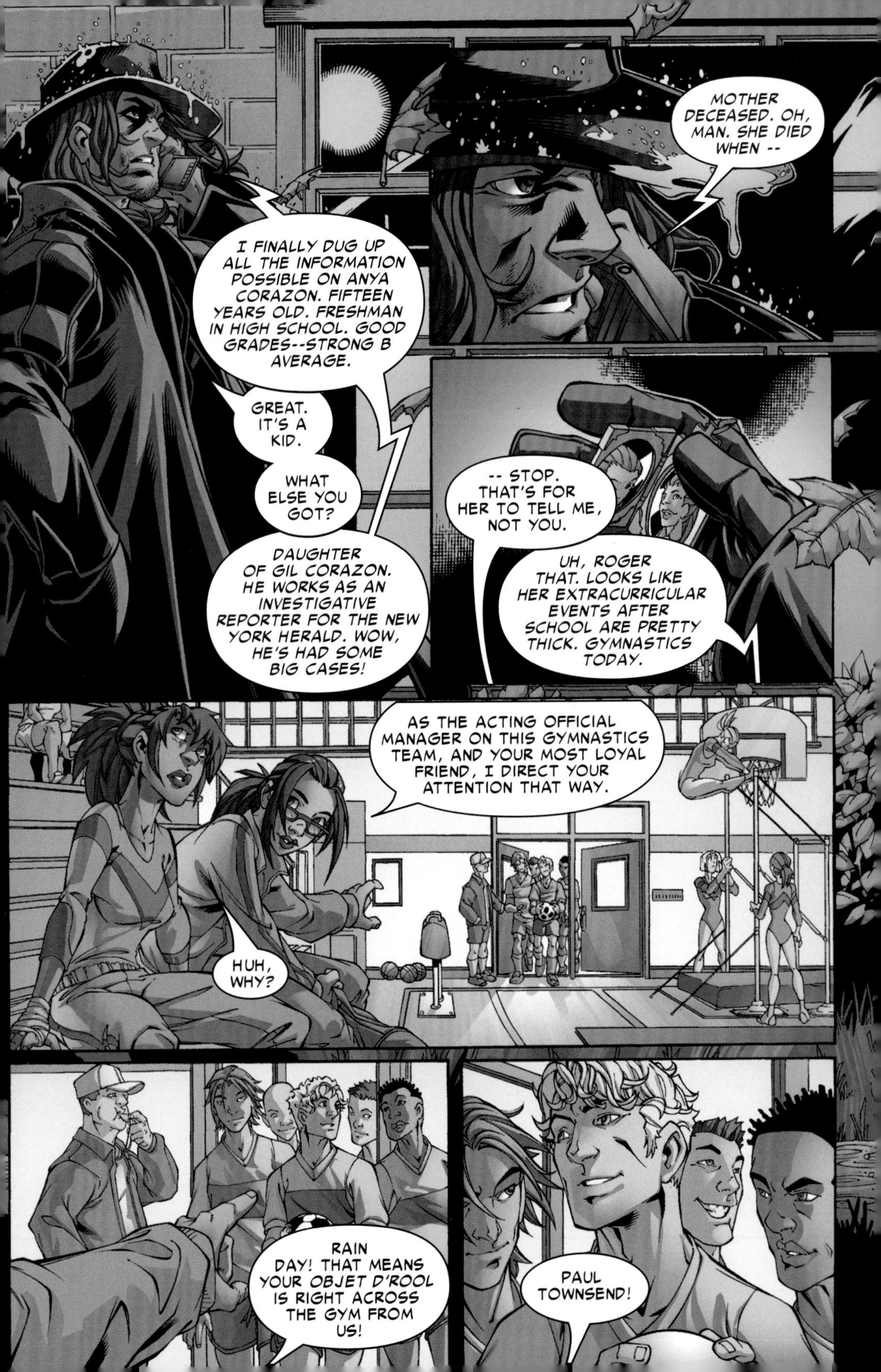
MOTHER DECEASED. OH, MAN. SHE DIED WHEN --
I FINALLY DUG UP ALL THE INFORMATION POSSIBLE ON ANYA CORAZON. FIFTEEN YEARS OLD. FRESHMAN IN HIGH SCHOOL. GOOD GRADES--STRONG B AVERAGE.
GREAT. IT'S A KID.
WHAT ELSE YOU GOT?
DAUGHTER OF GIL CORAZON. HE WORKS AS AN INVESTIGATIVE REPORTER FOR THE NEW YORK HERALD. WOW, HE'S HAD SOME BIG CASES!
-- STOP. THAT'S FOR HER TO TELL ME, NOT YOU.
UH, ROGER THAT. LOOKS LIKE HER EXTRACURRICULAR EVENTS AFTER SCHOOL ARE PRETTY THICK. GYMNASTICS TODAY.
AS THE ACTING OFFICIAL MANAGER ON THIS GYMNASTICS TEAM, AND YOUR MOST LOYAL FRIEND, I DIRECT YOUR ATTENTION THAT WAY.
HUH, WHY?
RAIN DAY! THAT MEANS YOUR OBJET D'ROOL IS RIGHT ACROSS THE GYM FROM US!
PAUL TOWNSEND!

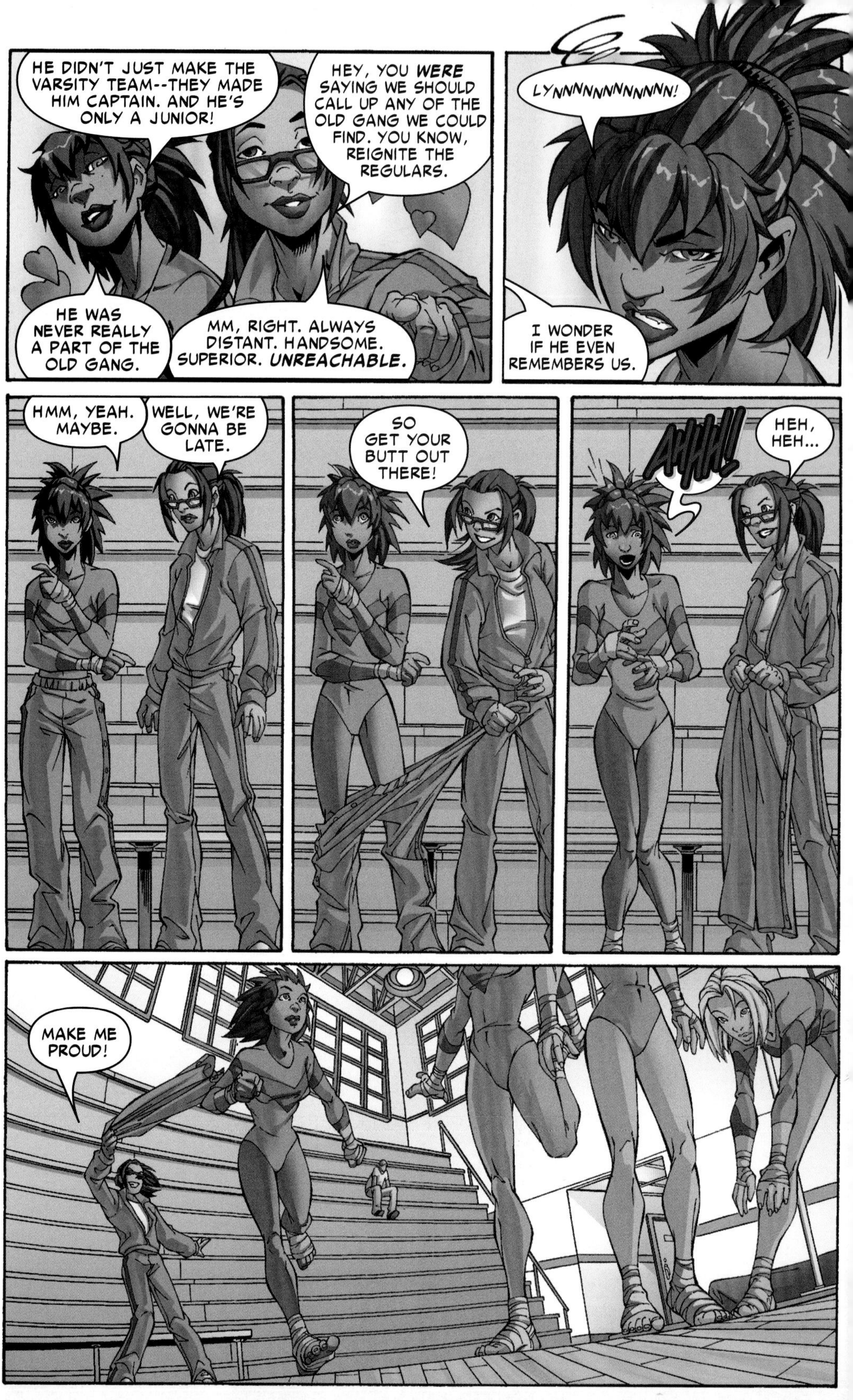
HE DIDN'T JUST MAKE THE VARSITY TEAM--THEY MADE HIM CAPTAIN. AND HE'S ONLY A JUNIOR!
HEY, YOU **WERE** SAYING WE SHOULD CALL UP ANY OF THE OLD GANG WE COULD FIND. YOU KNOW, REIGNITE THE REGULARS.
HE WAS NEVER REALLY A PART OF THE OLD GANG.
MM, RIGHT. ALWAYS DISTANT. HANDSOME. SUPERIOR. ***UNREACHABLE.***
LYNNNNNNNNNNNN!
I WONDER IF HE EVEN REMEMBERS US.
HMM, YEAH. MAYBE.
WELL, WE'RE GONNA BE LATE.
SO GET YOUR BUTT OUT THERE!
AHHH!!
HEH, HEH...
MAKE ME PROUD!

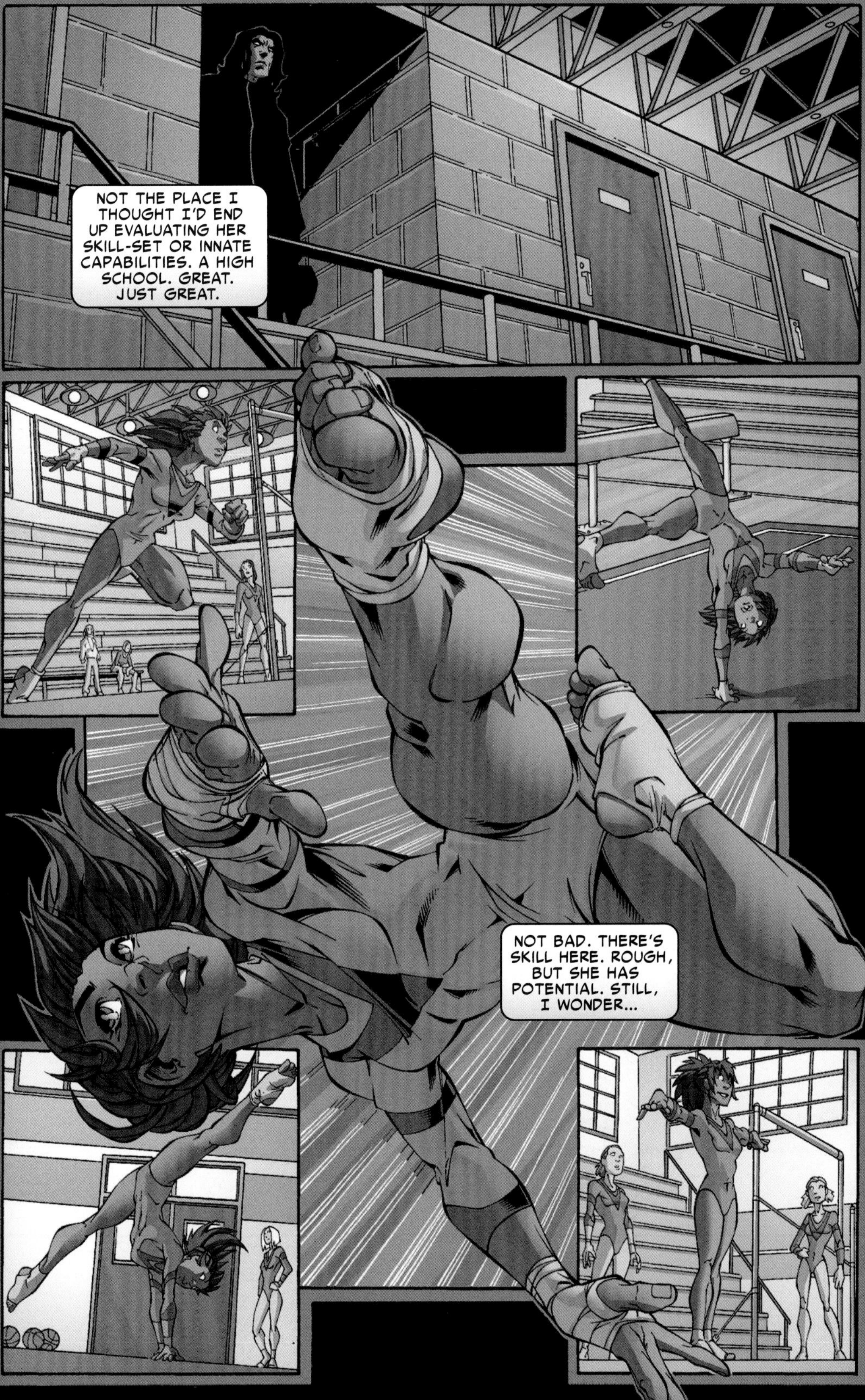
NOT THE PLACE I THOUGHT I'D END UP EVALUATING HER SKILL-SET OR INNATE CAPABILITIES. A HIGH SCHOOL. GREAT. JUST GREAT.
NOT BAD. THERE'S SKILL HERE. ROUGH, BUT SHE HAS POTENTIAL. STILL, I WONDER...

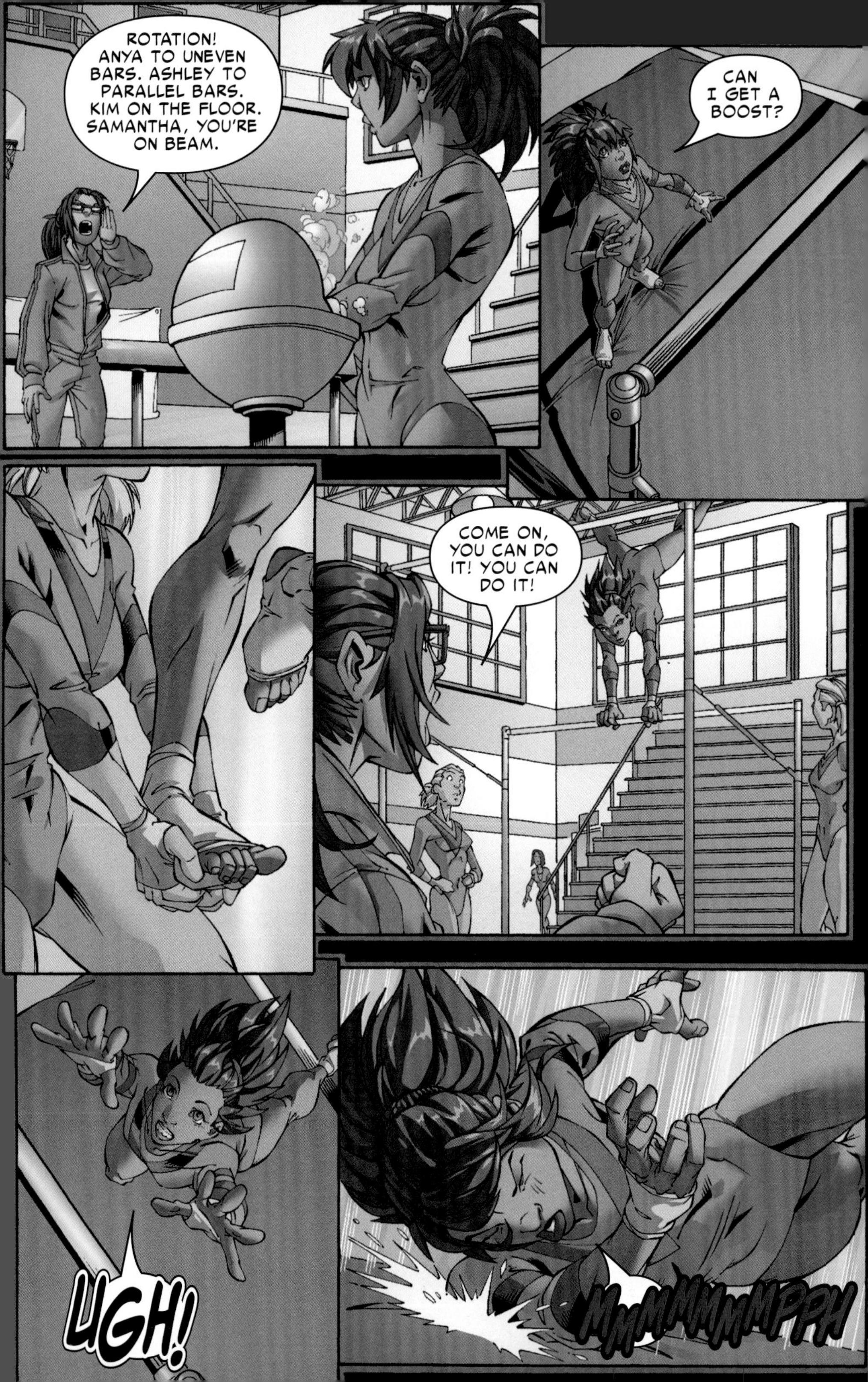
ROTATION! ANYA TO UNEVEN BARS. ASHLEY TO PARALLEL BARS. KIM ON THE FLOOR. SAMANTHA, YOU'RE ON BEAM.
CAN I GET A BOOST?
COME ON, YOU CAN DO IT! YOU CAN DO IT!
UGH!
MMMMMMMMPPH

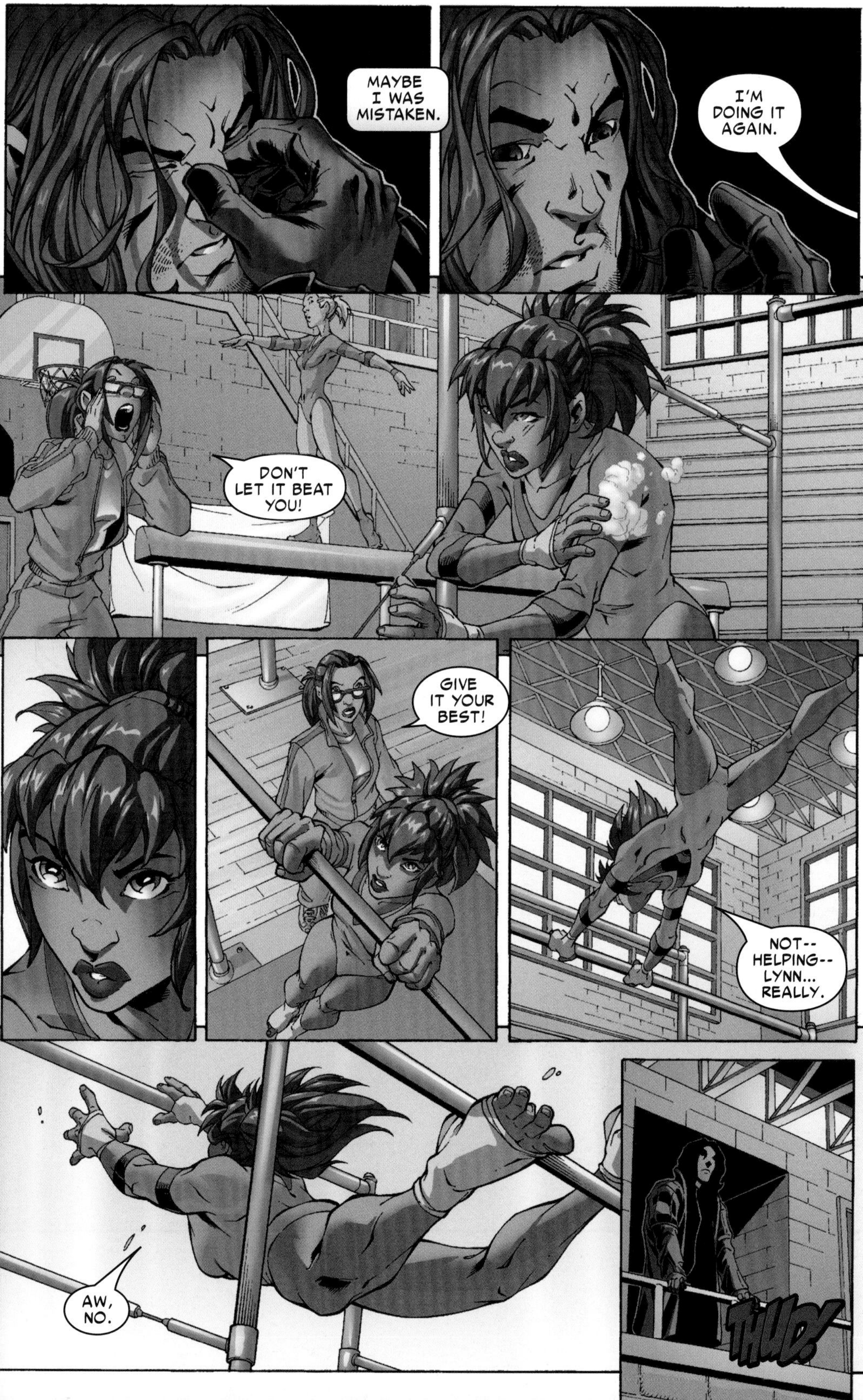
MAYBE I WAS MISTAKEN.
I'M DOING IT AGAIN.
DON'T LET IT BEAT YOU!
GIVE IT YOUR BEST!
NOT-- HELPING-- LYNN... REALLY.
AW, NO.
THUD!

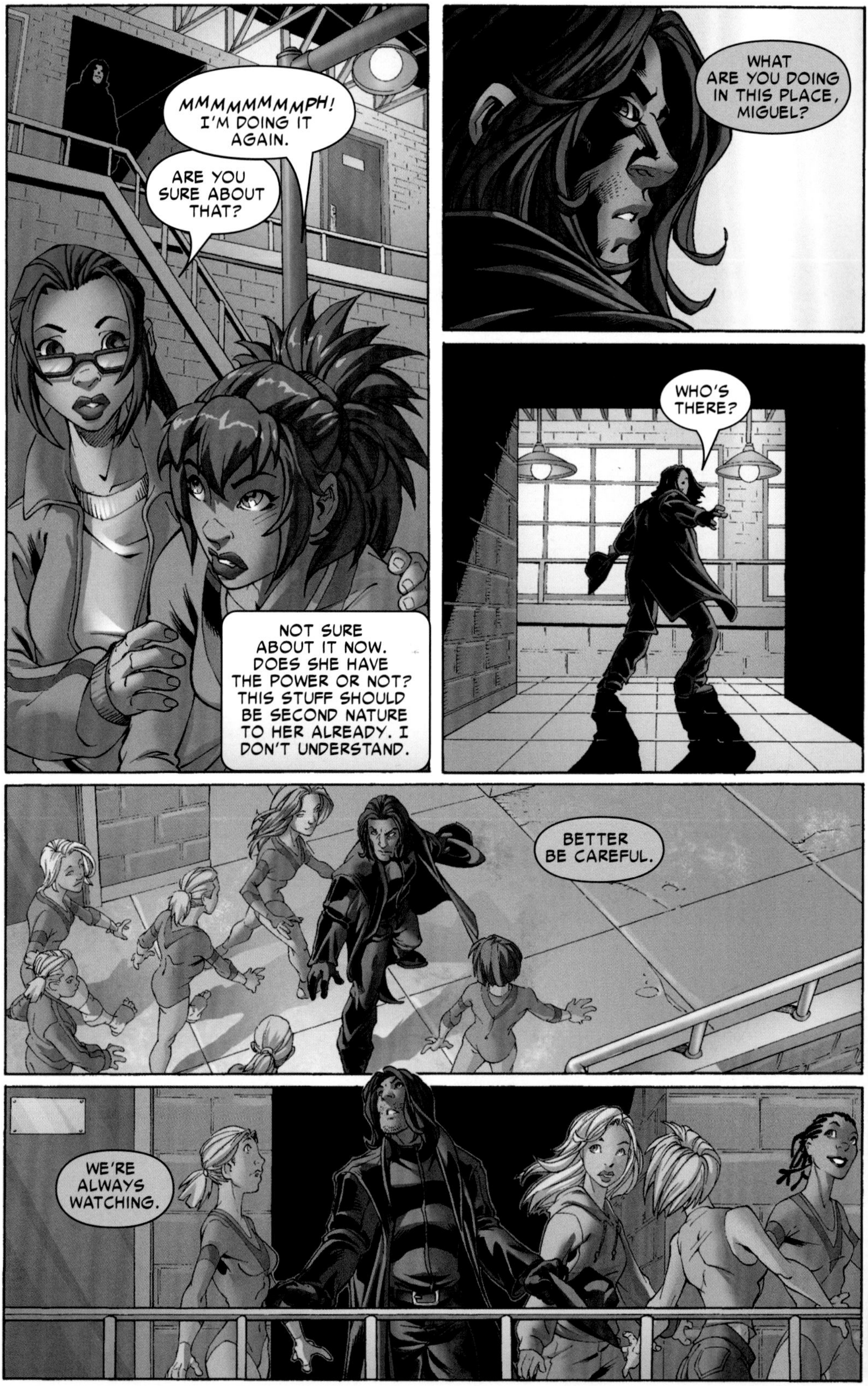
MMMMMMMMPH! I'M DOING IT AGAIN.
ARE YOU SURE ABOUT THAT?
NOT SURE ABOUT IT NOW. DOES SHE HAVE THE POWER OR NOT? THIS STUFF SHOULD BE SECOND NATURE TO HER ALREADY. I DON'T UNDERSTAND.
WHAT ARE YOU DOING IN THIS PLACE, MIGUEL?
WHO'S THERE?
BETTER BE CAREFUL.
WE'RE ALWAYS WATCHING.

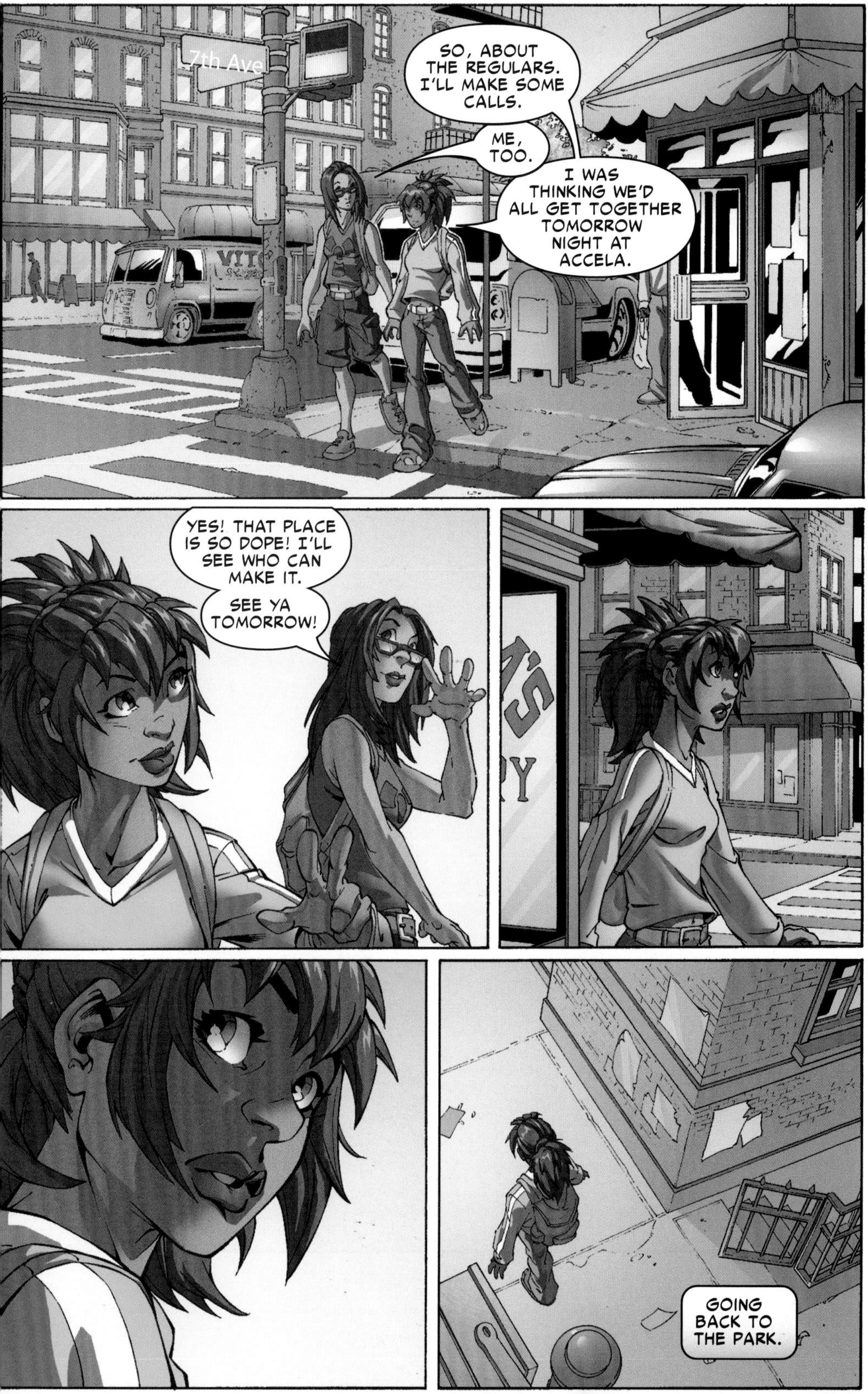
7th Ave
SO, ABOUT THE REGULARS. I'LL MAKE SOME CALLS.
ME, TOO.
I WAS THINKING WE'D ALL GET TOGETHER TOMORROW NIGHT AT ACCELA.
YES! THAT PLACE IS SO DOPE! I'LL SEE WHO CAN MAKE IT.
SEE YA TOMORROW!
GOING BACK TO THE PARK.

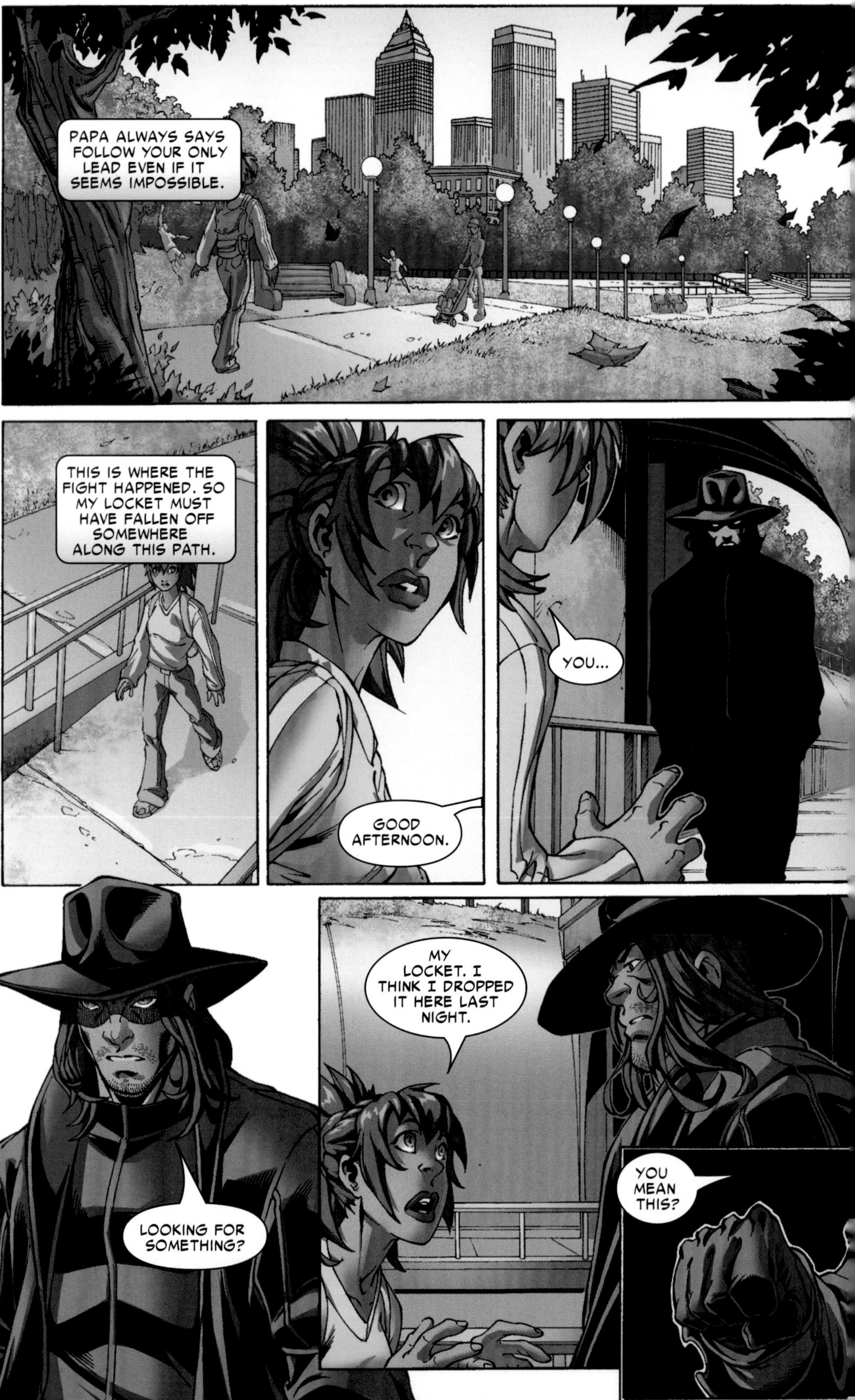
PAPA ALWAYS SAYS FOLLOW YOUR ONLY LEAD EVEN IF IT SEEMS IMPOSSIBLE.
THIS IS WHERE THE FIGHT HAPPENED. SO MY LOCKET MUST HAVE FALLEN OFF SOMEWHERE ALONG THIS PATH.
GOOD AFTERNOON.
YOU...
LOOKING FOR SOMETHING?
MY LOCKET. I THINK I DROPPED IT HERE LAST NIGHT.
YOU MEAN THIS?

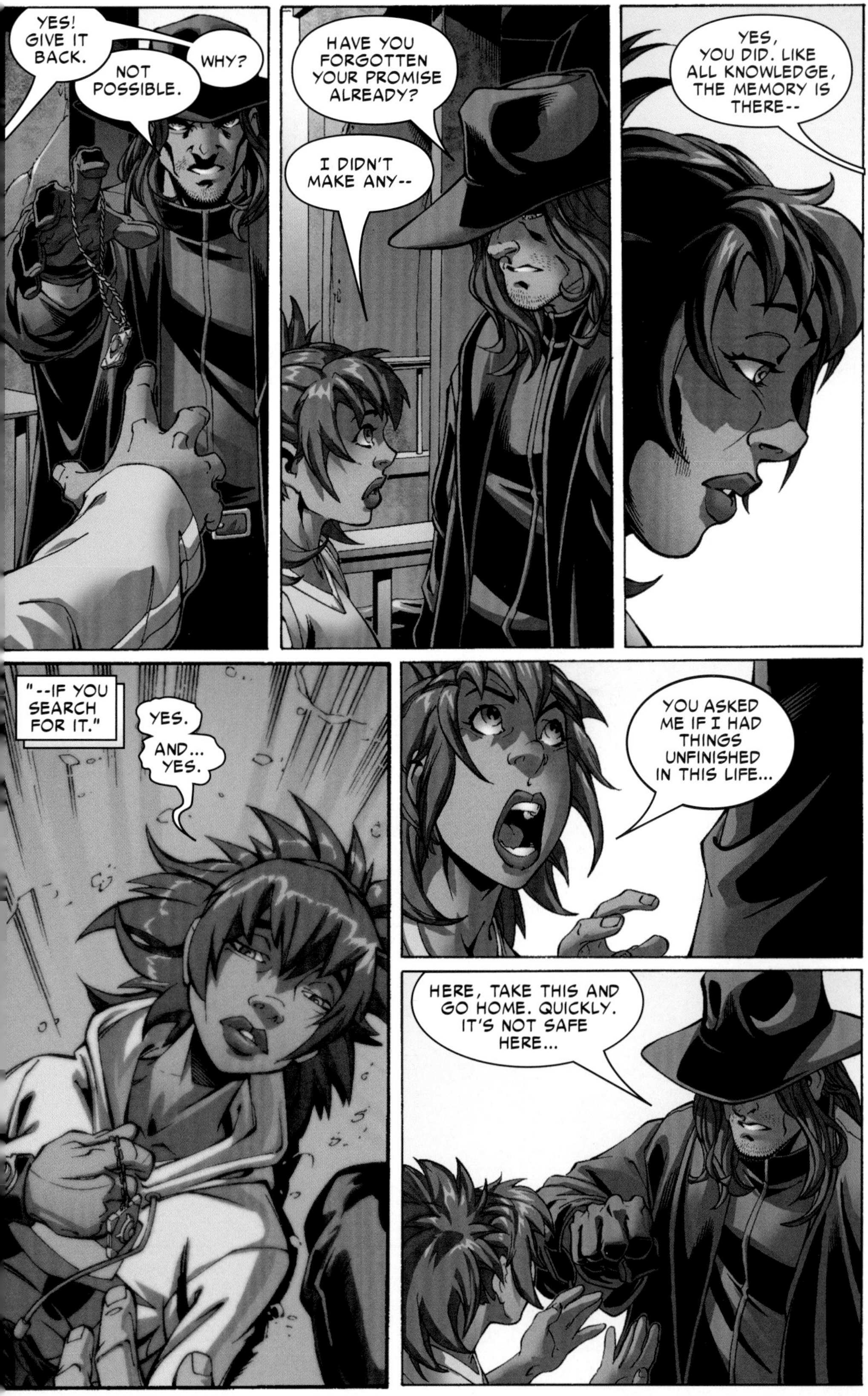
YES! GIVE IT BACK.
NOT POSSIBLE.
WHY?
HAVE YOU FORGOTTEN YOUR PROMISE ALREADY?
I DIDN'T MAKE ANY--
YES, YOU DID. LIKE ALL KNOWLEDGE, THE MEMORY IS THERE--
"--IF YOU SEARCH FOR IT."
YES.
AND... YES.
YOU ASKED ME IF I HAD THINGS UNFINISHED IN THIS LIFE...
HERE, TAKE THIS AND GO HOME. QUICKLY. IT'S NOT SAFE HERE...

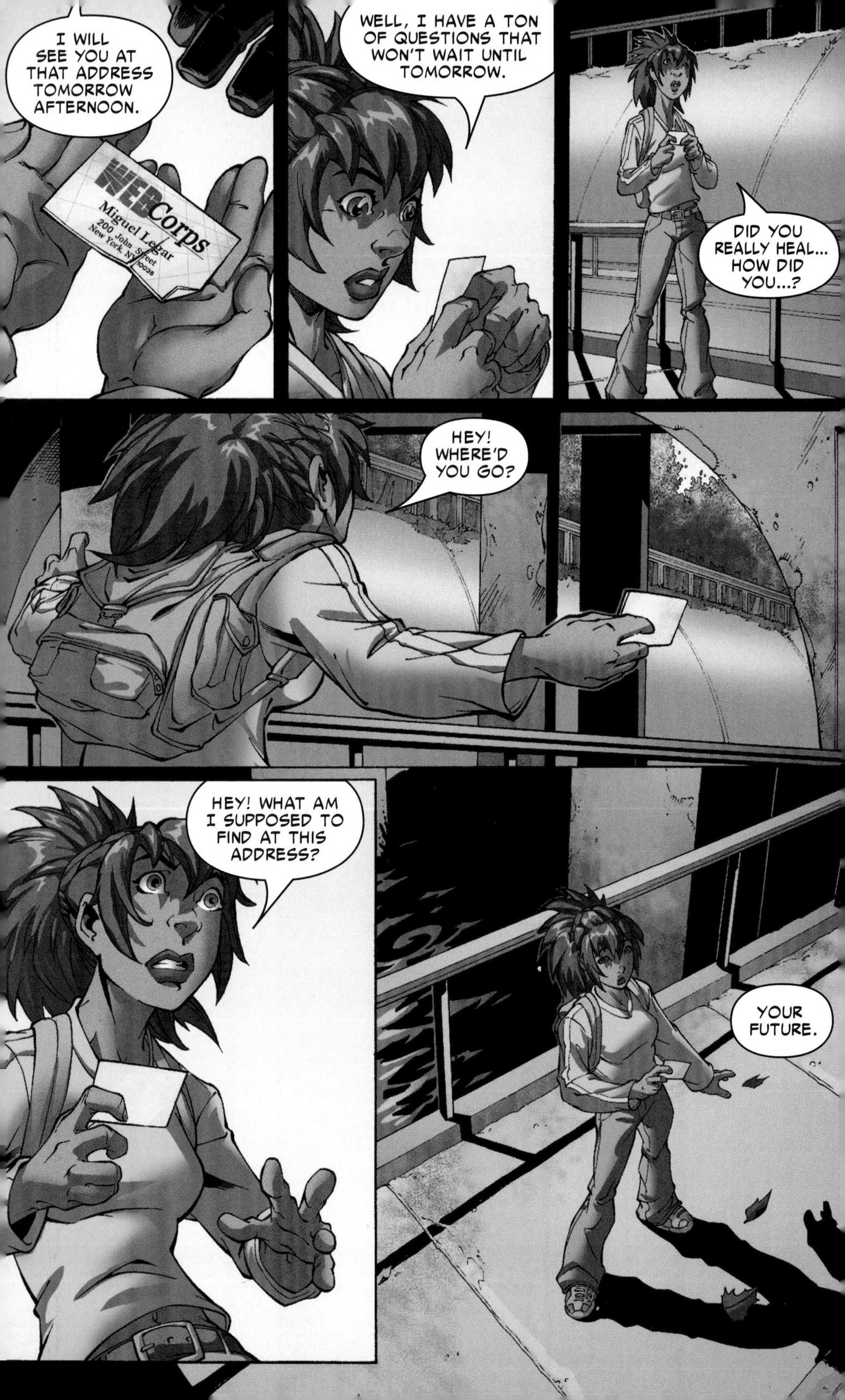
I WILL SEE YOU AT THAT ADDRESS TOMORROW AFTERNOON.
WEB Corps
Miguel Legar
200 John Street
WELL, I HAVE A TON OF QUESTIONS THAT WON'T WAIT UNTIL TOMORROW.
DID YOU REALLY HEAL... HOW DID YOU...?
HEY! WHERE'D YOU GO?
HEY! WHAT AM I SUPPOSED TO FIND AT THIS ADDRESS?
YOUR FUTURE.

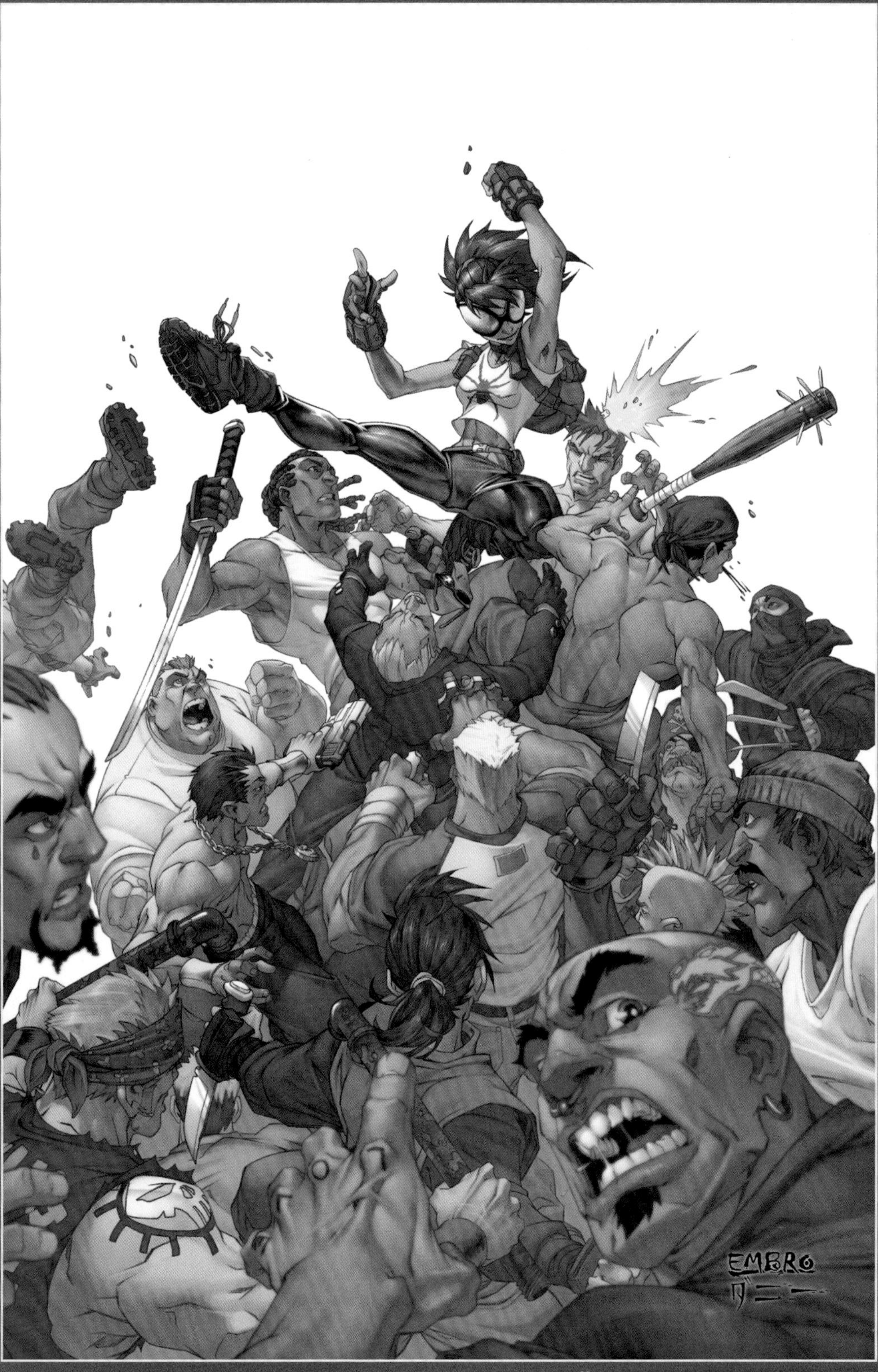
EMBRO

AMAZING FANTASY #3

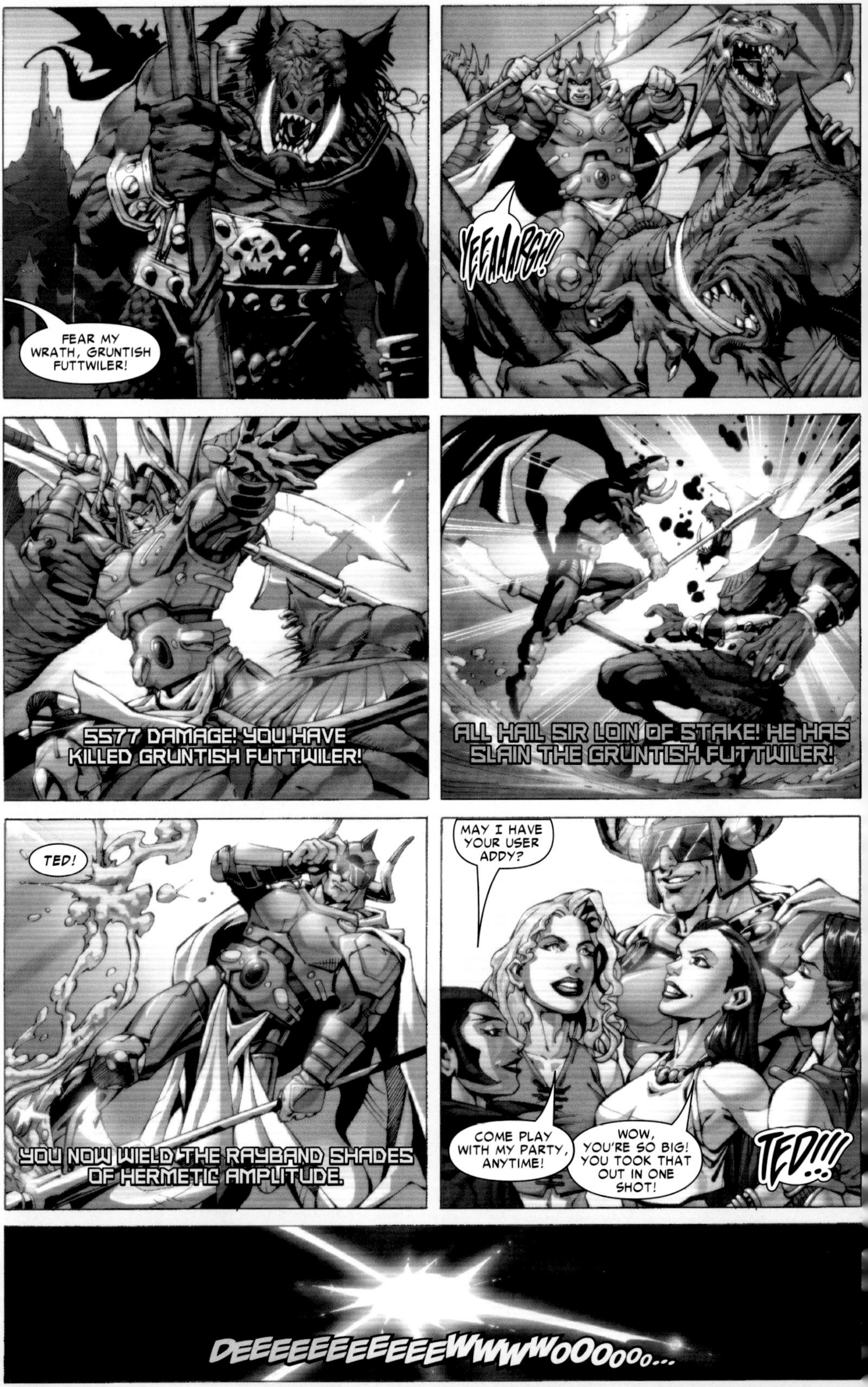
FEAR MY WRATH, GRUNTISH FUTTWILER!
YEEAAARGH!
5577 DAMAGE! YOU HAVE KILLED GRUNTISH FUTTWILER!
ALL HAIL SIR LOIN OF STAKE! HE HAS SLAIN THE GRUNTISH FUTTWILER!
TED!
YOU NOW WIELD THE RAYBAND SHADES OF HERMETIC AMPLITUDE.
MAY I HAVE YOUR USER ADDY?
COME PLAY WITH MY PARTY, ANYTIME!
WOW, YOU'RE SO BIG! YOU TOOK THAT OUT IN ONE SHOT!
TED!!!
DEEEEEEEEEEEEWWWWOOOOoo...

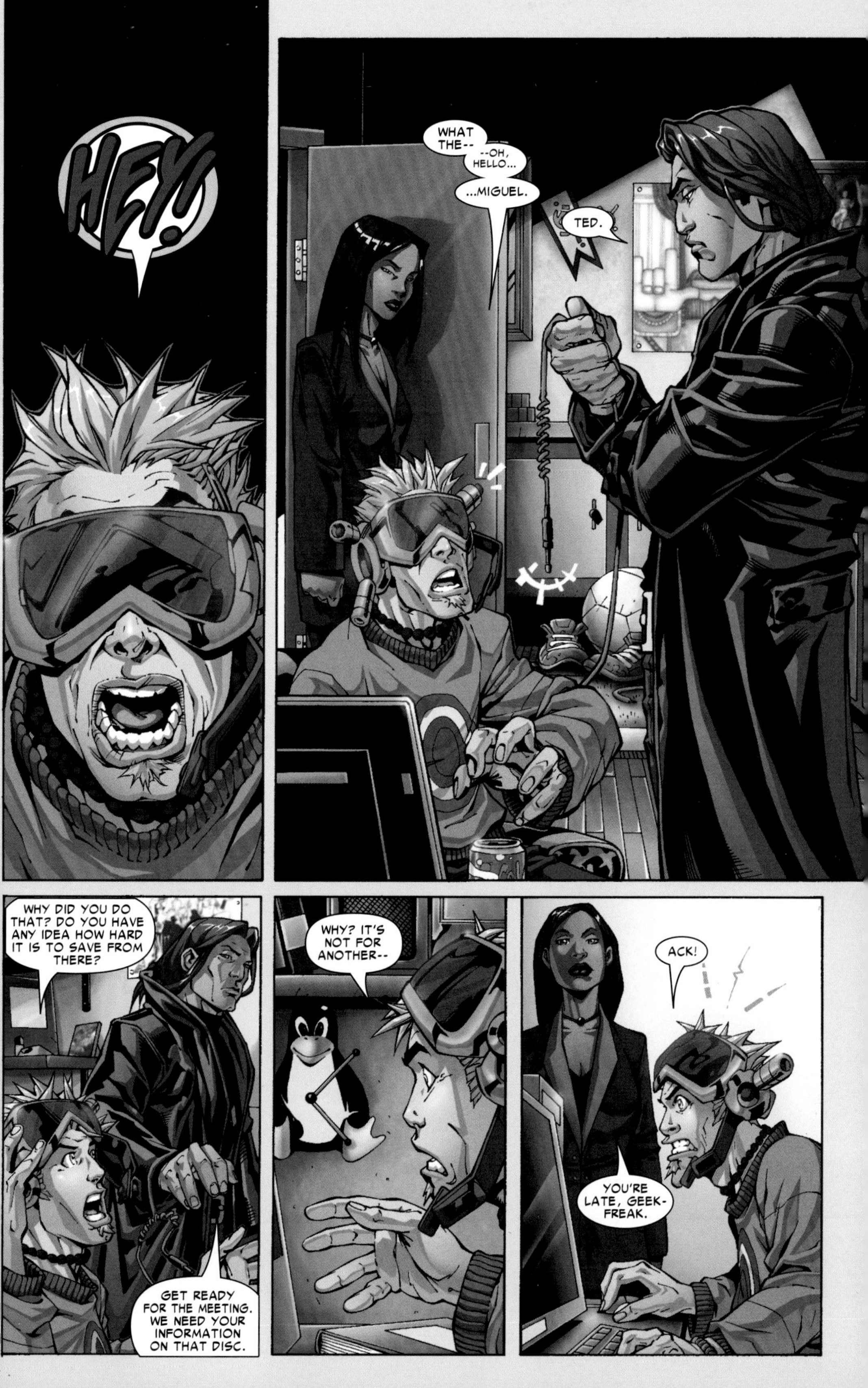
HEY!!
WHAT THE--
--OH, HELLO...
...MIGUEL.
TED.
WHY DID YOU DO THAT? DO YOU HAVE ANY IDEA HOW HARD IT IS TO SAVE FROM THERE?
GET READY FOR THE MEETING. WE NEED YOUR INFORMATION ON THAT DISC.
WHY? IT'S NOT FOR ANOTHER--
ACK!
YOU'RE LATE, GEEK-FREAK.

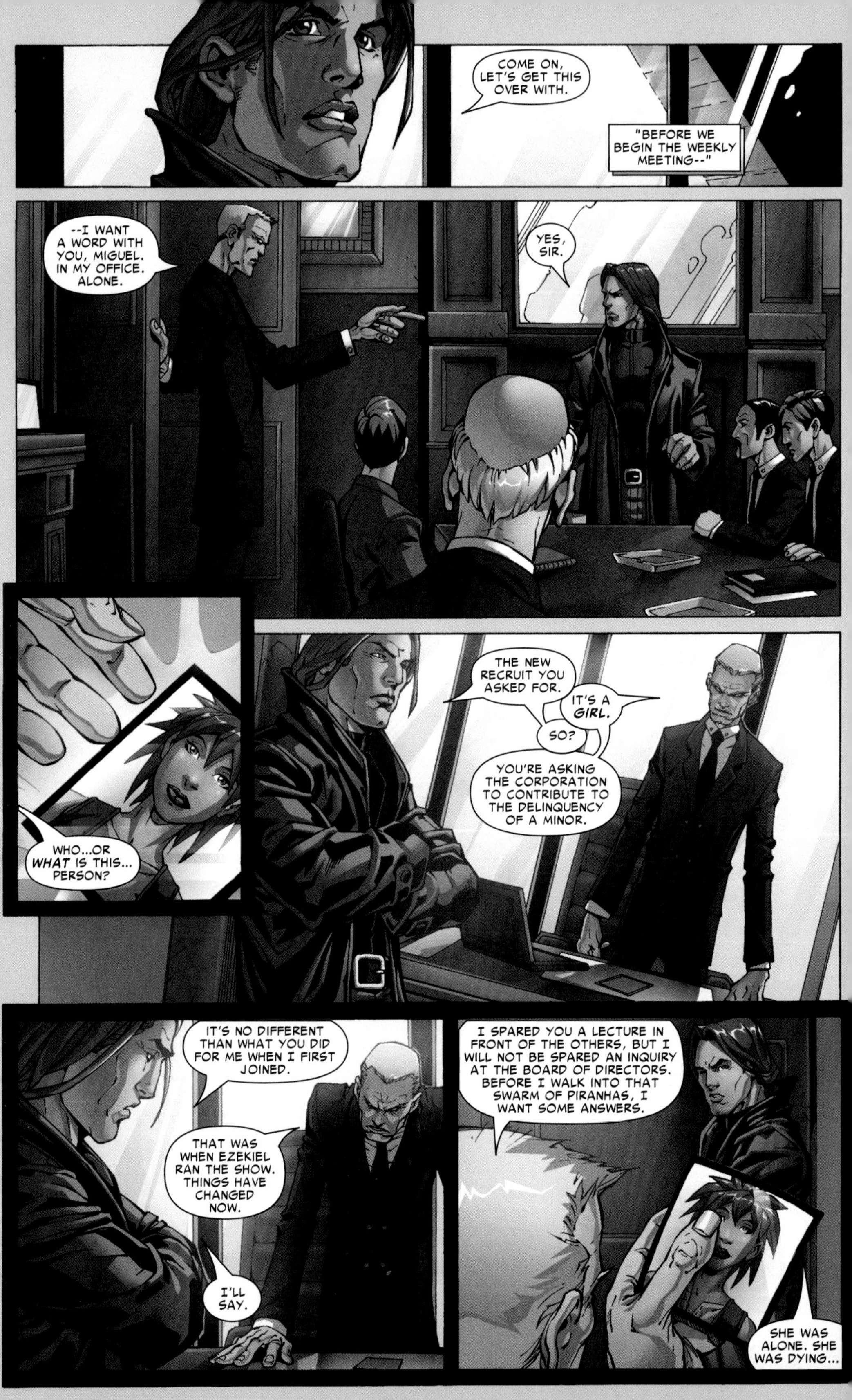
COME ON, LET'S GET THIS OVER WITH.
"BEFORE WE BEGIN THE WEEKLY MEETING--"
--I WANT A WORD WITH YOU, MIGUEL. IN MY OFFICE. ALONE.
YES, SIR.
WHO...OR WHAT IS THIS... PERSON?
THE NEW RECRUIT YOU ASKED FOR.
IT'S A GIRL.
SO?
YOU'RE ASKING THE CORPORATION TO CONTRIBUTE TO THE DELINQUENCY OF A MINOR.
IT'S NO DIFFERENT THAN WHAT YOU DID FOR ME WHEN I FIRST JOINED.
THAT WAS WHEN EZEKIEL RAN THE SHOW. THINGS HAVE CHANGED NOW.
I'LL SAY.
I SPARED YOU A LECTURE IN FRONT OF THE OTHERS, BUT I WILL NOT BE SPARED AN INQUIRY AT THE BOARD OF DIRECTORS. BEFORE I WALK INTO THAT SWARM OF PIRANHAS, I WANT SOME ANSWERS.
SHE WAS ALONE. SHE WAS DYING...

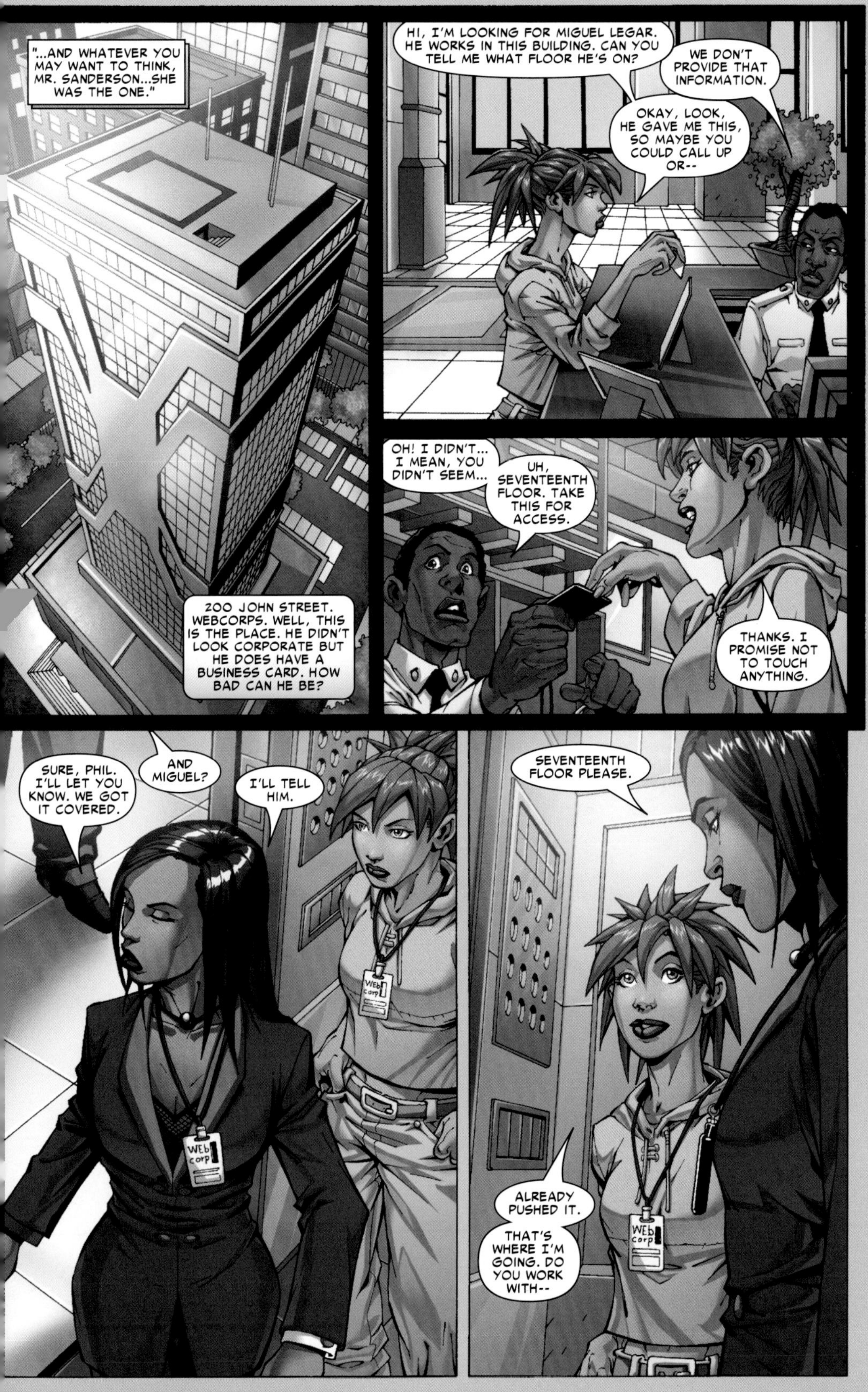
"...AND WHATEVER YOU MAY WANT TO THINK, MR. SANDERSON...SHE WAS THE ONE."
200 JOHN STREET. WEBCORPS. WELL, THIS IS THE PLACE. HE DIDN'T LOOK CORPORATE BUT HE DOES HAVE A BUSINESS CARD. HOW BAD CAN HE BE?
HI, I'M LOOKING FOR MIGUEL LEGAR. HE WORKS IN THIS BUILDING. CAN YOU TELL ME WHAT FLOOR HE'S ON?
WE DON'T PROVIDE THAT INFORMATION.
OKAY, LOOK, HE GAVE ME THIS, SO MAYBE YOU COULD CALL UP OR--
OH! I DIDN'T... I MEAN, YOU DIDN'T SEEM...
UH, SEVENTEENTH FLOOR. TAKE THIS FOR ACCESS.
THANKS. I PROMISE NOT TO TOUCH ANYTHING.
SURE, PHIL. I'LL LET YOU KNOW. WE GOT IT COVERED.
AND MIGUEL?
I'LL TELL HIM.
SEVENTEENTH FLOOR PLEASE.
ALREADY PUSHED IT.
THAT'S WHERE I'M GOING. DO YOU WORK WITH--

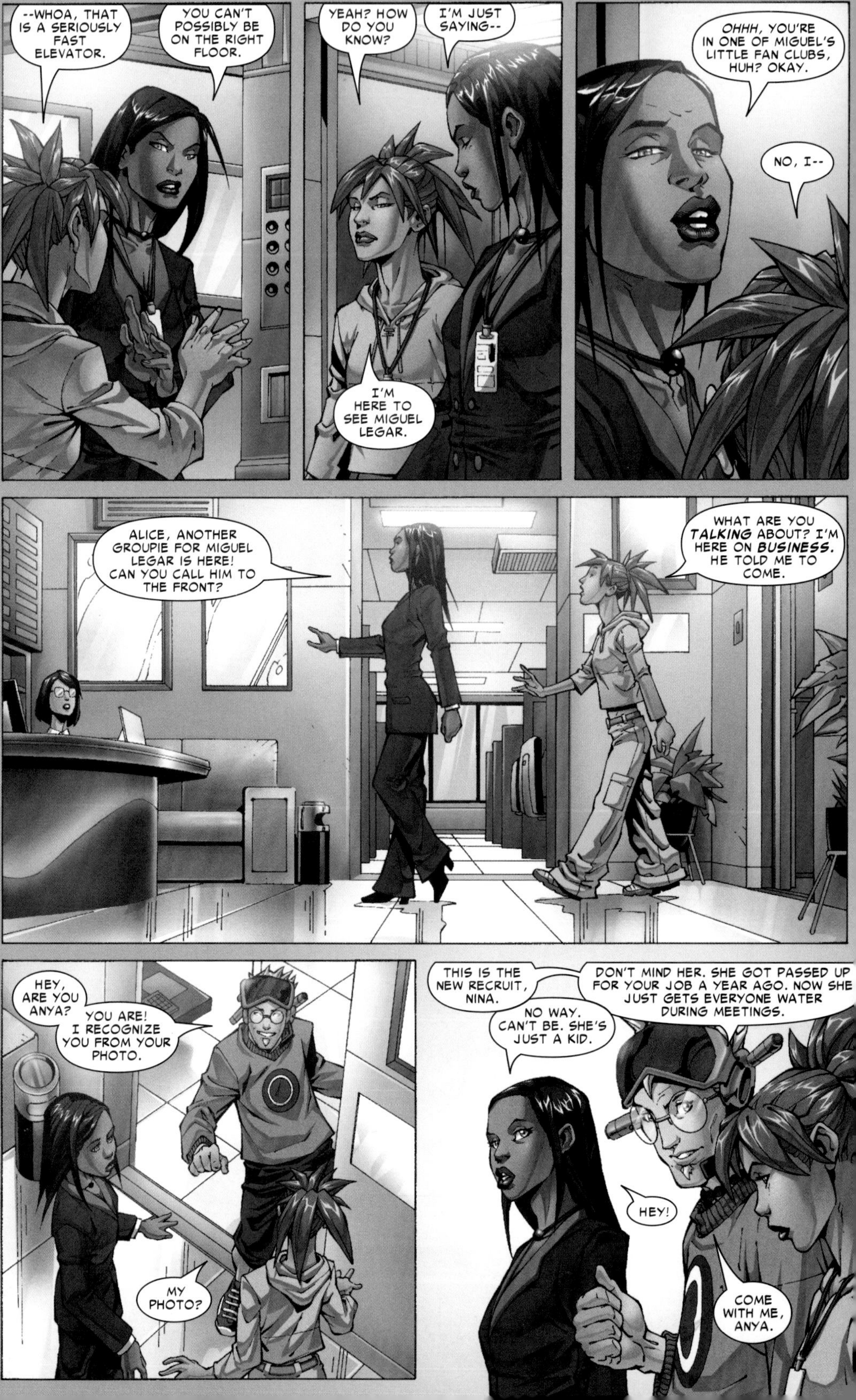
--WHOA, THAT IS A SERIOUSLY FAST ELEVATOR.
YOU CAN'T POSSIBLY BE ON THE RIGHT FLOOR.
YEAH? HOW DO YOU KNOW?
I'M JUST SAYING--
I'M HERE TO SEE MIGUEL LEGAR.
OHHH, YOU'RE IN ONE OF MIGUEL'S LITTLE FAN CLUBS, HUH? OKAY.
NO, I--
ALICE, ANOTHER GROUPIE FOR MIGUEL LEGAR IS HERE! CAN YOU CALL HIM TO THE FRONT?
WHAT ARE YOU TALKING ABOUT? I'M HERE ON BUSINESS. HE TOLD ME TO COME.
HEY, ARE YOU ANYA?
YOU ARE! I RECOGNIZE YOU FROM YOUR PHOTO.
MY PHOTO?
THIS IS THE NEW RECRUIT, NINA.
DON'T MIND HER. SHE GOT PASSED UP FOR YOUR JOB A YEAR AGO. NOW SHE JUST GETS EVERYONE WATER DURING MEETINGS.
NO WAY. CAN'T BE. SHE'S JUST A KID.
HEY!
COME WITH ME, ANYA.

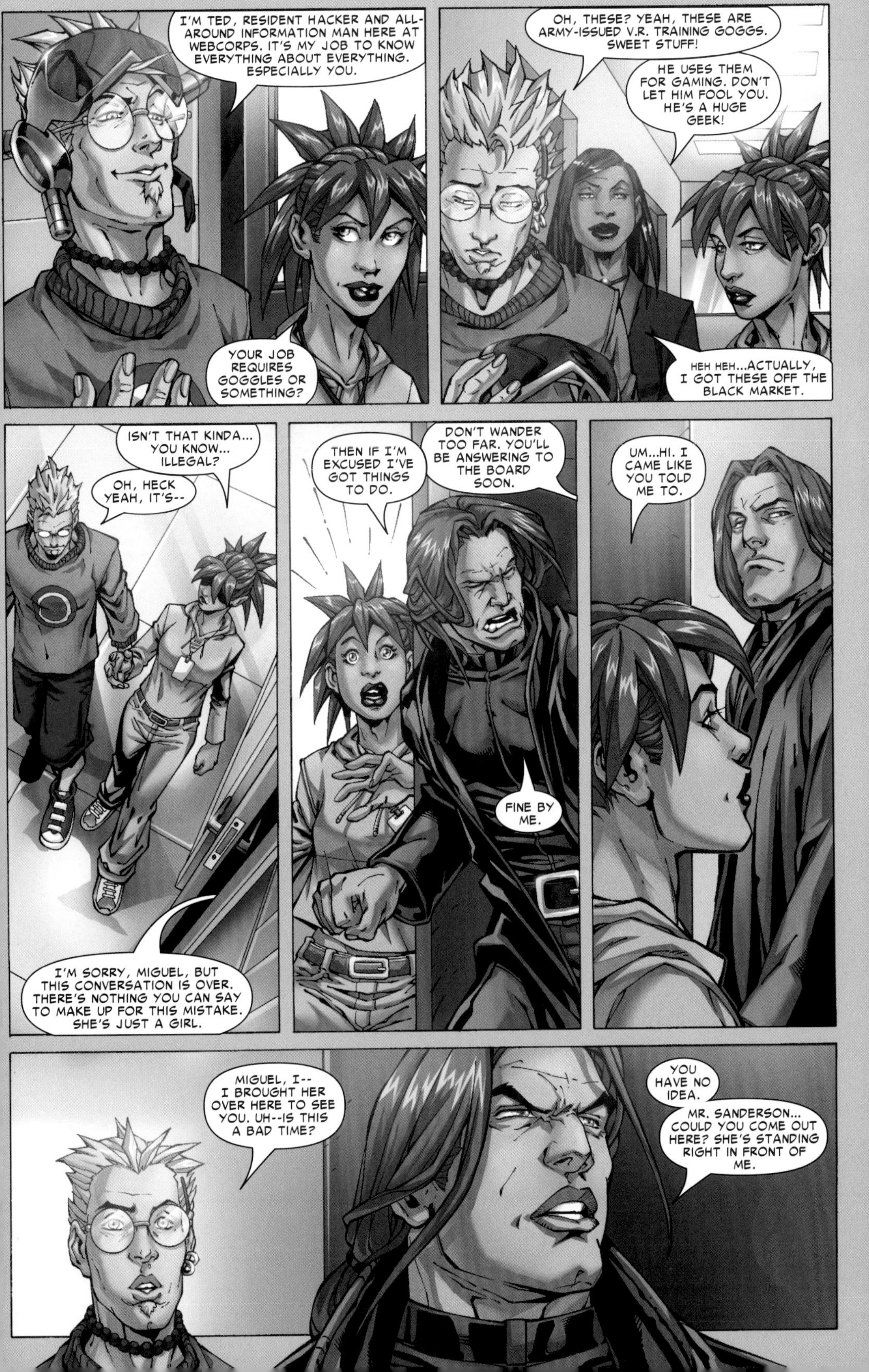

I'M TED, RESIDENT HACKER AND ALL-AROUND INFORMATION MAN HERE AT WEBCORPS. IT'S MY JOB TO KNOW EVERYTHING ABOUT EVERYTHING. ESPECIALLY YOU.
YOUR JOB REQUIRES GOGGLES OR SOMETHING?
OH, THESE? YEAH, THESE ARE ARMY-ISSUED V.R. TRAINING GOGGS. SWEET STUFF!
HE USES THEM FOR GAMING. DON'T LET HIM FOOL YOU. HE'S A HUGE GEEK!
HEH HEH...ACTUALLY, I GOT THESE OFF THE BLACK MARKET.
ISN'T THAT KINDA... YOU KNOW... ILLEGAL?
OH, HECK YEAH, IT'S--
I'M SORRY, MIGUEL, BUT THIS CONVERSATION IS OVER. THERE'S NOTHING YOU CAN SAY TO MAKE UP FOR THIS MISTAKE. SHE'S JUST A GIRL.
THEN IF I'M EXCUSED I'VE GOT THINGS TO DO.
DON'T WANDER TOO FAR. YOU'LL BE ANSWERING TO THE BOARD SOON.
FINE BY ME.
UM...HI. I CAME LIKE YOU TOLD ME TO.
MIGUEL, I-- I BROUGHT HER OVER HERE TO SEE YOU. UH--IS THIS A BAD TIME?
YOU HAVE NO IDEA.
MR. SANDERSON... COULD YOU COME OUT HERE? SHE'S STANDING RIGHT IN FRONT OF ME.

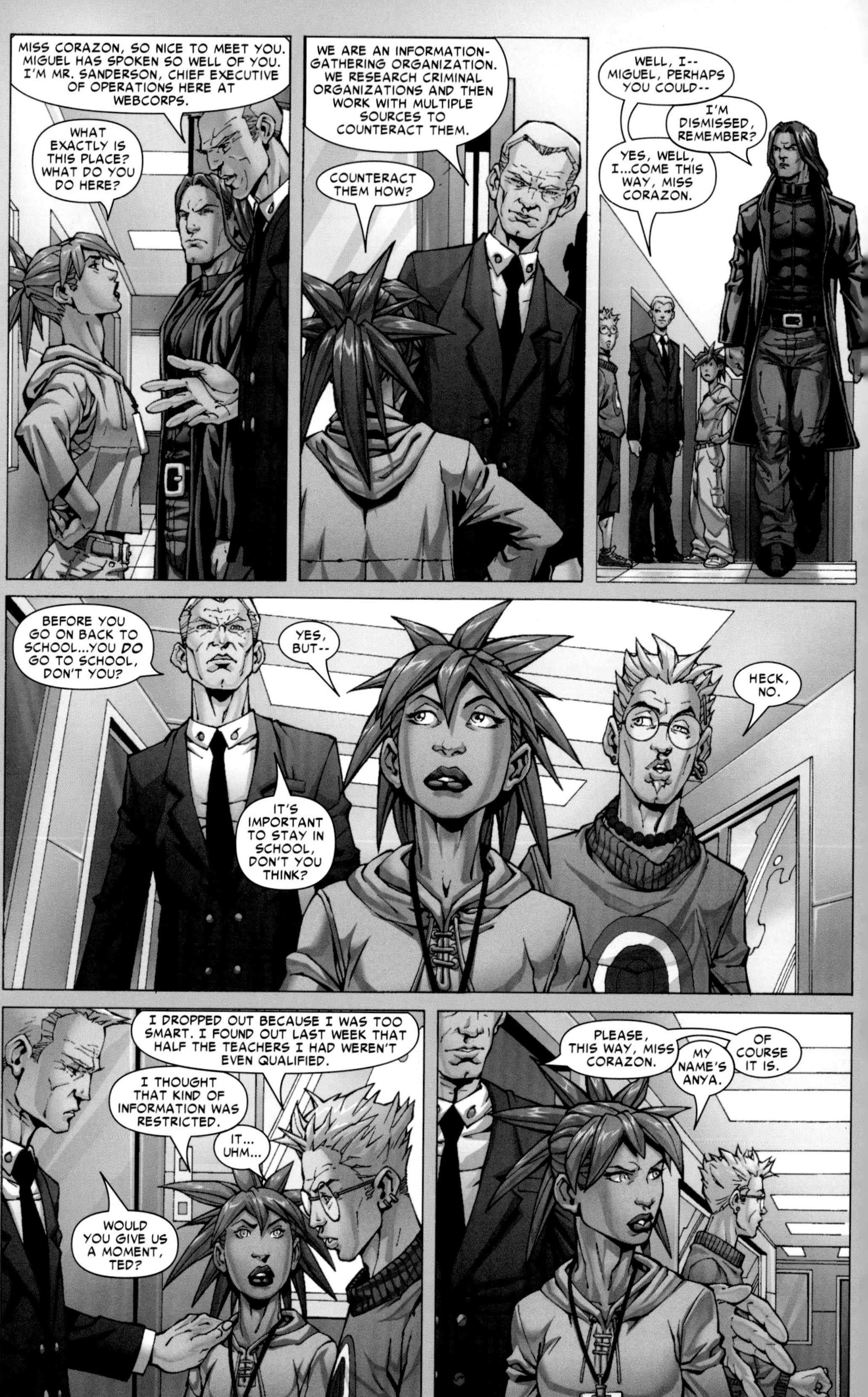
MISS CORAZON, SO NICE TO MEET YOU. MIGUEL HAS SPOKEN SO WELL OF YOU. I'M MR. SANDERSON, CHIEF EXECUTIVE OF OPERATIONS HERE AT WEBCORPS.
WHAT EXACTLY IS THIS PLACE? WHAT DO YOU DO HERE?
WE ARE AN INFORMATION-GATHERING ORGANIZATION. WE RESEARCH CRIMINAL ORGANIZATIONS AND THEN WORK WITH MULTIPLE SOURCES TO COUNTERACT THEM.
COUNTERACT THEM HOW?
WELL, I-- MIGUEL, PERHAPS YOU COULD--
I'M DISMISSED, REMEMBER?
YES, WELL, I...COME THIS WAY, MISS CORAZON.
BEFORE YOU GO ON BACK TO SCHOOL...YOU DO GO TO SCHOOL, DON'T YOU?
YES, BUT--
HECK, NO.
IT'S IMPORTANT TO STAY IN SCHOOL, DON'T YOU THINK?
I DROPPED OUT BECAUSE I WAS TOO SMART. I FOUND OUT LAST WEEK THAT HALF THE TEACHERS I HAD WEREN'T EVEN QUALIFIED.
I THOUGHT THAT KIND OF INFORMATION WAS RESTRICTED.
IT... UHM...
WOULD YOU GIVE US A MOMENT, TED?
PLEASE, THIS WAY, MISS CORAZON.
MY NAME'S ANYA.
OF COURSE IT IS.

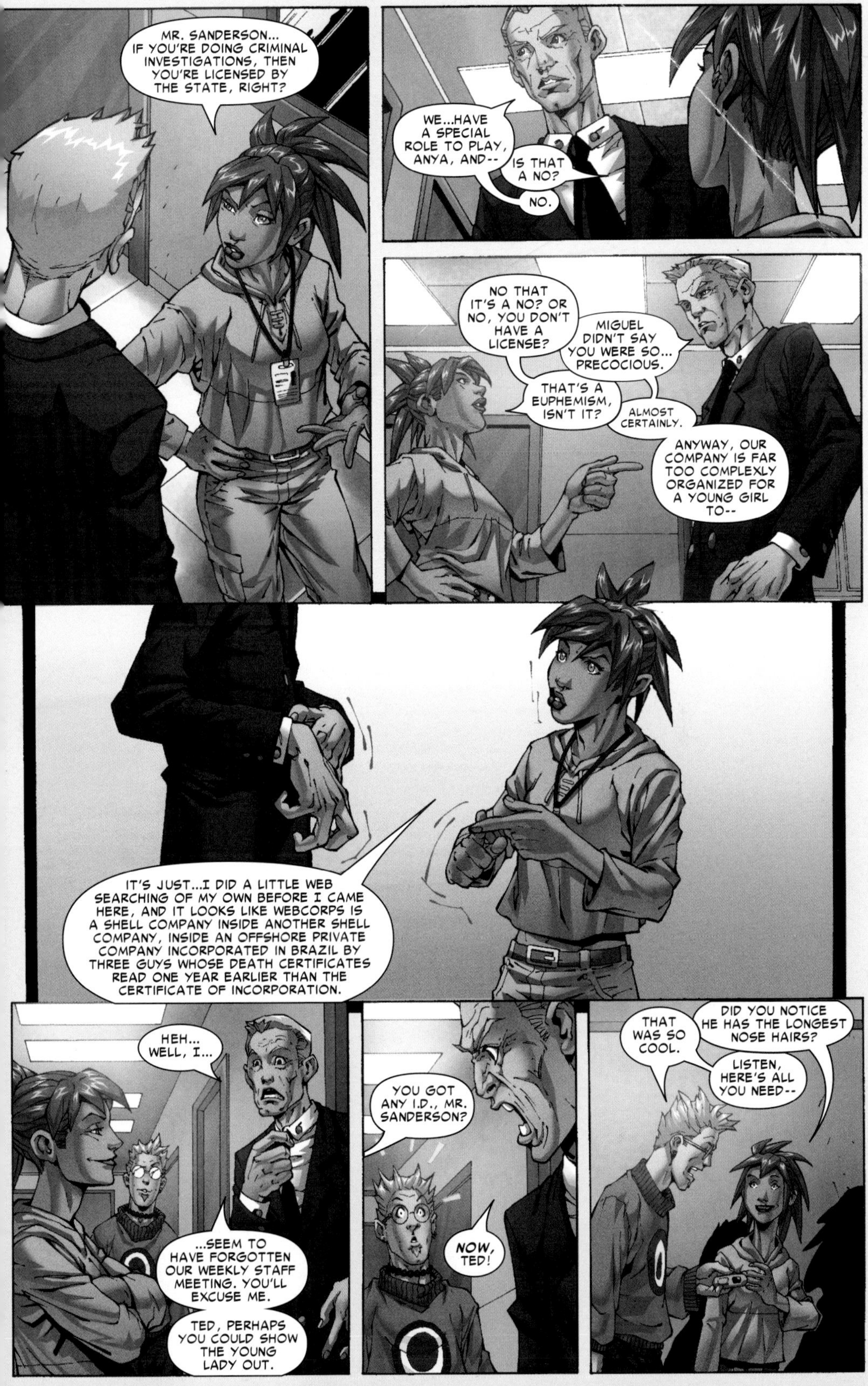
MR. SANDERSON... IF YOU'RE DOING CRIMINAL INVESTIGATIONS, THEN YOU'RE LICENSED BY THE STATE, RIGHT?
WE...HAVE A SPECIAL ROLE TO PLAY, ANYA, AND--
IS THAT A NO?
NO.
NO THAT IT'S A NO? OR NO, YOU DON'T HAVE A LICENSE?
MIGUEL DIDN'T SAY YOU WERE SO... PRECOCIOUS.
THAT'S A EUPHEMISM, ISN'T IT?
ALMOST CERTAINLY.
ANYWAY, OUR COMPANY IS FAR TOO COMPLEXLY ORGANIZED FOR A YOUNG GIRL TO--
IT'S JUST...I DID A LITTLE WEB SEARCHING OF MY OWN BEFORE I CAME HERE, AND IT LOOKS LIKE WEBCORPS IS A SHELL COMPANY INSIDE ANOTHER SHELL COMPANY, INSIDE AN OFFSHORE PRIVATE COMPANY INCORPORATED IN BRAZIL BY THREE GUYS WHOSE DEATH CERTIFICATES READ ONE YEAR EARLIER THAN THE CERTIFICATE OF INCORPORATION.
HEH... WELL, I...
...SEEM TO HAVE FORGOTTEN OUR WEEKLY STAFF MEETING. YOU'LL EXCUSE ME.
TED, PERHAPS YOU COULD SHOW THE YOUNG LADY OUT.
YOU GOT ANY I.D., MR. SANDERSON?
NOW, TED!
THAT WAS SO COOL.
DID YOU NOTICE HE HAS THE LONGEST NOSE HAIRS?
LISTEN, HERE'S ALL YOU NEED--

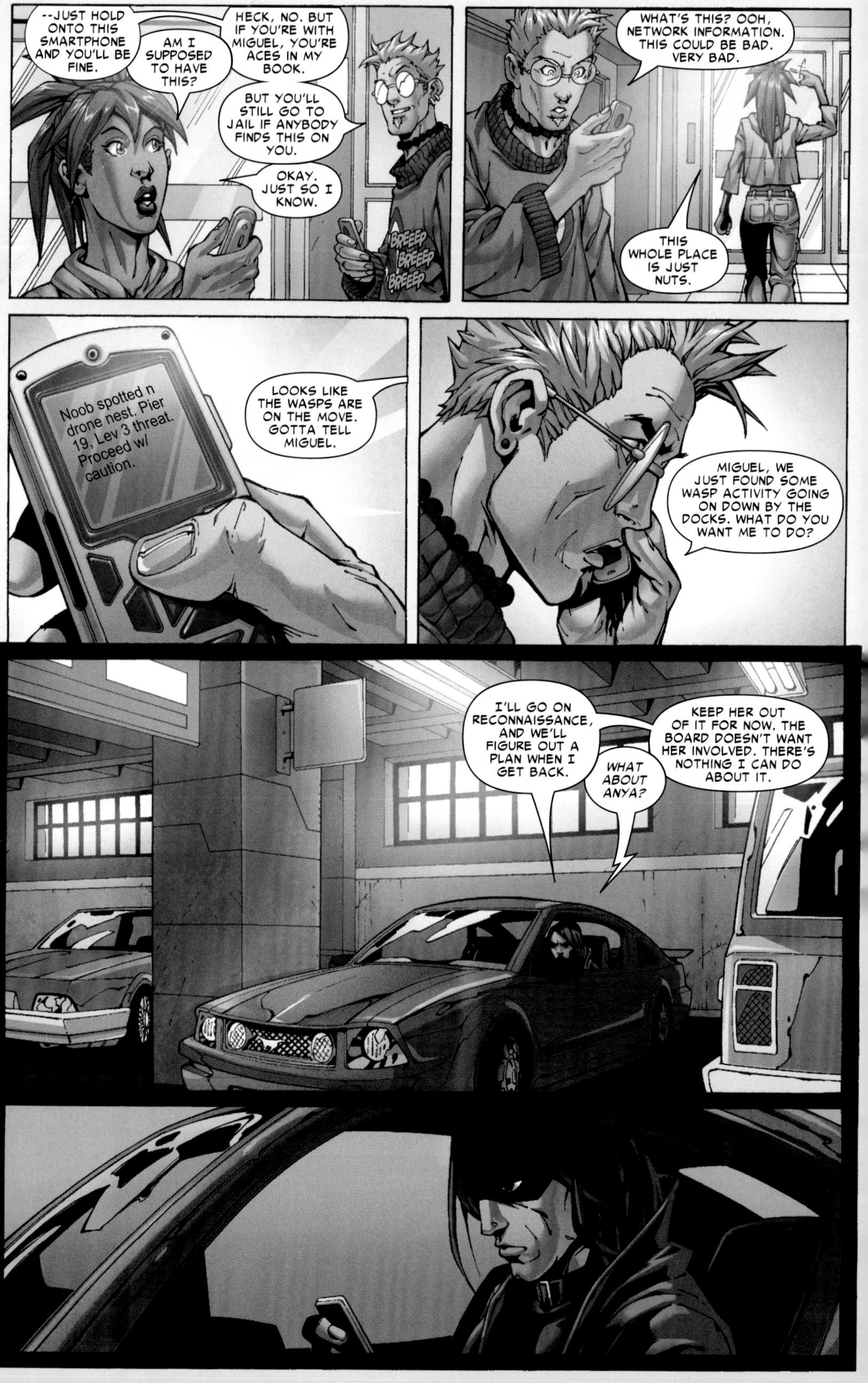
--JUST HOLD ONTO THIS SMARTPHONE AND YOU'LL BE FINE.
AM I SUPPOSED TO HAVE THIS?
HECK, NO. BUT IF YOU'RE WITH MIGUEL, YOU'RE ACES IN MY BOOK.
BUT YOU'LL STILL GO TO JAIL IF ANYBODY FINDS THIS ON YOU.
OKAY. JUST SO I KNOW.
BREEEP BREEEP BREEEP
WHAT'S THIS? OOH, NETWORK INFORMATION. THIS COULD BE BAD. VERY BAD.
THIS WHOLE PLACE IS JUST NUTS.
Noob spotted n drone nest. Pier 19, Lev 3 threat. Proceed w/ caution.
LOOKS LIKE THE WASPS ARE ON THE MOVE. GOTTA TELL MIGUEL.
MIGUEL, WE JUST FOUND SOME WASP ACTIVITY GOING ON DOWN BY THE DOCKS. WHAT DO YOU WANT ME TO DO?
I'LL GO ON RECONNAISSANCE, AND WE'LL FIGURE OUT A PLAN WHEN I GET BACK.
WHAT ABOUT ANYA?
KEEP HER OUT OF IT FOR NOW. THE BOARD DOESN'T WANT HER INVOLVED. THERE'S NOTHING I CAN DO ABOUT IT.

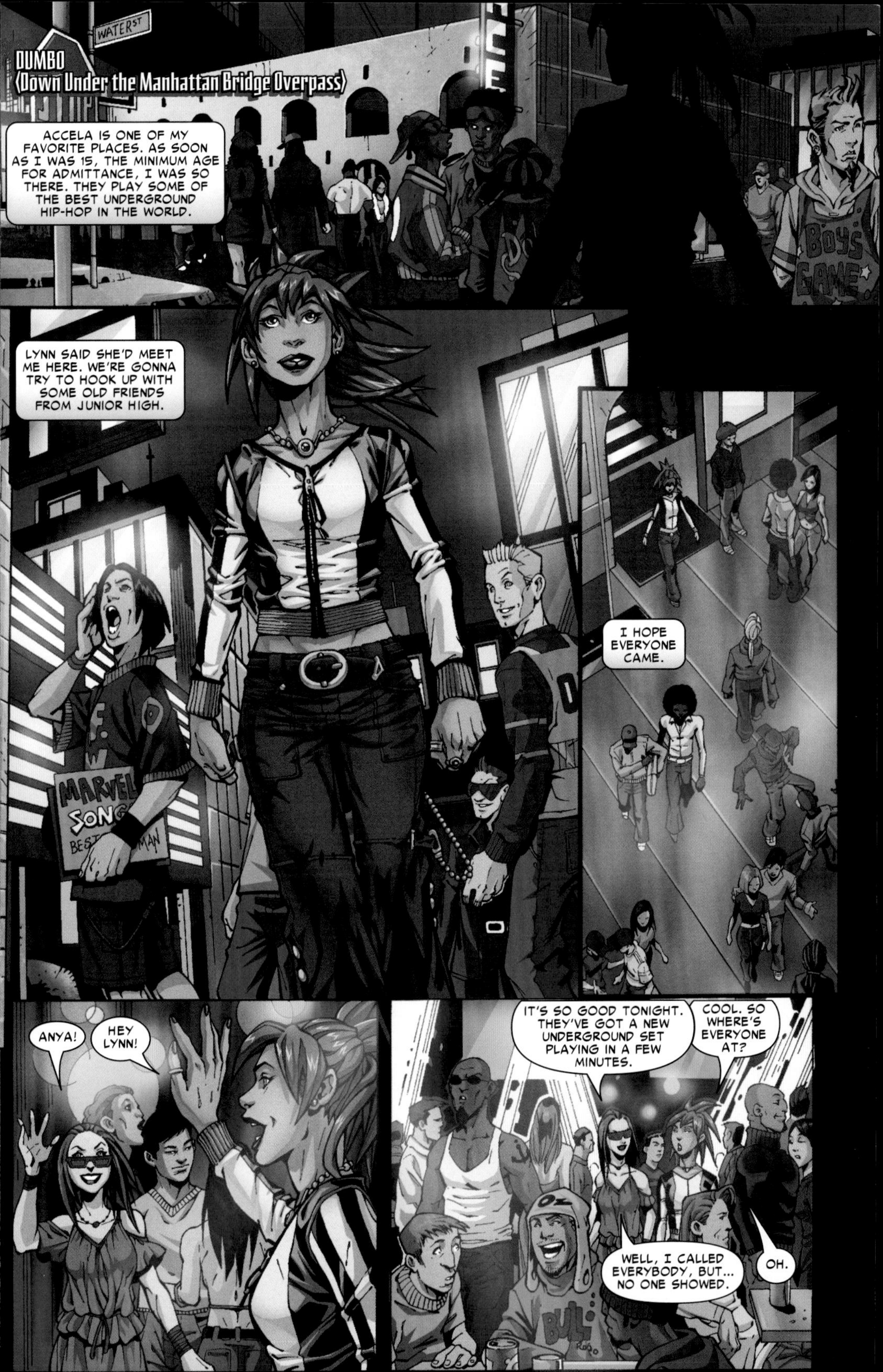
WATER ST
DUMBO
(Down Under the Manhattan Bridge Overpass)
ACCELA IS ONE OF MY FAVORITE PLACES. AS SOON AS I WAS 15, THE MINIMUM AGE FOR ADMITTANCE, I WAS SO THERE. THEY PLAY SOME OF THE BEST UNDERGROUND HIP-HOP IN THE WORLD.
BOYS GAME
LYNN SAID SHE'D MEET ME HERE. WE'RE GONNA TRY TO HOOK UP WITH SOME OLD FRIENDS FROM JUNIOR HIGH.
MARVEL SONG
I HOPE EVERYONE CAME.
ANYA!
HEY LYNN!
IT'S SO GOOD TONIGHT. THEY'VE GOT A NEW UNDERGROUND SET PLAYING IN A FEW MINUTES.
COOL. SO WHERE'S EVERYONE AT?
WELL, I CALLED EVERYBODY, BUT... NO ONE SHOWED.
OH.

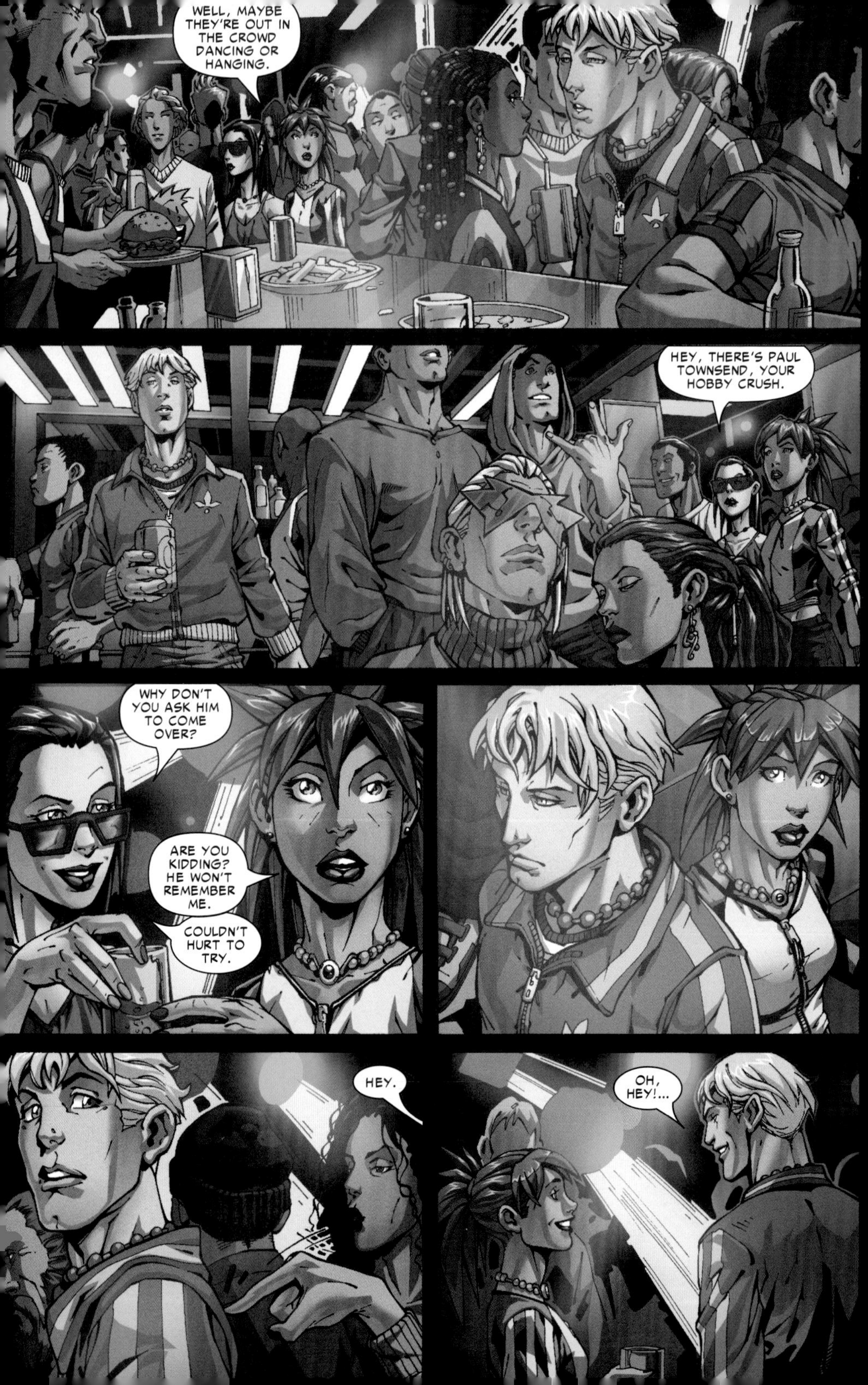
WELL, MAYBE THEY'RE OUT IN THE CROWD DANCING OR HANGING.
HEY, THERE'S PAUL TOWNSEND, YOUR HOBBY CRUSH.
WHY DON'T YOU ASK HIM TO COME OVER?
ARE YOU KIDDING? HE WON'T REMEMBER ME.
COULDN'T HURT TO TRY.
HEY.
OH, HEY!...

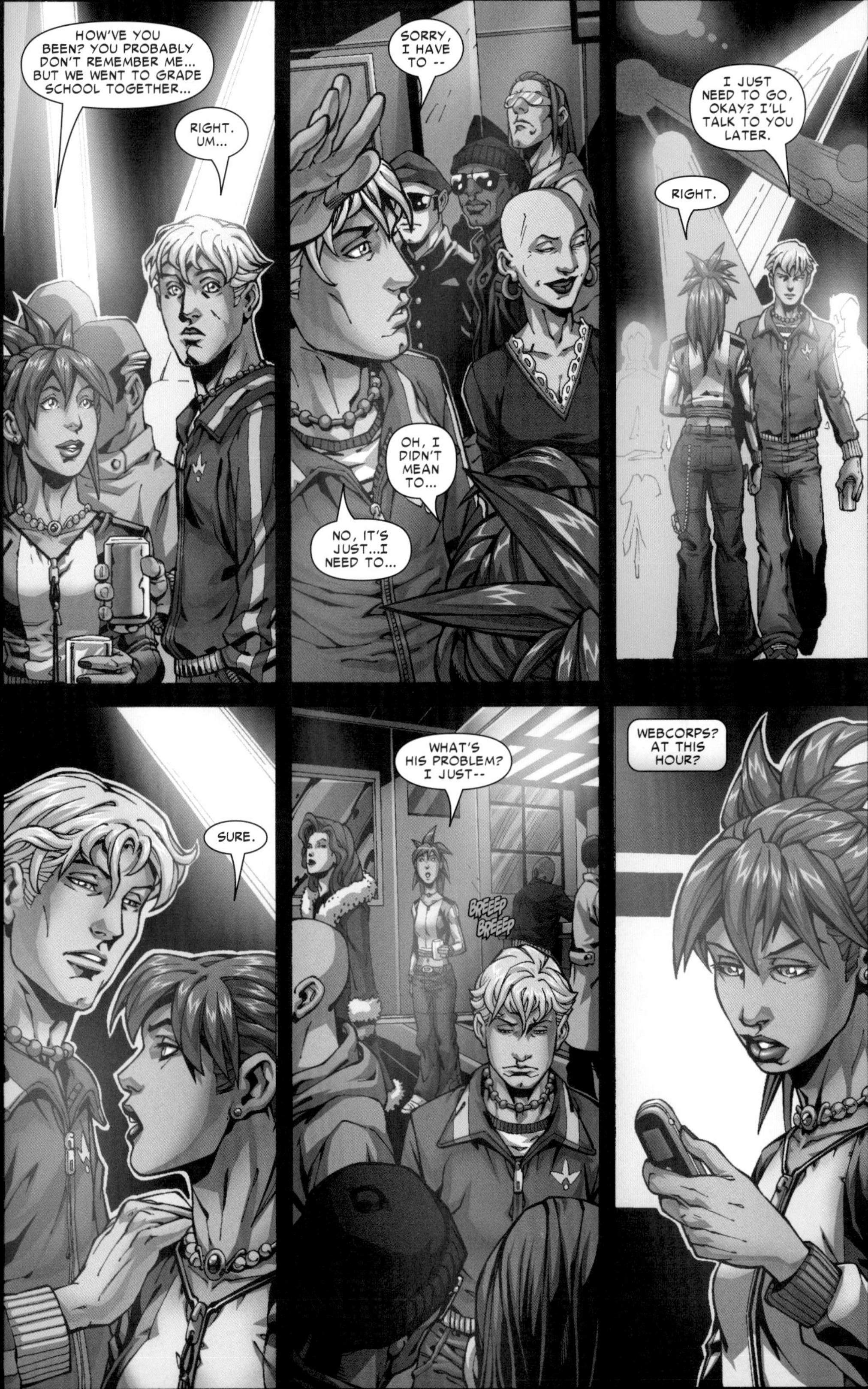
HOW'VE YOU BEEN? YOU PROBABLY DON'T REMEMBER ME... BUT WE WENT TO GRADE SCHOOL TOGETHER...
RIGHT. UM...
SORRY, I HAVE TO --
OH, I DIDN'T MEAN TO...
NO, IT'S JUST...I NEED TO...
I JUST NEED TO GO, OKAY? I'LL TALK TO YOU LATER.
RIGHT.
SURE.
WHAT'S HIS PROBLEM? I JUST--
BREEP BREEP
WEBCORPS? AT THIS HOUR?

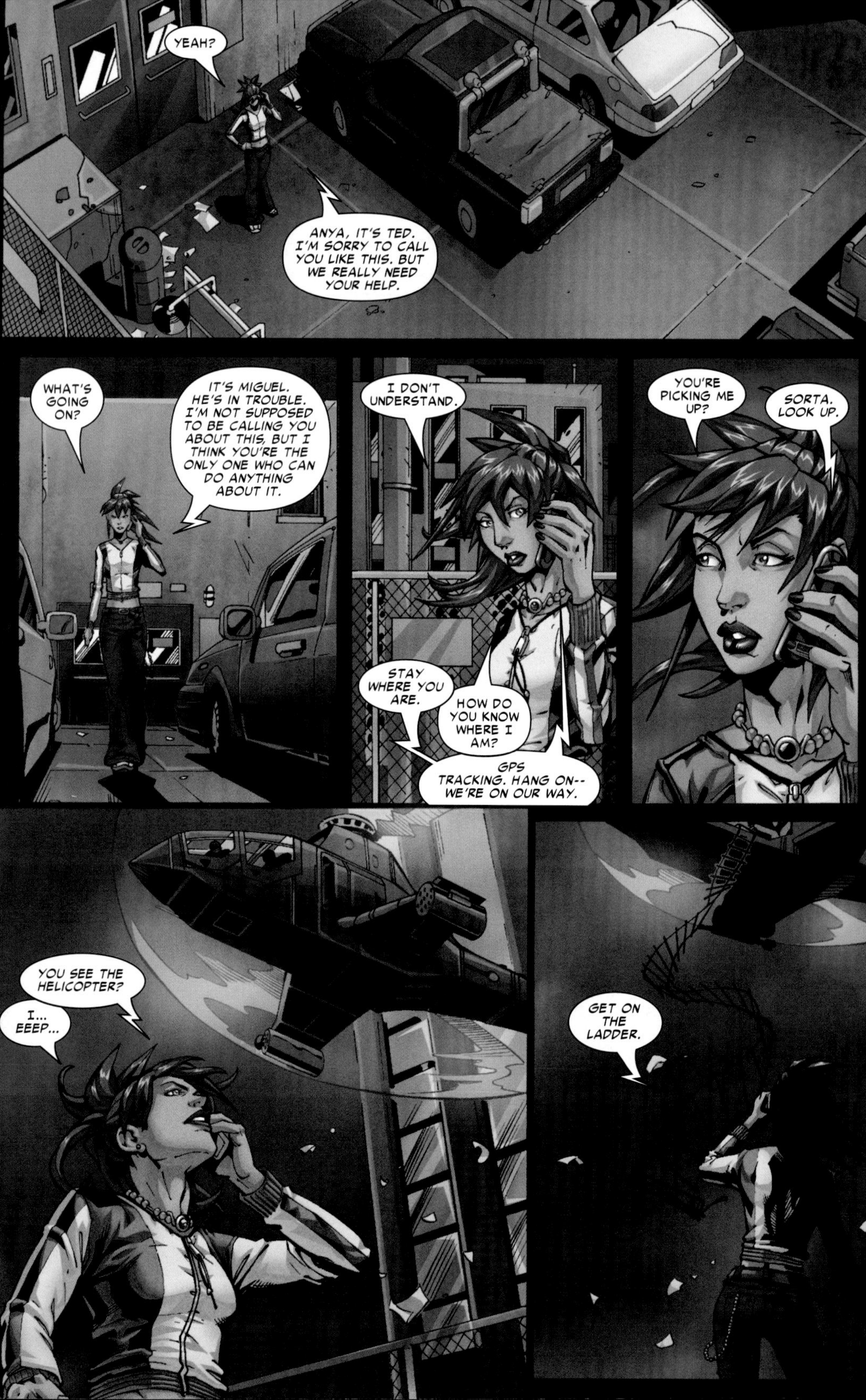
YEAH?
ANYA, IT'S TED. I'M SORRY TO CALL YOU LIKE THIS. BUT WE REALLY NEED YOUR HELP.
WHAT'S GOING ON?
IT'S MIGUEL. HE'S IN TROUBLE. I'M NOT SUPPOSED TO BE CALLING YOU ABOUT THIS, BUT I THINK YOU'RE THE ONLY ONE WHO CAN DO ANYTHING ABOUT IT.
I DON'T UNDERSTAND.
STAY WHERE YOU ARE.
HOW DO YOU KNOW WHERE I AM?
GPS TRACKING. HANG ON-- WE'RE ON OUR WAY.
YOU'RE PICKING ME UP?
SORTA. LOOK UP.
YOU SEE THE HELICOPTER?
I... EEEP...
GET ON THE LADDER.

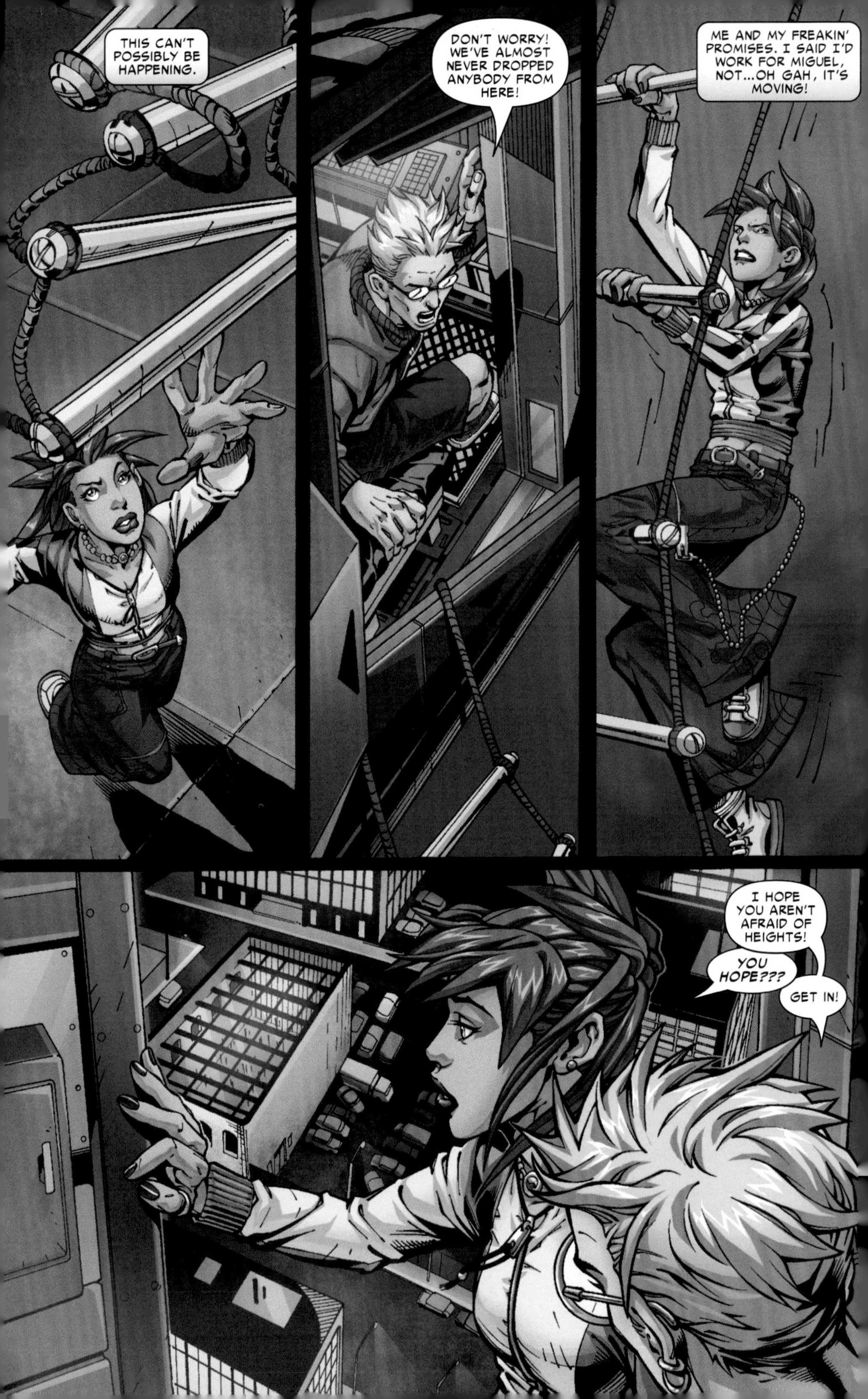
THIS CAN'T POSSIBLY BE HAPPENING.
DON'T WORRY! WE'VE ALMOST NEVER DROPPED ANYBODY FROM HERE!
ME AND MY FREAKIN' PROMISES. I SAID I'D WORK FOR MIGUEL, NOT...OH GAH, IT'S MOVING!
I HOPE YOU AREN'T AFRAID OF HEIGHTS!
YOU HOPE???
GET IN!

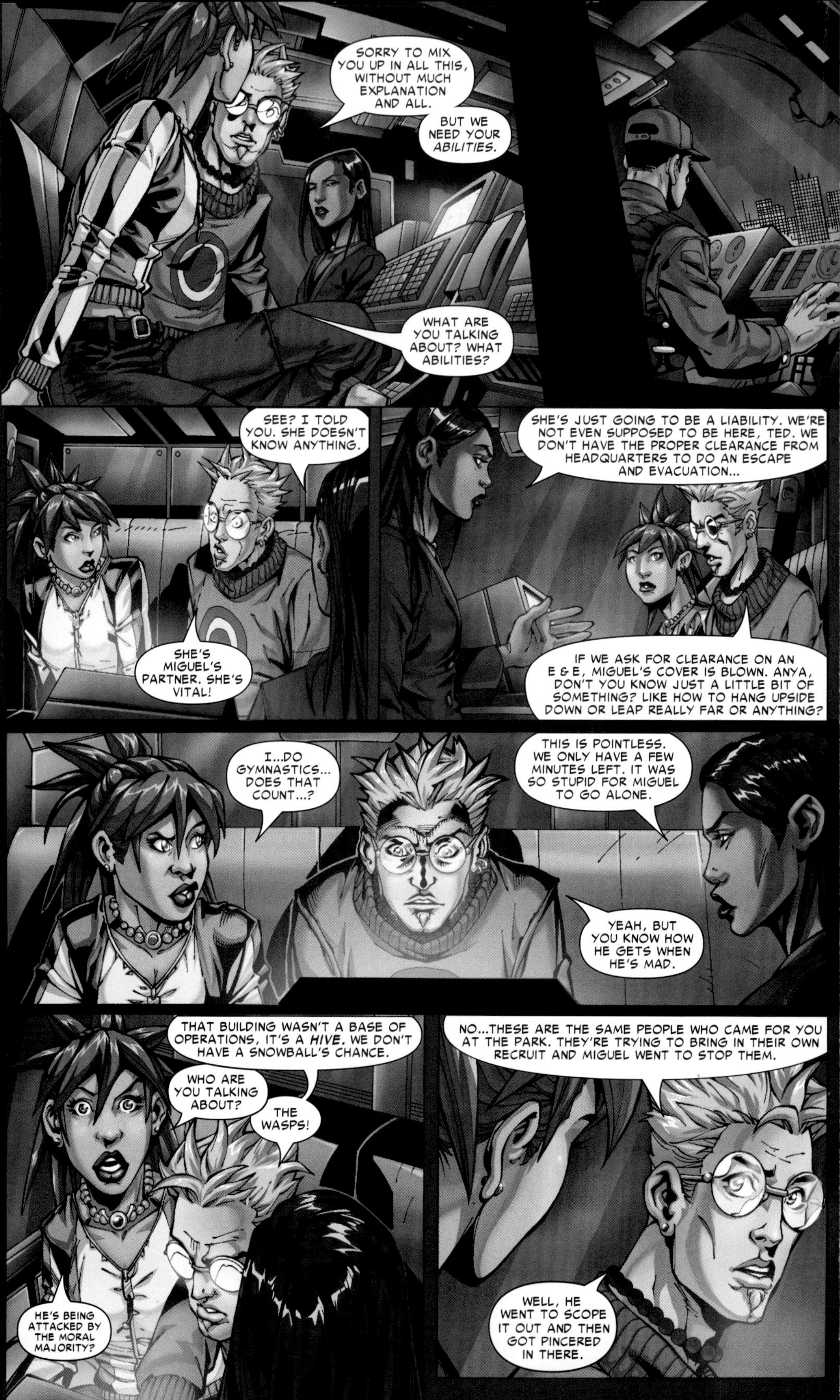
SORRY TO MIX YOU UP IN ALL THIS, WITHOUT MUCH EXPLANATION AND ALL.
BUT WE NEED YOUR ABILITIES.
WHAT ARE YOU TALKING ABOUT? WHAT ABILITIES?
SEE? I TOLD YOU. SHE DOESN'T KNOW ANYTHING.
SHE'S MIGUEL'S PARTNER. SHE'S VITAL!
SHE'S JUST GOING TO BE A LIABILITY. WE'RE NOT EVEN SUPPOSED TO BE HERE, TED. WE DON'T HAVE THE PROPER CLEARANCE FROM HEADQUARTERS TO DO AN ESCAPE AND EVACUATION...
IF WE ASK FOR CLEARANCE ON AN E & E, MIGUEL'S COVER IS BLOWN. ANYA, DON'T YOU KNOW JUST A LITTLE BIT OF SOMETHING? LIKE HOW TO HANG UPSIDE DOWN OR LEAP REALLY FAR OR ANYTHING?
I...DO GYMNASTICS... DOES THAT COUNT...?
THIS IS POINTLESS. WE ONLY HAVE A FEW MINUTES LEFT. IT WAS SO STUPID FOR MIGUEL TO GO ALONE.
YEAH, BUT YOU KNOW HOW HE GETS WHEN HE'S MAD.
THAT BUILDING WASN'T A BASE OF OPERATIONS, IT'S A HIVE. WE DON'T HAVE A SNOWBALL'S CHANCE.
WHO ARE YOU TALKING ABOUT?
THE WASPS!
HE'S BEING ATTACKED BY THE MORAL MAJORITY?
NO...THESE ARE THE SAME PEOPLE WHO CAME FOR YOU AT THE PARK. THEY'RE TRYING TO BRING IN THEIR OWN RECRUIT AND MIGUEL WENT TO STOP THEM.
WELL, HE WENT TO SCOPE IT OUT AND THEN GOT PINCERED IN THERE.

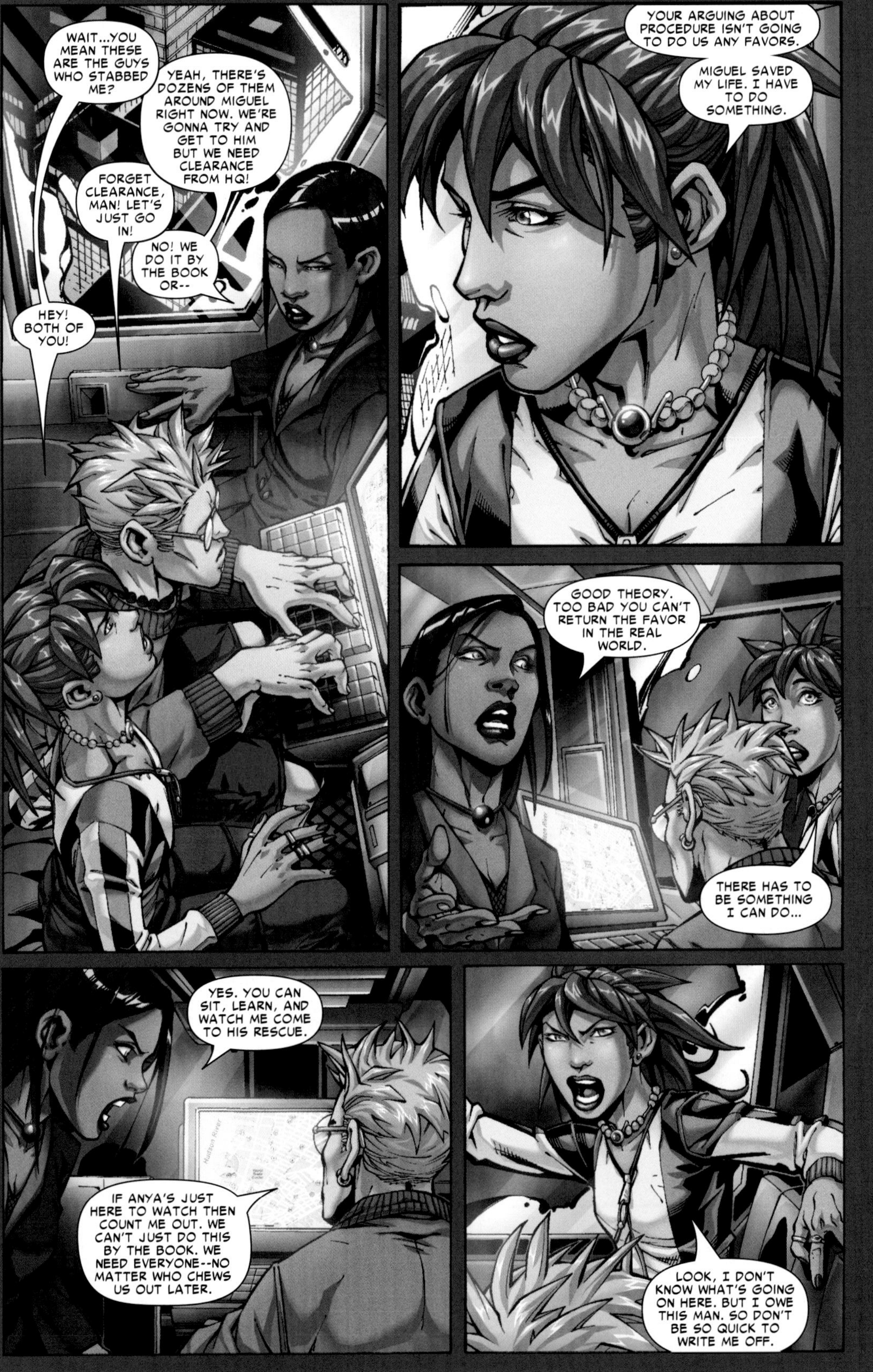
WAIT...YOU MEAN THESE ARE THE GUYS WHO STABBED ME?
YEAH, THERE'S DOZENS OF THEM AROUND MIGUEL RIGHT NOW. WE'RE GONNA TRY AND GET TO HIM BUT WE NEED CLEARANCE FROM HQ!
FORGET CLEARANCE, MAN! LET'S JUST GO IN!
NO! WE DO IT BY THE BOOK OR--
HEY! BOTH OF YOU!
YOUR ARGUING ABOUT PROCEDURE ISN'T GOING TO DO US ANY FAVORS.
MIGUEL SAVED MY LIFE. I HAVE TO DO SOMETHING.
GOOD THEORY. TOO BAD YOU CAN'T RETURN THE FAVOR IN THE REAL WORLD.
THERE HAS TO BE SOMETHING I CAN DO...
YES. YOU CAN SIT, LEARN, AND WATCH ME COME TO HIS RESCUE.
IF ANYA'S JUST HERE TO WATCH THEN COUNT ME OUT. WE CAN'T JUST DO THIS BY THE BOOK. WE NEED EVERYONE--NO MATTER WHO CHEWS US OUT LATER.
LOOK, I DON'T KNOW WHAT'S GOING ON HERE. BUT I OWE THIS MAN. SO DON'T BE SO QUICK TO WRITE ME OFF.

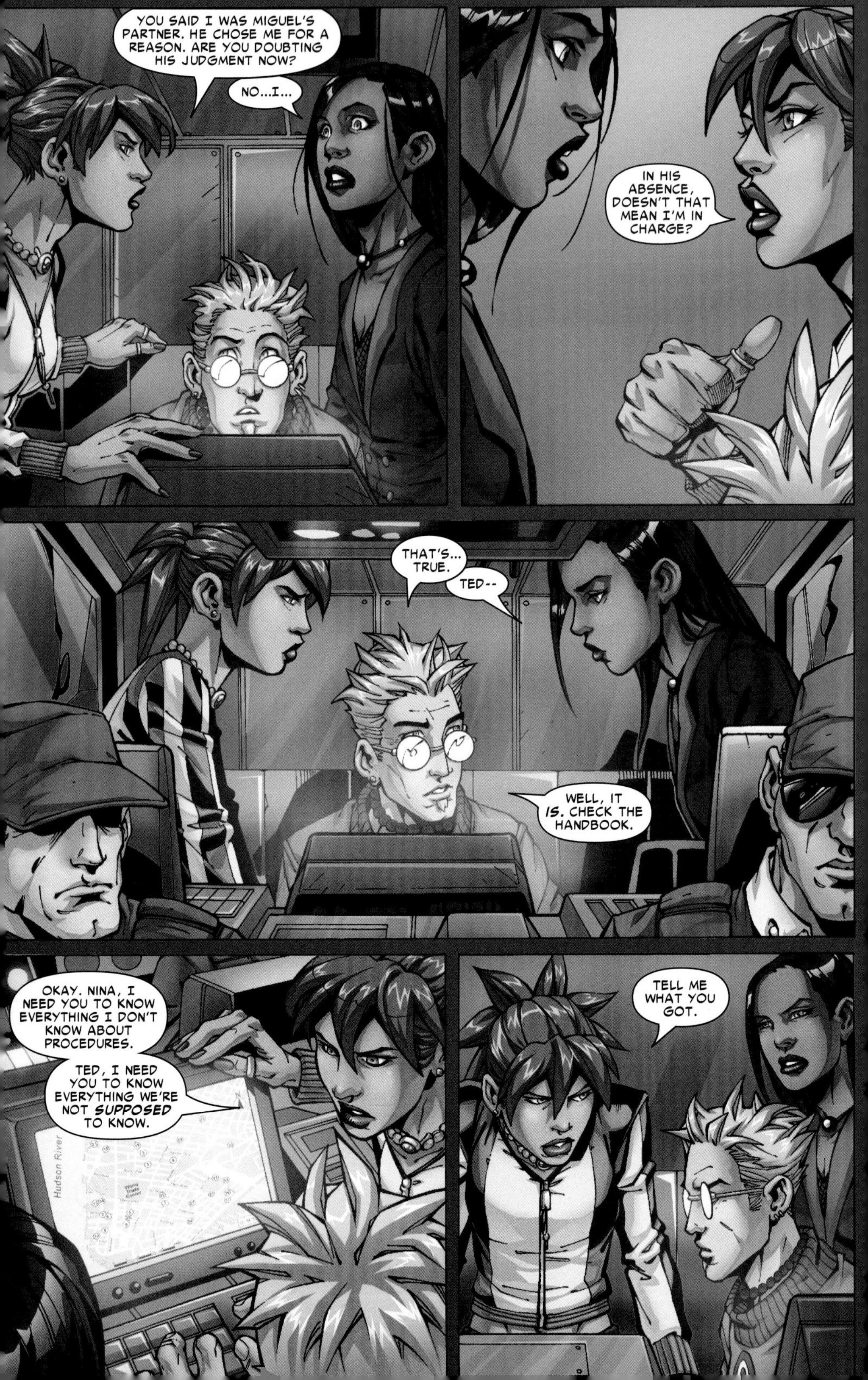
YOU SAID I WAS MIGUEL'S PARTNER. HE CHOSE ME FOR A REASON. ARE YOU DOUBTING HIS JUDGMENT NOW?
NO...I...
IN HIS ABSENCE, DOESN'T THAT MEAN I'M IN CHARGE?
THAT'S... TRUE.
TED--
WELL, IT *IS*. CHECK THE HANDBOOK.
OKAY. NINA, I NEED YOU TO KNOW EVERYTHING I DON'T KNOW ABOUT PROCEDURES.
TED, I NEED YOU TO KNOW EVERYTHING WE'RE NOT ***SUPPOSED*** TO KNOW.
Hudson River
TELL ME WHAT YOU GOT.

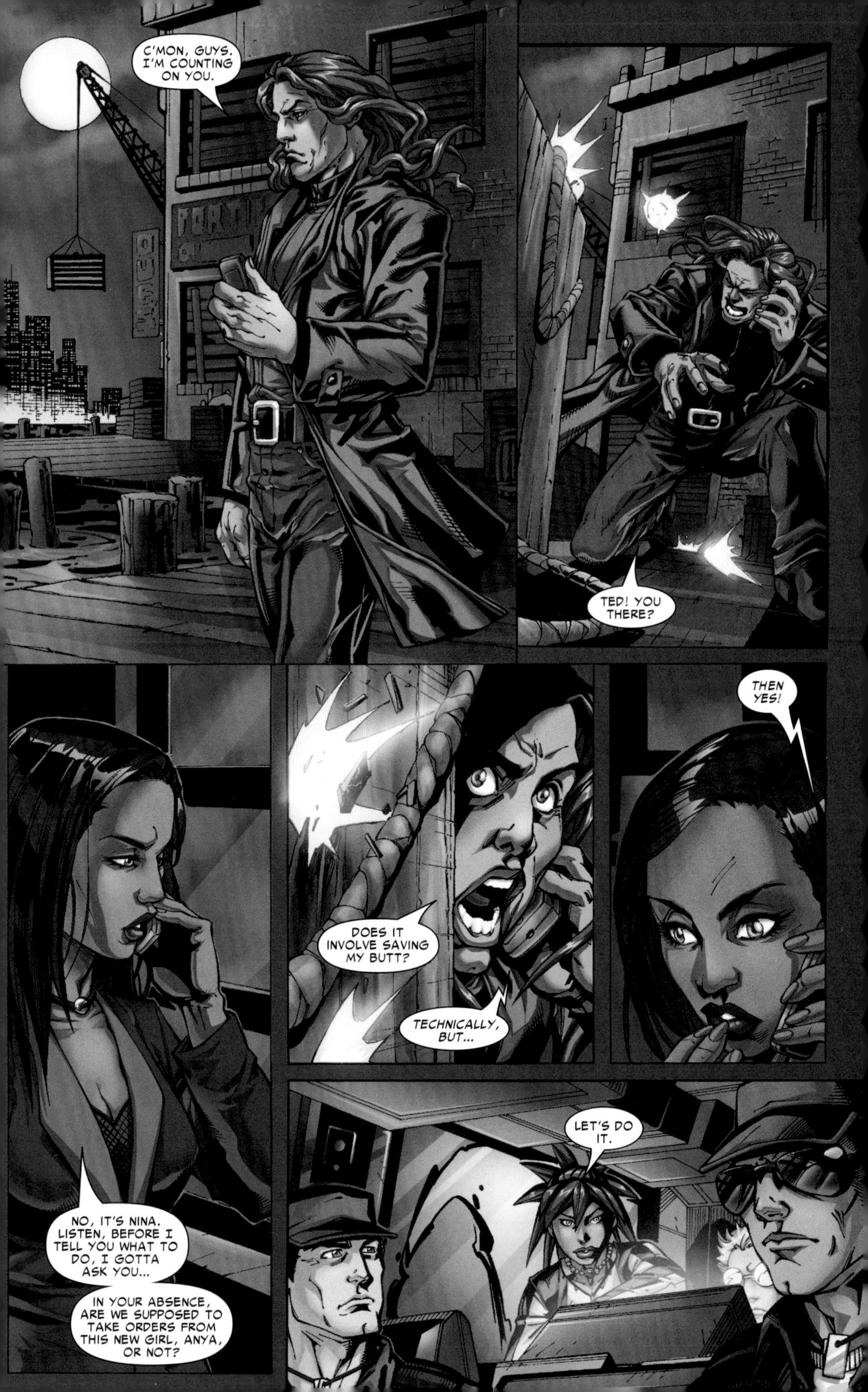
C'MON, GUYS. I'M COUNTING ON YOU.
TED! YOU THERE?
NO, IT'S NINA. LISTEN, BEFORE I TELL YOU WHAT TO DO, I GOTTA ASK YOU...
IN YOUR ABSENCE, ARE WE SUPPOSED TO TAKE ORDERS FROM THIS NEW GIRL, ANYA, OR NOT?
DOES IT INVOLVE SAVING MY BUTT?
TECHNICALLY, BUT...
THEN YES!
LET'S DO IT.

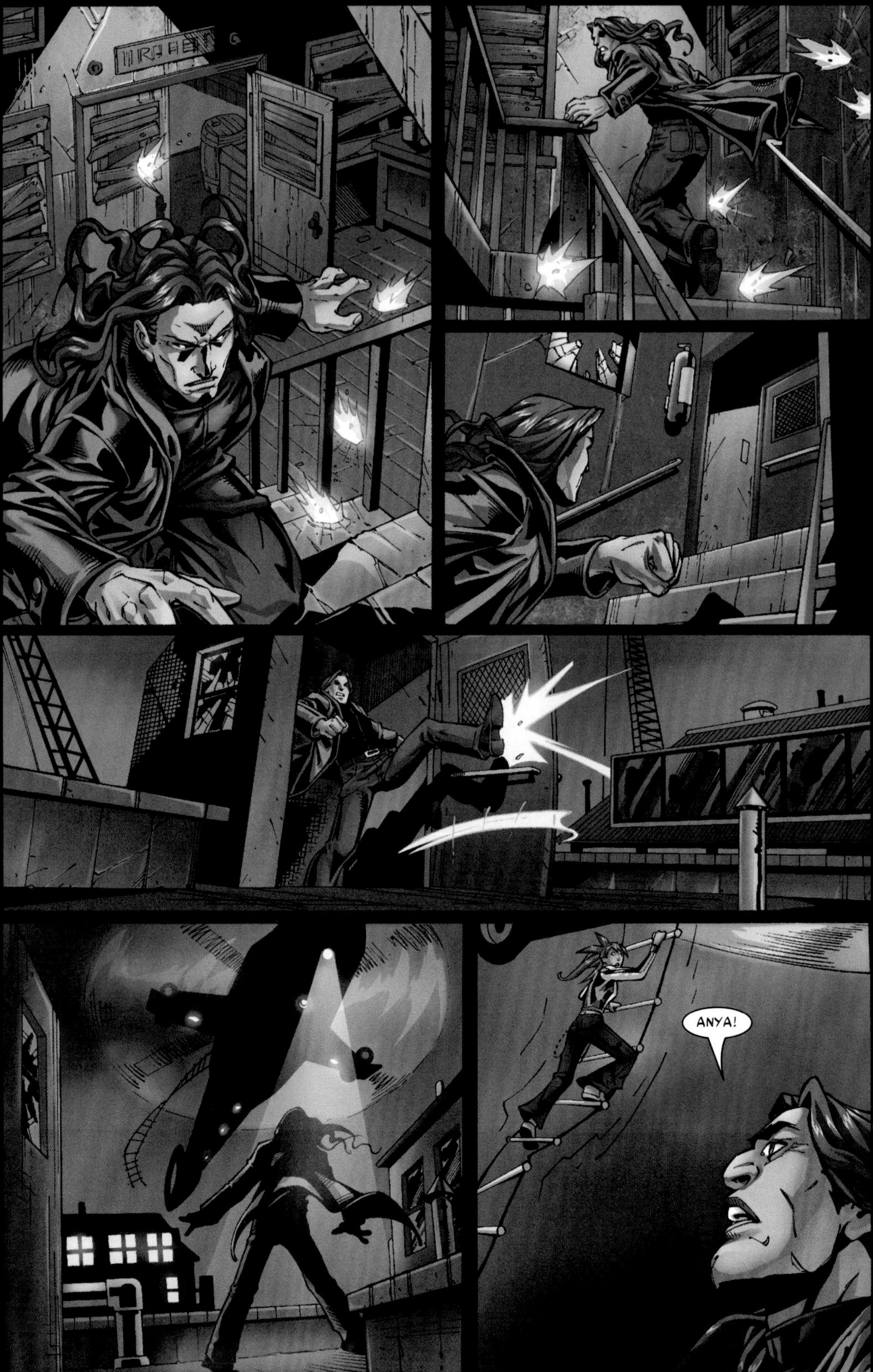
ANYA!

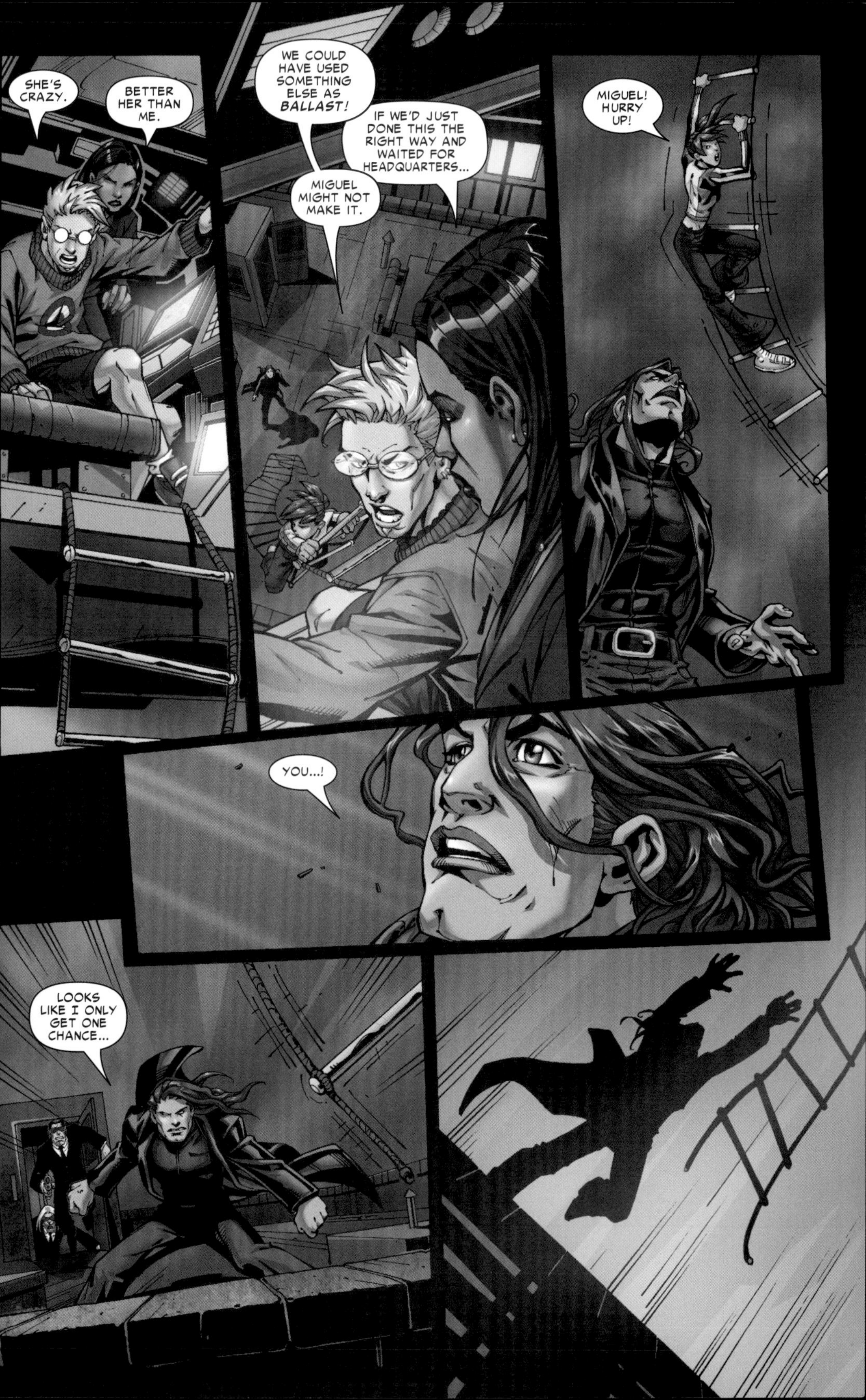
SHE'S CRAZY.
BETTER HER THAN ME.
WE COULD HAVE USED SOMETHING ELSE AS BALLAST!
IF WE'D JUST DONE THIS THE RIGHT WAY AND WAITED FOR HEADQUARTERS...
MIGUEL MIGHT NOT MAKE IT.
MIGUEL! HURRY UP!
YOU...!
LOOKS LIKE I ONLY GET ONE CHANCE...

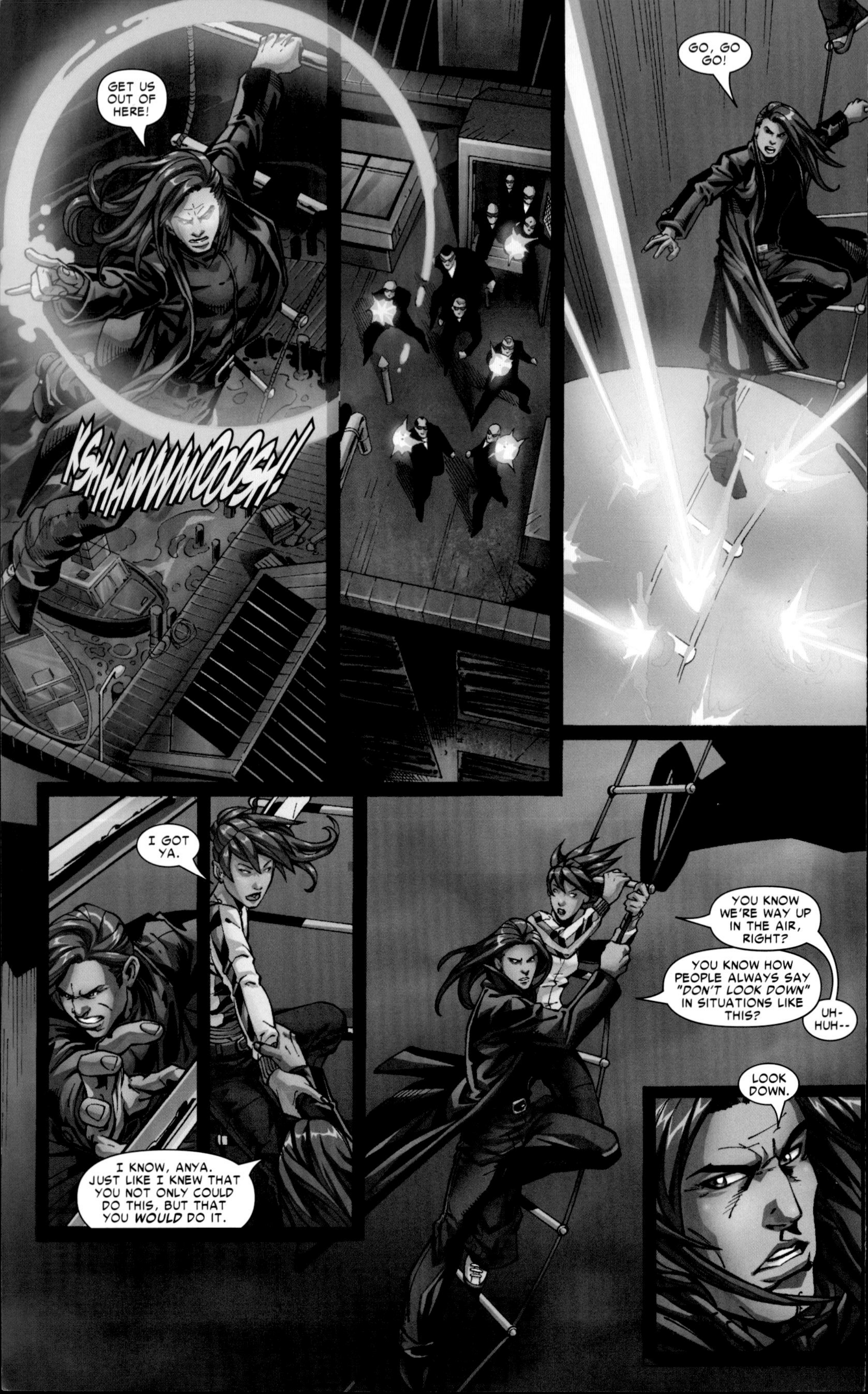
GET US OUT OF HERE!
KSHHWWWOOSH!
GO, GO GO!
I GOT YA.
I KNOW, ANYA. JUST LIKE I KNEW THAT YOU NOT ONLY COULD DO THIS, BUT THAT YOU *WOULD* DO IT.
YOU KNOW WE'RE WAY UP IN THE AIR, RIGHT?
UH-HUH--
YOU KNOW HOW PEOPLE ALWAYS SAY *"DON'T LOOK DOWN"* IN SITUATIONS LIKE THIS?
LOOK DOWN.

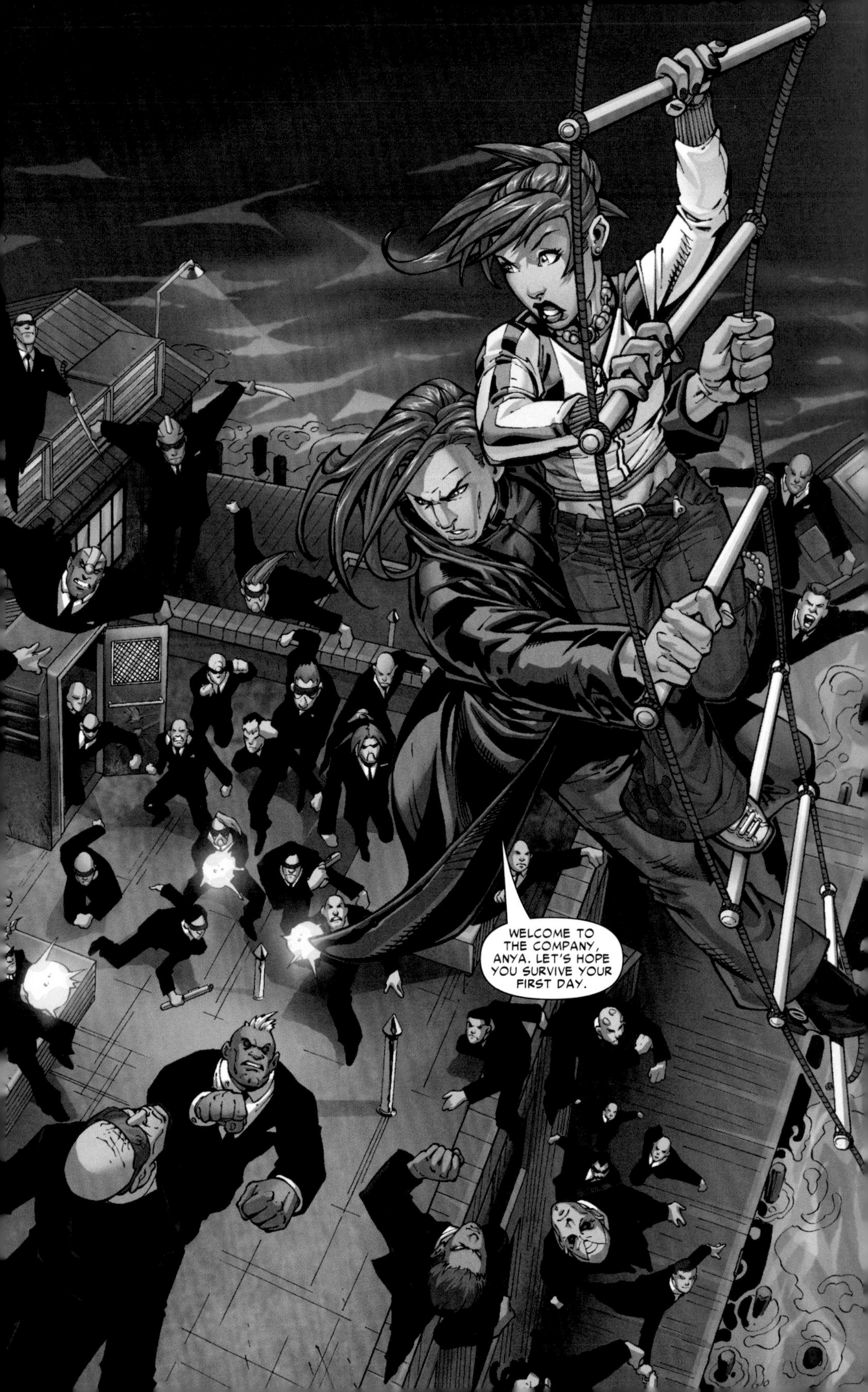
WELCOME TO THE COMPANY, ANYA. LET'S HOPE YOU SURVIVE YOUR FIRST DAY.

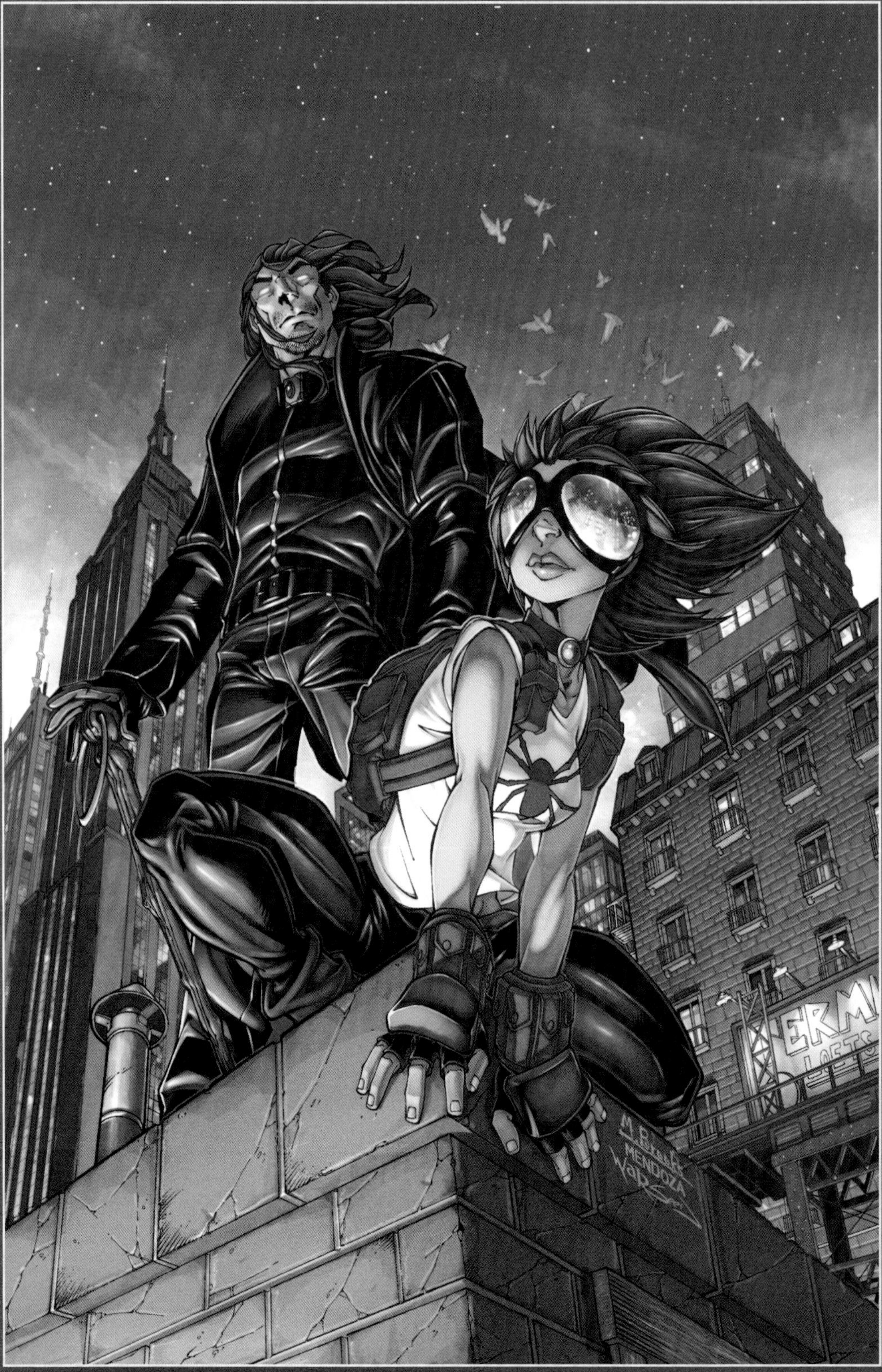
MENDOZA

AMAZING FANTASY #4

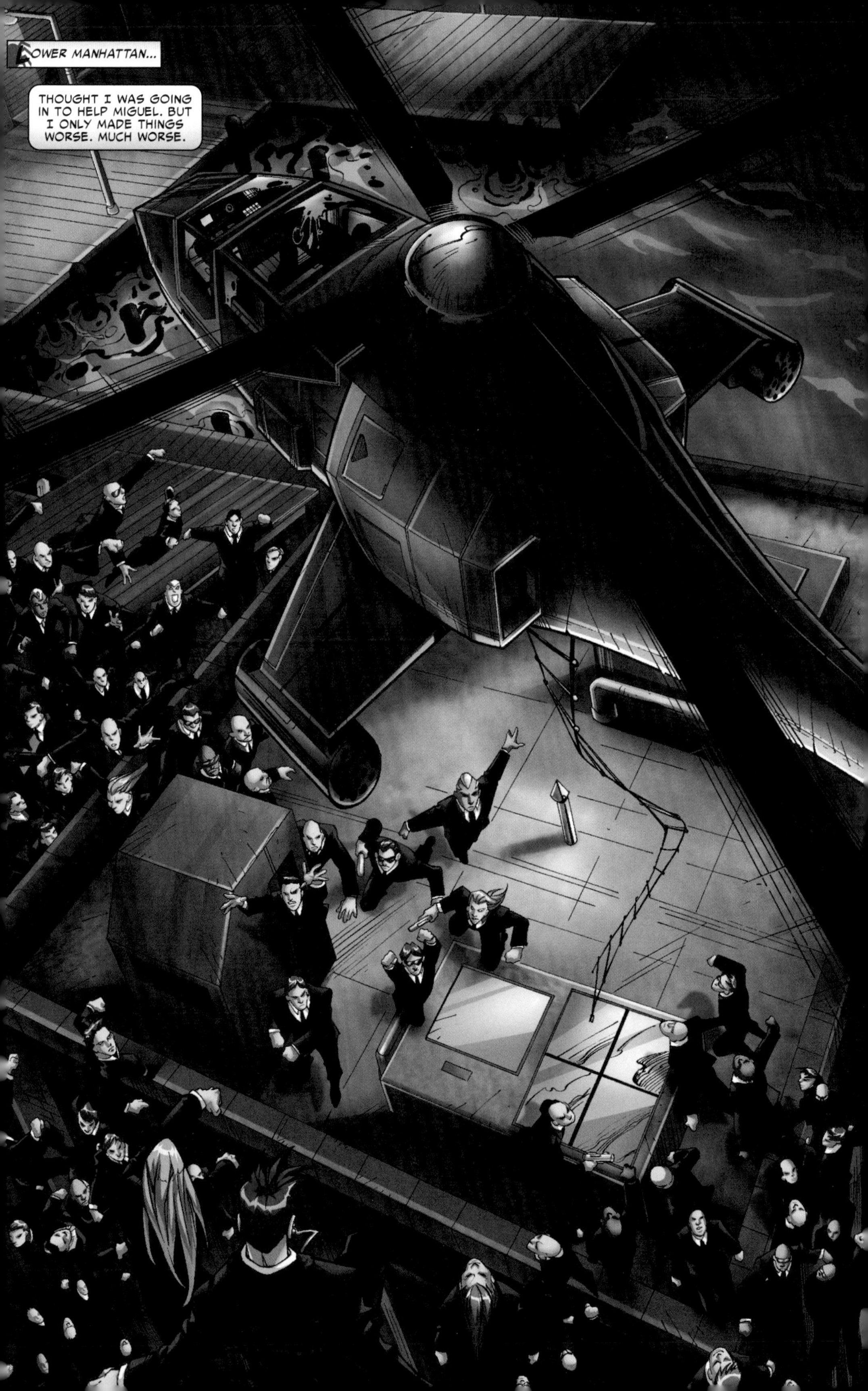
LOWER MANHATTAN...
THOUGHT I WAS GOING IN TO HELP MIGUEL. BUT I ONLY MADE THINGS WORSE. MUCH WORSE.

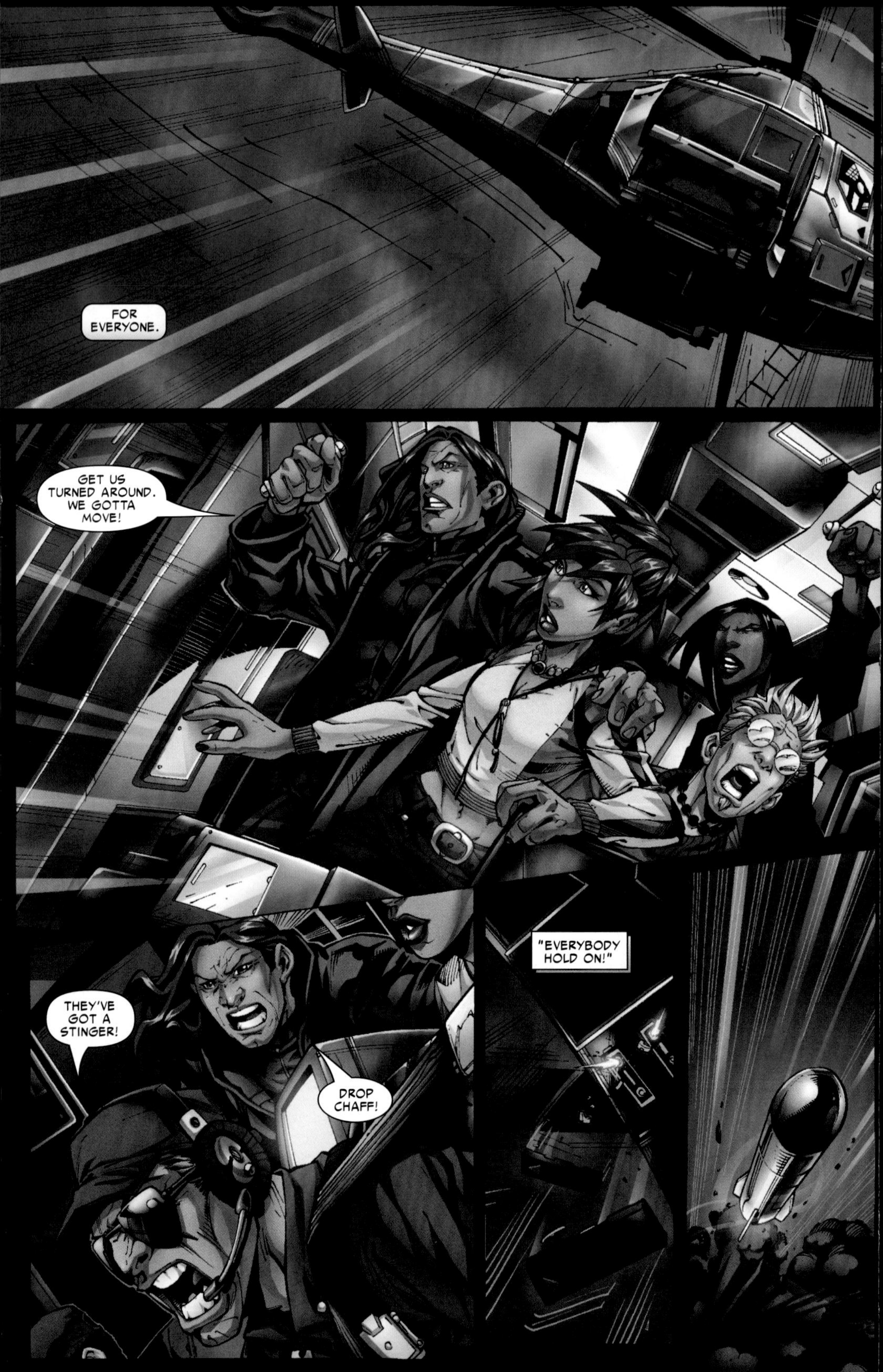
FOR EVERYONE.
GET US TURNED AROUND. WE GOTTA MOVE!
THEY'VE GOT A STINGER!
DROP CHAFF!
"EVERYBODY HOLD ON!"

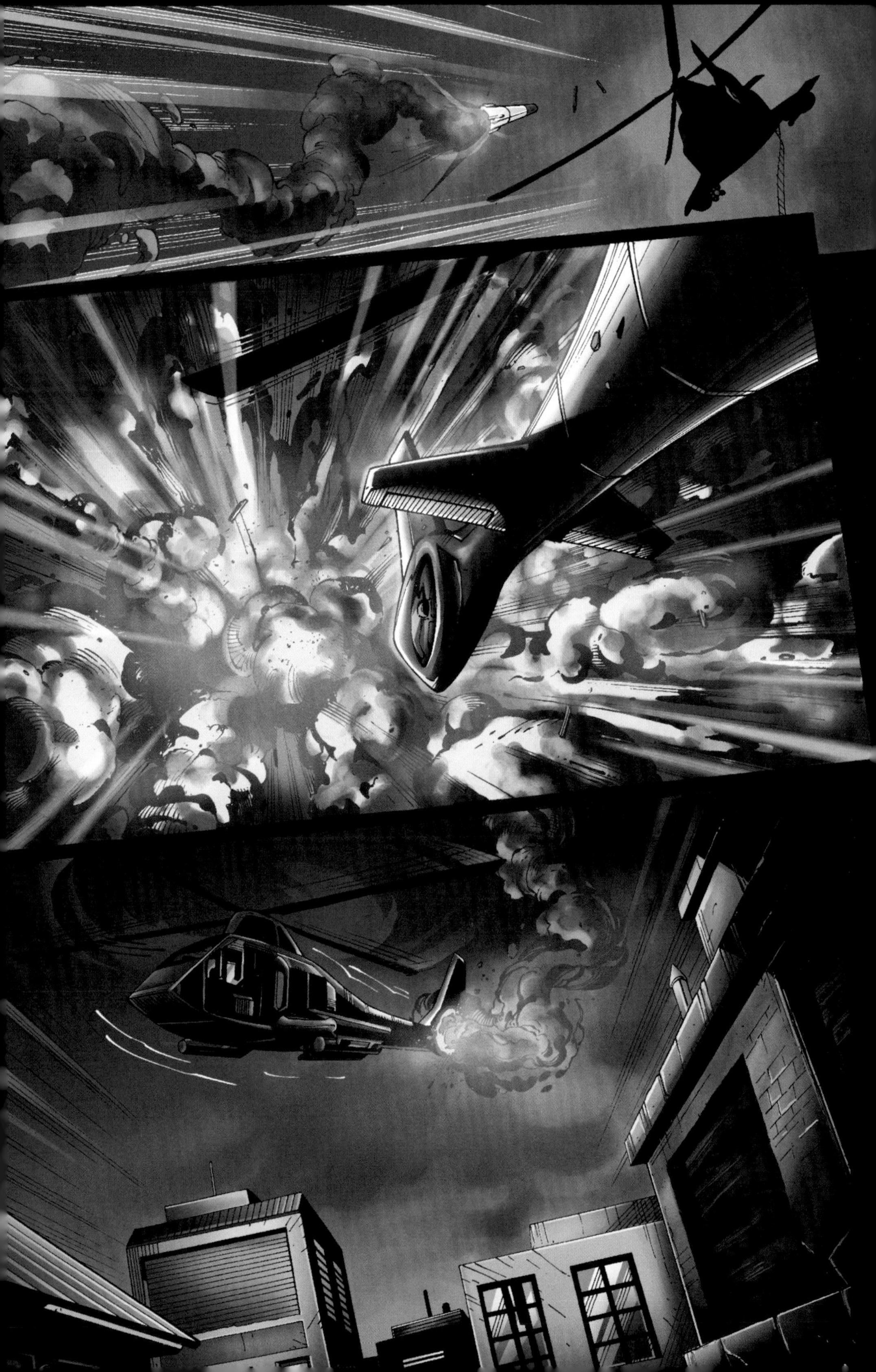

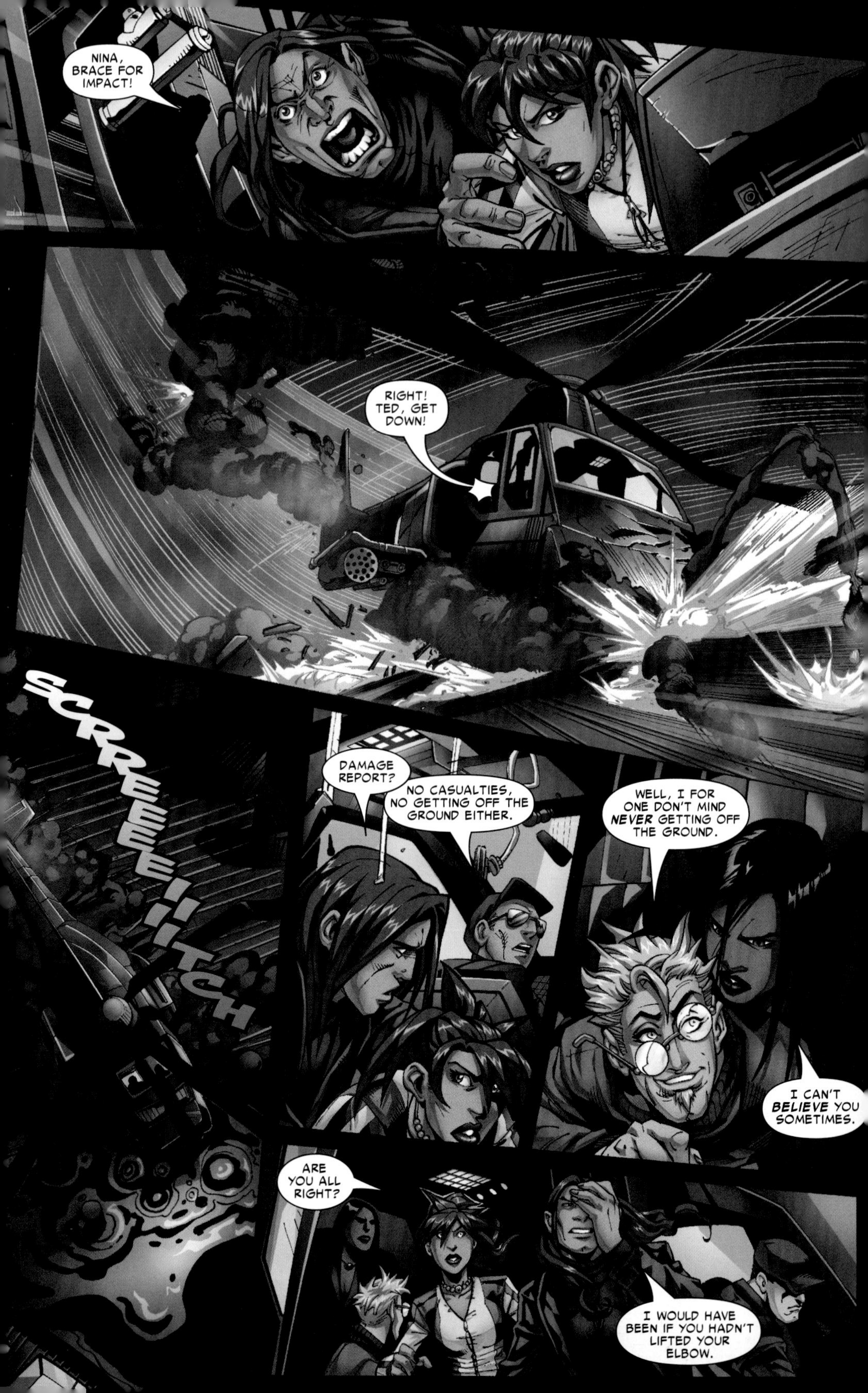
NINA, BRACE FOR IMPACT!
RIGHT! TED, GET DOWN!
SCREEEEE!!!ITCH
DAMAGE REPORT?
NO CASUALTIES, NO GETTING OFF THE GROUND EITHER.
WELL, I FOR ONE DON'T MIND NEVER GETTING OFF THE GROUND.
I CAN'T BELIEVE YOU SOMETIMES.
ARE YOU ALL RIGHT?
I WOULD HAVE BEEN IF YOU HADN'T LIFTED YOUR ELBOW.

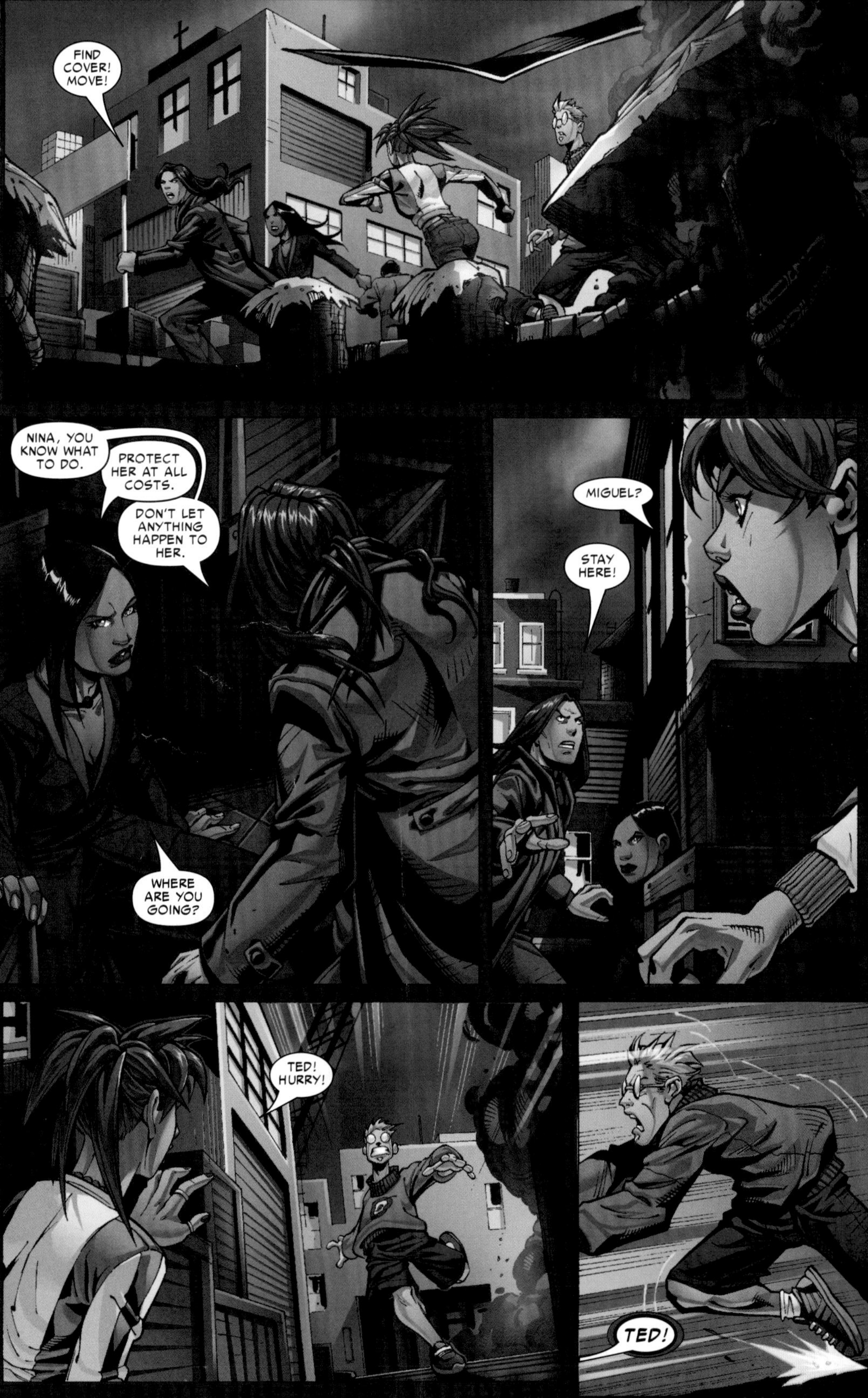
FIND COVER! MOVE!
NINA, YOU KNOW WHAT TO DO.
PROTECT HER AT ALL COSTS.
DON'T LET ANYTHING HAPPEN TO HER.
WHERE ARE YOU GOING?
MIGUEL?
STAY HERE!
TED! HURRY!
TED!

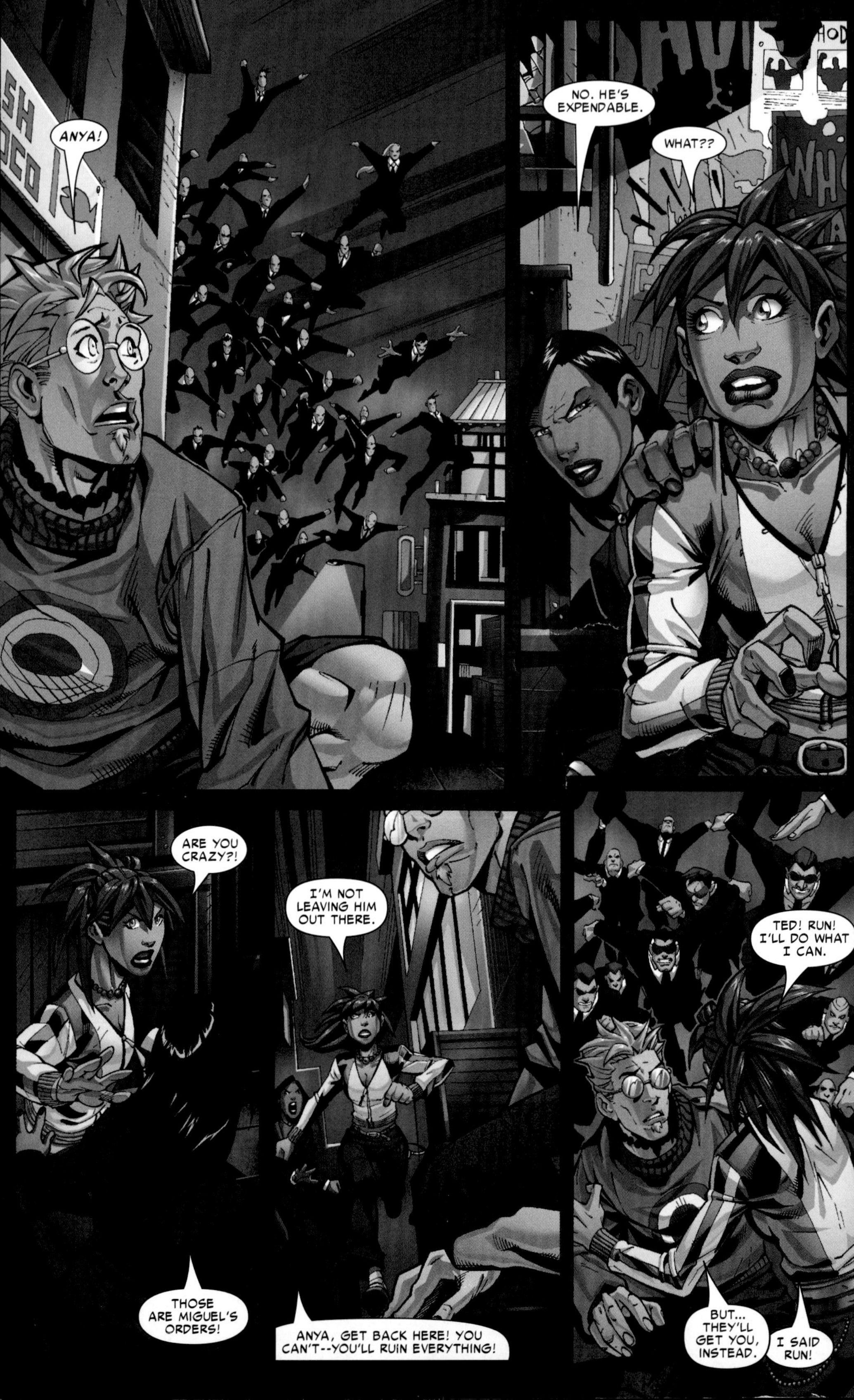
ANYA!
NO. HE'S EXPENDABLE.
WHAT??
ARE YOU CRAZY?!
THOSE ARE MIGUEL'S ORDERS!
I'M NOT LEAVING HIM OUT THERE.
ANYA, GET BACK HERE! YOU CAN'T--YOU'LL RUIN EVERYTHING!
TED! RUN! I'LL DO WHAT I CAN.
BUT... THEY'LL GET YOU, INSTEAD.
I SAID RUN!

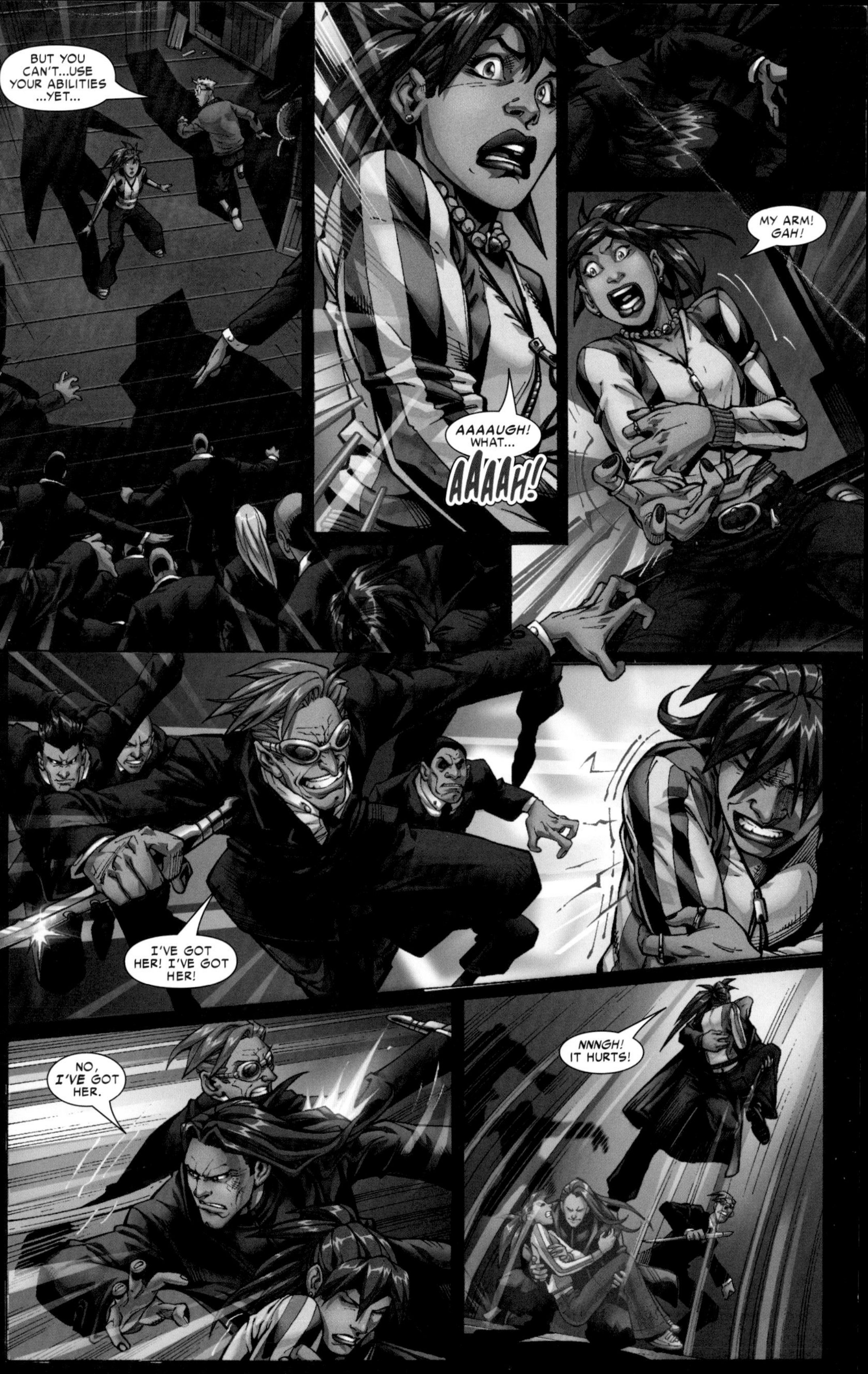
BUT YOU CAN'T...USE YOUR ABILITIES ...YET...
AAAAUGH! WHAT...
AAAAH!
MY ARM! GAH!
I'VE GOT HER! I'VE GOT HER!
NO, I'VE GOT HER.
NNNGH! IT HURTS!

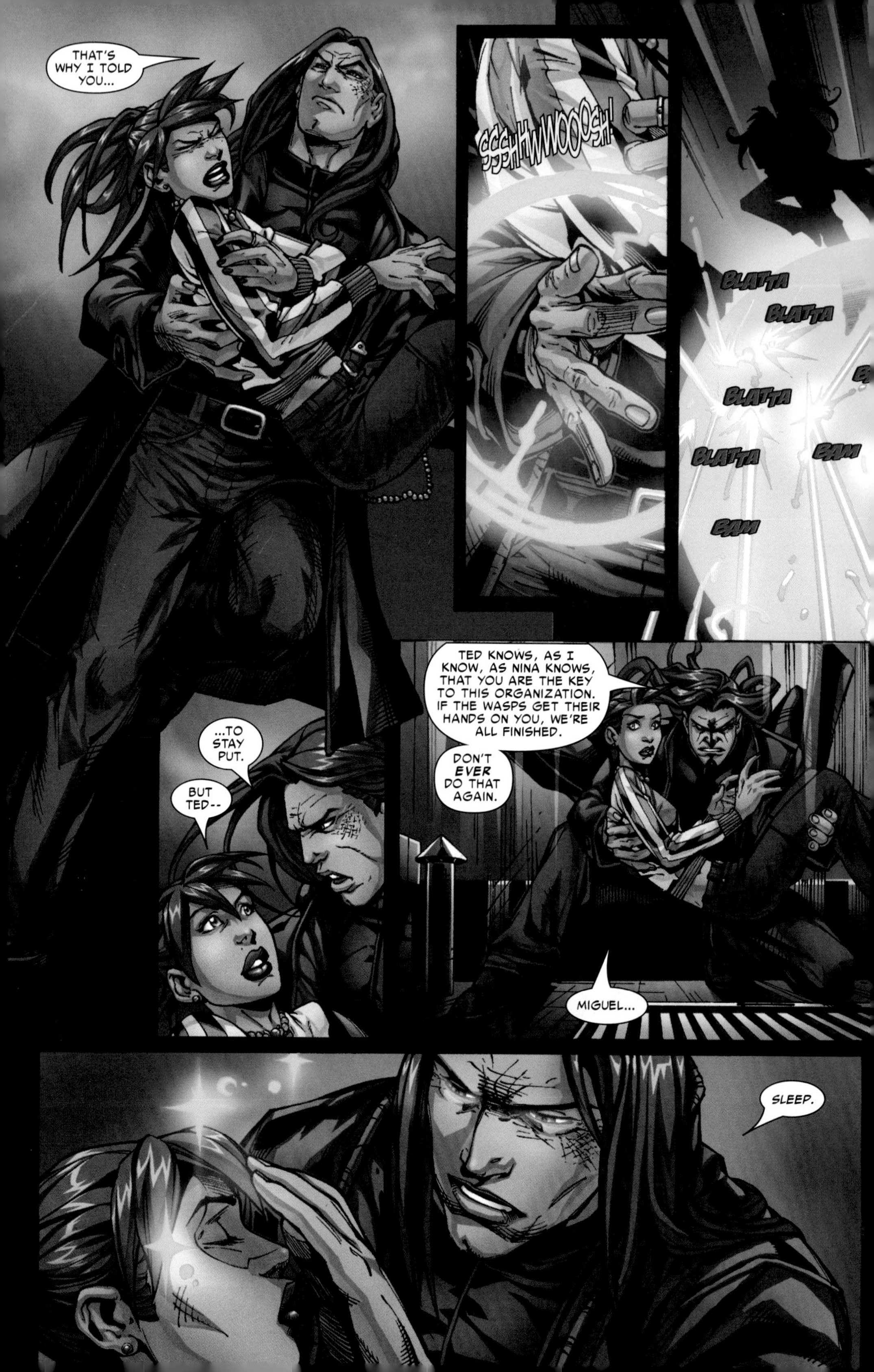
THAT'S WHY I TOLD YOU...
SSSHHWWOOOSH!
BLATTA
BLATTA
BLATTA
BLATTA
BAM
BAM
...TO STAY PUT.
BUT TED--
TED KNOWS, AS I KNOW, AS NINA KNOWS, THAT YOU ARE THE KEY TO THIS ORGANIZATION. IF THE WASPS GET THEIR HANDS ON YOU, WE'RE ALL FINISHED.
DON'T EVER DO THAT AGAIN.
MIGUEL...
SLEEP.

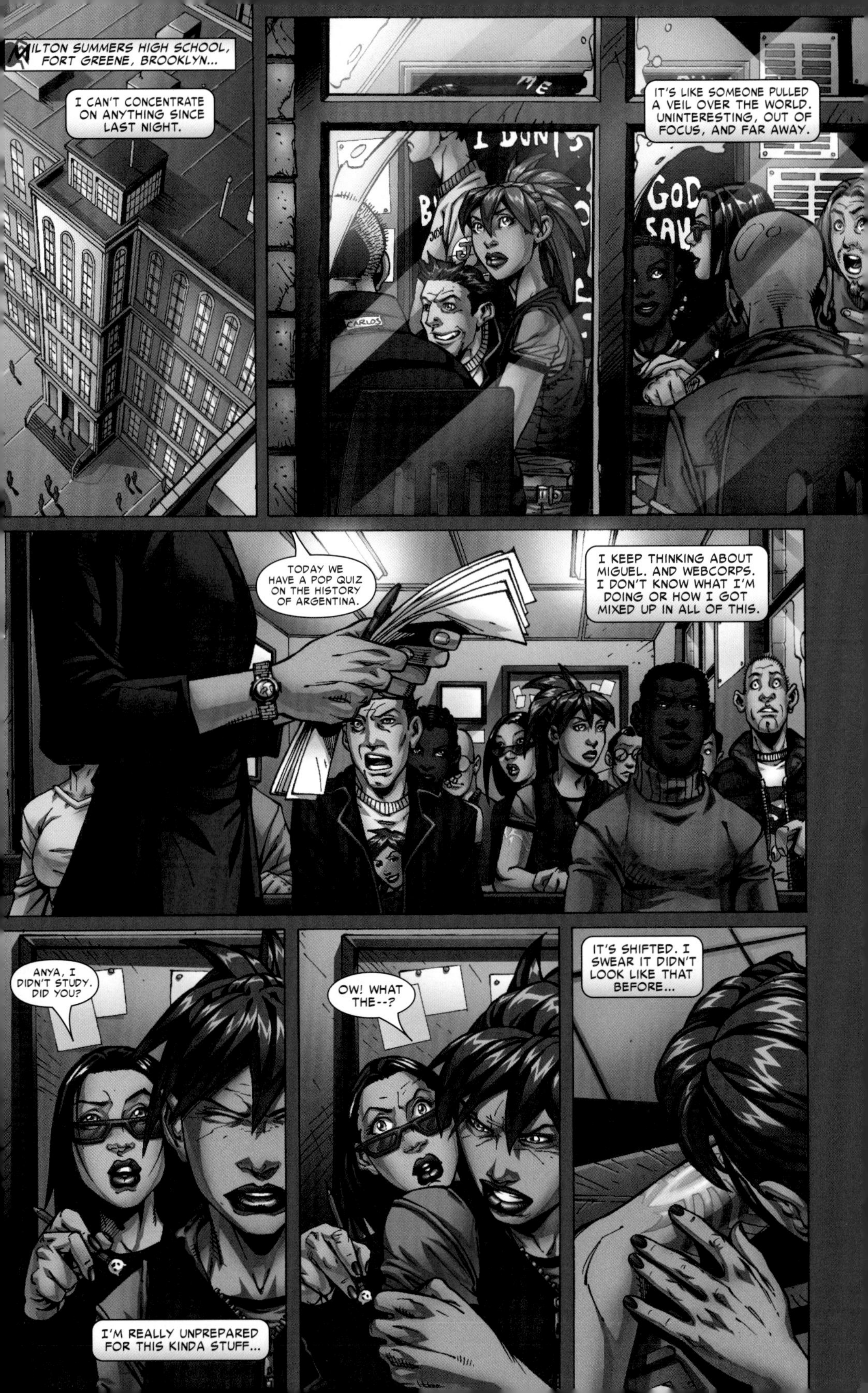
MILTON SUMMERS HIGH SCHOOL, FORT GREENE, BROOKLYN...
I CAN'T CONCENTRATE ON ANYTHING SINCE LAST NIGHT.
IT'S LIKE SOMEONE PULLED A VEIL OVER THE WORLD. UNINTERESTING, OUT OF FOCUS, AND FAR AWAY.
TODAY WE HAVE A POP QUIZ ON THE HISTORY OF ARGENTINA.
I KEEP THINKING ABOUT MIGUEL. AND WEBCORPS. I DON'T KNOW WHAT I'M DOING OR HOW I GOT MIXED UP IN ALL OF THIS.
ANYA, I DIDN'T STUDY. DID YOU?
I'M REALLY UNPREPARED FOR THIS KINDA STUFF...
OW! WHAT THE--?
IT'S SHIFTED. I SWEAR IT DIDN'T LOOK LIKE THAT BEFORE...

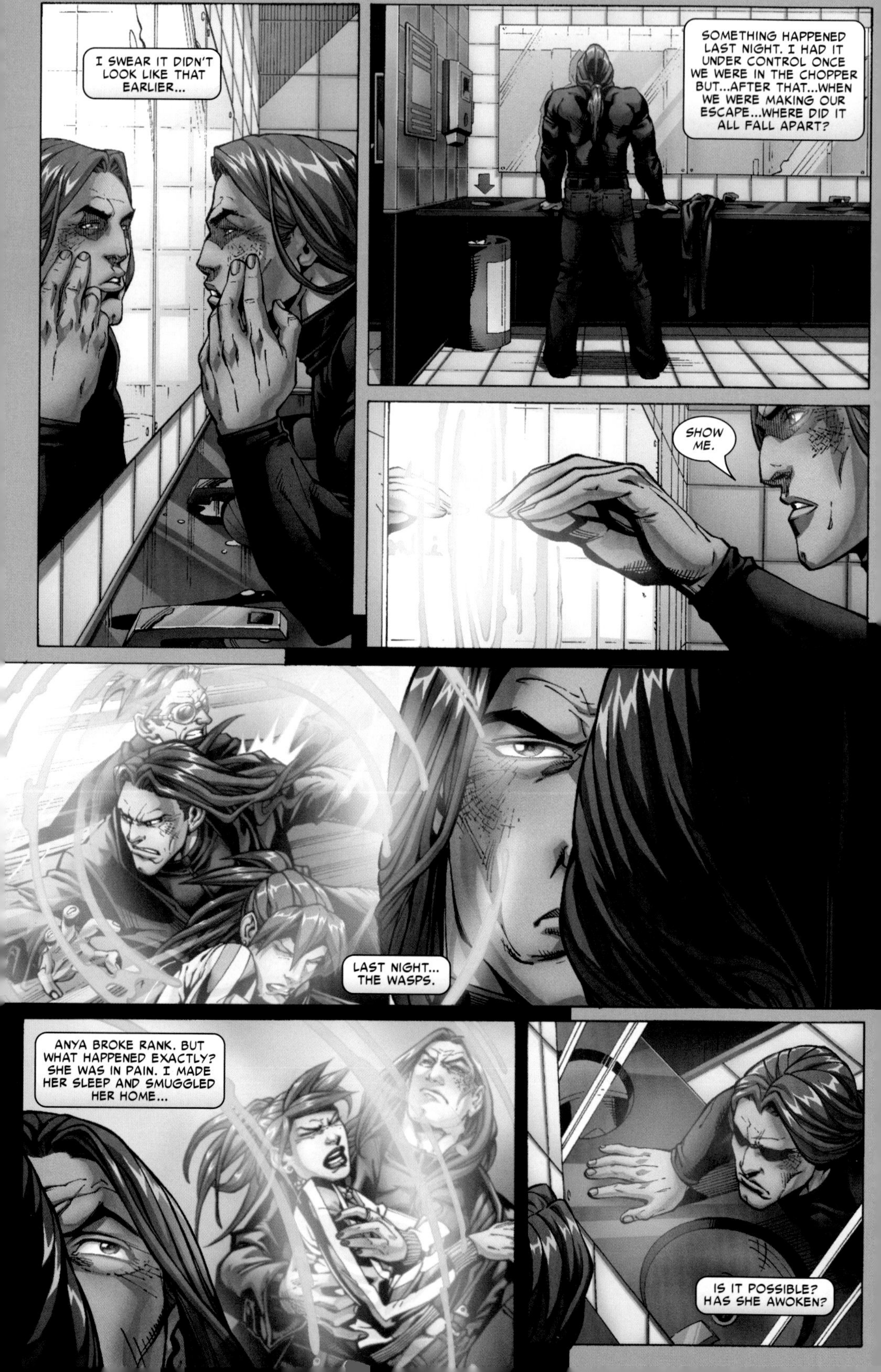
I SWEAR IT DIDN'T LOOK LIKE THAT EARLIER...
SOMETHING HAPPENED LAST NIGHT. I HAD IT UNDER CONTROL ONCE WE WERE IN THE CHOPPER BUT...AFTER THAT...WHEN WE WERE MAKING OUR ESCAPE...WHERE DID IT ALL FALL APART?
SHOW ME.
LAST NIGHT... THE WASPS.
ANYA BROKE RANK. BUT WHAT HAPPENED EXACTLY? SHE WAS IN PAIN. I MADE HER SLEEP AND SMUGGLED HER HOME...
IS IT POSSIBLE? HAS SHE AWOKEN?

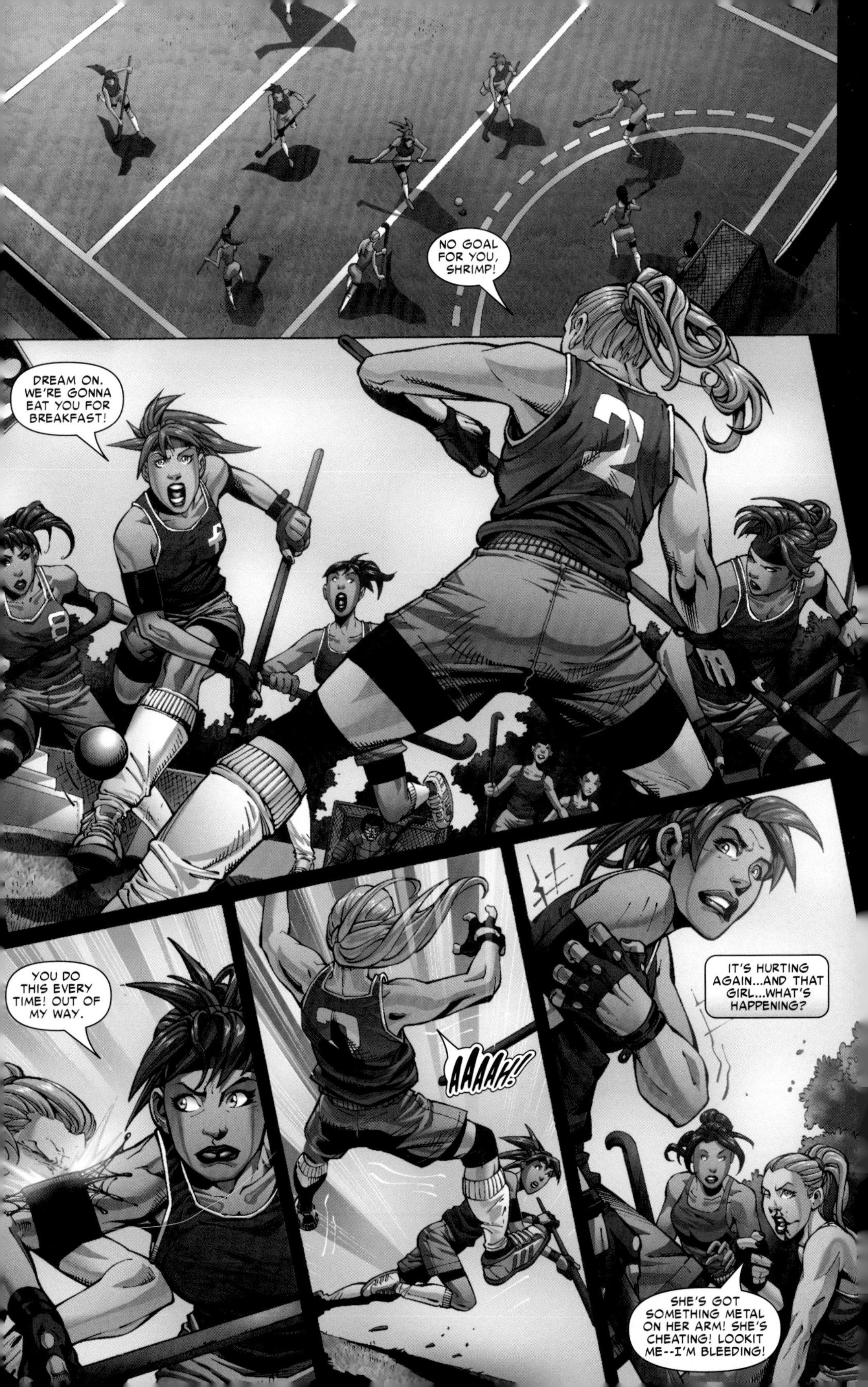
NO GOAL FOR YOU, SHRIMP!
DREAM ON. WE'RE GONNA EAT YOU FOR BREAKFAST!
YOU DO THIS EVERY TIME! OUT OF MY WAY.
AAAAH!
IT'S HURTING AGAIN...AND THAT GIRL...WHAT'S HAPPENING?
SHE'S GOT SOMETHING METAL ON HER ARM! SHE'S CHEATING! LOOKIT ME--I'M BLEEDING!

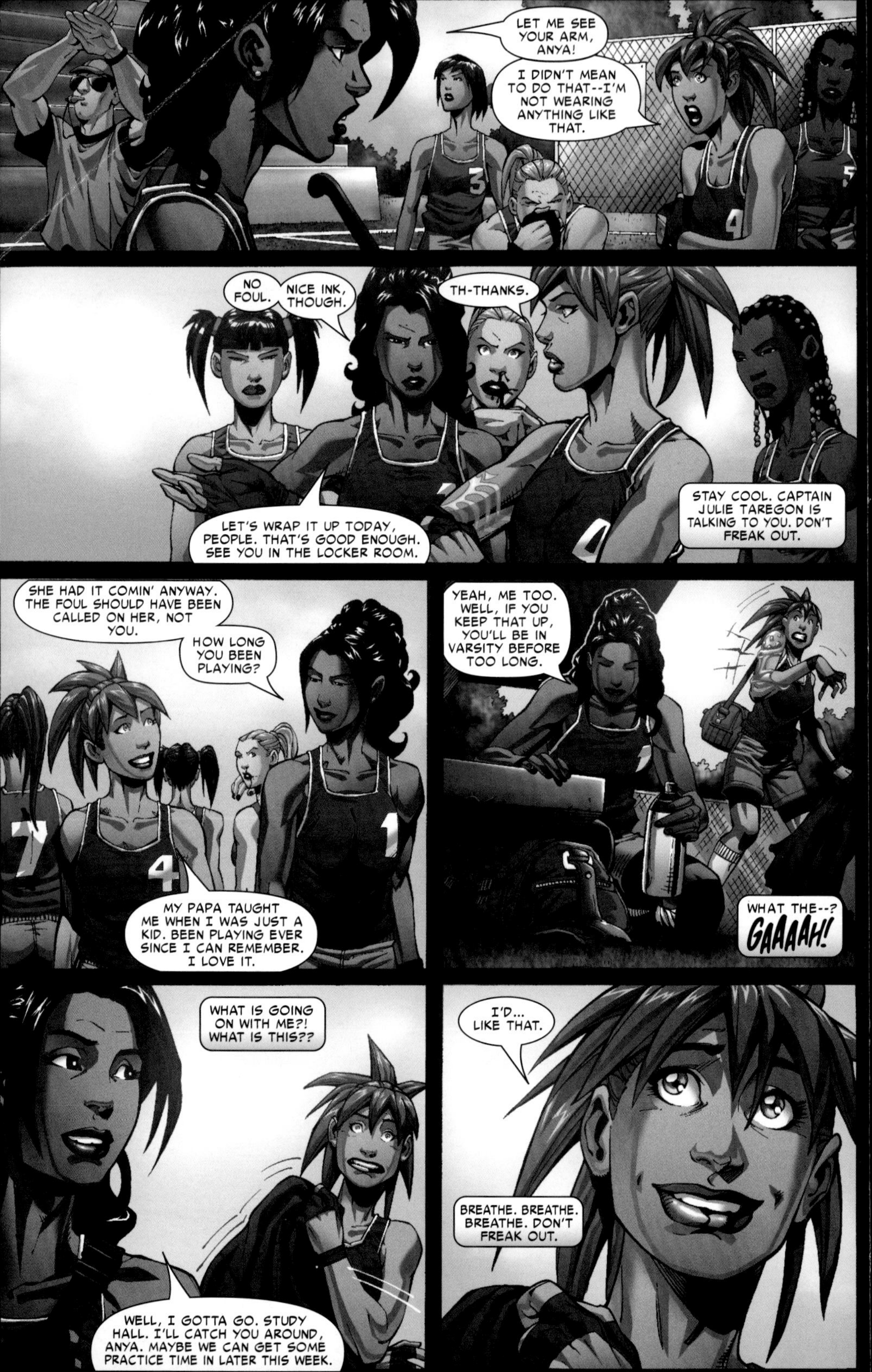
LET ME SEE YOUR ARM, ANYA!
I DIDN'T MEAN TO DO THAT--I'M NOT WEARING ANYTHING LIKE THAT.
NO FOUL.
NICE INK, THOUGH.
TH-THANKS.
LET'S WRAP IT UP TODAY, PEOPLE. THAT'S GOOD ENOUGH. SEE YOU IN THE LOCKER ROOM.
STAY COOL. CAPTAIN JULIE TAREGON IS TALKING TO YOU. DON'T FREAK OUT.
SHE HAD IT COMIN' ANYWAY. THE FOUL SHOULD HAVE BEEN CALLED ON HER, NOT YOU.
HOW LONG YOU BEEN PLAYING?
MY PAPA TAUGHT ME WHEN I WAS JUST A KID. BEEN PLAYING EVER SINCE I CAN REMEMBER. I LOVE IT.
YEAH, ME TOO. WELL, IF YOU KEEP THAT UP, YOU'LL BE IN VARSITY BEFORE TOO LONG.
WHAT THE--? GAAAAH!
WHAT IS GOING ON WITH ME?! WHAT IS THIS??
WELL, I GOTTA GO. STUDY HALL. I'LL CATCH YOU AROUND, ANYA. MAYBE WE CAN GET SOME PRACTICE TIME IN LATER THIS WEEK.
I'D... LIKE THAT.
BREATHE. BREATHE. BREATHE. DON'T FREAK OUT.

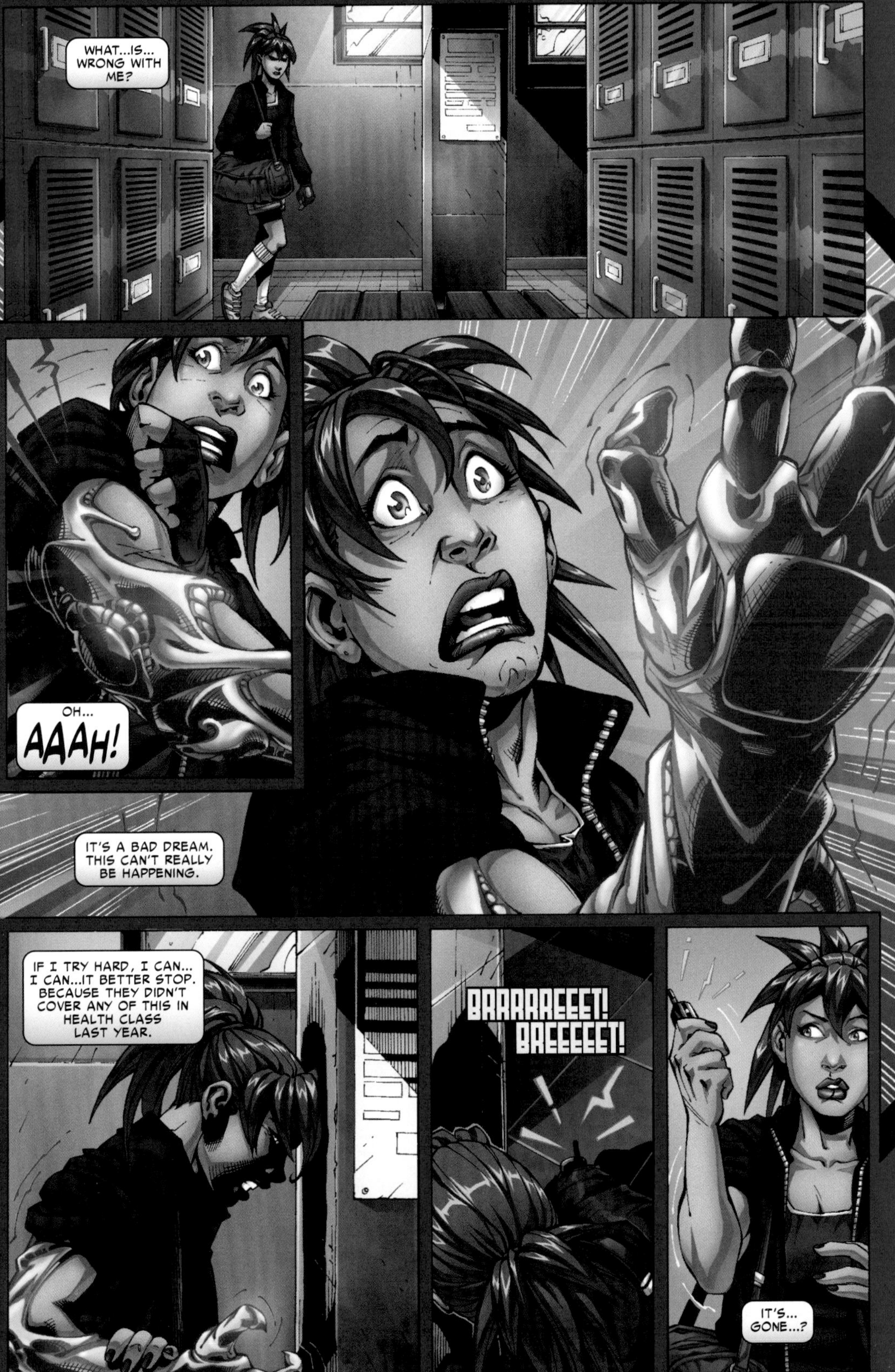
WHAT...IS... WRONG WITH ME?
OH... AAAH!
IT'S A BAD DREAM. THIS CAN'T REALLY BE HAPPENING.
IF I TRY HARD, I CAN... I CAN...IT BETTER STOP. BECAUSE THEY DIDN'T COVER ANY OF THIS IN HEALTH CLASS LAST YEAR.
BRRRRREEET! BREEEEET!
IT'S... GONE...?

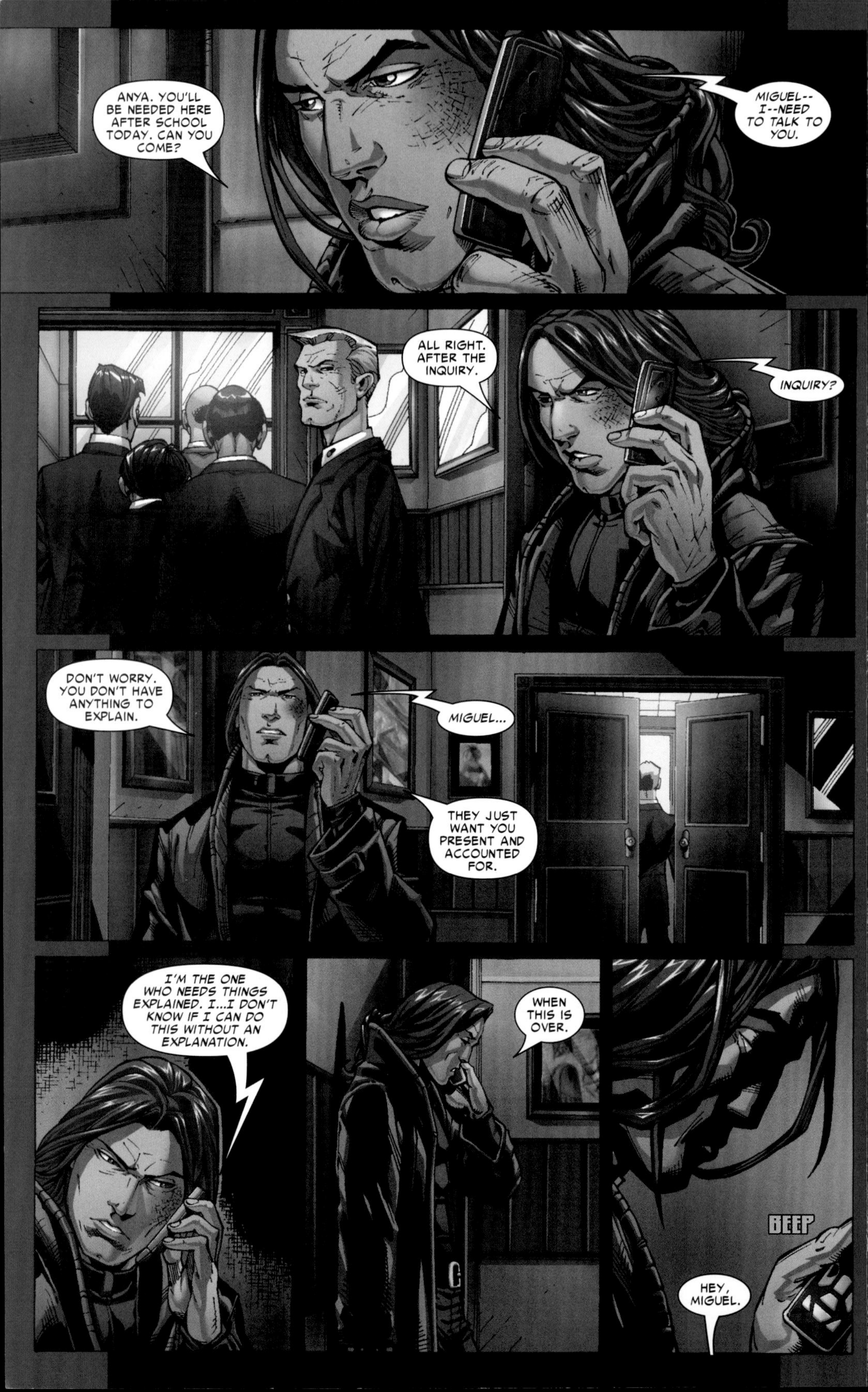
ANYA. YOU'LL BE NEEDED HERE AFTER SCHOOL TODAY. CAN YOU COME?
MIGUEL-- I--NEED TO TALK TO YOU.
ALL RIGHT. AFTER THE INQUIRY.
INQUIRY?
DON'T WORRY. YOU DON'T HAVE ANYTHING TO EXPLAIN.
MIGUEL...
THEY JUST WANT YOU PRESENT AND ACCOUNTED FOR.
I'M THE ONE WHO NEEDS THINGS EXPLAINED. I...I DON'T KNOW IF I CAN DO THIS WITHOUT AN EXPLANATION.
WHEN THIS IS OVER.
BEEP
HEY, MIGUEL.

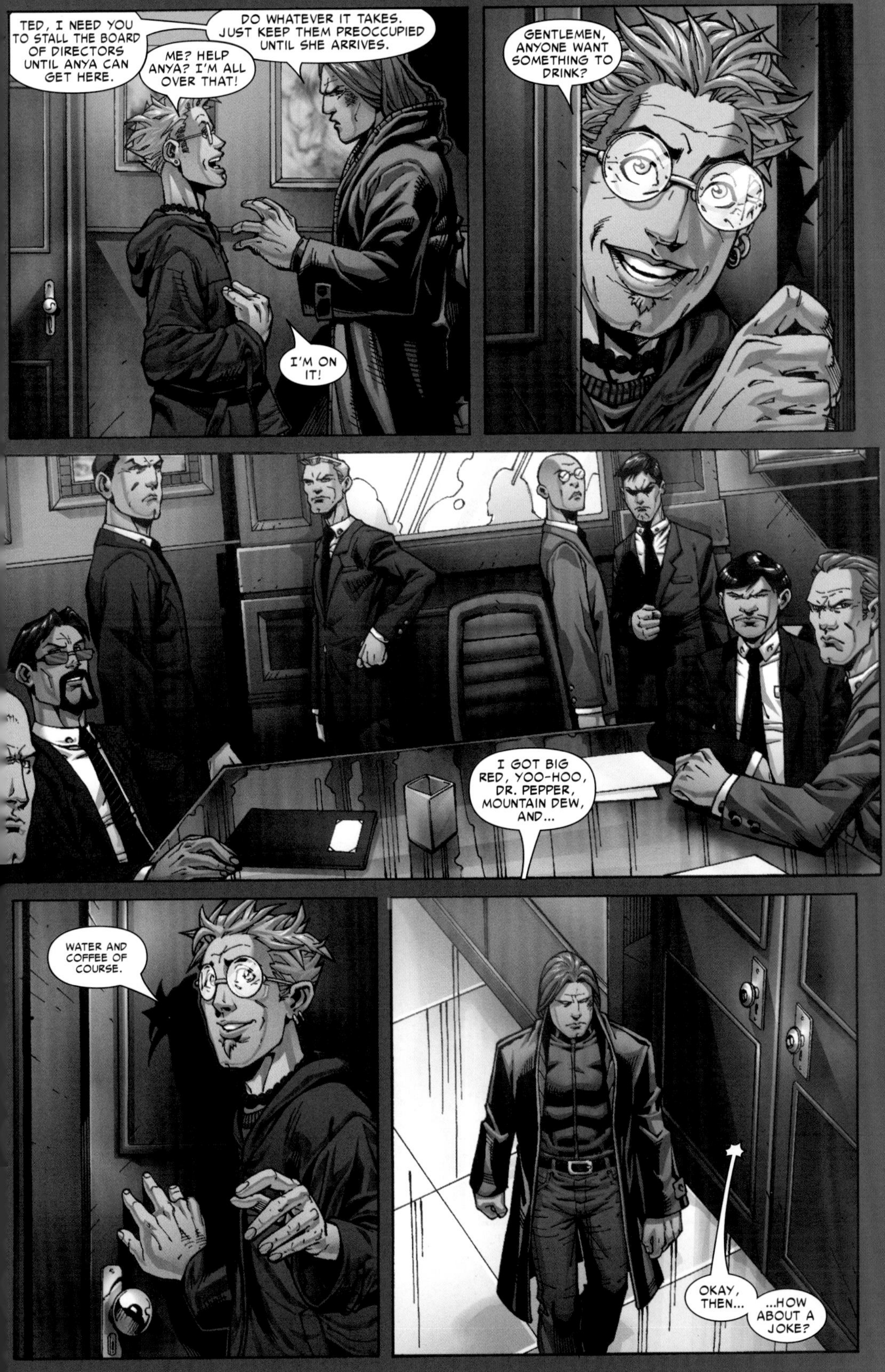

TED, I NEED YOU TO STALL THE BOARD OF DIRECTORS UNTIL ANYA CAN GET HERE.
ME? HELP ANYA? I'M ALL OVER THAT!
DO WHATEVER IT TAKES. JUST KEEP THEM PREOCCUPIED UNTIL SHE ARRIVES.
I'M ON IT!
GENTLEMEN, ANYONE WANT SOMETHING TO DRINK?
I GOT BIG RED, YOO-HOO, DR. PEPPER, MOUNTAIN DEW, AND...
WATER AND COFFEE OF COURSE.
OKAY, THEN...
...HOW ABOUT A JOKE?

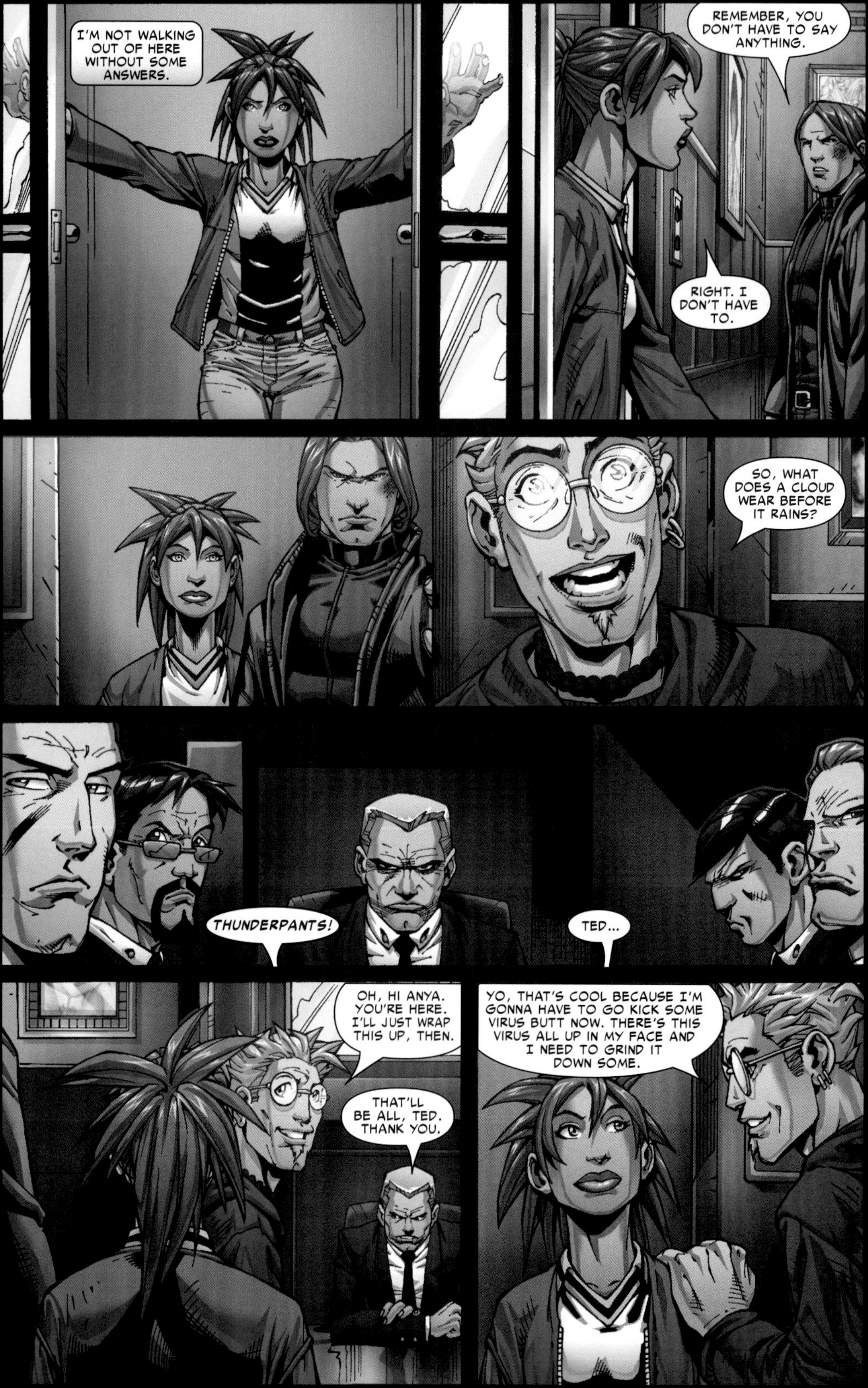
I'M NOT WALKING OUT OF HERE WITHOUT SOME ANSWERS.
REMEMBER, YOU DON'T HAVE TO SAY ANYTHING.
RIGHT. I DON'T HAVE TO.
SO, WHAT DOES A CLOUD WEAR BEFORE IT RAINS?
THUNDERPANTS!
TED...
OH, HI ANYA. YOU'RE HERE. I'LL JUST WRAP THIS UP, THEN.
THAT'LL BE ALL, TED. THANK YOU.
YO, THAT'S COOL BECAUSE I'M GONNA HAVE TO GO KICK SOME VIRUS BUTT NOW. THERE'S THIS VIRUS ALL UP IN MY FACE AND I NEED TO GRIND IT DOWN SOME.

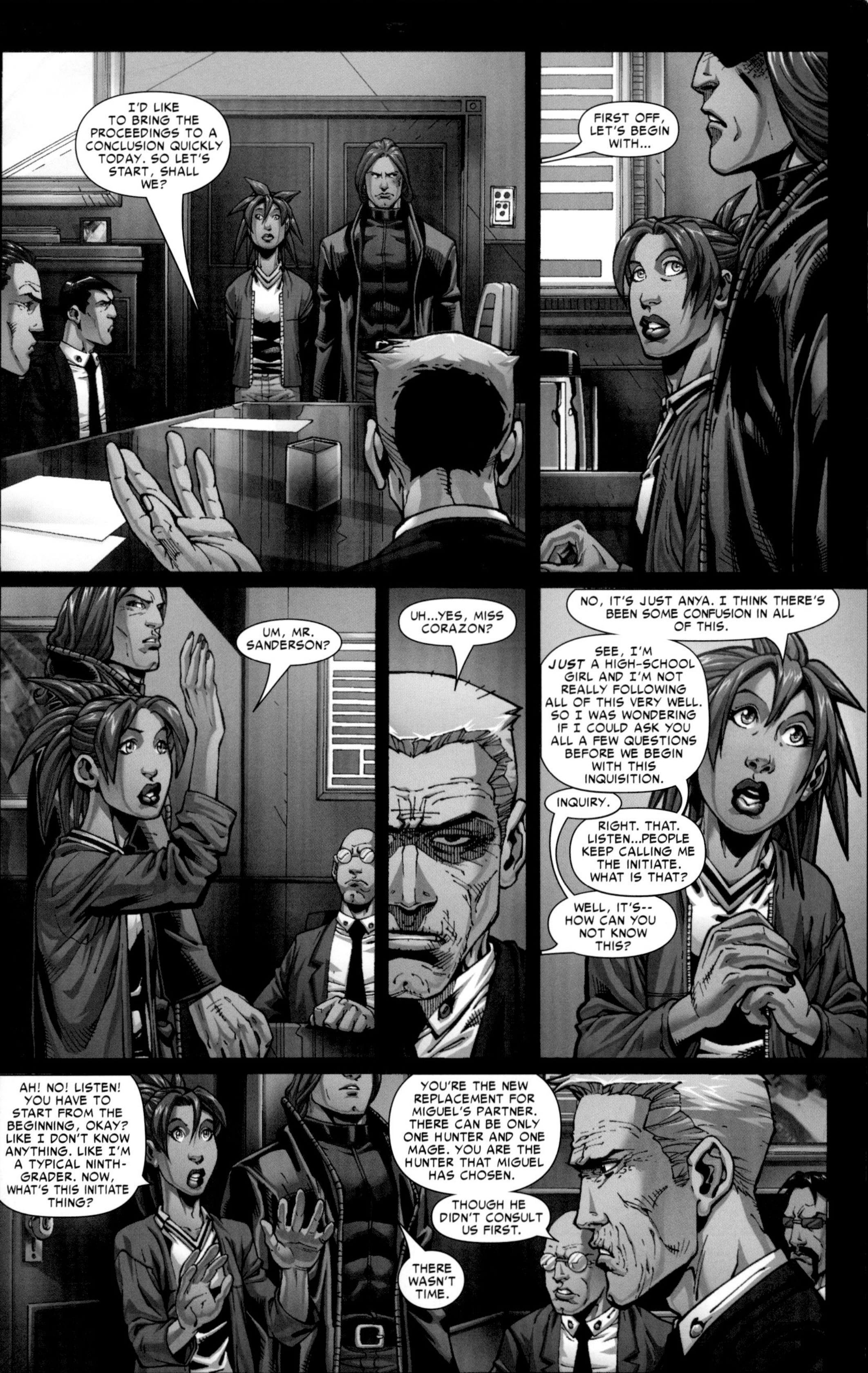
I'D LIKE TO BRING THE PROCEEDINGS TO A CONCLUSION QUICKLY TODAY. SO LET'S START, SHALL WE?
FIRST OFF, LET'S BEGIN WITH...
UM, MR. SANDERSON?
UH...YES, MISS CORAZON?
NO, IT'S JUST ANYA. I THINK THERE'S BEEN SOME CONFUSION IN ALL OF THIS.
SEE, I'M JUST A HIGH-SCHOOL GIRL AND I'M NOT REALLY FOLLOWING ALL OF THIS VERY WELL. SO I WAS WONDERING IF I COULD ASK YOU ALL A FEW QUESTIONS BEFORE WE BEGIN WITH THIS INQUISITION.
INQUIRY.
RIGHT. THAT. LISTEN...PEOPLE KEEP CALLING ME THE INITIATE. WHAT IS THAT?
WELL, IT'S-- HOW CAN YOU NOT KNOW THIS?
AH! NO! LISTEN! YOU HAVE TO START FROM THE BEGINNING, OKAY? LIKE I DON'T KNOW ANYTHING. LIKE I'M A TYPICAL NINTH-GRADER. NOW, WHAT'S THIS INITIATE THING?
YOU'RE THE NEW REPLACEMENT FOR MIGUEL'S PARTNER. THERE CAN BE ONLY ONE HUNTER AND ONE MAGE. YOU ARE THE HUNTER THAT MIGUEL HAS CHOSEN.
THOUGH HE DIDN'T CONSULT US FIRST.
THERE WASN'T TIME.

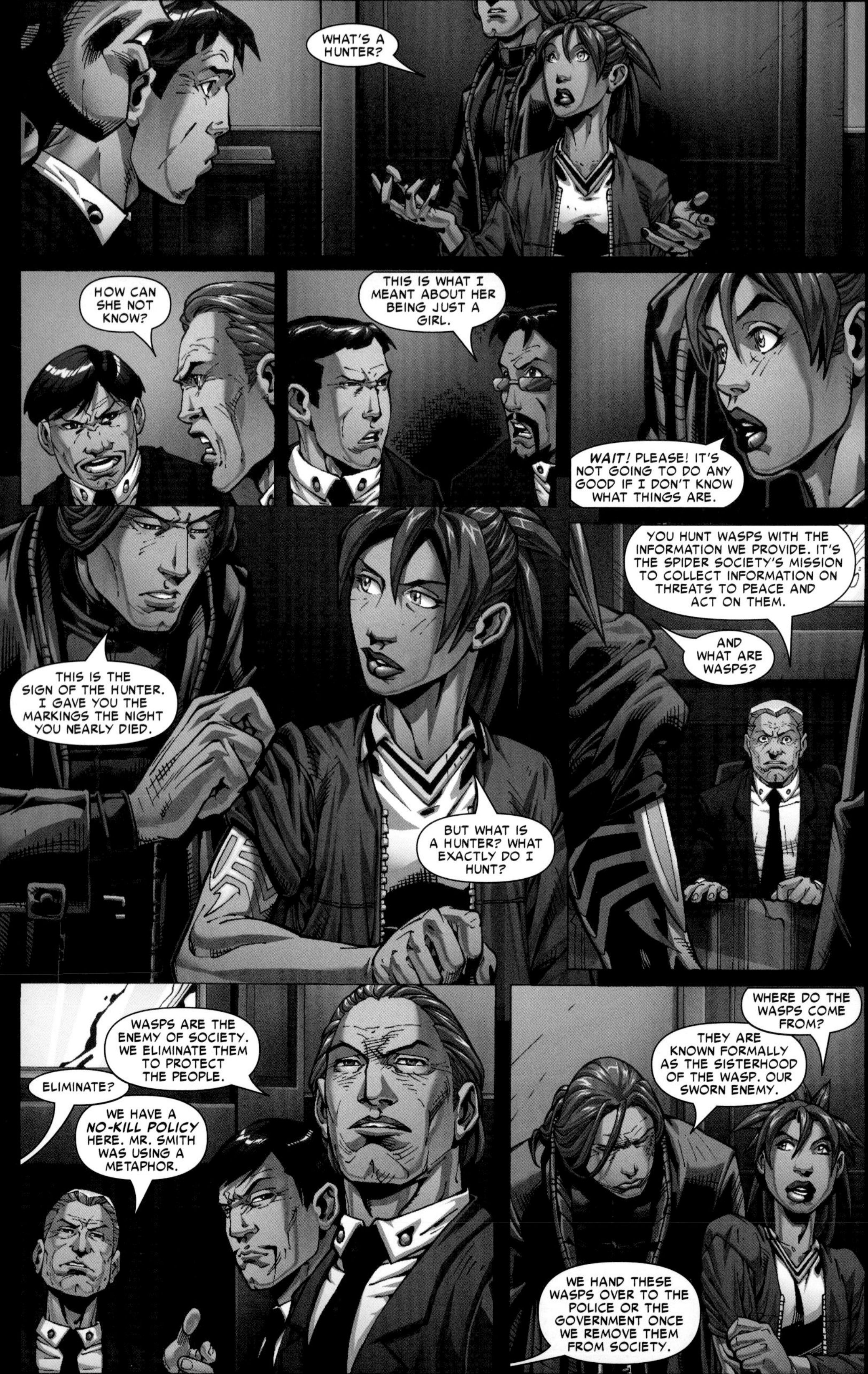
WHAT'S A HUNTER?
HOW CAN SHE NOT KNOW?
THIS IS WHAT I MEANT ABOUT HER BEING JUST A GIRL.
WAIT! PLEASE! IT'S NOT GOING TO DO ANY GOOD IF I DON'T KNOW WHAT THINGS ARE.
THIS IS THE SIGN OF THE HUNTER. I GAVE YOU THE MARKINGS THE NIGHT YOU NEARLY DIED.
BUT WHAT IS A HUNTER? WHAT EXACTLY DO I HUNT?
YOU HUNT WASPS WITH THE INFORMATION WE PROVIDE. IT'S THE SPIDER SOCIETY'S MISSION TO COLLECT INFORMATION ON THREATS TO PEACE AND ACT ON THEM.
AND WHAT ARE WASPS?
WASPS ARE THE ENEMY OF SOCIETY. WE ELIMINATE THEM TO PROTECT THE PEOPLE.
ELIMINATE?
WE HAVE A ***NO-KILL POLICY*** HERE. MR. SMITH WAS USING A METAPHOR.
WHERE DO THE WASPS COME FROM?
THEY ARE KNOWN FORMALLY AS THE SISTERHOOD OF THE WASP. OUR SWORN ENEMY.
WE HAND THESE WASPS OVER TO THE POLICE OR THE GOVERNMENT ONCE WE REMOVE THEM FROM SOCIETY.

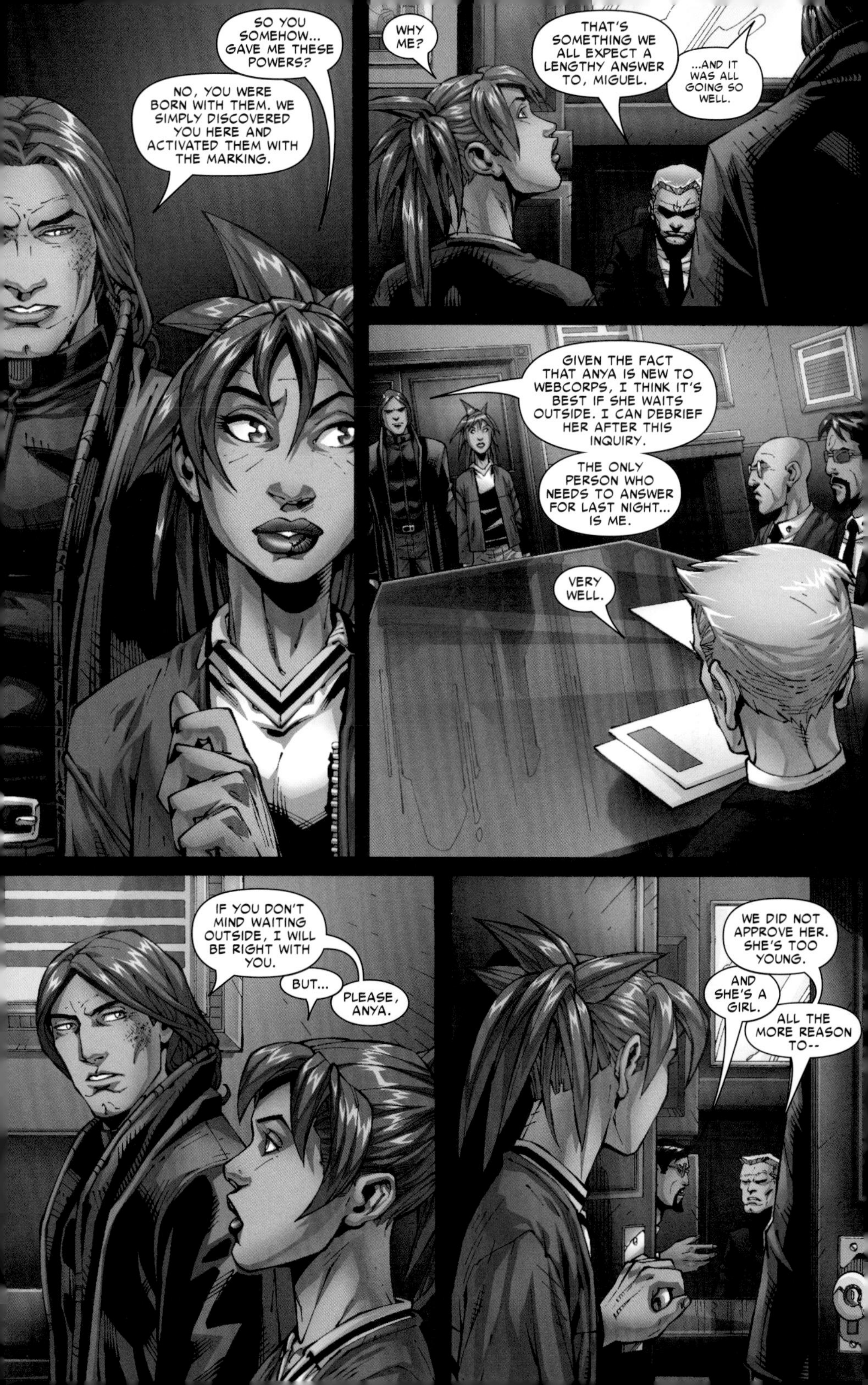
SO YOU SOMEHOW... GAVE ME THESE POWERS?
NO, YOU WERE BORN WITH THEM. WE SIMPLY DISCOVERED YOU HERE AND ACTIVATED THEM WITH THE MARKING.
WHY ME?
THAT'S SOMETHING WE ALL EXPECT A LENGTHY ANSWER TO, MIGUEL.
...AND IT WAS ALL GOING SO WELL.
GIVEN THE FACT THAT ANYA IS NEW TO WEBCORPS, I THINK IT'S BEST IF SHE WAITS OUTSIDE. I CAN DEBRIEF HER AFTER THIS INQUIRY.
THE ONLY PERSON WHO NEEDS TO ANSWER FOR LAST NIGHT... IS ME.
VERY WELL.
IF YOU DON'T MIND WAITING OUTSIDE, I WILL BE RIGHT WITH YOU.
BUT...
PLEASE, ANYA.
WE DID NOT APPROVE HER. SHE'S TOO YOUNG.
AND SHE'S A GIRL.
ALL THE MORE REASON TO--

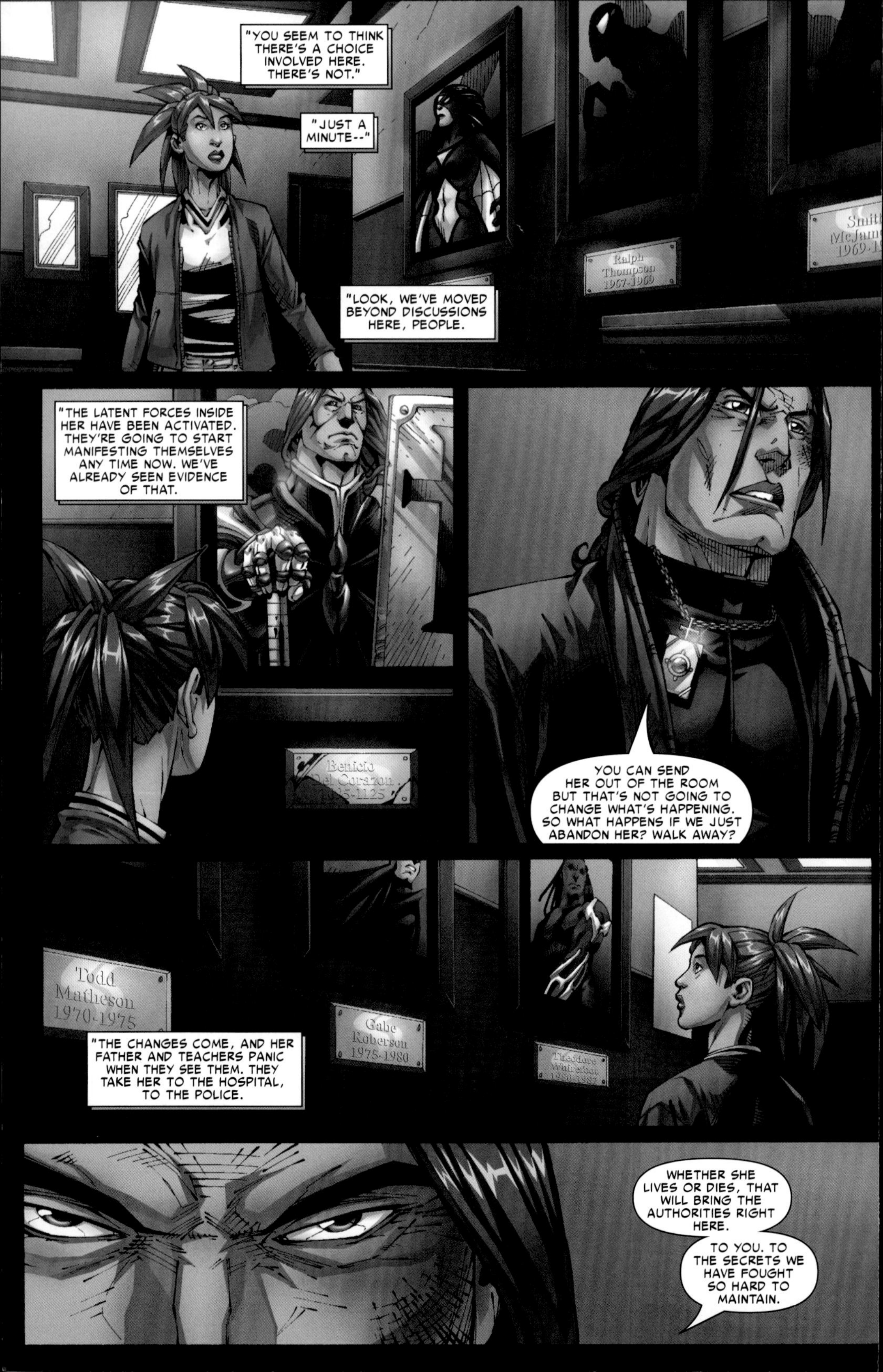
"YOU SEEM TO THINK THERE'S A CHOICE INVOLVED HERE. THERE'S NOT."
"JUST A MINUTE--"
Ralph Thompson 1967-1969
"LOOK, WE'VE MOVED BEYOND DISCUSSIONS HERE, PEOPLE.
"THE LATENT FORCES INSIDE HER HAVE BEEN ACTIVATED. THEY'RE GOING TO START MANIFESTING THEMSELVES ANY TIME NOW. WE'VE ALREADY SEEN EVIDENCE OF THAT.
YOU CAN SEND HER OUT OF THE ROOM BUT THAT'S NOT GOING TO CHANGE WHAT'S HAPPENING. SO WHAT HAPPENS IF WE JUST ABANDON HER? WALK AWAY?
Todd Matheson 1970-1975
Gabe Roberson 1975-1980
"THE CHANGES COME, AND HER FATHER AND TEACHERS PANIC WHEN THEY SEE THEM. THEY TAKE HER TO THE HOSPITAL, TO THE POLICE.
WHETHER SHE LIVES OR DIES, THAT WILL BRING THE AUTHORITIES RIGHT HERE.
TO YOU. TO THE SECRETS WE HAVE FOUGHT SO HARD TO MAINTAIN.

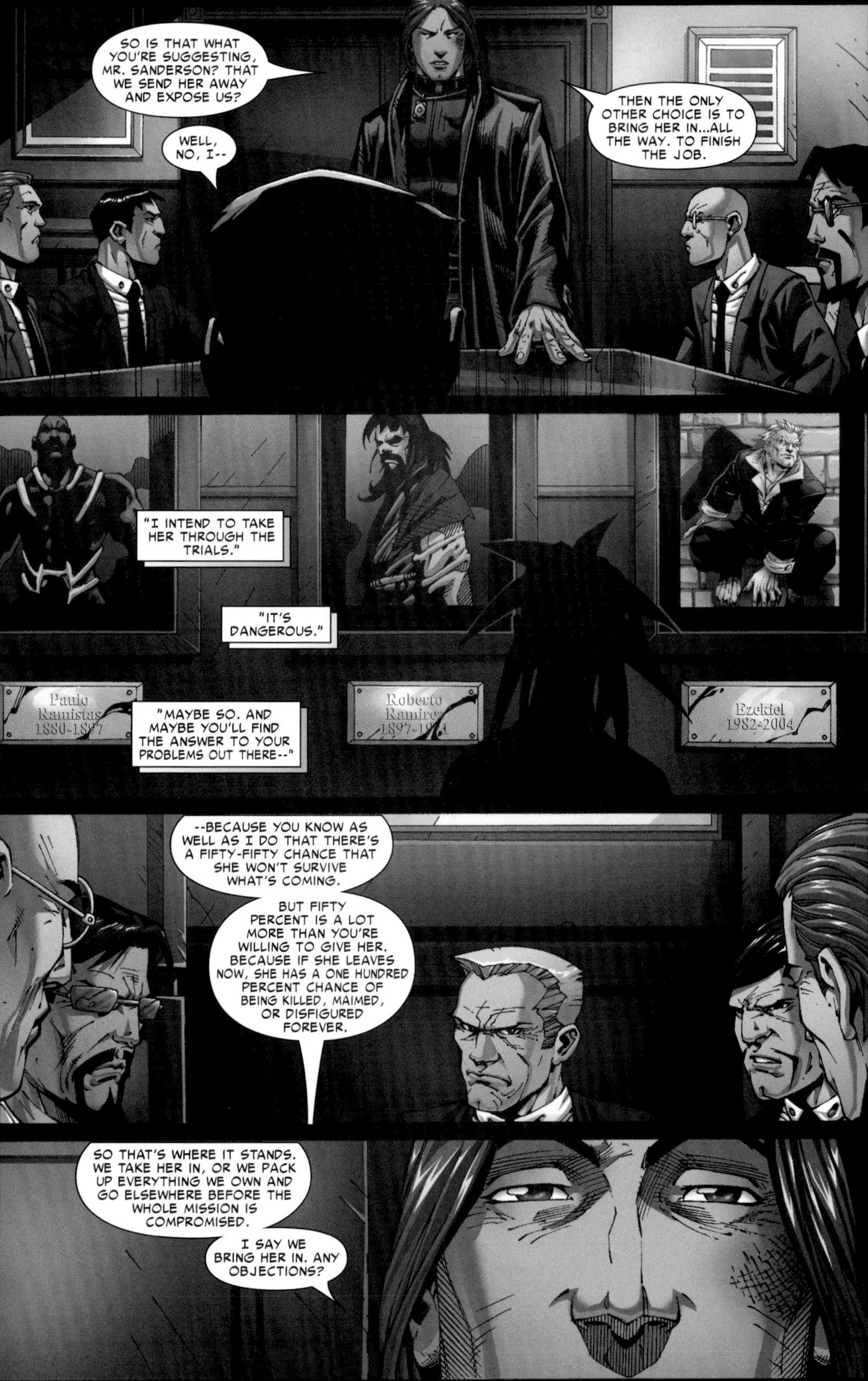
SO IS THAT WHAT YOU'RE SUGGESTING, MR. SANDERSON? THAT WE SEND HER AWAY AND EXPOSE US?
WELL, NO, I--
THEN THE ONLY OTHER CHOICE IS TO BRING HER IN...ALL THE WAY. TO FINISH THE JOB.
"I INTEND TO TAKE HER THROUGH THE TRIALS."
"IT'S DANGEROUS."
Paulo Ramistas 1880-1897
"MAYBE SO. AND MAYBE YOU'LL FIND THE ANSWER TO YOUR PROBLEMS OUT THERE--"
Roberto
Ezekiel 1982-2004
--BECAUSE YOU KNOW AS WELL AS I DO THAT THERE'S A FIFTY-FIFTY CHANCE THAT SHE WON'T SURVIVE WHAT'S COMING.
BUT FIFTY PERCENT IS A LOT MORE THAN YOU'RE WILLING TO GIVE HER. BECAUSE IF SHE LEAVES NOW, SHE HAS A ONE HUNDRED PERCENT CHANCE OF BEING KILLED, MAIMED, OR DISFIGURED FOREVER.
SO THAT'S WHERE IT STANDS. WE TAKE HER IN, OR WE PACK UP EVERYTHING WE OWN AND GO ELSEWHERE BEFORE THE WHOLE MISSION IS COMPROMISED.
I SAY WE BRING HER IN. ANY OBJECTIONS?

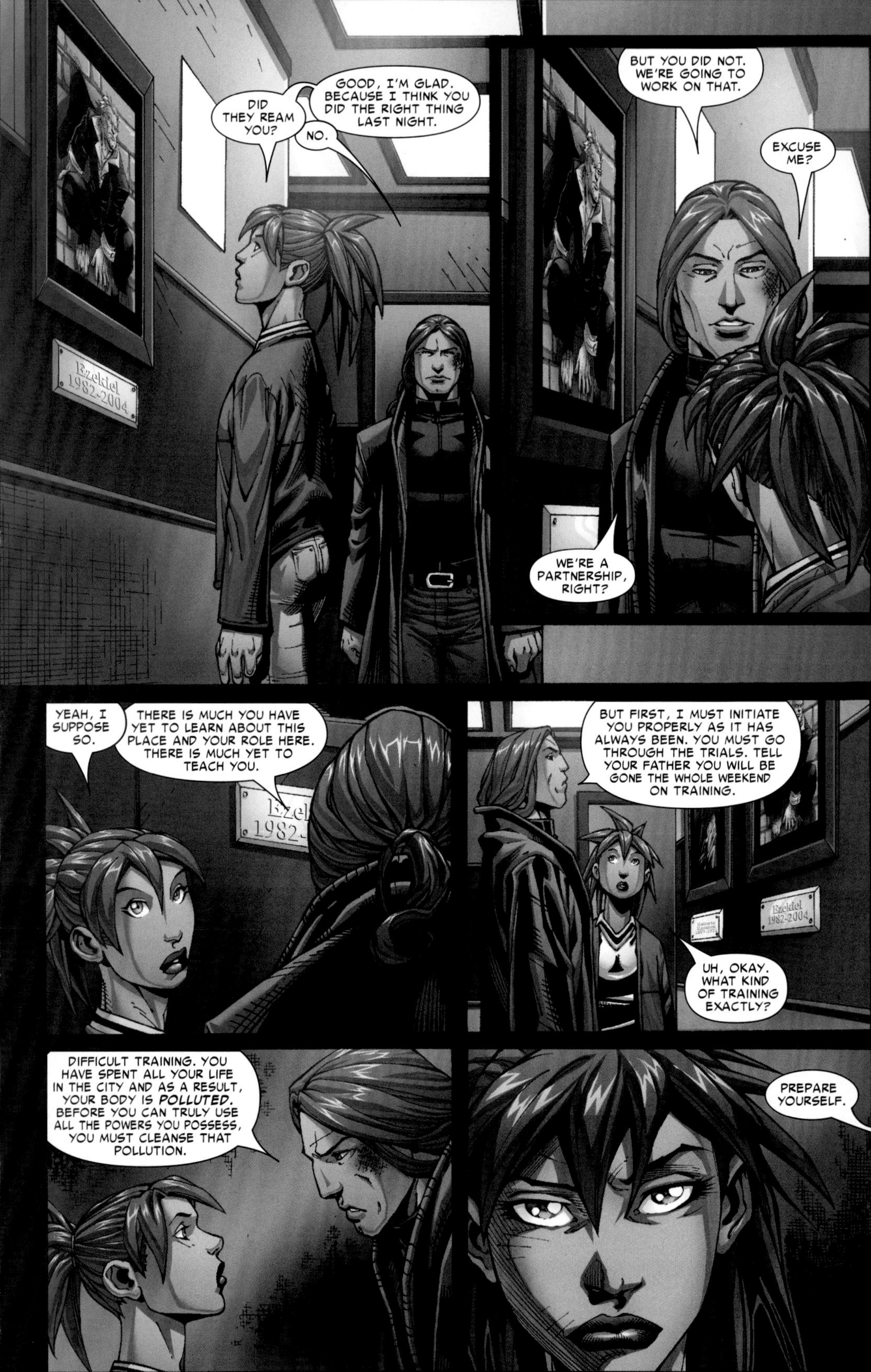

DID THEY REAM YOU?
NO.
GOOD, I'M GLAD. BECAUSE I THINK YOU DID THE RIGHT THING LAST NIGHT.
Ezekiel 1982-2004
BUT YOU DID NOT. WE'RE GOING TO WORK ON THAT.
EXCUSE ME?
WE'RE A PARTNERSHIP, RIGHT?
YEAH, I SUPPOSE SO.
THERE IS MUCH YOU HAVE YET TO LEARN ABOUT THIS PLACE AND YOUR ROLE HERE. THERE IS MUCH YET TO TEACH YOU.
BUT FIRST, I MUST INITIATE YOU PROPERLY AS IT HAS ALWAYS BEEN. YOU MUST GO THROUGH THE TRIALS. TELL YOUR FATHER YOU WILL BE GONE THE WHOLE WEEKEND ON TRAINING.
Ezekiel 1982-2004
UH, OKAY. WHAT KIND OF TRAINING EXACTLY?
DIFFICULT TRAINING. YOU HAVE SPENT ALL YOUR LIFE IN THE CITY AND AS A RESULT, YOUR BODY IS *POLLUTED*. BEFORE YOU CAN TRULY USE ALL THE POWERS YOU POSSESS, YOU MUST CLEANSE THAT POLLUTION.
PREPARE YOURSELF.

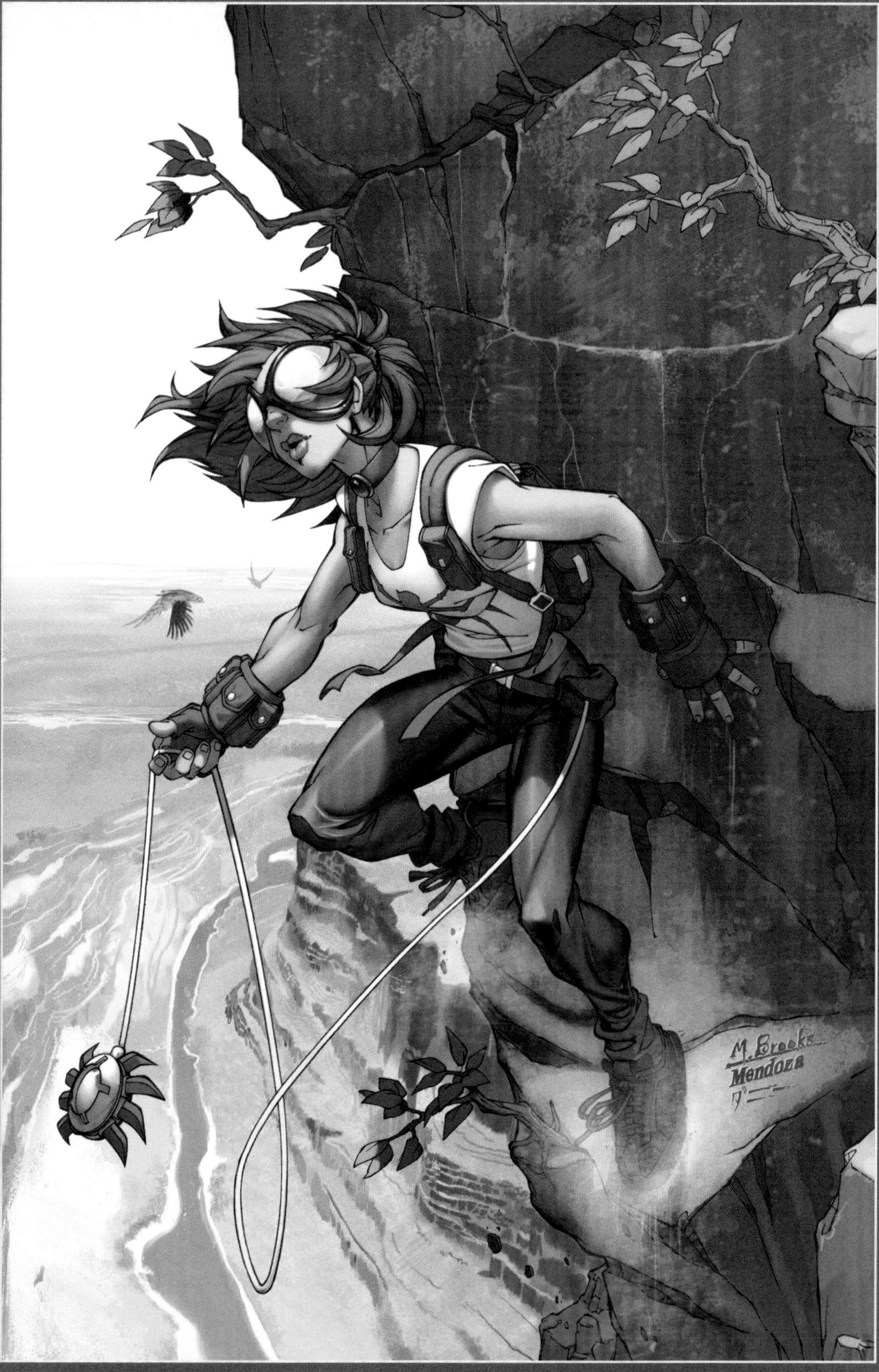
M. Brooks
Mendoza

AMAZING FANTASY #5

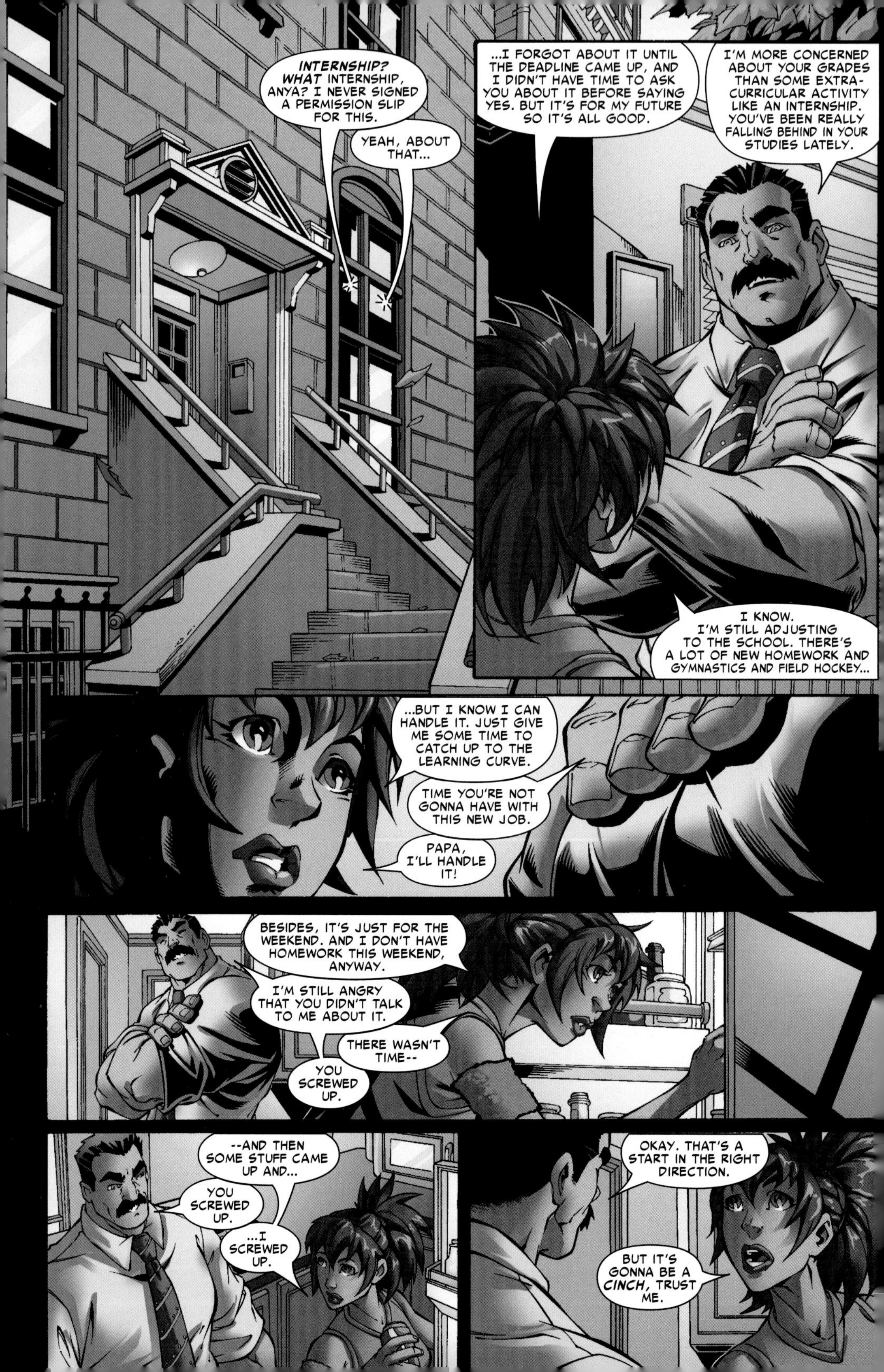
INTERNSHIP? WHAT INTERNSHIP, ANYA? I NEVER SIGNED A PERMISSION SLIP FOR THIS.
YEAH, ABOUT THAT...
...I FORGOT ABOUT IT UNTIL THE DEADLINE CAME UP, AND I DIDN'T HAVE TIME TO ASK YOU ABOUT IT BEFORE SAYING YES. BUT IT'S FOR MY FUTURE SO IT'S ALL GOOD.
I'M MORE CONCERNED ABOUT YOUR GRADES THAN SOME EXTRA-CURRICULAR ACTIVITY LIKE AN INTERNSHIP. YOU'VE BEEN REALLY FALLING BEHIND IN YOUR STUDIES LATELY.
I KNOW. I'M STILL ADJUSTING TO THE SCHOOL. THERE'S A LOT OF NEW HOMEWORK AND GYMNASTICS AND FIELD HOCKEY...
...BUT I KNOW I CAN HANDLE IT. JUST GIVE ME SOME TIME TO CATCH UP TO THE LEARNING CURVE.
TIME YOU'RE NOT GONNA HAVE WITH THIS NEW JOB.
PAPA, I'LL HANDLE IT!
BESIDES, IT'S JUST FOR THE WEEKEND. AND I DON'T HAVE HOMEWORK THIS WEEKEND, ANYWAY.
I'M STILL ANGRY THAT YOU DIDN'T TALK TO ME ABOUT IT.
THERE WASN'T TIME--
YOU SCREWED UP.
--AND THEN SOME STUFF CAME UP AND...
YOU SCREWED UP.
...I SCREWED UP.
OKAY. THAT'S A START IN THE RIGHT DIRECTION.
BUT IT'S GONNA BE A CINCH, TRUST ME.

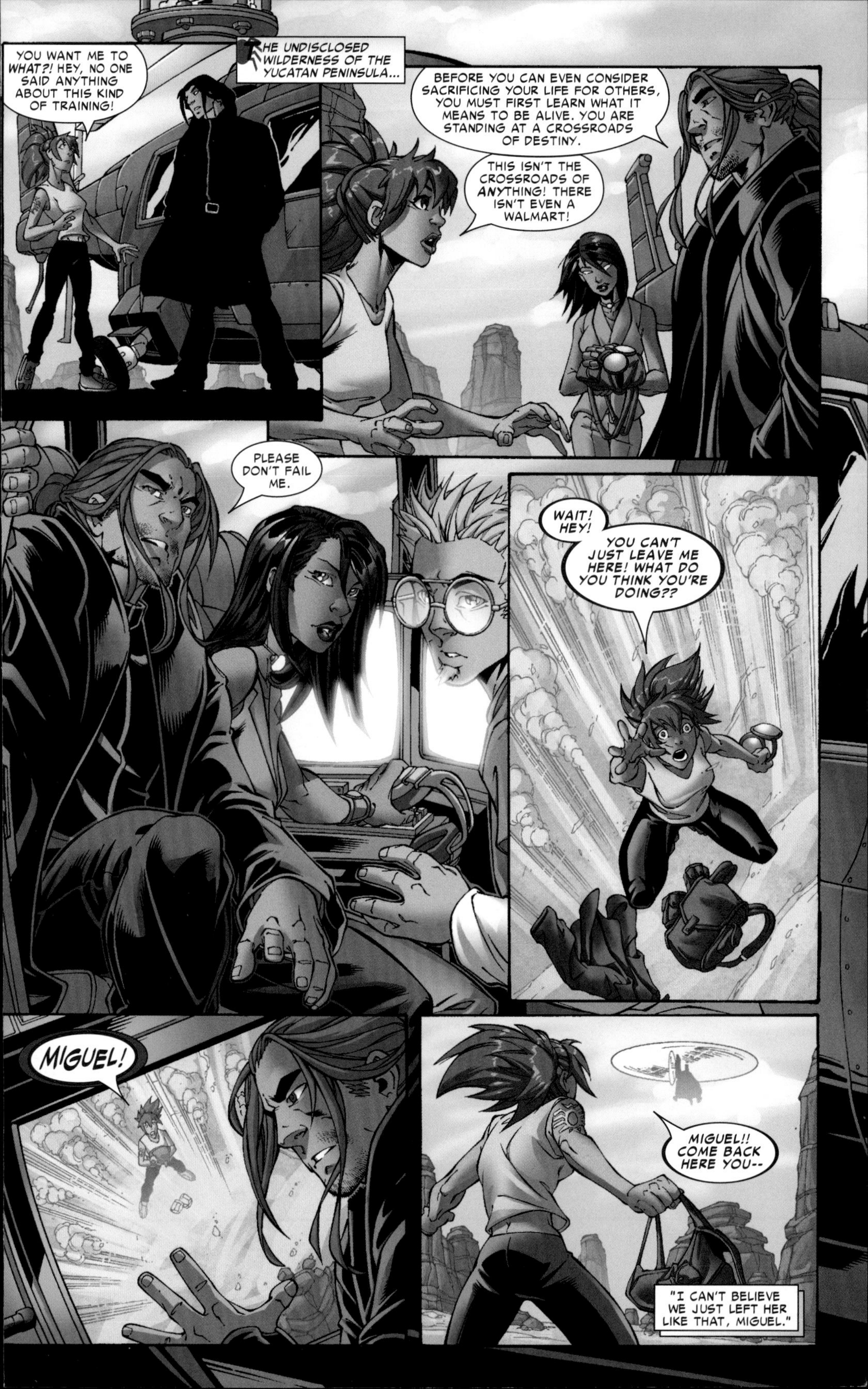
THE UNDISCLOSED WILDERNESS OF THE YUCATAN PENINSULA...
YOU WANT ME TO WHAT?! HEY, NO ONE SAID ANYTHING ABOUT THIS KIND OF TRAINING!
BEFORE YOU CAN EVEN CONSIDER SACRIFICING YOUR LIFE FOR OTHERS, YOU MUST FIRST LEARN WHAT IT MEANS TO BE ALIVE. YOU ARE STANDING AT A CROSSROADS OF DESTINY.
THIS ISN'T THE CROSSROADS OF ANYTHING! THERE ISN'T EVEN A WALMART!
PLEASE DON'T FAIL ME.
WAIT! HEY!
YOU CAN'T JUST LEAVE ME HERE! WHAT DO YOU THINK YOU'RE DOING??
MIGUEL!
MIGUEL!! COME BACK HERE YOU--
"I CAN'T BELIEVE WE JUST LEFT HER LIKE THAT, MIGUEL."

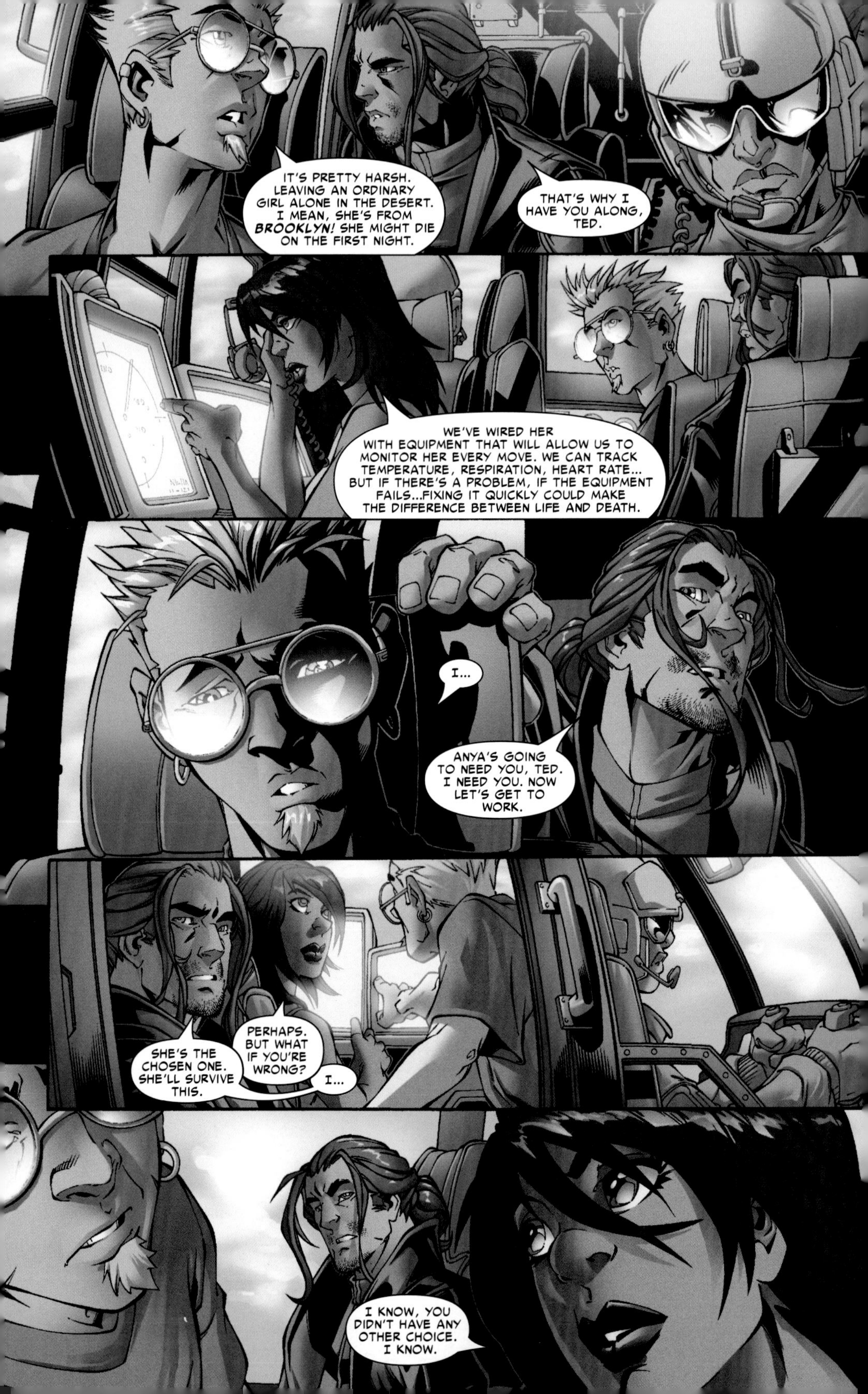
IT'S PRETTY HARSH. LEAVING AN ORDINARY GIRL ALONE IN THE DESERT. I MEAN, SHE'S FROM *BROOKLYN!* SHE MIGHT DIE ON THE FIRST NIGHT.
THAT'S WHY I HAVE YOU ALONG, TED.
WE'VE WIRED HER WITH EQUIPMENT THAT WILL ALLOW US TO MONITOR HER EVERY MOVE. WE CAN TRACK TEMPERATURE, RESPIRATION, HEART RATE... BUT IF THERE'S A PROBLEM, IF THE EQUIPMENT FAILS...FIXING IT QUICKLY COULD MAKE THE DIFFERENCE BETWEEN LIFE AND DEATH.
I...
ANYA'S GOING TO NEED YOU, TED. I NEED YOU. NOW LET'S GET TO WORK.
SHE'S THE CHOSEN ONE. SHE'LL SURVIVE THIS.
PERHAPS. BUT WHAT IF YOU'RE WRONG?
I...
I KNOW, YOU DIDN'T HAVE ANY OTHER CHOICE. I KNOW.

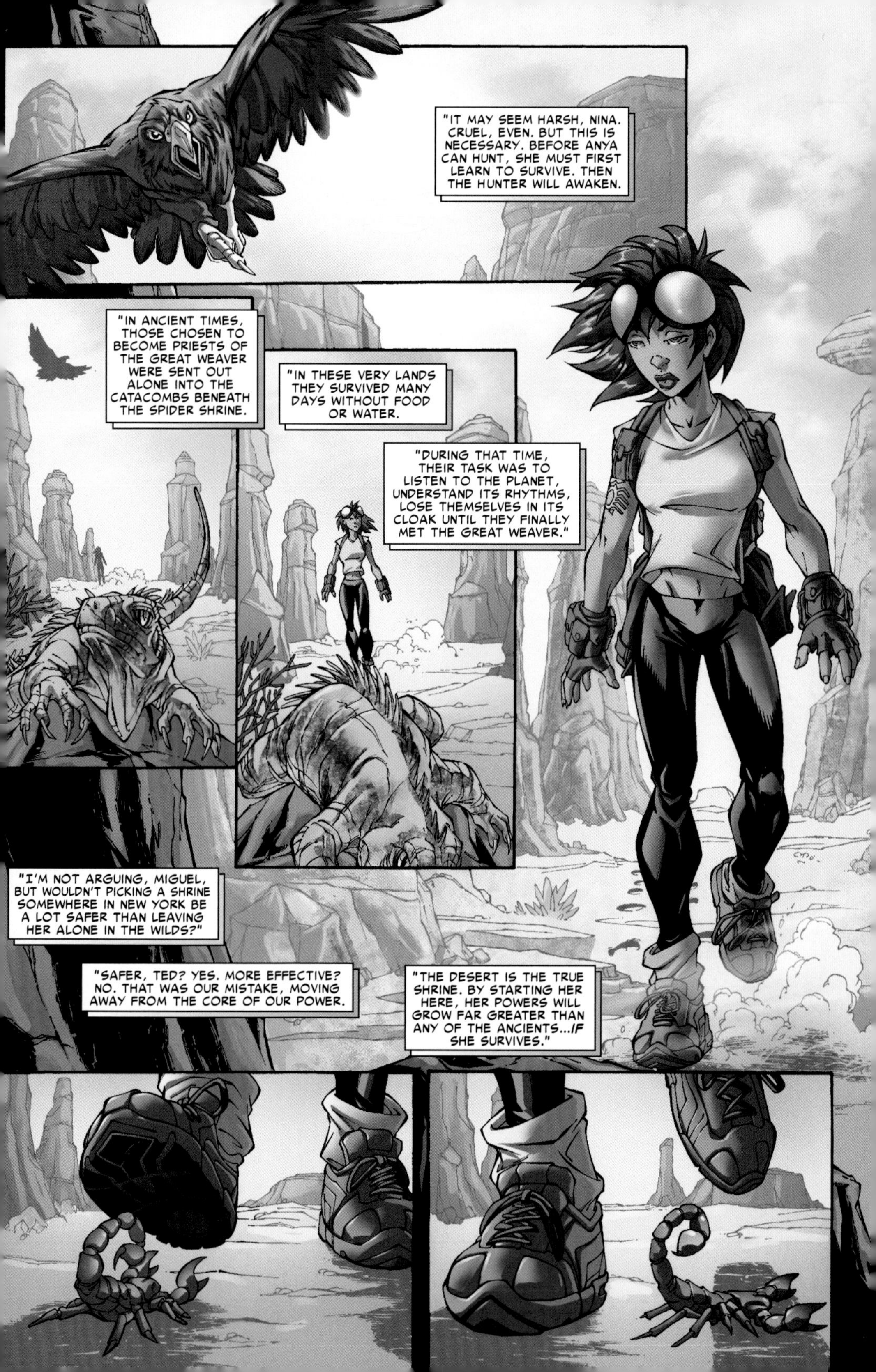
"IT MAY SEEM HARSH, NINA. CRUEL, EVEN. BUT THIS IS NECESSARY. BEFORE ANYA CAN HUNT, SHE MUST FIRST LEARN TO SURVIVE. THEN THE HUNTER WILL AWAKEN.
"IN ANCIENT TIMES, THOSE CHOSEN TO BECOME PRIESTS OF THE GREAT WEAVER WERE SENT OUT ALONE INTO THE CATACOMBS BENEATH THE SPIDER SHRINE.
"IN THESE VERY LANDS THEY SURVIVED MANY DAYS WITHOUT FOOD OR WATER.
"DURING THAT TIME, THEIR TASK WAS TO LISTEN TO THE PLANET, UNDERSTAND ITS RHYTHMS, LOSE THEMSELVES IN ITS CLOAK UNTIL THEY FINALLY MET THE GREAT WEAVER."
"I'M NOT ARGUING, MIGUEL, BUT WOULDN'T PICKING A SHRINE SOMEWHERE IN NEW YORK BE A LOT SAFER THAN LEAVING HER ALONE IN THE WILDS?"
"SAFER, TED? YES. MORE EFFECTIVE? NO. THAT WAS OUR MISTAKE, MOVING AWAY FROM THE CORE OF OUR POWER.
"THE DESERT IS THE TRUE SHRINE. BY STARTING HER HERE, HER POWERS WILL GROW FAR GREATER THAN ANY OF THE ANCIENTS...*IF* SHE SURVIVES."

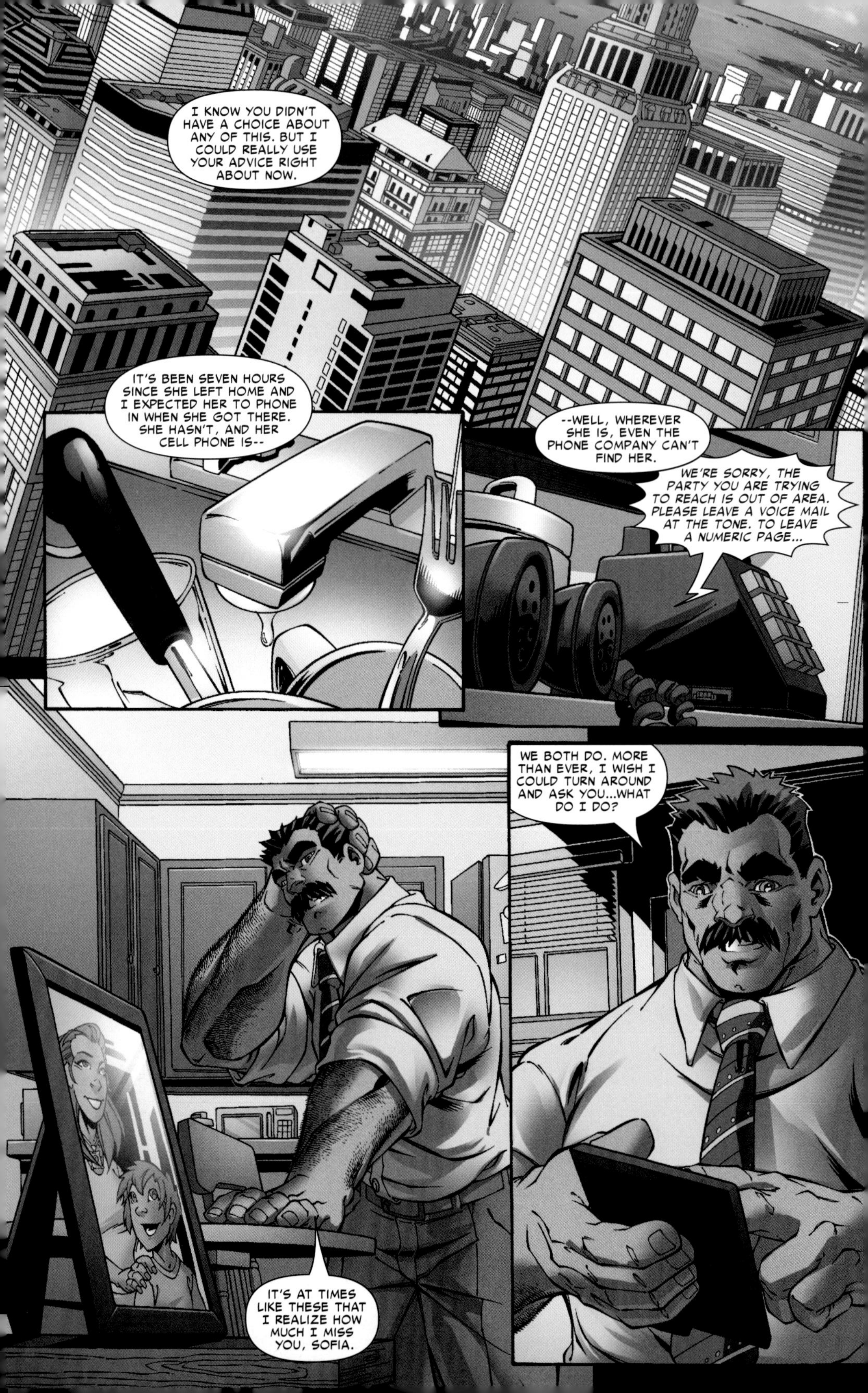
I KNOW YOU DIDN'T HAVE A CHOICE ABOUT ANY OF THIS. BUT I COULD REALLY USE YOUR ADVICE RIGHT ABOUT NOW.
IT'S BEEN SEVEN HOURS SINCE SHE LEFT HOME AND I EXPECTED HER TO PHONE IN WHEN SHE GOT THERE. SHE HASN'T, AND HER CELL PHONE IS--
--WELL, WHEREVER SHE IS, EVEN THE PHONE COMPANY CAN'T FIND HER.
WE'RE SORRY, THE PARTY YOU ARE TRYING TO REACH IS OUT OF AREA. PLEASE LEAVE A VOICE MAIL AT THE TONE. TO LEAVE A NUMERIC PAGE...
IT'S AT TIMES LIKE THESE THAT I REALIZE HOW MUCH I MISS YOU, SOFIA.
WE BOTH DO. MORE THAN EVER, I WISH I COULD TURN AROUND AND ASK YOU...WHAT DO I DO?

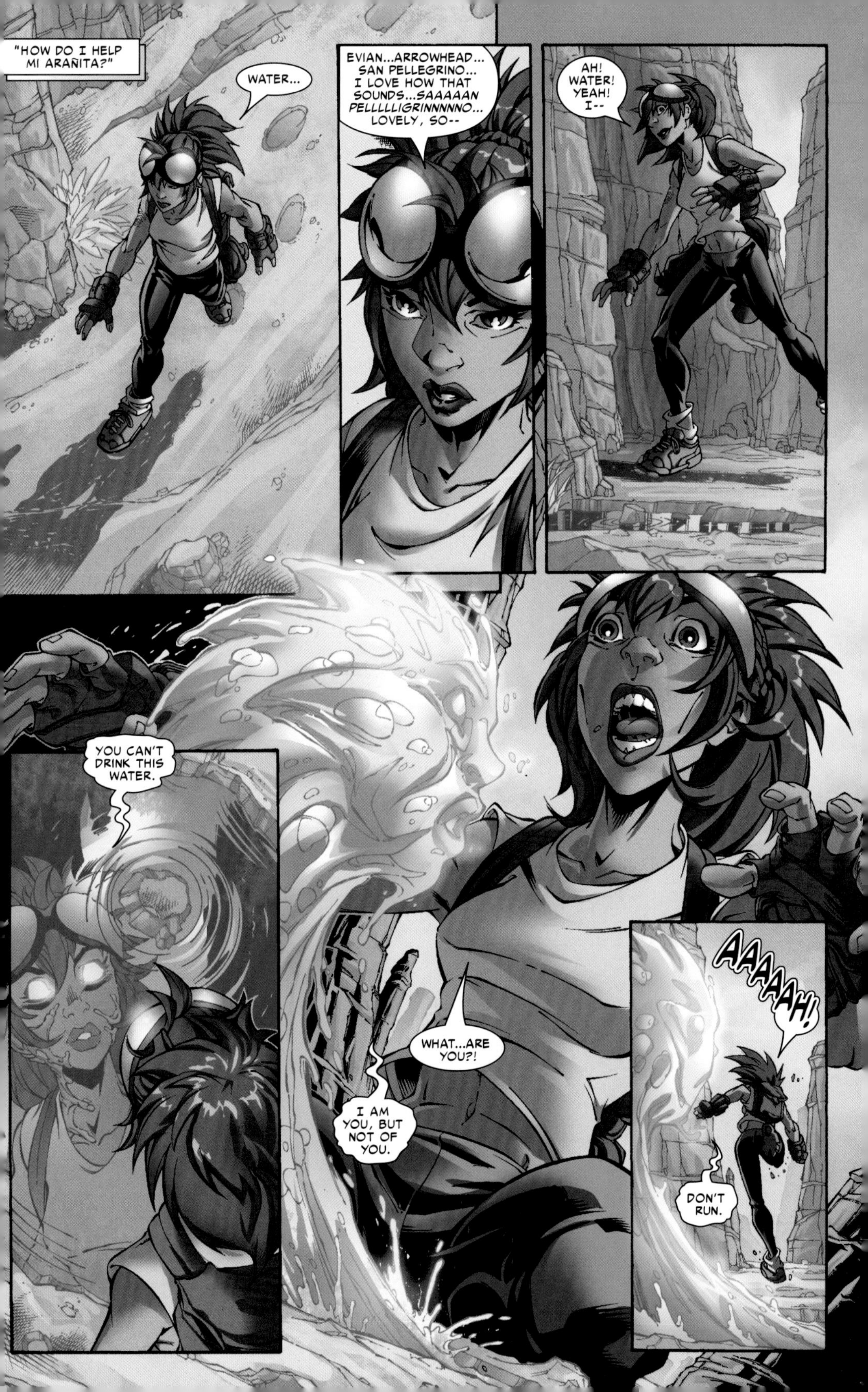
"HOW DO I HELP MI ARAÑITA?"
WATER...
EVIAN...ARROWHEAD... SAN PELLEGRINO... I LOVE HOW THAT SOUNDS...SAAAAAN PELLLLLIGRINNNNNO... LOVELY, SO--
AH! WATER! YEAH! I--
YOU CAN'T DRINK THIS WATER.
WHAT...ARE YOU?!
I AM YOU, BUT NOT OF YOU.
AAAAAAH!
DON'T RUN.

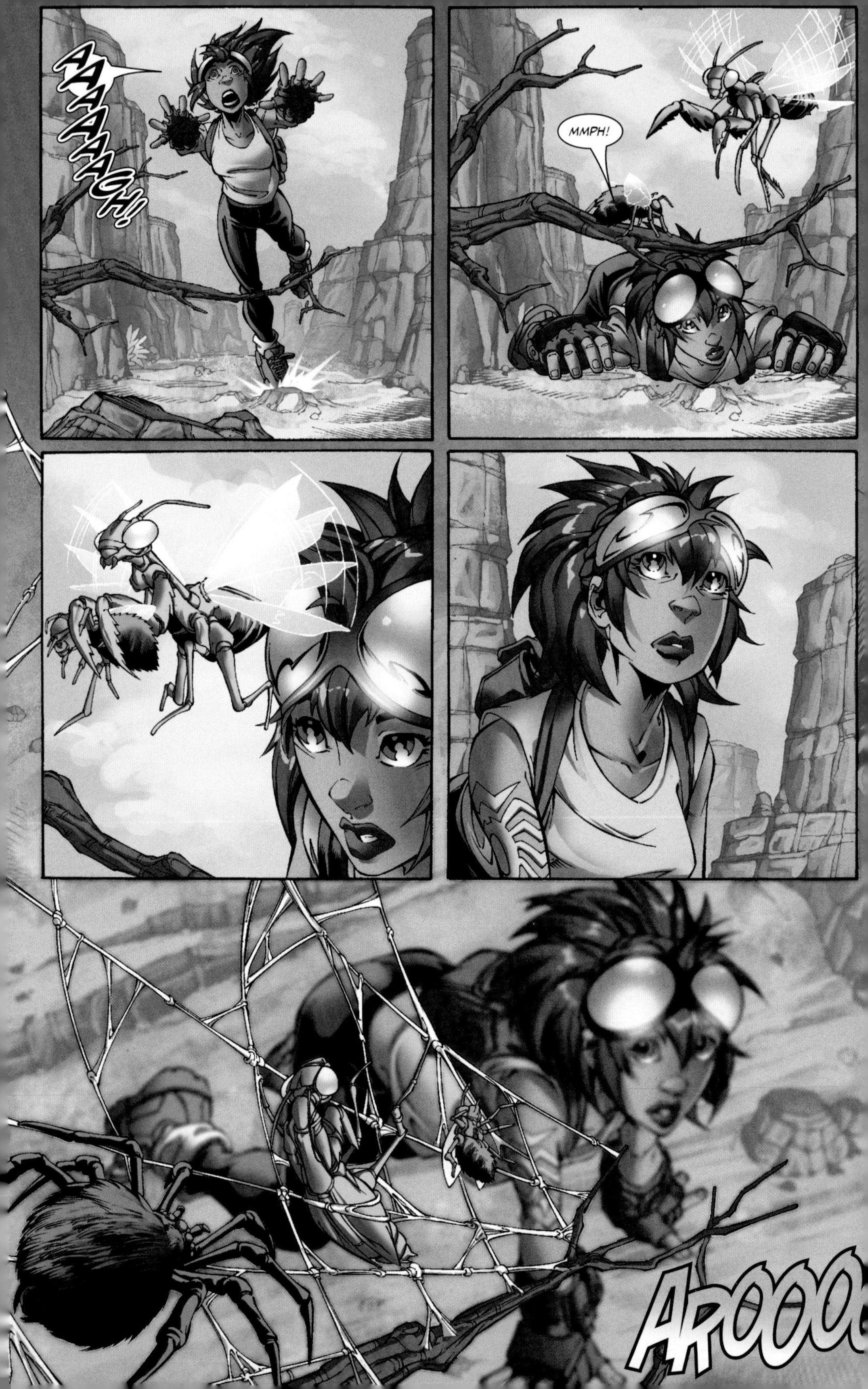
AAAAAAGH!
MMPH!
AROOO

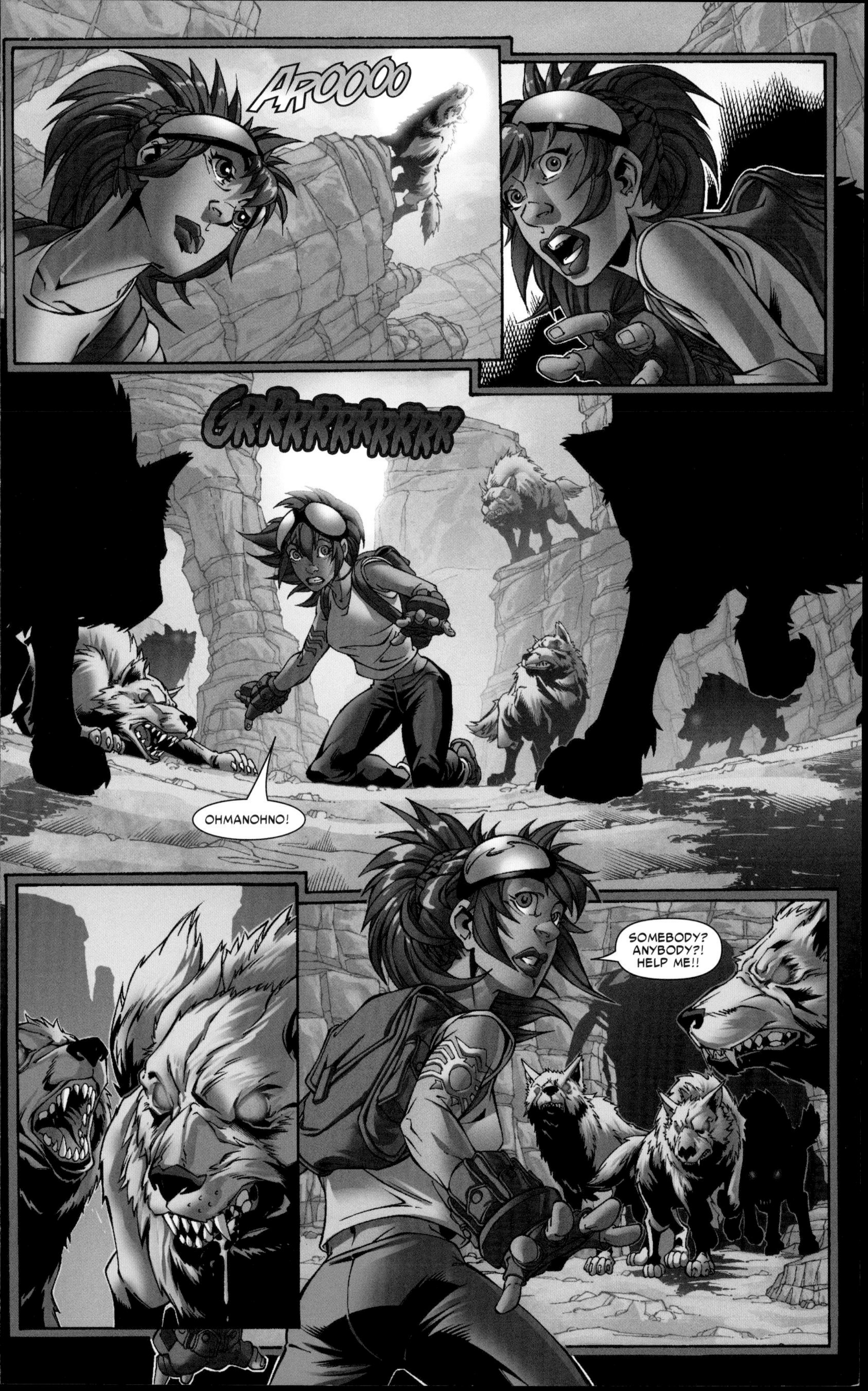
AROOOO
GRRRRRRRRRR
OHMANOHNO!
SOMEBODY? ANYBODY?! HELP ME!!

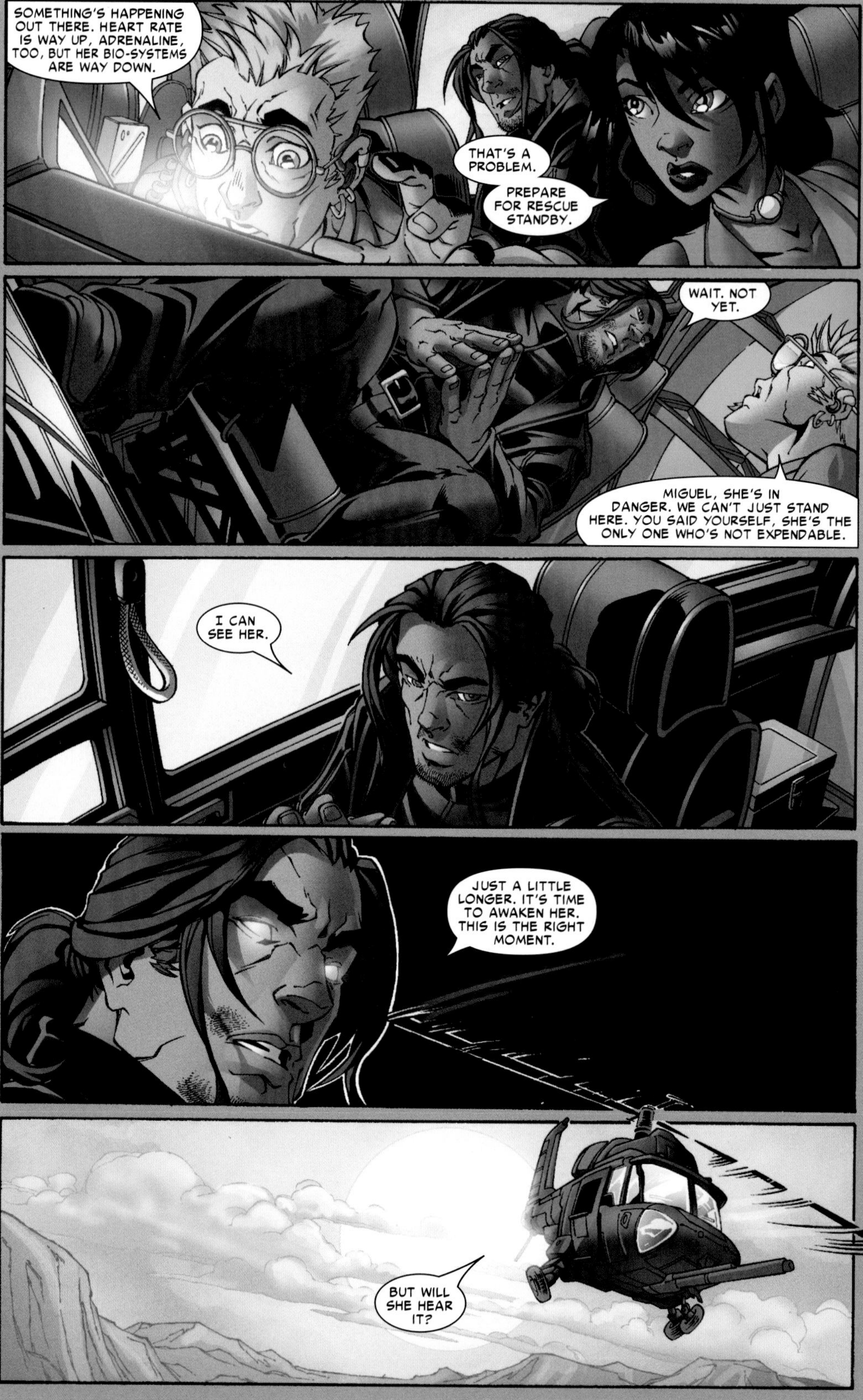
SOMETHING'S HAPPENING OUT THERE. HEART RATE IS WAY UP, ADRENALINE, TOO, BUT HER BIO-SYSTEMS ARE WAY DOWN.
THAT'S A PROBLEM.
PREPARE FOR RESCUE STANDBY.
WAIT. NOT YET.
MIGUEL, SHE'S IN DANGER. WE CAN'T JUST STAND HERE. YOU SAID YOURSELF, SHE'S THE ONLY ONE WHO'S NOT EXPENDABLE.
I CAN SEE HER.
JUST A LITTLE LONGER. IT'S TIME TO AWAKEN HER. THIS IS THE RIGHT MOMENT.
BUT WILL SHE HEAR IT?

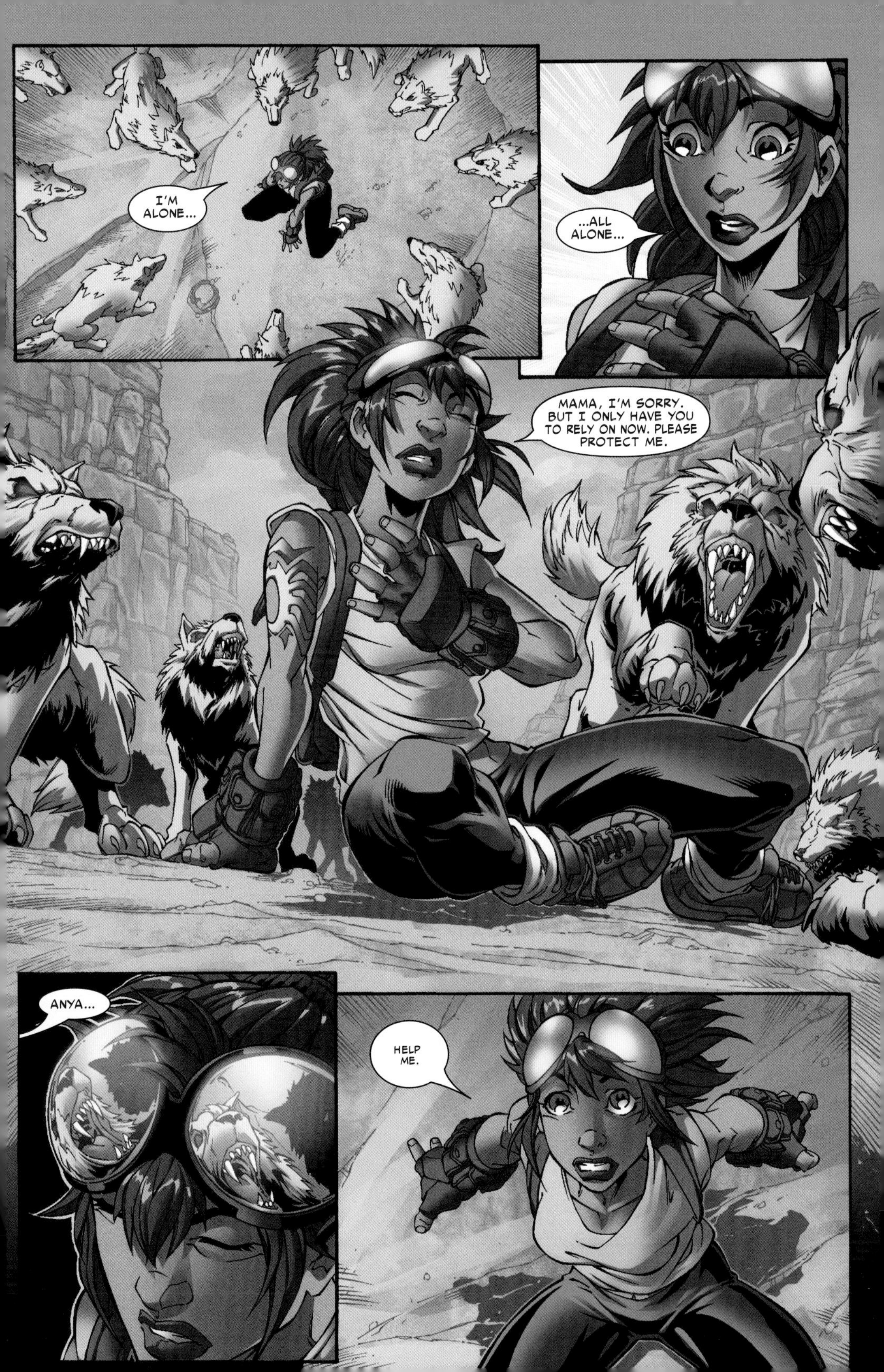
I'M ALONE...
...ALL ALONE...
MAMA, I'M SORRY. BUT I ONLY HAVE YOU TO RELY ON NOW. PLEASE PROTECT ME.
ANYA...
HELP ME.

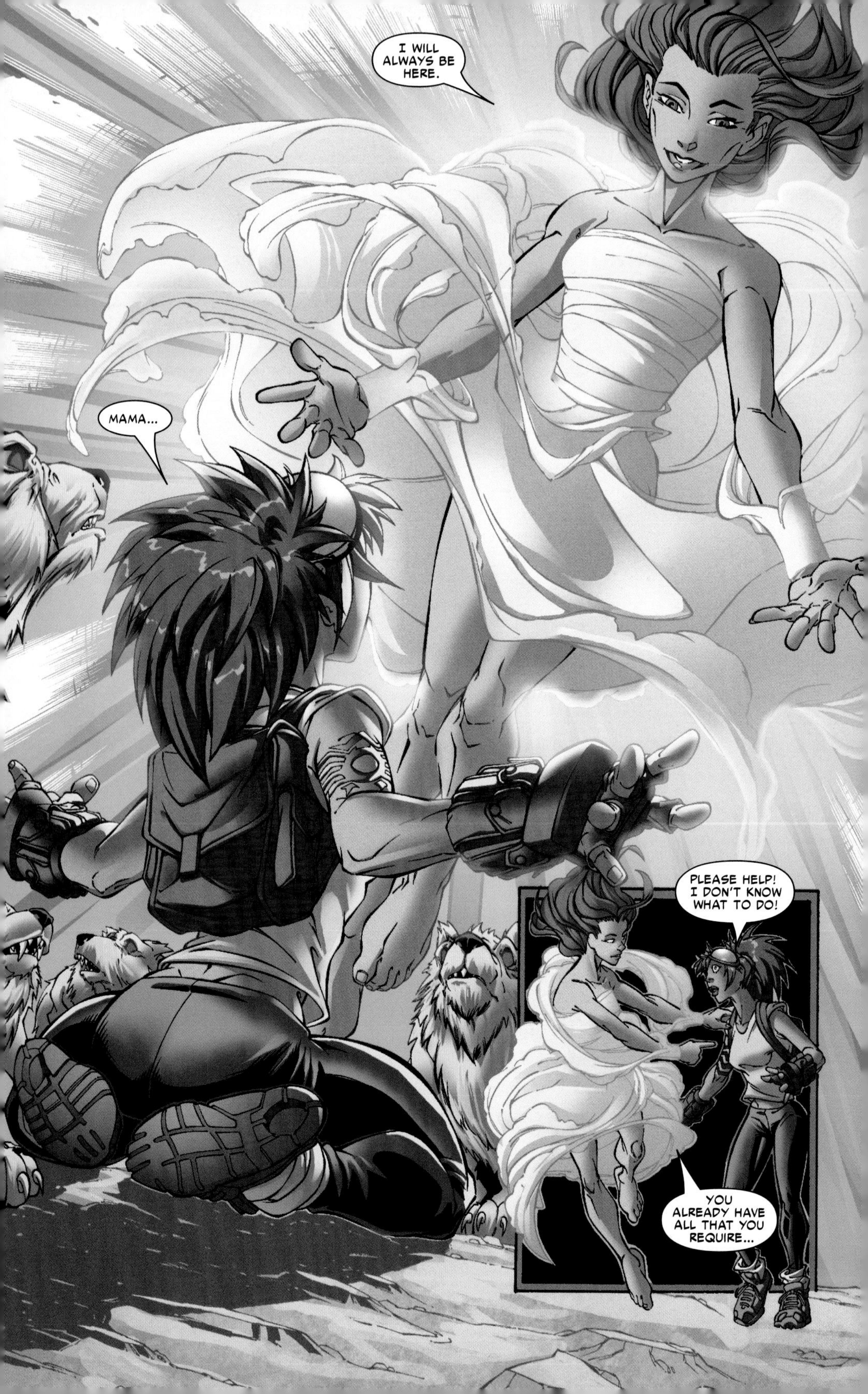
I WILL ALWAYS BE HERE.
MAMA...
PLEASE HELP! I DON'T KNOW WHAT TO DO!
YOU ALREADY HAVE ALL THAT YOU REQUIRE...

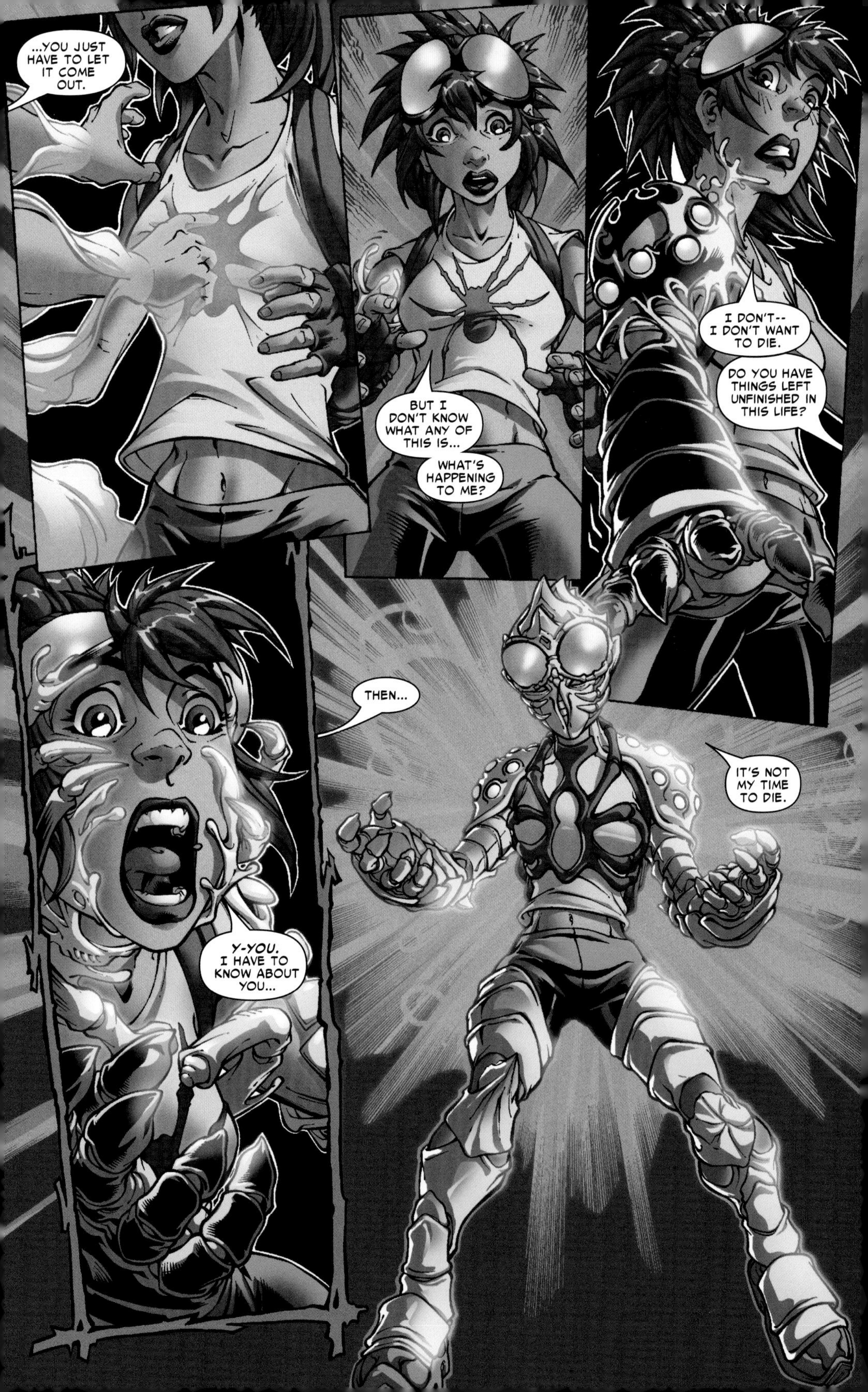
...YOU JUST HAVE TO LET IT COME OUT.
BUT I DON'T KNOW WHAT ANY OF THIS IS...
WHAT'S HAPPENING TO ME?
I DON'T-- I DON'T WANT TO DIE.
DO YOU HAVE THINGS LEFT UNFINISHED IN THIS LIFE?
Y-YOU. I HAVE TO KNOW ABOUT YOU...
THEN...
IT'S NOT MY TIME TO DIE.

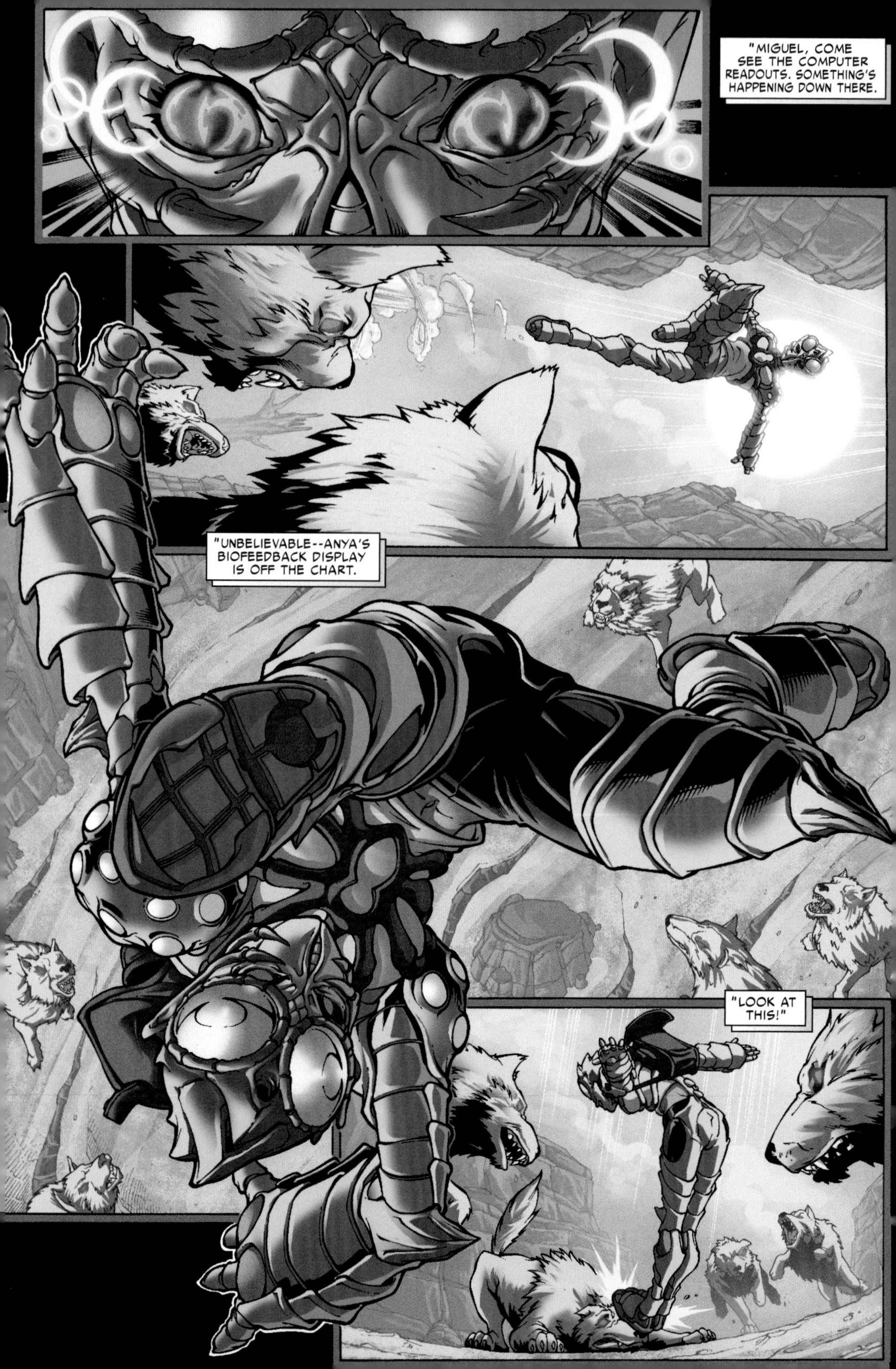
"MIGUEL, COME SEE THE COMPUTER READOUTS. SOMETHING'S HAPPENING DOWN THERE.
"UNBELIEVABLE--ANYA'S BIOFEEDBACK DISPLAY IS OFF THE CHART.
"LOOK AT THIS!"

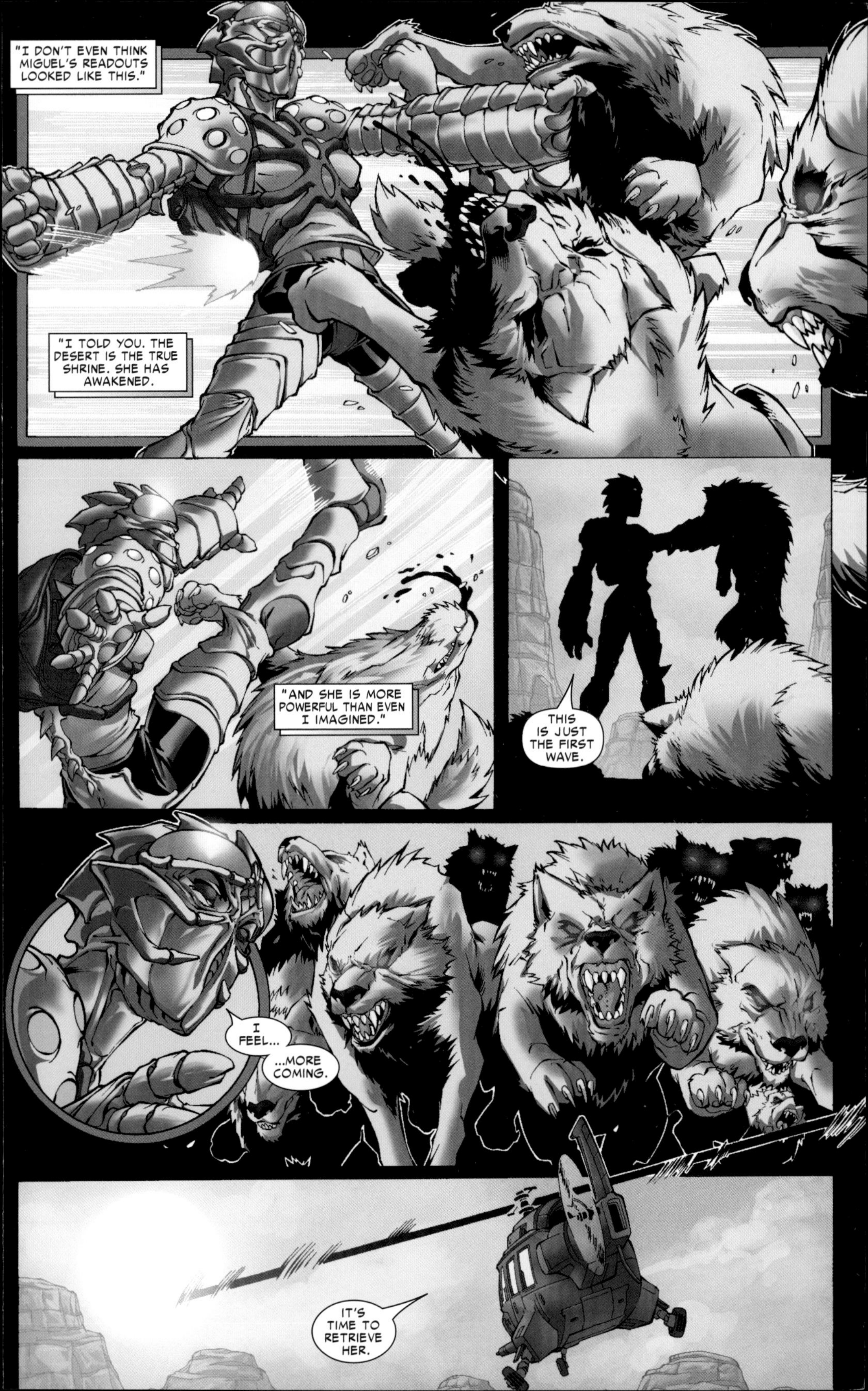
"I DON'T EVEN THINK MIGUEL'S READOUTS LOOKED LIKE THIS."
"I TOLD YOU. THE DESERT IS THE TRUE SHRINE. SHE HAS AWAKENED.
"AND SHE IS MORE POWERFUL THAN EVEN I IMAGINED."
THIS IS JUST THE FIRST WAVE.
I FEEL...
...MORE COMING.
IT'S TIME TO RETRIEVE HER.

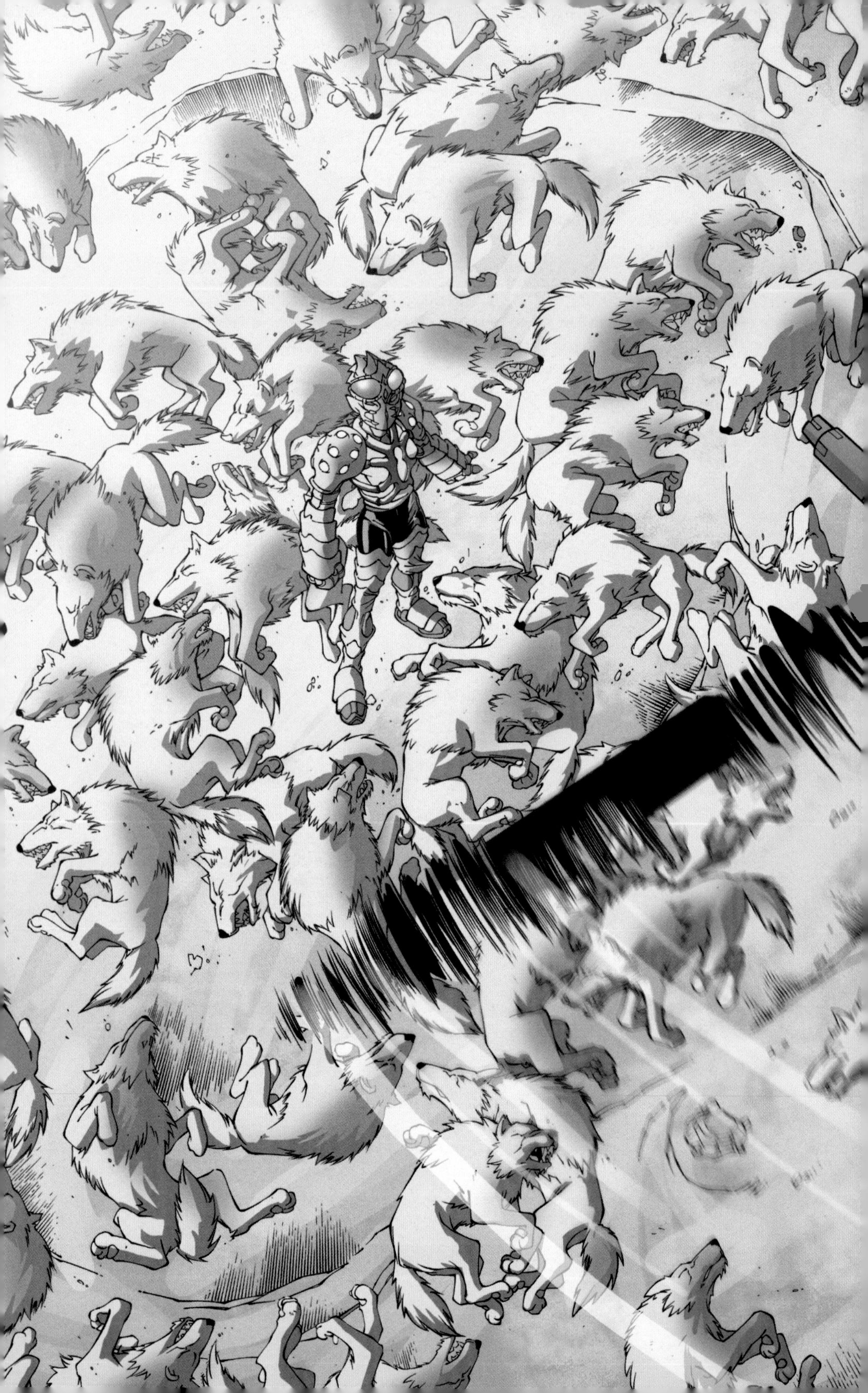

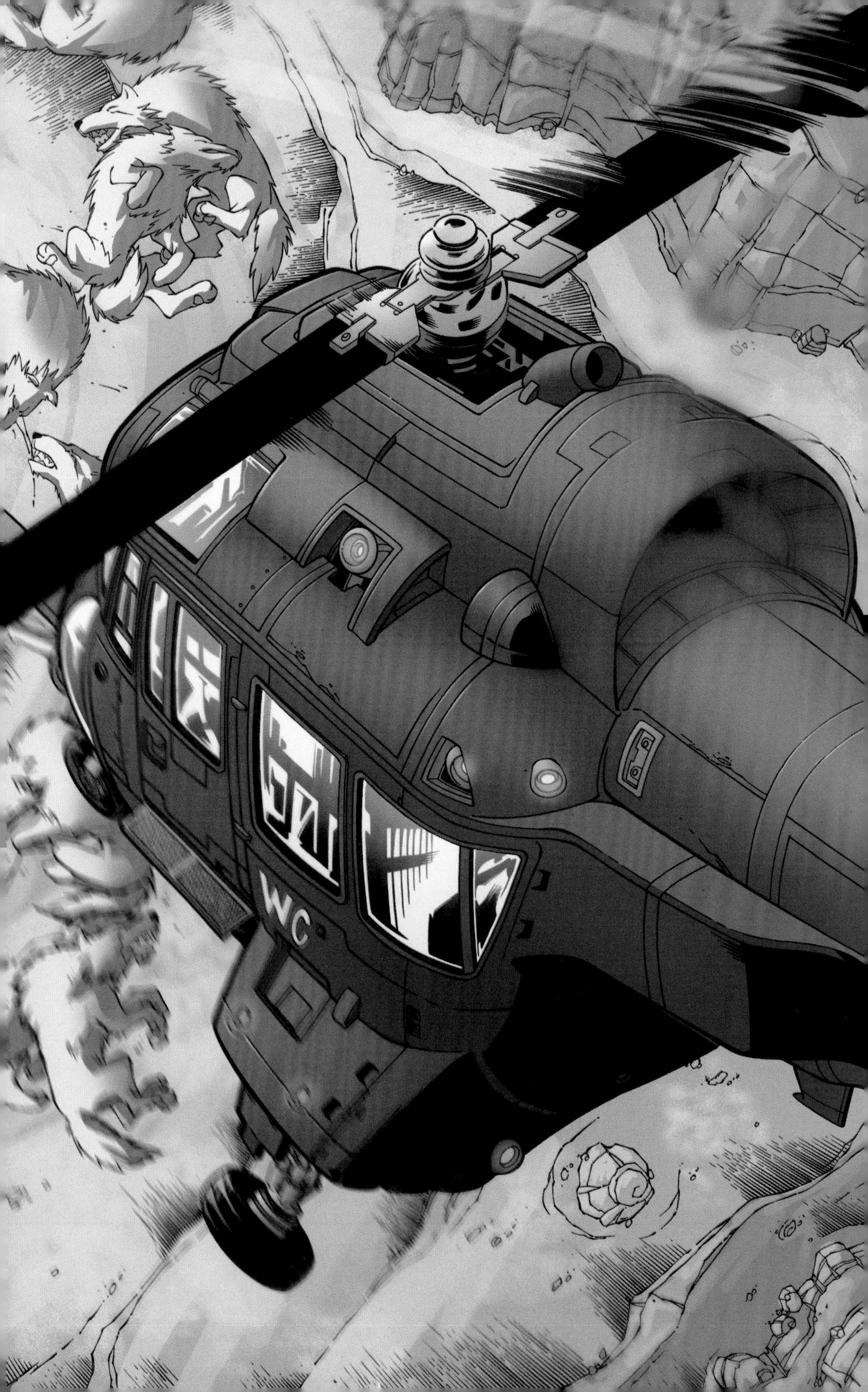
WC

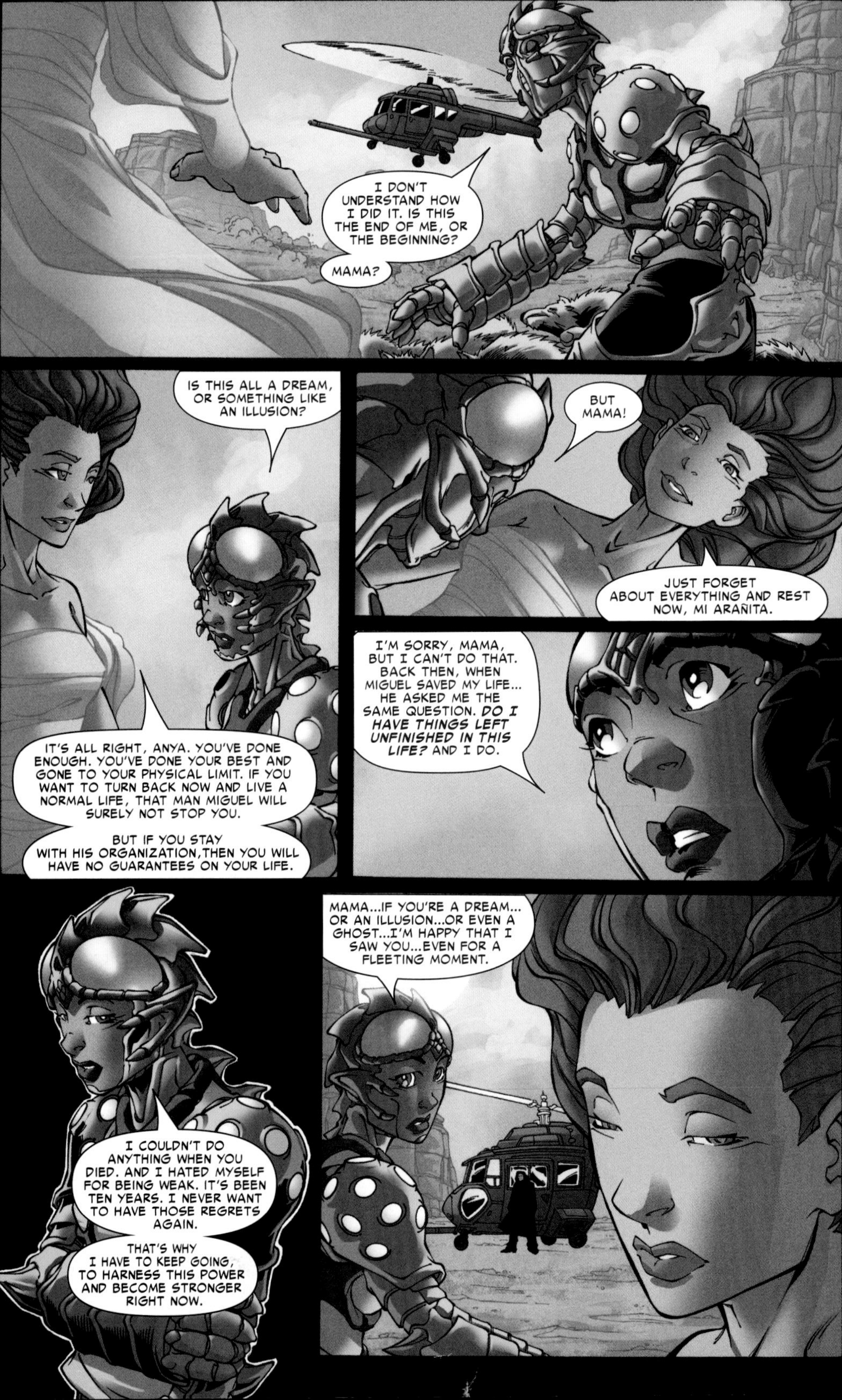
I DON'T UNDERSTAND HOW I DID IT. IS THIS THE END OF ME, OR THE BEGINNING?
MAMA?
IS THIS ALL A DREAM, OR SOMETHING LIKE AN ILLUSION?
IT'S ALL RIGHT, ANYA. YOU'VE DONE ENOUGH. YOU'VE DONE YOUR BEST AND GONE TO YOUR PHYSICAL LIMIT. IF YOU WANT TO TURN BACK NOW AND LIVE A NORMAL LIFE, THAT MAN MIGUEL WILL SURELY NOT STOP YOU.
BUT IF YOU STAY WITH HIS ORGANIZATION, THEN YOU WILL HAVE NO GUARANTEES ON YOUR LIFE.
BUT MAMA!
JUST FORGET ABOUT EVERYTHING AND REST NOW, MI ARAÑITA.
I'M SORRY, MAMA, BUT I CAN'T DO THAT. BACK THEN, WHEN MIGUEL SAVED MY LIFE... HE ASKED ME THE SAME QUESTION. *DO I HAVE THINGS LEFT UNFINISHED IN THIS LIFE?* AND I DO.
I COULDN'T DO ANYTHING WHEN YOU DIED. AND I HATED MYSELF FOR BEING WEAK. IT'S BEEN TEN YEARS. I NEVER WANT TO HAVE THOSE REGRETS AGAIN.
THAT'S WHY I HAVE TO KEEP GOING, TO HARNESS THIS POWER AND BECOME STRONGER RIGHT NOW.
MAMA...IF YOU'RE A DREAM... OR AN ILLUSION...OR EVEN A GHOST...I'M HAPPY THAT I SAW YOU...EVEN FOR A FLEETING MOMENT.

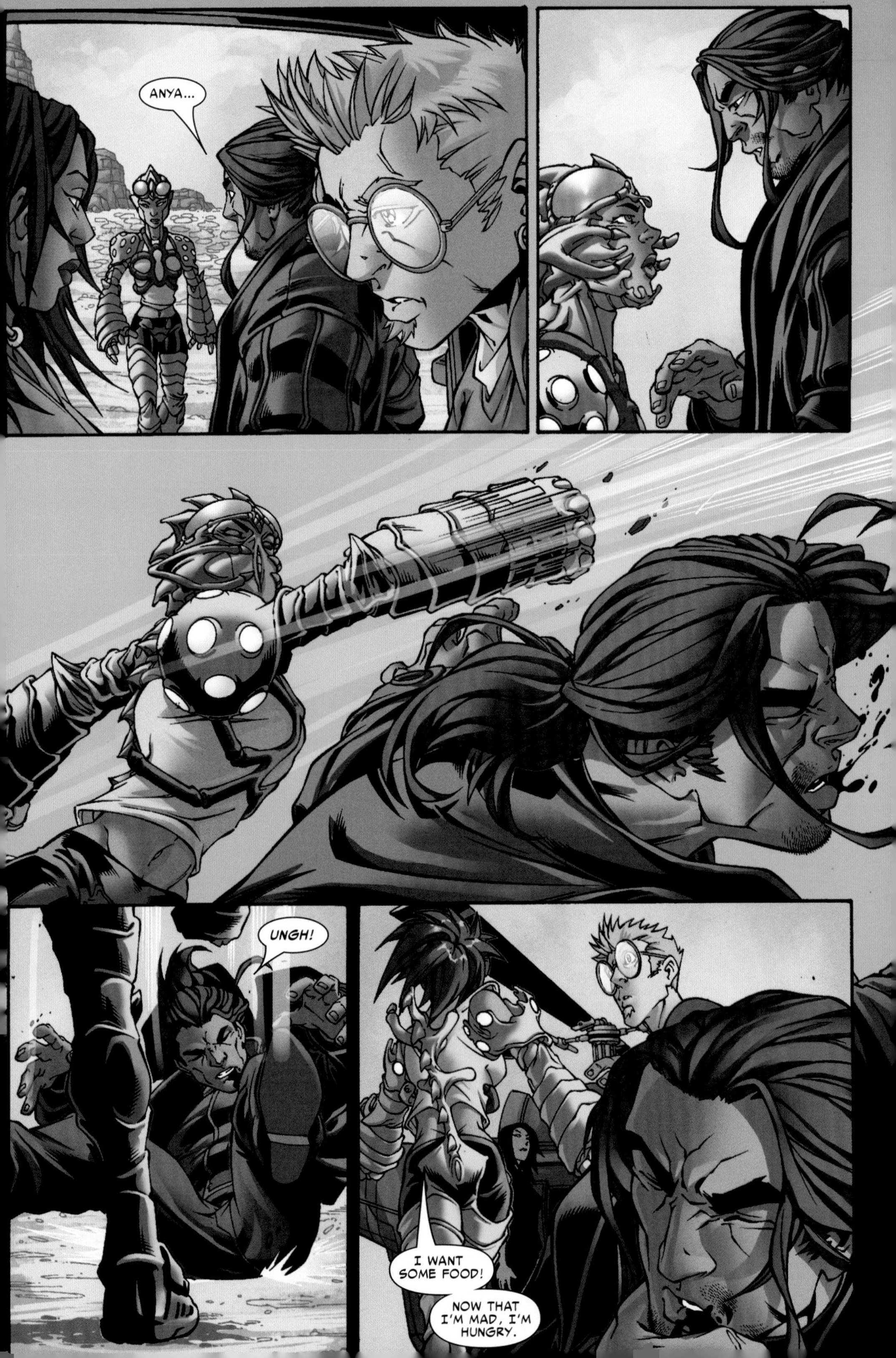
ANYA...
UNGH!
I WANT SOME FOOD!
NOW THAT I'M MAD, I'M HUNGRY.

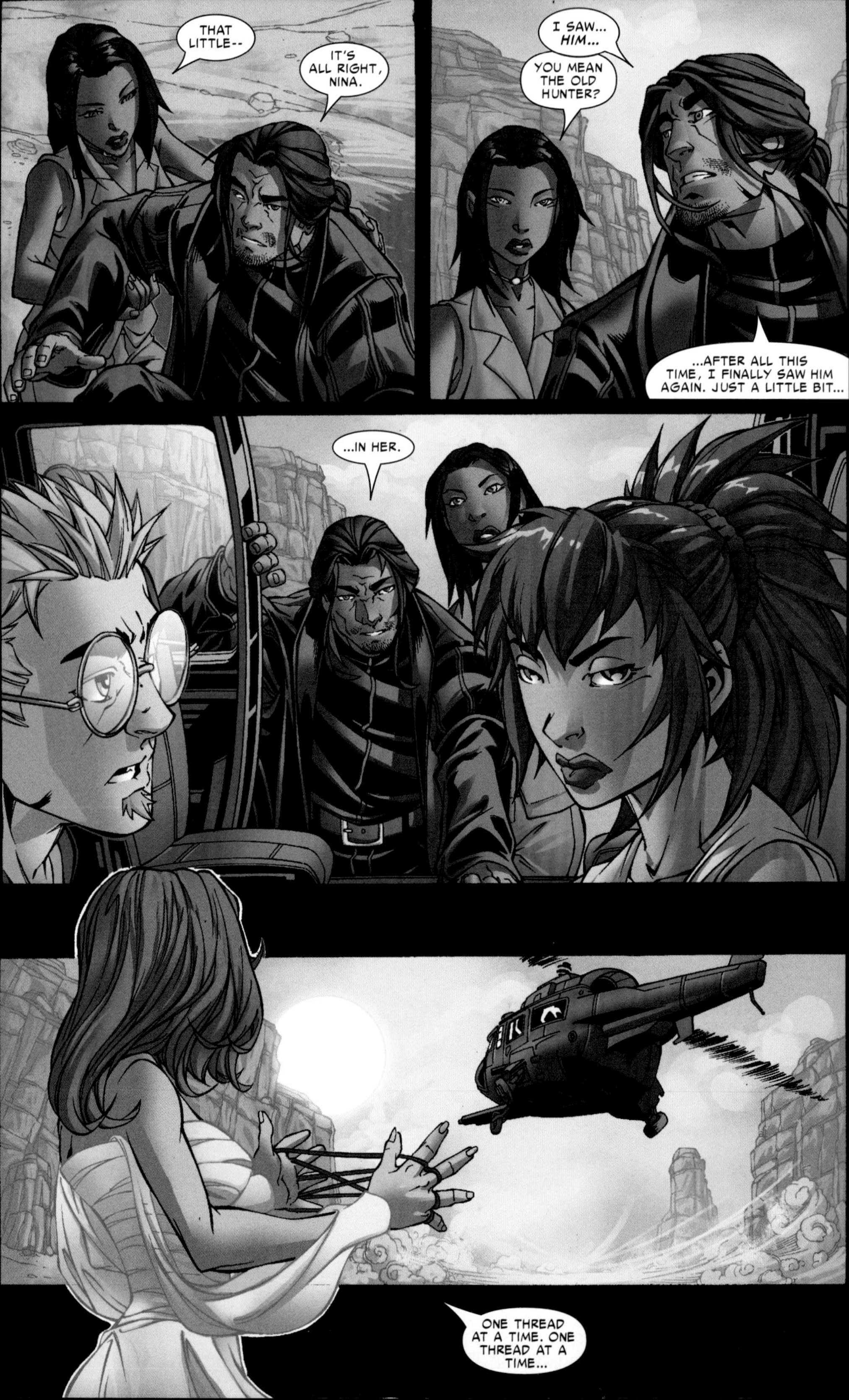
THAT LITTLE--
IT'S ALL RIGHT, NINA.
I SAW... HIM...
YOU MEAN THE OLD HUNTER?
...AFTER ALL THIS TIME, I FINALLY SAW HIM AGAIN. JUST A LITTLE BIT...
...IN HER.
ONE THREAD AT A TIME. ONE THREAD AT A TIME...

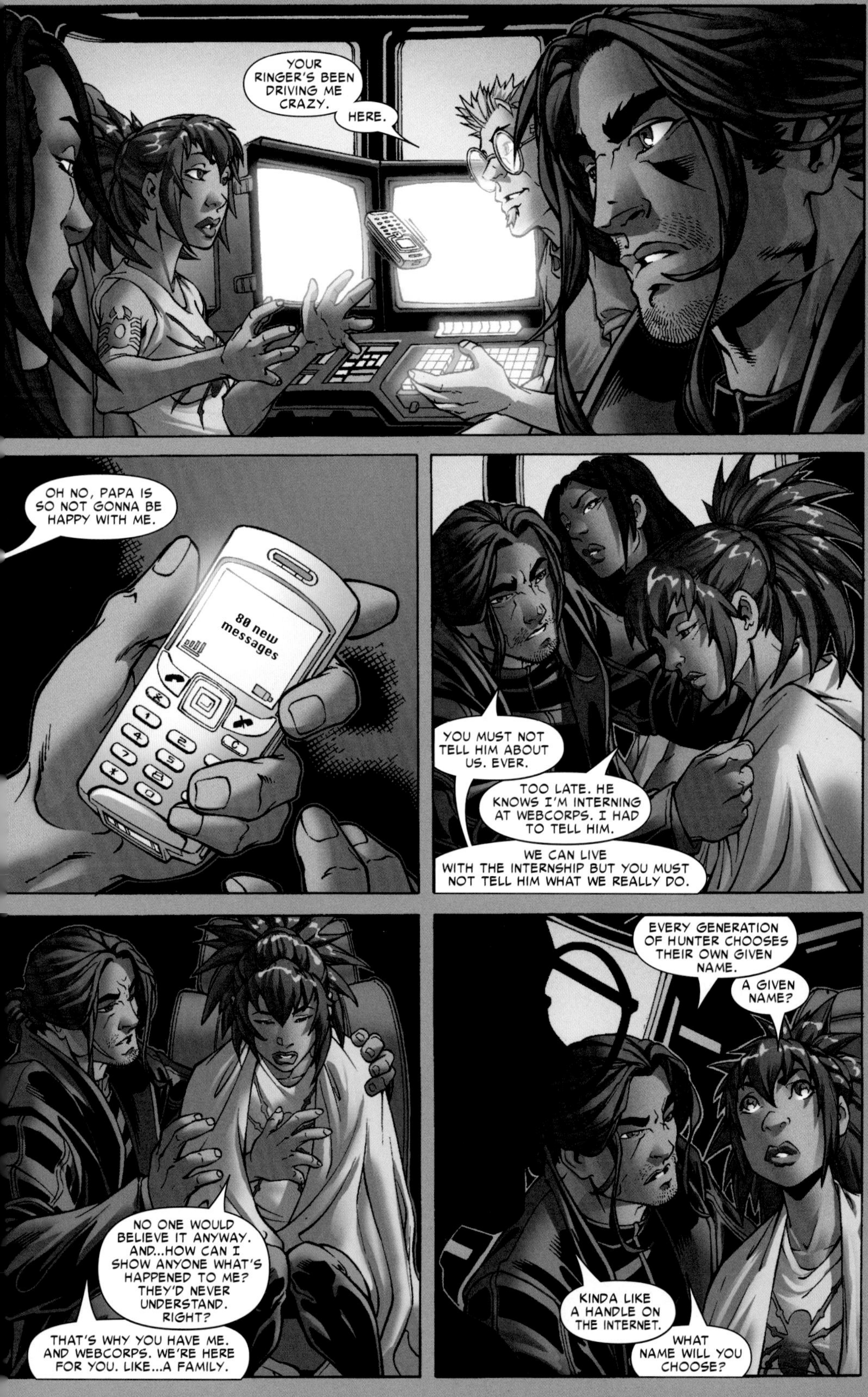
YOUR RINGER'S BEEN DRIVING ME CRAZY.
HERE.
OH NO, PAPA IS SO NOT GONNA BE HAPPY WITH ME.
80 new messages
YOU MUST NOT TELL HIM ABOUT US. EVER.
TOO LATE. HE KNOWS I'M INTERNING AT WEBCORPS. I HAD TO TELL HIM.
WE CAN LIVE WITH THE INTERNSHIP BUT YOU MUST NOT TELL HIM WHAT WE REALLY DO.
NO ONE WOULD BELIEVE IT ANYWAY. AND...HOW CAN I SHOW ANYONE WHAT'S HAPPENED TO ME? THEY'D NEVER UNDERSTAND. RIGHT?
THAT'S WHY YOU HAVE ME. AND WEBCORPS. WE'RE HERE FOR YOU. LIKE...A FAMILY.
EVERY GENERATION OF HUNTER CHOOSES THEIR OWN GIVEN NAME.
A GIVEN NAME?
KINDA LIKE A HANDLE ON THE INTERNET.
WHAT NAME WILL YOU CHOOSE?

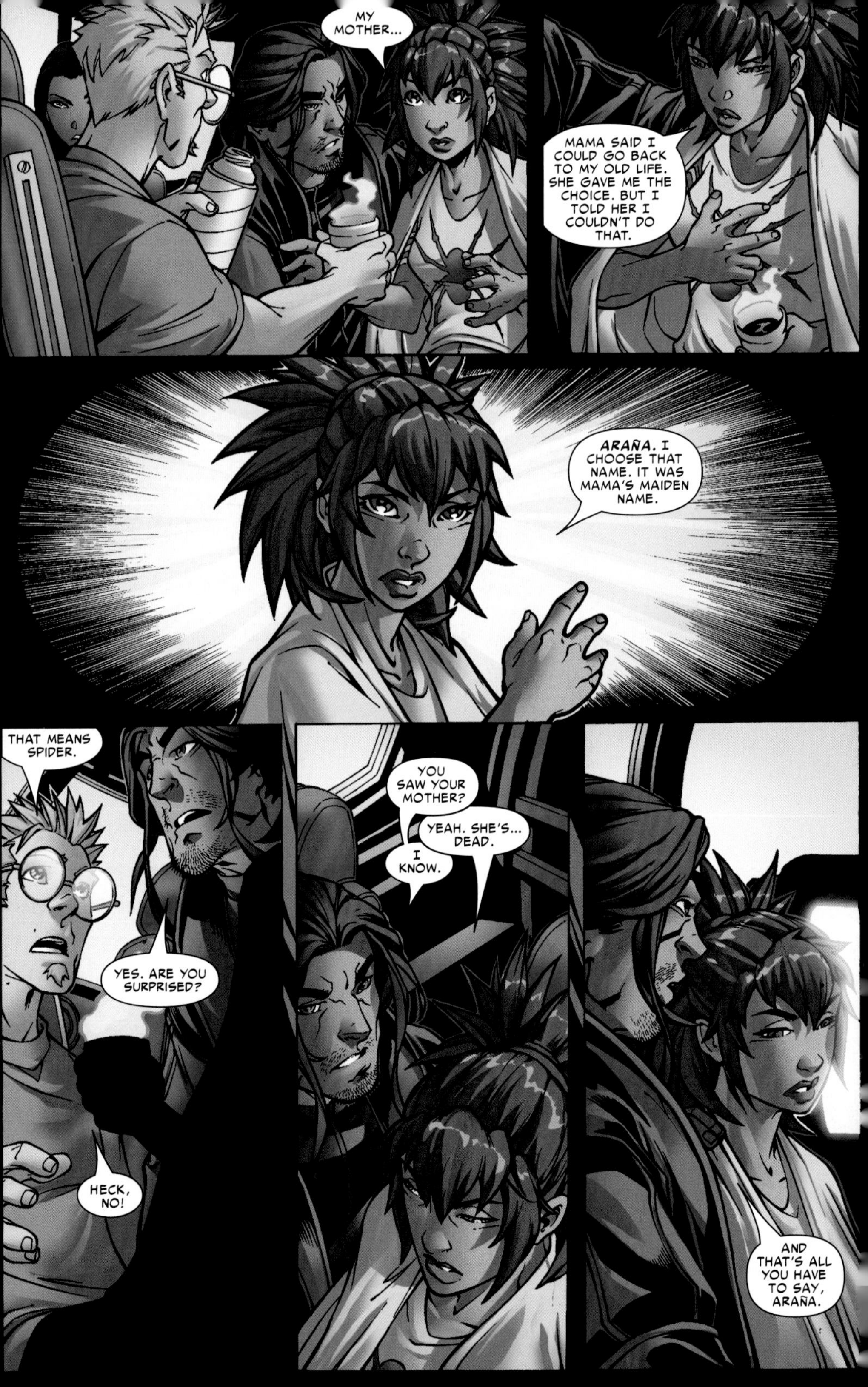
MY MOTHER...
MAMA SAID I COULD GO BACK TO MY OLD LIFE. SHE GAVE ME THE CHOICE. BUT I TOLD HER I COULDN'T DO THAT.
ARAÑA. I CHOOSE THAT NAME. IT WAS MAMA'S MAIDEN NAME.
THAT MEANS SPIDER.
YES. ARE YOU SURPRISED?
HECK, NO!
YOU SAW YOUR MOTHER?
YEAH. SHE'S... DEAD.
I KNOW.
AND THAT'S ALL YOU HAVE TO SAY, ARAÑA.

I'M HOME.

I KNOW YOU'RE UPSET, PAPA. I'M SORRY. I SHOULD HAVE ANSWERED THE PHONE BUT I WAS OUT OF THE AREA ALL WEEKEND.

AND YOU COULDN'T FIND ANOTHER PHONE TO CALL FROM?

I WAS SO BUSY I... DIDN'T REALLY THINK ABOUT IT.

YOU WERE SUPPOSED TO CALL ME WITH HOTEL AND SEMINAR INFORMATION. I SHOULD HAVE HAD THE NUMBER TO BOTH IN CASE OF AN EMERGENCY. WHAT WERE YOU THINKING?

I REALLY WASN'T THINKING. NO JOKE.

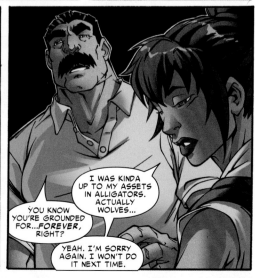

I WAS KINDA UP TO MY ASSETS IN ALLIGATORS. ACTUALLY WOLVES...

YOU KNOW YOU'RE GROUNDED FOR...FOREVER, RIGHT?

YEAH. I'M SORRY AGAIN. I WON'T DO IT NEXT TIME.

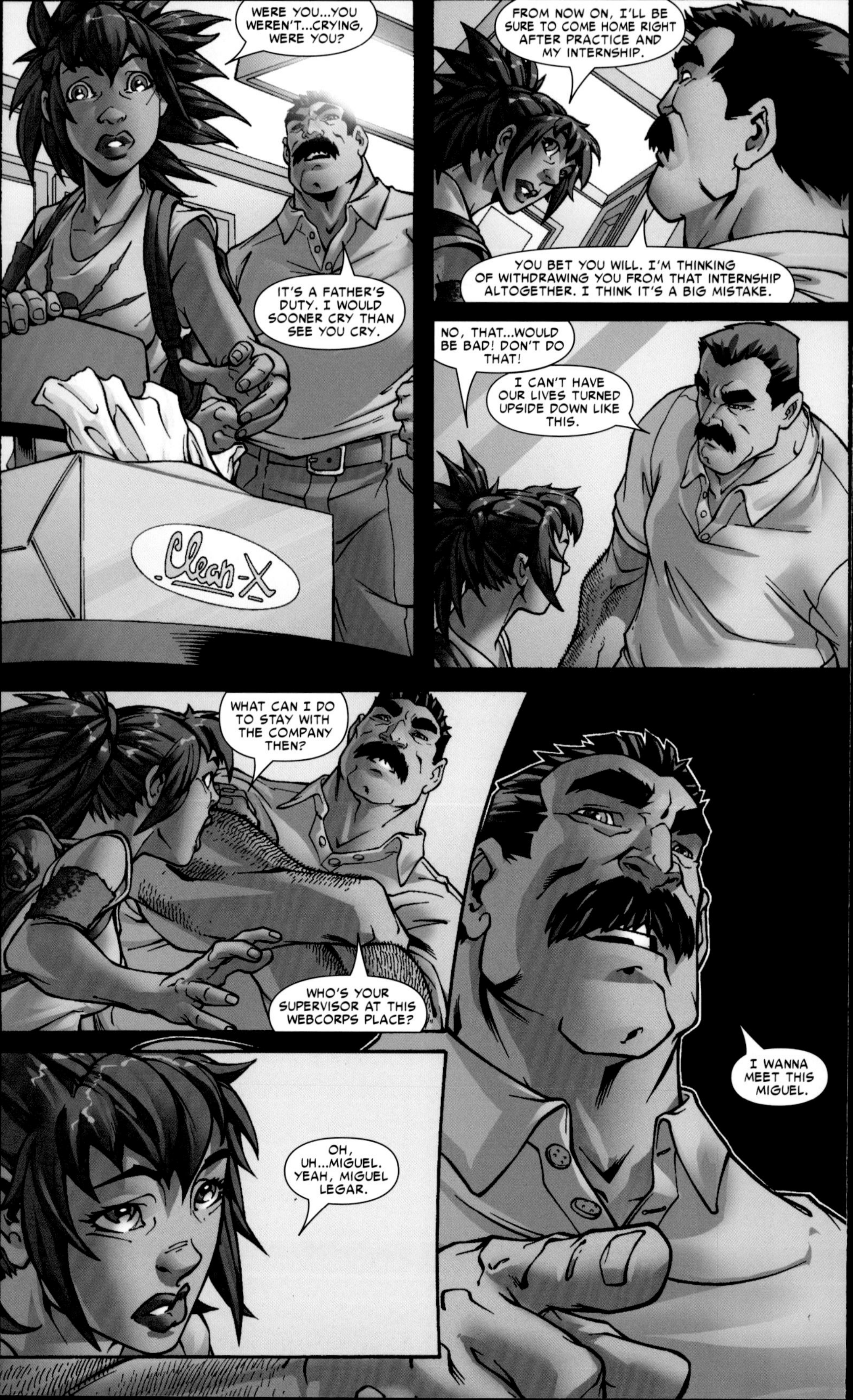
WERE YOU...YOU WEREN'T...CRYING, WERE YOU?
IT'S A FATHER'S DUTY. I WOULD SOONER CRY THAN SEE YOU CRY.
Clean-X
FROM NOW ON, I'LL BE SURE TO COME HOME RIGHT AFTER PRACTICE AND MY INTERNSHIP.
YOU BET YOU WILL. I'M THINKING OF WITHDRAWING YOU FROM THAT INTERNSHIP ALTOGETHER. I THINK IT'S A BIG MISTAKE.
NO, THAT...WOULD BE BAD! DON'T DO THAT!
I CAN'T HAVE OUR LIVES TURNED UPSIDE DOWN LIKE THIS.
WHAT CAN I DO TO STAY WITH THE COMPANY THEN?
WHO'S YOUR SUPERVISOR AT THIS WEBCORPS PLACE?
OH, UH...MIGUEL. YEAH, MIGUEL LEGAR.
I WANNA MEET THIS MIGUEL.

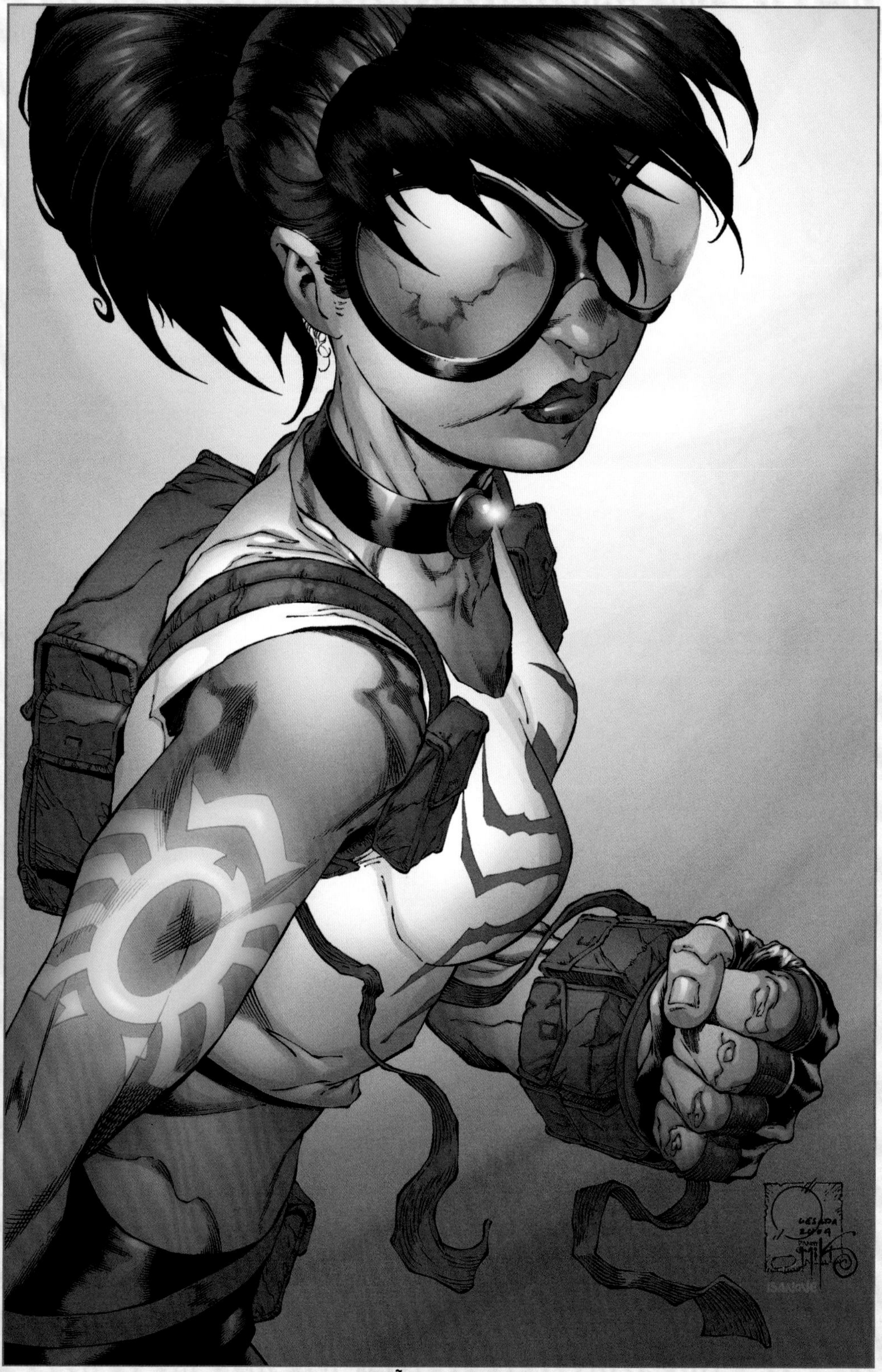

ARAÑA #1 VARIANT

BY JOE QUESADA, DANNY MIKI & RICHARD ISANOVE

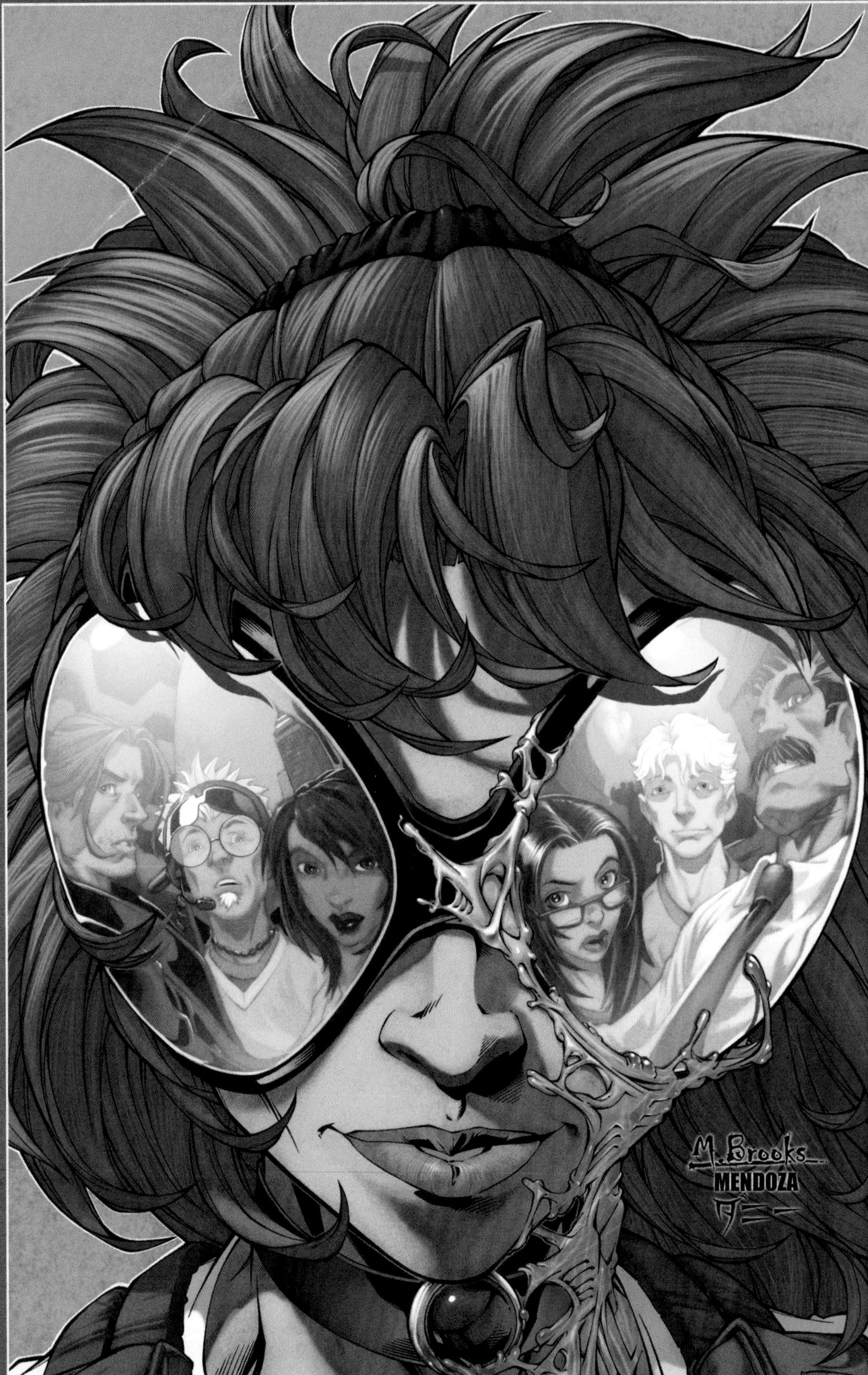
M. Brooks
MENDOZA

AMAZING FANTASY #6

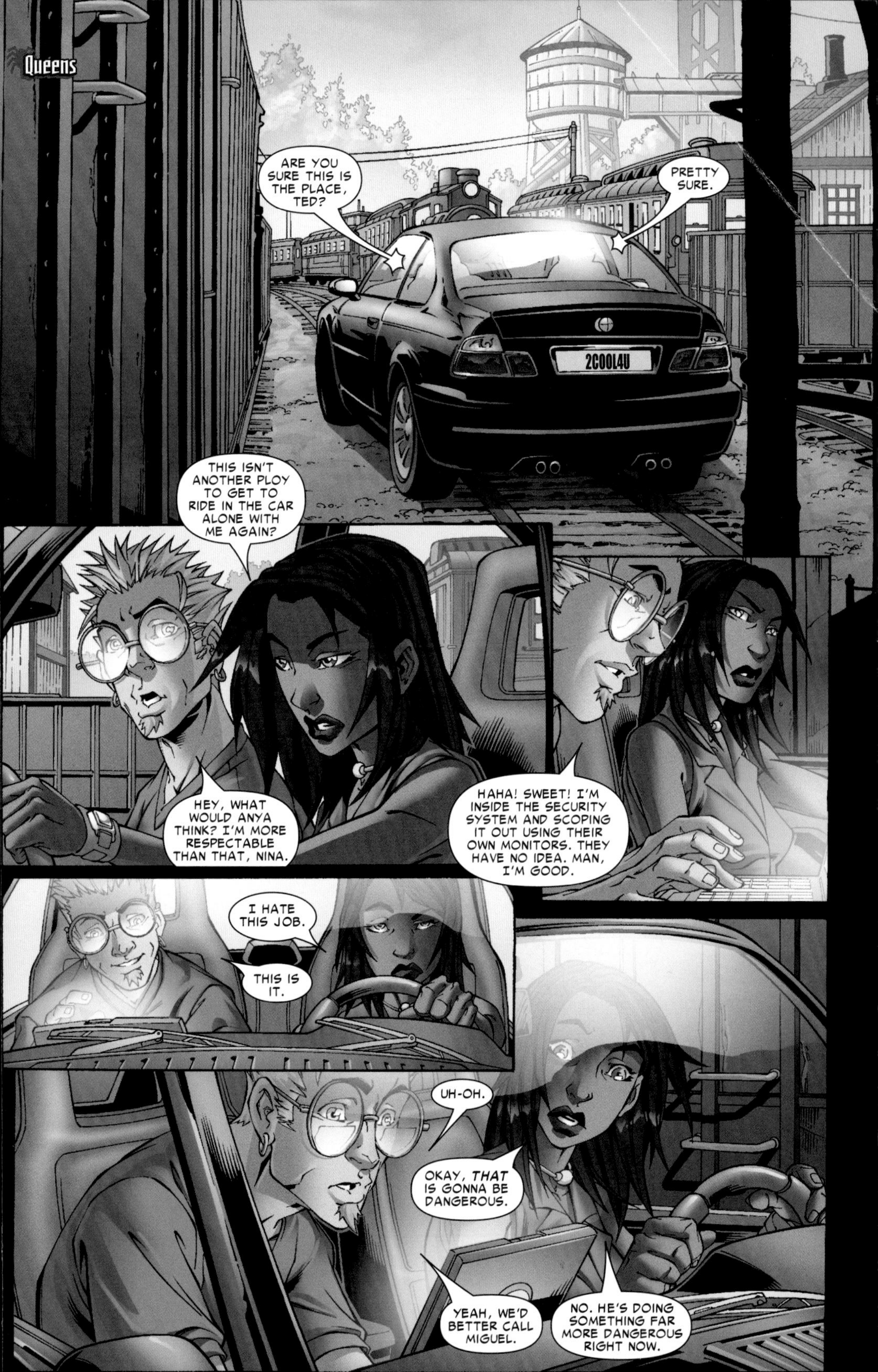
Queens
ARE YOU SURE THIS IS THE PLACE, TED?
PRETTY SURE.
2COOL4U
THIS ISN'T ANOTHER PLOY TO GET TO RIDE IN THE CAR ALONE WITH ME AGAIN?
HEY, WHAT WOULD ANYA THINK? I'M MORE RESPECTABLE THAN THAT, NINA.
HAHA! SWEET! I'M INSIDE THE SECURITY SYSTEM AND SCOPING IT OUT USING THEIR OWN MONITORS. THEY HAVE NO IDEA. MAN, I'M GOOD.
I HATE THIS JOB.
THIS IS IT.
UH-OH.
OKAY, *THAT* IS GONNA BE DANGEROUS.
YEAH, WE'D BETTER CALL MIGUEL.
NO. HE'S DOING SOMETHING FAR MORE DANGEROUS RIGHT NOW.

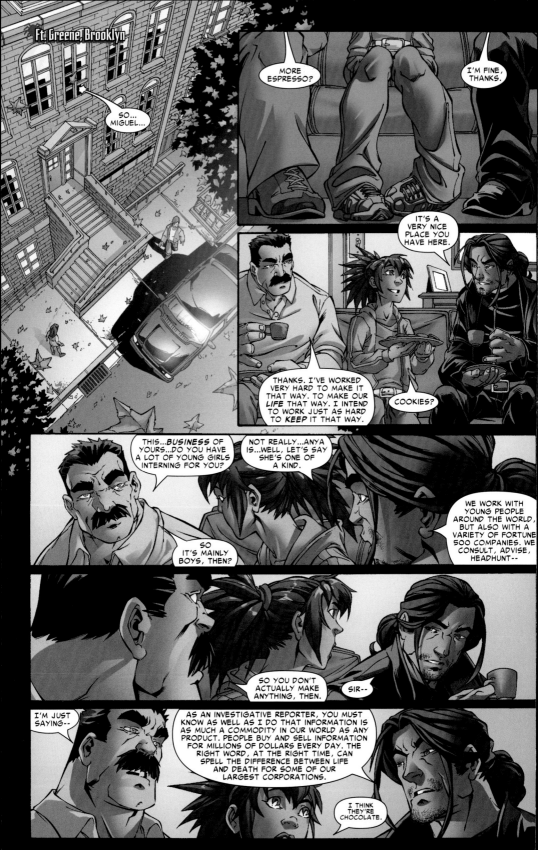

SO... MIGUEL...

MORE ESPRESSO?

I'M FINE, THANKS.

IT'S A VERY NICE PLACE YOU HAVE HERE.

COOKIES?

THANKS. I'VE WORKED VERY HARD TO MAKE IT THAT WAY. TO MAKE OUR *LIFE* THAT WAY. I INTEND TO WORK JUST AS HARD TO *KEEP* IT THAT WAY.

THIS...*BUSINESS* OF YOURS...DO YOU HAVE A LOT OF YOUNG GIRLS INTERNING FOR YOU?

NOT REALLY...ANYA IS...WELL, LET'S SAY SHE'S ONE OF A KIND.

WE WORK WITH YOUNG PEOPLE AROUND THE WORLD, BUT ALSO WITH A VARIETY OF FORTUNE 500 COMPANIES. WE CONSULT, ADVISE, HEADHUNT--

SO IT'S MAINLY BOYS, THEN?

SO YOU DON'T ACTUALLY MAKE ANYTHING, THEN.

SIR--

I'M JUST SAYING--

AS AN INVESTIGATIVE REPORTER, YOU MUST KNOW AS WELL AS I DO THAT INFORMATION IS AS MUCH A COMMODITY IN OUR WORLD AS ANY PRODUCT. PEOPLE BUY AND SELL INFORMATION FOR MILLIONS OF DOLLARS EVERY DAY. THE RIGHT WORD, AT THE RIGHT TIME, CAN SPELL THE DIFFERENCE BETWEEN LIFE AND DEATH FOR SOME OF OUR LARGEST CORPORATIONS.

I THINK THEY'RE CHOCOLATE.

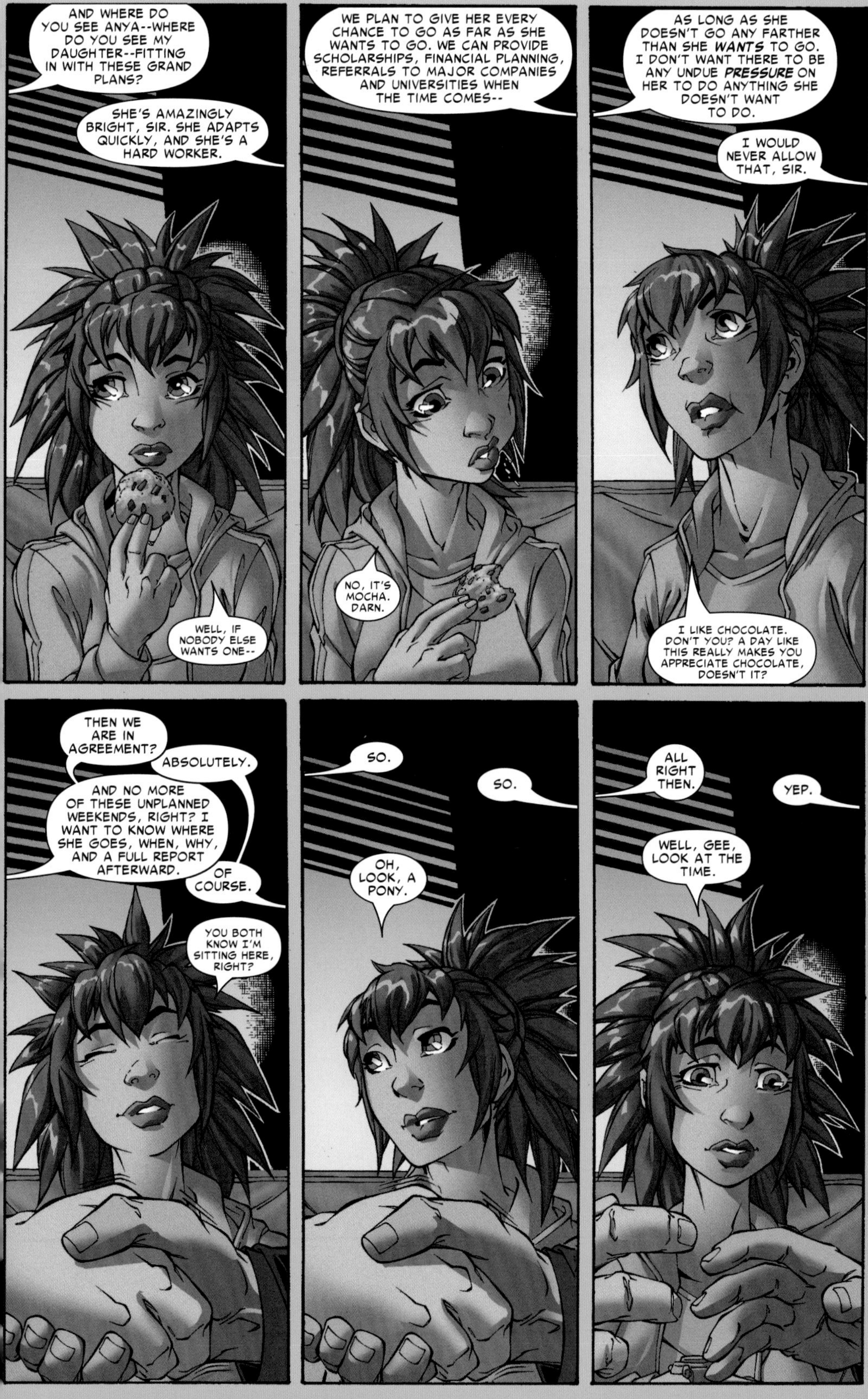
AND WHERE DO YOU SEE ANYA--WHERE DO YOU SEE MY DAUGHTER--FITTING IN WITH THESE GRAND PLANS?
SHE'S AMAZINGLY BRIGHT, SIR. SHE ADAPTS QUICKLY, AND SHE'S A HARD WORKER.
WELL, IF NOBODY ELSE WANTS ONE--
WE PLAN TO GIVE HER EVERY CHANCE TO GO AS FAR AS SHE WANTS TO GO. WE CAN PROVIDE SCHOLARSHIPS, FINANCIAL PLANNING, REFERRALS TO MAJOR COMPANIES AND UNIVERSITIES WHEN THE TIME COMES--
NO, IT'S MOCHA. DARN.
AS LONG AS SHE DOESN'T GO ANY FARTHER THAN SHE *WANTS* TO GO. I DON'T WANT THERE TO BE ANY UNDUE *PRESSURE* ON HER TO DO ANYTHING SHE DOESN'T WANT TO DO.
I WOULD NEVER ALLOW THAT, SIR.
I LIKE CHOCOLATE. DON'T YOU? A DAY LIKE THIS REALLY MAKES YOU APPRECIATE CHOCOLATE, DOESN'T IT?
THEN WE ARE IN AGREEMENT?
ABSOLUTELY.
AND NO MORE OF THESE UNPLANNED WEEKENDS, RIGHT? I WANT TO KNOW WHERE SHE GOES, WHEN, WHY, AND A FULL REPORT AFTERWARD.
OF COURSE.
YOU BOTH KNOW I'M SITTING HERE, RIGHT?
SO.
SO.
OH, LOOK, A PONY.
ALL RIGHT THEN.
YEP.
WELL, GEE, LOOK AT THE TIME.

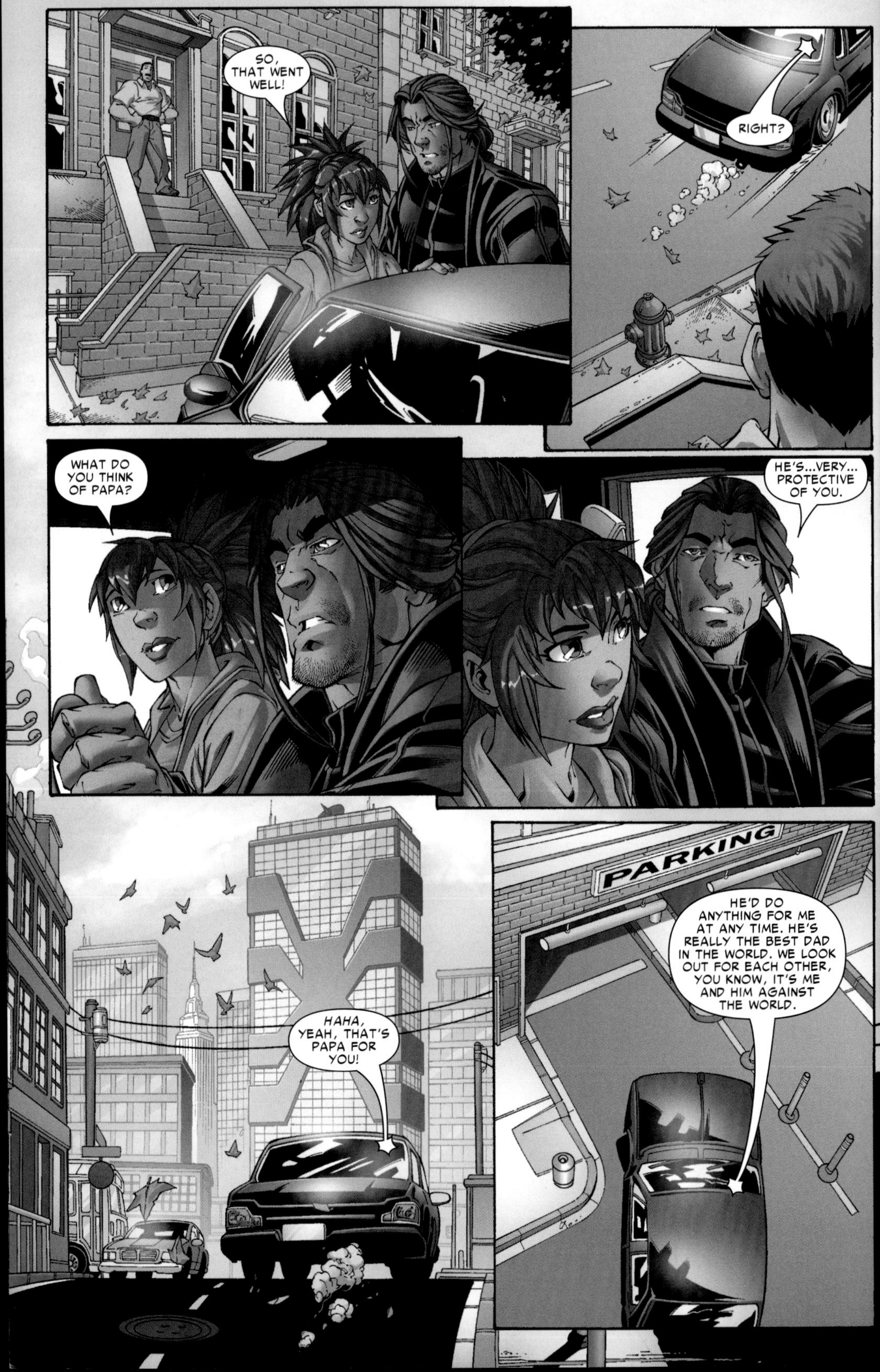
SO, THAT WENT WELL!
RIGHT?
WHAT DO YOU THINK OF PAPA?
HE'S...VERY... PROTECTIVE OF YOU.
HAHA, YEAH, THAT'S PAPA FOR YOU!
PARKING
HE'D DO ANYTHING FOR ME AT ANY TIME. HE'S REALLY THE BEST DAD IN THE WORLD. WE LOOK OUT FOR EACH OTHER, YOU KNOW, IT'S ME AND HIM AGAINST THE WORLD.

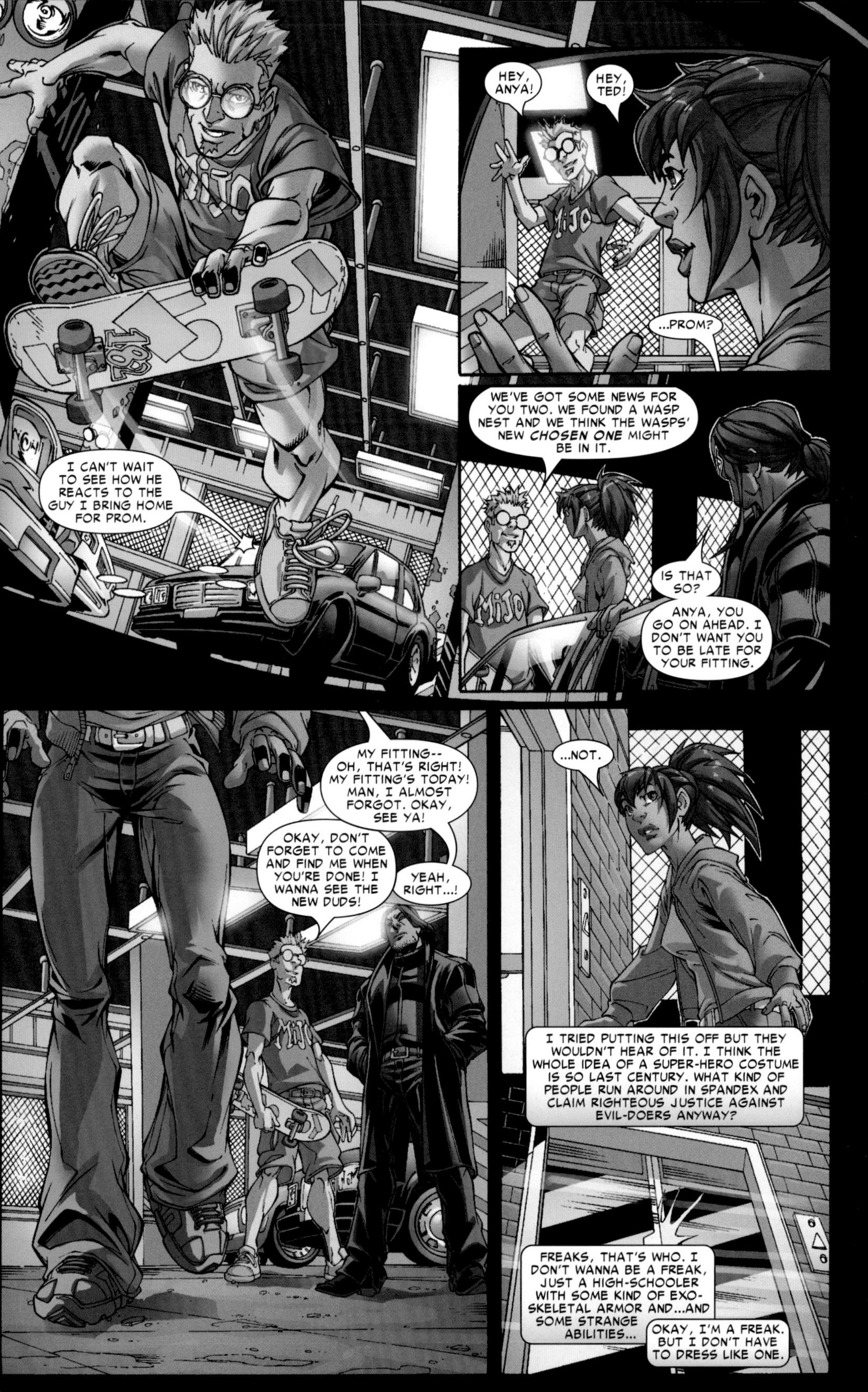
HEY, ANYA!
HEY, TED!
...PROM?
I CAN'T WAIT TO SEE HOW HE REACTS TO THE GUY I BRING HOME FOR PROM.
WE'VE GOT SOME NEWS FOR YOU TWO. WE FOUND A WASP NEST AND WE THINK THE WASPS' NEW CHOSEN ONE MIGHT BE IN IT.
IS THAT SO?
ANYA, YOU GO ON AHEAD. I DON'T WANT YOU TO BE LATE FOR YOUR FITTING.
MY FITTING-- OH, THAT'S RIGHT! MY FITTING'S TODAY! MAN, I ALMOST FORGOT. OKAY, SEE YA!
OKAY, DON'T FORGET TO COME AND FIND ME WHEN YOU'RE DONE! I WANNA SEE THE NEW DUDS!
YEAH, RIGHT...!
...NOT.
I TRIED PUTTING THIS OFF BUT THEY WOULDN'T HEAR OF IT. I THINK THE WHOLE IDEA OF A SUPER-HERO COSTUME IS SO LAST CENTURY. WHAT KIND OF PEOPLE RUN AROUND IN SPANDEX AND CLAIM RIGHTEOUS JUSTICE AGAINST EVIL-DOERS ANYWAY?
FREAKS, THAT'S WHO. I DON'T WANNA BE A FREAK, JUST A HIGH-SCHOOLER WITH SOME KIND OF EXO-SKELETAL ARMOR AND...AND SOME STRANGE ABILITIES...
OKAY, I'M A FREAK. BUT I DON'T HAVE TO DRESS LIKE ONE.

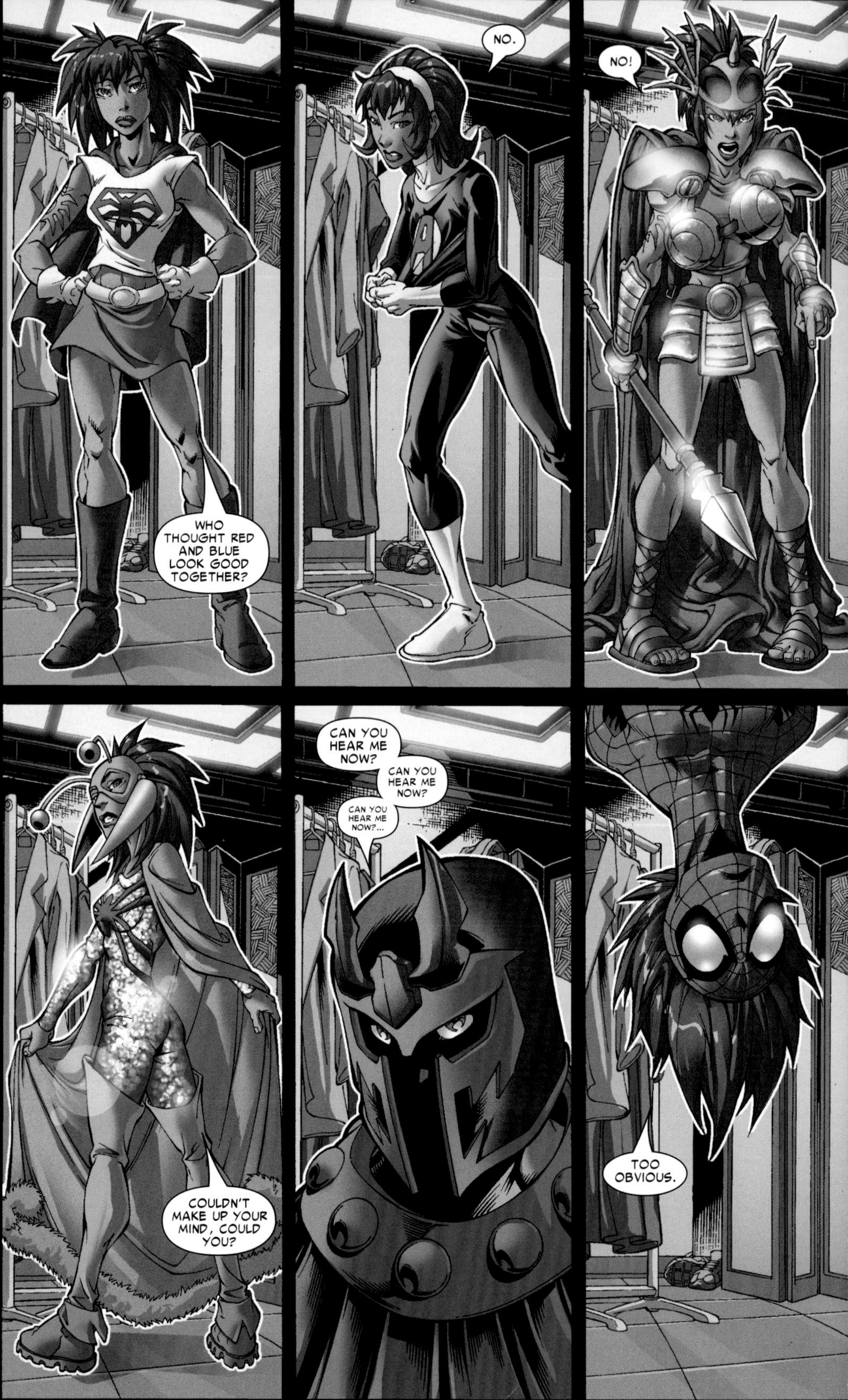
WHO THOUGHT RED AND BLUE LOOK GOOD TOGETHER?
NO.
NO!
COULDN'T MAKE UP YOUR MIND, COULD YOU?
CAN YOU HEAR ME NOW?
CAN YOU HEAR ME NOW?
CAN YOU HEAR ME NOW?...
TOO OBVIOUS.

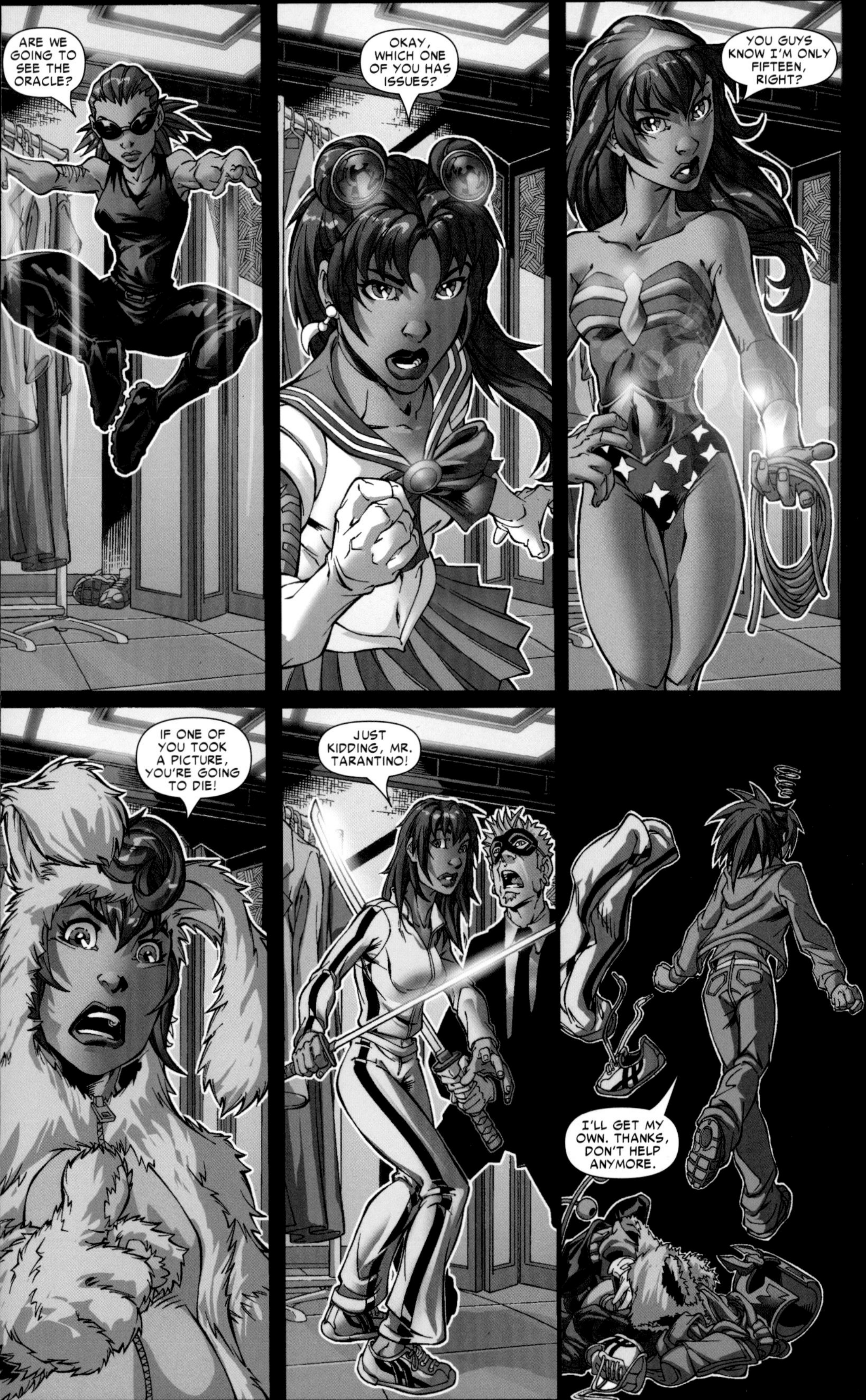
ARE WE GOING TO SEE THE ORACLE?
OKAY, WHICH ONE OF YOU HAS ISSUES?
YOU GUYS KNOW I'M ONLY FIFTEEN, RIGHT?
IF ONE OF YOU TOOK A PICTURE, YOU'RE GOING TO DIE!
JUST KIDDING, MR. TARANTINO!
I'LL GET MY OWN. THANKS, DON'T HELP ANYMORE.

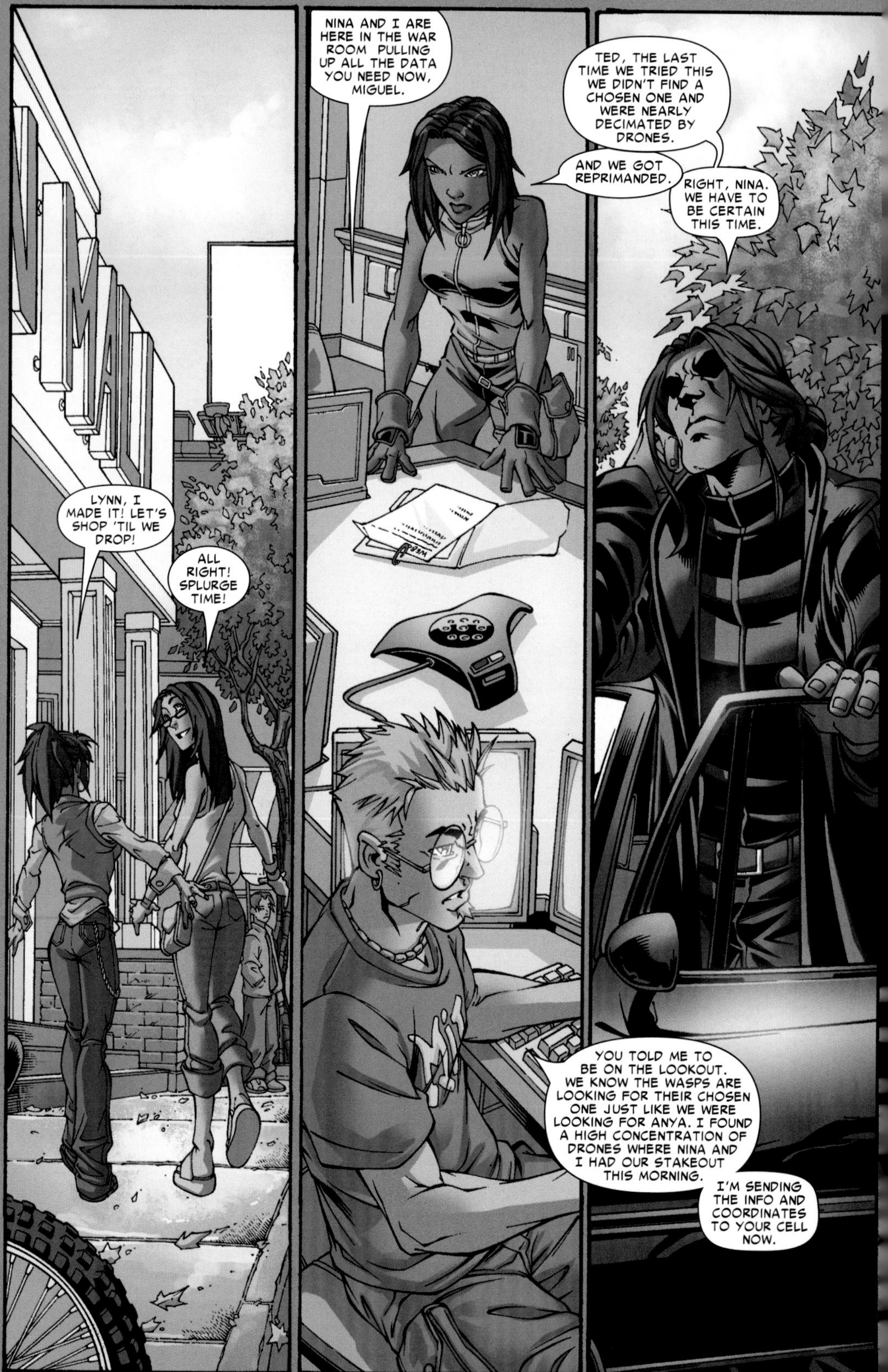
LYNN, I MADE IT! LET'S SHOP 'TIL WE DROP!
ALL RIGHT! SPLURGE TIME!
NINA AND I ARE HERE IN THE WAR ROOM PULLING UP ALL THE DATA YOU NEED NOW, MIGUEL.
TED, THE LAST TIME WE TRIED THIS WE DIDN'T FIND A CHOSEN ONE AND WERE NEARLY DECIMATED BY DRONES.
AND WE GOT REPRIMANDED.
RIGHT, NINA. WE HAVE TO BE CERTAIN THIS TIME.
YOU TOLD ME TO BE ON THE LOOKOUT. WE KNOW THE WASPS ARE LOOKING FOR THEIR CHOSEN ONE JUST LIKE WE WERE LOOKING FOR ANYA. I FOUND A HIGH CONCENTRATION OF DRONES WHERE NINA AND I HAD OUR STAKEOUT THIS MORNING.
I'M SENDING THE INFO AND COORDINATES TO YOUR CELL NOW.

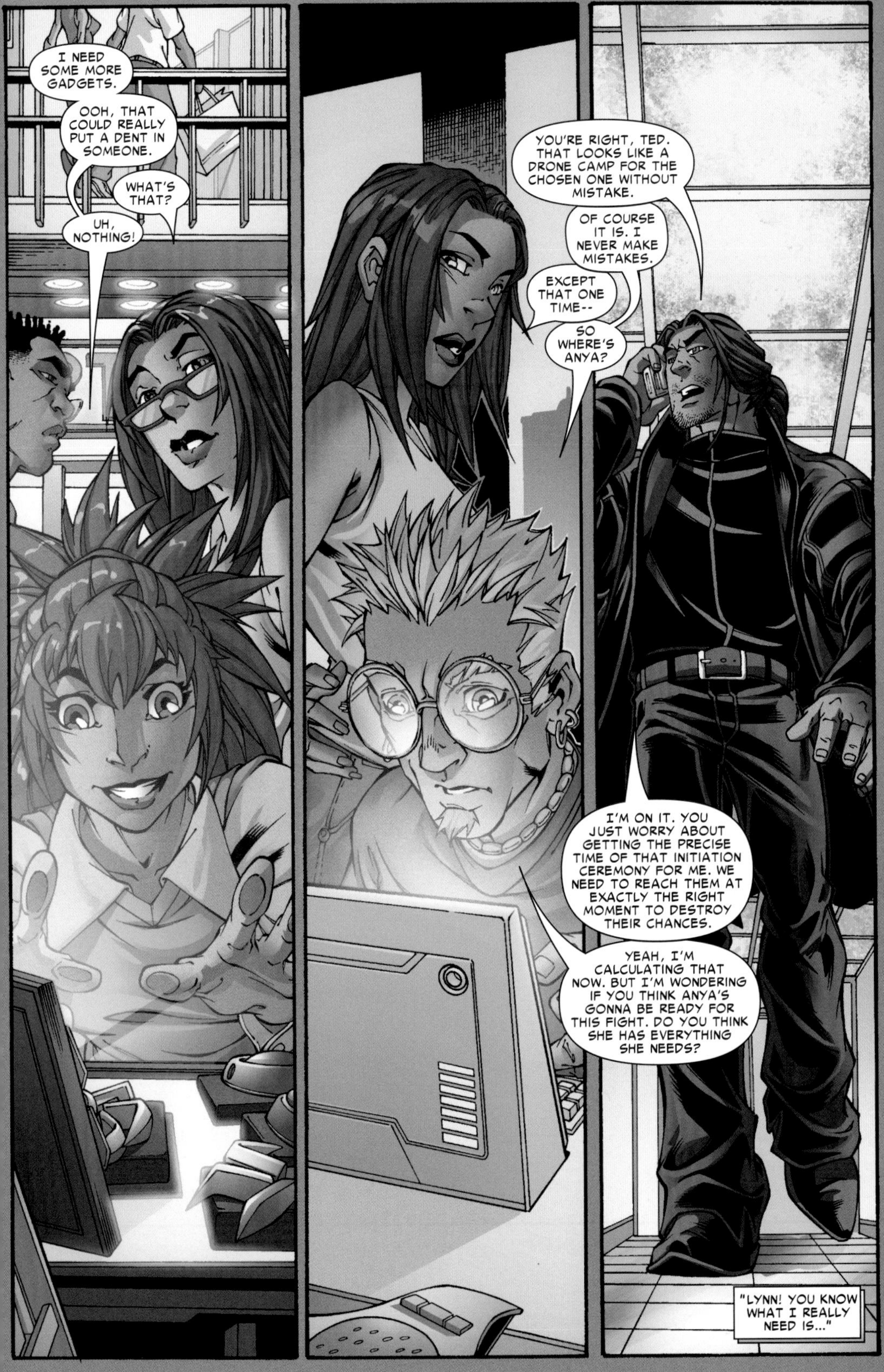
I NEED SOME MORE GADGETS.
OOH, THAT COULD REALLY PUT A DENT IN SOMEONE.
WHAT'S THAT?
UH, NOTHING!
YOU'RE RIGHT, TED. THAT LOOKS LIKE A DRONE CAMP FOR THE CHOSEN ONE WITHOUT MISTAKE.
OF COURSE IT IS. I NEVER MAKE MISTAKES.
EXCEPT THAT ONE TIME--
SO WHERE'S ANYA?
I'M ON IT. YOU JUST WORRY ABOUT GETTING THE PRECISE TIME OF THAT INITIATION CEREMONY FOR ME. WE NEED TO REACH THEM AT EXACTLY THE RIGHT MOMENT TO DESTROY THEIR CHANCES.
YEAH, I'M CALCULATING THAT NOW. BUT I'M WONDERING IF YOU THINK ANYA'S GONNA BE READY FOR THIS FIGHT. DO YOU THINK SHE HAS EVERYTHING SHE NEEDS?
"LYNN! YOU KNOW WHAT I REALLY NEED IS..."

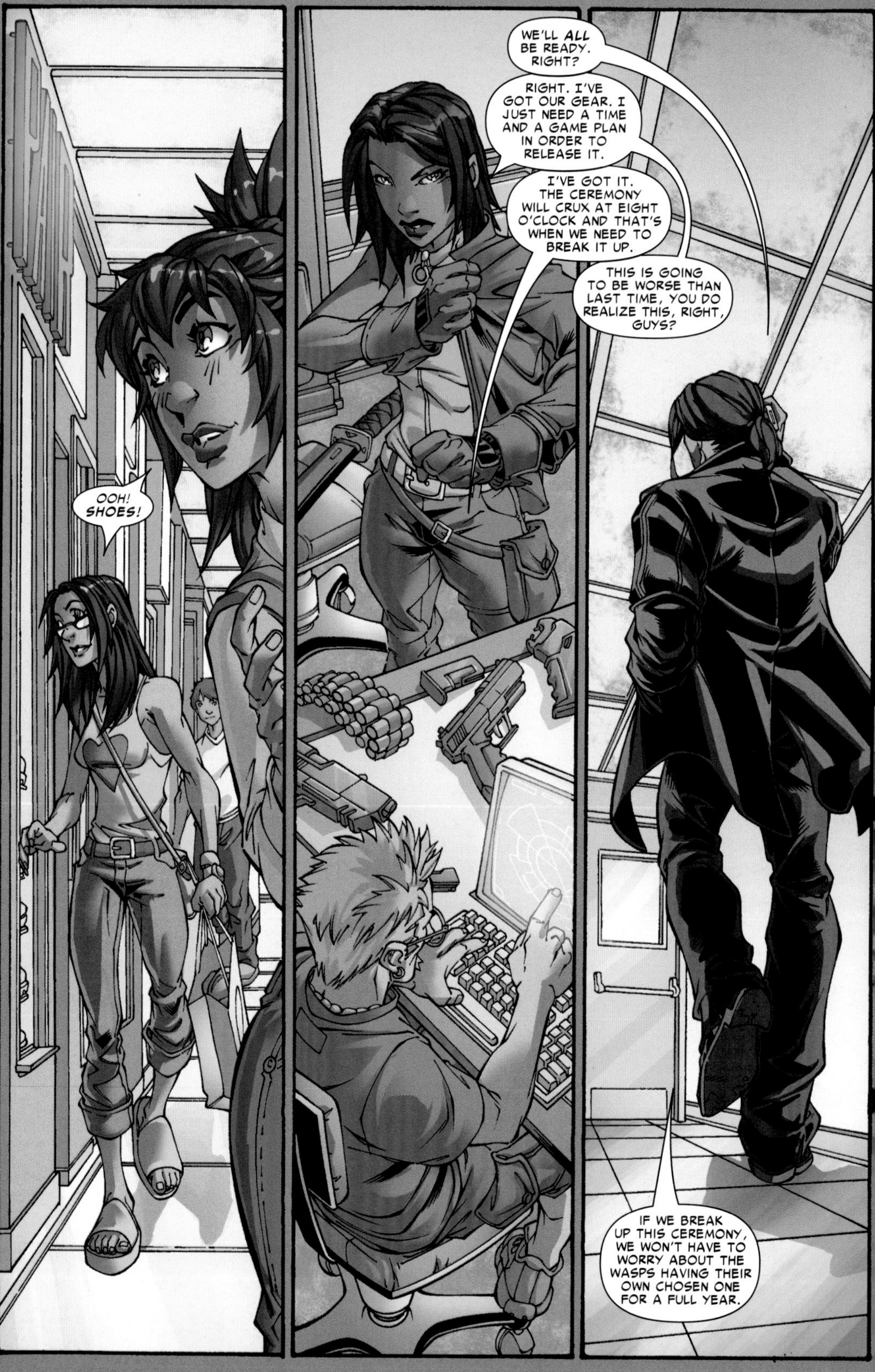
OOH! SHOES!
WE'LL ALL BE READY. RIGHT?
RIGHT. I'VE GOT OUR GEAR. I JUST NEED A TIME AND A GAME PLAN IN ORDER TO RELEASE IT.
I'VE GOT IT. THE CEREMONY WILL CRUX AT EIGHT O'CLOCK AND THAT'S WHEN WE NEED TO BREAK IT UP.
THIS IS GOING TO BE WORSE THAN LAST TIME, YOU DO REALIZE THIS, RIGHT, GUYS?
IF WE BREAK UP THIS CEREMONY, WE WON'T HAVE TO WORRY ABOUT THE WASPS HAVING THEIR OWN CHOSEN ONE FOR A FULL YEAR.

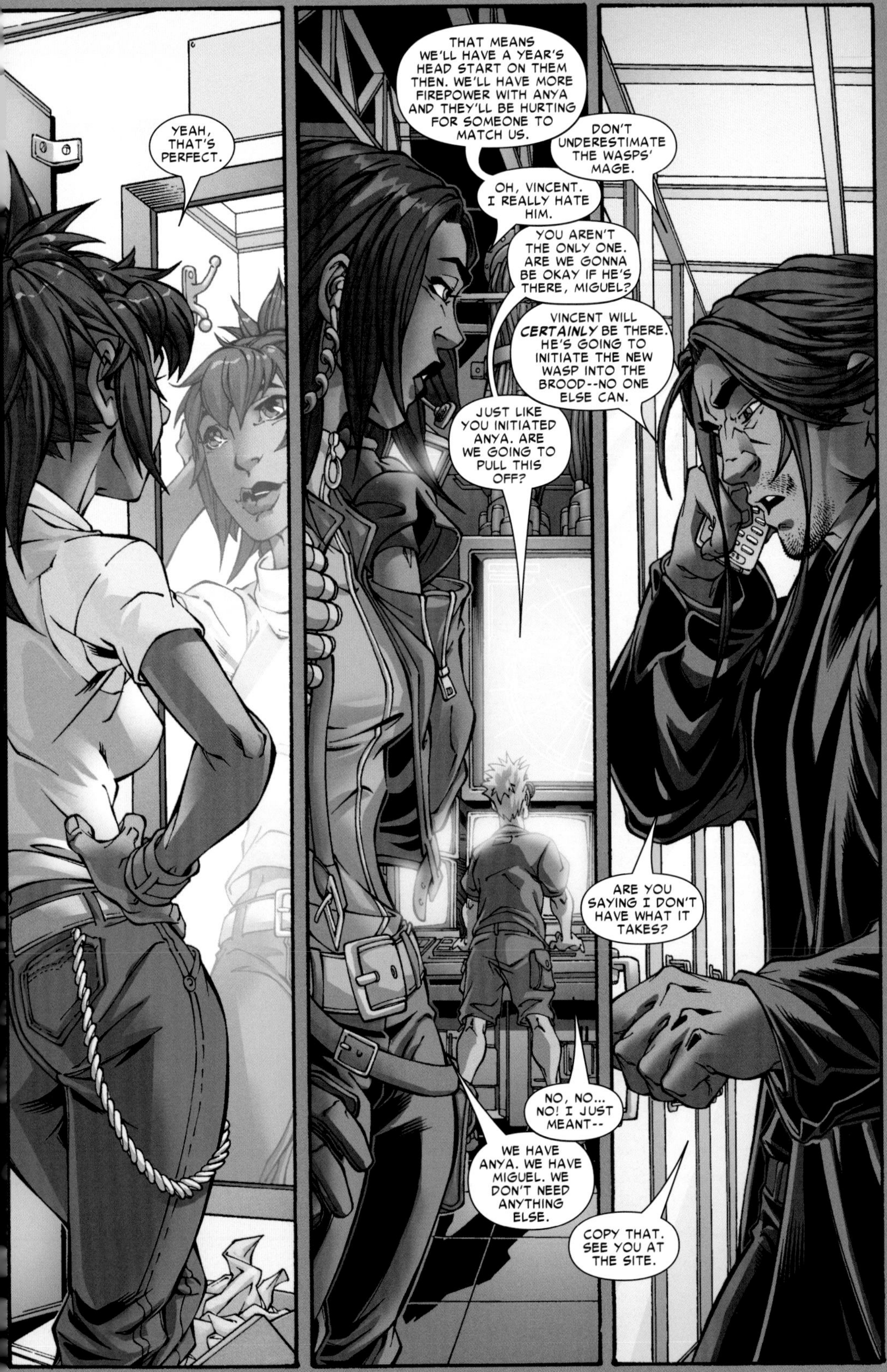
YEAH, THAT'S PERFECT.
THAT MEANS WE'LL HAVE A YEAR'S HEAD START ON THEM THEN. WE'LL HAVE MORE FIREPOWER WITH ANYA AND THEY'LL BE HURTING FOR SOMEONE TO MATCH US.
DON'T UNDERESTIMATE THE WASPS' MAGE.
OH, VINCENT. I REALLY HATE HIM.
YOU AREN'T THE ONLY ONE. ARE WE GONNA BE OKAY IF HE'S THERE, MIGUEL?
VINCENT WILL *CERTAINLY* BE THERE. HE'S GOING TO INITIATE THE NEW WASP INTO THE BROOD--NO ONE ELSE CAN.
JUST LIKE YOU INITIATED ANYA. ARE WE GOING TO PULL THIS OFF?
ARE YOU SAYING I DON'T HAVE WHAT IT TAKES?
NO, NO... NO! I JUST MEANT--
WE HAVE ANYA. WE HAVE MIGUEL. WE DON'T NEED ANYTHING ELSE.
COPY THAT. SEE YOU AT THE SITE.

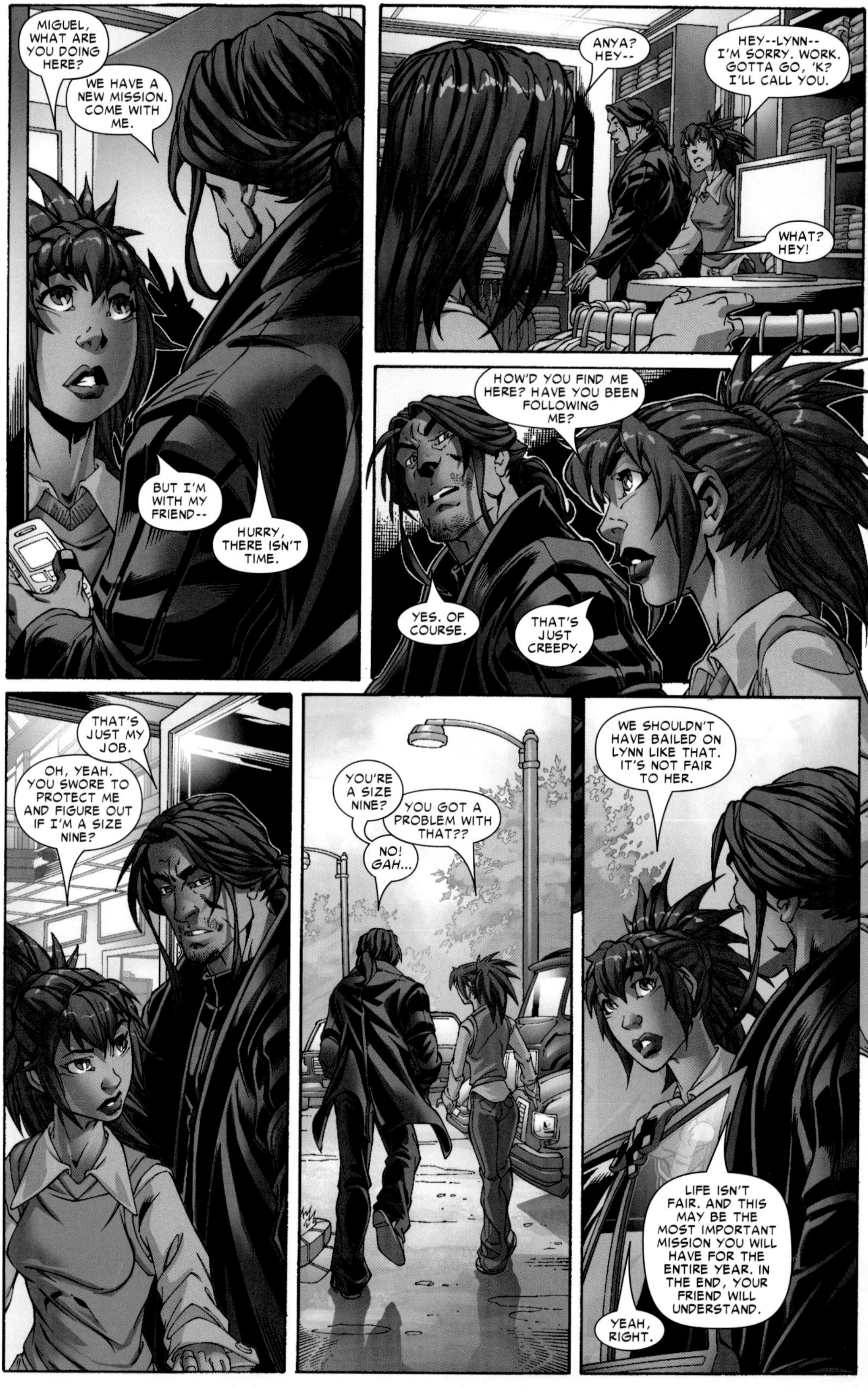
MIGUEL, WHAT ARE YOU DOING HERE?
WE HAVE A NEW MISSION. COME WITH ME.
BUT I'M WITH MY FRIEND--
HURRY, THERE ISN'T TIME.
ANYA? HEY--
HEY--LYNN-- I'M SORRY. WORK. GOTTA GO, 'K? I'LL CALL YOU.
WHAT? HEY!
HOW'D YOU FIND ME HERE? HAVE YOU BEEN FOLLOWING ME?
YES. OF COURSE.
THAT'S JUST CREEPY.
THAT'S JUST MY JOB.
OH, YEAH. YOU SWORE TO PROTECT ME AND FIGURE OUT IF I'M A SIZE NINE?
YOU'RE A SIZE NINE?
YOU GOT A PROBLEM WITH THAT??
NO! GAH...
WE SHOULDN'T HAVE BAILED ON LYNN LIKE THAT. IT'S NOT FAIR TO HER.
LIFE ISN'T FAIR. AND THIS MAY BE THE MOST IMPORTANT MISSION YOU WILL HAVE FOR THE ENTIRE YEAR. IN THE END, YOUR FRIEND WILL UNDERSTAND.
YEAH, RIGHT.

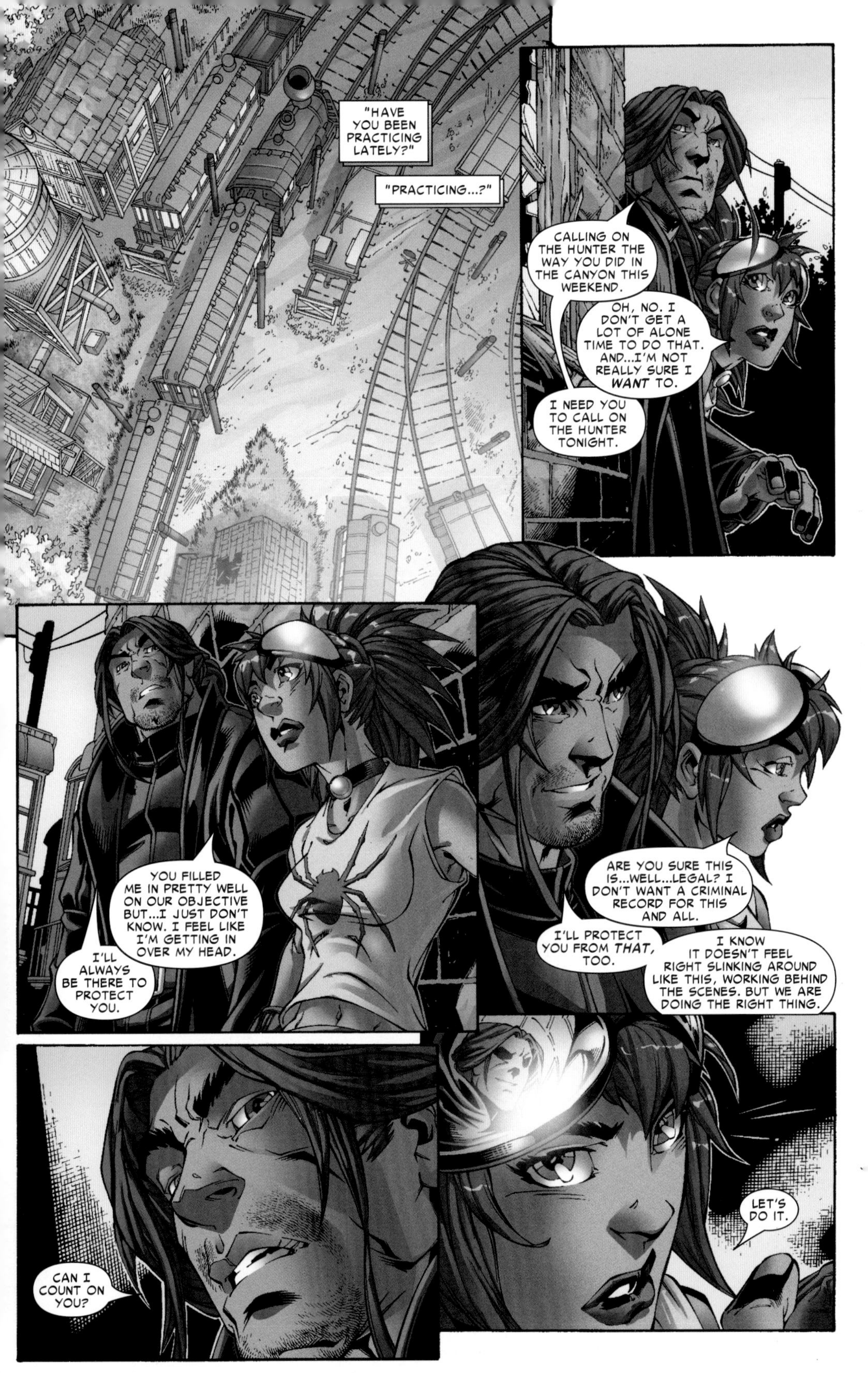
"HAVE YOU BEEN PRACTICING LATELY?"
"PRACTICING...?"
CALLING ON THE HUNTER THE WAY YOU DID IN THE CANYON THIS WEEKEND.
OH, NO. I DON'T GET A LOT OF ALONE TIME TO DO THAT. AND...I'M NOT REALLY SURE I *WANT* TO.
I NEED YOU TO CALL ON THE HUNTER TONIGHT.
YOU FILLED ME IN PRETTY WELL ON OUR OBJECTIVE BUT...I JUST DON'T KNOW. I FEEL LIKE I'M GETTING IN OVER MY HEAD.
I'LL ALWAYS BE THERE TO PROTECT YOU.
ARE YOU SURE THIS IS...WELL...LEGAL? I DON'T WANT A CRIMINAL RECORD FOR THIS AND ALL.
I'LL PROTECT YOU FROM *THAT*, TOO.
I KNOW IT DOESN'T FEEL RIGHT SLINKING AROUND LIKE THIS, WORKING BEHIND THE SCENES. BUT WE ARE DOING THE RIGHT THING.
CAN I COUNT ON YOU?
LET'S DO IT.

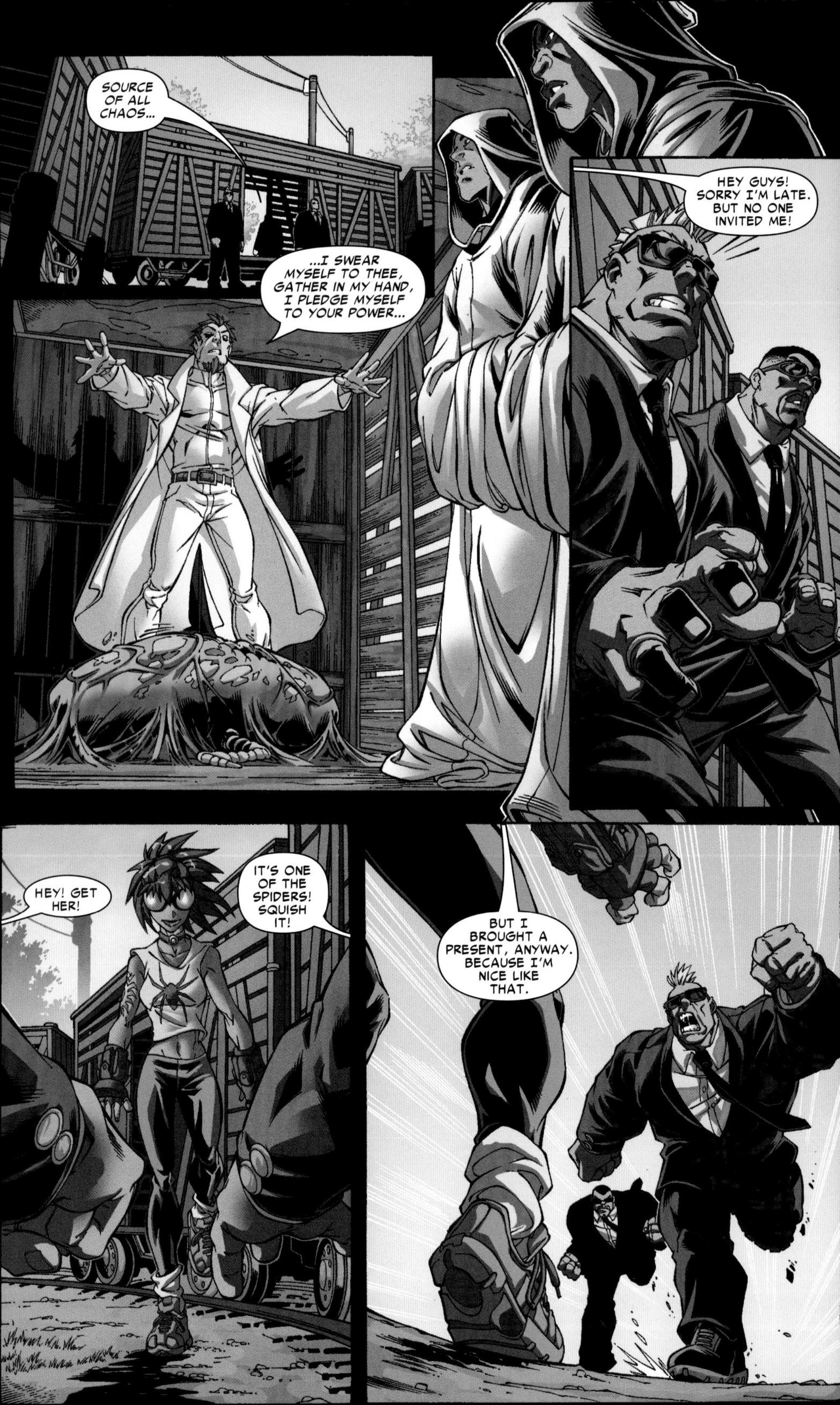
SOURCE OF ALL CHAOS...
...I SWEAR MYSELF TO THEE, GATHER IN MY HAND, I PLEDGE MYSELF TO YOUR POWER...
HEY GUYS! SORRY I'M LATE. BUT NO ONE INVITED ME!
HEY! GET HER!
IT'S ONE OF THE SPIDERS! SQUISH IT!
BUT I BROUGHT A PRESENT, ANYWAY. BECAUSE I'M NICE LIKE THAT.

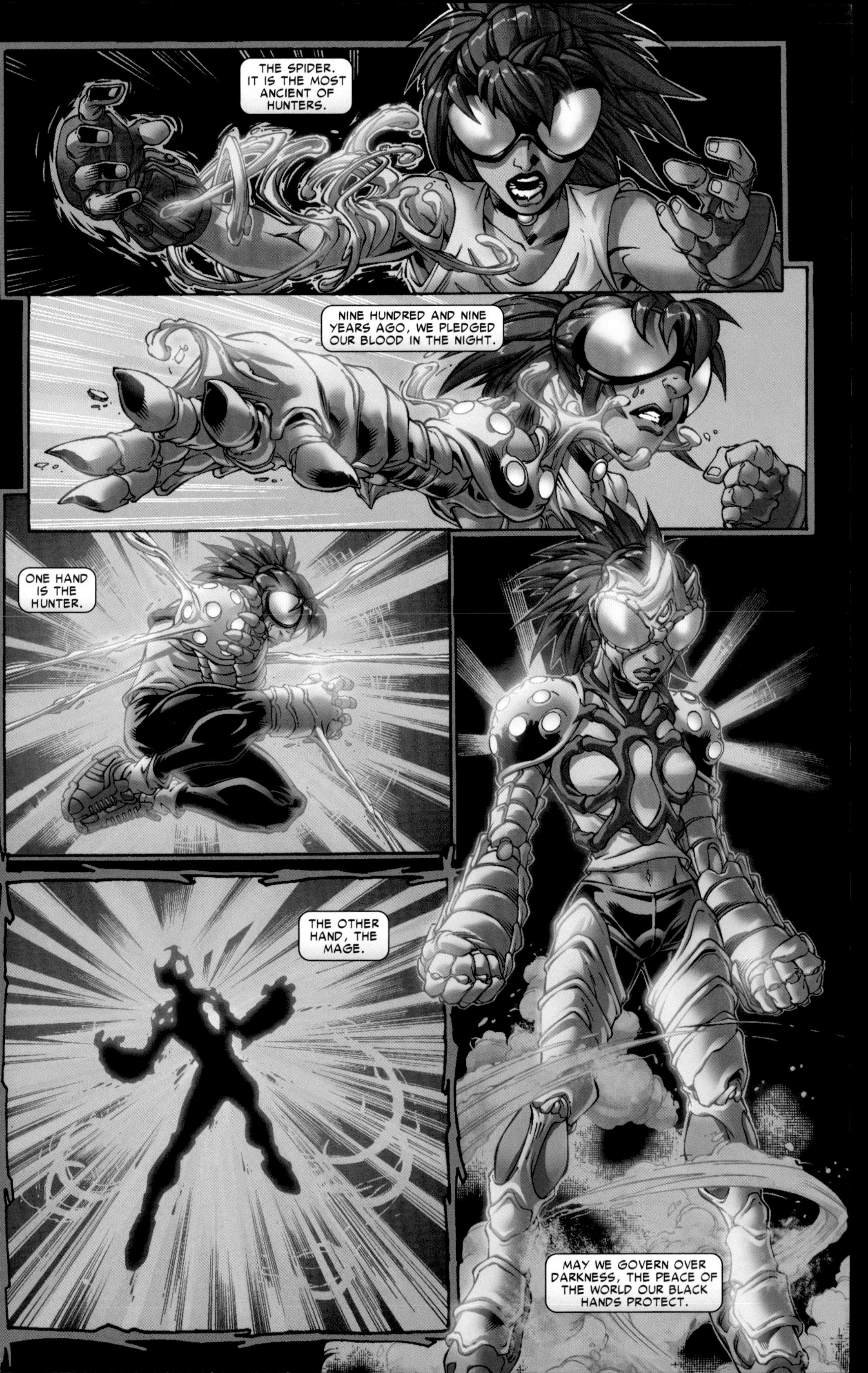

THE SPIDER. IT IS THE MOST ANCIENT OF HUNTERS.
NINE HUNDRED AND NINE YEARS AGO, WE PLEDGED OUR BLOOD IN THE NIGHT.
ONE HAND IS THE HUNTER.
THE OTHER HAND, THE MAGE.
MAY WE GOVERN OVER DARKNESS, THE PEACE OF THE WORLD OUR BLACK HANDS PROTECT.

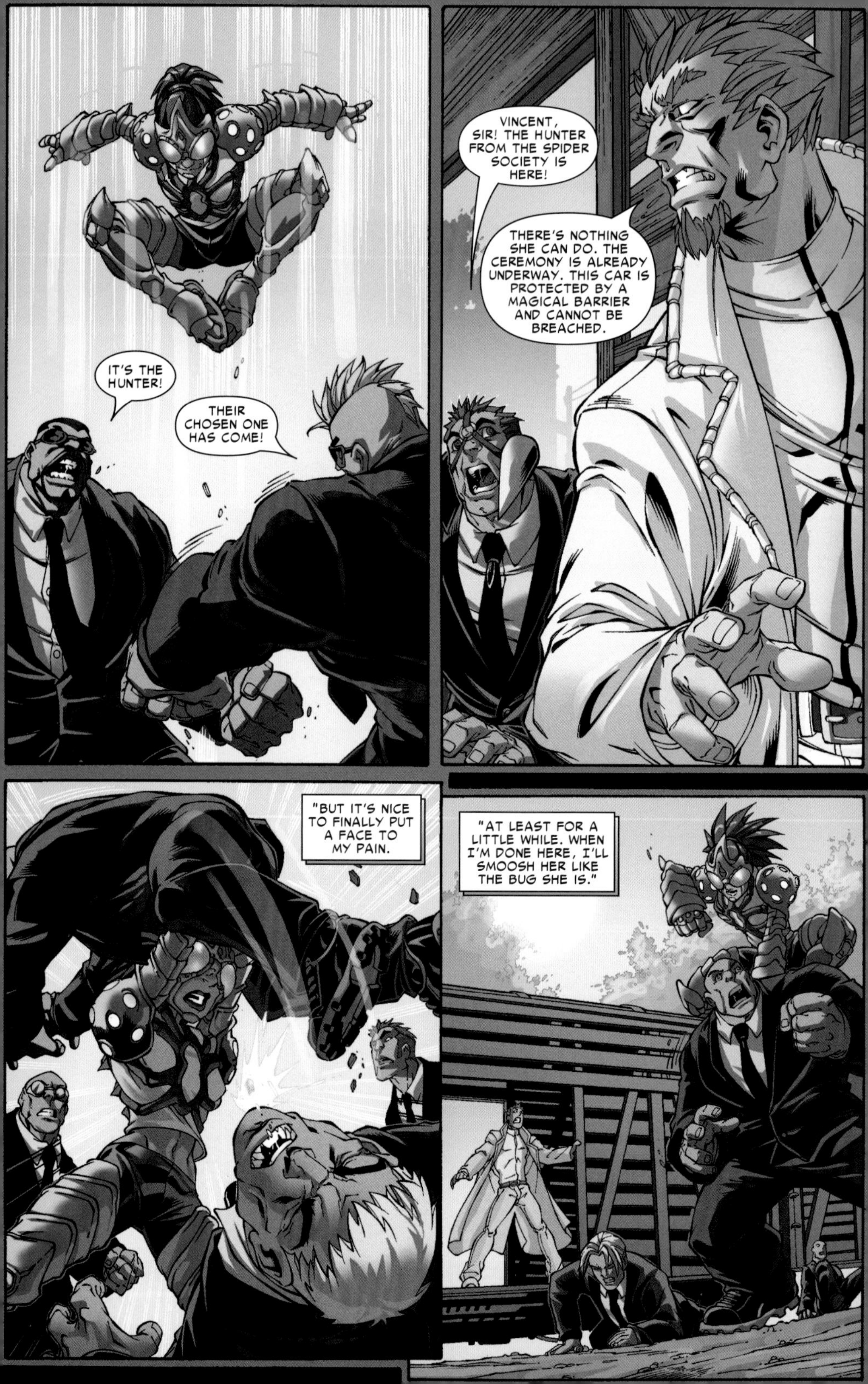
IT'S THE HUNTER!
THEIR CHOSEN ONE HAS COME!
VINCENT, SIR! THE HUNTER FROM THE SPIDER SOCIETY IS HERE!
THERE'S NOTHING SHE CAN DO. THE CEREMONY IS ALREADY UNDERWAY. THIS CAR IS PROTECTED BY A MAGICAL BARRIER AND CANNOT BE BREACHED.
"BUT IT'S NICE TO FINALLY PUT A FACE TO MY PAIN.
"AT LEAST FOR A LITTLE WHILE. WHEN I'M DONE HERE, I'LL SMOOSH HER LIKE THE BUG SHE IS."

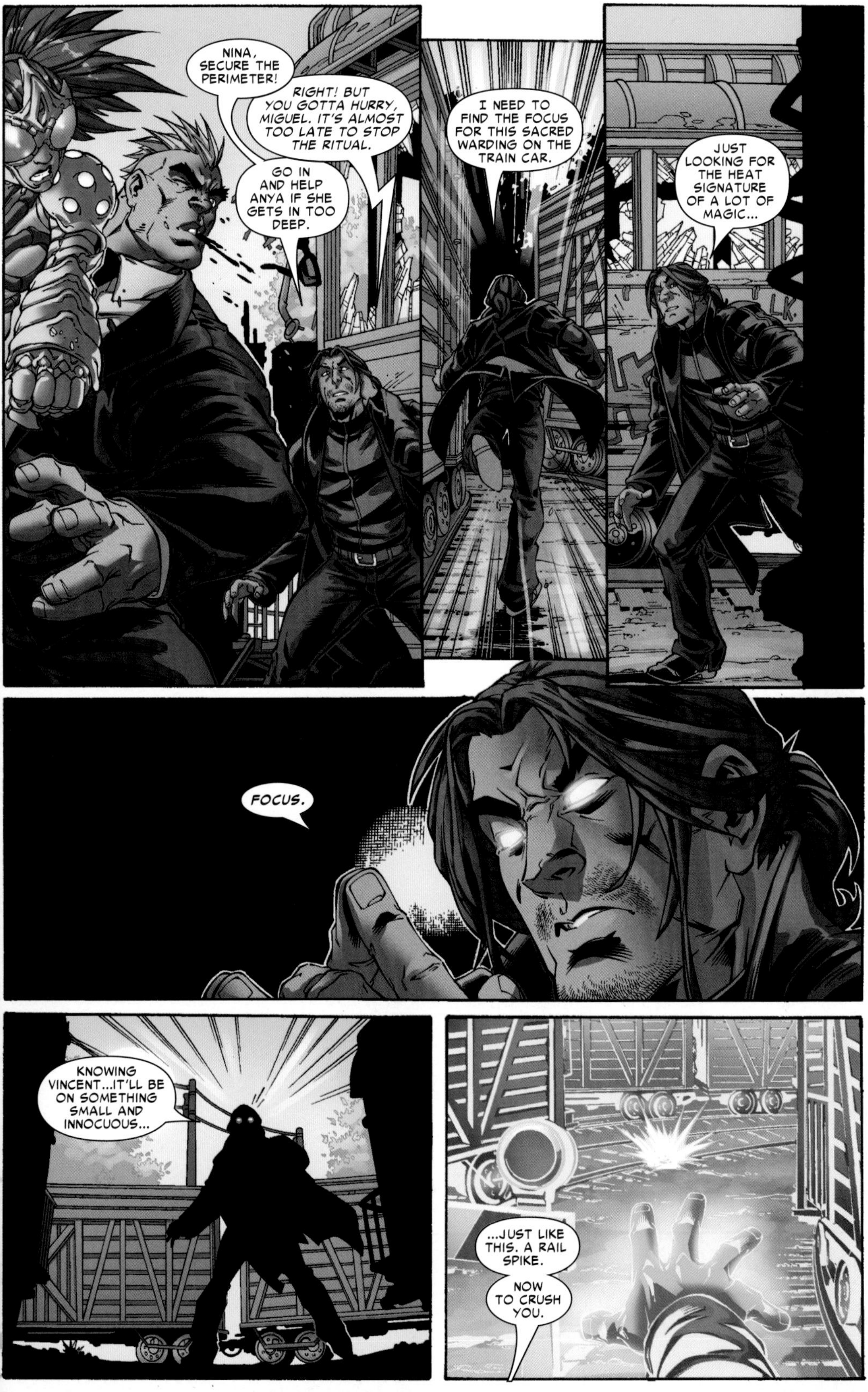
NINA, SECURE THE PERIMETER!
RIGHT! BUT YOU GOTTA HURRY, MIGUEL. IT'S ALMOST TOO LATE TO STOP THE RITUAL.
GO IN AND HELP ANYA IF SHE GETS IN TOO DEEP.
I NEED TO FIND THE FOCUS FOR THIS SACRED WARDING ON THE TRAIN CAR.
JUST LOOKING FOR THE HEAT SIGNATURE OF A LOT OF MAGIC...
FOCUS.
KNOWING VINCENT...IT'LL BE ON SOMETHING SMALL AND INNOCUOUS...
...JUST LIKE THIS. A RAIL SPIKE.
NOW TO CRUSH YOU.

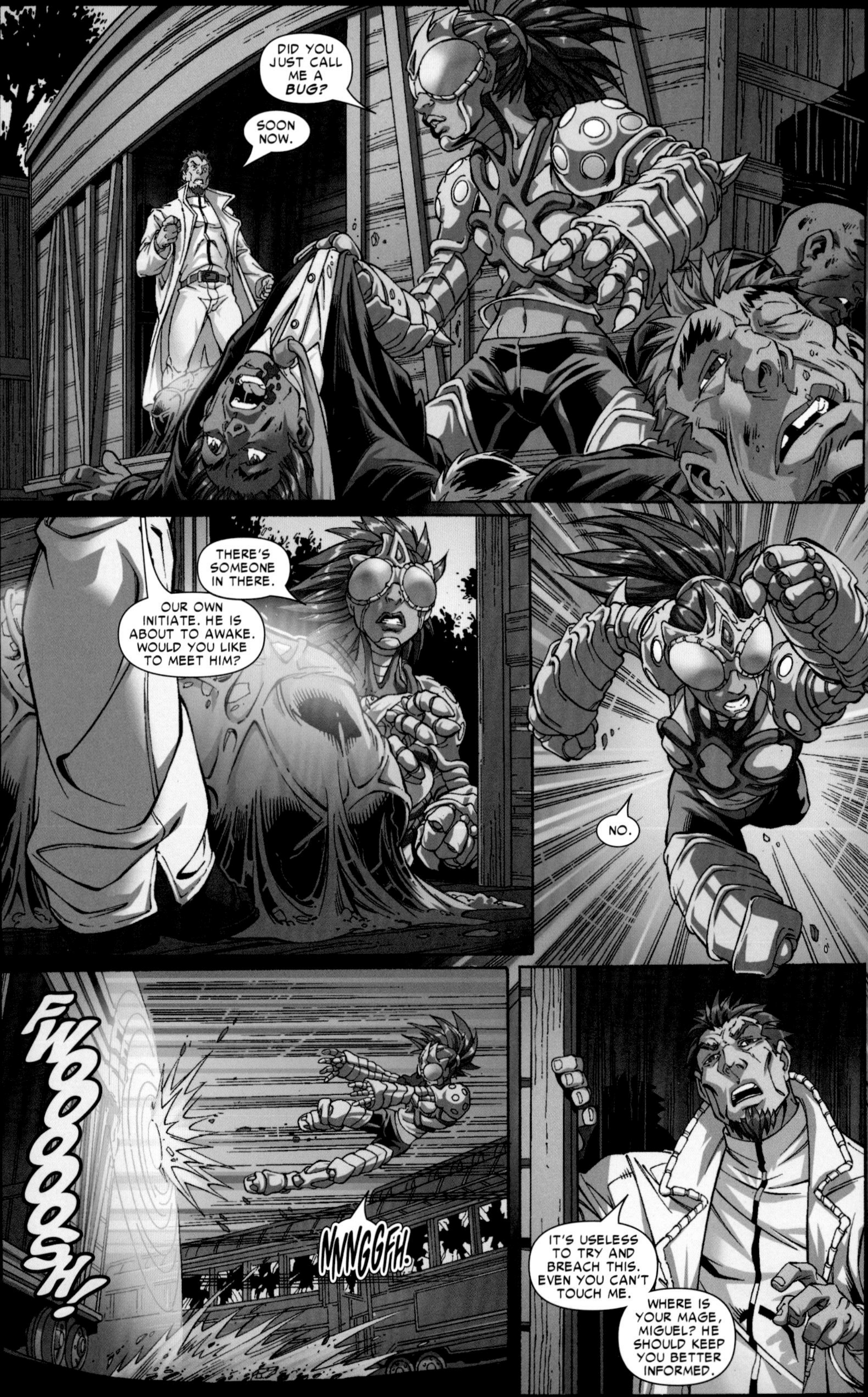
DID YOU JUST CALL ME A *BUG?*
SOON NOW.
THERE'S SOMEONE IN THERE.
OUR OWN INITIATE. HE IS ABOUT TO AWAKE. WOULD YOU LIKE TO MEET HIM?
NO.
FWOOOOOOSH!
MNNGGFH.
IT'S USELESS TO TRY AND BREACH THIS. EVEN YOU CAN'T TOUCH ME.
WHERE IS YOUR MAGE, MIGUEL? HE SHOULD KEEP YOU BETTER INFORMED.

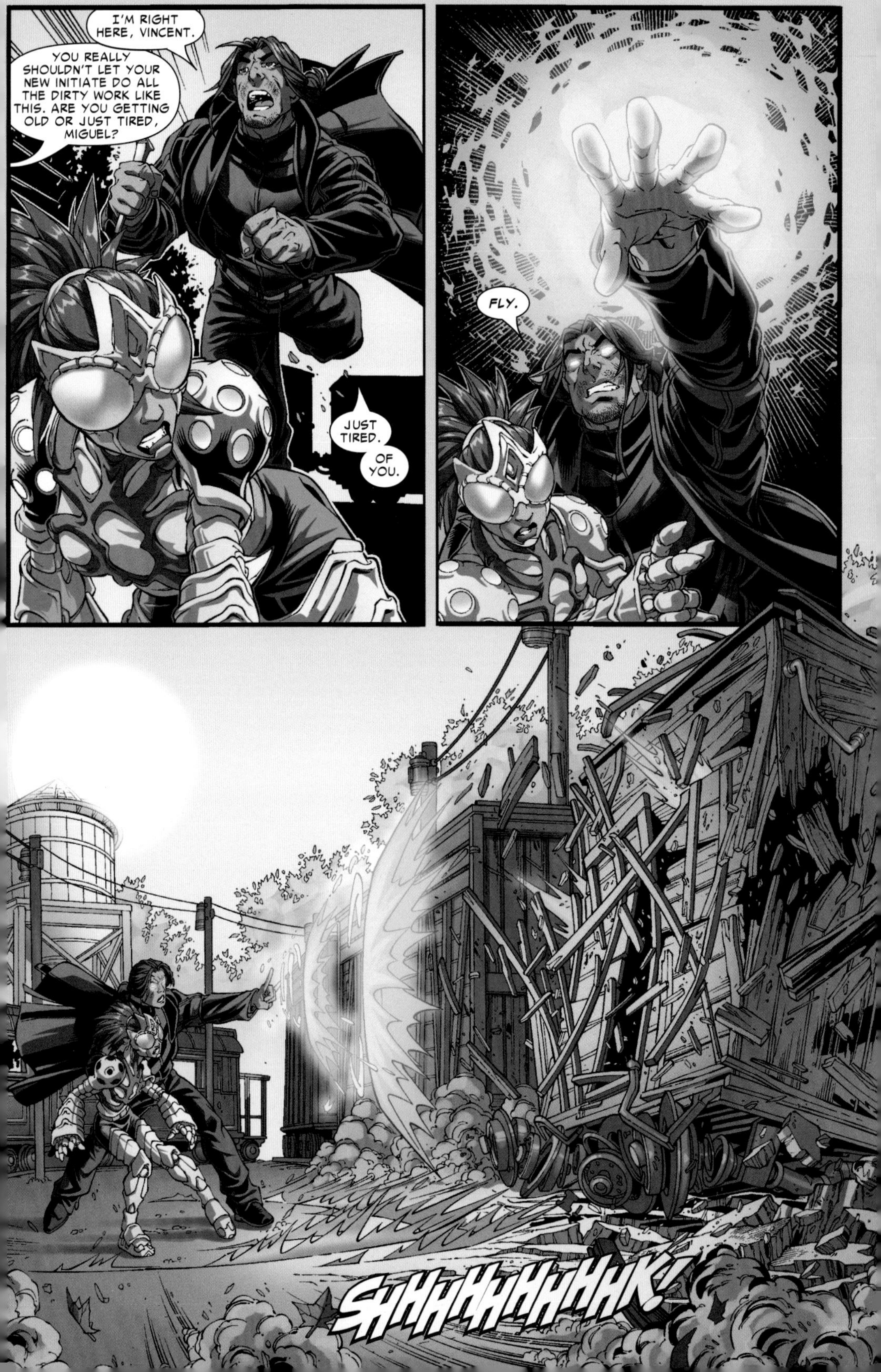

I'M RIGHT HERE, VINCENT.
YOU REALLY SHOULDN'T LET YOUR NEW INITIATE DO ALL THE DIRTY WORK LIKE THIS. ARE YOU GETTING OLD OR JUST TIRED, MIGUEL?
JUST TIRED.
OF YOU.
FLY.
SHHHHHHHHHK!

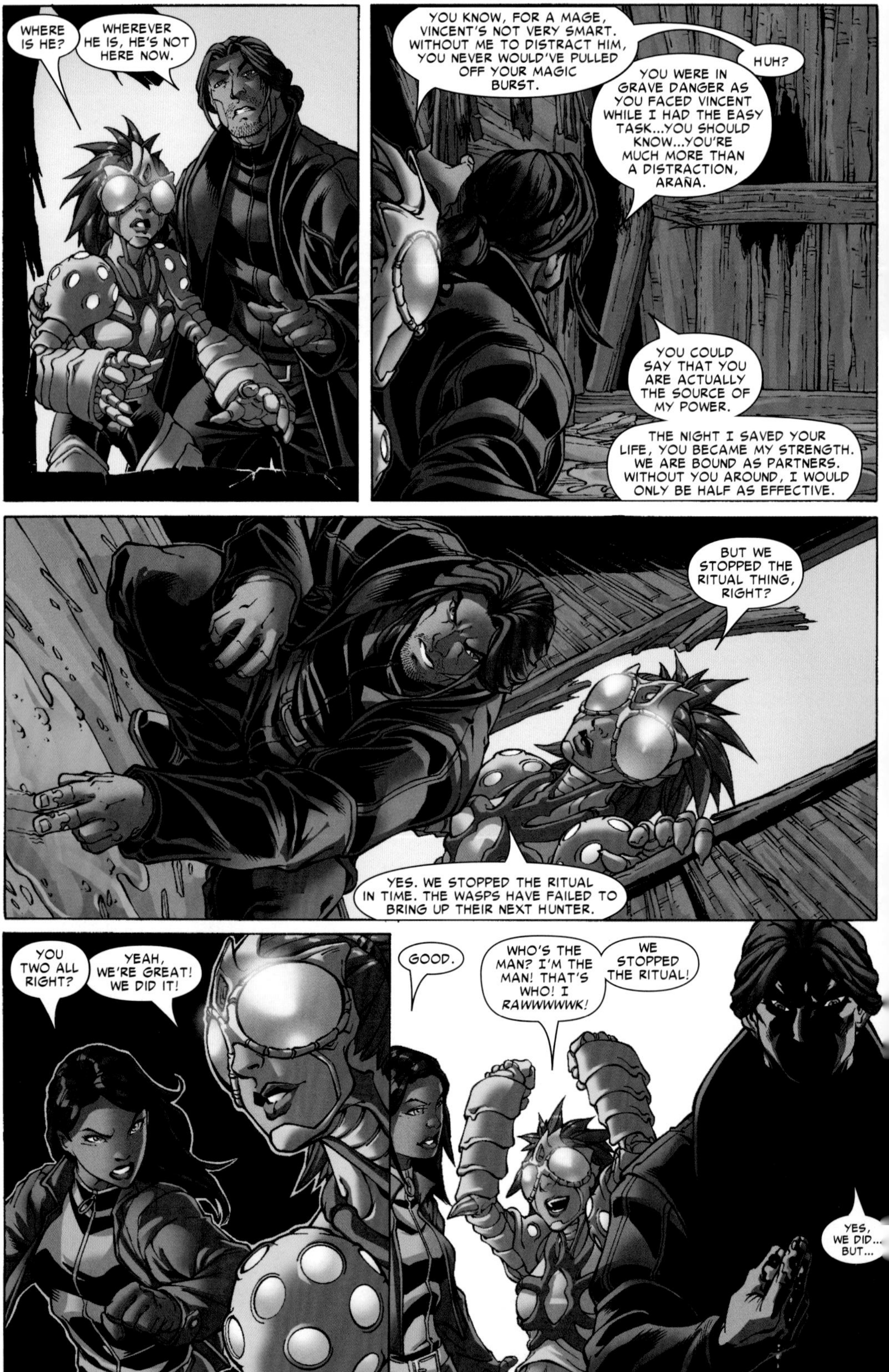
WHERE IS HE?
WHEREVER HE IS, HE'S NOT HERE NOW.
YOU KNOW, FOR A MAGE, VINCENT'S NOT VERY SMART. WITHOUT ME TO DISTRACT HIM, YOU NEVER WOULD'VE PULLED OFF YOUR MAGIC BURST.
HUH?
YOU WERE IN GRAVE DANGER AS YOU FACED VINCENT WHILE I HAD THE EASY TASK...YOU SHOULD KNOW...YOU'RE MUCH MORE THAN A DISTRACTION, ARAÑA.
YOU COULD SAY THAT YOU ARE ACTUALLY THE SOURCE OF MY POWER.
THE NIGHT I SAVED YOUR LIFE, YOU BECAME MY STRENGTH. WE ARE BOUND AS PARTNERS. WITHOUT YOU AROUND, I WOULD ONLY BE HALF AS EFFECTIVE.
BUT WE STOPPED THE RITUAL THING, RIGHT?
YES. WE STOPPED THE RITUAL IN TIME. THE WASPS HAVE FAILED TO BRING UP THEIR NEXT HUNTER.
YOU TWO ALL RIGHT?
YEAH, WE'RE GREAT! WE DID IT!
GOOD.
WHO'S THE MAN? I'M THE MAN! THAT'S WHO! I RAWWWWWK!
WE STOPPED THE RITUAL!
YES, WE DID... BUT...

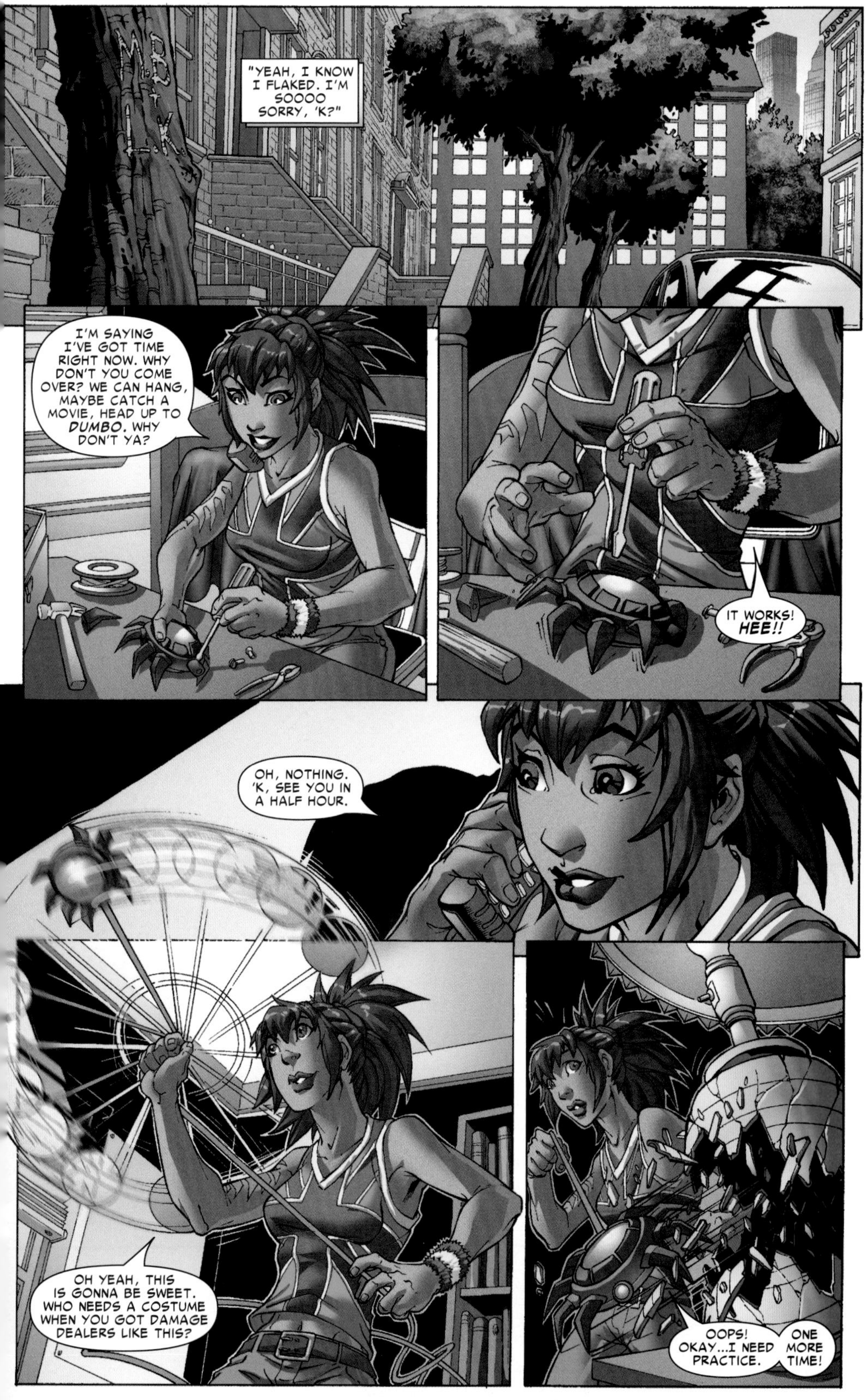
"YEAH, I KNOW I FLAKED. I'M SOOOO SORRY, 'K?"
I'M SAYING I'VE GOT TIME RIGHT NOW. WHY DON'T YOU COME OVER? WE CAN HANG, MAYBE CATCH A MOVIE, HEAD UP TO DUMBO. WHY DON'T YA?
IT WORKS! HEE!!
OH, NOTHING. 'K, SEE YOU IN A HALF HOUR.
OH YEAH, THIS IS GONNA BE SWEET. WHO NEEDS A COSTUME WHEN YOU GOT DAMAGE DEALERS LIKE THIS?
OOPS! OKAY...I NEED PRACTICE.
ONE MORE TIME!

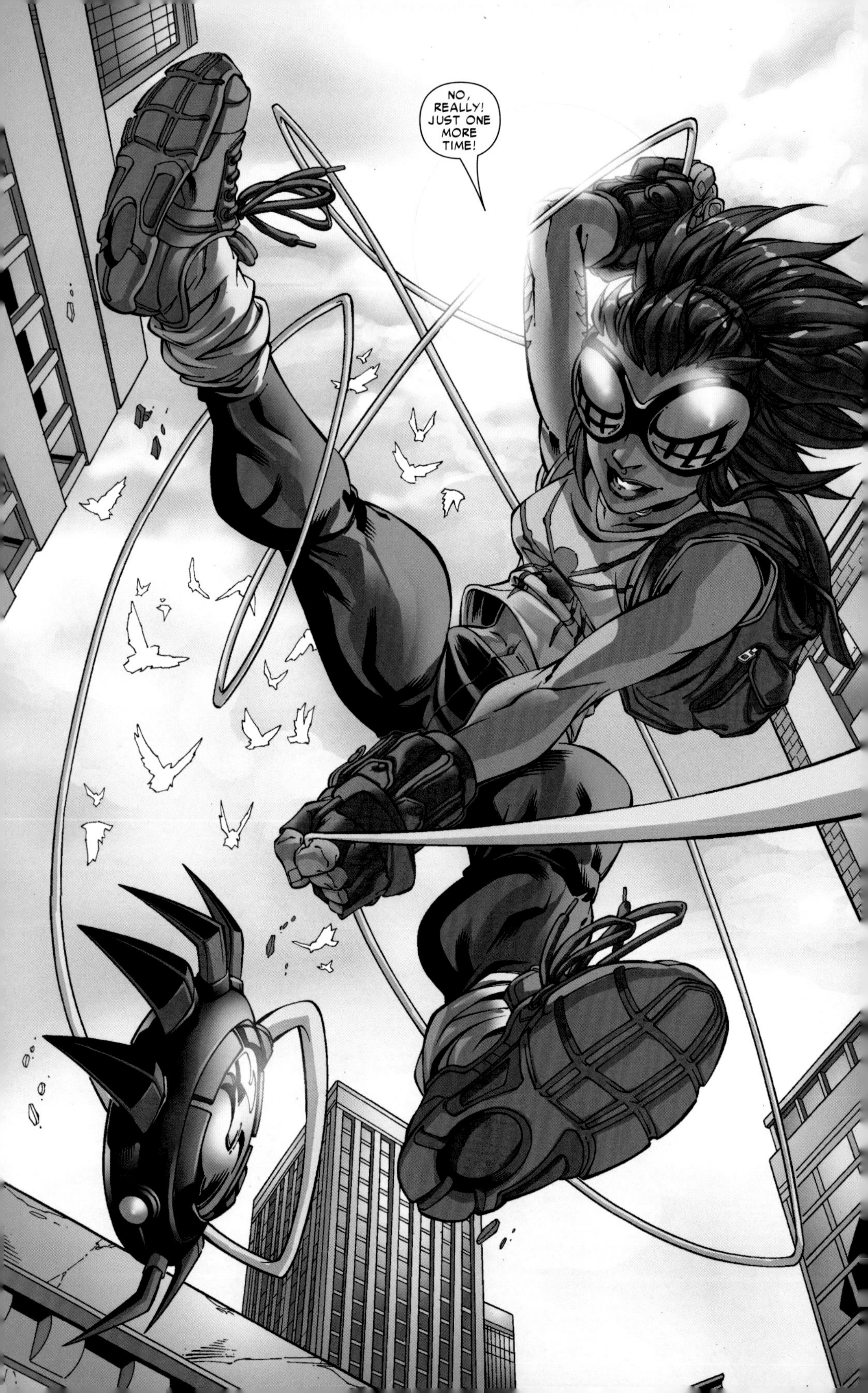
NO, REALLY! JUST ONE MORE TIME!

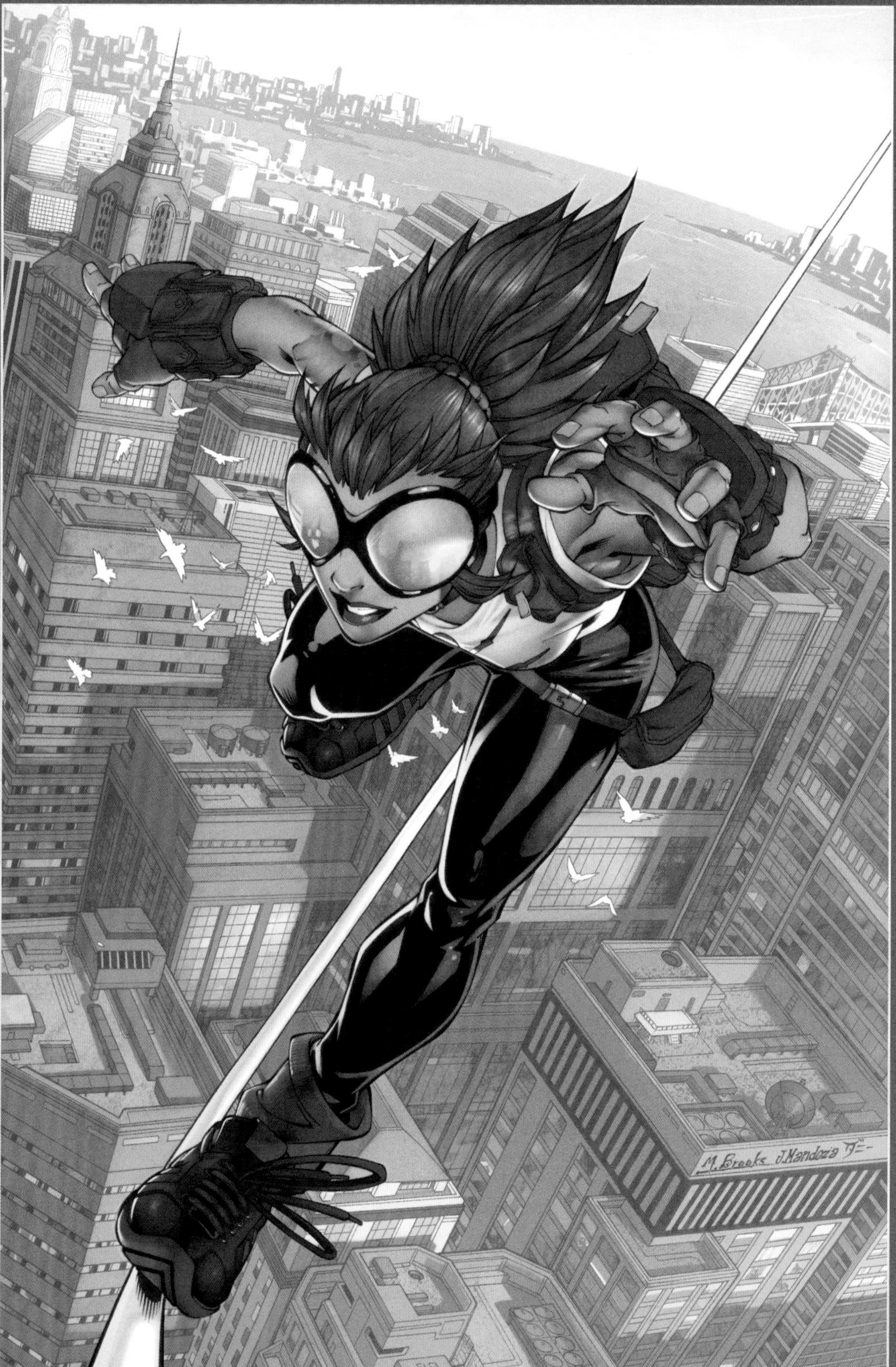
M. Brooks J.Mendoza

ARAÑA #1

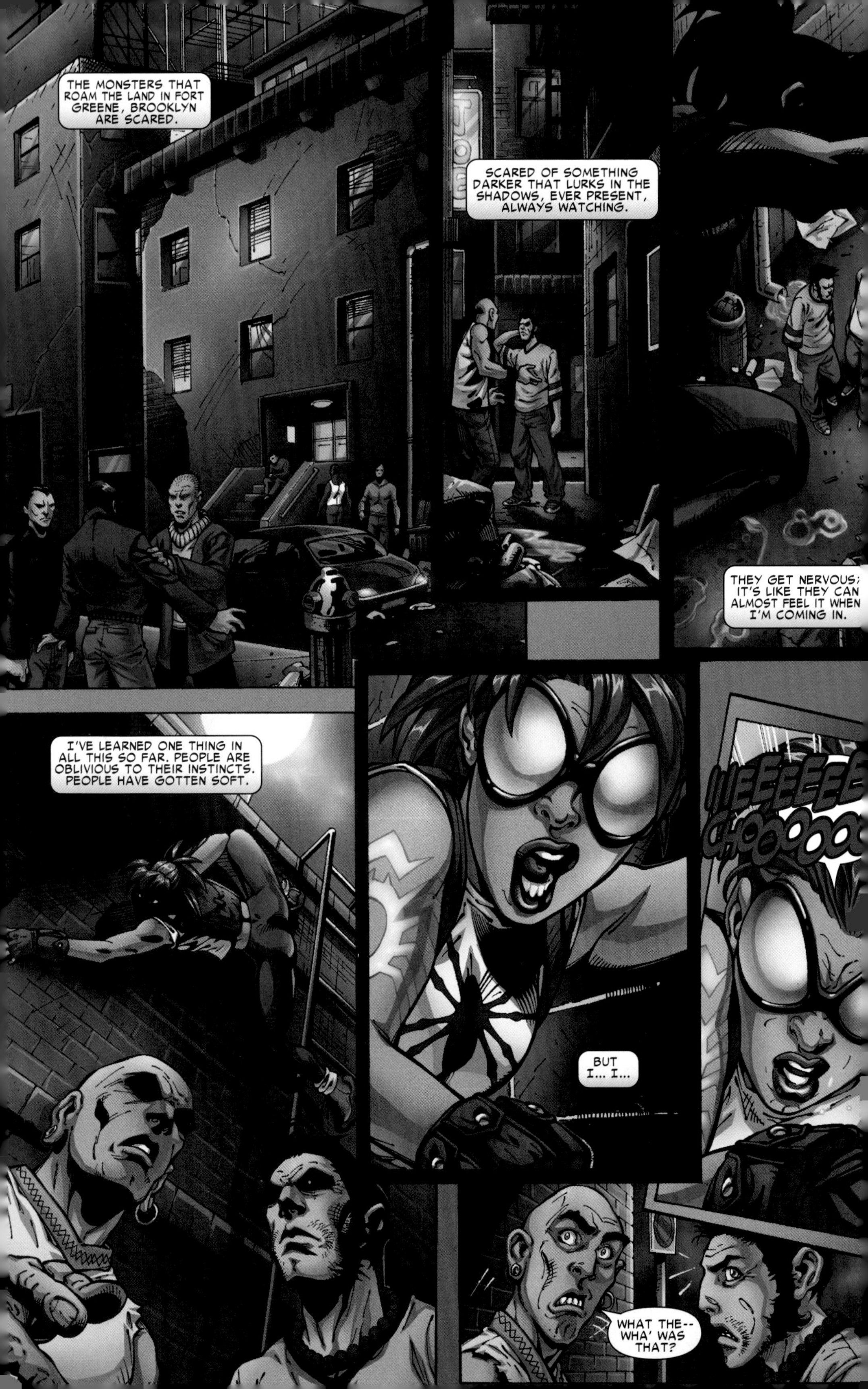
THE MONSTERS THAT ROAM THE LAND IN FORT GREENE, BROOKLYN ARE SCARED.
SCARED OF SOMETHING DARKER THAT LURKS IN THE SHADOWS, EVER PRESENT, ALWAYS WATCHING.
THEY GET NERVOUS; IT'S LIKE THEY CAN ALMOST FEEL IT WHEN I'M COMING IN.
I'VE LEARNED ONE THING IN ALL THIS SO FAR. PEOPLE ARE OBLIVIOUS TO THEIR INSTINCTS. PEOPLE HAVE GOTTEN SOFT.
BUT I... I...
WHAT THE-- WHA' WAS THAT?

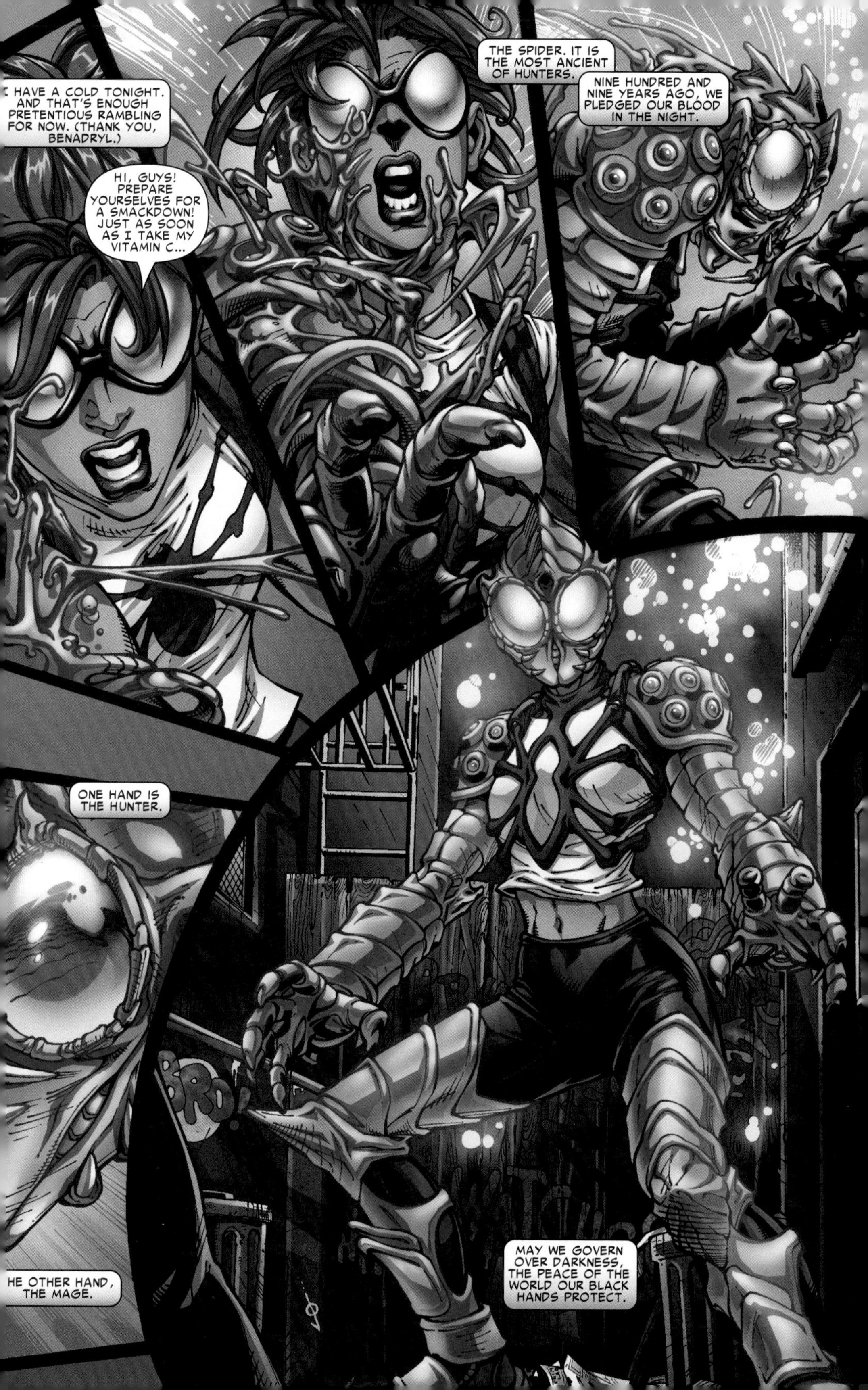
I HAVE A COLD TONIGHT. AND THAT'S ENOUGH PRETENTIOUS RAMBLING FOR NOW. (THANK YOU, BENADRYL.)
HI, GUYS! PREPARE YOURSELVES FOR A SMACKDOWN! JUST AS SOON AS I TAKE MY VITAMIN C...
THE SPIDER. IT IS THE MOST ANCIENT OF HUNTERS.
NINE HUNDRED AND NINE YEARS AGO, WE PLEDGED OUR BLOOD IN THE NIGHT.
ONE HAND IS THE HUNTER.
THE OTHER HAND, THE MAGE.
MAY WE GOVERN OVER DARKNESS, THE PEACE OF THE WORLD OUR BLACK HANDS PROTECT.

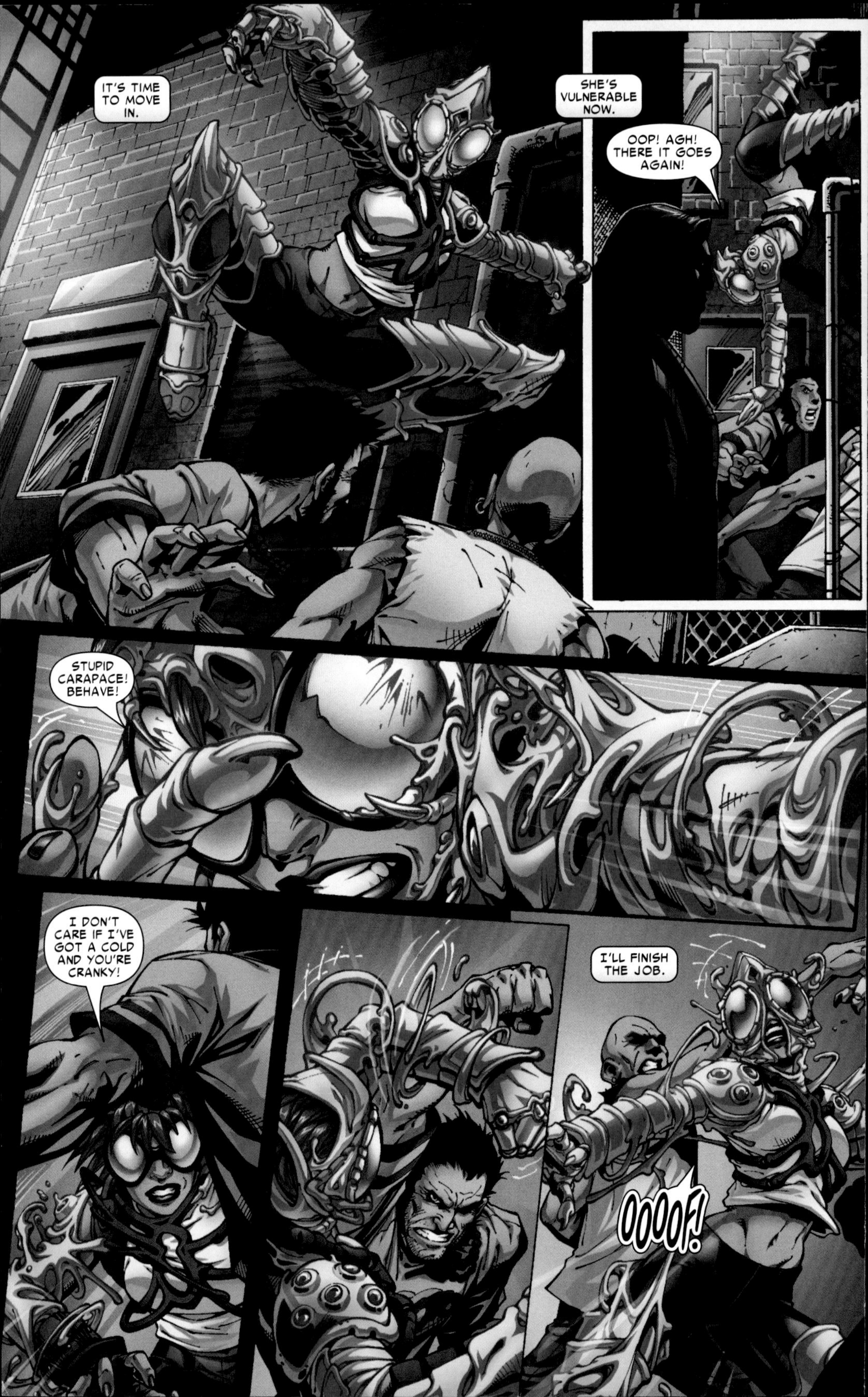
IT'S TIME TO MOVE IN.
SHE'S VULNERABLE NOW.
OOP! AGH! THERE IT GOES AGAIN!
STUPID CARAPACE! BEHAVE!
I DON'T CARE IF I'VE GOT A COLD AND YOU'RE CRANKY!
I'LL FINISH THE JOB.
OOOOF!

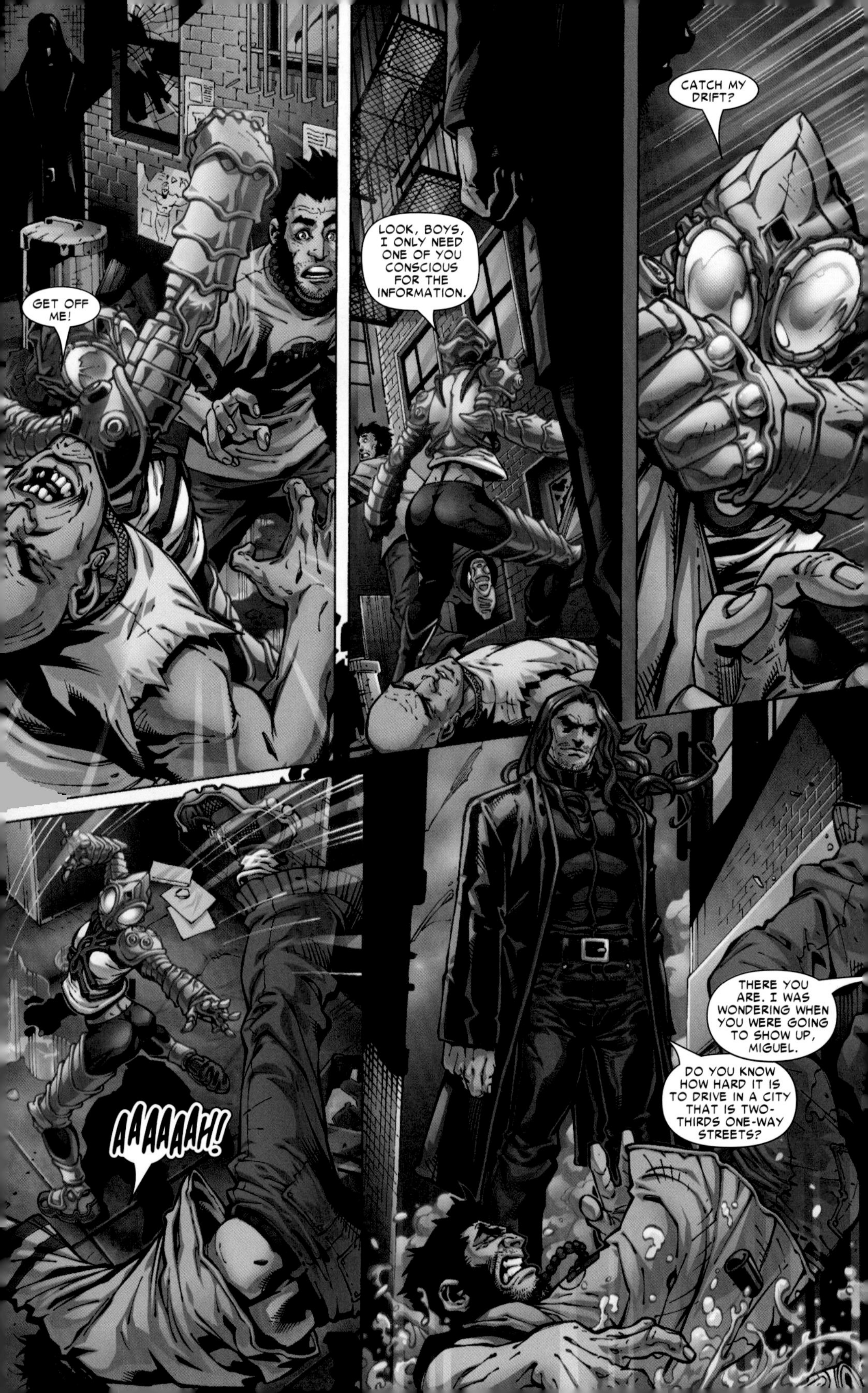
GET OFF ME!
LOOK, BOYS, I ONLY NEED ONE OF YOU CONSCIOUS FOR THE INFORMATION.
CATCH MY DRIFT?
AAAAAAH!
THERE YOU ARE. I WAS WONDERING WHEN YOU WERE GOING TO SHOW UP, MIGUEL.
DO YOU KNOW HOW HARD IT IS TO DRIVE IN A CITY THAT IS TWO-THIRDS ONE-WAY STREETS?

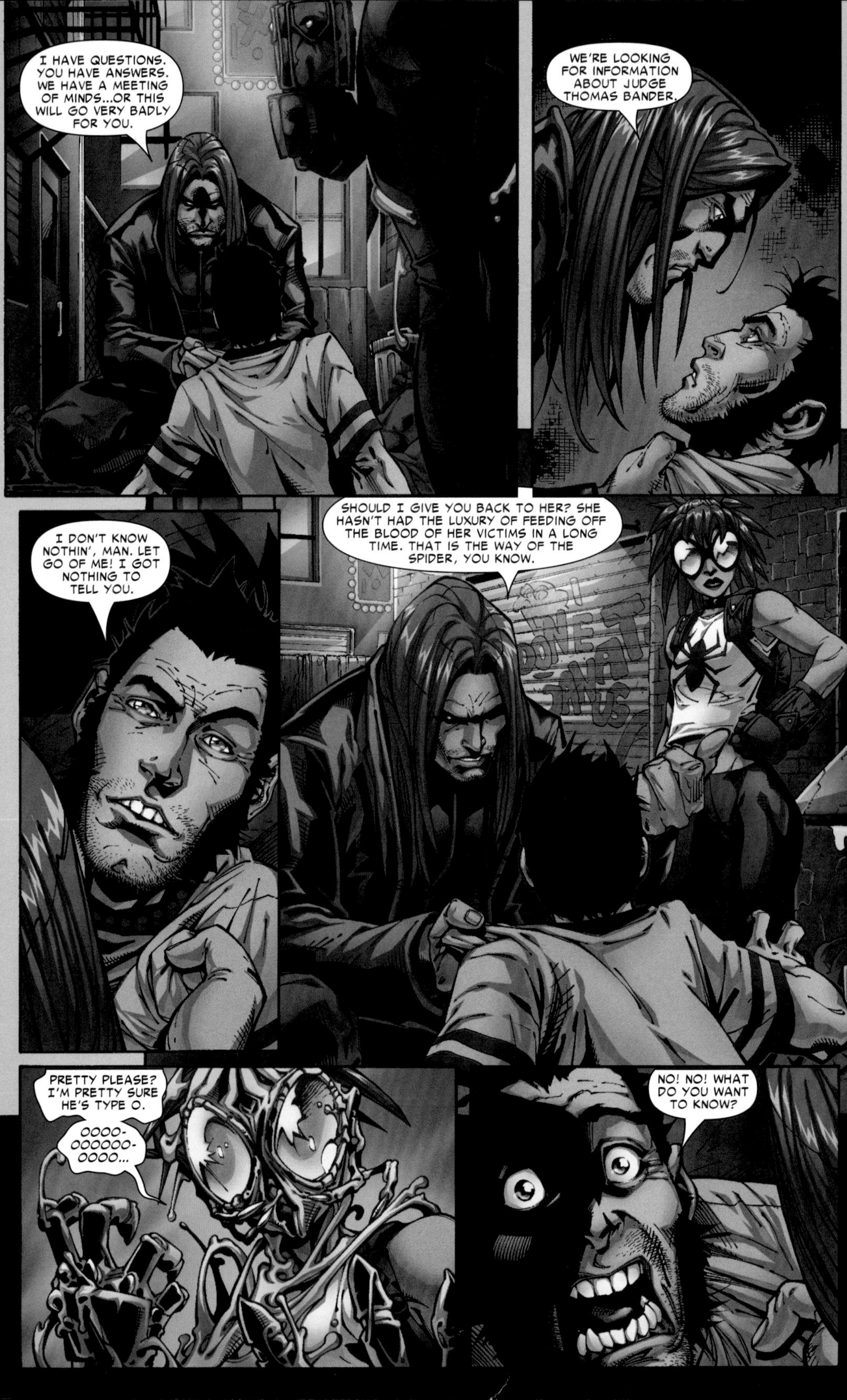
I HAVE QUESTIONS. YOU HAVE ANSWERS. WE HAVE A MEETING OF MINDS...OR THIS WILL GO VERY BADLY FOR YOU.
WE'RE LOOKING FOR INFORMATION ABOUT JUDGE THOMAS BANDER.
I DON'T KNOW NOTHIN', MAN. LET GO OF ME! I GOT NOTHING TO TELL YOU.
SHOULD I GIVE YOU BACK TO HER? SHE HASN'T HAD THE LUXURY OF FEEDING OFF THE BLOOD OF HER VICTIMS IN A LONG TIME. THAT IS THE WAY OF THE SPIDER, YOU KNOW.
PRETTY PLEASE? I'M PRETTY SURE HE'S TYPE O.
OOOO-OOOOOOO-OOOO...
NO! NO! WHAT DO YOU WANT TO KNOW?

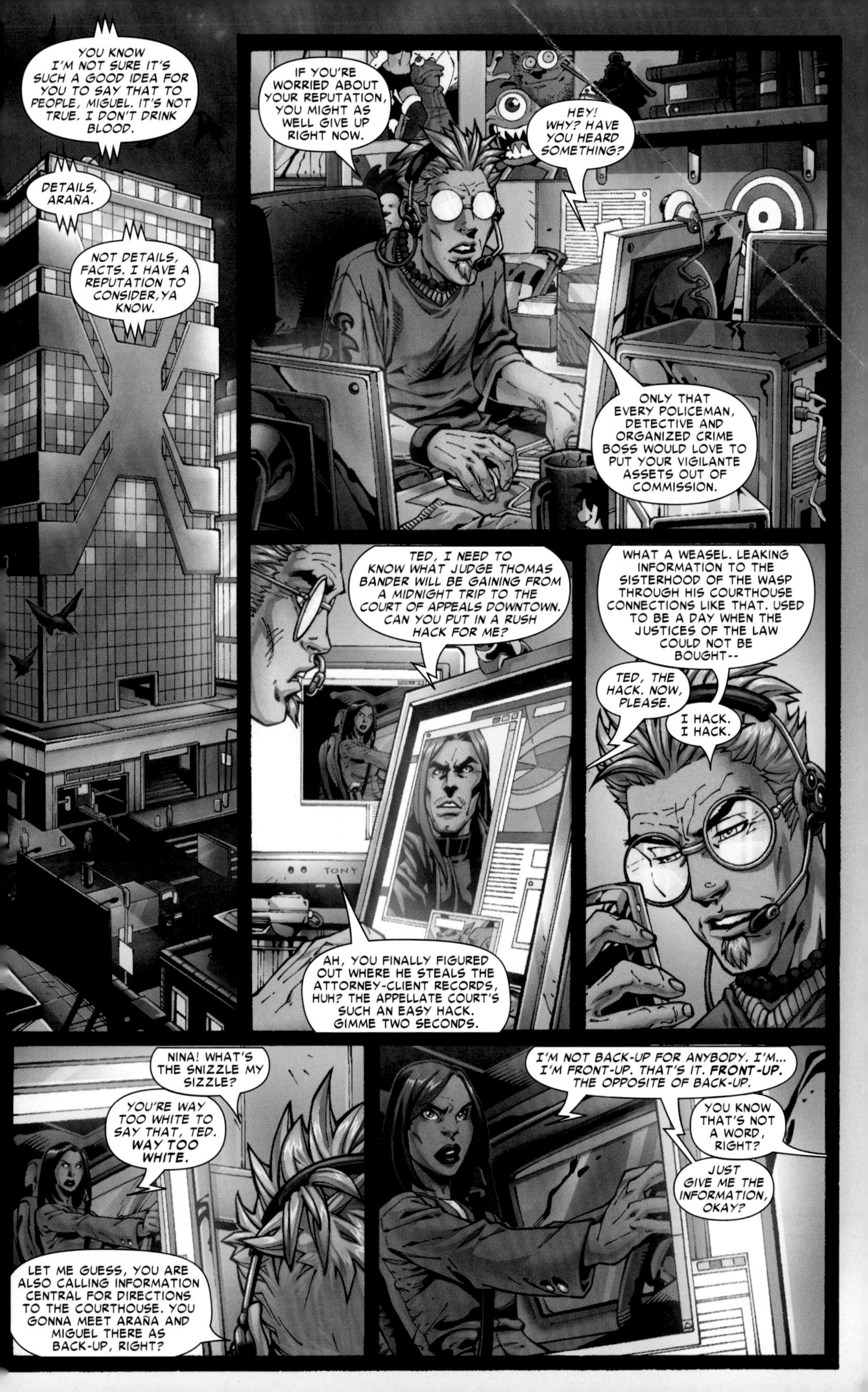
YOU KNOW I'M NOT SURE IT'S SUCH A GOOD IDEA FOR YOU TO SAY THAT TO PEOPLE, MIGUEL. IT'S NOT TRUE. I DON'T DRINK BLOOD.
DETAILS, ARAÑA.
NOT DETAILS, FACTS. I HAVE A REPUTATION TO CONSIDER,YA KNOW.
IF YOU'RE WORRIED ABOUT YOUR REPUTATION, YOU MIGHT AS WELL GIVE UP RIGHT NOW.
HEY! WHY? HAVE YOU HEARD SOMETHING?
ONLY THAT EVERY POLICEMAN, DETECTIVE AND ORGANIZED CRIME BOSS WOULD LOVE TO PUT YOUR VIGILANTE ASSETS OUT OF COMMISSION.
TED, I NEED TO KNOW WHAT JUDGE THOMAS BANDER WILL BE GAINING FROM A MIDNIGHT TRIP TO THE COURT OF APPEALS DOWNTOWN. CAN YOU PUT IN A RUSH HACK FOR ME?
TONY
AH, YOU FINALLY FIGURED OUT WHERE HE STEALS THE ATTORNEY-CLIENT RECORDS, HUH? THE APPELLATE COURT'S SUCH AN EASY HACK. GIMME TWO SECONDS.
WHAT A WEASEL. LEAKING INFORMATION TO THE SISTERHOOD OF THE WASP THROUGH HIS COURTHOUSE CONNECTIONS LIKE THAT. USED TO BE A DAY WHEN THE JUSTICES OF THE LAW COULD NOT BE BOUGHT--
TED, THE HACK. NOW, PLEASE.
I HACK. I HACK.
NINA! WHAT'S THE SNIZZLE MY SIZZLE?
YOU'RE WAY TOO WHITE TO SAY THAT, TED. **WAY TOO WHITE.**
LET ME GUESS, YOU ARE ALSO CALLING INFORMATION CENTRAL FOR DIRECTIONS TO THE COURTHOUSE. YOU GONNA MEET ARAÑA AND MIGUEL THERE AS BACK-UP, RIGHT?
I'M NOT BACK-UP FOR ANYBODY. I'M... I'M FRONT-UP. THAT'S IT. **FRONT-UP.** THE OPPOSITE OF BACK-UP.
YOU KNOW THAT'S NOT A WORD, RIGHT?
JUST GIVE ME THE INFORMATION, OKAY?

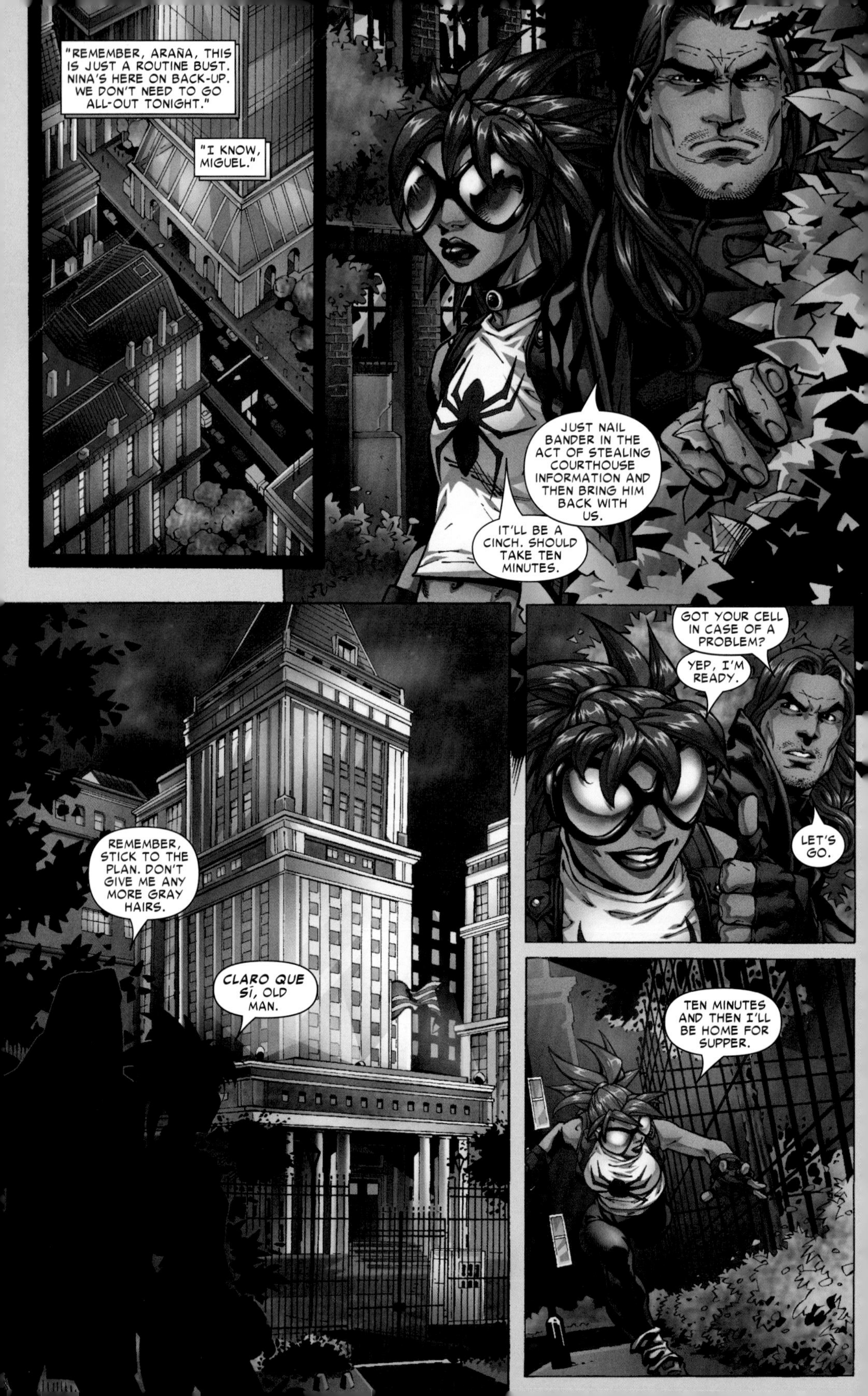
"REMEMBER, ARAÑA, THIS IS JUST A ROUTINE BUST. NINA'S HERE ON BACK-UP. WE DON'T NEED TO GO ALL-OUT TONIGHT."
"I KNOW, MIGUEL."
JUST NAIL BANDER IN THE ACT OF STEALING COURTHOUSE INFORMATION AND THEN BRING HIM BACK WITH US.
IT'LL BE A CINCH. SHOULD TAKE TEN MINUTES.
REMEMBER, STICK TO THE PLAN. DON'T GIVE ME ANY MORE GRAY HAIRS.
CLARO QUE SÍ, OLD MAN.
GOT YOUR CELL IN CASE OF A PROBLEM?
YEP, I'M READY.
LET'S GO.
TEN MINUTES AND THEN I'LL BE HOME FOR SUPPER.

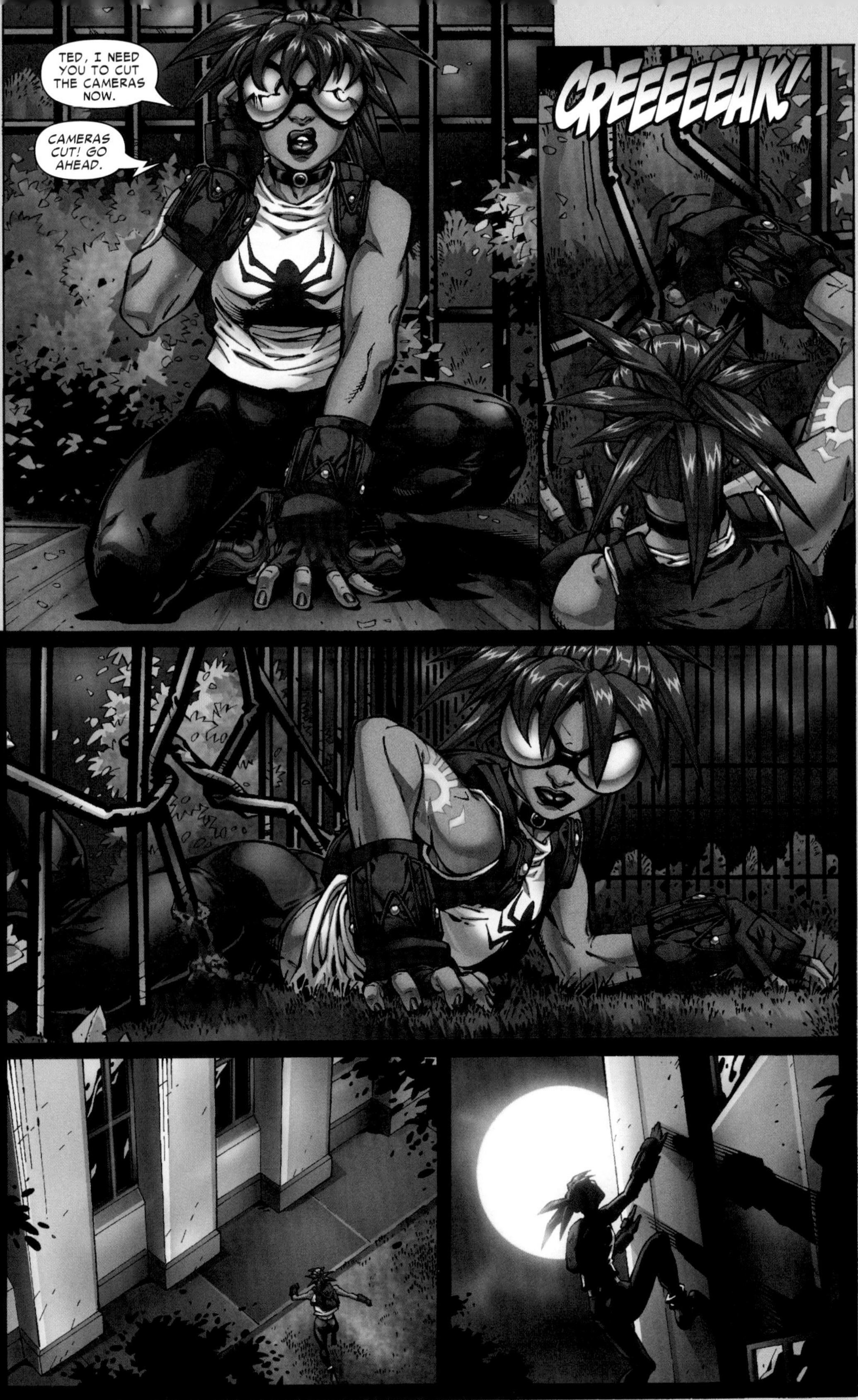
TED, I NEED YOU TO CUT THE CAMERAS NOW.
CAMERAS CUT! GO AHEAD.
CREEEEEAK!

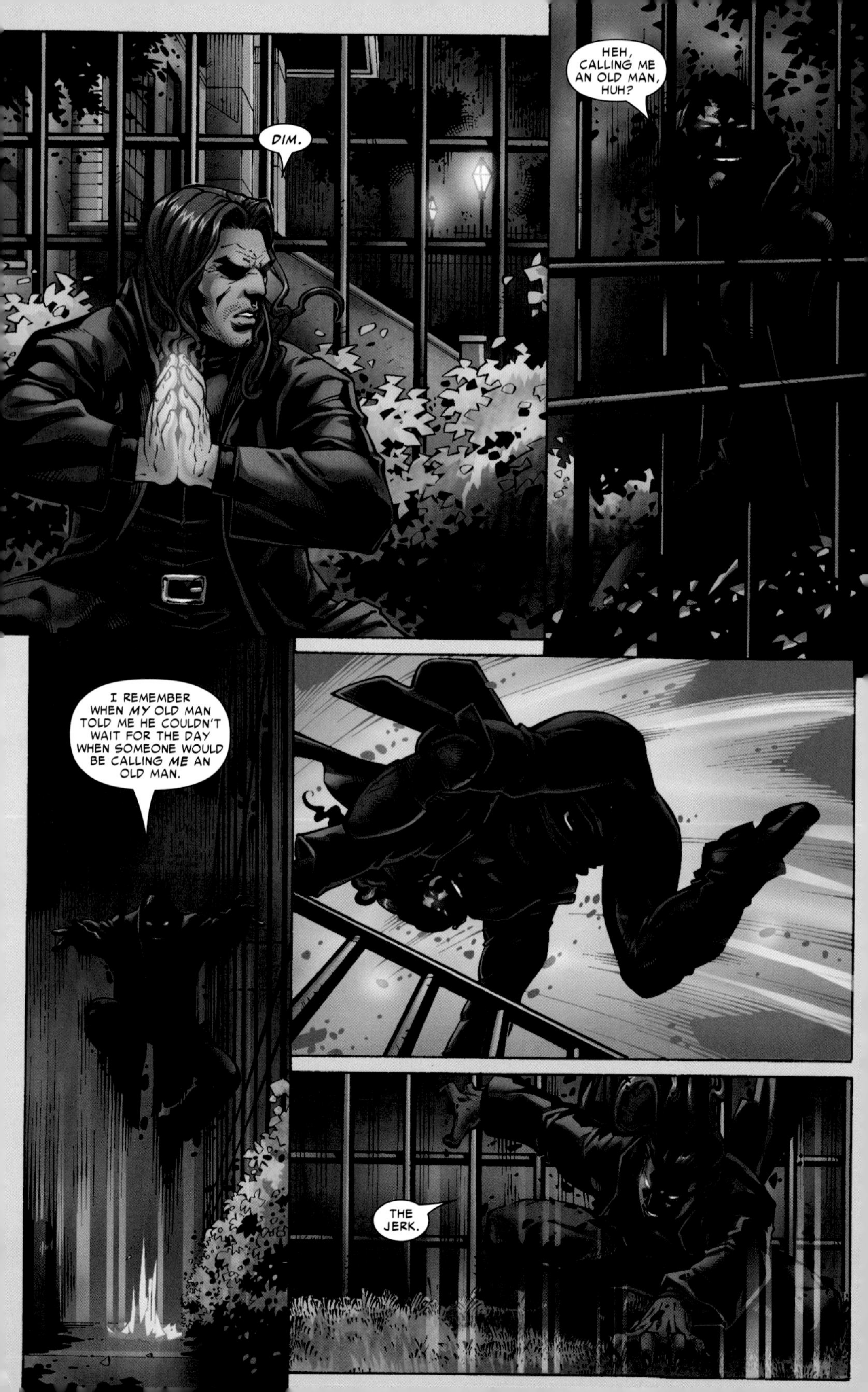
DIM.
HEH, CALLING ME AN OLD MAN, HUH?
I REMEMBER WHEN MY OLD MAN TOLD ME HE COULDN'T WAIT FOR THE DAY WHEN SOMEONE WOULD BE CALLING ME AN OLD MAN.
THE JERK.

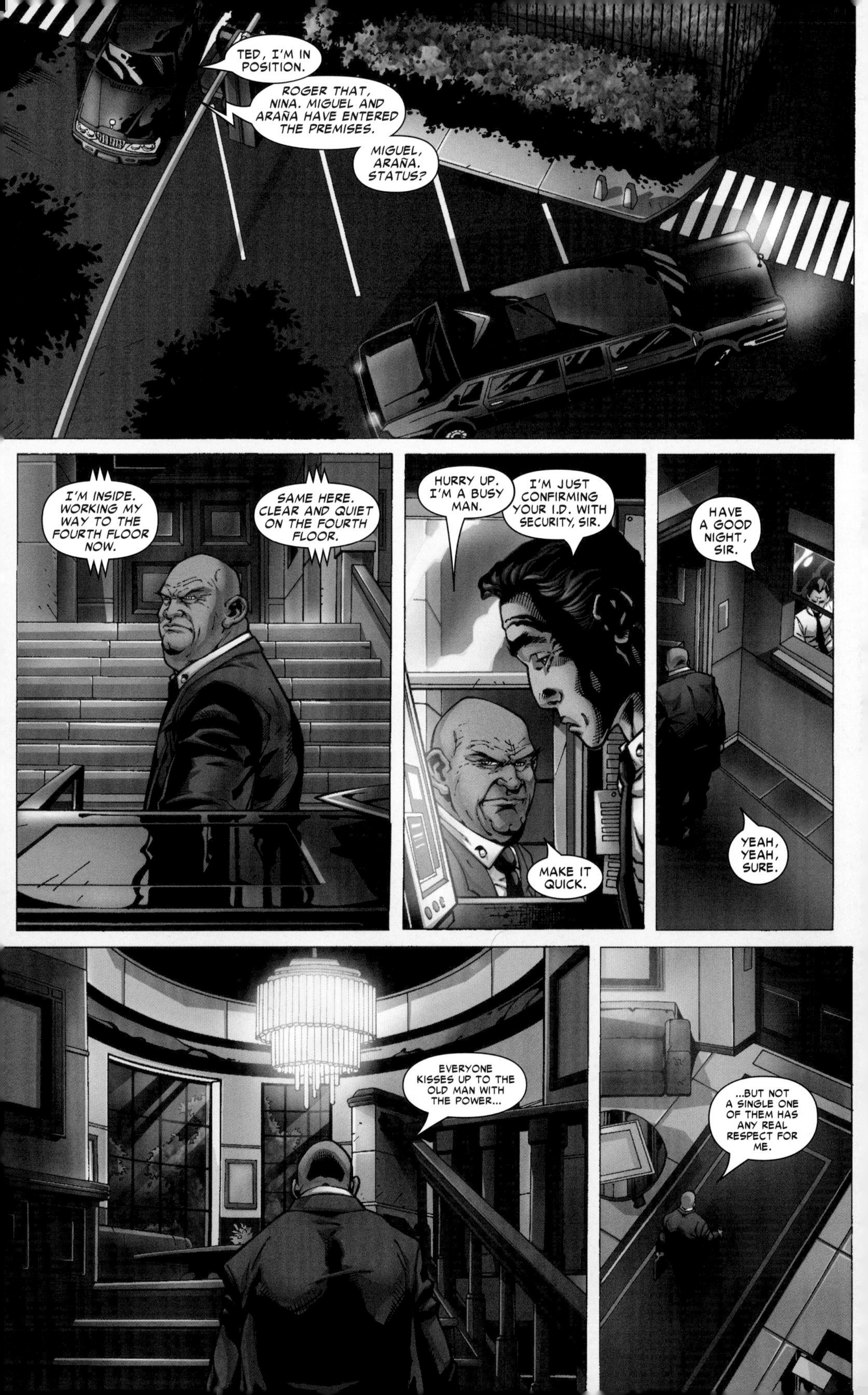
TED, I'M IN POSITION.
ROGER THAT, NINA. MIGUEL AND ARAÑA HAVE ENTERED THE PREMISES.
MIGUEL, ARAÑA. STATUS?
I'M INSIDE. WORKING MY WAY TO THE FOURTH FLOOR NOW.
SAME HERE. CLEAR AND QUIET ON THE FOURTH FLOOR.
HURRY UP. I'M A BUSY MAN.
I'M JUST CONFIRMING YOUR I.D. WITH SECURITY, SIR.
MAKE IT QUICK.
HAVE A GOOD NIGHT, SIR.
YEAH, YEAH, SURE.
EVERYONE KISSES UP TO THE OLD MAN WITH THE POWER...
...BUT NOT A SINGLE ONE OF THEM HAS ANY REAL RESPECT FOR ME.

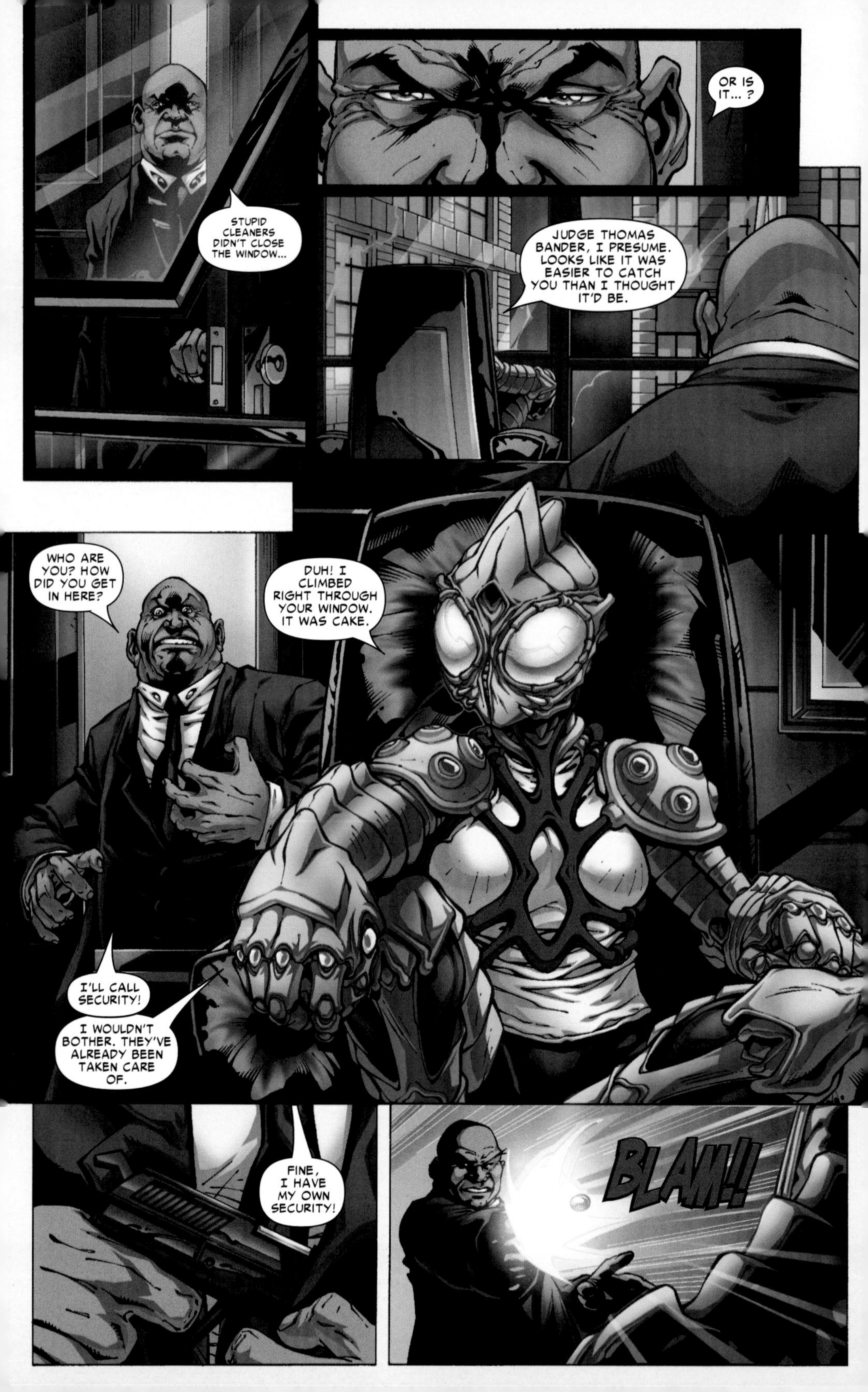
STUPID CLEANERS DIDN'T CLOSE THE WINDOW...
OR IS IT... ?
JUDGE THOMAS BANDER, I PRESUME. LOOKS LIKE IT WAS EASIER TO CATCH YOU THAN I THOUGHT IT'D BE.
WHO ARE YOU? HOW DID YOU GET IN HERE?
DUH! I CLIMBED RIGHT THROUGH YOUR WINDOW. IT WAS CAKE.
I'LL CALL SECURITY!
I WOULDN'T BOTHER. THEY'VE ALREADY BEEN TAKEN CARE OF.
FINE, I HAVE MY OWN SECURITY!
BLAM!!

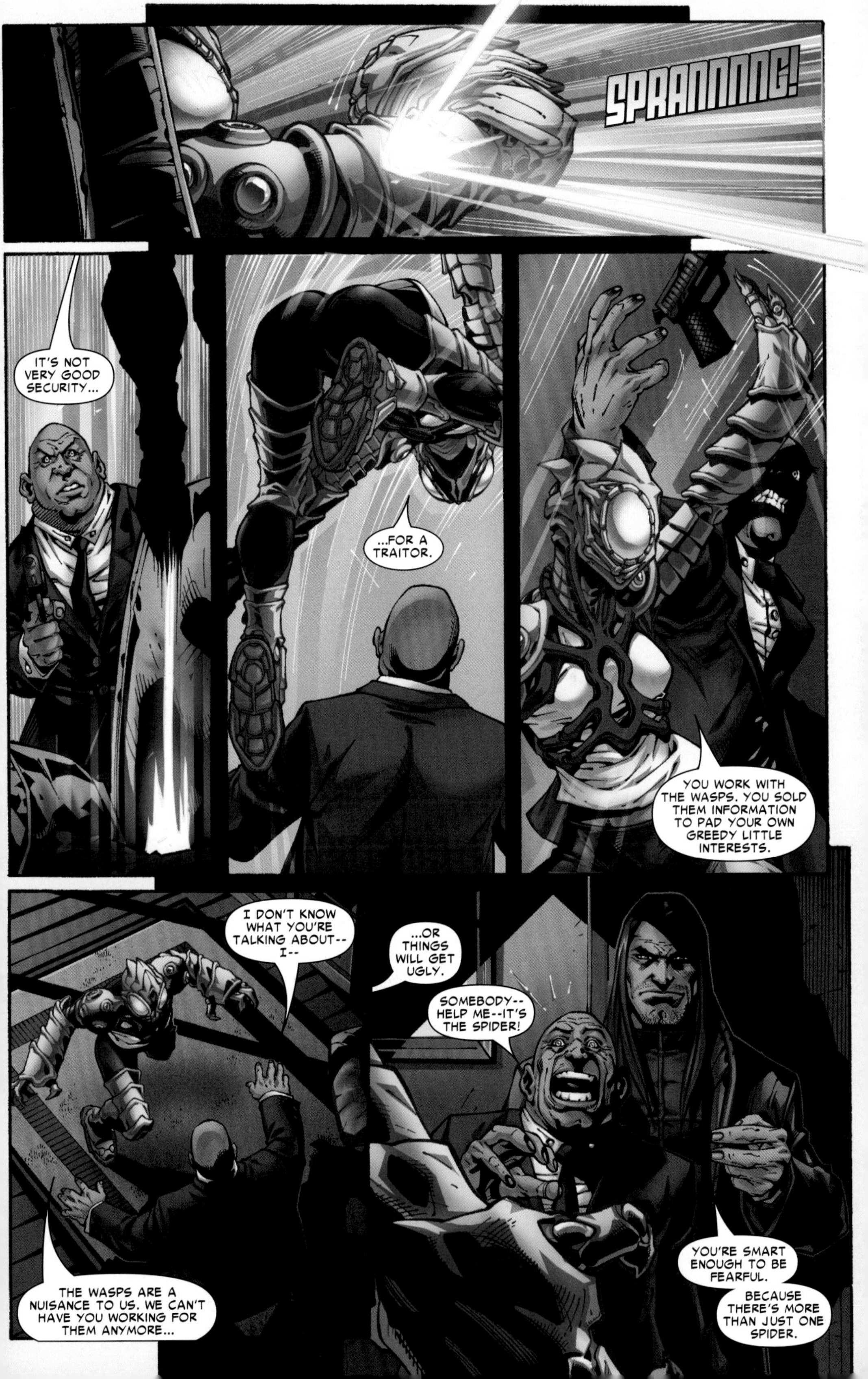
SPRANNNNG!
IT'S NOT VERY GOOD SECURITY...
...FOR A TRAITOR.
YOU WORK WITH THE WASPS. YOU SOLD THEM INFORMATION TO PAD YOUR OWN GREEDY LITTLE INTERESTS.
I DON'T KNOW WHAT YOU'RE TALKING ABOUT-- I--
THE WASPS ARE A NUISANCE TO US. WE CAN'T HAVE YOU WORKING FOR THEM ANYMORE...
...OR THINGS WILL GET UGLY.
SOMEBODY-- HELP ME--IT'S THE SPIDER!
YOU'RE SMART ENOUGH TO BE FEARFUL.
BECAUSE THERE'S MORE THAN JUST ONE SPIDER.

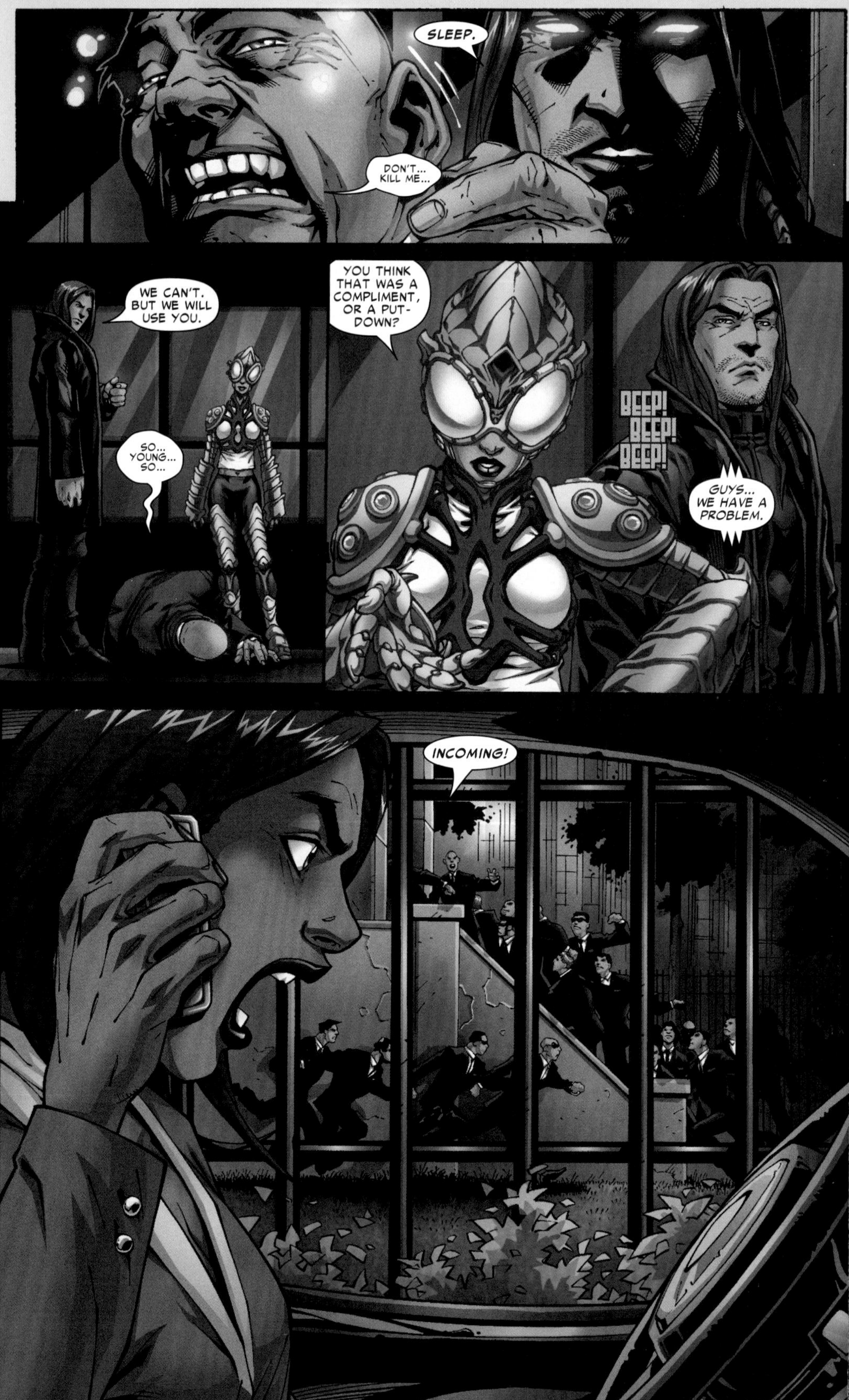
SLEEP.
DON'T... KILL ME...
WE CAN'T. BUT WE WILL USE YOU.
SO... YOUNG... SO...
YOU THINK THAT WAS A COMPLIMENT, OR A PUT-DOWN?
BEEP! BEEP! BEEP!
GUYS... WE HAVE A PROBLEM.
INCOMING!

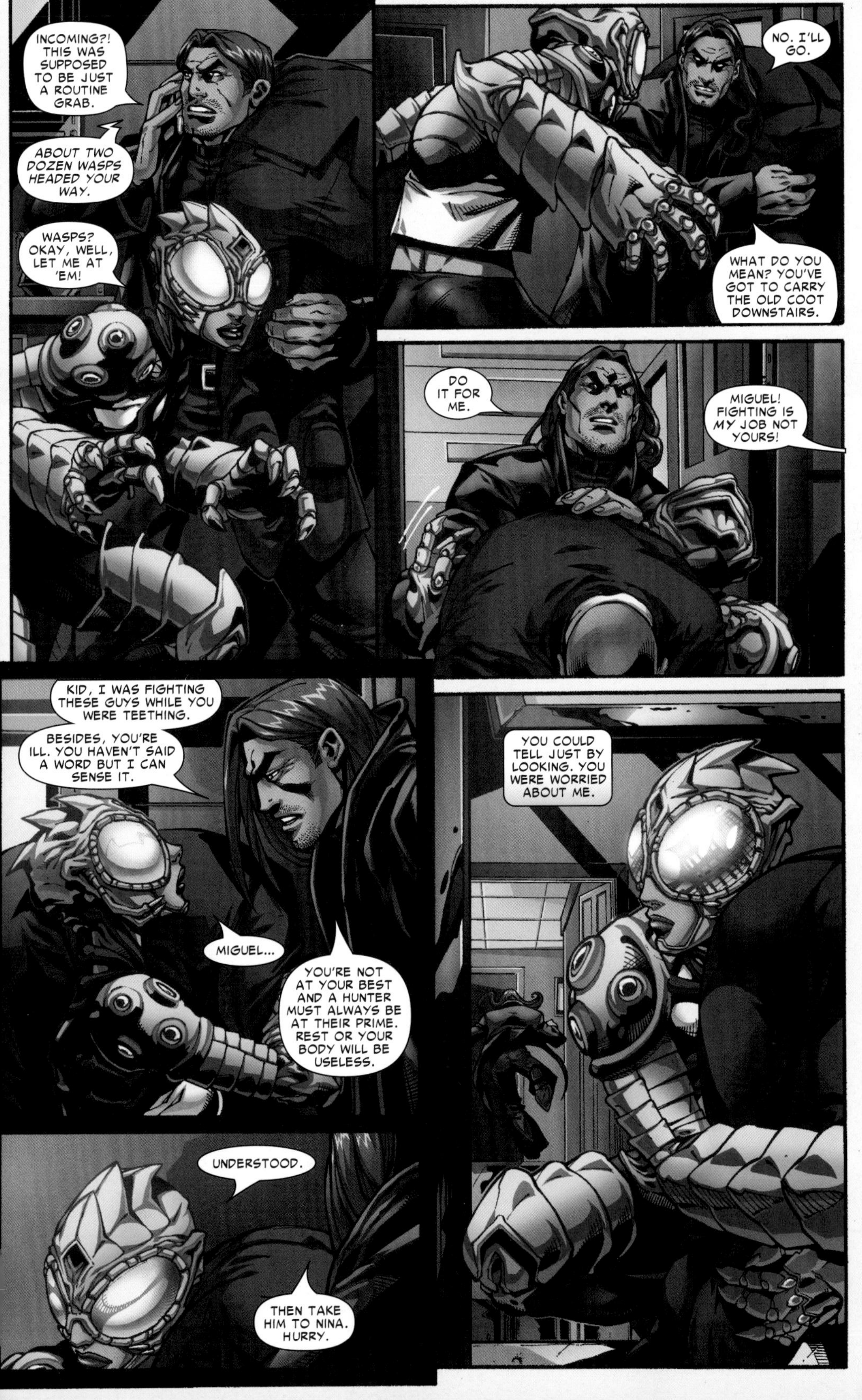
INCOMING?! THIS WAS SUPPOSED TO BE JUST A ROUTINE GRAB.
ABOUT TWO DOZEN WASPS HEADED YOUR WAY.
WASPS? OKAY, WELL, LET ME AT 'EM!
NO. I'LL GO.
WHAT DO YOU MEAN? YOU'VE GOT TO CARRY THE OLD COOT DOWNSTAIRS.
DO IT FOR ME.
MIGUEL! FIGHTING IS MY JOB NOT YOURS!
KID, I WAS FIGHTING THESE GUYS WHILE YOU WERE TEETHING.
BESIDES, YOU'RE ILL. YOU HAVEN'T SAID A WORD BUT I CAN SENSE IT.
MIGUEL...
YOU'RE NOT AT YOUR BEST AND A HUNTER MUST ALWAYS BE AT THEIR PRIME. REST OR YOUR BODY WILL BE USELESS.
UNDERSTOOD.
THEN TAKE HIM TO NINA. HURRY.
YOU COULD TELL JUST BY LOOKING. YOU WERE WORRIED ABOUT ME.

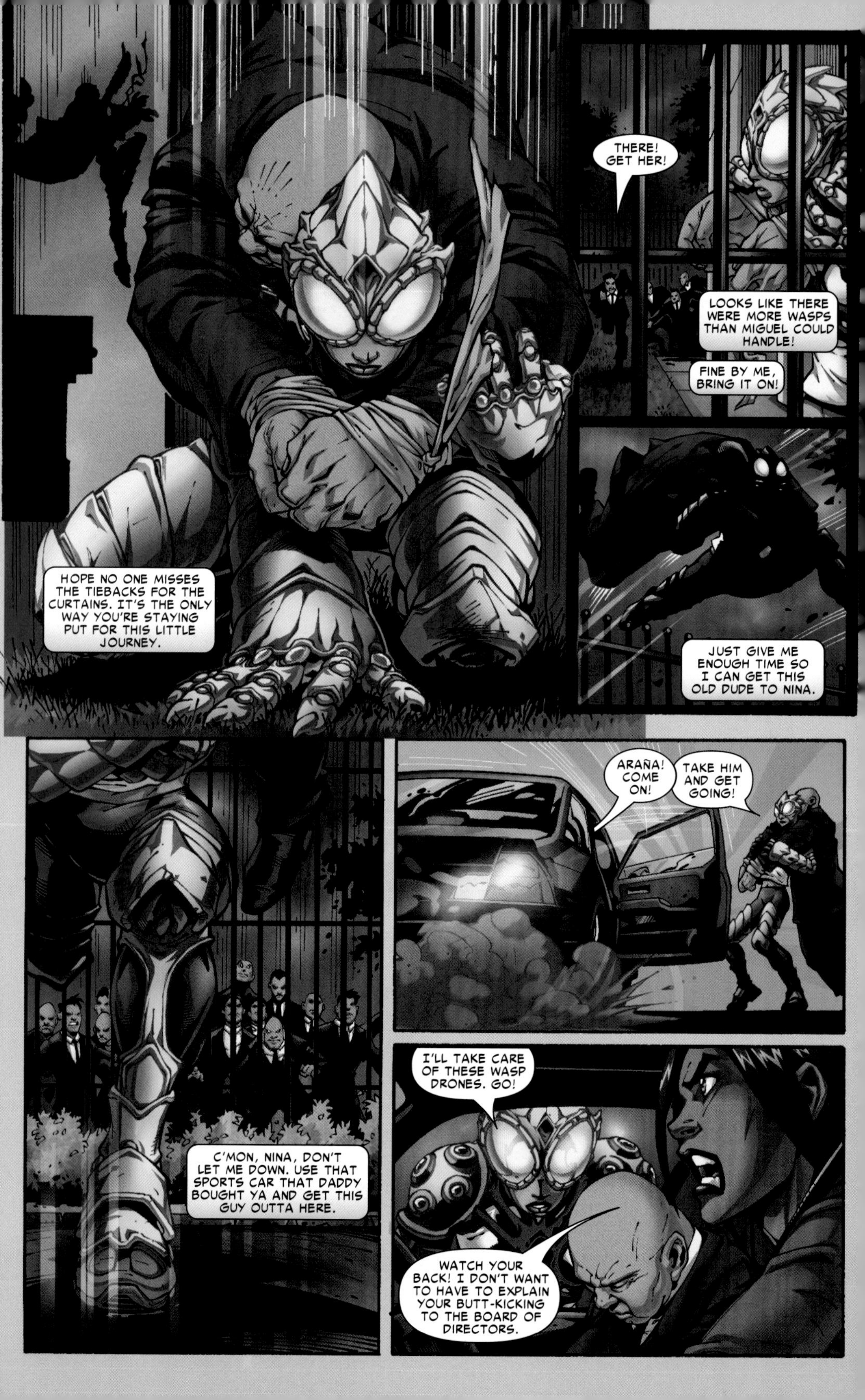

HOPE NO ONE MISSES THE TIEBACKS FOR THE CURTAINS. IT'S THE ONLY WAY YOU'RE STAYING PUT FOR THIS LITTLE JOURNEY.
THERE! GET HER!
LOOKS LIKE THERE WERE MORE WASPS THAN MIGUEL COULD HANDLE!
FINE BY ME, BRING IT ON!
JUST GIVE ME ENOUGH TIME SO I CAN GET THIS OLD DUDE TO NINA.
C'MON, NINA, DON'T LET ME DOWN. USE THAT SPORTS CAR THAT DADDY BOUGHT YA AND GET THIS GUY OUTTA HERE.
ARAÑA! COME ON!
TAKE HIM AND GET GOING!
I'LL TAKE CARE OF THESE WASP DRONES. GO!
WATCH YOUR BACK! I DON'T WANT TO HAVE TO EXPLAIN YOUR BUTT-KICKING TO THE BOARD OF DIRECTORS.

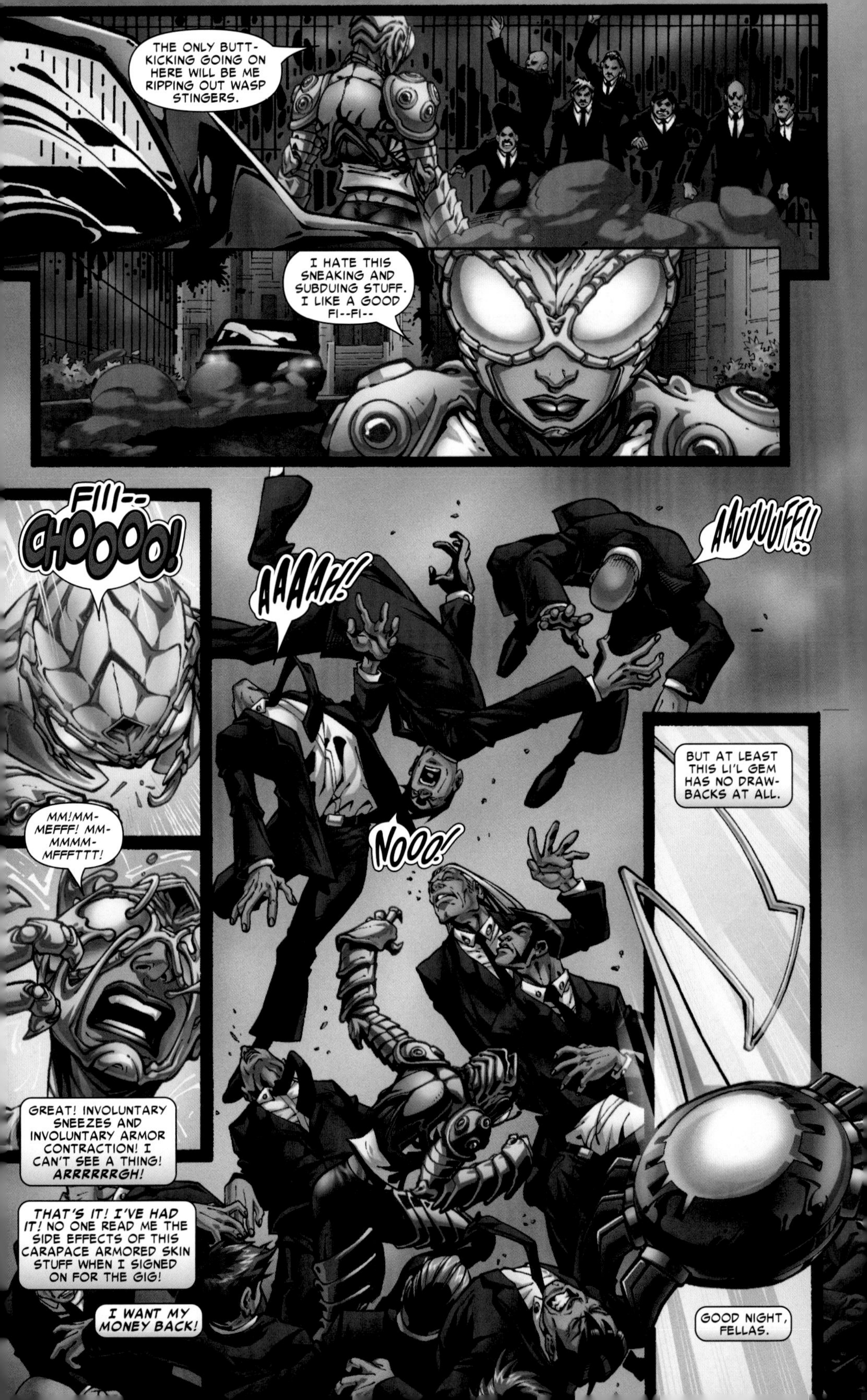
THE ONLY BUTT-KICKING GOING ON HERE WILL BE ME RIPPING OUT WASP STINGERS.
I HATE THIS SNEAKING AND SUBDUING STUFF. I LIKE A GOOD FI--FI--
FIII--CHOOOOO!
AAAAAH!
AAUUUUFF!!
MM!MM-MEFFF! MM-MMMM-MFFFTTT!
NOOO!
BUT AT LEAST THIS LI'L GEM HAS NO DRAW-BACKS AT ALL.
GREAT! INVOLUNTARY SNEEZES AND INVOLUNTARY ARMOR CONTRACTION! I CAN'T SEE A THING! ARRRRRRGH!
THAT'S IT! I'VE HAD IT! NO ONE READ ME THE SIDE EFFECTS OF THIS CARAPACE ARMORED SKIN STUFF WHEN I SIGNED ON FOR THE GIG!
I WANT MY MONEY BACK!
GOOD NIGHT, FELLAS.

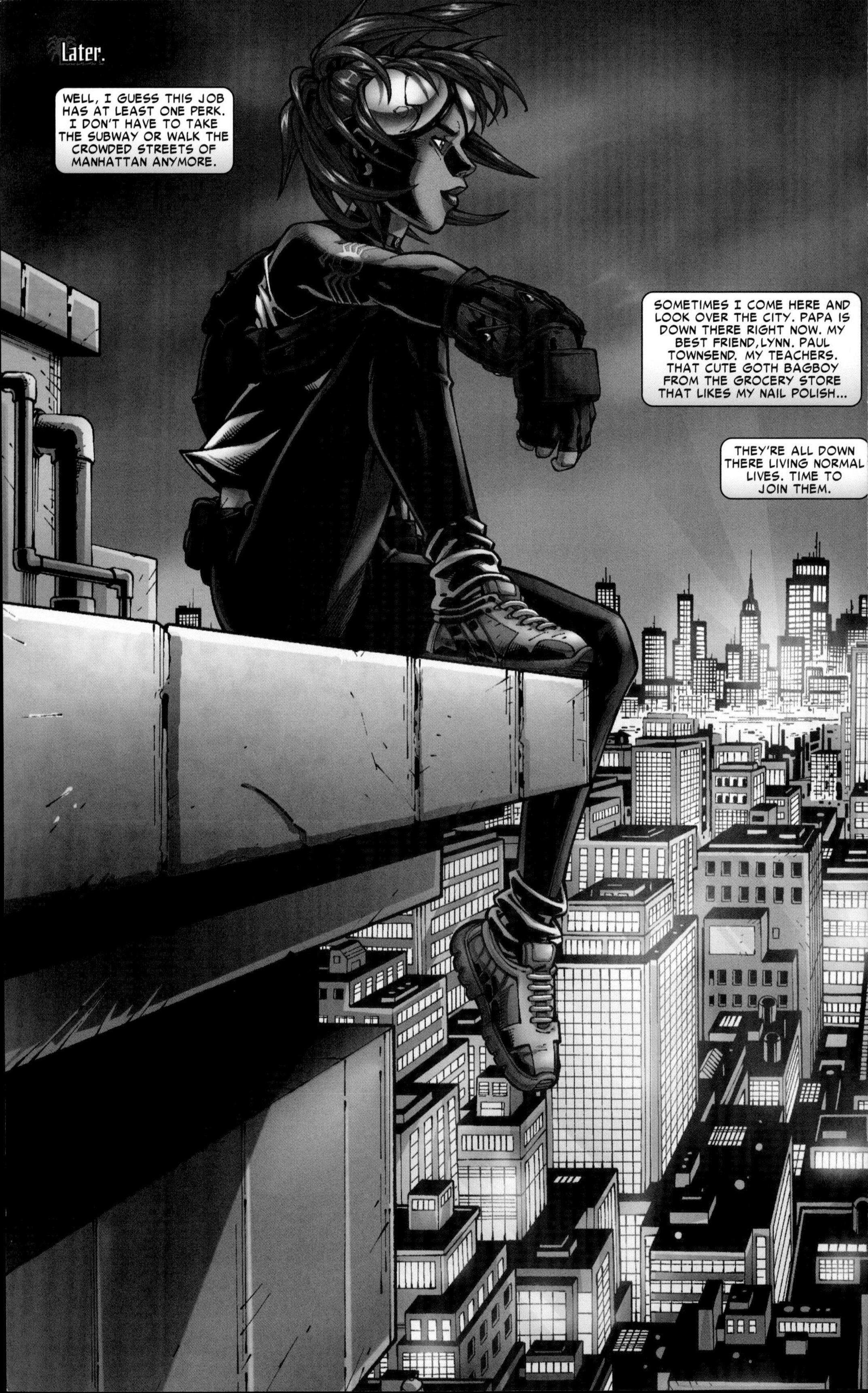
Later.
WELL, I GUESS THIS JOB HAS AT LEAST ONE PERK. I DON'T HAVE TO TAKE THE SUBWAY OR WALK THE CROWDED STREETS OF MANHATTAN ANYMORE.
SOMETIMES I COME HERE AND LOOK OVER THE CITY. PAPA IS DOWN THERE RIGHT NOW. MY BEST FRIEND, LYNN. PAUL TOWNSEND. MY TEACHERS. THAT CUTE GOTH BAGBOY FROM THE GROCERY STORE THAT LIKES MY NAIL POLISH...
THEY'RE ALL DOWN THERE LIVING NORMAL LIVES. TIME TO JOIN THEM.

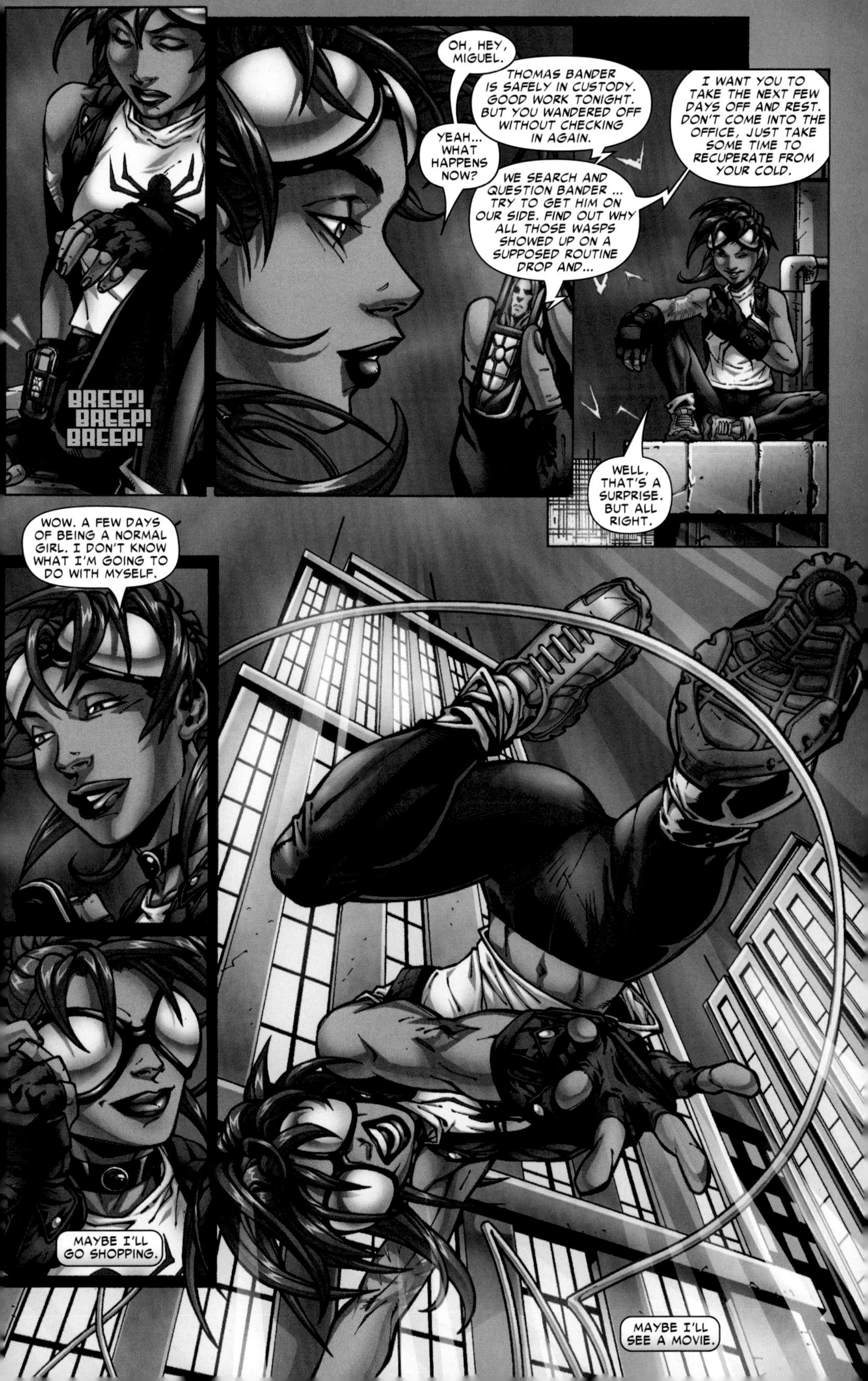
BREEP! BREEP! BREEP!
OH, HEY, MIGUEL.
THOMAS BANDER IS SAFELY IN CUSTODY. GOOD WORK TONIGHT. BUT YOU WANDERED OFF WITHOUT CHECKING IN AGAIN.
YEAH... WHAT HAPPENS NOW?
WE SEARCH AND QUESTION BANDER ... TRY TO GET HIM ON OUR SIDE. FIND OUT WHY ALL THOSE WASPS SHOWED UP ON A SUPPOSED ROUTINE DROP AND...
I WANT YOU TO TAKE THE NEXT FEW DAYS OFF AND REST. DON'T COME INTO THE OFFICE, JUST TAKE SOME TIME TO RECUPERATE FROM YOUR COLD.
WELL, THAT'S A SURPRISE. BUT ALL RIGHT.
WOW. A FEW DAYS OF BEING A NORMAL GIRL. I DON'T KNOW WHAT I'M GOING TO DO WITH MYSELF.
MAYBE I'LL GO SHOPPING.
MAYBE I'LL SEE A MOVIE.

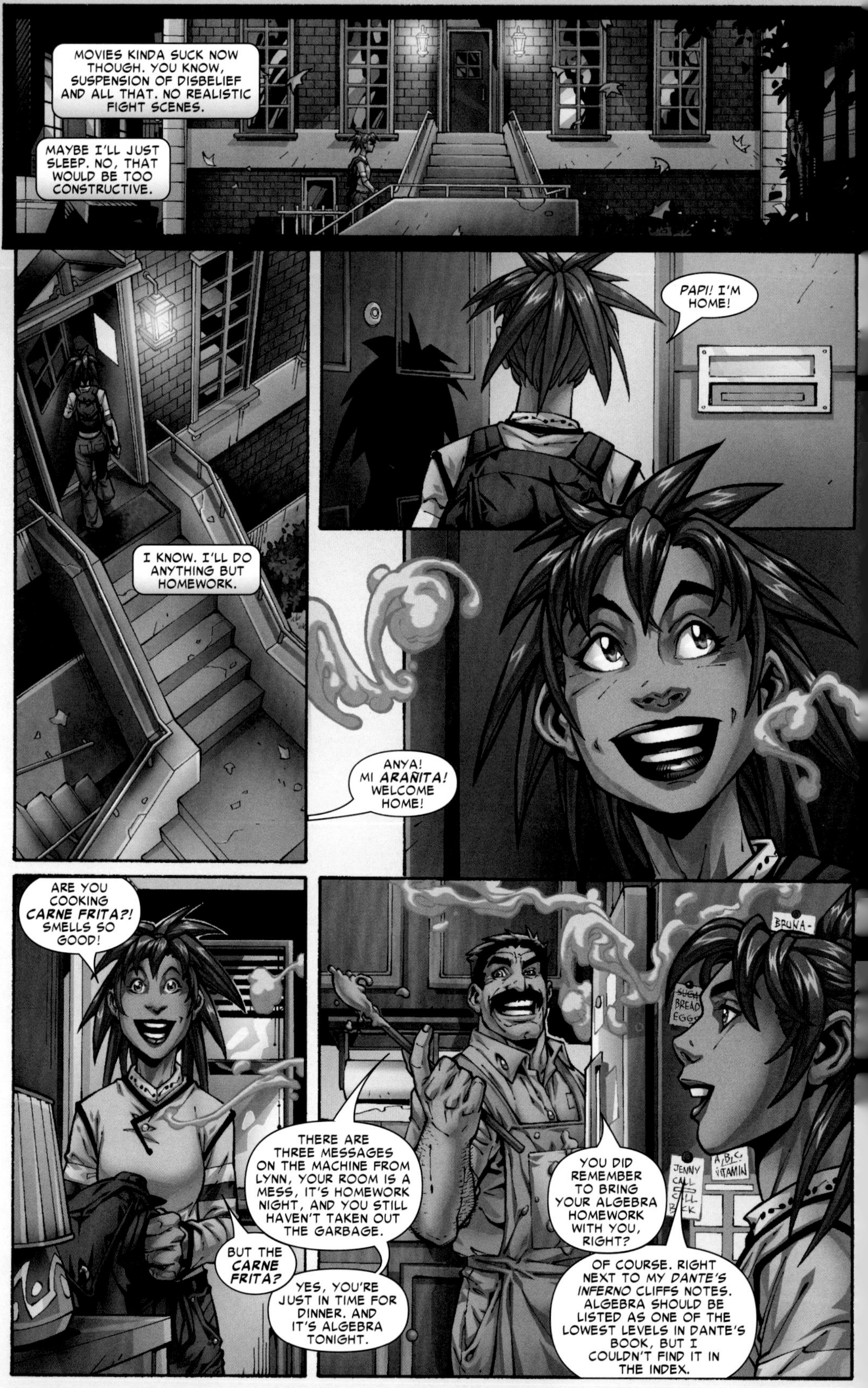
MOVIES KINDA SUCK NOW THOUGH. YOU KNOW, SUSPENSION OF DISBELIEF AND ALL THAT. NO REALISTIC FIGHT SCENES.
MAYBE I'LL JUST SLEEP. NO, THAT WOULD BE TOO CONSTRUCTIVE.
I KNOW. I'LL DO ANYTHING BUT HOMEWORK.
PAPI! I'M HOME!
ANYA! MI ARAÑITA! WELCOME HOME!
ARE YOU COOKING CARNE FRITA?! SMELLS SO GOOD!
THERE ARE THREE MESSAGES ON THE MACHINE FROM LYNN, YOUR ROOM IS A MESS, IT'S HOMEWORK NIGHT, AND YOU STILL HAVEN'T TAKEN OUT THE GARBAGE.
BUT THE CARNE FRITA?
YES, YOU'RE JUST IN TIME FOR DINNER. AND IT'S ALGEBRA TONIGHT.
YOU DID REMEMBER TO BRING YOUR ALGEBRA HOMEWORK WITH YOU, RIGHT?
OF COURSE. RIGHT NEXT TO MY DANTE'S INFERNO CLIFFS NOTES. ALGEBRA SHOULD BE LISTED AS ONE OF THE LOWEST LEVELS IN DANTE'S BOOK, BUT I COULDN'T FIND IT IN THE INDEX.

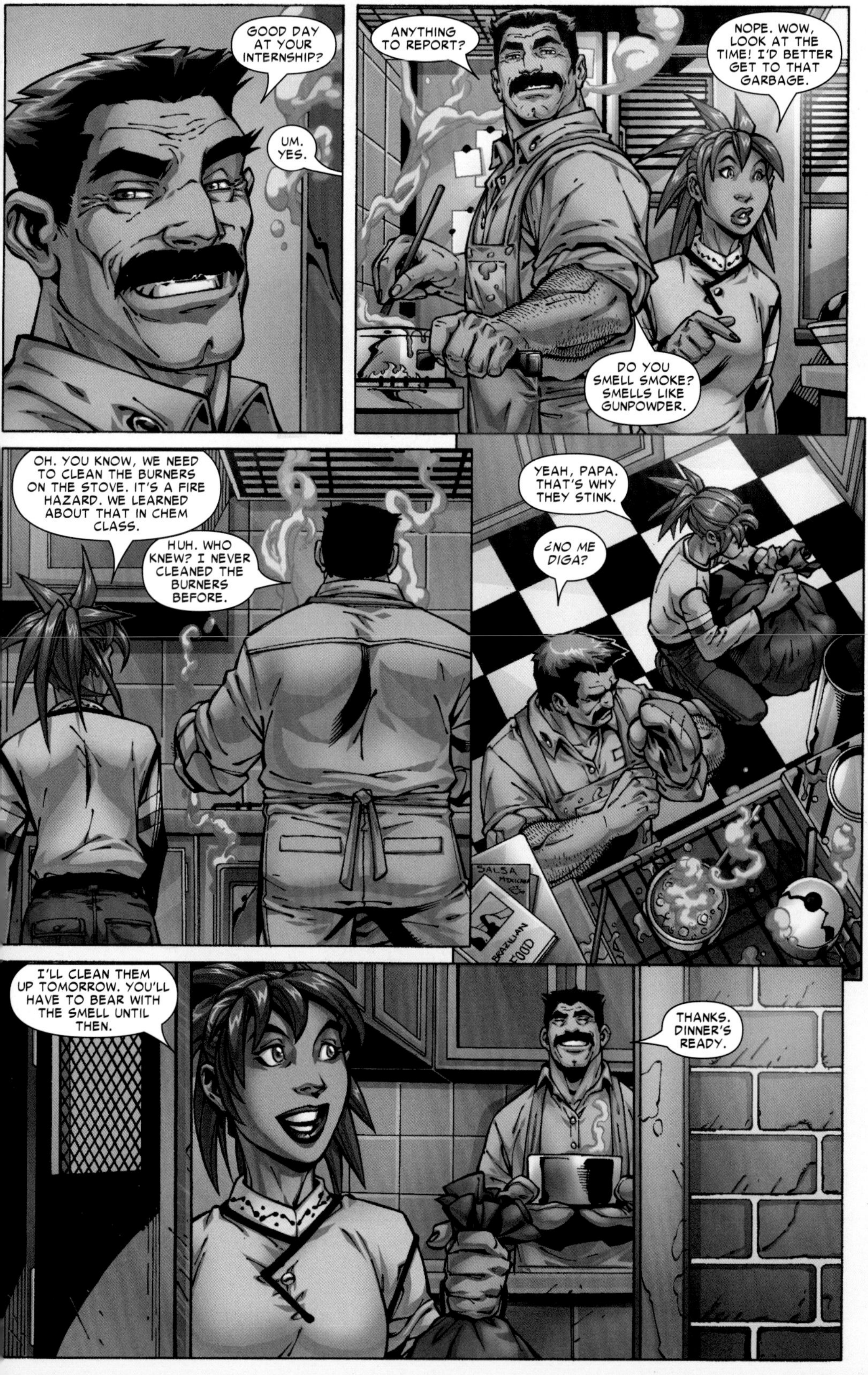
GOOD DAY AT YOUR INTERNSHIP?
UM. YES.
ANYTHING TO REPORT?
NOPE. WOW, LOOK AT THE TIME! I'D BETTER GET TO THAT GARBAGE.
DO YOU SMELL SMOKE? SMELLS LIKE GUNPOWDER.
OH. YOU KNOW, WE NEED TO CLEAN THE BURNERS ON THE STOVE. IT'S A FIRE HAZARD. WE LEARNED ABOUT THAT IN CHEM CLASS.
HUH. WHO KNEW? I NEVER CLEANED THE BURNERS BEFORE.
YEAH, PAPA. THAT'S WHY THEY STINK.
¿NO ME DIGA?
SALSA
BRAZILIAN FOOD
I'LL CLEAN THEM UP TOMORROW. YOU'LL HAVE TO BEAR WITH THE SMELL UNTIL THEN.
THANKS. DINNER'S READY.

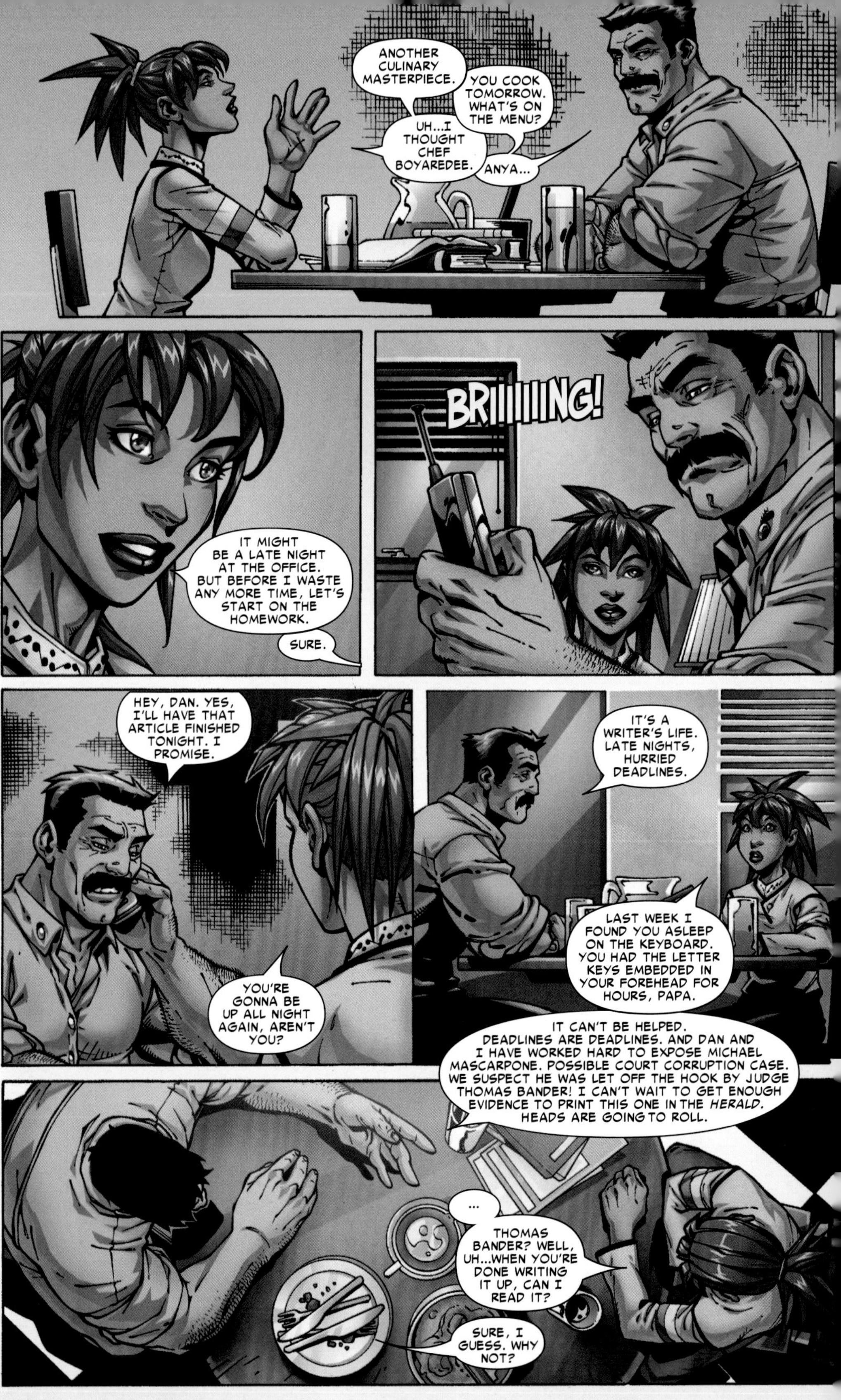
ANOTHER CULINARY MASTERPIECE.
UH...I THOUGHT CHEF BOYAREDEE.
YOU COOK TOMORROW. WHAT'S ON THE MENU?
ANYA...
IT MIGHT BE A LATE NIGHT AT THE OFFICE. BUT BEFORE I WASTE ANY MORE TIME, LET'S START ON THE HOMEWORK.
SURE.
BRIIIIIING!
HEY, DAN. YES, I'LL HAVE THAT ARTICLE FINISHED TONIGHT. I PROMISE.
YOU'RE GONNA BE UP ALL NIGHT AGAIN, AREN'T YOU?
IT'S A WRITER'S LIFE. LATE NIGHTS, HURRIED DEADLINES.
LAST WEEK I FOUND YOU ASLEEP ON THE KEYBOARD. YOU HAD THE LETTER KEYS EMBEDDED IN YOUR FOREHEAD FOR HOURS, PAPA.
IT CAN'T BE HELPED. DEADLINES ARE DEADLINES. AND DAN AND I HAVE WORKED HARD TO EXPOSE MICHAEL MASCARPONE. POSSIBLE COURT CORRUPTION CASE. WE SUSPECT HE WAS LET OFF THE HOOK BY JUDGE THOMAS BANDER! I CAN'T WAIT TO GET ENOUGH EVIDENCE TO PRINT THIS ONE IN THE *HERALD*. HEADS ARE GOING TO ROLL.
...
THOMAS BANDER? WELL, UH...WHEN YOU'RE DONE WRITING IT UP, CAN I READ IT?
SURE, I GUESS. WHY NOT?

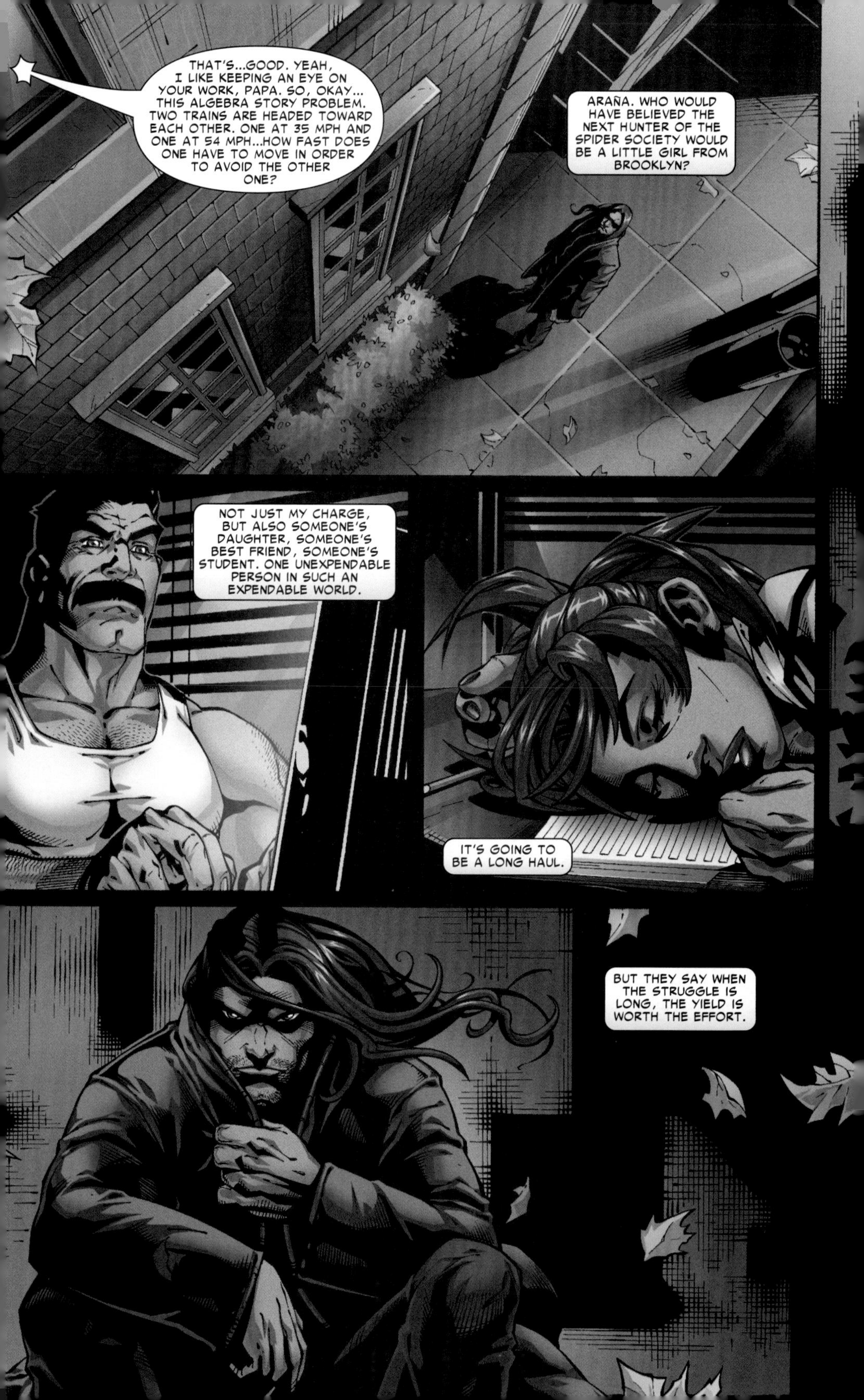
THAT'S...GOOD. YEAH, I LIKE KEEPING AN EYE ON YOUR WORK, PAPA. SO, OKAY... THIS ALGEBRA STORY PROBLEM. TWO TRAINS ARE HEADED TOWARD EACH OTHER. ONE AT 35 MPH AND ONE AT 54 MPH...HOW FAST DOES ONE HAVE TO MOVE IN ORDER TO AVOID THE OTHER ONE?
ARAÑA. WHO WOULD HAVE BELIEVED THE NEXT HUNTER OF THE SPIDER SOCIETY WOULD BE A LITTLE GIRL FROM BROOKLYN?
NOT JUST MY CHARGE, BUT ALSO SOMEONE'S DAUGHTER, SOMEONE'S BEST FRIEND, SOMEONE'S STUDENT. ONE UNEXPENDABLE PERSON IN SUCH AN EXPENDABLE WORLD.
IT'S GOING TO BE A LONG HAUL.
BUT THEY SAY WHEN THE STRUGGLE IS LONG, THE YIELD IS WORTH THE EFFORT.

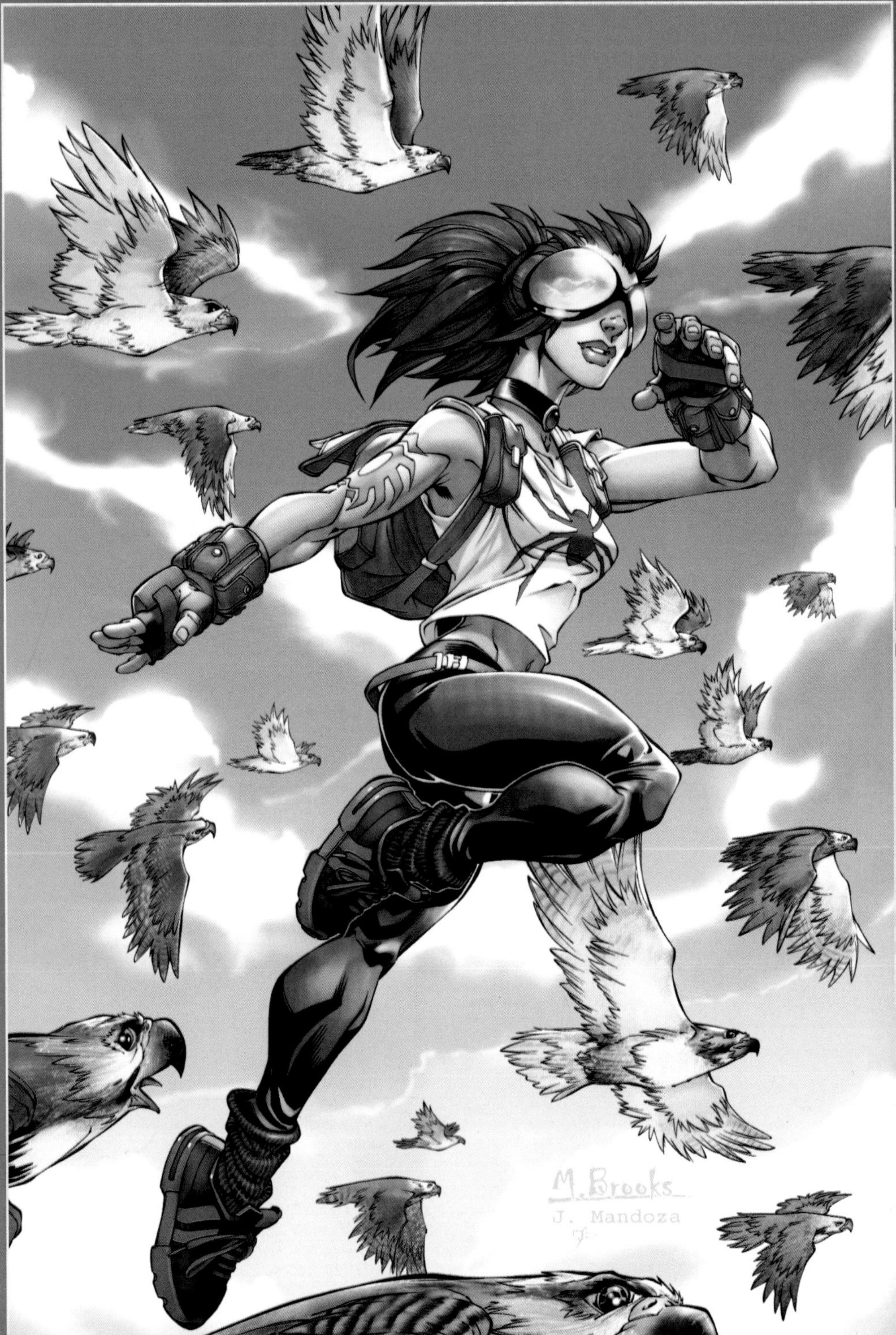
M. Brooks
J. Mandoza

ARAÑA #2

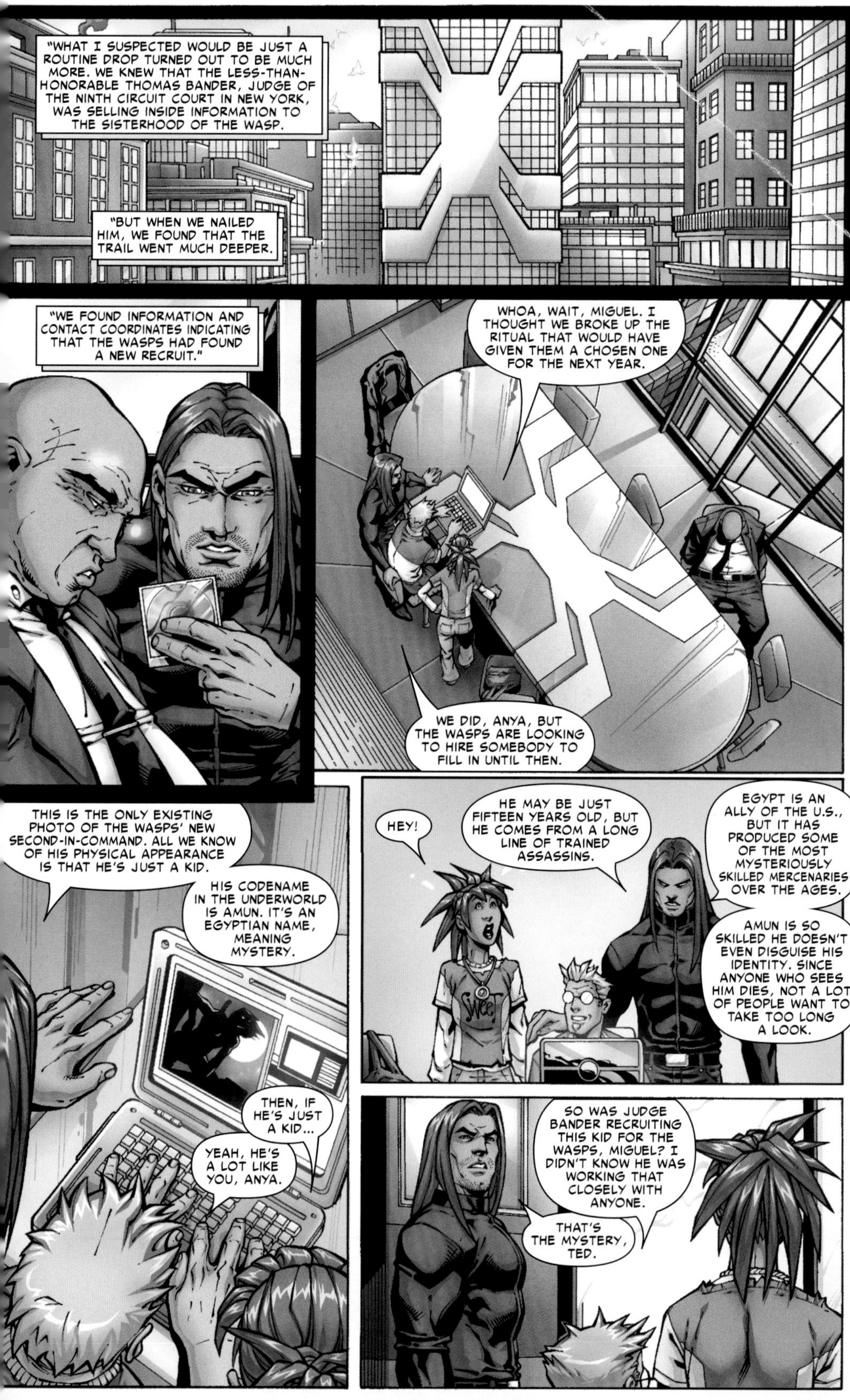
"WHAT I SUSPECTED WOULD BE JUST A ROUTINE DROP TURNED OUT TO BE MUCH MORE. WE KNEW THAT THE LESS-THAN-HONORABLE THOMAS BANDER, JUDGE OF THE NINTH CIRCUIT COURT IN NEW YORK, WAS SELLING INSIDE INFORMATION TO THE SISTERHOOD OF THE WASP.
"BUT WHEN WE NAILED HIM, WE FOUND THAT THE TRAIL WENT MUCH DEEPER.
"WE FOUND INFORMATION AND CONTACT COORDINATES INDICATING THAT THE WASPS HAD FOUND A NEW RECRUIT."
WHOA, WAIT, MIGUEL. I THOUGHT WE BROKE UP THE RITUAL THAT WOULD HAVE GIVEN THEM A CHOSEN ONE FOR THE NEXT YEAR.
WE DID, ANYA, BUT THE WASPS ARE LOOKING TO HIRE SOMEBODY TO FILL IN UNTIL THEN.
THIS IS THE ONLY EXISTING PHOTO OF THE WASPS' NEW SECOND-IN-COMMAND. ALL WE KNOW OF HIS PHYSICAL APPEARANCE IS THAT HE'S JUST A KID.
HIS CODENAME IN THE UNDERWORLD IS AMUN. IT'S AN EGYPTIAN NAME, MEANING MYSTERY.
THEN, IF HE'S JUST A KID...
YEAH, HE'S A LOT LIKE YOU, ANYA.
HEY!
HE MAY BE JUST FIFTEEN YEARS OLD, BUT HE COMES FROM A LONG LINE OF TRAINED ASSASSINS.
EGYPT IS AN ALLY OF THE U.S., BUT IT HAS PRODUCED SOME OF THE MOST MYSTERIOUSLY SKILLED MERCENARIES OVER THE AGES.
AMUN IS SO SKILLED HE DOESN'T EVEN DISGUISE HIS IDENTITY. SINCE ANYONE WHO SEES HIM DIES, NOT A LOT OF PEOPLE WANT TO TAKE TOO LONG A LOOK.
SO WAS JUDGE BANDER RECRUITING THIS KID FOR THE WASPS, MIGUEL? I DIDN'T KNOW HE WAS WORKING THAT CLOSELY WITH ANYONE.
THAT'S THE MYSTERY, TED.

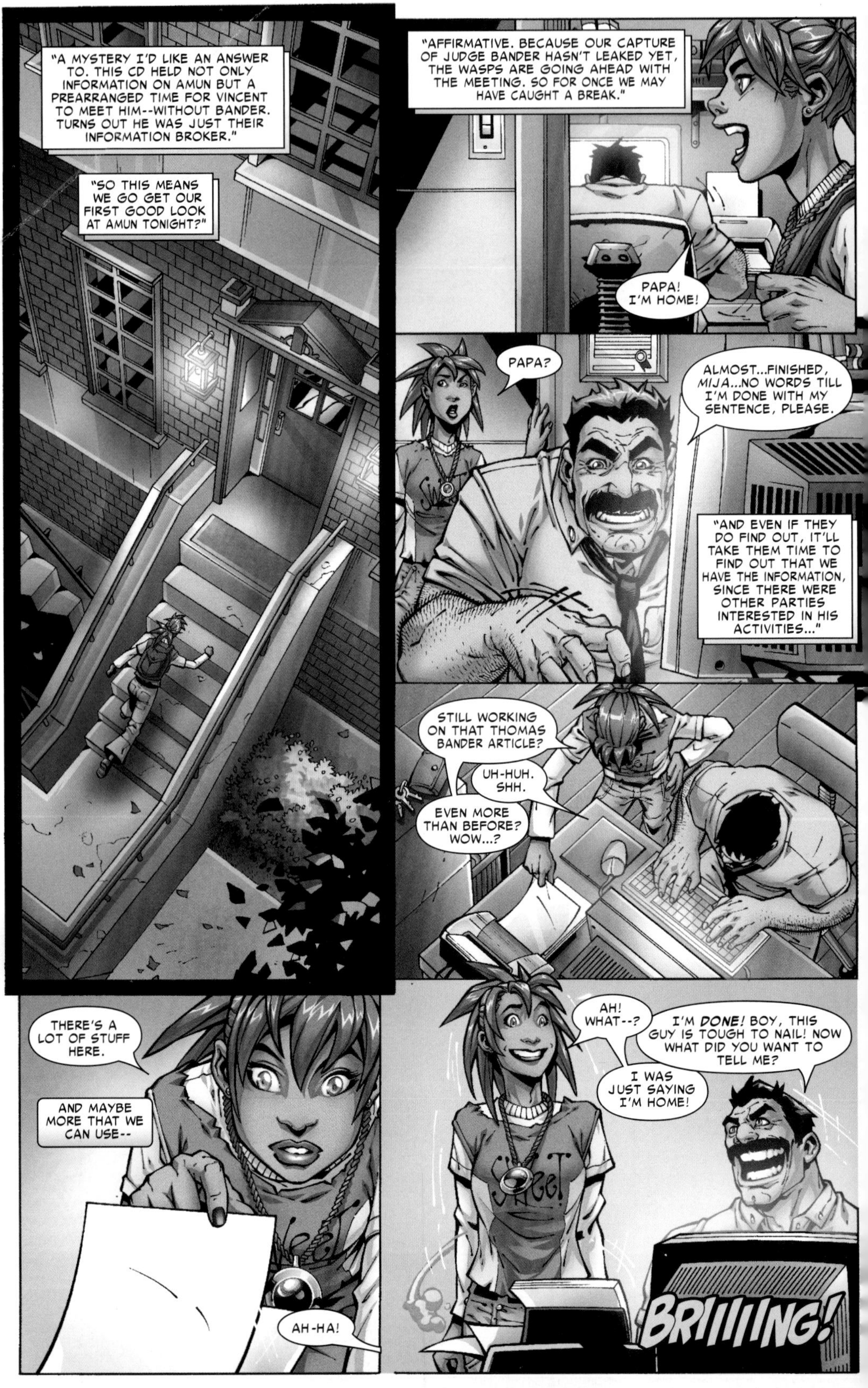

"A MYSTERY I'D LIKE AN ANSWER TO. THIS CD HELD NOT ONLY INFORMATION ON AMUN BUT A PREARRANGED TIME FOR VINCENT TO MEET HIM--WITHOUT BANDER. TURNS OUT HE WAS JUST THEIR INFORMATION BROKER."
"SO THIS MEANS WE GO GET OUR FIRST GOOD LOOK AT AMUN TONIGHT?"
"AFFIRMATIVE. BECAUSE OUR CAPTURE OF JUDGE BANDER HASN'T LEAKED YET, THE WASPS ARE GOING AHEAD WITH THE MEETING. SO FOR ONCE WE MAY HAVE CAUGHT A BREAK."
PAPA! I'M HOME!
PAPA?
ALMOST...FINISHED, MIJA...NO WORDS TILL I'M DONE WITH MY SENTENCE, PLEASE.
"AND EVEN IF THEY DO FIND OUT, IT'LL TAKE THEM TIME TO FIND OUT THAT WE HAVE THE INFORMATION, SINCE THERE WERE OTHER PARTIES INTERESTED IN HIS ACTIVITIES..."
STILL WORKING ON THAT THOMAS BANDER ARTICLE?
UH-HUH. SHH.
EVEN MORE THAN BEFORE? WOW...?
THERE'S A LOT OF STUFF HERE.
AND MAYBE MORE THAT WE CAN USE--
AH-HA!
AH! WHAT--?
I'M DONE! BOY, THIS GUY IS TOUGH TO NAIL! NOW WHAT DID YOU WANT TO TELL ME?
I WAS JUST SAYING I'M HOME!
BRIIIIING!

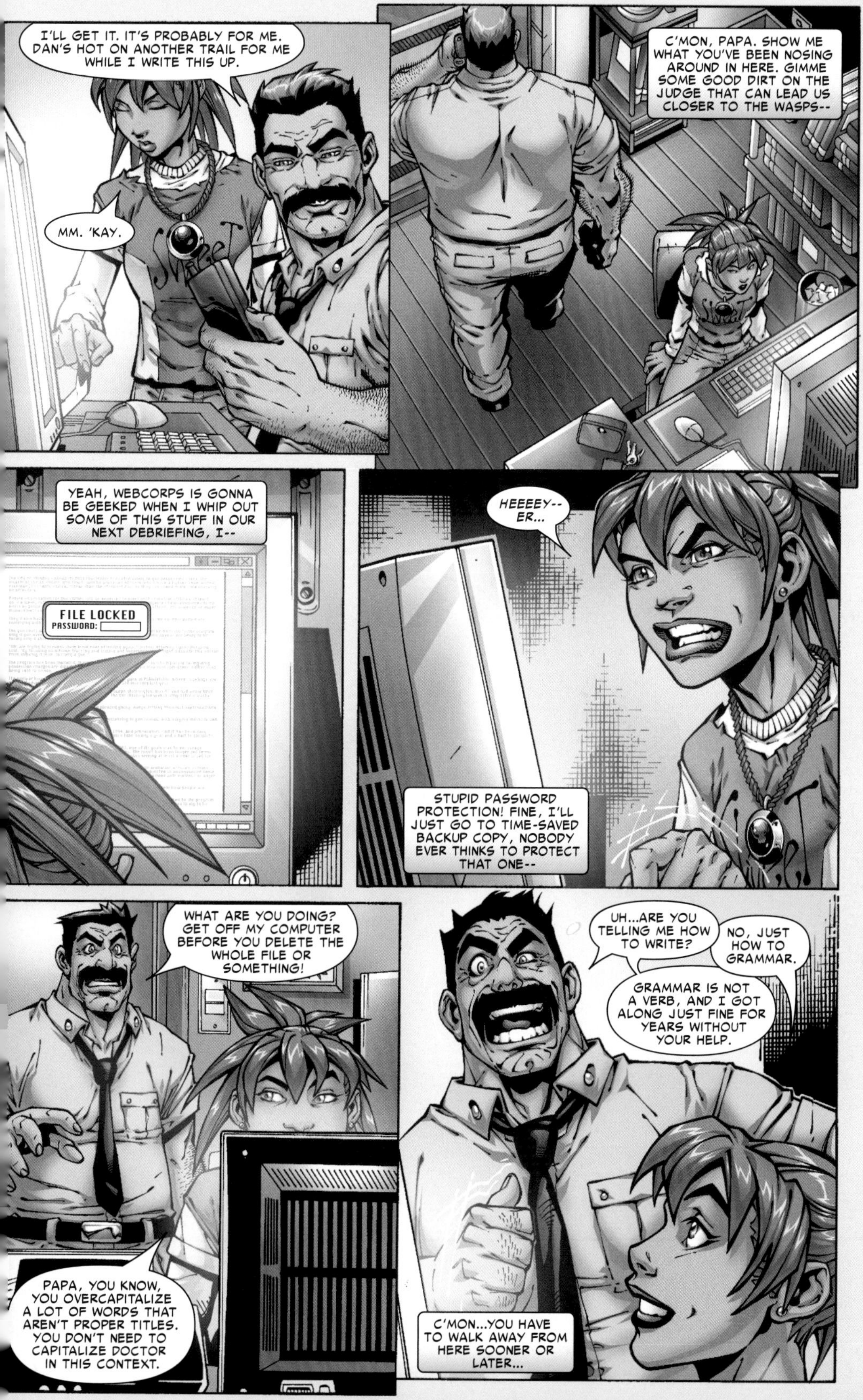
I'LL GET IT. IT'S PROBABLY FOR ME. DAN'S HOT ON ANOTHER TRAIL FOR ME WHILE I WRITE THIS UP.
MM. 'KAY.
C'MON, PAPA. SHOW ME WHAT YOU'VE BEEN NOSING AROUND IN HERE. GIMME SOME GOOD DIRT ON THE JUDGE THAT CAN LEAD US CLOSER TO THE WASPS--
YEAH, WEBCORPS IS GONNA BE GEEKED WHEN I WHIP OUT SOME OF THIS STUFF IN OUR NEXT DEBRIEFING, I--
FILE LOCKED
PASSWORD:
HEEEEY-- ER...
STUPID PASSWORD PROTECTION! FINE, I'LL JUST GO TO TIME-SAVED BACKUP COPY, NOBODY EVER THINKS TO PROTECT THAT ONE--
WHAT ARE YOU DOING? GET OFF MY COMPUTER BEFORE YOU DELETE THE WHOLE FILE OR SOMETHING!
PAPA, YOU KNOW, YOU OVERCAPITALIZE A LOT OF WORDS THAT AREN'T PROPER TITLES. YOU DON'T NEED TO CAPITALIZE DOCTOR IN THIS CONTEXT.
UH...ARE YOU TELLING ME HOW TO WRITE?
NO, JUST HOW TO GRAMMAR.
GRAMMAR IS NOT A VERB, AND I GOT ALONG JUST FINE FOR YEARS WITHOUT YOUR HELP.
C'MON...YOU HAVE TO WALK AWAY FROM HERE SOONER OR LATER...

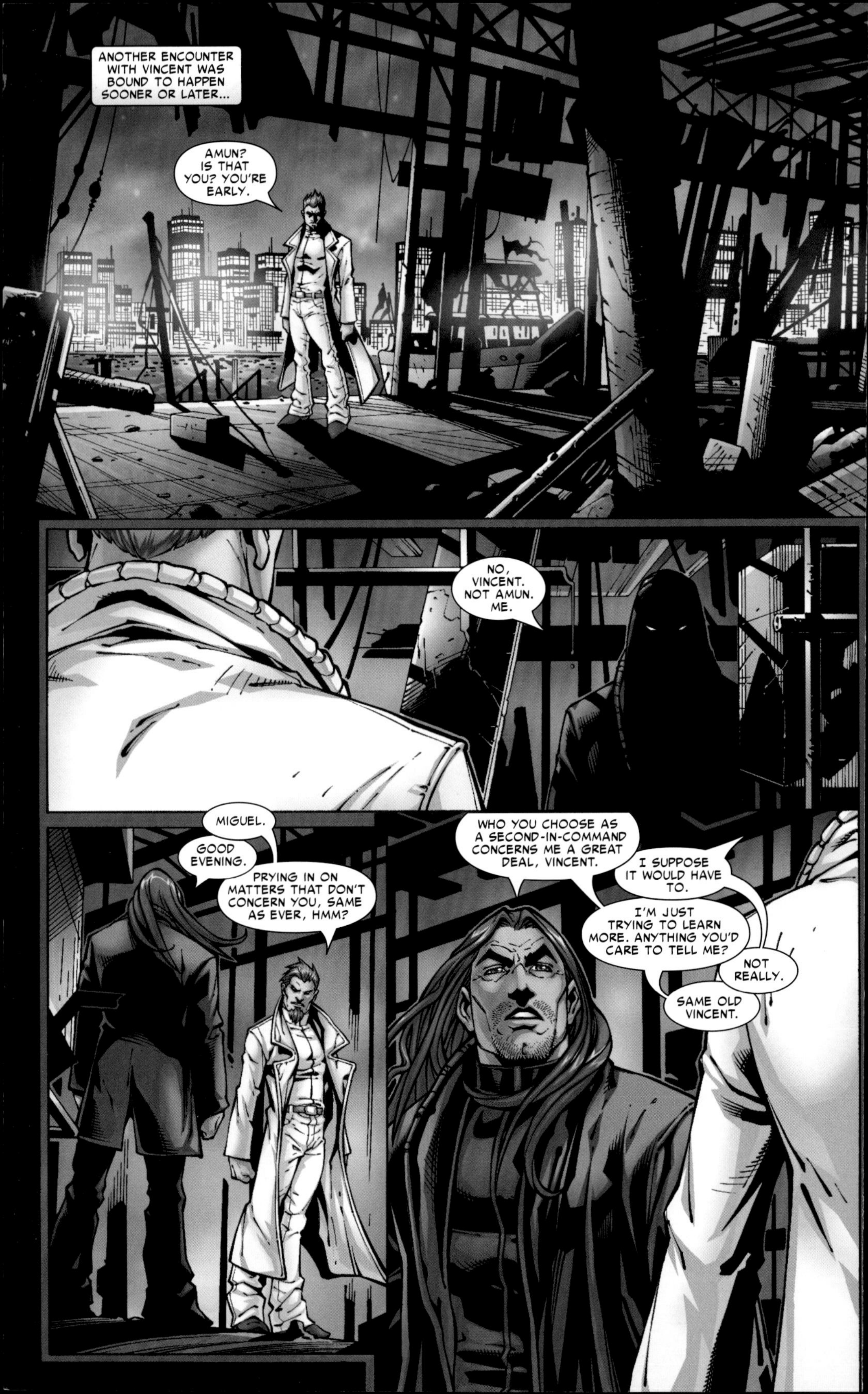
ANOTHER ENCOUNTER WITH VINCENT WAS BOUND TO HAPPEN SOONER OR LATER...
AMUN? IS THAT YOU? YOU'RE EARLY.
NO, VINCENT. NOT AMUN. ME.
MIGUEL.
GOOD EVENING.
PRYING IN ON MATTERS THAT DON'T CONCERN YOU, SAME AS EVER, HMM?
WHO YOU CHOOSE AS A SECOND-IN-COMMAND CONCERNS ME A GREAT DEAL, VINCENT.
I SUPPOSE IT WOULD HAVE TO.
I'M JUST TRYING TO LEARN MORE. ANYTHING YOU'D CARE TO TELL ME?
NOT REALLY.
SAME OLD VINCENT.

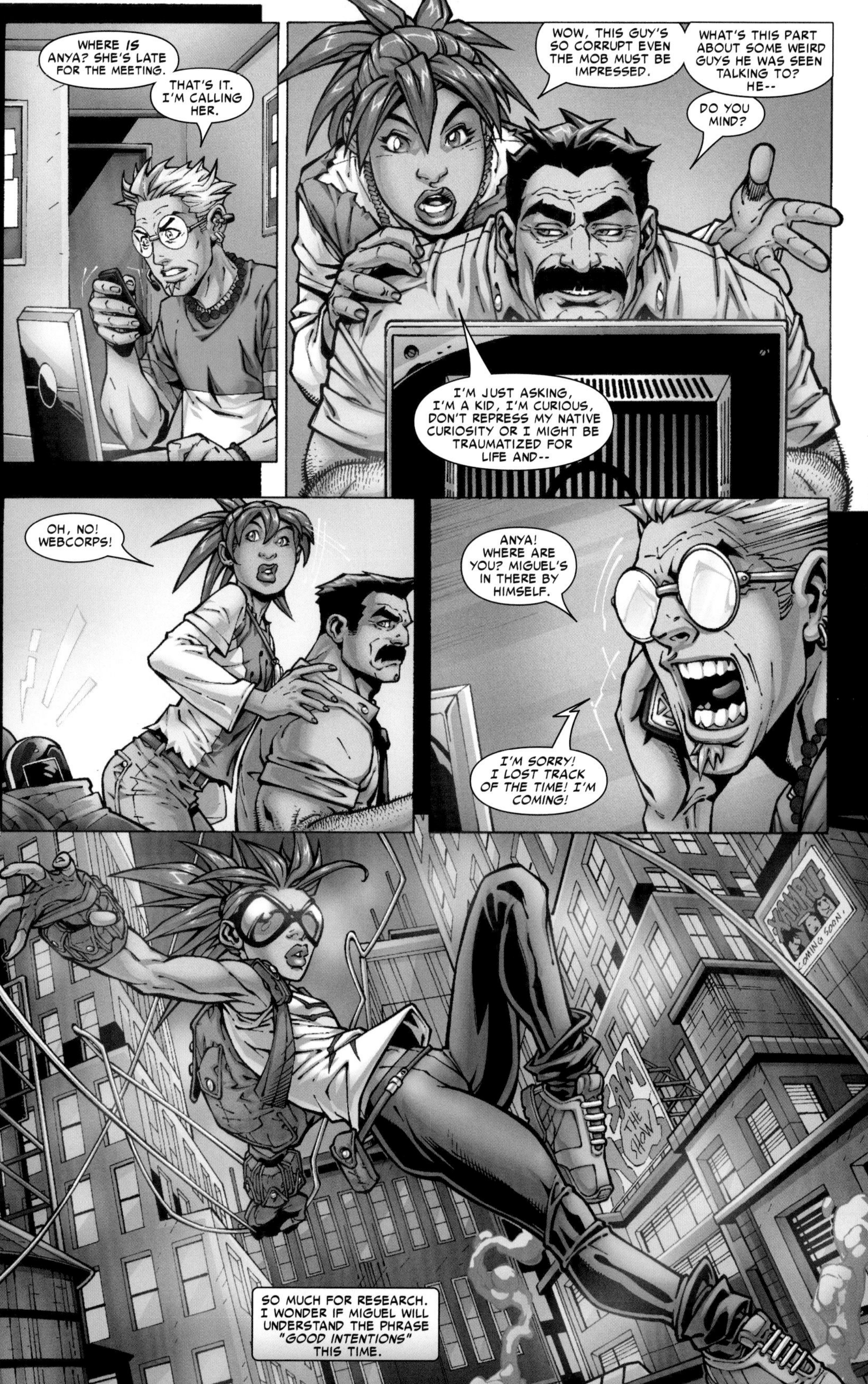
WHERE *IS* ANYA? SHE'S LATE FOR THE MEETING.
THAT'S IT. I'M CALLING HER.
WOW, THIS GUY'S SO CORRUPT EVEN THE MOB MUST BE IMPRESSED.
WHAT'S THIS PART ABOUT SOME WEIRD GUYS HE WAS SEEN TALKING TO? HE--
DO YOU MIND?
I'M JUST ASKING, I'M A KID, I'M CURIOUS, DON'T REPRESS MY NATIVE CURIOSITY OR I MIGHT BE TRAUMATIZED FOR LIFE AND--
OH, NO! WEBCORPS!
ANYA! WHERE ARE YOU? MIGUEL'S IN THERE BY HIMSELF.
I'M SORRY! I LOST TRACK OF THE TIME! I'M COMING!
COMING SOON
SO MUCH FOR RESEARCH. I WONDER IF MIGUEL WILL UNDERSTAND THE PHRASE *"GOOD INTENTIONS"* THIS TIME.

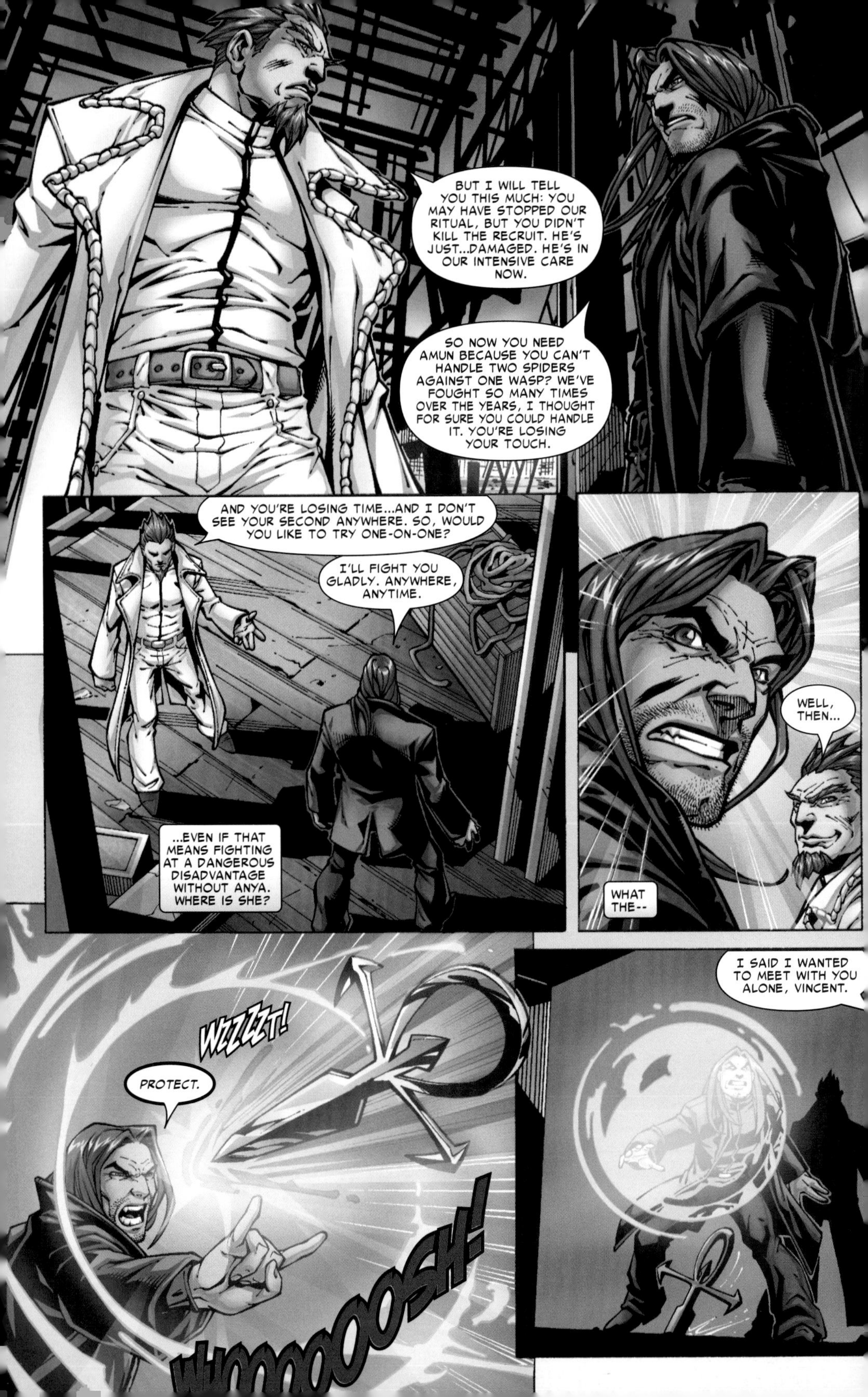
BUT I WILL TELL YOU THIS MUCH: YOU MAY HAVE STOPPED OUR RITUAL, BUT YOU DIDN'T KILL THE RECRUIT. HE'S JUST...DAMAGED. HE'S IN OUR INTENSIVE CARE NOW.
SO NOW YOU NEED AMUN BECAUSE YOU CAN'T HANDLE TWO SPIDERS AGAINST ONE WASP? WE'VE FOUGHT SO MANY TIMES OVER THE YEARS, I THOUGHT FOR SURE YOU COULD HANDLE IT. YOU'RE LOSING YOUR TOUCH.
AND YOU'RE LOSING TIME...AND I DON'T SEE YOUR SECOND ANYWHERE. SO, WOULD YOU LIKE TO TRY ONE-ON-ONE?
I'LL FIGHT YOU GLADLY. ANYWHERE, ANYTIME.
...EVEN IF THAT MEANS FIGHTING AT A DANGEROUS DISADVANTAGE WITHOUT ANYA. WHERE IS SHE?
WELL, THEN...
WHAT THE--
WZZZZT!
PROTECT.
WHOOOOOOSH!
I SAID I WANTED TO MEET WITH YOU ALONE, VINCENT.

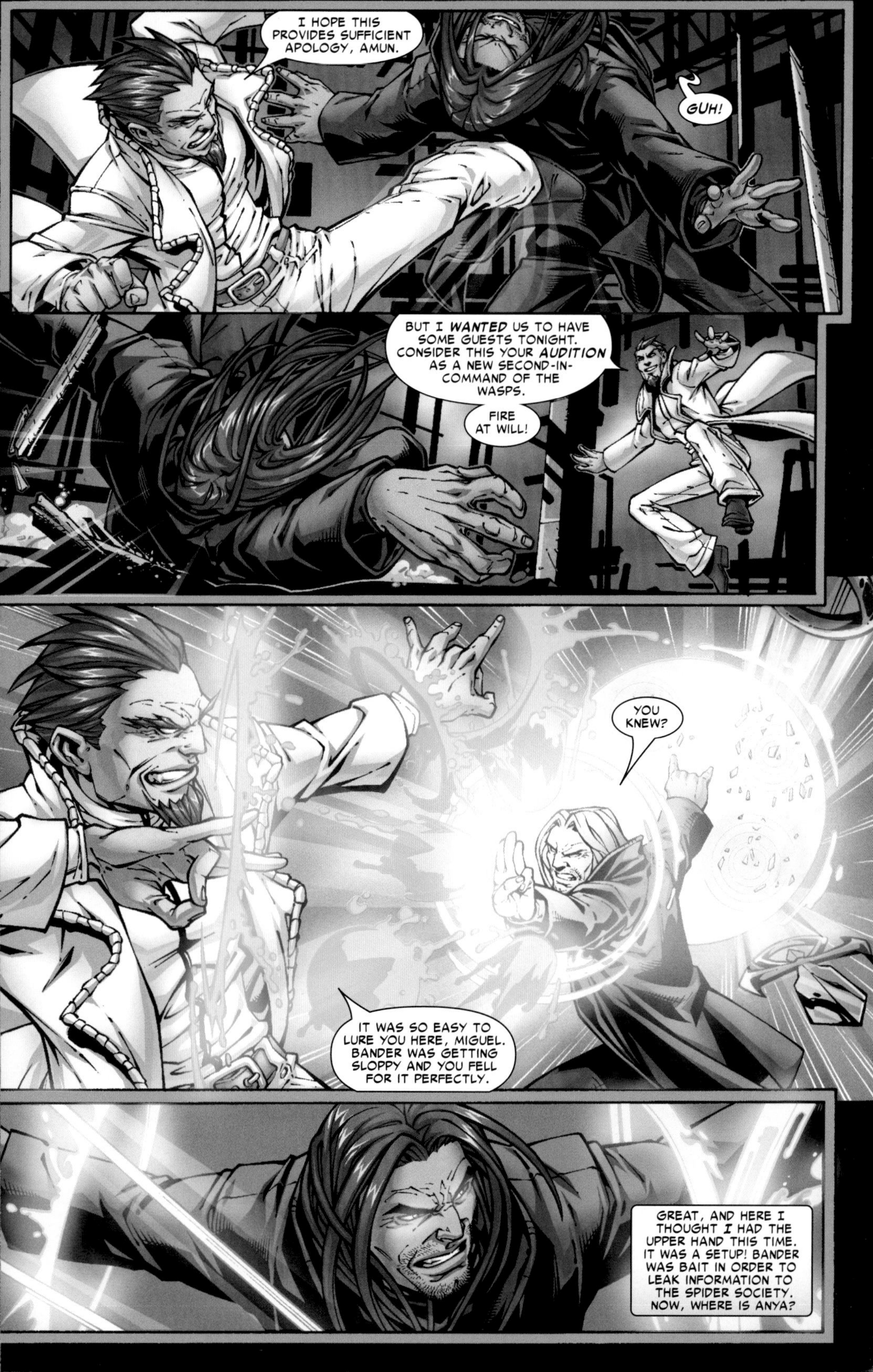
I HOPE THIS PROVIDES SUFFICIENT APOLOGY, AMUN.
GUH!
BUT I WANTED US TO HAVE SOME GUESTS TONIGHT. CONSIDER THIS YOUR AUDITION AS A NEW SECOND-IN-COMMAND OF THE WASPS.
FIRE AT WILL!
YOU KNEW?
IT WAS SO EASY TO LURE YOU HERE, MIGUEL. BANDER WAS GETTING SLOPPY AND YOU FELL FOR IT PERFECTLY.
GREAT, AND HERE I THOUGHT I HAD THE UPPER HAND THIS TIME. IT WAS A SETUP! BANDER WAS BAIT IN ORDER TO LEAK INFORMATION TO THE SPIDER SOCIETY. NOW, WHERE IS ANYA?

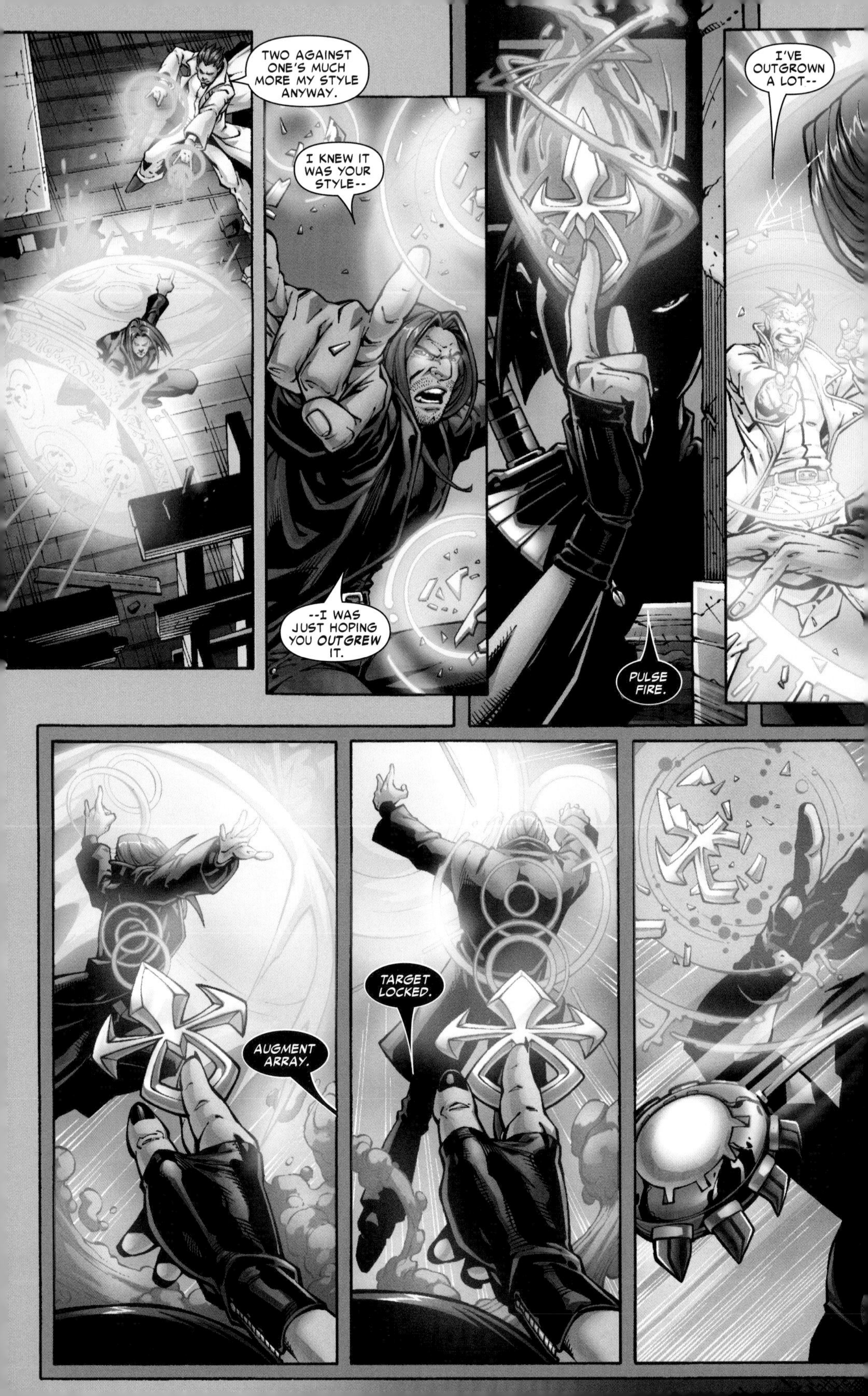

TWO AGAINST ONE'S MUCH MORE MY STYLE ANYWAY.
I KNEW IT WAS YOUR STYLE--
--I WAS JUST HOPING YOU OUTGREW IT.
PULSE FIRE.
I'VE OUTGROWN A LOT--
AUGMENT ARRAY.
TARGET LOCKED.

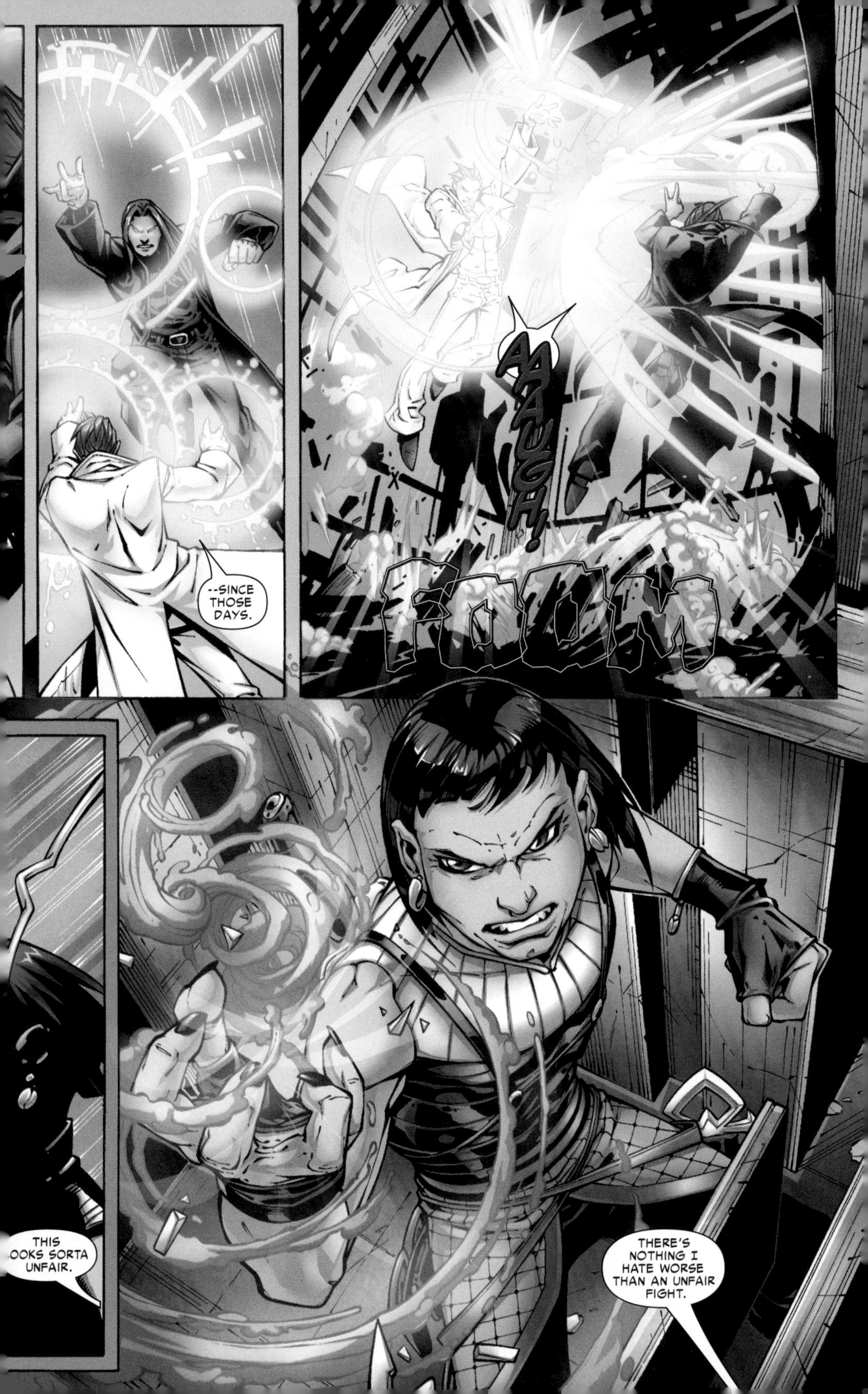
--SINCE THOSE DAYS.
AAAUGH!
FOOM
THIS LOOKS SORTA UNFAIR.
THERE'S NOTHING I HATE WORSE THAN AN UNFAIR FIGHT.

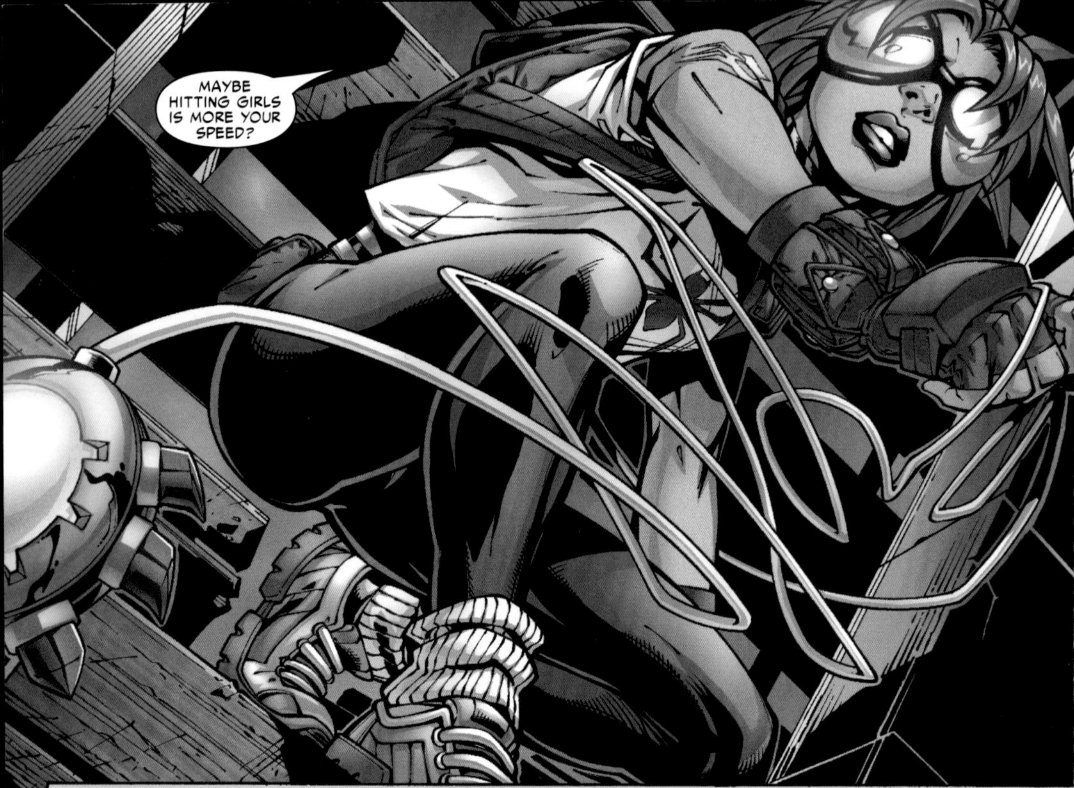
MAYBE HITTING GIRLS IS MORE YOUR SPEED?

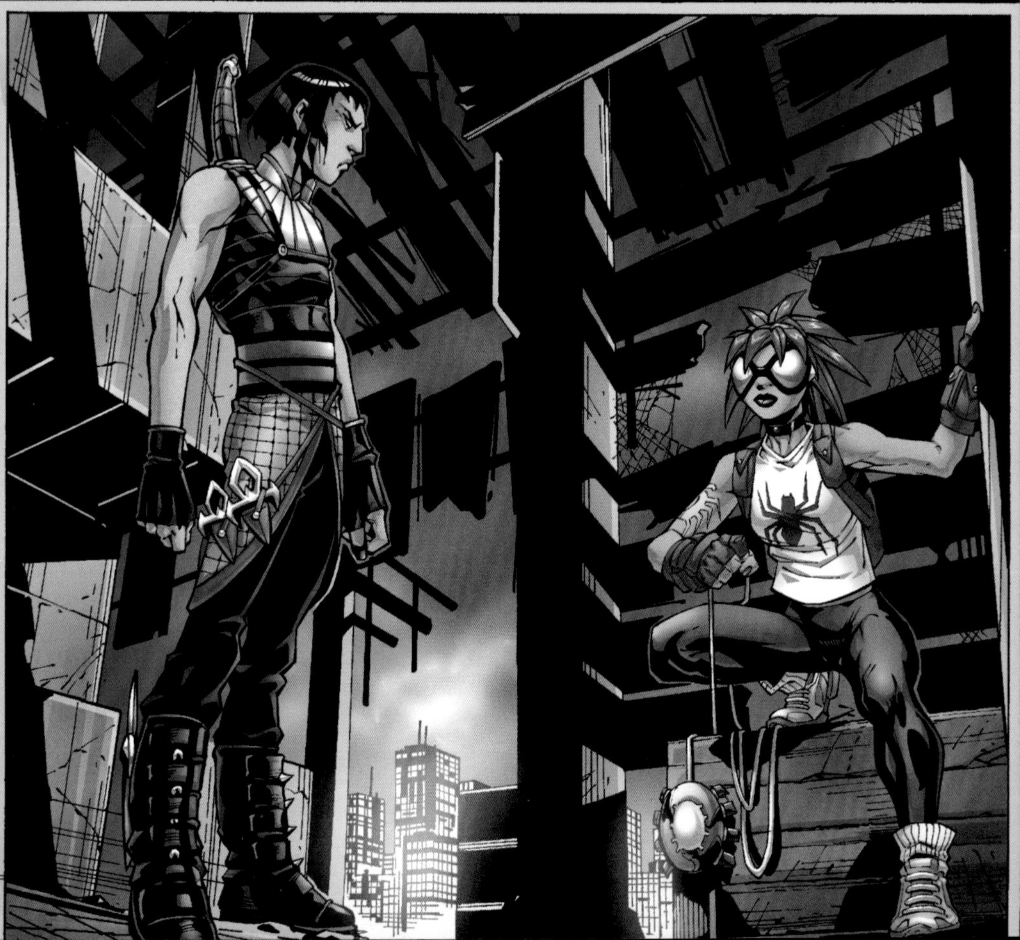

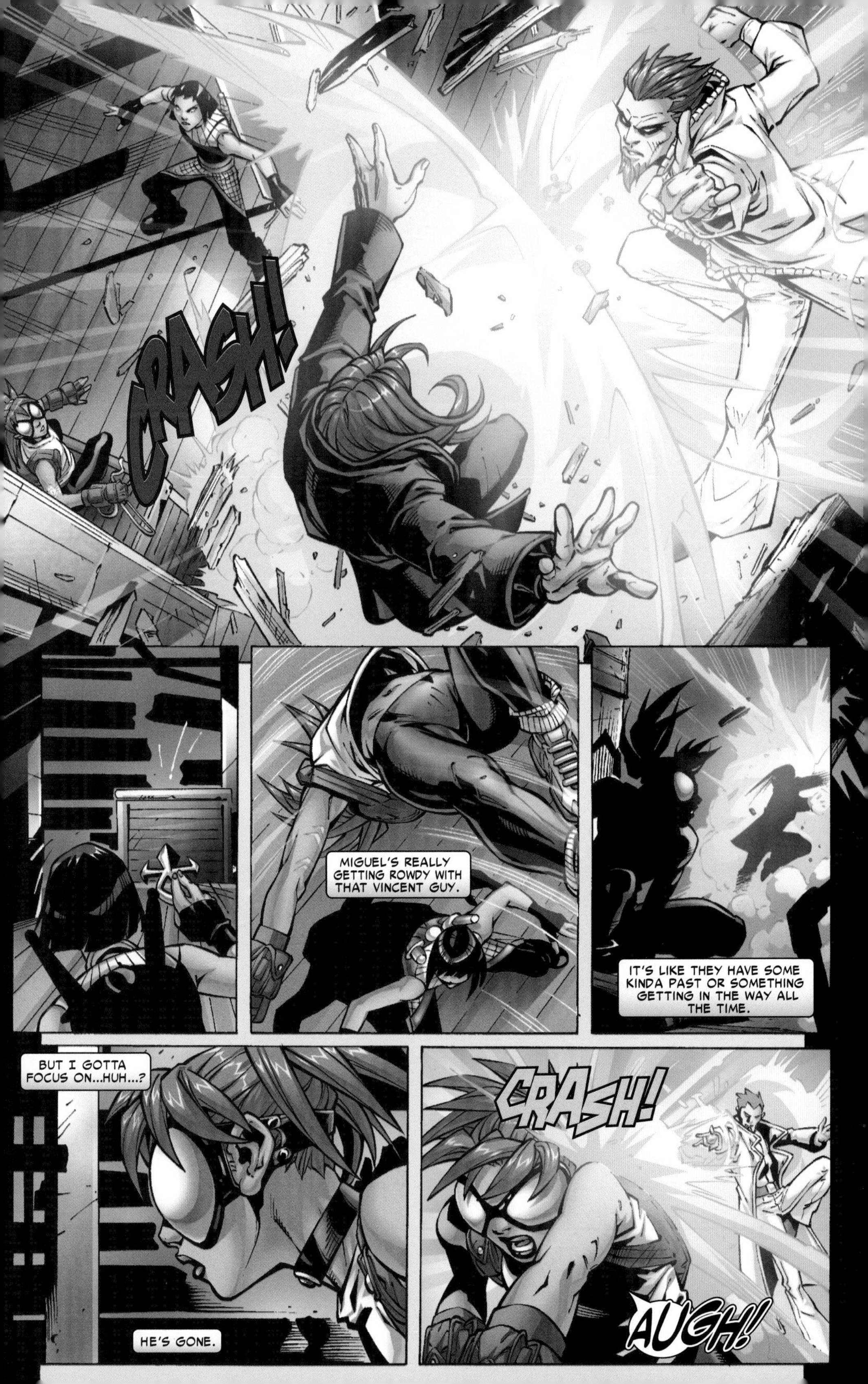
CRASH!
MIGUEL'S REALLY GETTING ROWDY WITH THAT VINCENT GUY.
IT'S LIKE THEY HAVE SOME KINDA PAST OR SOMETHING GETTING IN THE WAY ALL THE TIME.
BUT I GOTTA FOCUS ON...HUH...?
HE'S GONE.
CRASH!
AUGH!

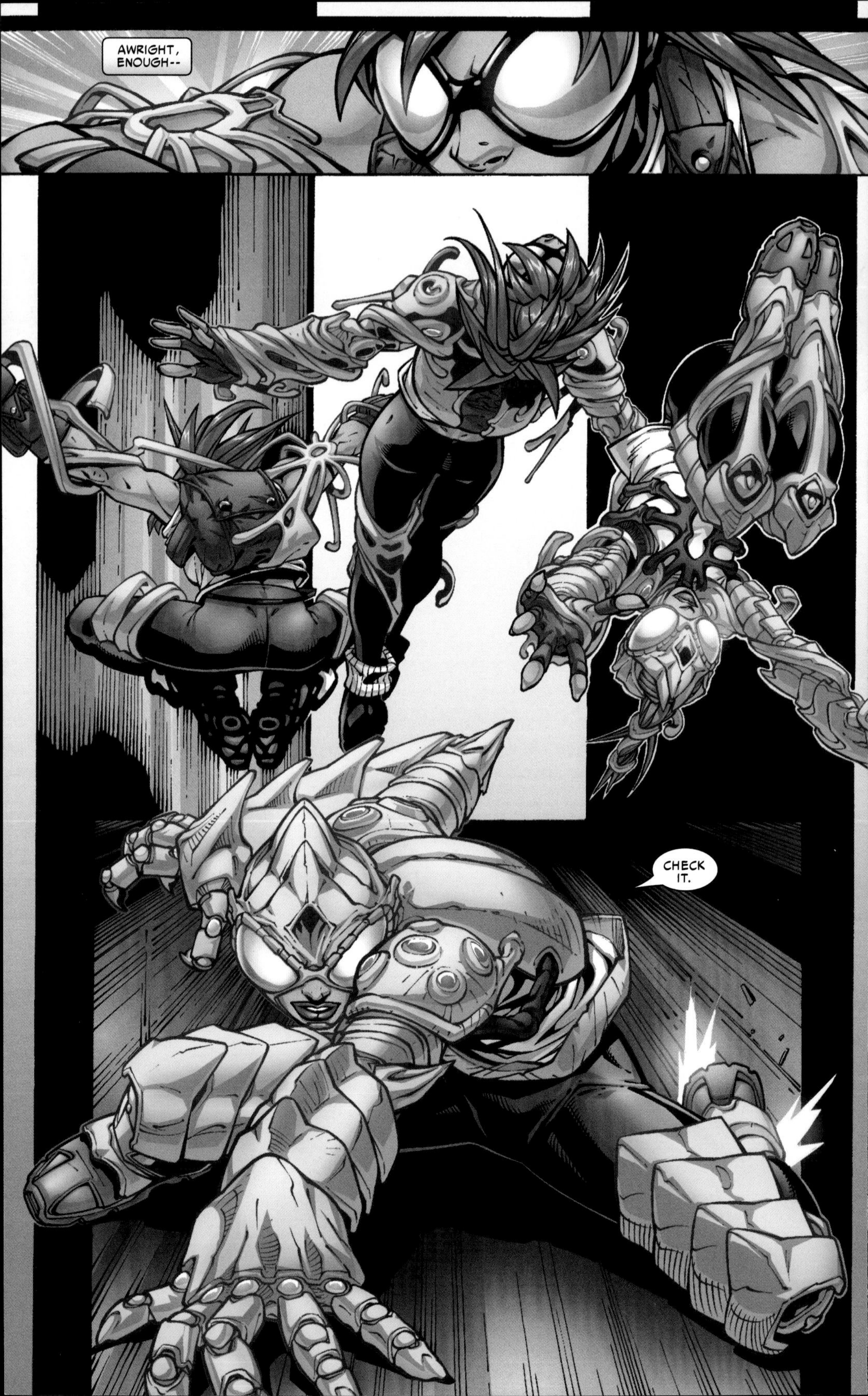
AWRIGHT, ENOUGH--
CHECK IT.

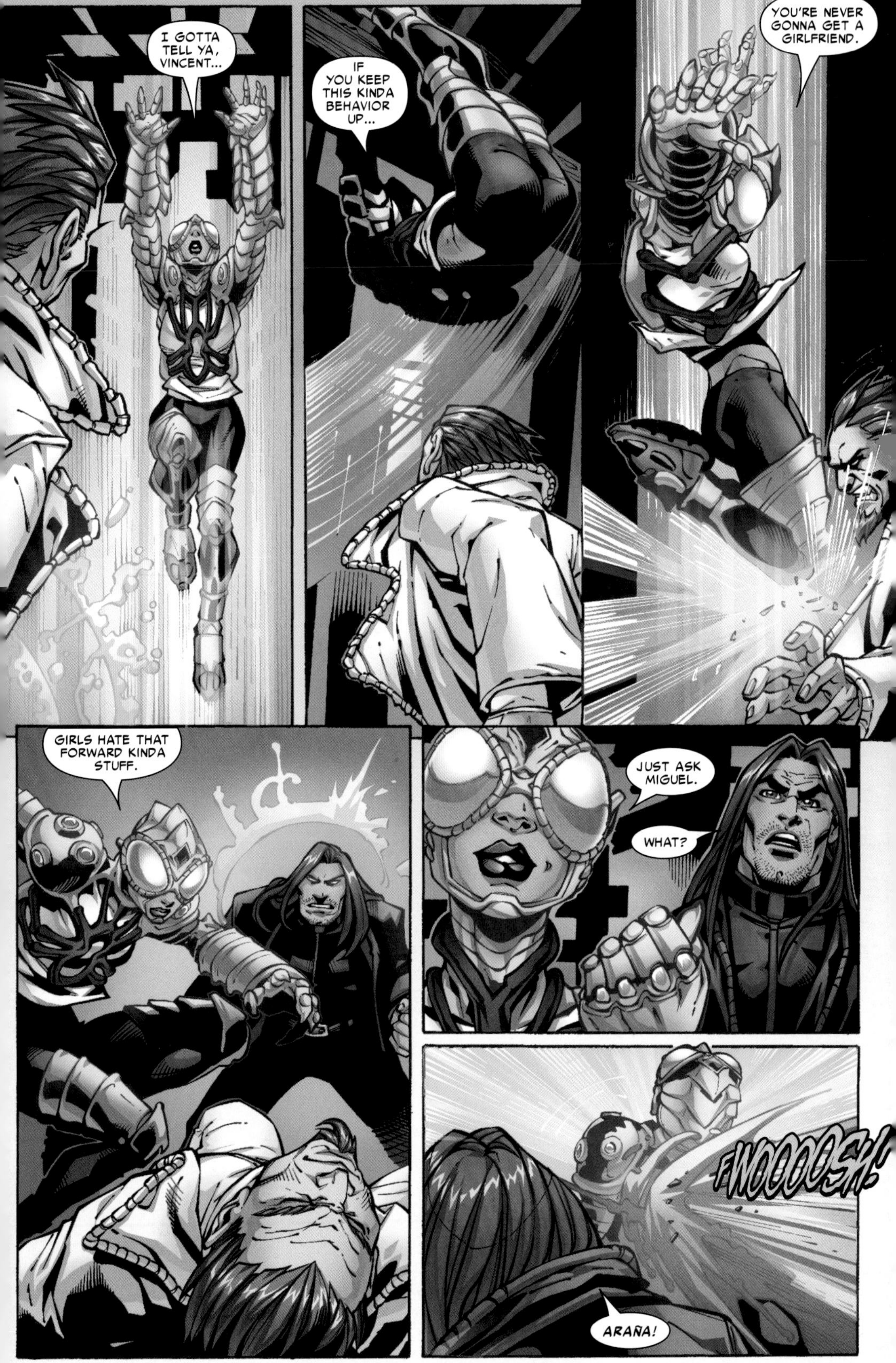
I GOTTA TELL YA, VINCENT...
IF YOU KEEP THIS KINDA BEHAVIOR UP...
YOU'RE NEVER GONNA GET A GIRLFRIEND.
GIRLS HATE THAT FORWARD KINDA STUFF.
JUST ASK MIGUEL.
WHAT?
FWOOOOSH!
ARAÑA!

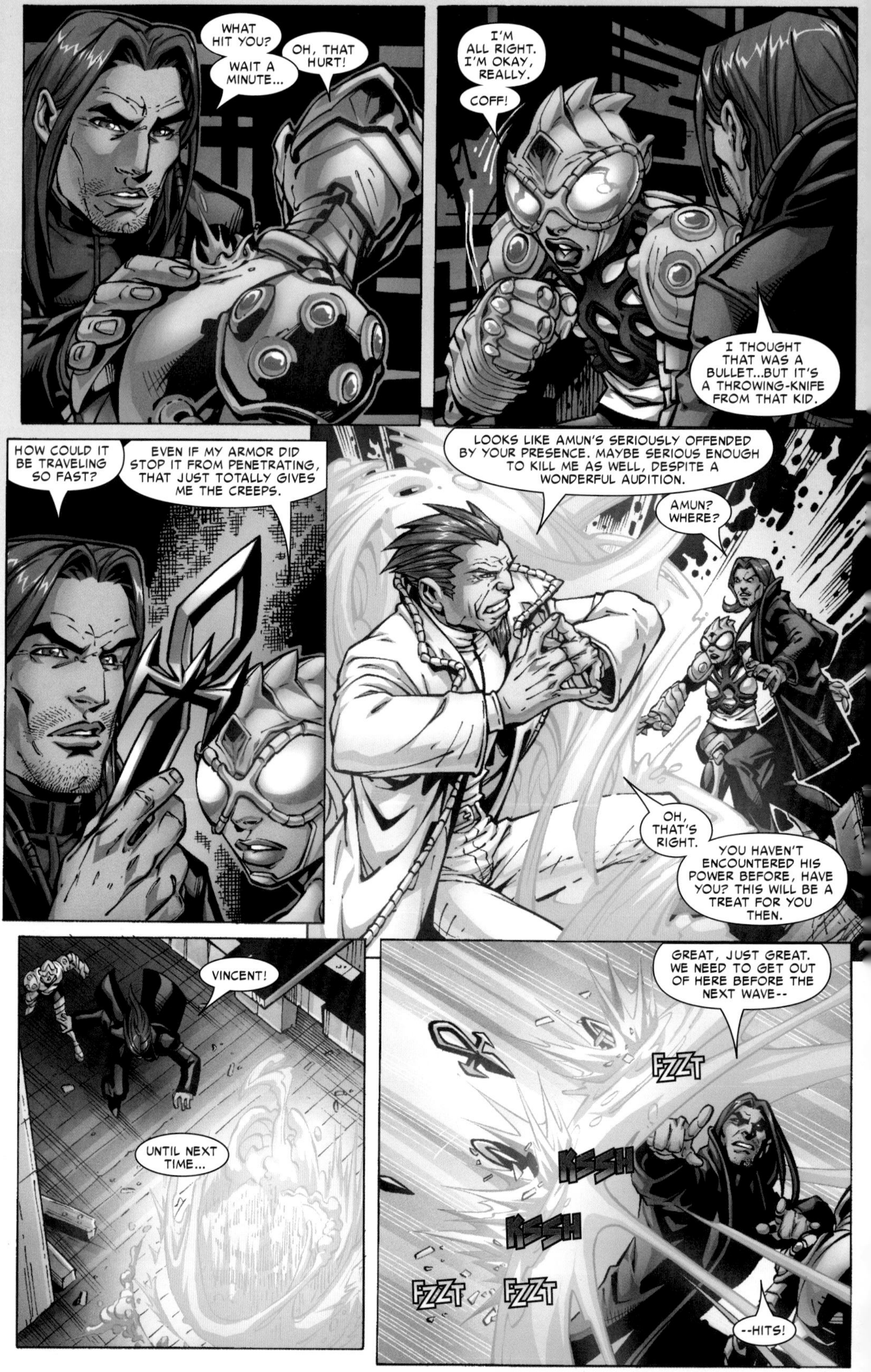
WHAT HIT YOU?
WAIT A MINUTE...
OH, THAT HURT!
I'M ALL RIGHT. I'M OKAY, REALLY.
COFF!
I THOUGHT THAT WAS A BULLET...BUT IT'S A THROWING-KNIFE FROM THAT KID.
HOW COULD IT BE TRAVELING SO FAST?
EVEN IF MY ARMOR DID STOP IT FROM PENETRATING, THAT JUST TOTALLY GIVES ME THE CREEPS.
LOOKS LIKE AMUN'S SERIOUSLY OFFENDED BY YOUR PRESENCE. MAYBE SERIOUS ENOUGH TO KILL ME AS WELL, DESPITE A WONDERFUL AUDITION.
AMUN? WHERE?
OH, THAT'S RIGHT.
YOU HAVEN'T ENCOUNTERED HIS POWER BEFORE, HAVE YOU? THIS WILL BE A TREAT FOR YOU THEN.
VINCENT!
UNTIL NEXT TIME...
GREAT, JUST GREAT. WE NEED TO GET OUT OF HERE BEFORE THE NEXT WAVE--
FZZT
KSSH
KSSH
FZZT
FZZT
--HITS!

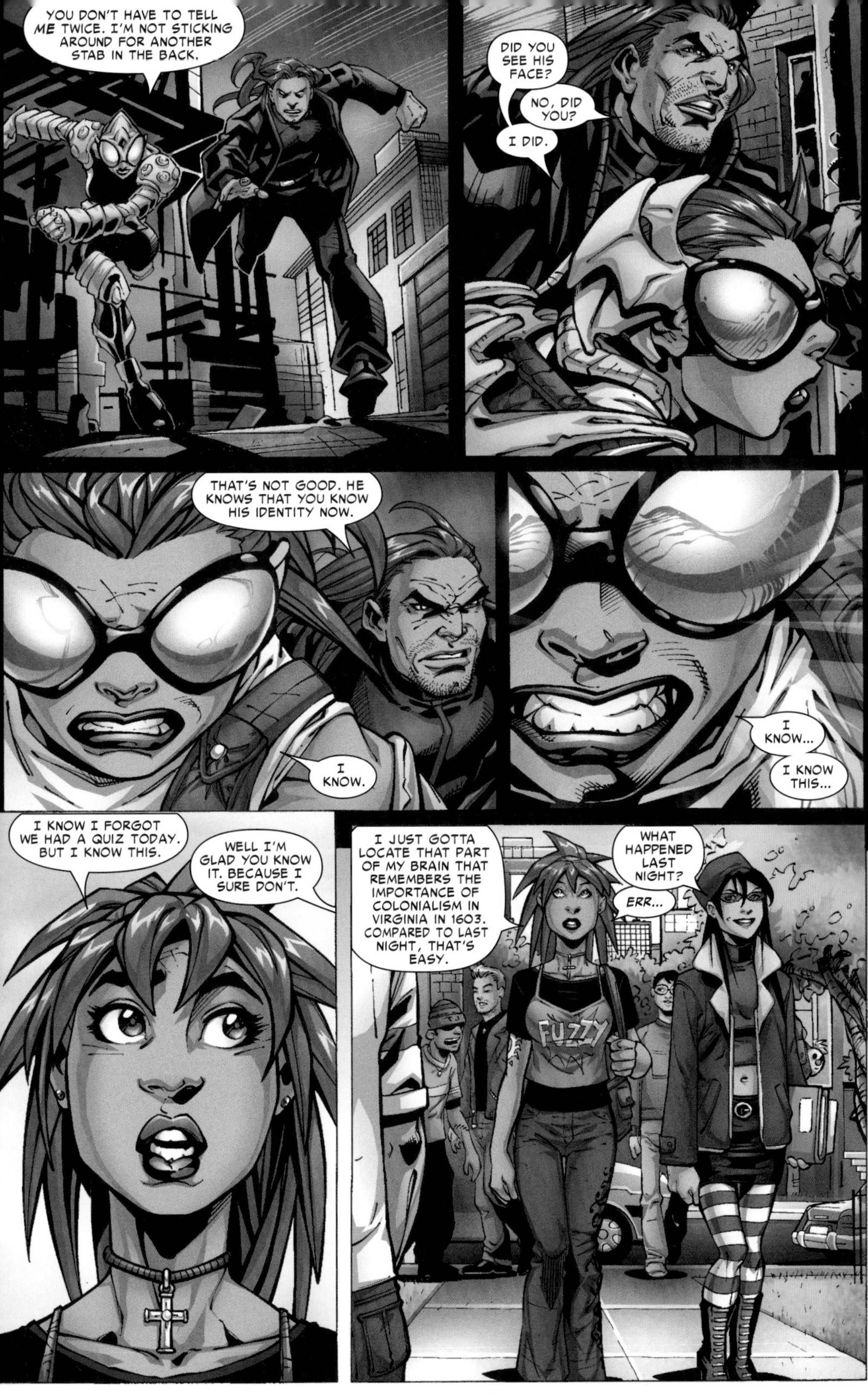
YOU DON'T HAVE TO TELL ME TWICE. I'M NOT STICKING AROUND FOR ANOTHER STAB IN THE BACK.
DID YOU SEE HIS FACE?
NO, DID YOU?
I DID.
THAT'S NOT GOOD. HE KNOWS THAT YOU KNOW HIS IDENTITY NOW.
I KNOW.
I KNOW...
I KNOW THIS...
I KNOW I FORGOT WE HAD A QUIZ TODAY. BUT I KNOW THIS.
WELL I'M GLAD YOU KNOW IT. BECAUSE I SURE DON'T.
I JUST GOTTA LOCATE THAT PART OF MY BRAIN THAT REMEMBERS THE IMPORTANCE OF COLONIALISM IN VIRGINIA IN 1603. COMPARED TO LAST NIGHT, THAT'S EASY.
WHAT HAPPENED LAST NIGHT?
ERR...
FUZZY

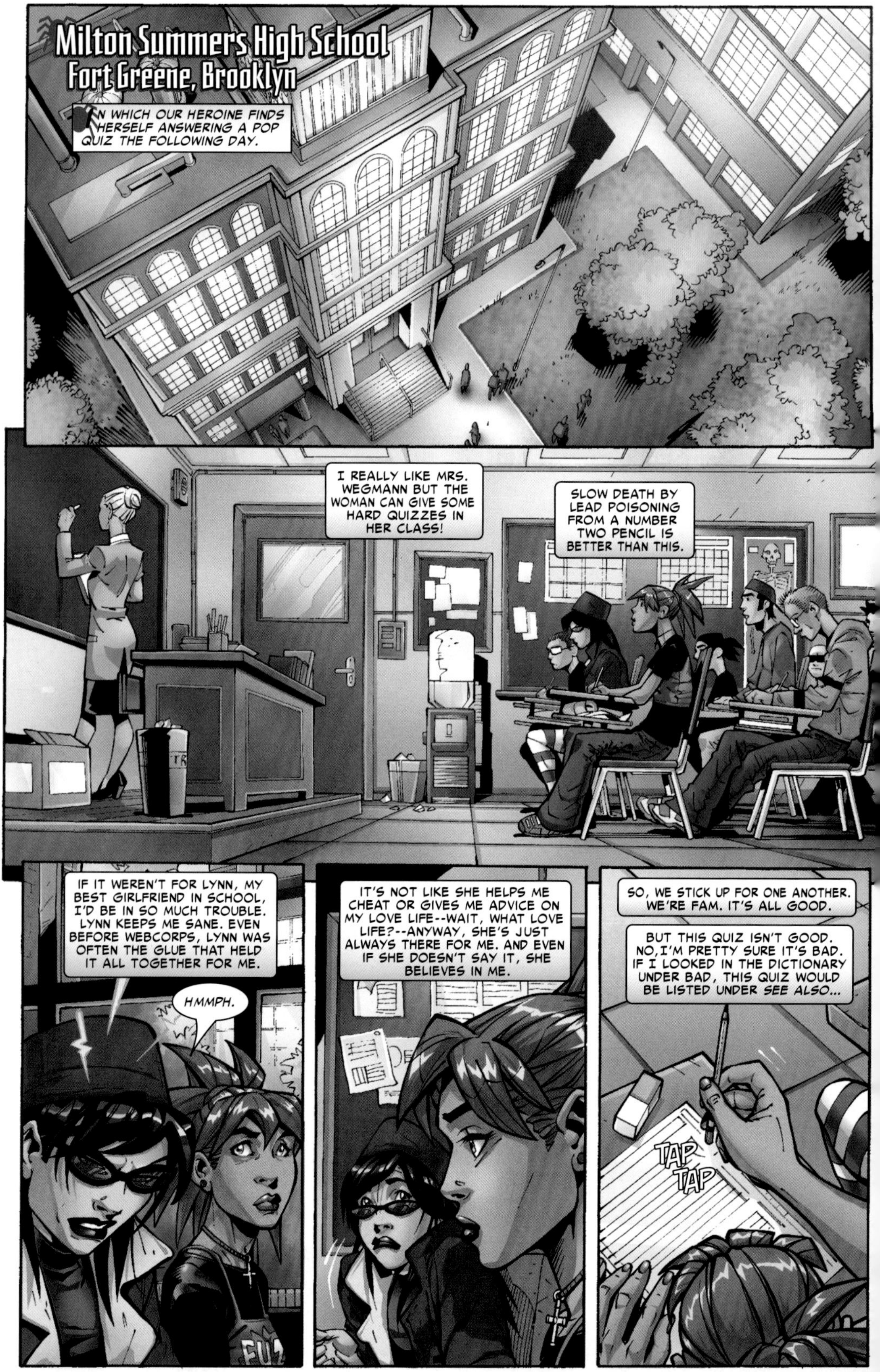
Milton Summers High School
Fort Greene, Brooklyn
IN WHICH OUR HEROINE FINDS HERSELF ANSWERING A POP QUIZ THE FOLLOWING DAY.
I REALLY LIKE MRS. WEGMANN BUT THE WOMAN CAN GIVE SOME HARD QUIZZES IN HER CLASS!
SLOW DEATH BY LEAD POISONING FROM A NUMBER TWO PENCIL IS BETTER THAN THIS.
IF IT WEREN'T FOR LYNN, MY BEST GIRLFRIEND IN SCHOOL, I'D BE IN SO MUCH TROUBLE. LYNN KEEPS ME SANE. EVEN BEFORE WEBCORPS, LYNN WAS OFTEN THE GLUE THAT HELD IT ALL TOGETHER FOR ME.
HMMPH.
IT'S NOT LIKE SHE HELPS ME CHEAT OR GIVES ME ADVICE ON MY LOVE LIFE--WAIT, WHAT LOVE LIFE?--ANYWAY, SHE'S JUST ALWAYS THERE FOR ME. AND EVEN IF SHE DOESN'T SAY IT, SHE BELIEVES IN ME.
SO, WE STICK UP FOR ONE ANOTHER. WE'RE FAM. IT'S ALL GOOD.
BUT THIS QUIZ ISN'T GOOD. NO, I'M PRETTY SURE IT'S BAD. IF I LOOKED IN THE DICTIONARY UNDER BAD, THIS QUIZ WOULD BE LISTED UNDER SEE ALSO...
TAP
TAP

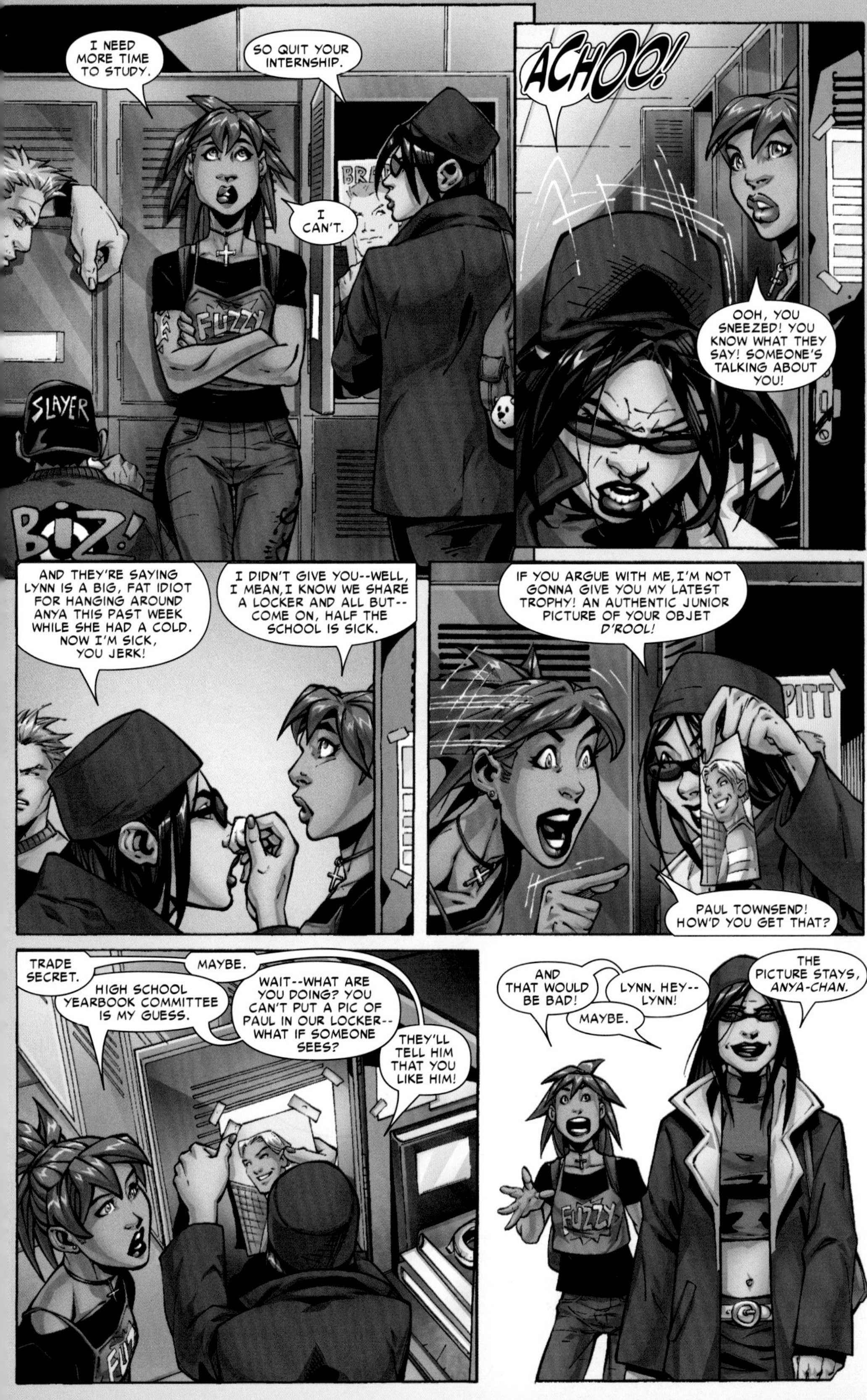
I NEED MORE TIME TO STUDY.
SO QUIT YOUR INTERNSHIP.
I CAN'T.
SLAYER
BIZ!
ACHOO!
OOH, YOU SNEEZED! YOU KNOW WHAT THEY SAY! SOMEONE'S TALKING ABOUT YOU!
AND THEY'RE SAYING LYNN IS A BIG, FAT IDIOT FOR HANGING AROUND ANYA THIS PAST WEEK WHILE SHE HAD A COLD. NOW I'M SICK, YOU JERK!
I DIDN'T GIVE YOU--WELL, I MEAN, I KNOW WE SHARE A LOCKER AND ALL BUT--COME ON, HALF THE SCHOOL IS SICK.
IF YOU ARGUE WITH ME, I'M NOT GONNA GIVE YOU MY LATEST TROPHY! AN AUTHENTIC JUNIOR PICTURE OF YOUR OBJET *D'ROOL!*
PITT
PAUL TOWNSEND! HOW'D YOU GET THAT?
TRADE SECRET.
MAYBE.
HIGH SCHOOL YEARBOOK COMMITTEE IS MY GUESS.
WAIT--WHAT ARE YOU DOING? YOU CAN'T PUT A PIC OF PAUL IN OUR LOCKER--WHAT IF SOMEONE SEES?
THEY'LL TELL HIM THAT YOU LIKE HIM!
AND THAT WOULD BE BAD!
LYNN. HEY--LYNN!
MAYBE.
THE PICTURE STAYS, *ANYA-CHAN.*

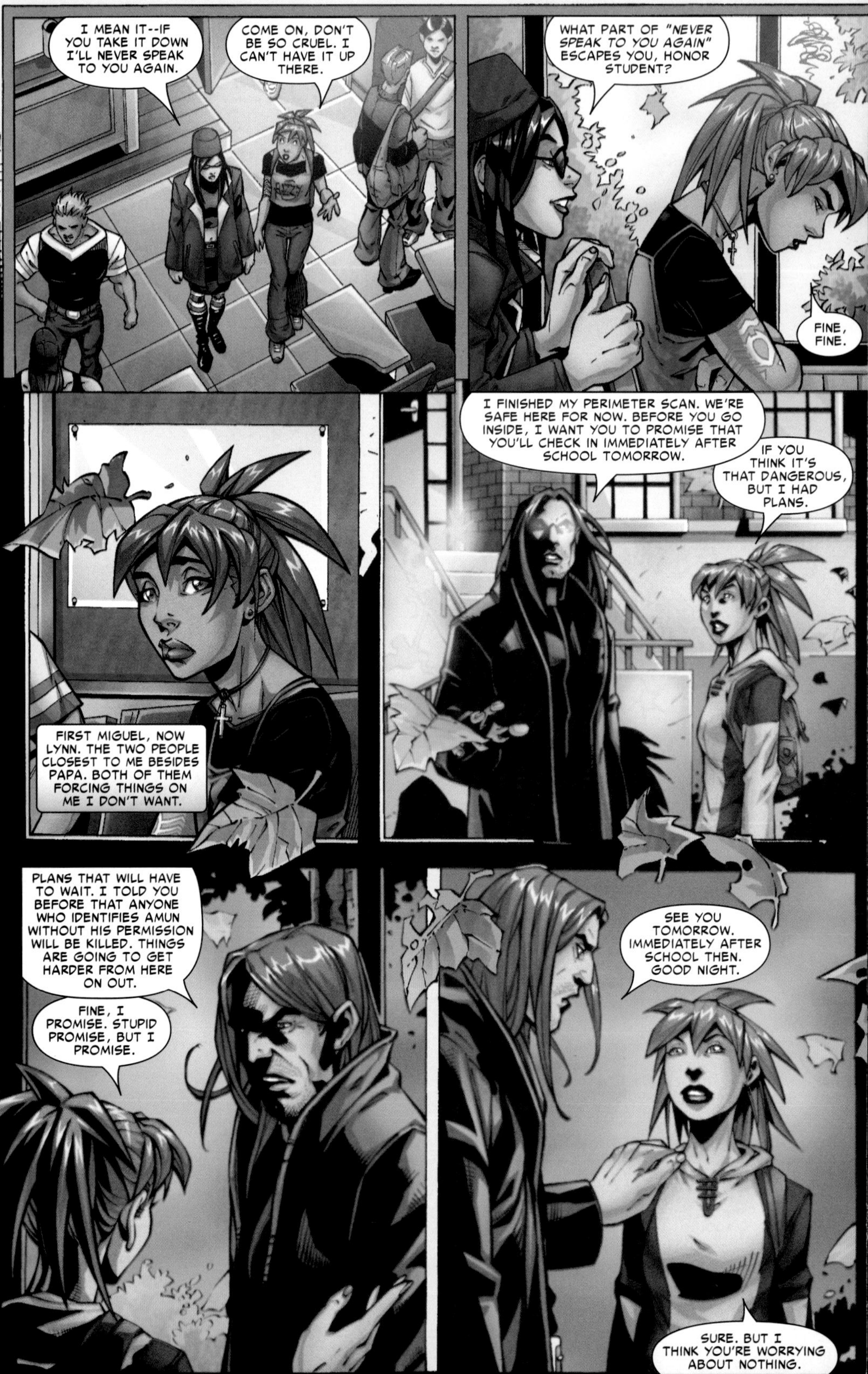
I MEAN IT--IF YOU TAKE IT DOWN I'LL NEVER SPEAK TO YOU AGAIN.
COME ON, DON'T BE SO CRUEL. I CAN'T HAVE IT UP THERE.
WHAT PART OF "NEVER SPEAK TO YOU AGAIN" ESCAPES YOU, HONOR STUDENT?
FINE, FINE.
FIRST MIGUEL, NOW LYNN. THE TWO PEOPLE CLOSEST TO ME BESIDES PAPA. BOTH OF THEM FORCING THINGS ON ME I DON'T WANT.
I FINISHED MY PERIMETER SCAN. WE'RE SAFE HERE FOR NOW. BEFORE YOU GO INSIDE, I WANT YOU TO PROMISE THAT YOU'LL CHECK IN IMMEDIATELY AFTER SCHOOL TOMORROW.
IF YOU THINK IT'S THAT DANGEROUS, BUT I HAD PLANS.
PLANS THAT WILL HAVE TO WAIT. I TOLD YOU BEFORE THAT ANYONE WHO IDENTIFIES AMUN WITHOUT HIS PERMISSION WILL BE KILLED. THINGS ARE GOING TO GET HARDER FROM HERE ON OUT.
FINE, I PROMISE. STUPID PROMISE, BUT I PROMISE.
SEE YOU TOMORROW. IMMEDIATELY AFTER SCHOOL THEN. GOOD NIGHT.
SURE. BUT I THINK YOU'RE WORRYING ABOUT NOTHING.

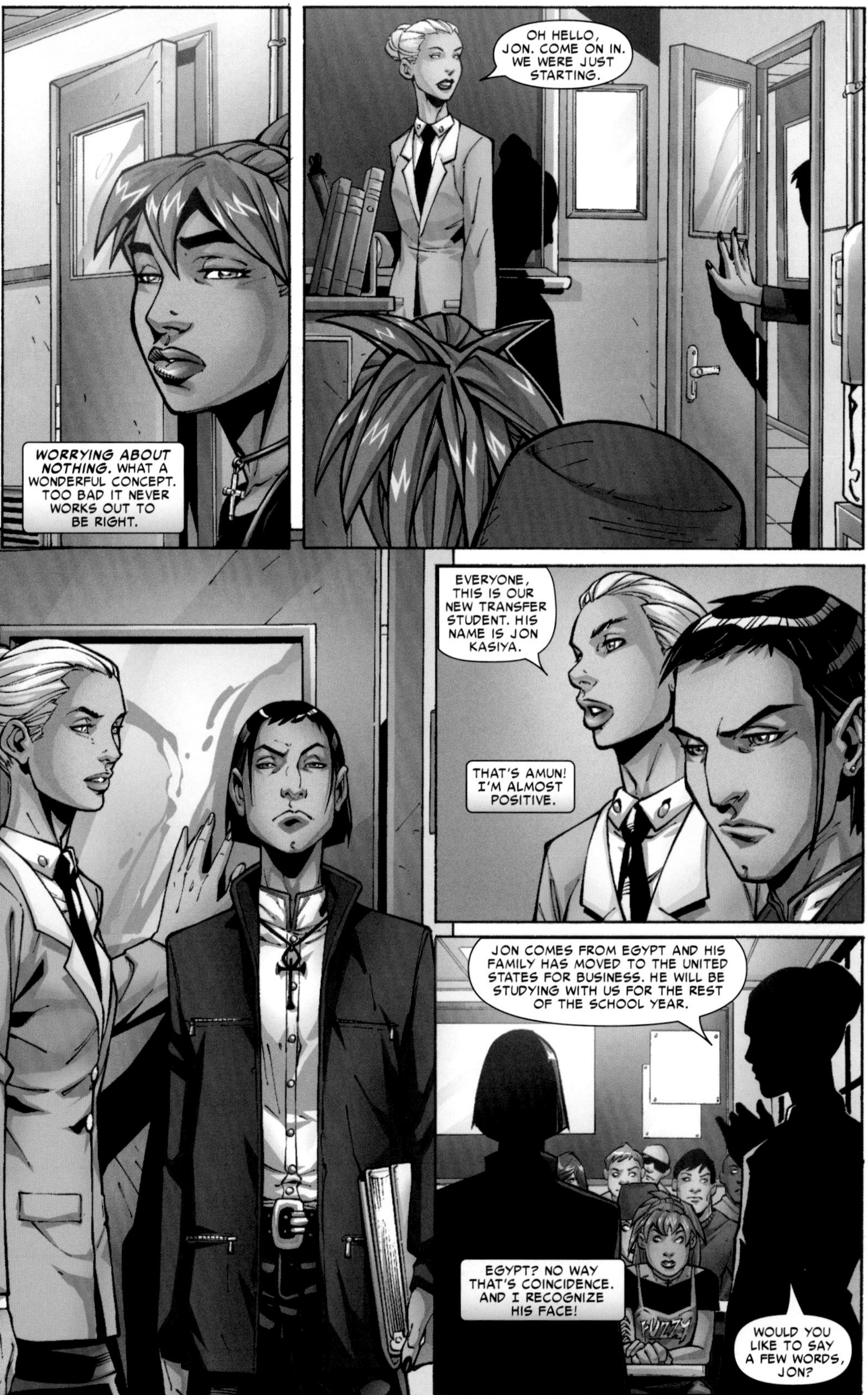
WORRYING ABOUT NOTHING. WHAT A WONDERFUL CONCEPT. TOO BAD IT NEVER WORKS OUT TO BE RIGHT.
OH HELLO, JON. COME ON IN. WE WERE JUST STARTING.
EVERYONE, THIS IS OUR NEW TRANSFER STUDENT. HIS NAME IS JON KASIYA.
THAT'S AMUN! I'M ALMOST POSITIVE.
JON COMES FROM EGYPT AND HIS FAMILY HAS MOVED TO THE UNITED STATES FOR BUSINESS. HE WILL BE STUDYING WITH US FOR THE REST OF THE SCHOOL YEAR.
EGYPT? NO WAY THAT'S COINCIDENCE. AND I RECOGNIZE HIS FACE!
WOULD YOU LIKE TO SAY A FEW WORDS, JON?

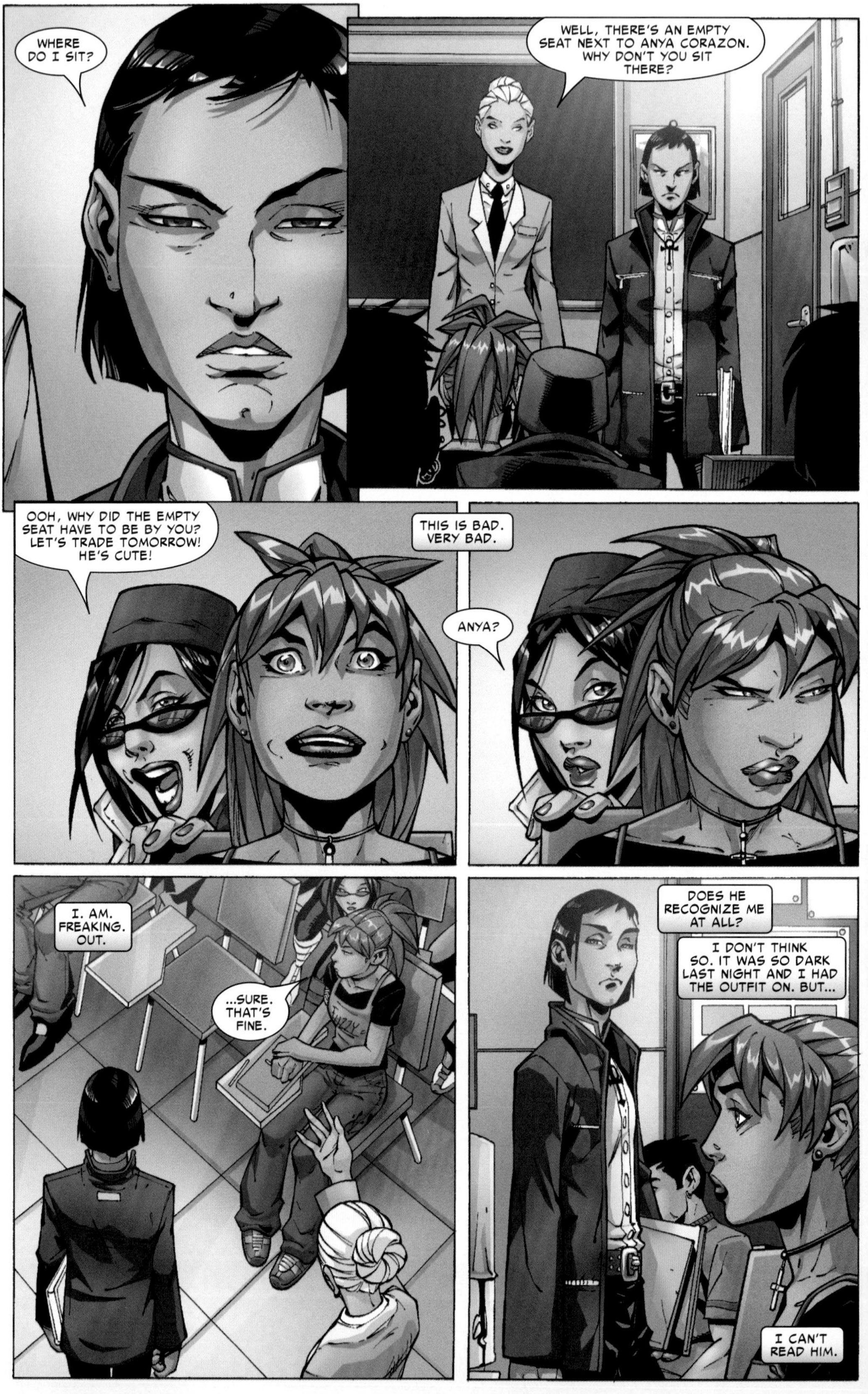
WHERE DO I SIT?
WELL, THERE'S AN EMPTY SEAT NEXT TO ANYA CORAZON. WHY DON'T YOU SIT THERE?
OOH, WHY DID THE EMPTY SEAT HAVE TO BE BY YOU? LET'S TRADE TOMORROW! HE'S CUTE!
THIS IS BAD. VERY BAD.
ANYA?
I. AM. FREAKING. OUT.
...SURE. THAT'S FINE.
DOES HE RECOGNIZE ME AT ALL?
I DON'T THINK SO. IT WAS SO DARK LAST NIGHT AND I HAD THE OUTFIT ON. BUT...
I CAN'T READ HIM.

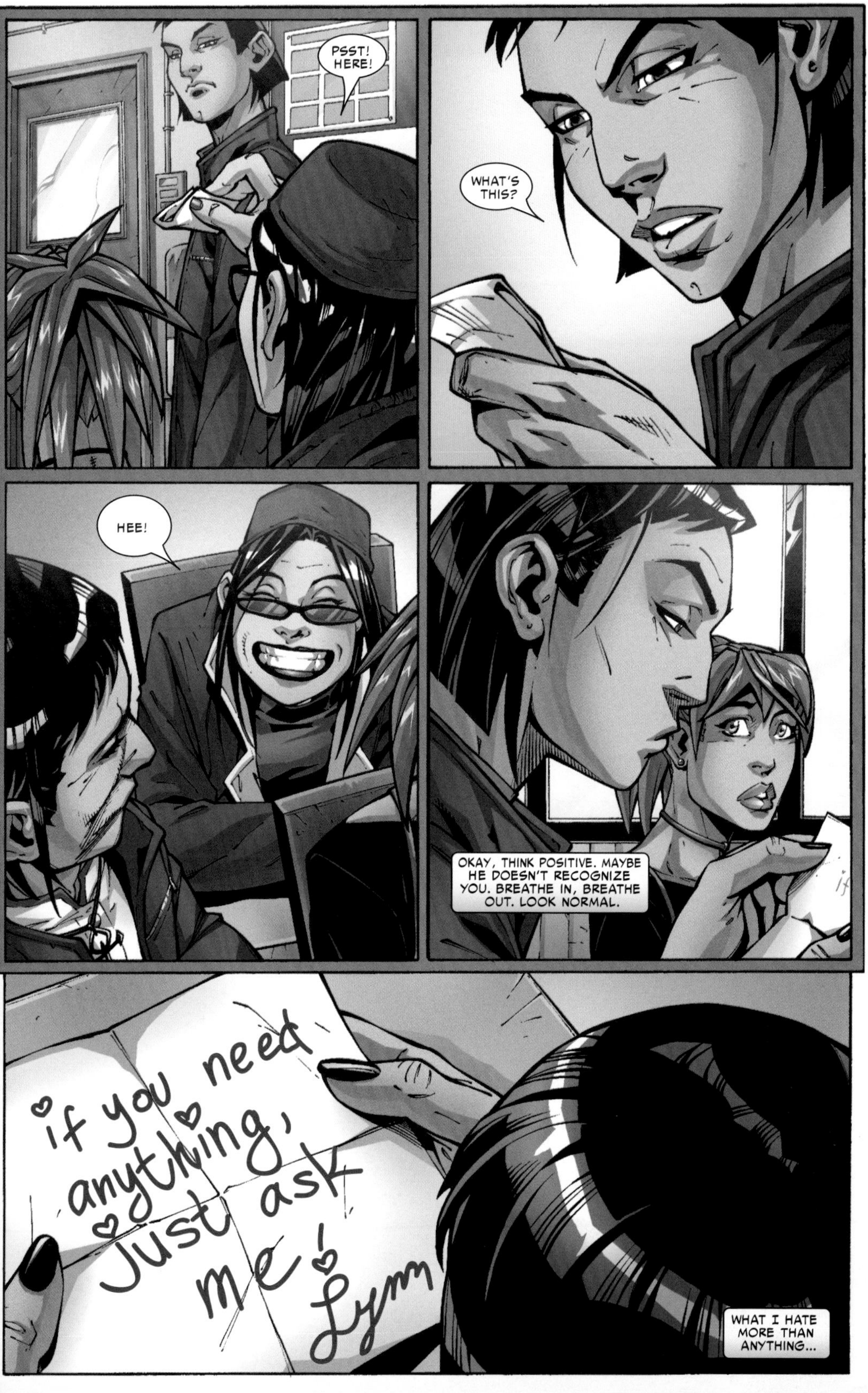
PSST! HERE!
WHAT'S THIS?
HEE!
OKAY, THINK POSITIVE. MAYBE HE DOESN'T RECOGNIZE YOU. BREATHE IN, BREATHE OUT. LOOK NORMAL.
if you need anything, just ask me! Lynn
WHAT I HATE MORE THAN ANYTHING...

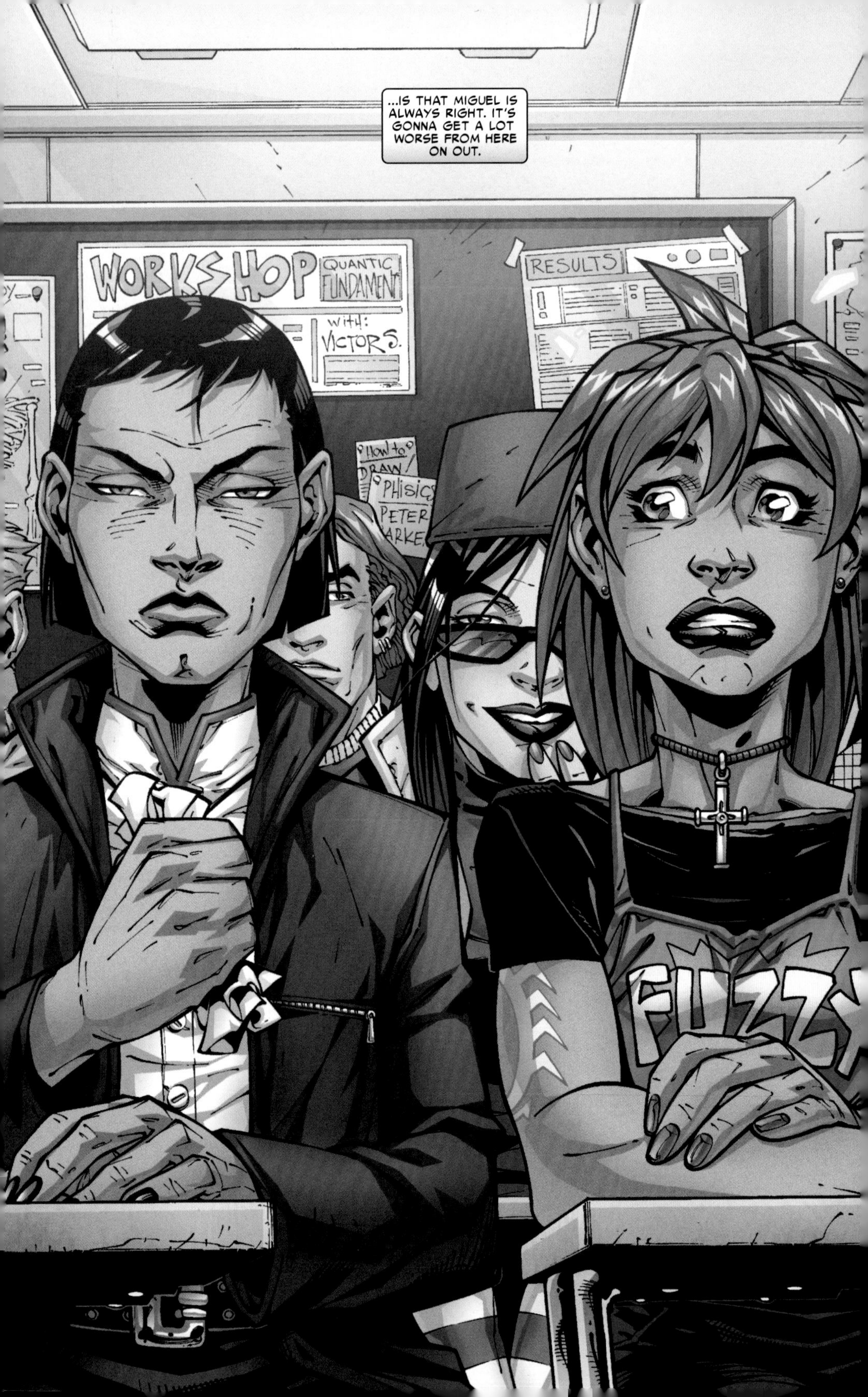
...IS THAT MIGUEL IS ALWAYS RIGHT. IT'S GONNA GET A LOT WORSE FROM HERE ON OUT.
WORKSHOP
QUANTIC FUNDAMENT
with: VICTOR S.
RESULTS
How to DRAW
PHISICS
PETER

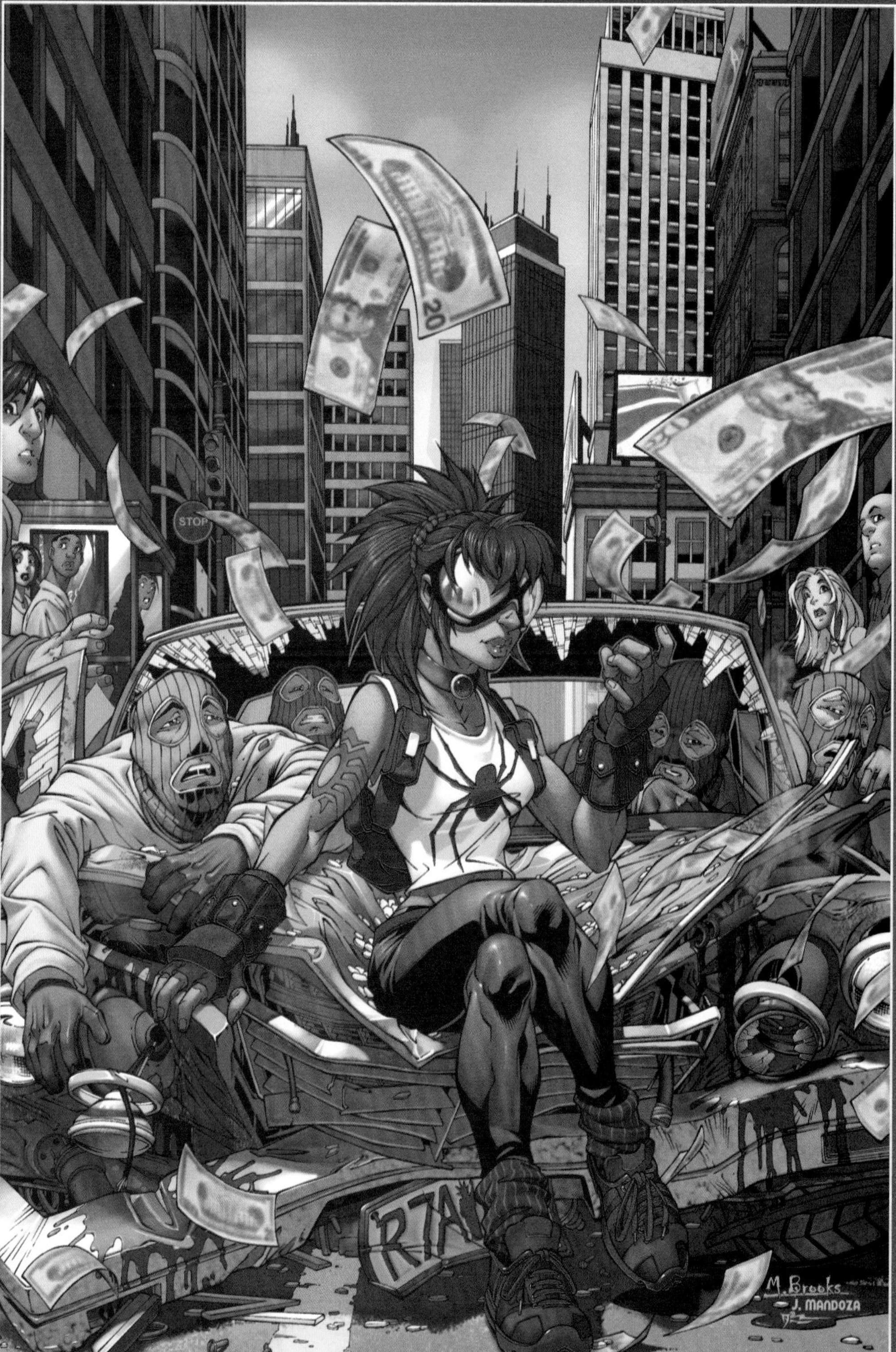

STOP
20
RZA
M. Brooks
J. MANDOZA

ARAÑA #3

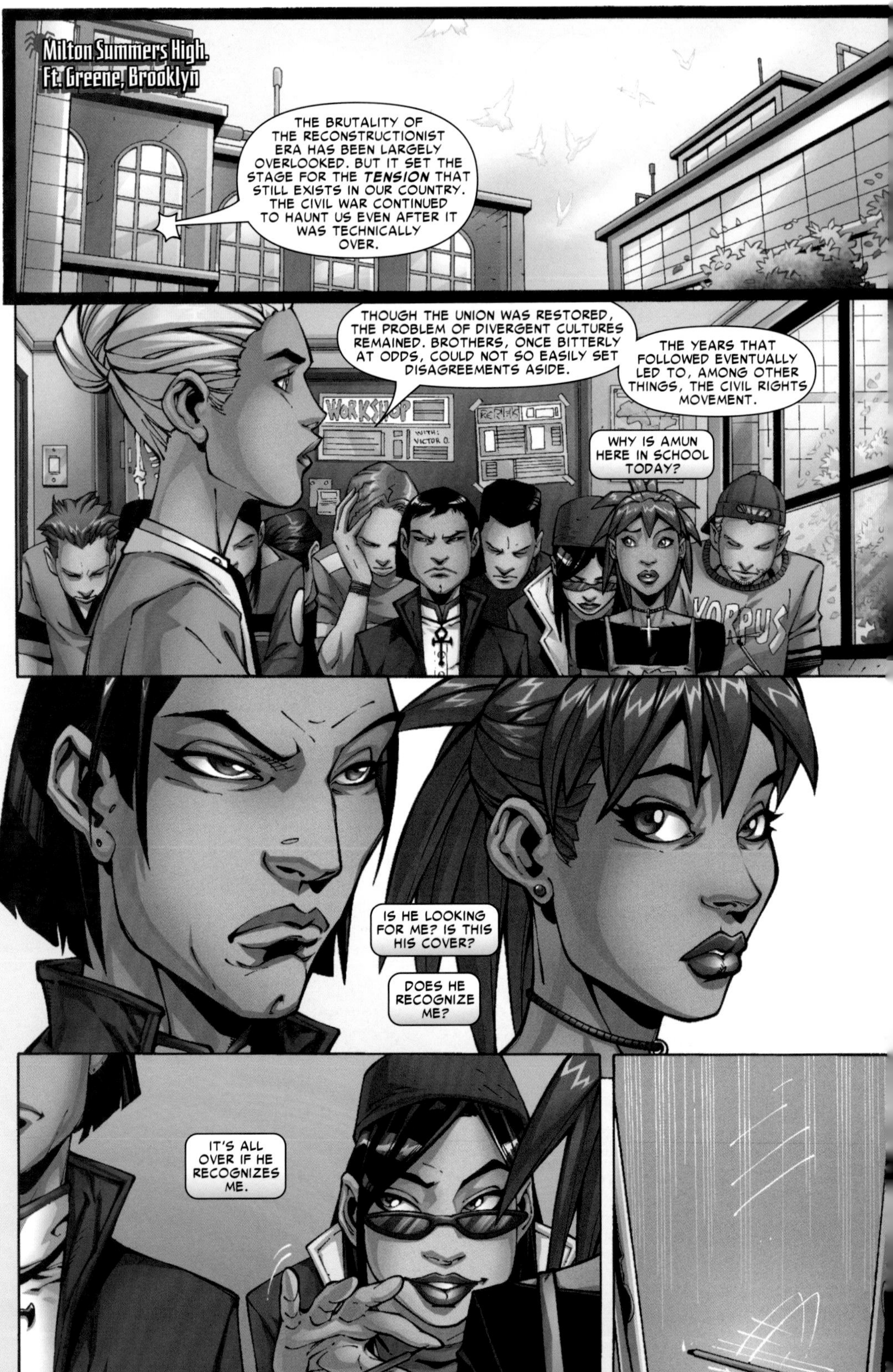
Milton Summers High. Ft. Greene, Brooklyn
THE BRUTALITY OF THE RECONSTRUCTIONIST ERA HAS BEEN LARGELY OVERLOOKED. BUT IT SET THE STAGE FOR THE TENSION THAT STILL EXISTS IN OUR COUNTRY. THE CIVIL WAR CONTINUED TO HAUNT US EVEN AFTER IT WAS TECHNICALLY OVER.
THOUGH THE UNION WAS RESTORED, THE PROBLEM OF DIVERGENT CULTURES REMAINED. BROTHERS, ONCE BITTERLY AT ODDS, COULD NOT SO EASILY SET DISAGREEMENTS ASIDE.
THE YEARS THAT FOLLOWED EVENTUALLY LED TO, AMONG OTHER THINGS, THE CIVIL RIGHTS MOVEMENT.
WORKSHOP
WITH: VICTOR O.
WHY IS AMUN HERE IN SCHOOL TODAY?
IS HE LOOKING FOR ME? IS THIS HIS COVER?
DOES HE RECOGNIZE ME?
IT'S ALL OVER IF HE RECOGNIZES ME.

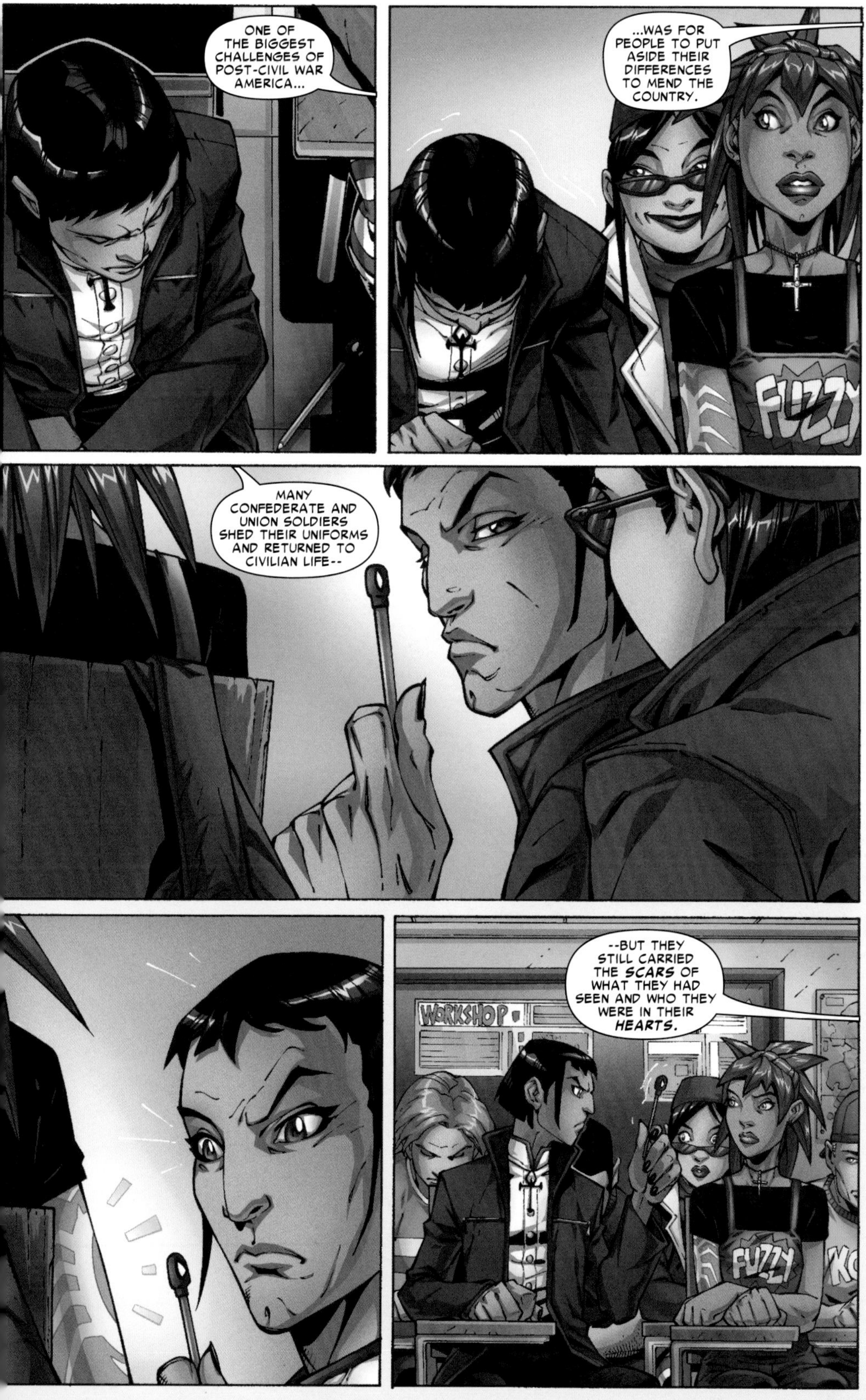
ONE OF THE BIGGEST CHALLENGES OF POST-CIVIL WAR AMERICA...
...WAS FOR PEOPLE TO PUT ASIDE THEIR DIFFERENCES TO MEND THE COUNTRY.
FUZZY
MANY CONFEDERATE AND UNION SOLDIERS SHED THEIR UNIFORMS AND RETURNED TO CIVILIAN LIFE--
--BUT THEY STILL CARRIED THE SCARS OF WHAT THEY HAD SEEN AND WHO THEY WERE IN THEIR HEARTS.
WORKSHOP
FUZZY

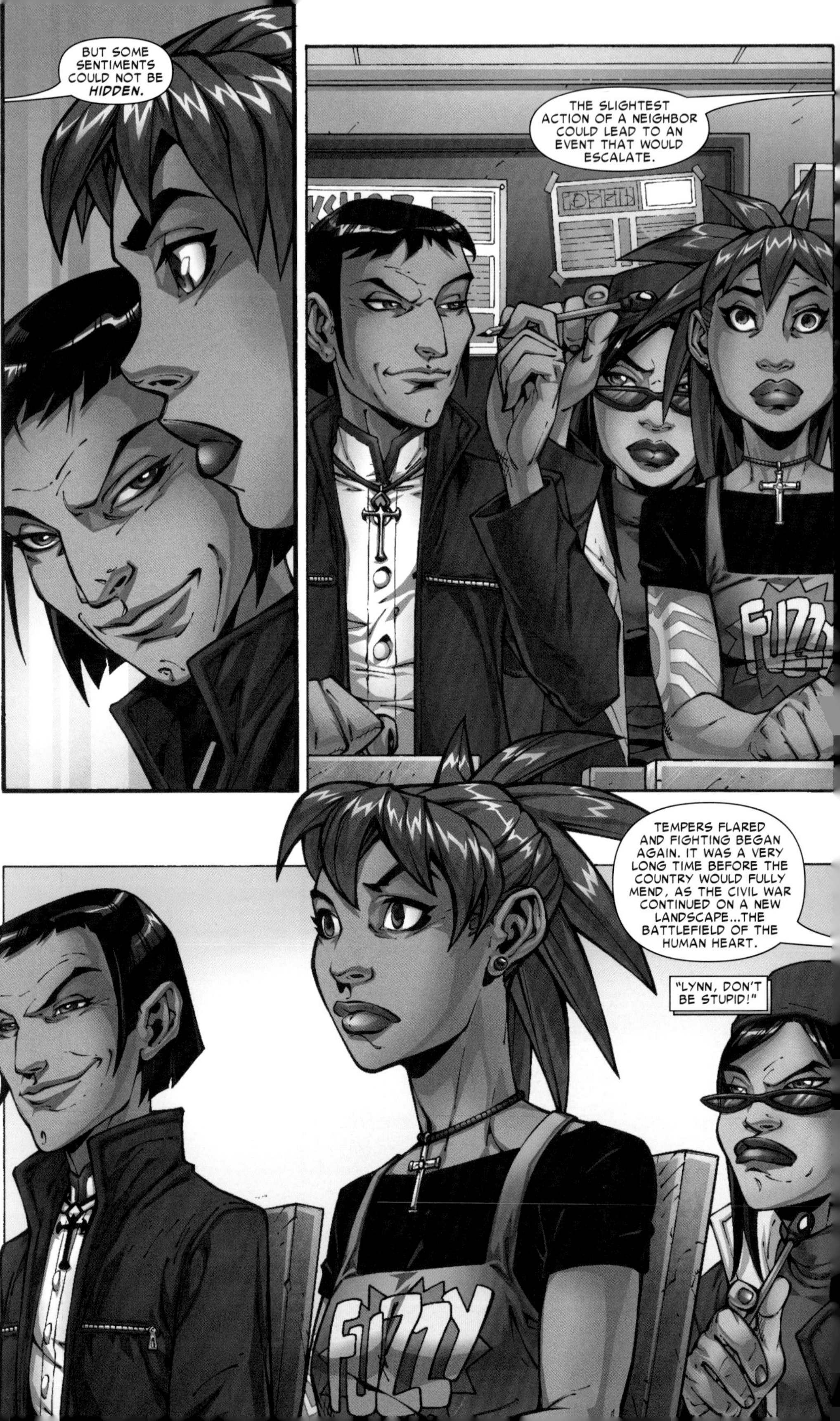
BUT SOME SENTIMENTS COULD NOT BE *HIDDEN.*
THE SLIGHTEST ACTION OF A NEIGHBOR COULD LEAD TO AN EVENT THAT WOULD ESCALATE.
TEMPERS FLARED AND FIGHTING BEGAN AGAIN. IT WAS A VERY LONG TIME BEFORE THE COUNTRY WOULD FULLY MEND, AS THE CIVIL WAR CONTINUED ON A NEW LANDSCAPE...THE BATTLEFIELD OF THE HUMAN HEART.
"LYNN, DON'T BE STUPID!"
FIZZY

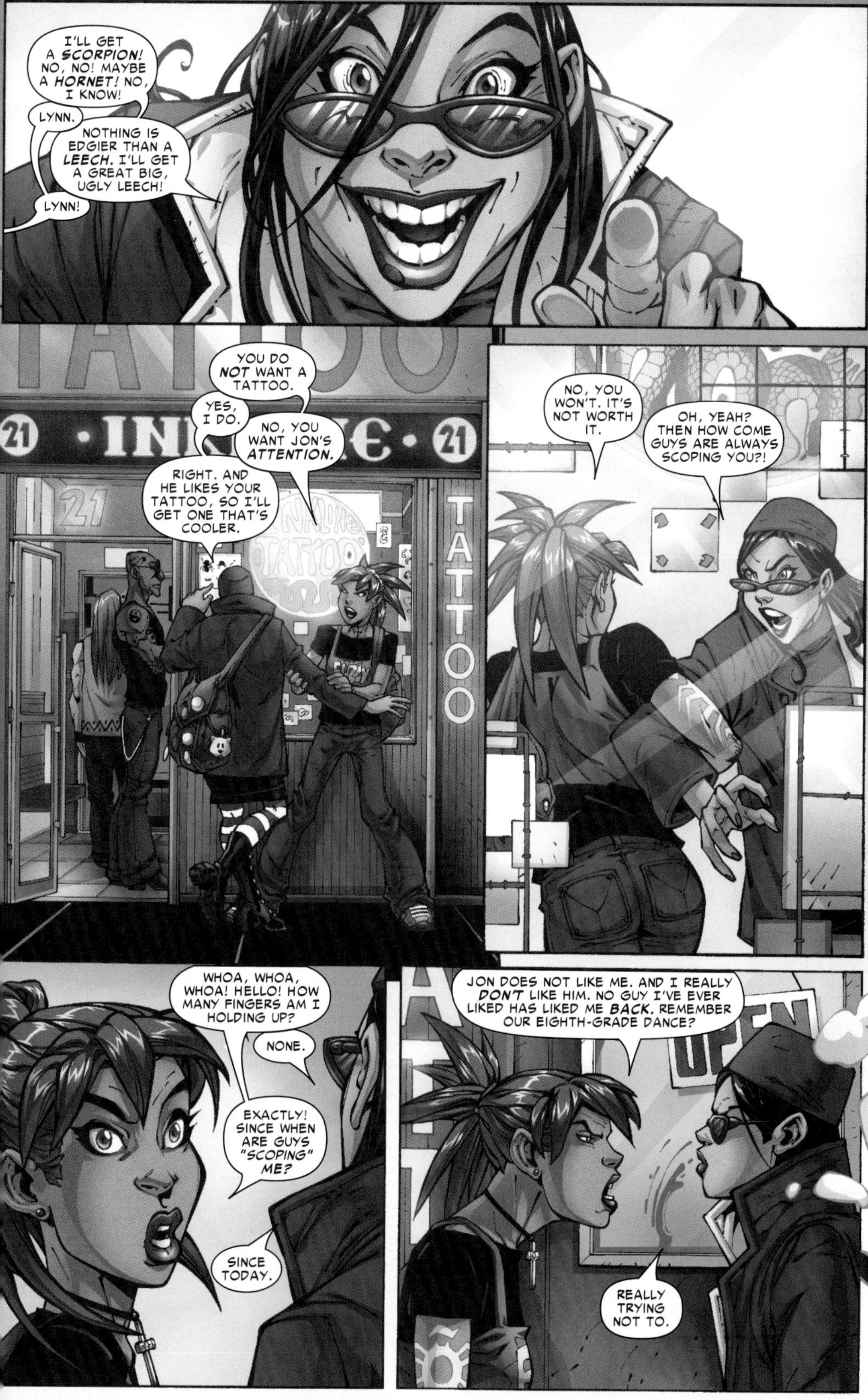
I'LL GET A *SCORPION!* NO, NO! MAYBE A *HORNET!* NO, I KNOW!
LYNN.
NOTHING IS EDGIER THAN A *LEECH.* I'LL GET A GREAT BIG, UGLY LEECH!
LYNN!
TATTOO
21 · INKLINE · 21
YOU DO *NOT* WANT A TATTOO.
YES, I DO.
NO, YOU WANT JON'S *ATTENTION.*
RIGHT. AND HE LIKES YOUR TATTOO, SO I'LL GET ONE THAT'S COOLER.
TATTOO
NO, YOU WON'T. IT'S NOT WORTH IT.
OH, YEAH? THEN HOW COME GUYS ARE ALWAYS SCOPING YOU?!
WHOA, WHOA, WHOA! HELLO! HOW MANY FINGERS AM I HOLDING UP?
NONE.
EXACTLY! SINCE WHEN ARE GUYS *"SCOPING" ME?*
SINCE TODAY.
JON DOES NOT LIKE ME. AND I REALLY *DON'T* LIKE HIM. NO GUY I'VE EVER LIKED HAS LIKED ME *BACK.* REMEMBER OUR EIGHTH-GRADE DANCE?
REALLY TRYING NOT TO.

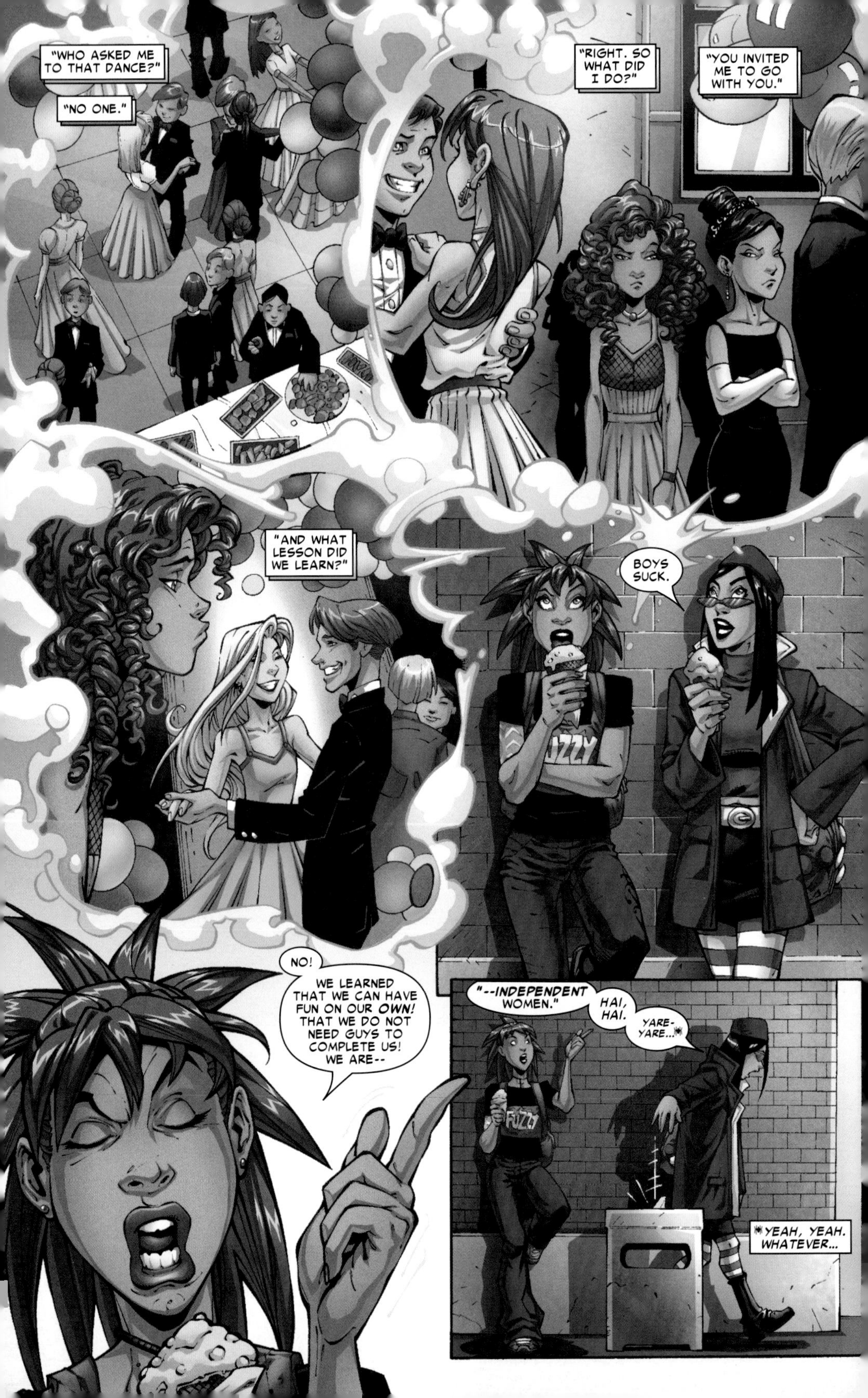
"WHO ASKED ME TO THAT DANCE?"
"NO ONE."
"RIGHT. SO WHAT DID I DO?"
"YOU INVITED ME TO GO WITH YOU."
"AND WHAT LESSON DID WE LEARN?"
BOYS SUCK.
NO!
WE LEARNED THAT WE CAN HAVE FUN ON OUR OWN! THAT WE DO NOT NEED GUYS TO COMPLETE US! WE ARE--
"--INDEPENDENT WOMEN."
HAI, HAI.
YARE-YARE...
YEAH, YEAH. WHATEVER...

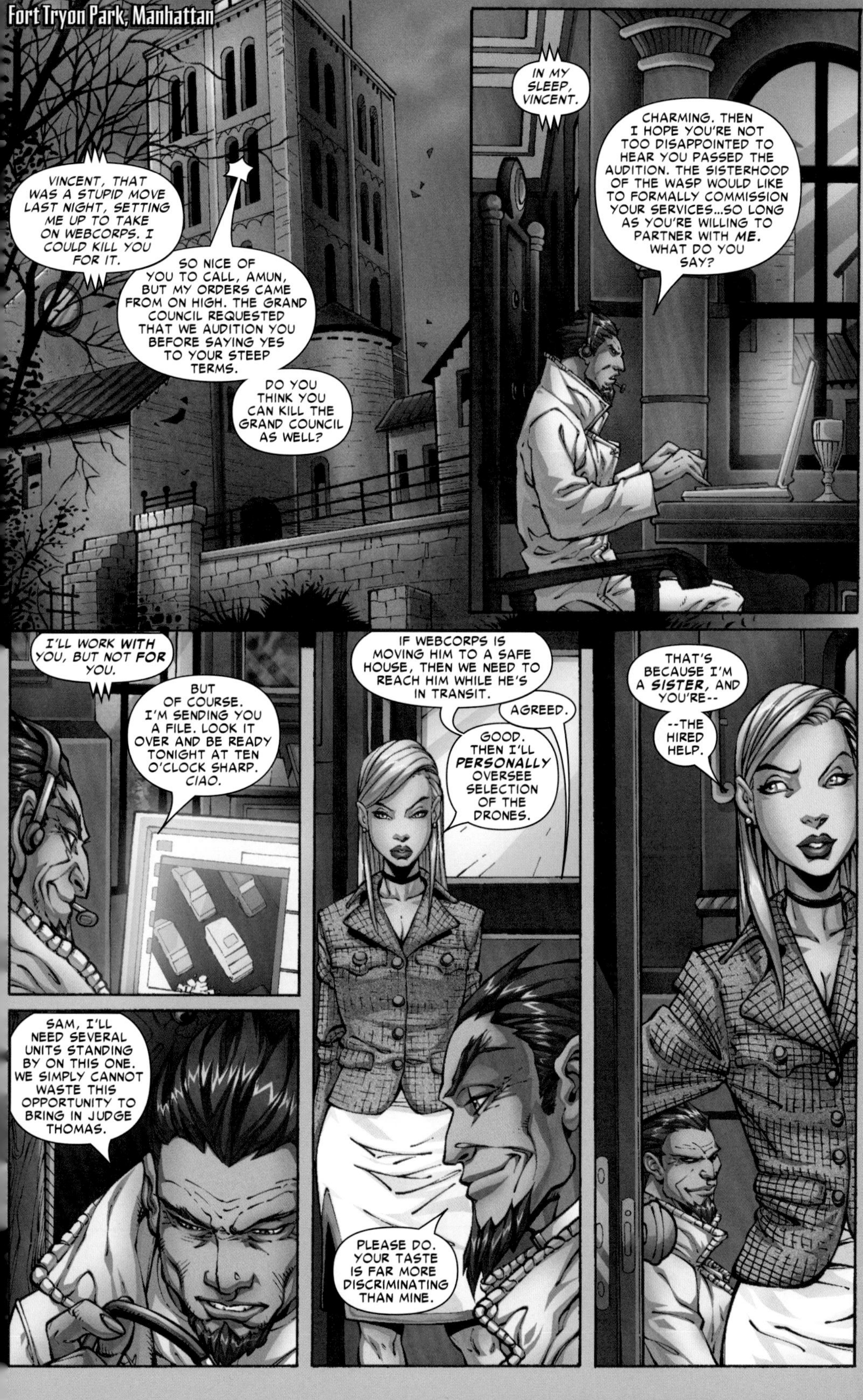
Fort Tryon Park, Manhattan
VINCENT, THAT WAS A STUPID MOVE LAST NIGHT, SETTING ME UP TO TAKE ON WEBCORPS. I COULD KILL YOU FOR IT.
SO NICE OF YOU TO CALL, AMUN, BUT MY ORDERS CAME FROM ON HIGH. THE GRAND COUNCIL REQUESTED THAT WE AUDITION YOU BEFORE SAYING YES TO YOUR STEEP TERMS.
DO YOU THINK YOU CAN KILL THE GRAND COUNCIL AS WELL?
IN MY SLEEP, VINCENT.
CHARMING. THEN I HOPE YOU'RE NOT TOO DISAPPOINTED TO HEAR YOU PASSED THE AUDITION. THE SISTERHOOD OF THE WASP WOULD LIKE TO FORMALLY COMMISSION YOUR SERVICES...SO LONG AS YOU'RE WILLING TO PARTNER WITH ME. WHAT DO YOU SAY?
I'LL WORK WITH YOU, BUT NOT FOR YOU.
BUT OF COURSE. I'M SENDING YOU A FILE. LOOK IT OVER AND BE READY TONIGHT AT TEN O'CLOCK SHARP. CIAO.
SAM, I'LL NEED SEVERAL UNITS STANDING BY ON THIS ONE. WE SIMPLY CANNOT WASTE THIS OPPORTUNITY TO BRING IN JUDGE THOMAS.
IF WEBCORPS IS MOVING HIM TO A SAFE HOUSE, THEN WE NEED TO REACH HIM WHILE HE'S IN TRANSIT.
AGREED.
GOOD. THEN I'LL PERSONALLY OVERSEE SELECTION OF THE DRONES.
PLEASE DO. YOUR TASTE IS FAR MORE DISCRIMINATING THAN MINE.
THAT'S BECAUSE I'M A SISTER, AND YOU'RE--
--THE HIRED HELP.

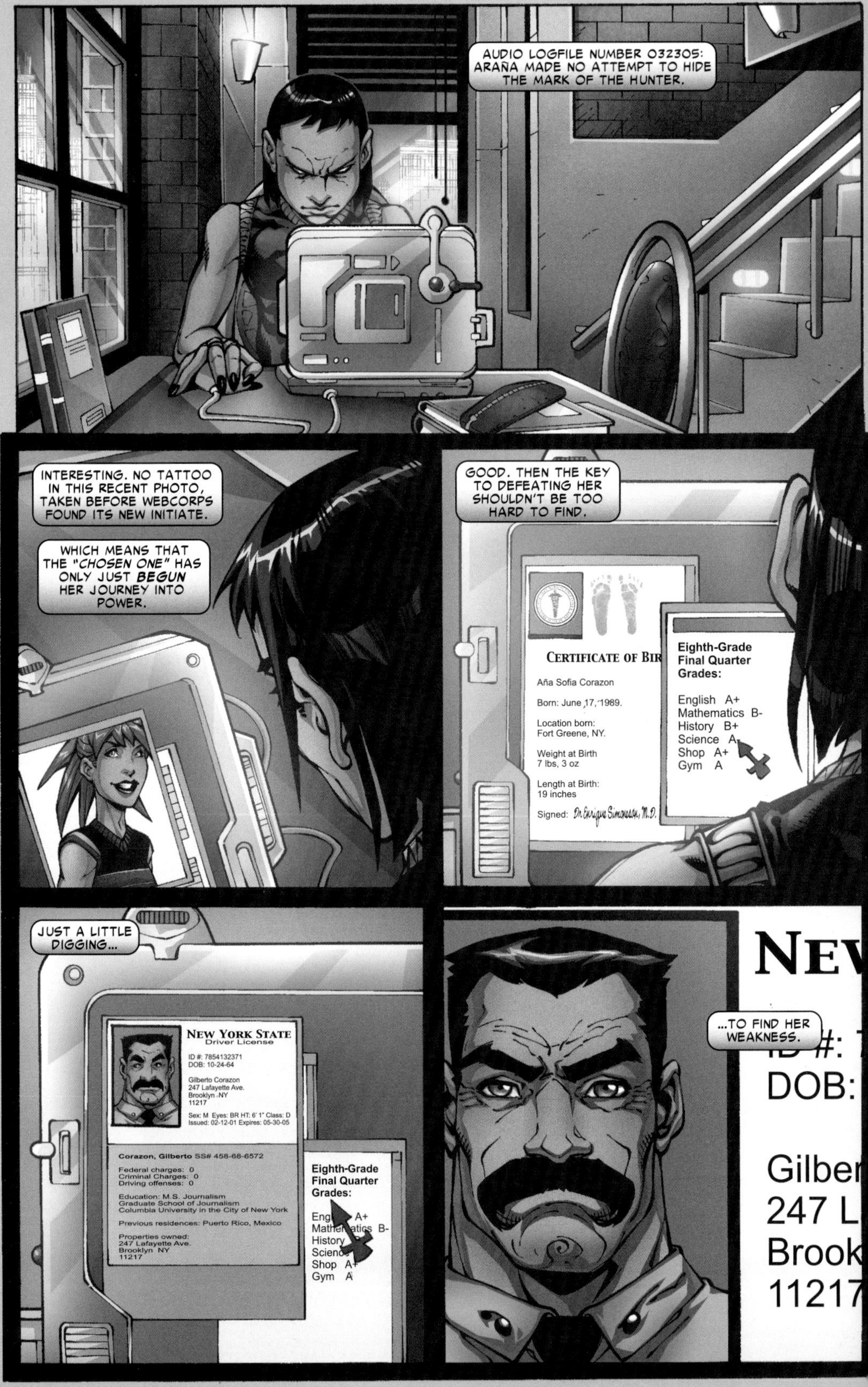
AUDIO LOGFILE NUMBER 032305: ARAÑA MADE NO ATTEMPT TO HIDE THE MARK OF THE HUNTER.
INTERESTING. NO TATTOO IN THIS RECENT PHOTO, TAKEN BEFORE WEBCORPS FOUND ITS NEW INITIATE.
WHICH MEANS THAT THE "CHOSEN ONE" HAS ONLY JUST BEGUN HER JOURNEY INTO POWER.
GOOD. THEN THE KEY TO DEFEATING HER SHOULDN'T BE TOO HARD TO FIND.
CERTIFICATE OF BIR
Aña Sofia Corazon
Born: June 17, 1989.
Location born: Fort Greene, NY.
Weight at Birth 7 lbs, 3 oz
Length at Birth: 19 inches
Signed: Dr. Enrique Simonsson, M.D.
Eighth-Grade Final Quarter Grades:
English A+
Mathematics B-
History B+
Science A
Shop A+
Gym A
JUST A LITTLE DIGGING...
NEW YORK STATE Driver License
ID #: 7854132371
DOB: 10-24-64
Gilberto Corazon
247 Lafayette Ave.
Brooklyn NY
11217
Sex: M Eyes: BR HT: 6' 1" Class: D
Issued: 02-12-01 Expires: 05-30-05
Corazon, Gilberto SS# 458-68-6572
Federal charges: 0
Criminal Charges: 0
Driving offenses: 0
Education: M.S. Journalism
Graduate School of Journalism
Columbia University in the City of New York
Previous residences: Puerto Rico, Mexico
Properties owned:
247 Lafayette Ave.
Brooklyn NY
11217
...TO FIND HER WEAKNESS.

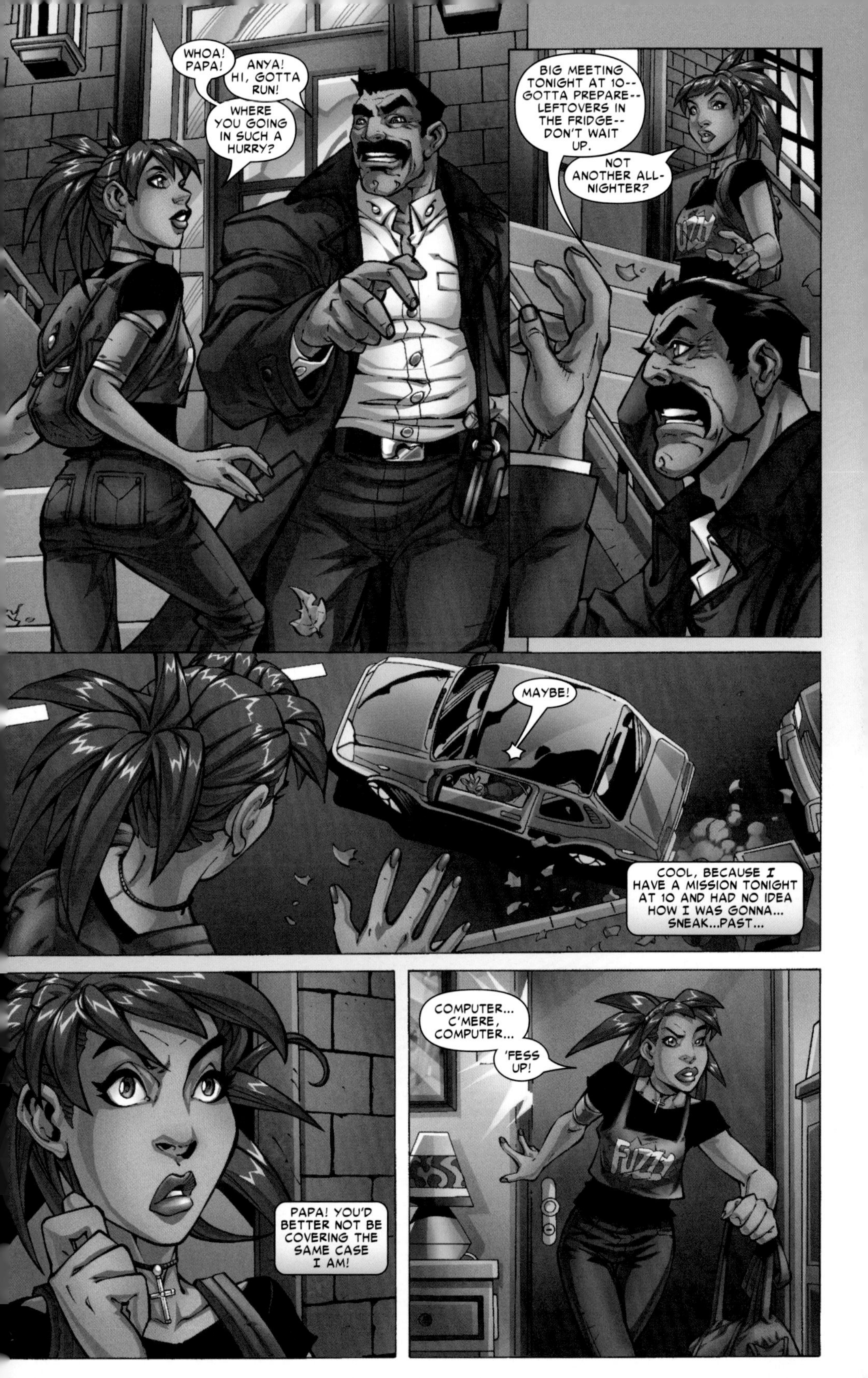
WHOA! PAPA!
ANYA! HI, GOTTA RUN!
WHERE YOU GOING IN SUCH A HURRY?
BIG MEETING TONIGHT AT 10-- GOTTA PREPARE-- LEFTOVERS IN THE FRIDGE-- DON'T WAIT UP.
NOT ANOTHER ALL-NIGHTER?
MAYBE!
COOL, BECAUSE I HAVE A MISSION TONIGHT AT 10 AND HAD NO IDEA HOW I WAS GONNA... SNEAK...PAST...
PAPA! YOU'D BETTER NOT BE COVERING THE SAME CASE I AM!
COMPUTER... C'MERE, COMPUTER...
'FESS UP!
FUZZY

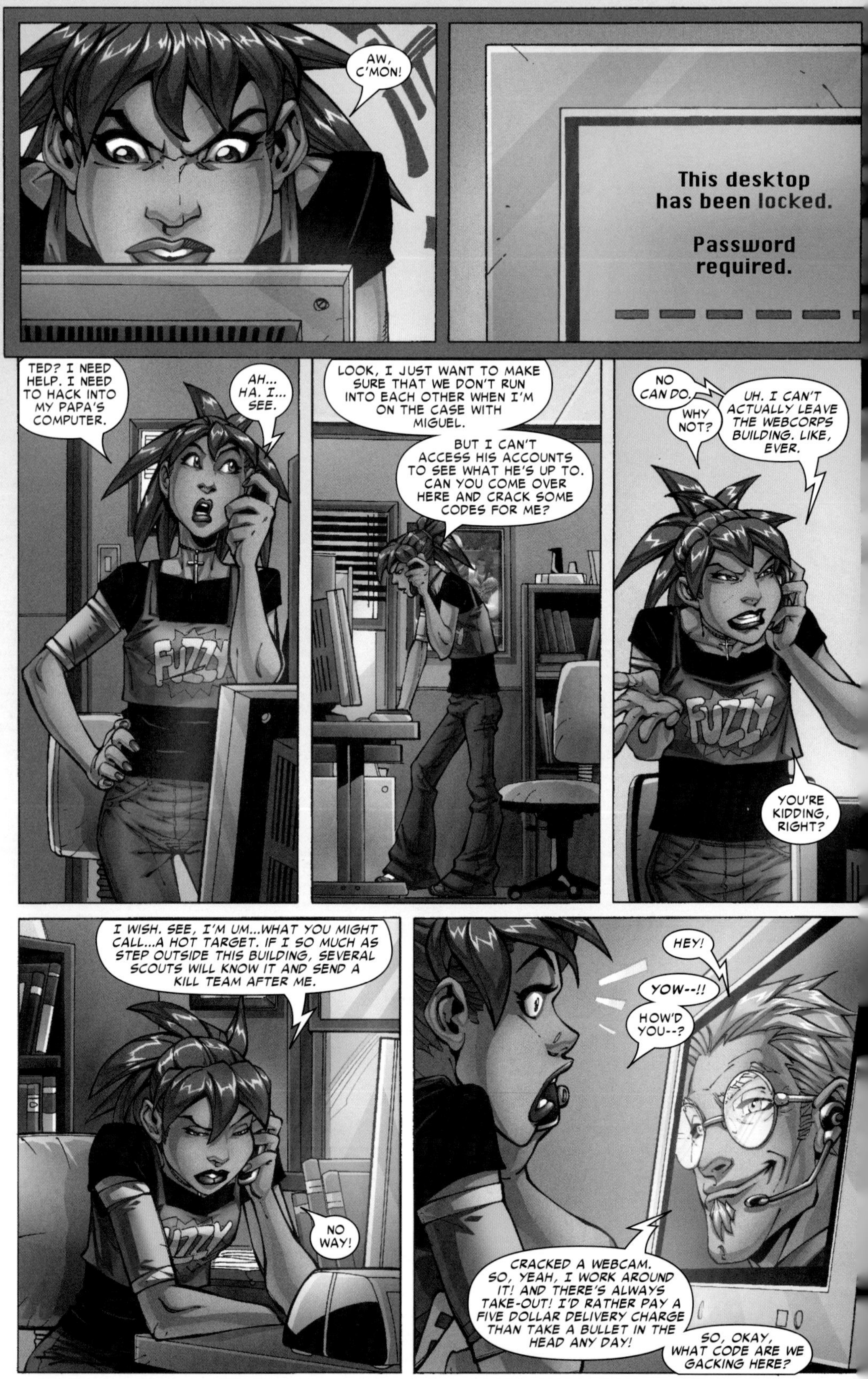
AW, C'MON!
This desktop has been locked.
Password required.
TED? I NEED HELP. I NEED TO HACK INTO MY PAPA'S COMPUTER.
AH... HA. I... SEE.
LOOK, I JUST WANT TO MAKE SURE THAT WE DON'T RUN INTO EACH OTHER WHEN I'M ON THE CASE WITH MIGUEL.
BUT I CAN'T ACCESS HIS ACCOUNTS TO SEE WHAT HE'S UP TO. CAN YOU COME OVER HERE AND CRACK SOME CODES FOR ME?
NO CAN DO.
WHY NOT?
UH. I CAN'T ACTUALLY LEAVE THE WEBCORPS BUILDING. LIKE, EVER.
YOU'RE KIDDING, RIGHT?
I WISH. SEE, I'M UM...WHAT YOU MIGHT CALL...A HOT TARGET. IF I SO MUCH AS STEP OUTSIDE THIS BUILDING, SEVERAL SCOUTS WILL KNOW IT AND SEND A KILL TEAM AFTER ME.
NO WAY!
HEY!
YOW--!!
HOW'D YOU--?
CRACKED A WEBCAM. SO, YEAH, I WORK AROUND IT! AND THERE'S ALWAYS TAKE-OUT! I'D RATHER PAY A FIVE DOLLAR DELIVERY CHARGE THAN TAKE A BULLET IN THE HEAD ANY DAY!
SO, OKAY, WHAT CODE ARE WE GACKING HERE?

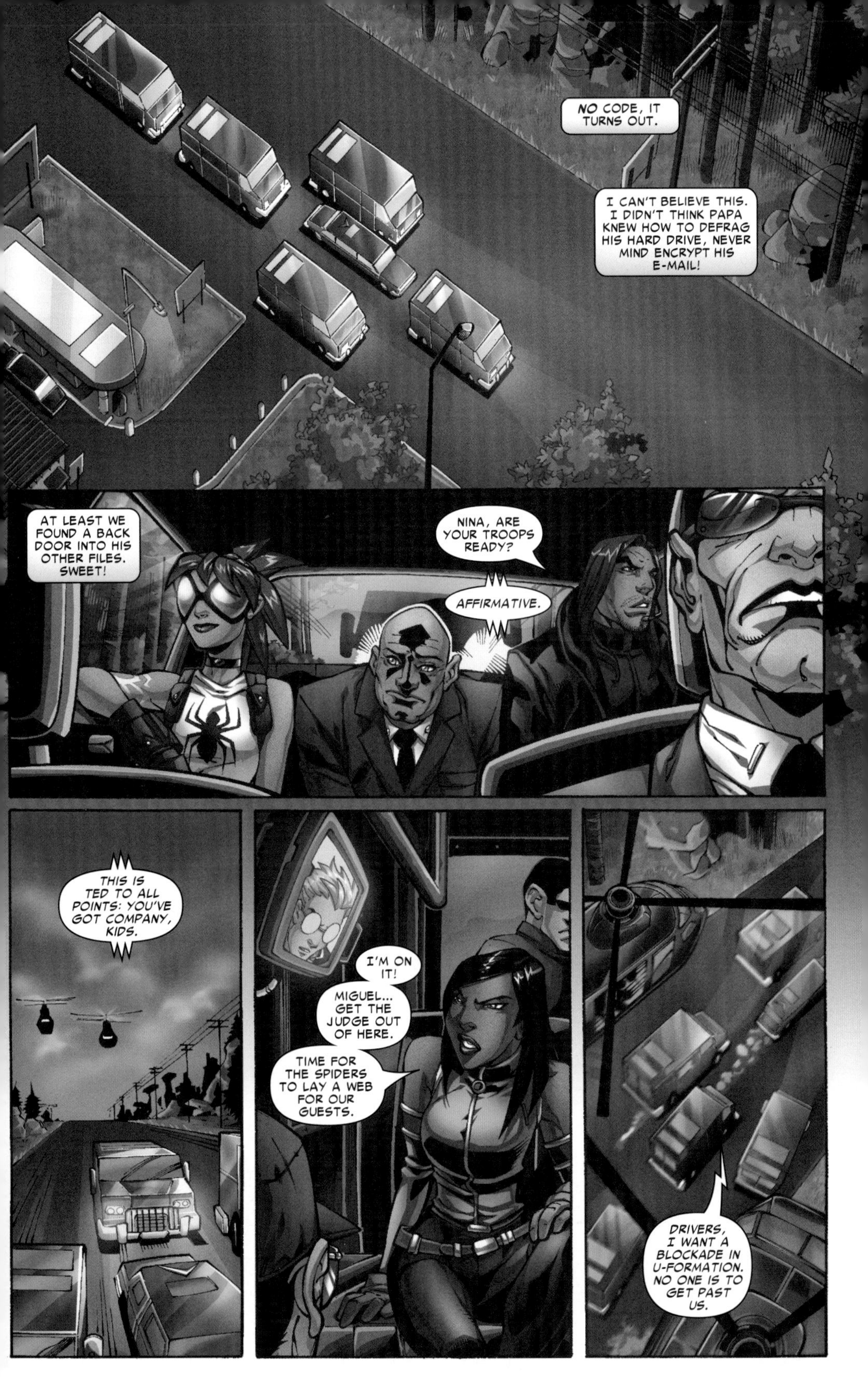
NO CODE, IT TURNS OUT.
I CAN'T BELIEVE THIS. I DIDN'T THINK PAPA KNEW HOW TO DEFRAG HIS HARD DRIVE, NEVER MIND ENCRYPT HIS E-MAIL!
AT LEAST WE FOUND A BACK DOOR INTO HIS OTHER FILES. SWEET!
NINA, ARE YOUR TROOPS READY?
AFFIRMATIVE.
THIS IS TED TO ALL POINTS: YOU'VE GOT COMPANY, KIDS.
I'M ON IT!
MIGUEL... GET THE JUDGE OUT OF HERE.
TIME FOR THE SPIDERS TO LAY A WEB FOR OUR GUESTS.
DRIVERS, I WANT A BLOCKADE IN U-FORMATION. NO ONE IS TO GET PAST US.

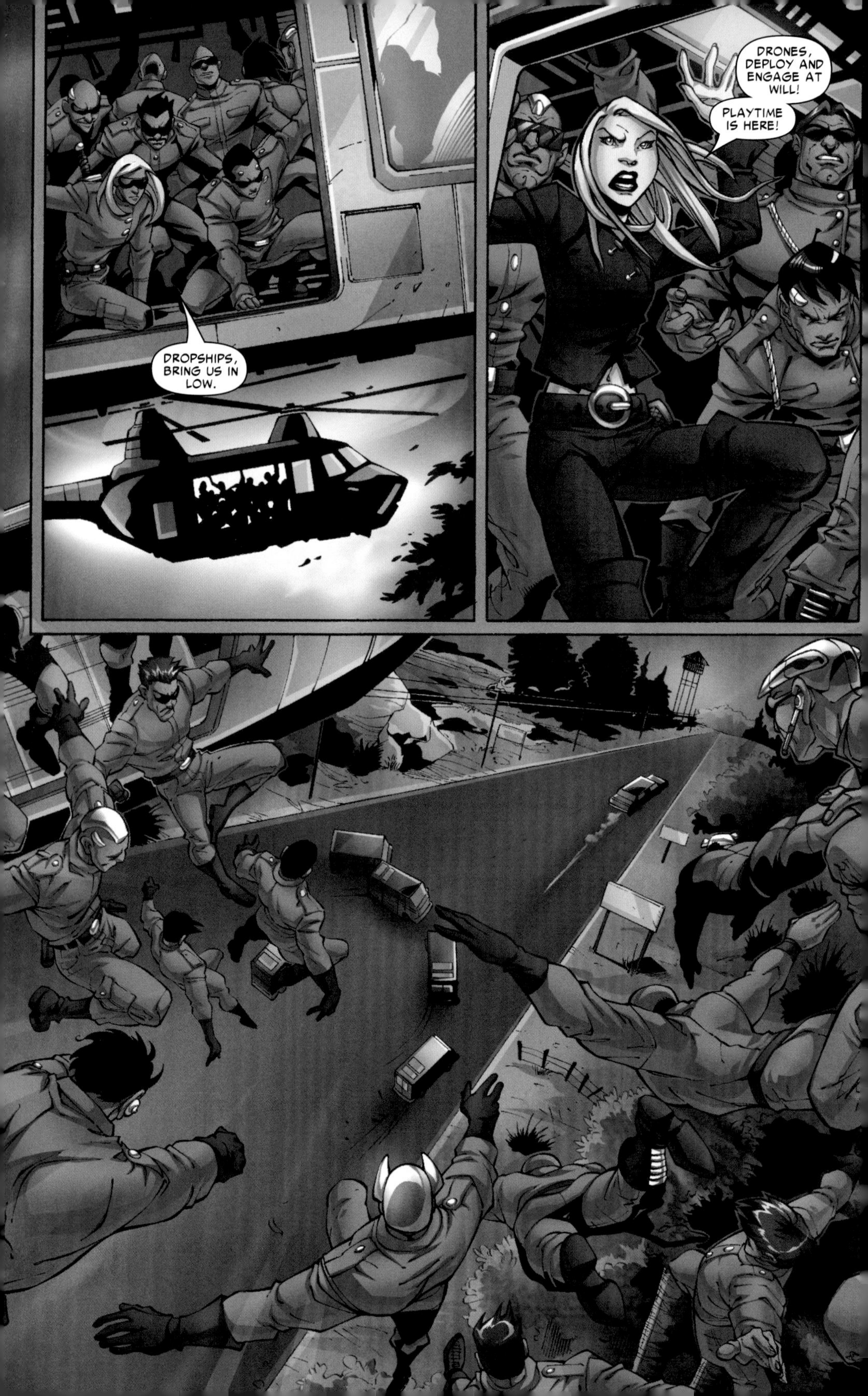
DROPSHIPS, BRING US IN LOW.
DRONES, DEPLOY AND ENGAGE AT WILL!
PLAYTIME IS HERE!

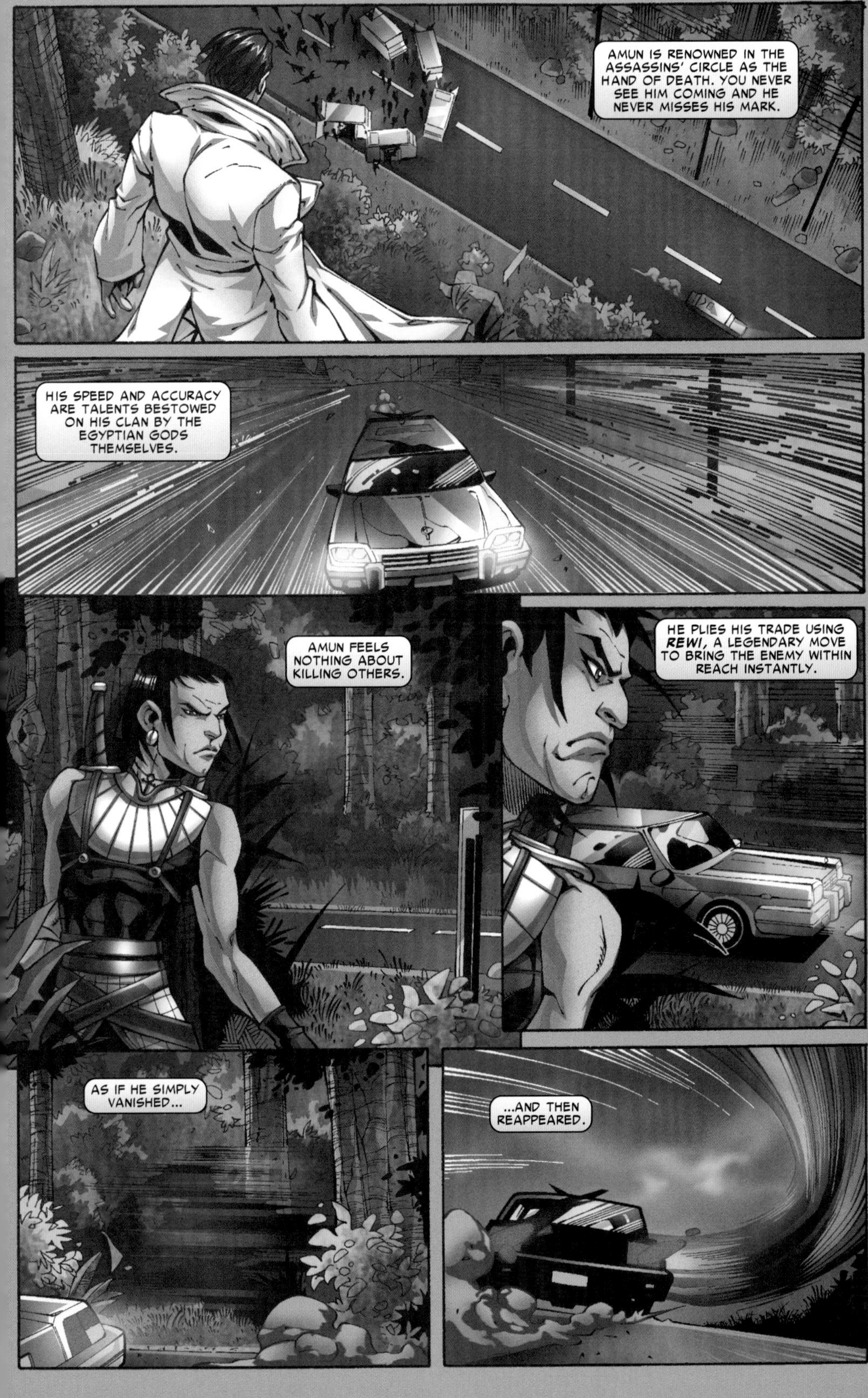
AMUN IS RENOWNED IN THE ASSASSINS' CIRCLE AS THE HAND OF DEATH. YOU NEVER SEE HIM COMING AND HE NEVER MISSES HIS MARK.
HIS SPEED AND ACCURACY ARE TALENTS BESTOWED ON HIS CLAN BY THE EGYPTIAN GODS THEMSELVES.
AMUN FEELS NOTHING ABOUT KILLING OTHERS.
HE PLIES HIS TRADE USING ***REWI,*** A LEGENDARY MOVE TO BRING THE ENEMY WITHIN REACH INSTANTLY.
AS IF HE SIMPLY VANISHED...
...AND THEN REAPPEARED.

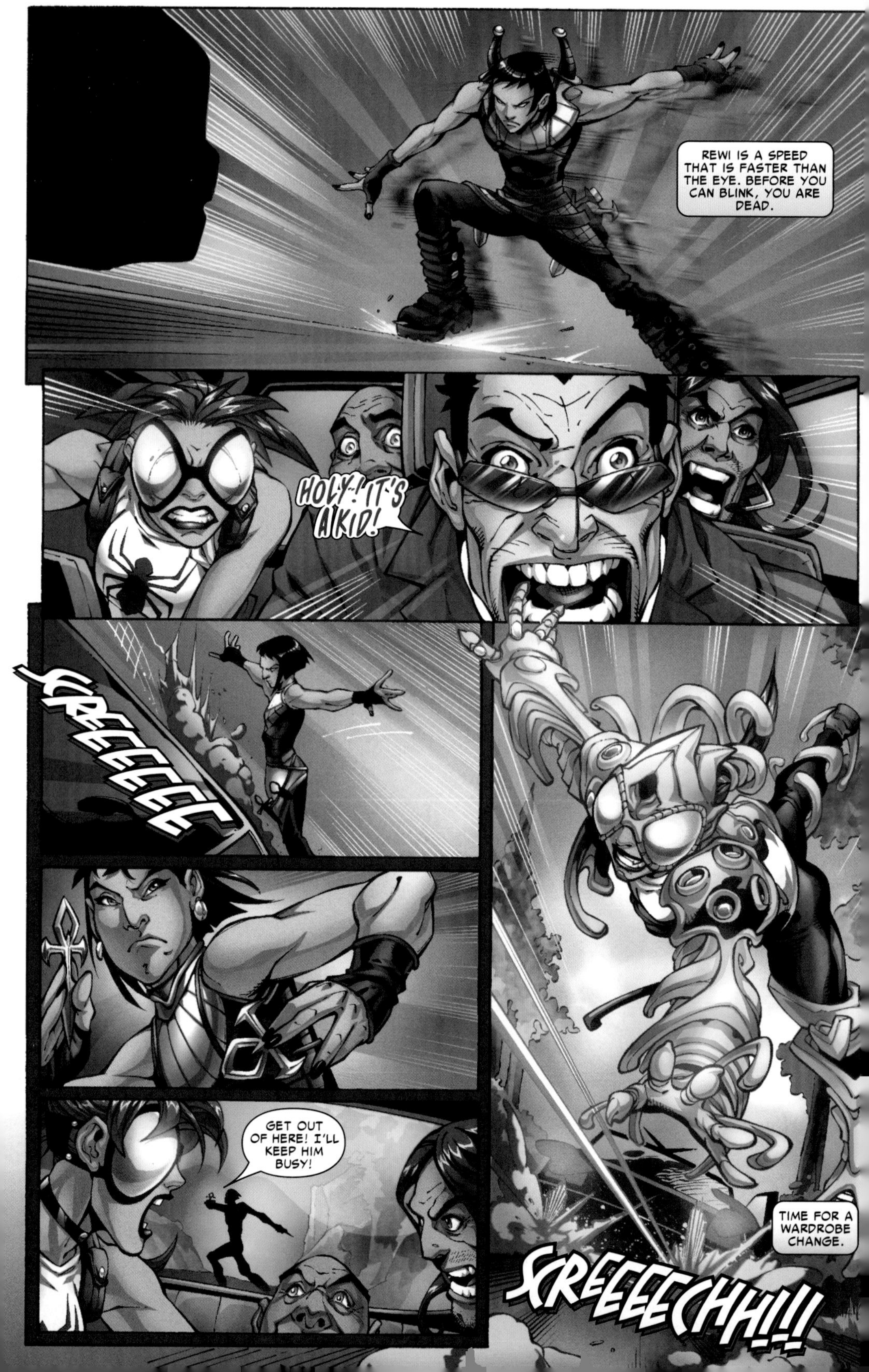
REWI IS A SPEED THAT IS FASTER THAN THE EYE. BEFORE YOU CAN BLINK, YOU ARE DEAD.
HOLY-! IT'S A KID!
SCREEEEE
GET OUT OF HERE! I'LL KEEP HIM BUSY!
TIME FOR A WARDROBE CHANGE.
SCREEEECHH!!!

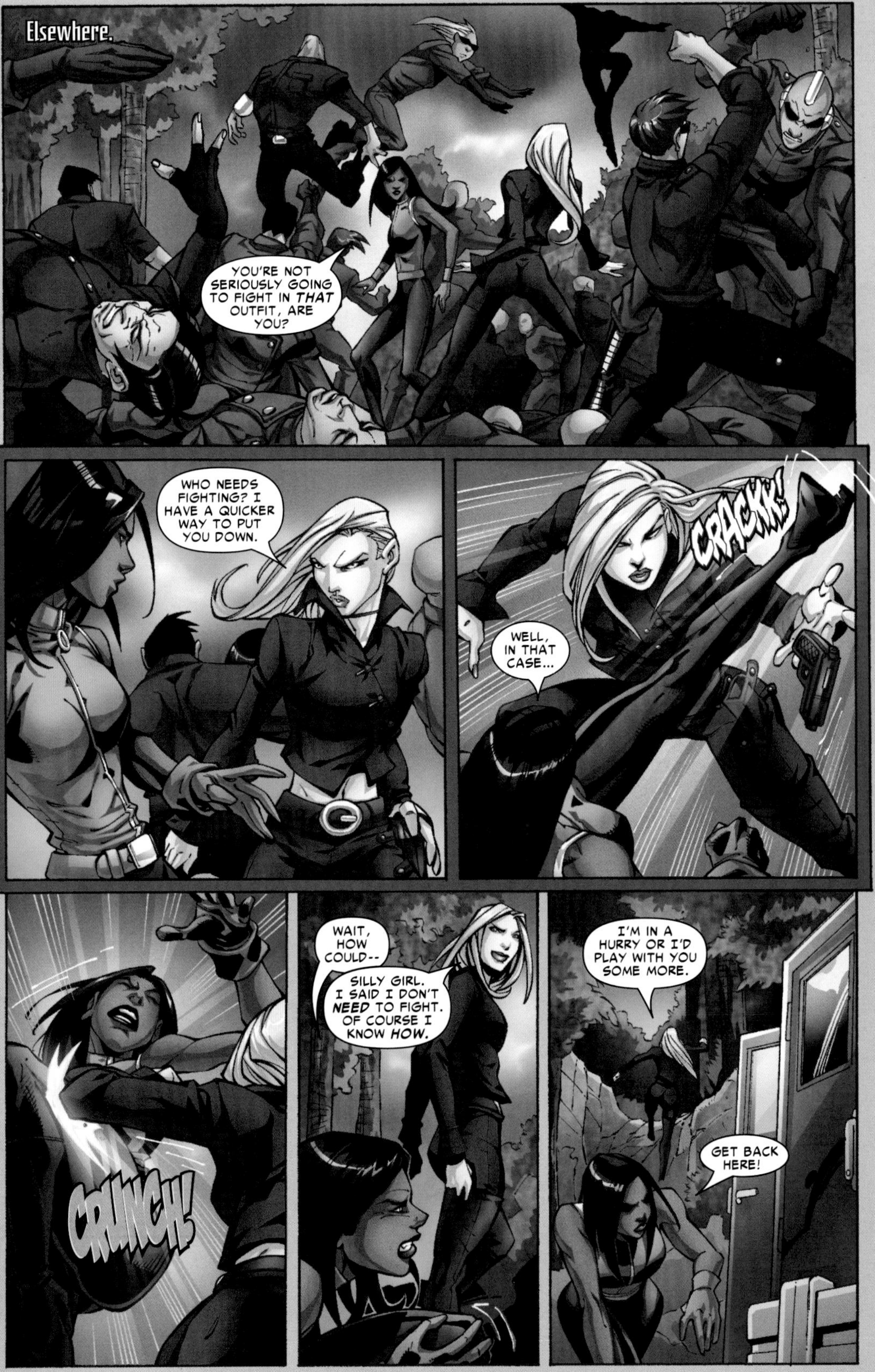
Elsewhere.
YOU'RE NOT SERIOUSLY GOING TO FIGHT IN *THAT* OUTFIT, ARE YOU?
WHO NEEDS FIGHTING? I HAVE A QUICKER WAY TO PUT YOU DOWN.
WELL, IN THAT CASE...
CRACKK!
CRUNCH!
WAIT, HOW COULD--
SILLY GIRL. I SAID I DON'T *NEED* TO FIGHT. OF COURSE I KNOW *HOW*.
I'M IN A HURRY OR I'D PLAY WITH YOU SOME MORE.
GET BACK HERE!

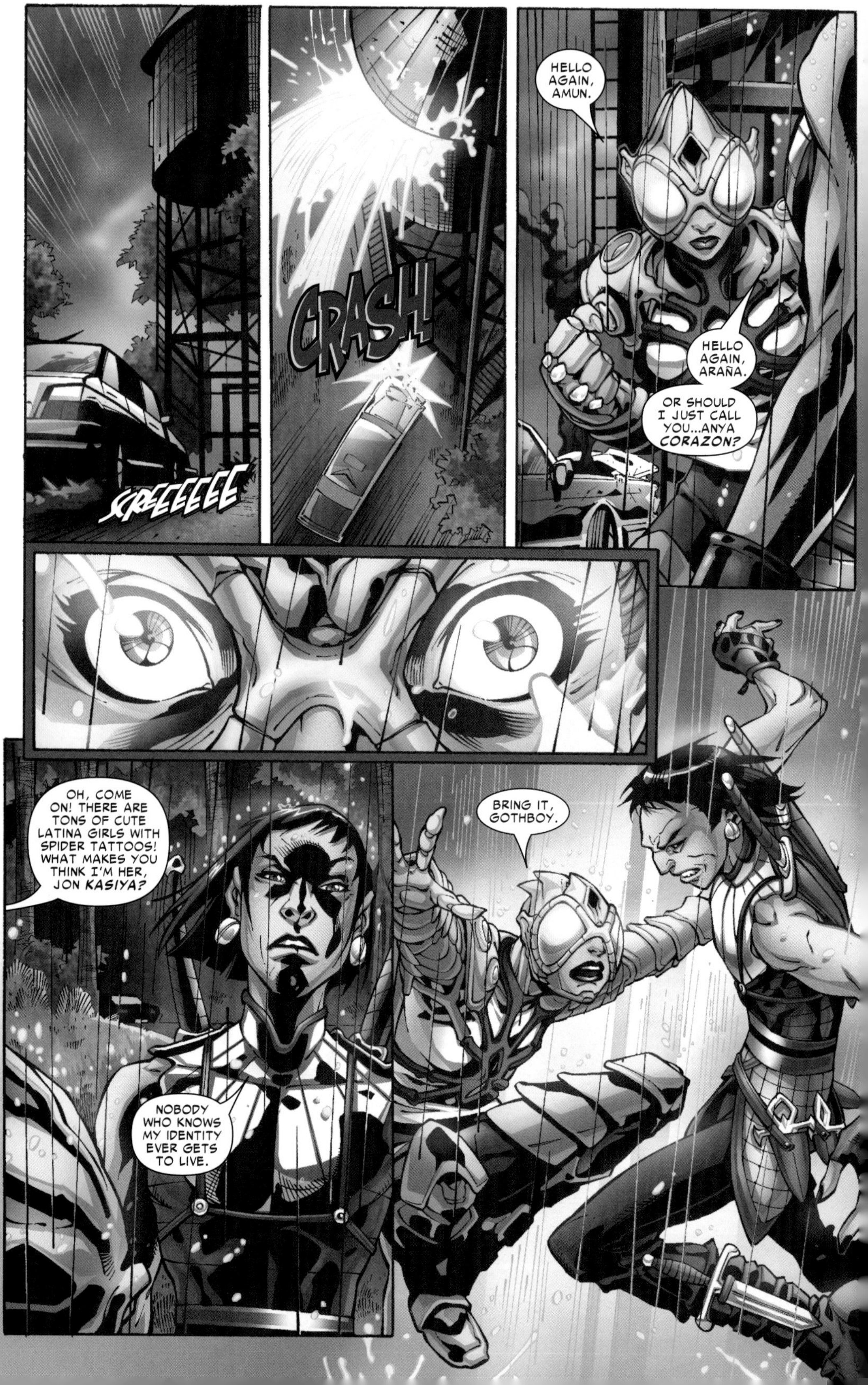
SCREEEEEEE
CRASH!
HELLO AGAIN, AMUN.
HELLO AGAIN, ARAÑA.
OR SHOULD I JUST CALL YOU...ANYA CORAZON?
OH, COME ON! THERE ARE TONS OF CUTE LATINA GIRLS WITH SPIDER TATTOOS! WHAT MAKES YOU THINK I'M HER, JON KASIYA?
BRING IT, GOTHBOY.
NOBODY WHO KNOWS MY IDENTITY EVER GETS TO LIVE.

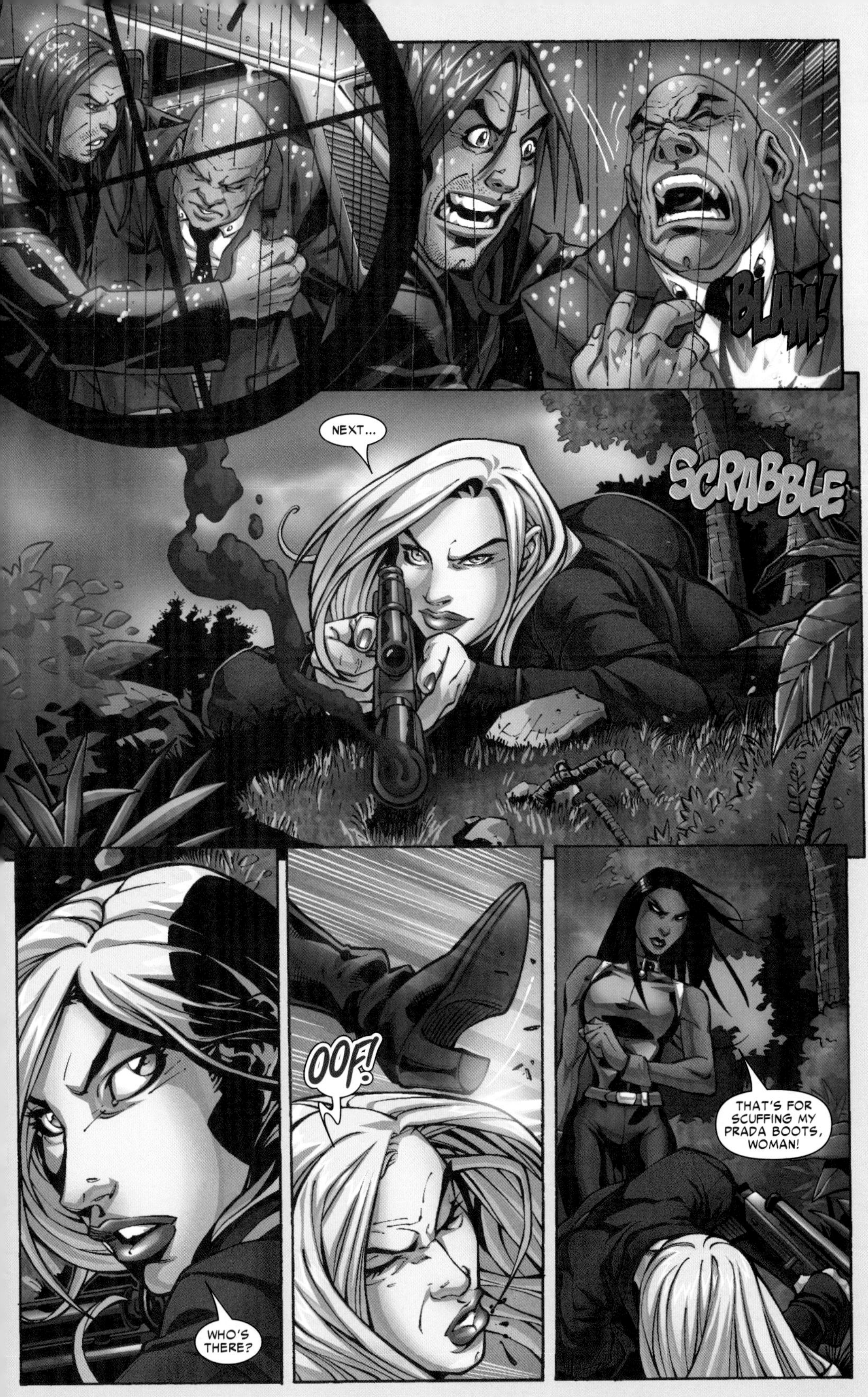
BLAM!
NEXT...
SCRABBLE
WHO'S THERE?
OOF!
THAT'S FOR SCUFFING MY PRADA BOOTS, WOMAN!

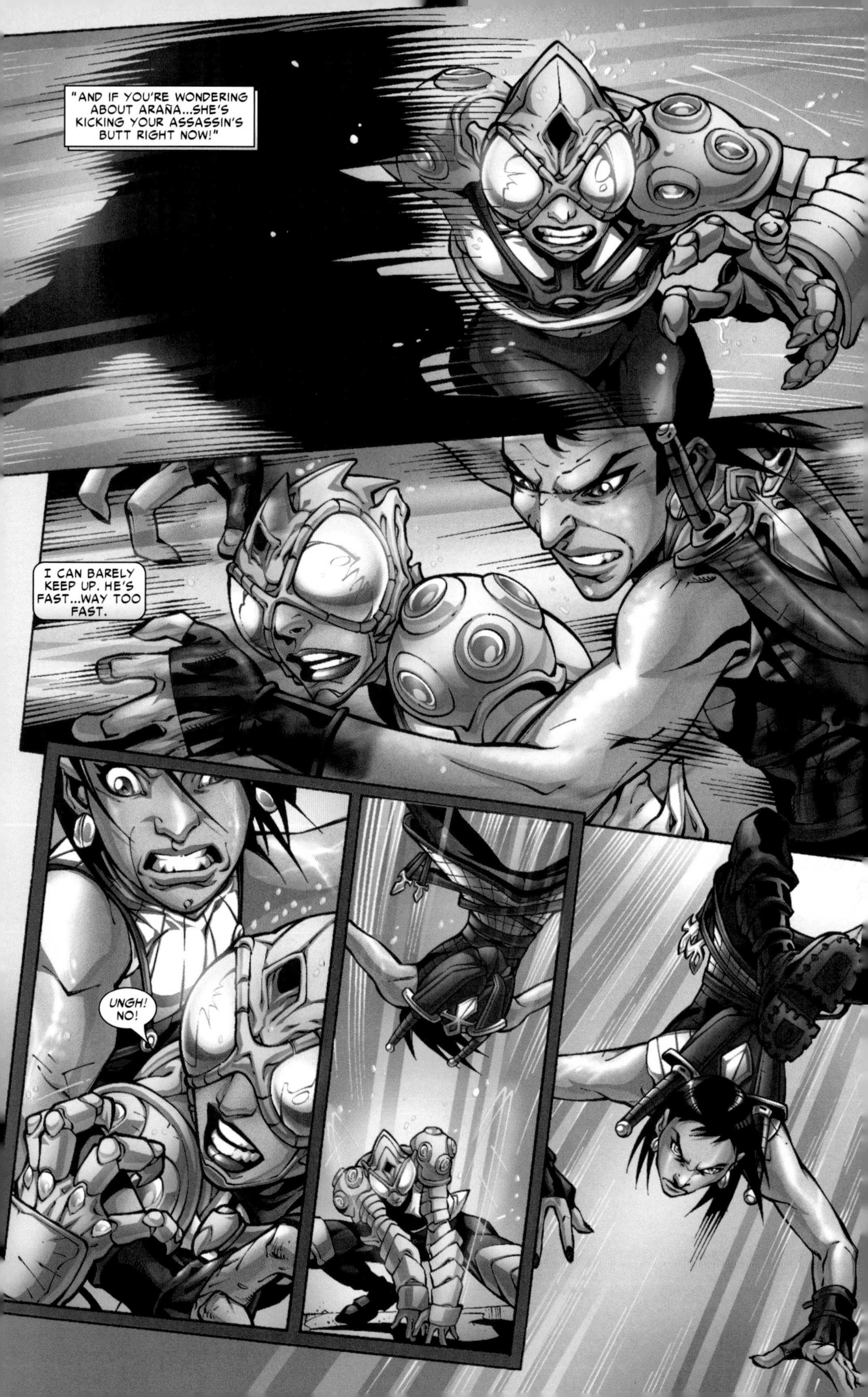
"AND IF YOU'RE WONDERING ABOUT ARAÑA...SHE'S KICKING YOUR ASSASSIN'S BUTT RIGHT NOW!"
I CAN BARELY KEEP UP. HE'S FAST...WAY TOO FAST.
UNGH! NO!

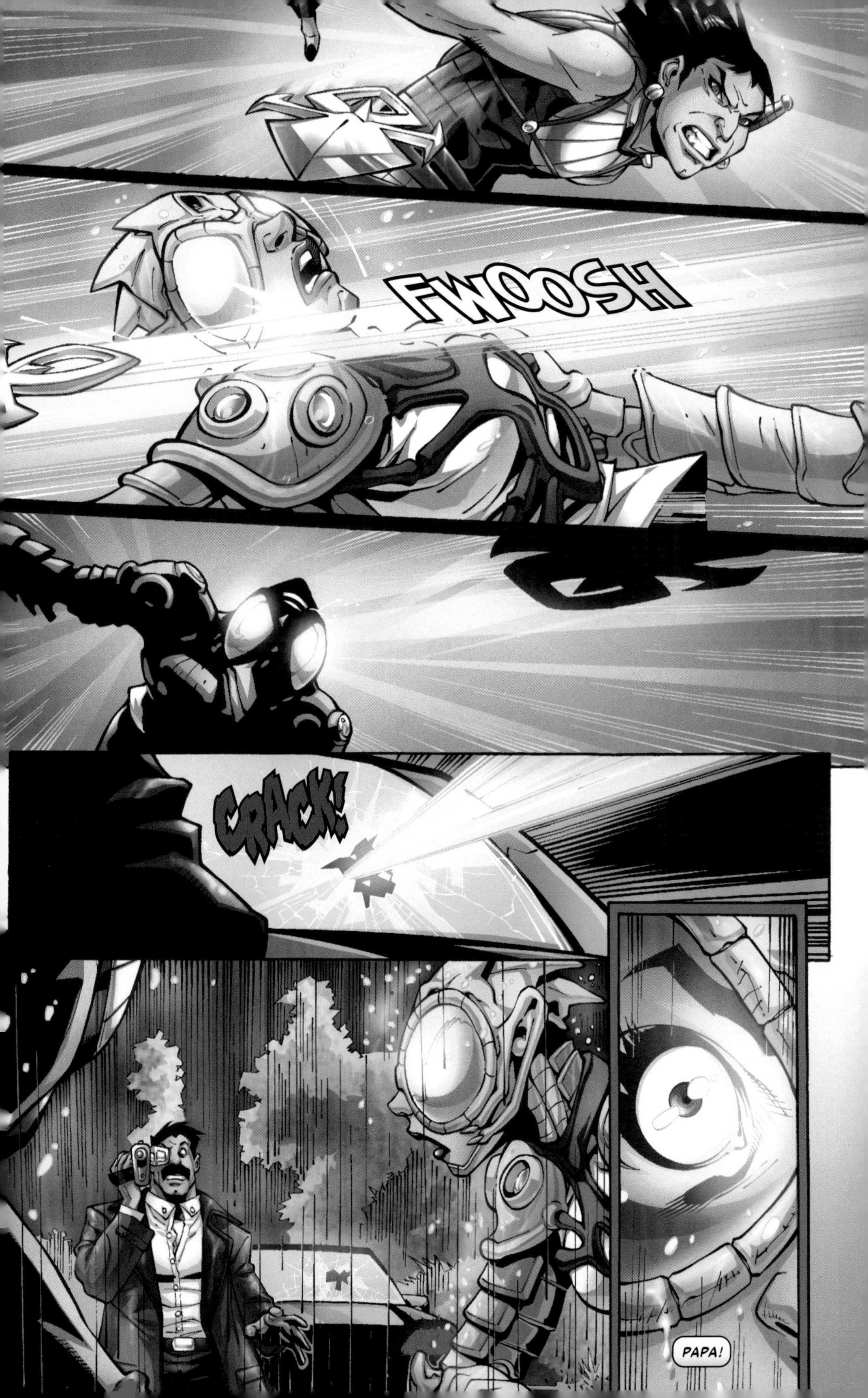
FWOOSH
CRACK!
PAPA!

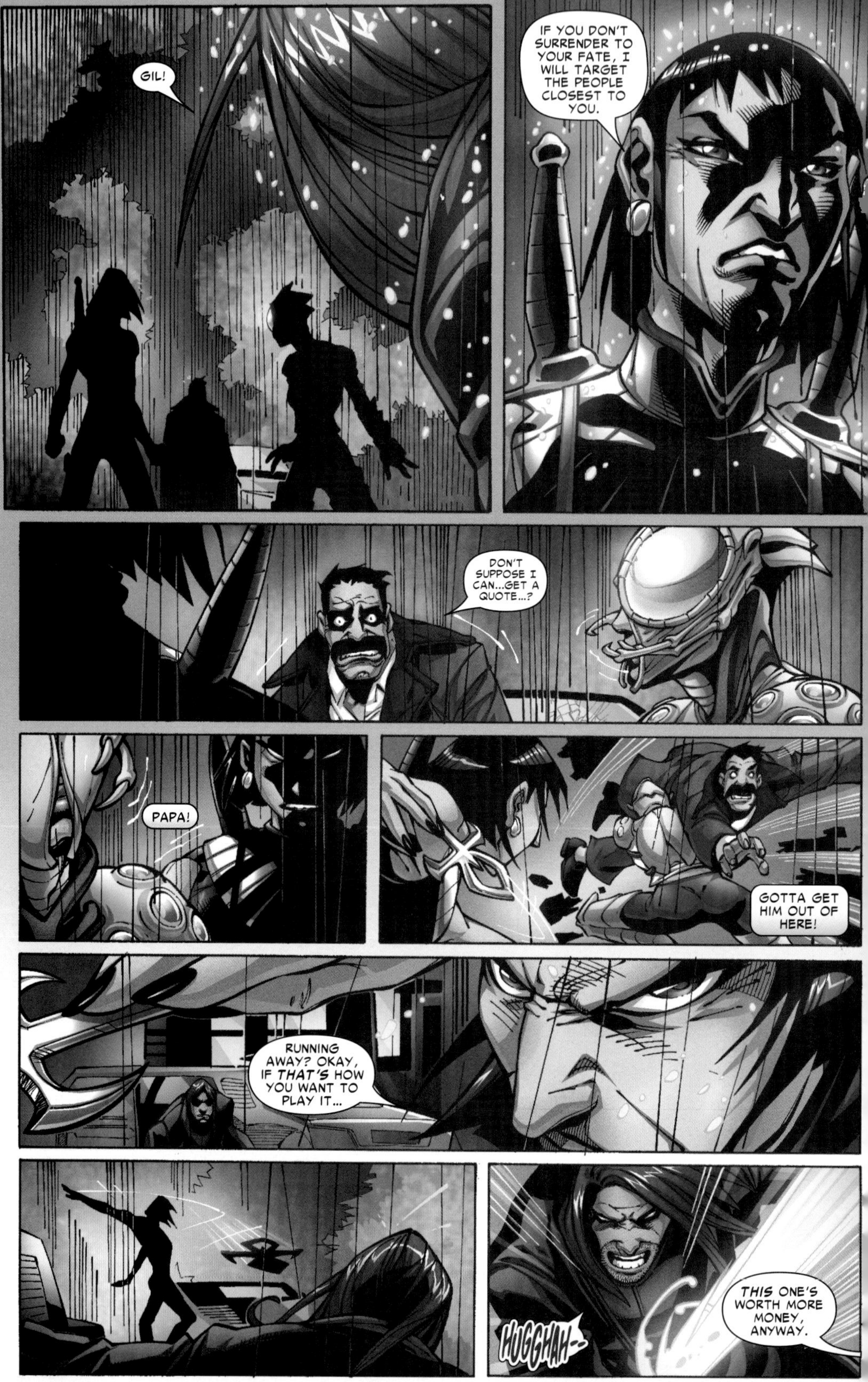
GIL!
IF YOU DON'T SURRENDER TO YOUR FATE, I WILL TARGET THE PEOPLE CLOSEST TO YOU.
DON'T SUPPOSE I CAN...GET A QUOTE...?
PAPA!
GOTTA GET HIM OUT OF HERE!
RUNNING AWAY? OKAY, IF *THAT'S* HOW YOU WANT TO PLAY IT...
HUGGHAH-
THIS ONE'S WORTH MORE MONEY, ANYWAY.

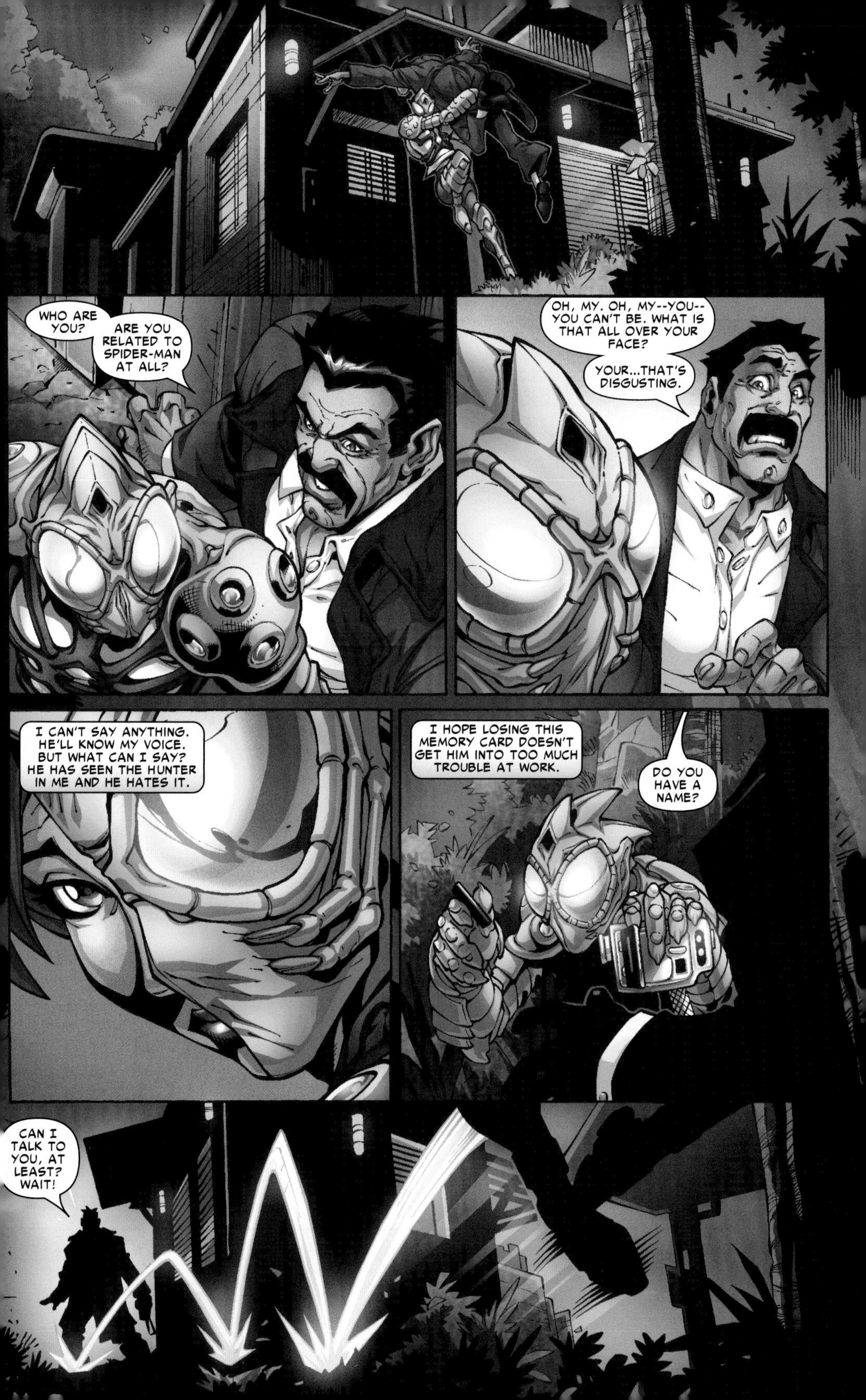
WHO ARE YOU?
ARE YOU RELATED TO SPIDER-MAN AT ALL?
OH, MY. OH, MY--YOU--YOU CAN'T BE. WHAT IS THAT ALL OVER YOUR FACE?
YOUR...THAT'S DISGUSTING.
I CAN'T SAY ANYTHING. HE'LL KNOW MY VOICE. BUT WHAT CAN I SAY? HE HAS SEEN THE HUNTER IN ME AND HE HATES IT.
I HOPE LOSING THIS MEMORY CARD DOESN'T GET HIM INTO TOO MUCH TROUBLE AT WORK.
DO YOU HAVE A NAME?
CAN I TALK TO YOU, AT LEAST? WAIT!

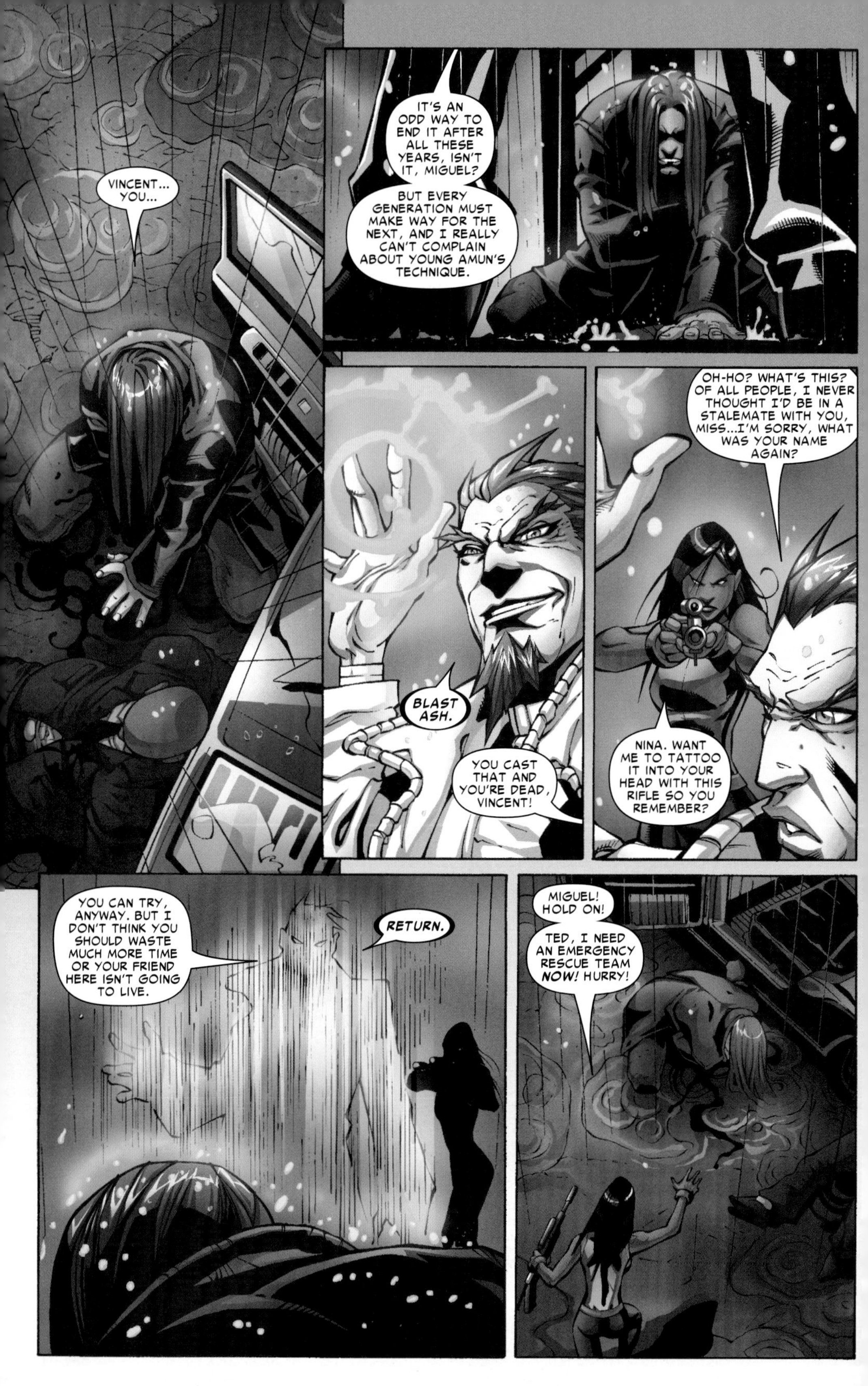
VINCENT... YOU...
IT'S AN ODD WAY TO END IT AFTER ALL THESE YEARS, ISN'T IT, MIGUEL?
BUT EVERY GENERATION MUST MAKE WAY FOR THE NEXT, AND I REALLY CAN'T COMPLAIN ABOUT YOUNG AMUN'S TECHNIQUE.
BLAST ASH.
YOU CAST THAT AND YOU'RE DEAD, VINCENT!
OH-HO? WHAT'S THIS? OF ALL PEOPLE, I NEVER THOUGHT I'D BE IN A STALEMATE WITH YOU, MISS...I'M SORRY, WHAT WAS YOUR NAME AGAIN?
NINA. WANT ME TO TATTOO IT INTO YOUR HEAD WITH THIS RIFLE SO YOU REMEMBER?
YOU CAN TRY, ANYWAY. BUT I DON'T THINK YOU SHOULD WASTE MUCH MORE TIME OR YOUR FRIEND HERE ISN'T GOING TO LIVE.
RETURN.
MIGUEL! HOLD ON!
TED, I NEED AN EMERGENCY RESCUE TEAM NOW! HURRY!

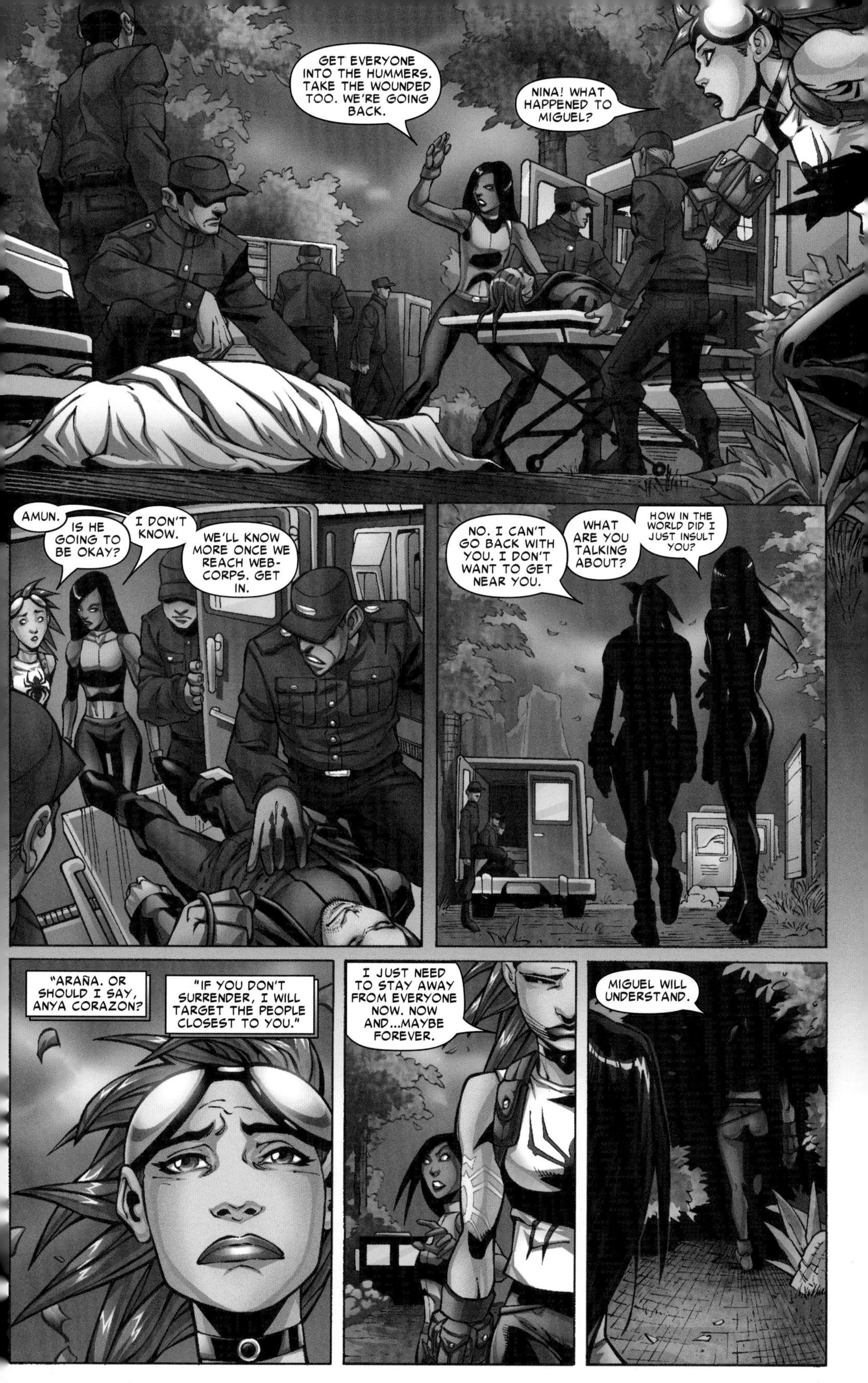
GET EVERYONE INTO THE HUMMERS. TAKE THE WOUNDED TOO. WE'RE GOING BACK.
NINA! WHAT HAPPENED TO MIGUEL?
AMUN.
IS HE GOING TO BE OKAY?
I DON'T KNOW.
WE'LL KNOW MORE ONCE WE REACH WEB-CORPS. GET IN.
NO. I CAN'T GO BACK WITH YOU. I DON'T WANT TO GET NEAR YOU.
WHAT ARE YOU TALKING ABOUT?
HOW IN THE WORLD DID I JUST INSULT YOU?
"ARAÑA. OR SHOULD I SAY, ANYA CORAZON?
"IF YOU DON'T SURRENDER, I WILL TARGET THE PEOPLE CLOSEST TO YOU."
I JUST NEED TO STAY AWAY FROM EVERYONE NOW. NOW AND...MAYBE FOREVER.
MIGUEL WILL UNDERSTAND.

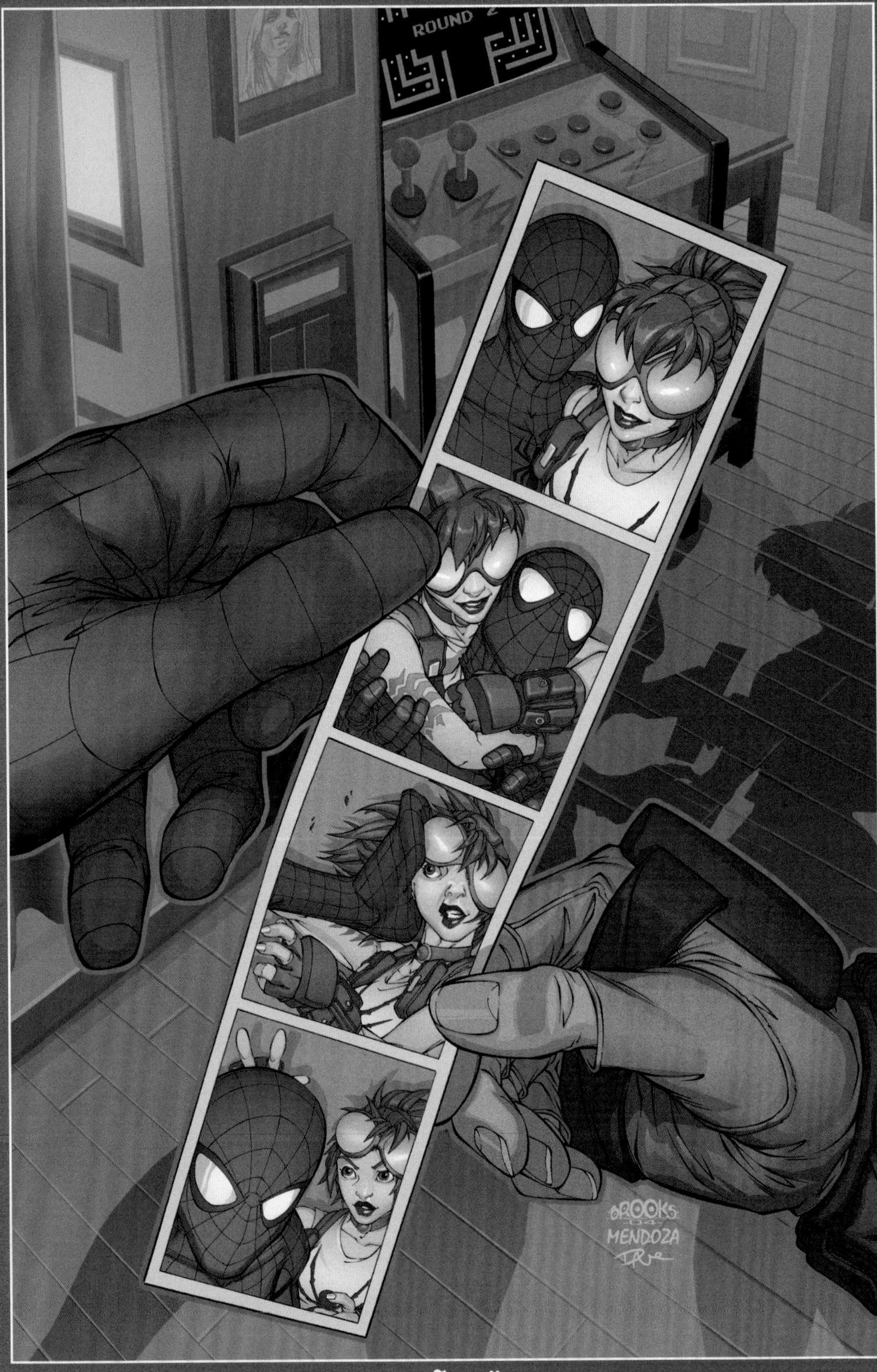
ROUND 2
BROOKS 04
MENDOZA

ARAÑA #4

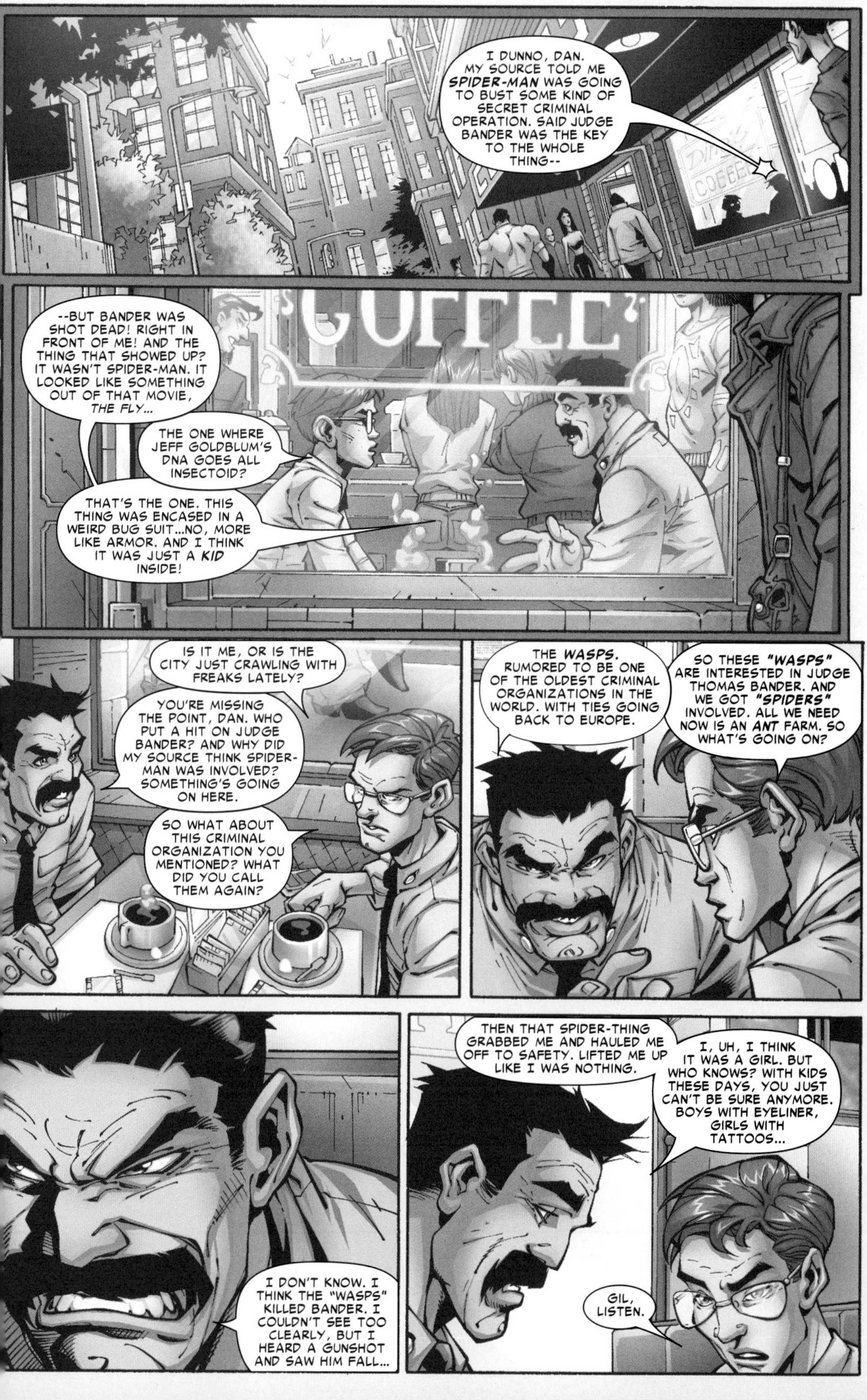

I DUNNO, DAN. MY SOURCE TOLD ME SPIDER-MAN WAS GOING TO BUST SOME KIND OF SECRET CRIMINAL OPERATION. SAID JUDGE BANDER WAS THE KEY TO THE WHOLE THING--
COFFEE
--BUT BANDER WAS SHOT DEAD! RIGHT IN FRONT OF ME! AND THE THING THAT SHOWED UP? IT WASN'T SPIDER-MAN. IT LOOKED LIKE SOMETHING OUT OF THAT MOVIE, THE FLY...
THE ONE WHERE JEFF GOLDBLUM'S DNA GOES ALL INSECTOID?
THAT'S THE ONE. THIS THING WAS ENCASED IN A WEIRD BUG SUIT...NO, MORE LIKE ARMOR. AND I THINK IT WAS JUST A KID INSIDE!
IS IT ME, OR IS THE CITY JUST CRAWLING WITH FREAKS LATELY?
YOU'RE MISSING THE POINT, DAN. WHO PUT A HIT ON JUDGE BANDER? AND WHY DID MY SOURCE THINK SPIDER-MAN WAS INVOLVED? SOMETHING'S GOING ON HERE.
SO WHAT ABOUT THIS CRIMINAL ORGANIZATION YOU MENTIONED? WHAT DID YOU CALL THEM AGAIN?
THE WASPS. RUMORED TO BE ONE OF THE OLDEST CRIMINAL ORGANIZATIONS IN THE WORLD. WITH TIES GOING BACK TO EUROPE.
SO THESE "WASPS" ARE INTERESTED IN JUDGE THOMAS BANDER. AND WE GOT "SPIDERS" INVOLVED. ALL WE NEED NOW IS AN ANT FARM. SO WHAT'S GOING ON?
I DON'T KNOW. I THINK THE "WASPS" KILLED BANDER. I COULDN'T SEE TOO CLEARLY, BUT I HEARD A GUNSHOT AND SAW HIM FALL...
THEN THAT SPIDER-THING GRABBED ME AND HAULED ME OFF TO SAFETY. LIFTED ME UP LIKE I WAS NOTHING.
I, UH, I THINK IT WAS A GIRL. BUT WHO KNOWS? WITH KIDS THESE DAYS, YOU JUST CAN'T BE SURE ANYMORE. BOYS WITH EYELINER, GIRLS WITH TATTOOS...
GIL, LISTEN.

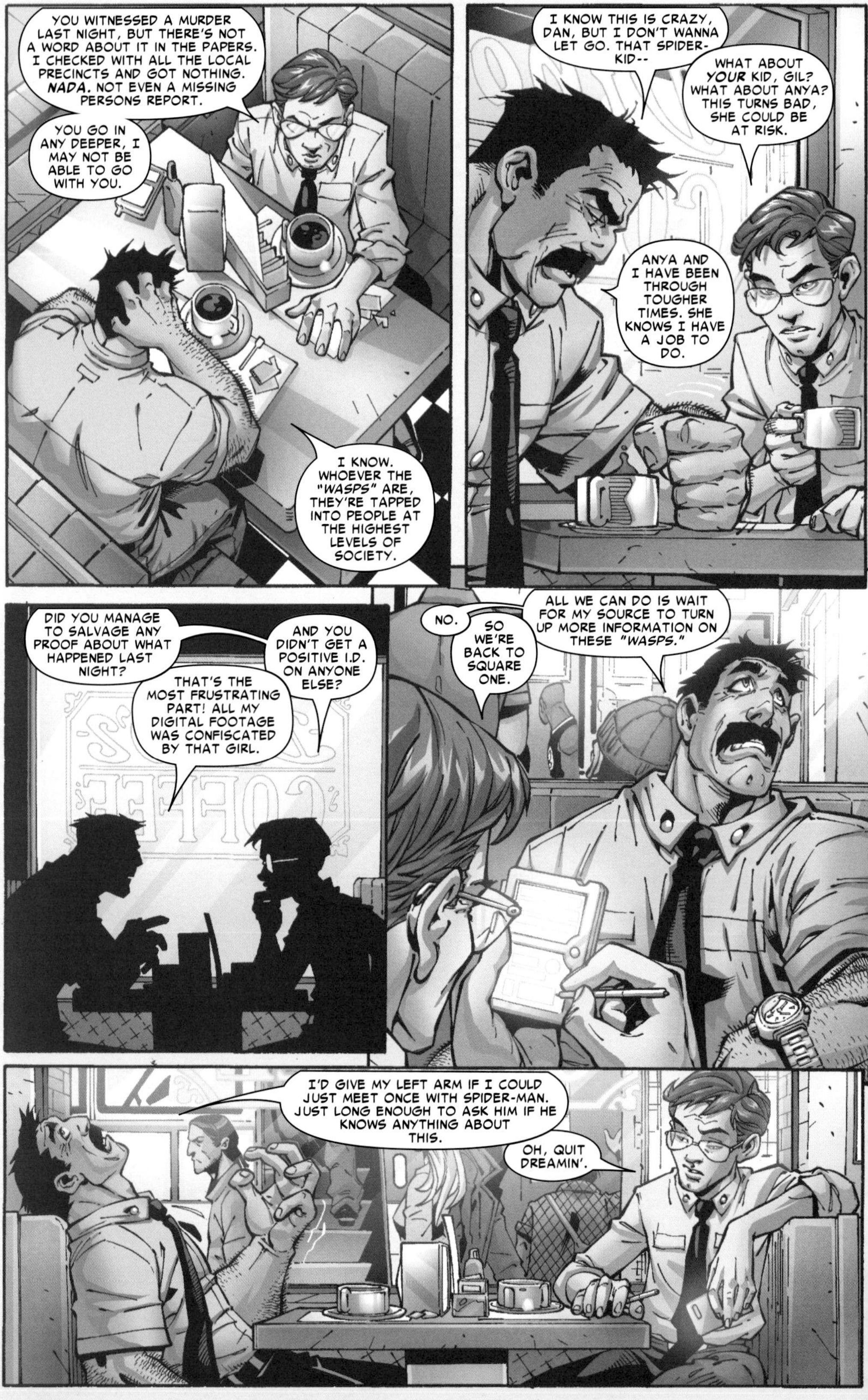
YOU WITNESSED A MURDER LAST NIGHT, BUT THERE'S NOT A WORD ABOUT IT IN THE PAPERS. I CHECKED WITH ALL THE LOCAL PRECINCTS AND GOT NOTHING. NADA. NOT EVEN A MISSING PERSONS REPORT.
YOU GO IN ANY DEEPER, I MAY NOT BE ABLE TO GO WITH YOU.
I KNOW. WHOEVER THE "WASPS" ARE, THEY'RE TAPPED INTO PEOPLE AT THE HIGHEST LEVELS OF SOCIETY.
I KNOW THIS IS CRAZY, DAN, BUT I DON'T WANNA LET GO. THAT SPIDER-KID--
WHAT ABOUT YOUR KID, GIL? WHAT ABOUT ANYA? THIS TURNS BAD, SHE COULD BE AT RISK.
ANYA AND I HAVE BEEN THROUGH TOUGHER TIMES. SHE KNOWS I HAVE A JOB TO DO.
DID YOU MANAGE TO SALVAGE ANY PROOF ABOUT WHAT HAPPENED LAST NIGHT?
AND YOU DIDN'T GET A POSITIVE I.D. ON ANYONE ELSE?
THAT'S THE MOST FRUSTRATING PART! ALL MY DIGITAL FOOTAGE WAS CONFISCATED BY THAT GIRL.
NO.
SO WE'RE BACK TO SQUARE ONE.
ALL WE CAN DO IS WAIT FOR MY SOURCE TO TURN UP MORE INFORMATION ON THESE "WASPS."
I'D GIVE MY LEFT ARM IF I COULD JUST MEET ONCE WITH SPIDER-MAN. JUST LONG ENOUGH TO ASK HIM IF HE KNOWS ANYTHING ABOUT THIS.
OH, QUIT DREAMIN'.

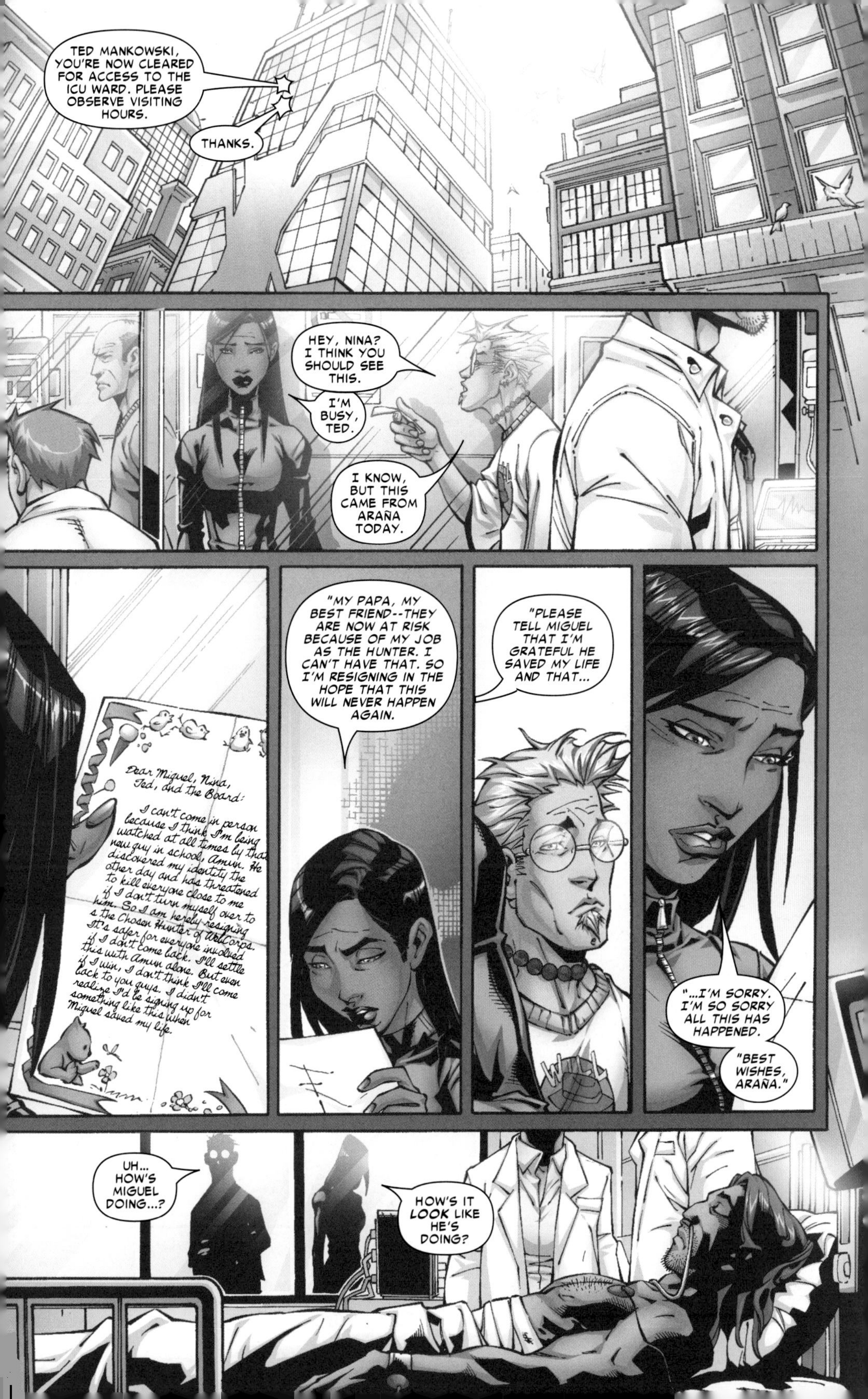
TED MANKOWSKI, YOU'RE NOW CLEARED FOR ACCESS TO THE ICU WARD. PLEASE OBSERVE VISITING HOURS.
THANKS.
HEY, NINA? I THINK YOU SHOULD SEE THIS.
I'M BUSY, TED.
I KNOW, BUT THIS CAME FROM ARAÑA TODAY.
Dear Miguel, Nina, Ted, and the Board:
I can't come in person because I think I'm being watched at all times by tha new guy in school, Amun. He discovered my identity the other day and has threatened to kill everyone close to me if I don't turn myself over to him. So I am hereby resigning s the Chosen Hunter of WebCorps. It's safer for everyone involved if I don't come back. I'll settle this with Amun alone. But even if I win, I don't think I'll come back to you guys. I didn't realize I'd be signing up for something like this when Miguel saved my life.
"MY PAPA, MY BEST FRIEND--THEY ARE NOW AT RISK BECAUSE OF MY JOB AS THE HUNTER. I CAN'T HAVE THAT. SO I'M RESIGNING IN THE HOPE THAT THIS WILL NEVER HAPPEN AGAIN.
"PLEASE TELL MIGUEL THAT I'M GRATEFUL HE SAVED MY LIFE AND THAT...
"...I'M SORRY. I'M SO SORRY ALL THIS HAS HAPPENED.
"BEST WISHES, ARAÑA."
UH... HOW'S MIGUEL DOING...?
HOW'S IT LOOK LIKE HE'S DOING?

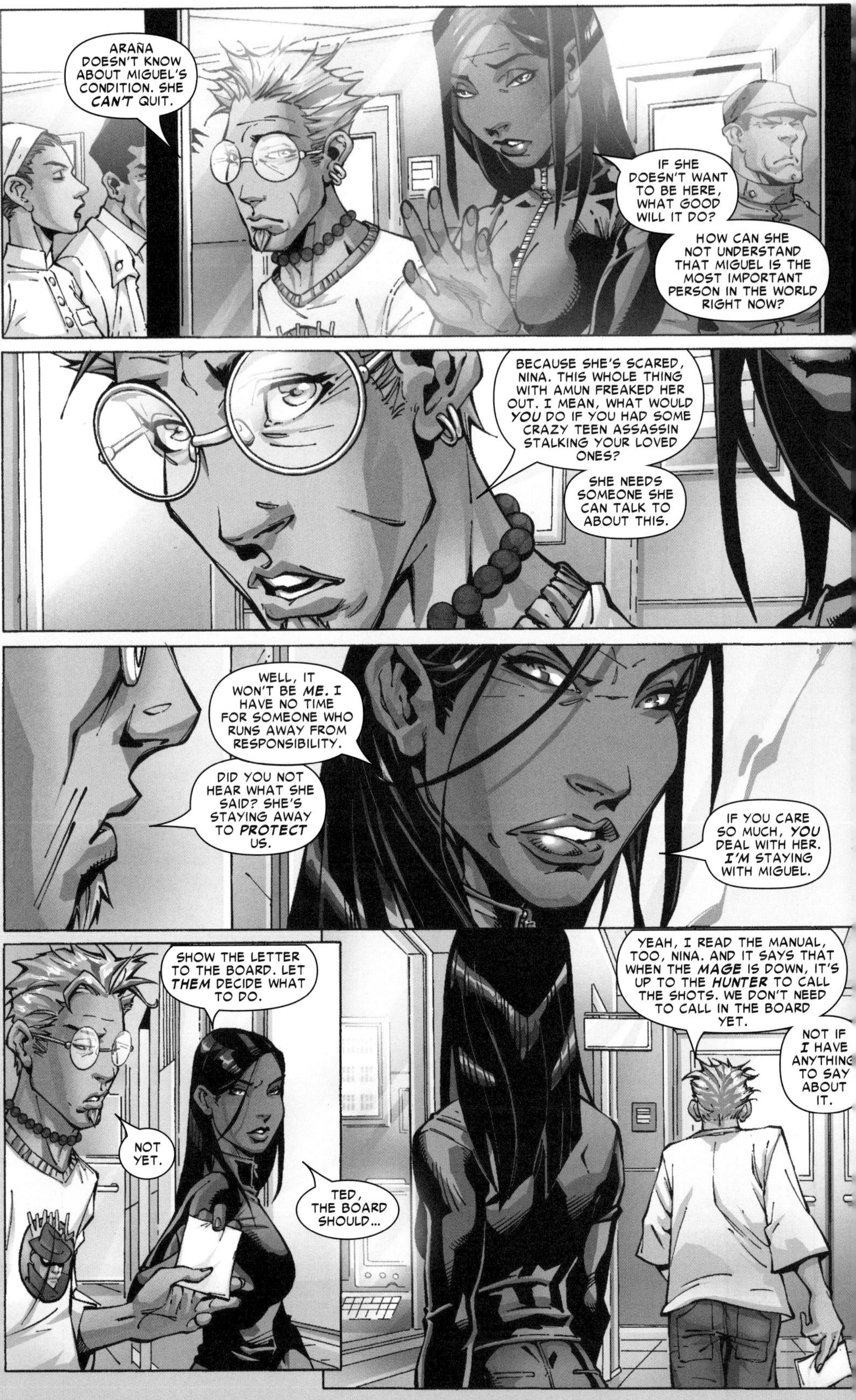
ARAÑA DOESN'T KNOW ABOUT MIGUEL'S CONDITION. SHE *CAN'T* QUIT.
IF SHE DOESN'T WANT TO BE HERE, WHAT GOOD WILL IT DO?
HOW CAN SHE NOT UNDERSTAND THAT MIGUEL IS THE MOST IMPORTANT PERSON IN THE WORLD RIGHT NOW?
BECAUSE SHE'S SCARED, NINA. THIS WHOLE THING WITH AMUN FREAKED HER OUT. I MEAN, WHAT WOULD *YOU* DO IF YOU HAD SOME CRAZY TEEN ASSASSIN STALKING YOUR LOVED ONES?
SHE NEEDS SOMEONE SHE CAN TALK TO ABOUT THIS.
WELL, IT WON'T BE *ME.* I HAVE NO TIME FOR SOMEONE WHO RUNS AWAY FROM RESPONSIBILITY.
DID YOU NOT HEAR WHAT SHE SAID? SHE'S STAYING AWAY TO *PROTECT* US.
IF YOU CARE SO MUCH, *YOU* DEAL WITH HER. *I'M* STAYING WITH MIGUEL.
SHOW THE LETTER TO THE BOARD. LET *THEM* DECIDE WHAT TO DO.
NOT YET.
TED, THE BOARD SHOULD...
YEAH, I READ THE MANUAL, TOO, NINA. AND IT SAYS THAT WHEN THE *MAGE* IS DOWN, IT'S UP TO THE *HUNTER* TO CALL THE SHOTS. WE DON'T NEED TO CALL IN THE BOARD YET.
NOT IF *I* HAVE ANYTHING TO SAY ABOUT IT.

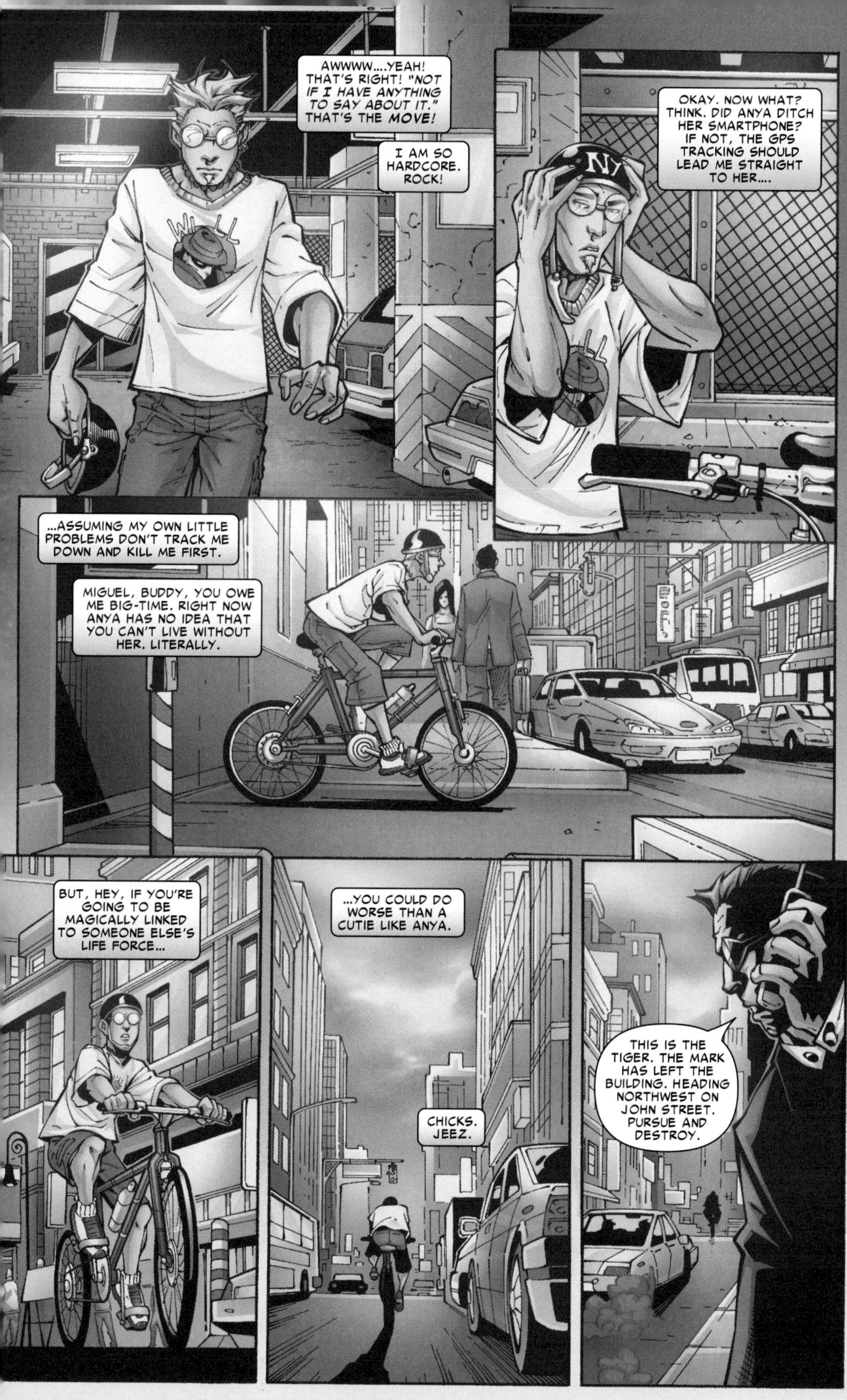
AWWWW....YEAH! THAT'S RIGHT! "NOT IF I HAVE ANYTHING TO SAY ABOUT IT." THAT'S THE MOVE!
I AM SO HARDCORE. ROCK!
OKAY. NOW WHAT? THINK. DID ANYA DITCH HER SMARTPHONE? IF NOT, THE GPS TRACKING SHOULD LEAD ME STRAIGHT TO HER....
NY
...ASSUMING MY OWN LITTLE PROBLEMS DON'T TRACK ME DOWN AND KILL ME FIRST.
MIGUEL, BUDDY, YOU OWE ME BIG-TIME. RIGHT NOW ANYA HAS NO IDEA THAT YOU CAN'T LIVE WITHOUT HER. LITERALLY.
BUT, HEY, IF YOU'RE GOING TO BE MAGICALLY LINKED TO SOMEONE ELSE'S LIFE FORCE...
...YOU COULD DO WORSE THAN A CUTIE LIKE ANYA.
CHICKS. JEEZ.
THIS IS THE TIGER. THE MARK HAS LEFT THE BUILDING. HEADING NORTHWEST ON JOHN STREET. PURSUE AND DESTROY.

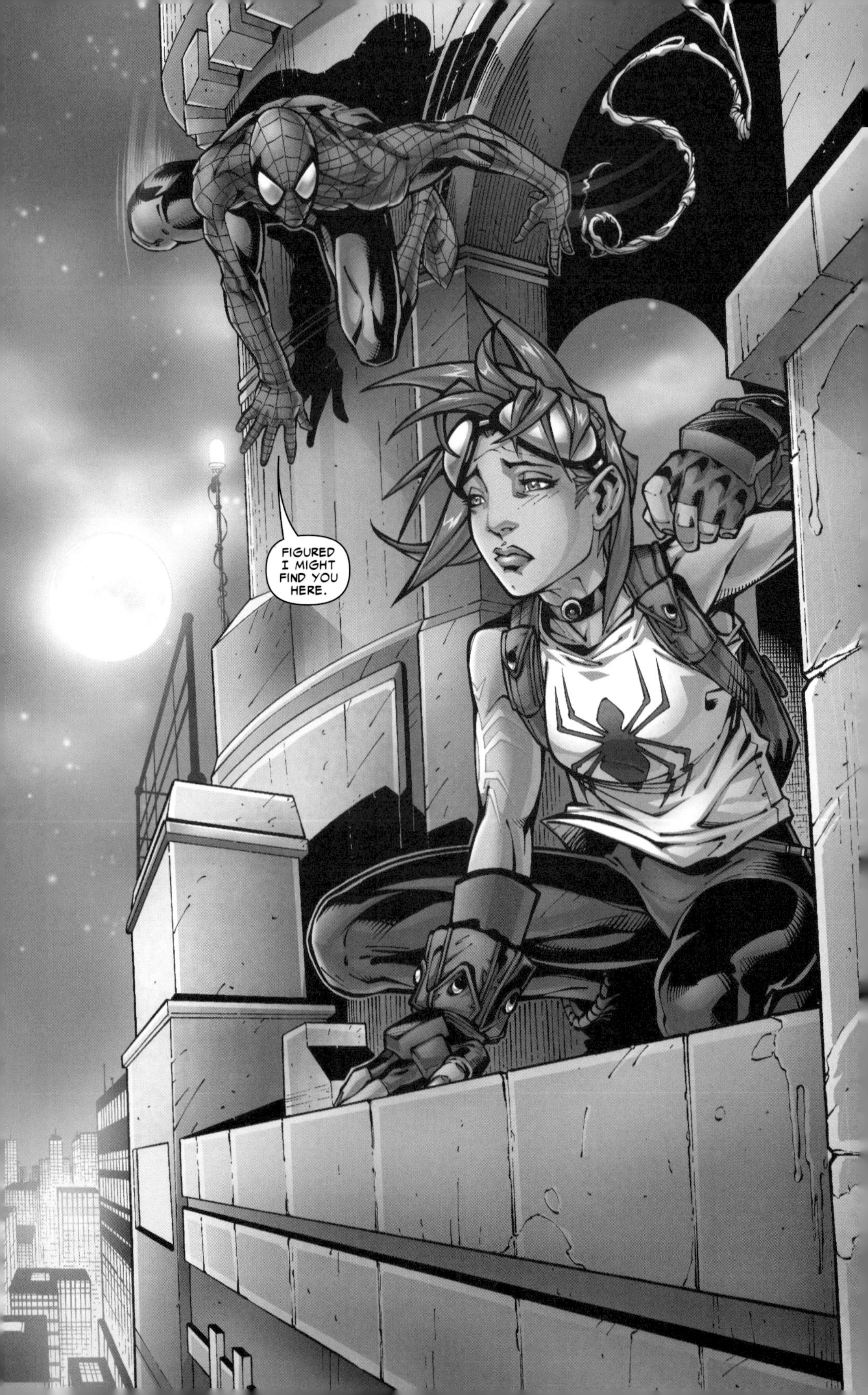
FIGURED I MIGHT FIND YOU HERE.

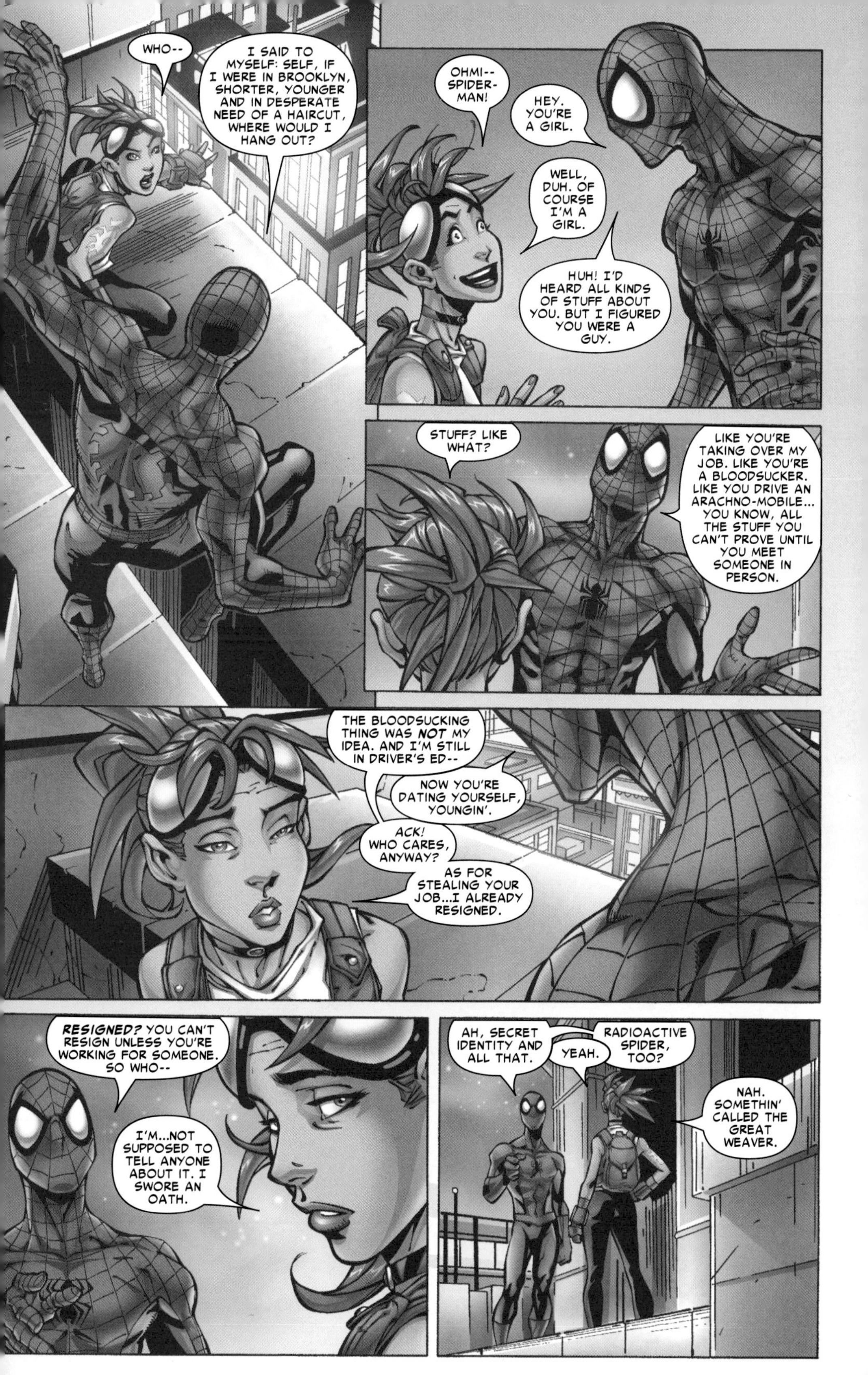
WHO--
I SAID TO MYSELF: SELF, IF I WERE IN BROOKLYN, SHORTER, YOUNGER AND IN DESPERATE NEED OF A HAIRCUT, WHERE WOULD I HANG OUT?
OHMI-- SPIDER-MAN!
HEY. YOU'RE A GIRL.
WELL, DUH. OF COURSE I'M A GIRL.
HUH! I'D HEARD ALL KINDS OF STUFF ABOUT YOU. BUT I FIGURED YOU WERE A GUY.
STUFF? LIKE WHAT?
LIKE YOU'RE TAKING OVER MY JOB. LIKE YOU'RE A BLOODSUCKER. LIKE YOU DRIVE AN ARACHNO-MOBILE... YOU KNOW, ALL THE STUFF YOU CAN'T PROVE UNTIL YOU MEET SOMEONE IN PERSON.
THE BLOODSUCKING THING WAS ***NOT*** MY IDEA. AND I'M STILL IN DRIVER'S ED--
NOW YOU'RE DATING YOURSELF, YOUNGIN'.
ACK! WHO CARES, ANYWAY?
AS FOR STEALING YOUR JOB...I ALREADY RESIGNED.
RESIGNED? YOU CAN'T RESIGN UNLESS YOU'RE WORKING FOR SOMEONE. SO WHO--
I'M...NOT SUPPOSED TO TELL ANYONE ABOUT IT. I SWORE AN OATH.
AH, SECRET IDENTITY AND ALL THAT.
YEAH.
RADIOACTIVE SPIDER, TOO?
NAH. SOMETHIN' CALLED THE GREAT WEAVER.

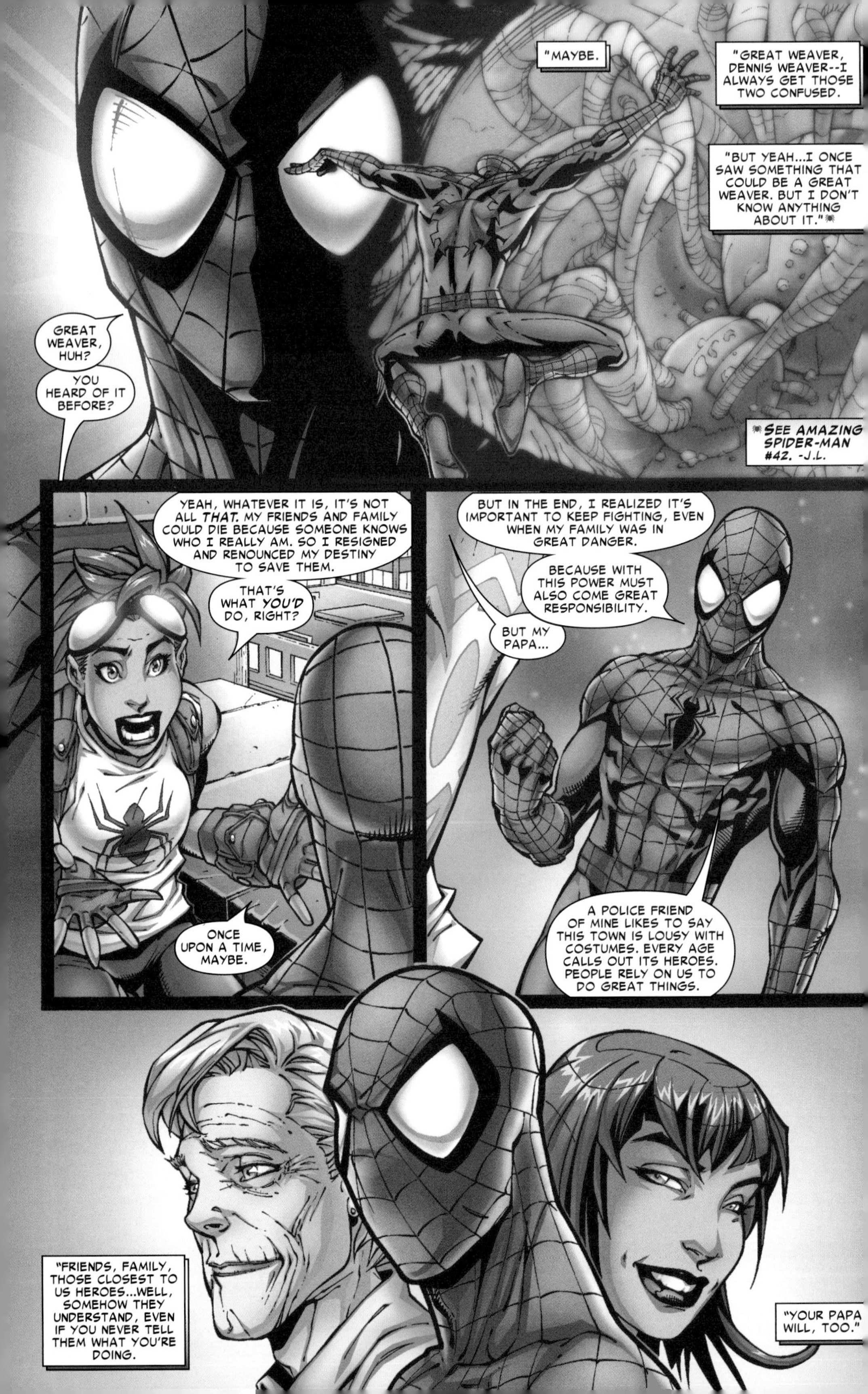
"MAYBE.
"GREAT WEAVER, DENNIS WEAVER--I ALWAYS GET THOSE TWO CONFUSED.
"BUT YEAH...I ONCE SAW SOMETHING THAT COULD BE A GREAT WEAVER. BUT I DON'T KNOW ANYTHING ABOUT IT."
GREAT WEAVER, HUH?
YOU HEARD OF IT BEFORE?
SEE AMAZING SPIDER-MAN #42. -J.L.
YEAH, WHATEVER IT IS, IT'S NOT ALL THAT. MY FRIENDS AND FAMILY COULD DIE BECAUSE SOMEONE KNOWS WHO I REALLY AM. SO I RESIGNED AND RENOUNCED MY DESTINY TO SAVE THEM.
THAT'S WHAT YOU'D DO, RIGHT?
ONCE UPON A TIME, MAYBE.
BUT IN THE END, I REALIZED IT'S IMPORTANT TO KEEP FIGHTING, EVEN WHEN MY FAMILY WAS IN GREAT DANGER.
BECAUSE WITH THIS POWER MUST ALSO COME GREAT RESPONSIBILITY.
BUT MY PAPA...
A POLICE FRIEND OF MINE LIKES TO SAY THIS TOWN IS LOUSY WITH COSTUMES. EVERY AGE CALLS OUT ITS HEROES. PEOPLE RELY ON US TO DO GREAT THINGS.
"FRIENDS, FAMILY, THOSE CLOSEST TO US HEROES...WELL, SOMEHOW THEY UNDERSTAND, EVEN IF YOU NEVER TELL THEM WHAT YOU'RE DOING.
"YOUR PAPA WILL, TOO."

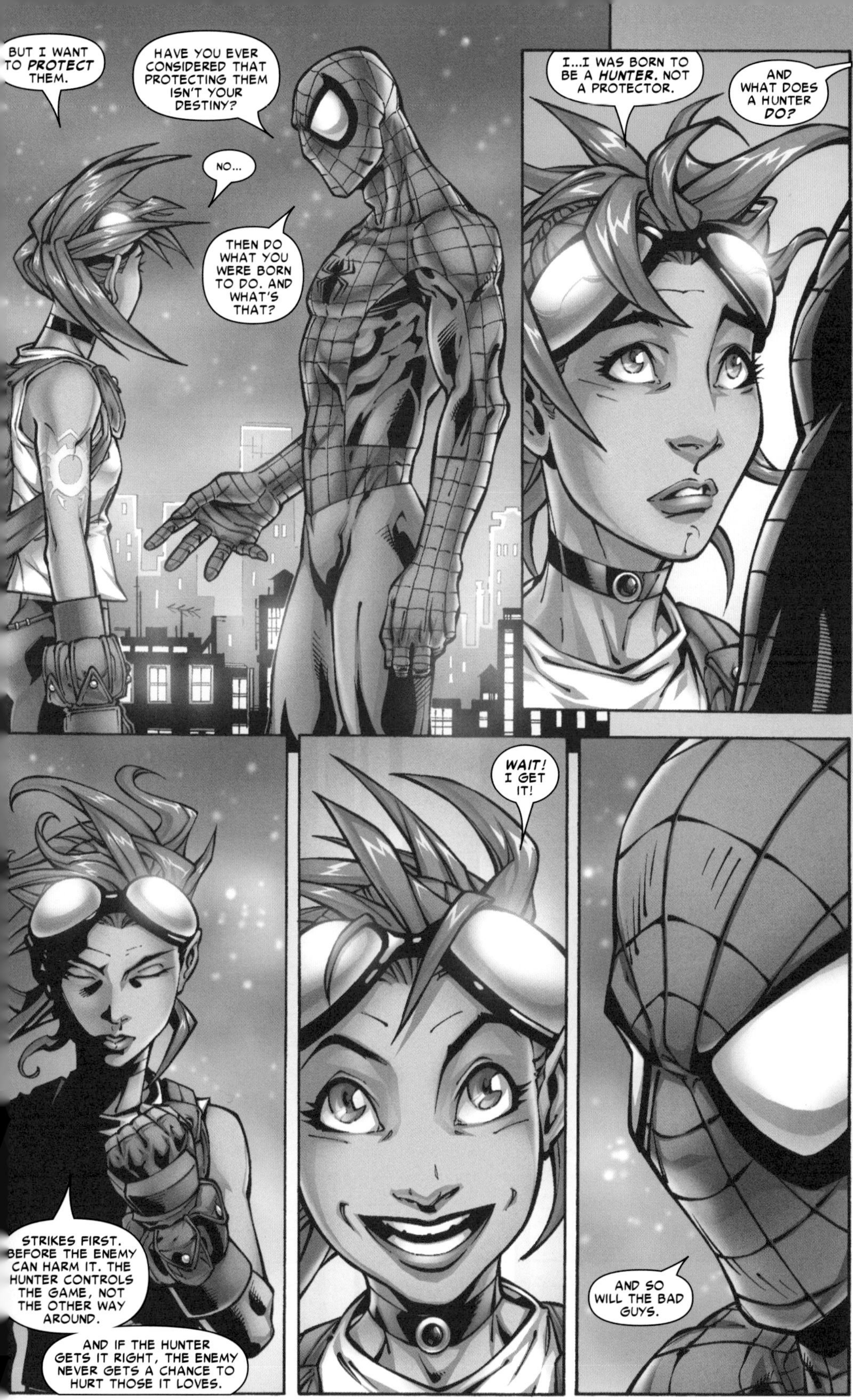
BUT I WANT TO *PROTECT* THEM.
HAVE YOU EVER CONSIDERED THAT PROTECTING THEM ISN'T YOUR DESTINY?
NO...
THEN DO WHAT YOU WERE BORN TO DO. AND WHAT'S THAT?
I...I WAS BORN TO BE A *HUNTER.* NOT A PROTECTOR.
AND WHAT DOES A HUNTER *DO?*
STRIKES FIRST. BEFORE THE ENEMY CAN HARM IT. THE HUNTER CONTROLS THE GAME, NOT THE OTHER WAY AROUND.
AND IF THE HUNTER GETS IT RIGHT, THE ENEMY NEVER GETS A CHANCE TO HURT THOSE IT LOVES.
WAIT! I GET IT!
AND SO WILL THE BAD GUYS.

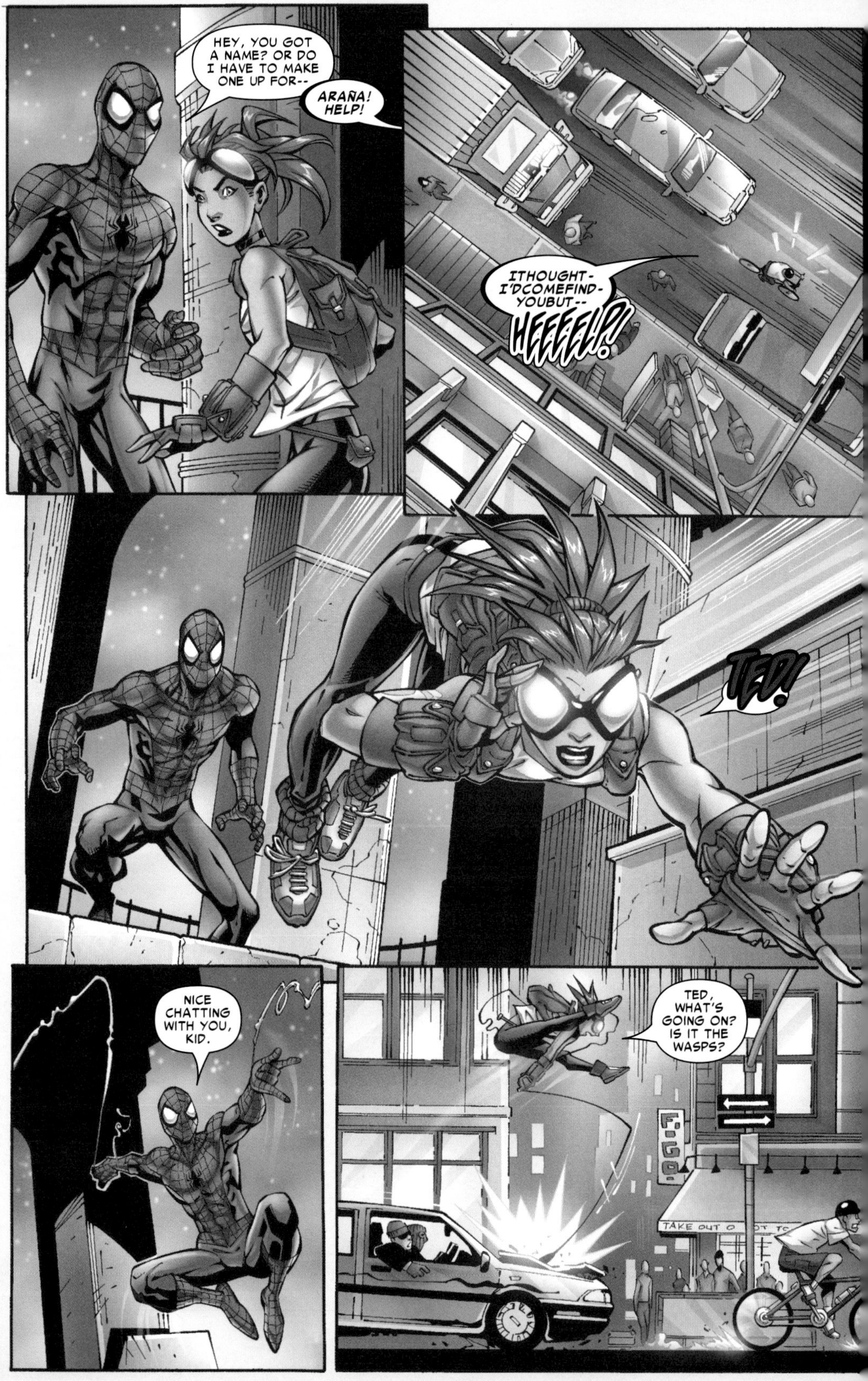
HEY, YOU GOT A NAME? OR DO I HAVE TO MAKE ONE UP FOR--
ARAÑA! HELP!
ITHOUGHT-I'DCOMEFIND-YOUBUT--
HEEEELP!
TED!
NICE CHATTING WITH YOU, KID.
TED, WHAT'S GOING ON? IS IT THE WASPS?
TAKE OUT

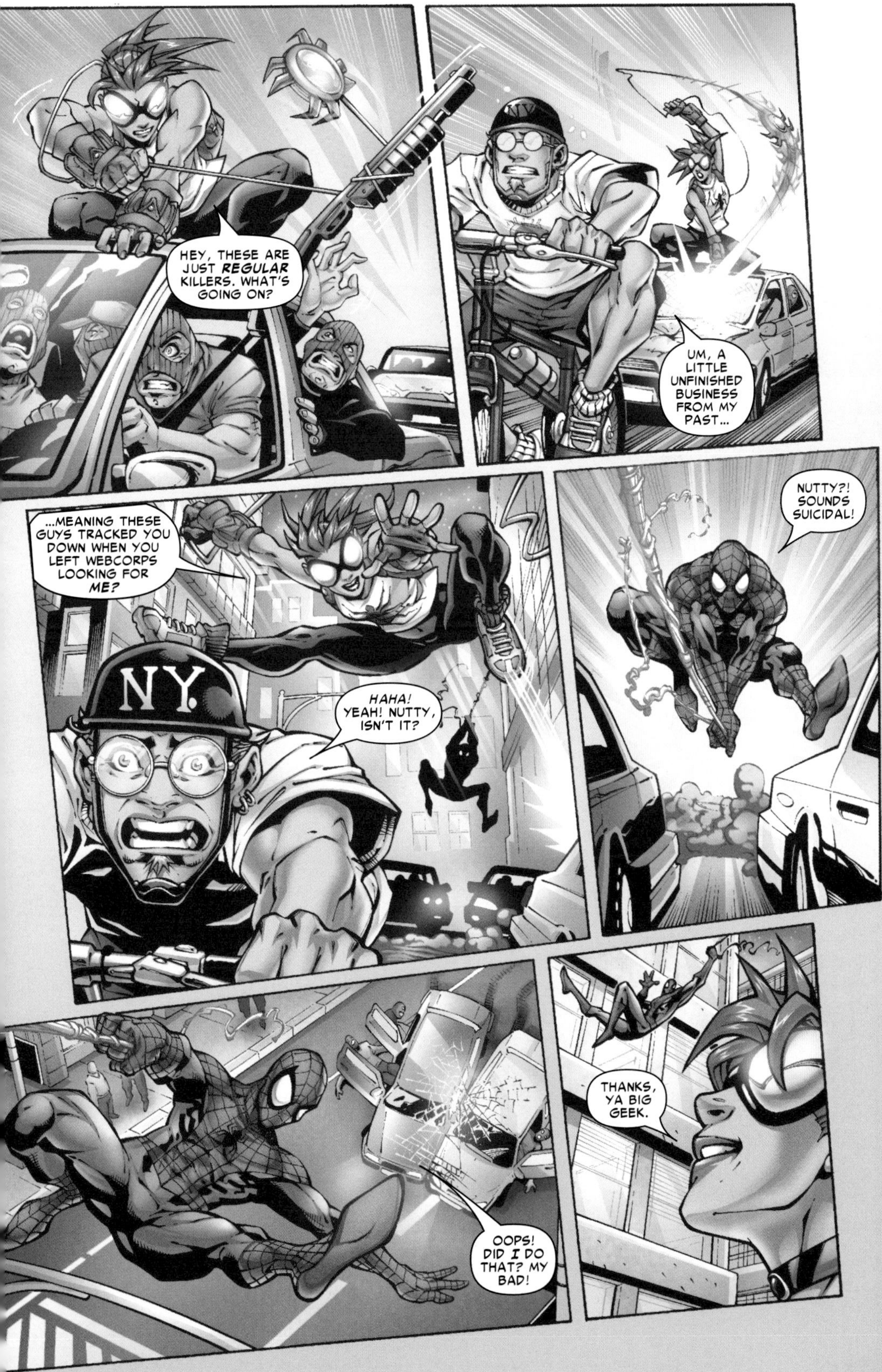
HEY, THESE ARE JUST REGULAR KILLERS. WHAT'S GOING ON?
UM, A LITTLE UNFINISHED BUSINESS FROM MY PAST...
...MEANING THESE GUYS TRACKED YOU DOWN WHEN YOU LEFT WEBCORPS LOOKING FOR ME?
HAHA! YEAH! NUTTY, ISN'T IT?
NUTTY?! SOUNDS SUICIDAL!
OOPS! DID I DO THAT? MY BAD!
THANKS, YA BIG GEEK.

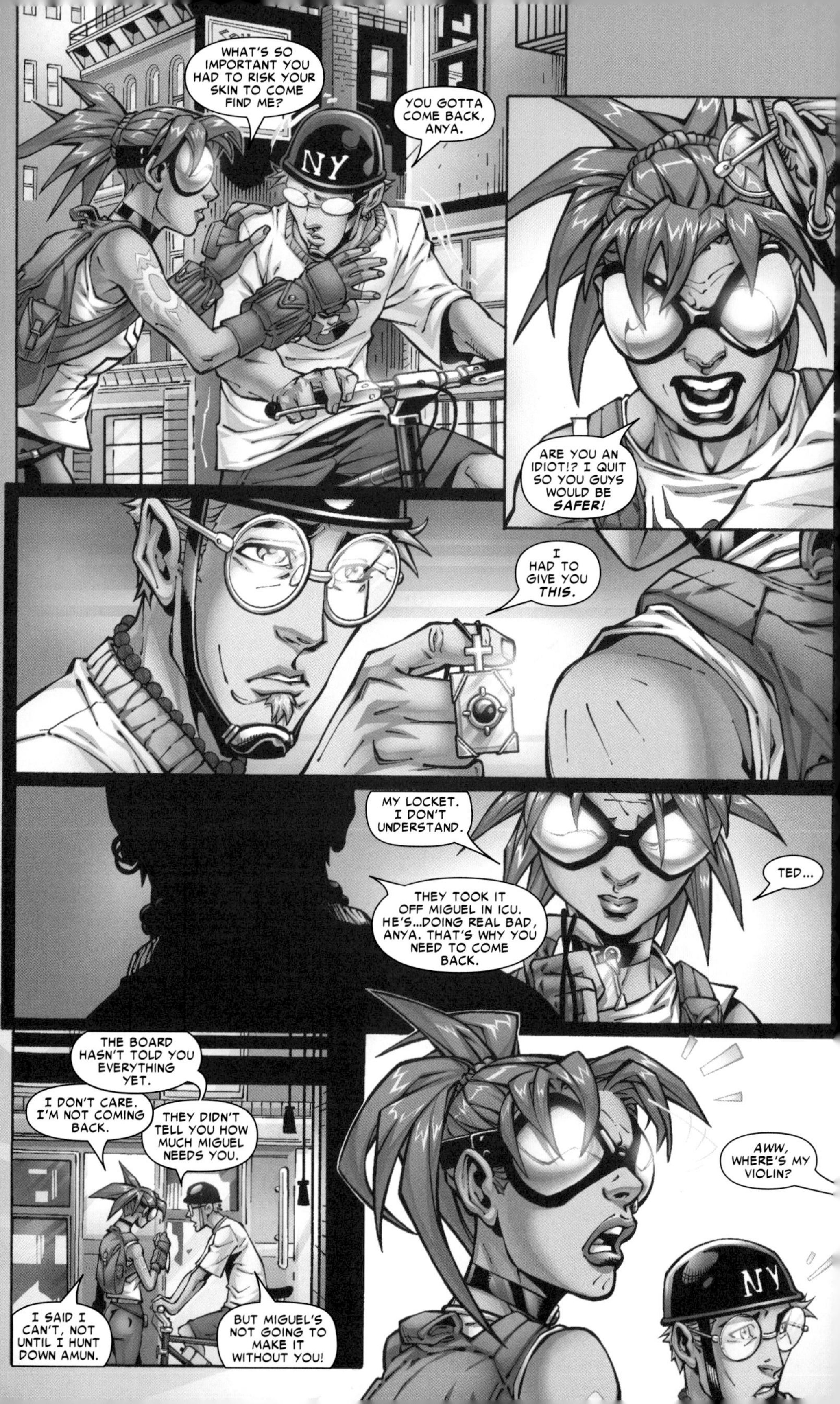
WHAT'S SO IMPORTANT YOU HAD TO RISK YOUR SKIN TO COME FIND ME?
YOU GOTTA COME BACK, ANYA.
NY
ARE YOU AN IDIOT!? I QUIT SO YOU GUYS WOULD BE *SAFER!*
I HAD TO GIVE YOU *THIS.*
MY LOCKET. I DON'T UNDERSTAND.
THEY TOOK IT OFF MIGUEL IN ICU. HE'S...DOING REAL BAD, ANYA. THAT'S WHY YOU NEED TO COME BACK.
TED...
THE BOARD HASN'T TOLD YOU EVERYTHING YET.
I DON'T CARE. I'M NOT COMING BACK.
THEY DIDN'T TELL YOU HOW MUCH MIGUEL NEEDS YOU.
I SAID I CAN'T, NOT UNTIL I HUNT DOWN AMUN.
BUT MIGUEL'S NOT GOING TO MAKE IT WITHOUT YOU!
AWW, WHERE'S MY VIOLIN?
NY

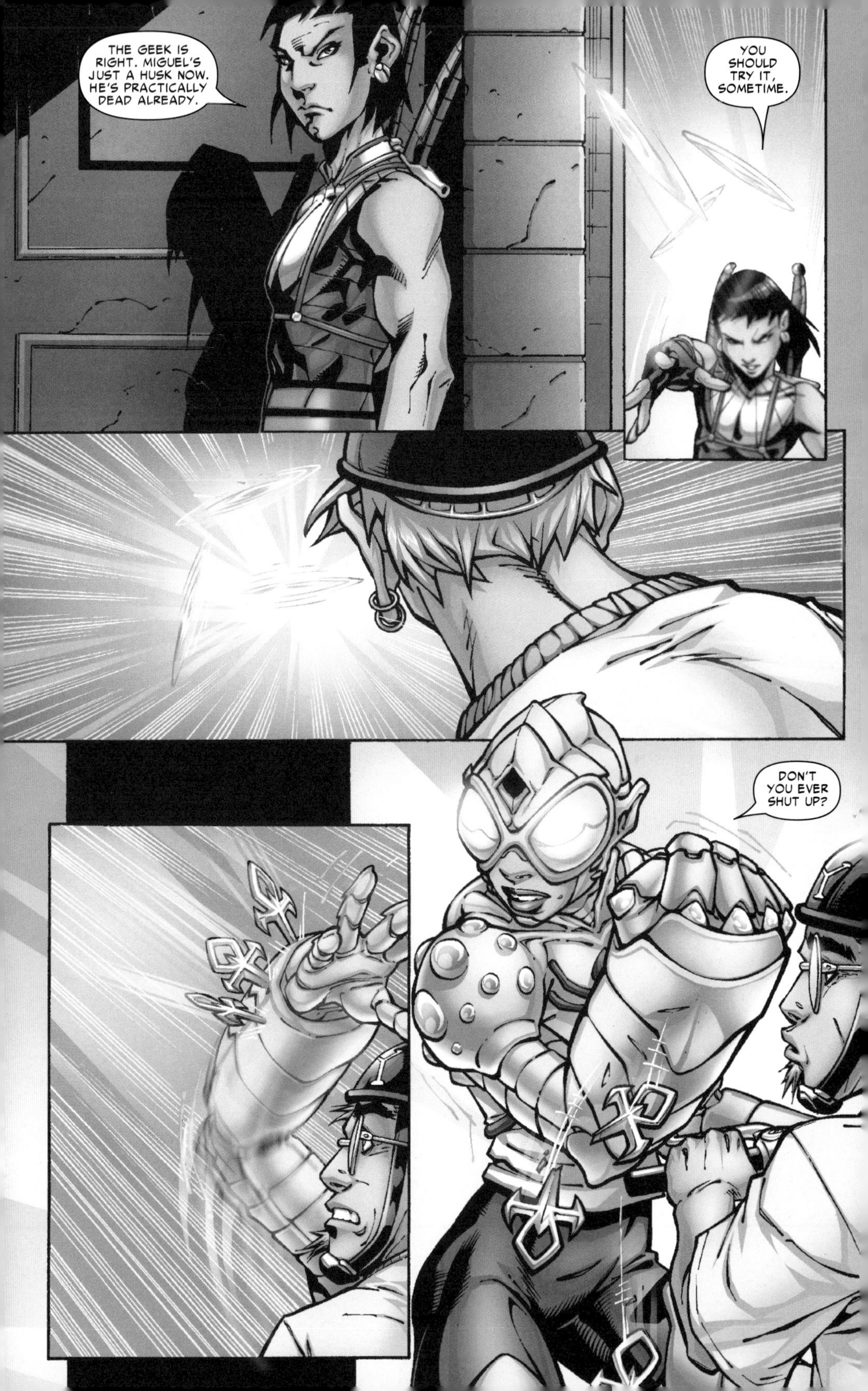
THE GEEK IS RIGHT. MIGUEL'S JUST A HUSK NOW. HE'S PRACTICALLY DEAD ALREADY.
YOU SHOULD TRY IT, SOMETIME.
DON'T YOU EVER SHUT UP?

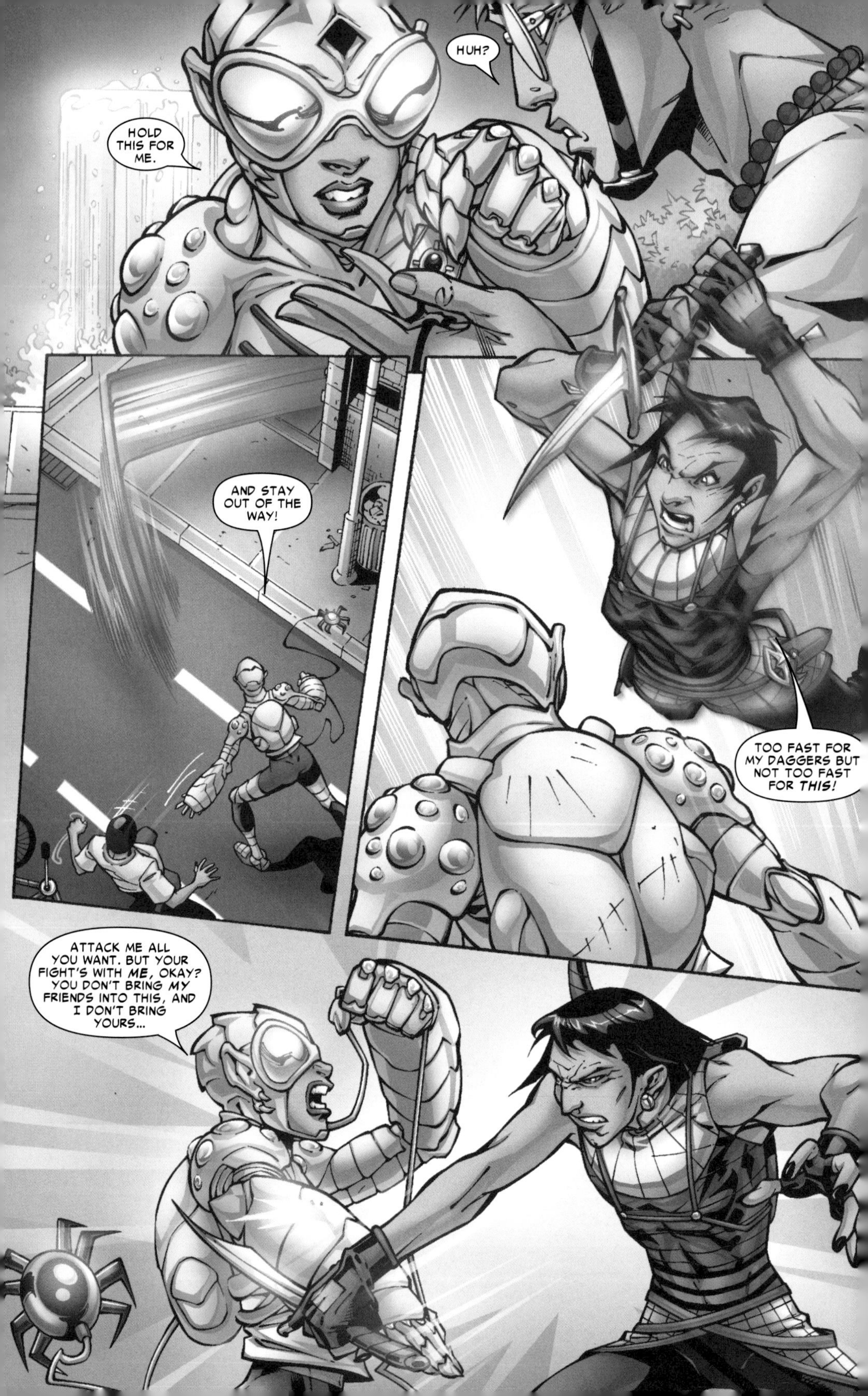
HUH?
HOLD THIS FOR ME.
AND STAY OUT OF THE WAY!
TOO FAST FOR MY DAGGERS BUT NOT TOO FAST FOR *THIS!*
ATTACK ME ALL YOU WANT. BUT YOUR FIGHT'S WITH *ME*, OKAY? YOU DON'T BRING *MY* FRIENDS INTO THIS, AND I DON'T BRING YOURS...

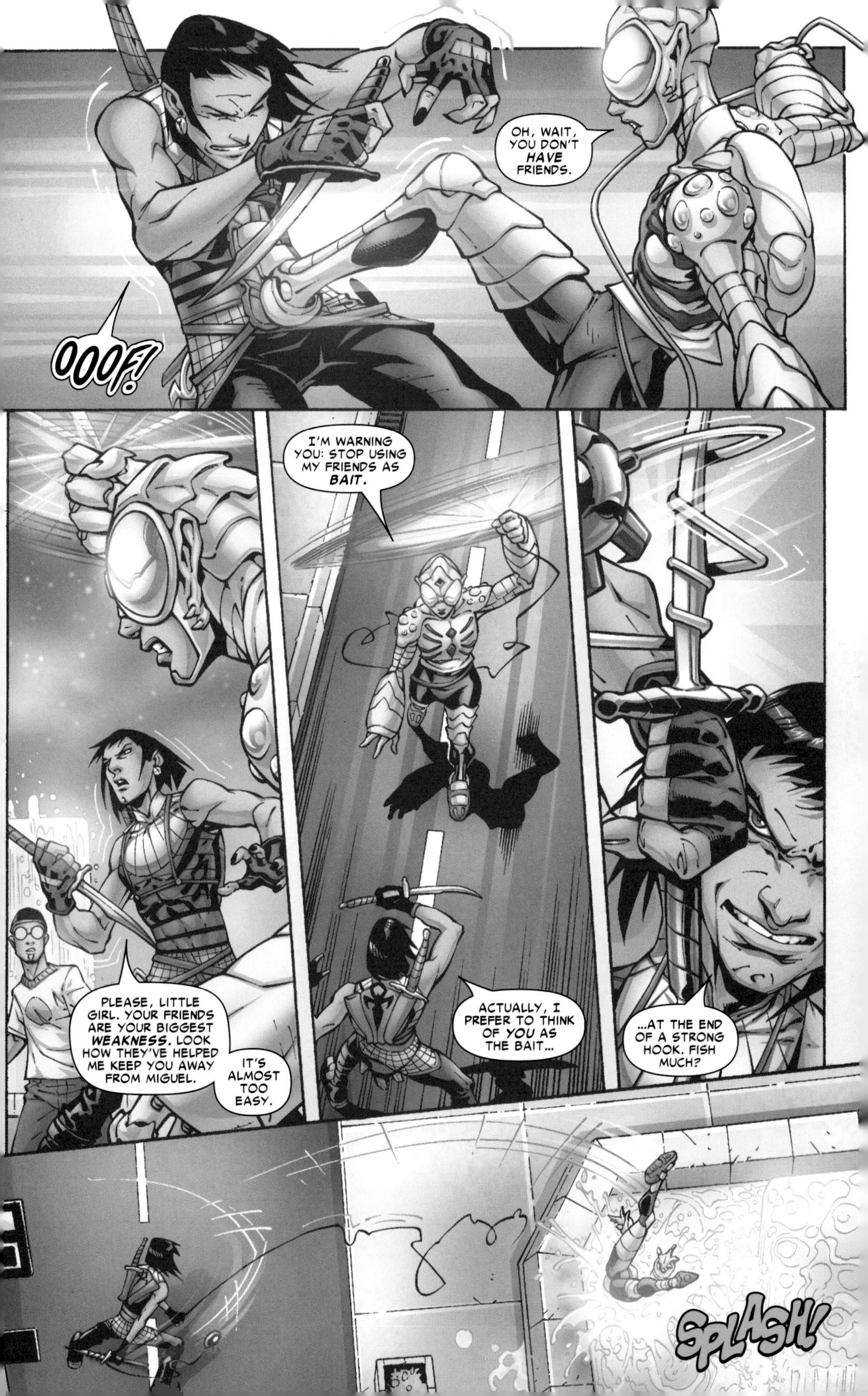
OH, WAIT, YOU DON'T HAVE FRIENDS.
OOOF!
PLEASE, LITTLE GIRL. YOUR FRIENDS ARE YOUR BIGGEST WEAKNESS. LOOK HOW THEY'VE HELPED ME KEEP YOU AWAY FROM MIGUEL.
IT'S ALMOST TOO EASY.
I'M WARNING YOU: STOP USING MY FRIENDS AS BAIT.
ACTUALLY, I PREFER TO THINK OF YOU AS THE BAIT...
...AT THE END OF A STRONG HOOK. FISH MUCH?
SPLASH!

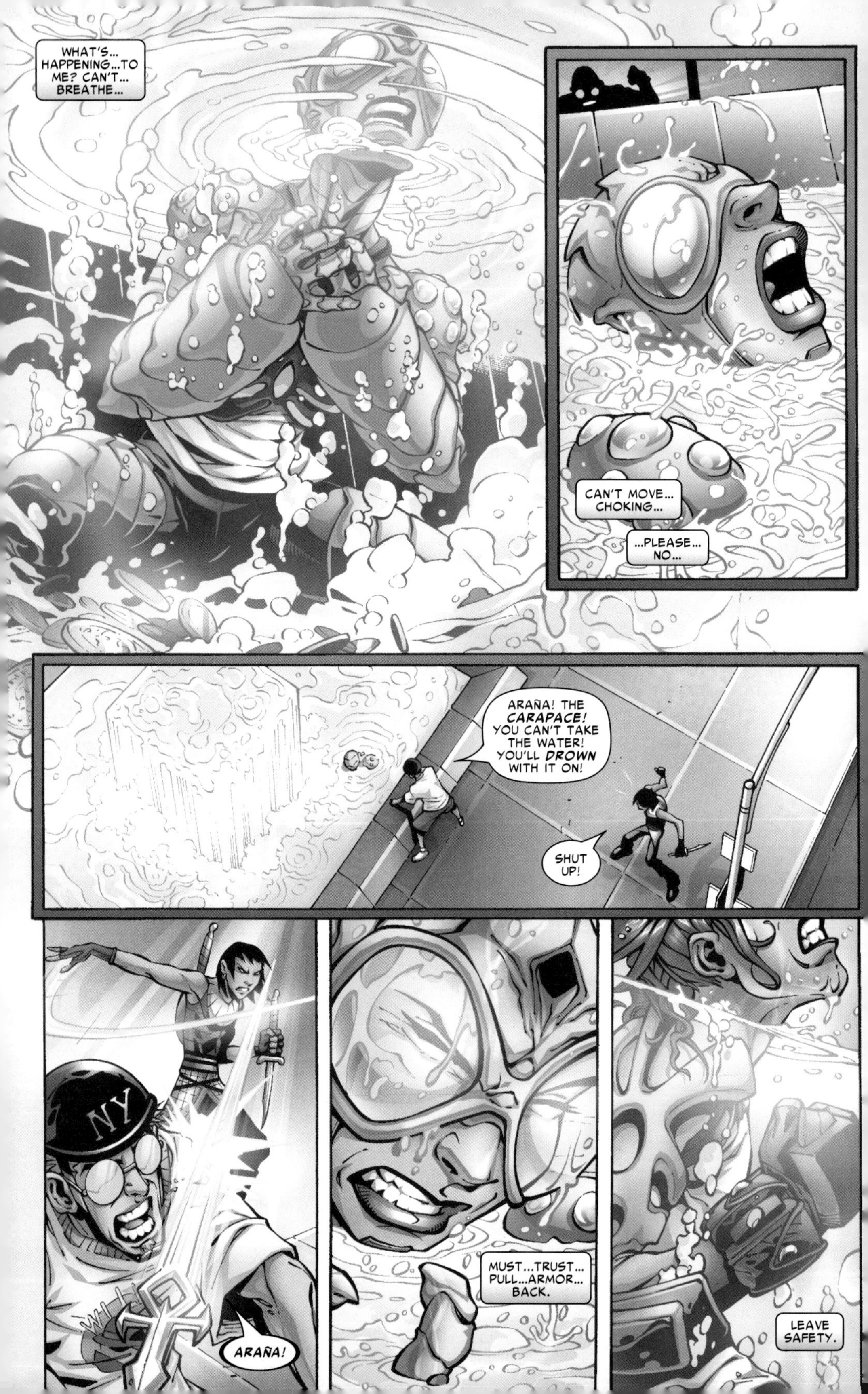
WHAT'S... HAPPENING...TO ME? CAN'T... BREATHE...
CAN'T MOVE... CHOKING...
...PLEASE... NO...
ARAÑA! THE *CARAPACE!* YOU CAN'T TAKE THE WATER! YOU'LL *DROWN* WITH IT ON!
SHUT UP!
ARAÑA!
MUST...TRUST... PULL...ARMOR... BACK.
LEAVE SAFETY.

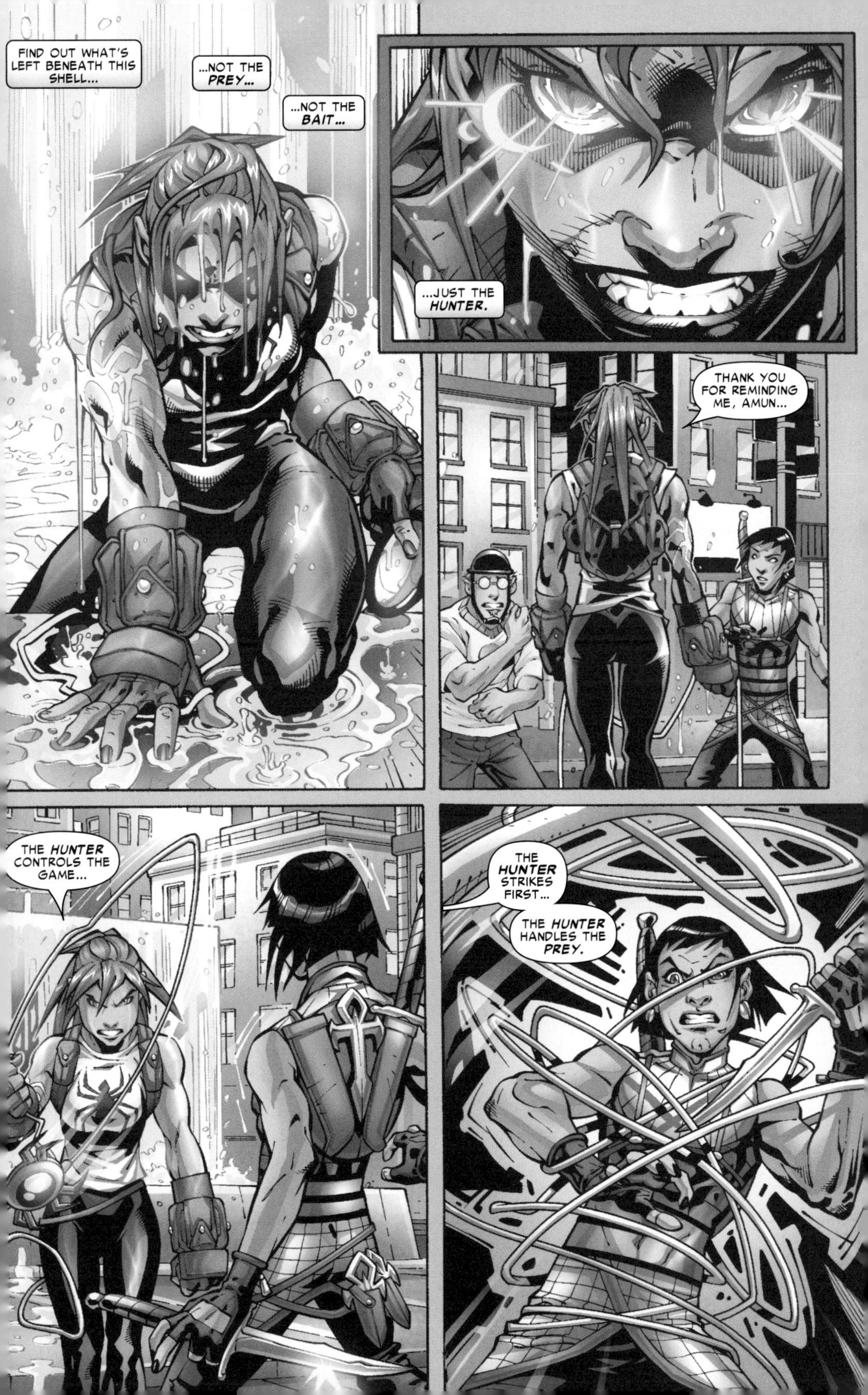

FIND OUT WHAT'S LEFT BENEATH THIS SHELL...
...NOT THE *PREY*...
...NOT THE *BAIT*...
...JUST THE *HUNTER*.
THANK YOU FOR REMINDING ME, AMUN...
THE *HUNTER* CONTROLS THE GAME...
THE *HUNTER* STRIKES FIRST...
THE *HUNTER* HANDLES THE *PREY*.

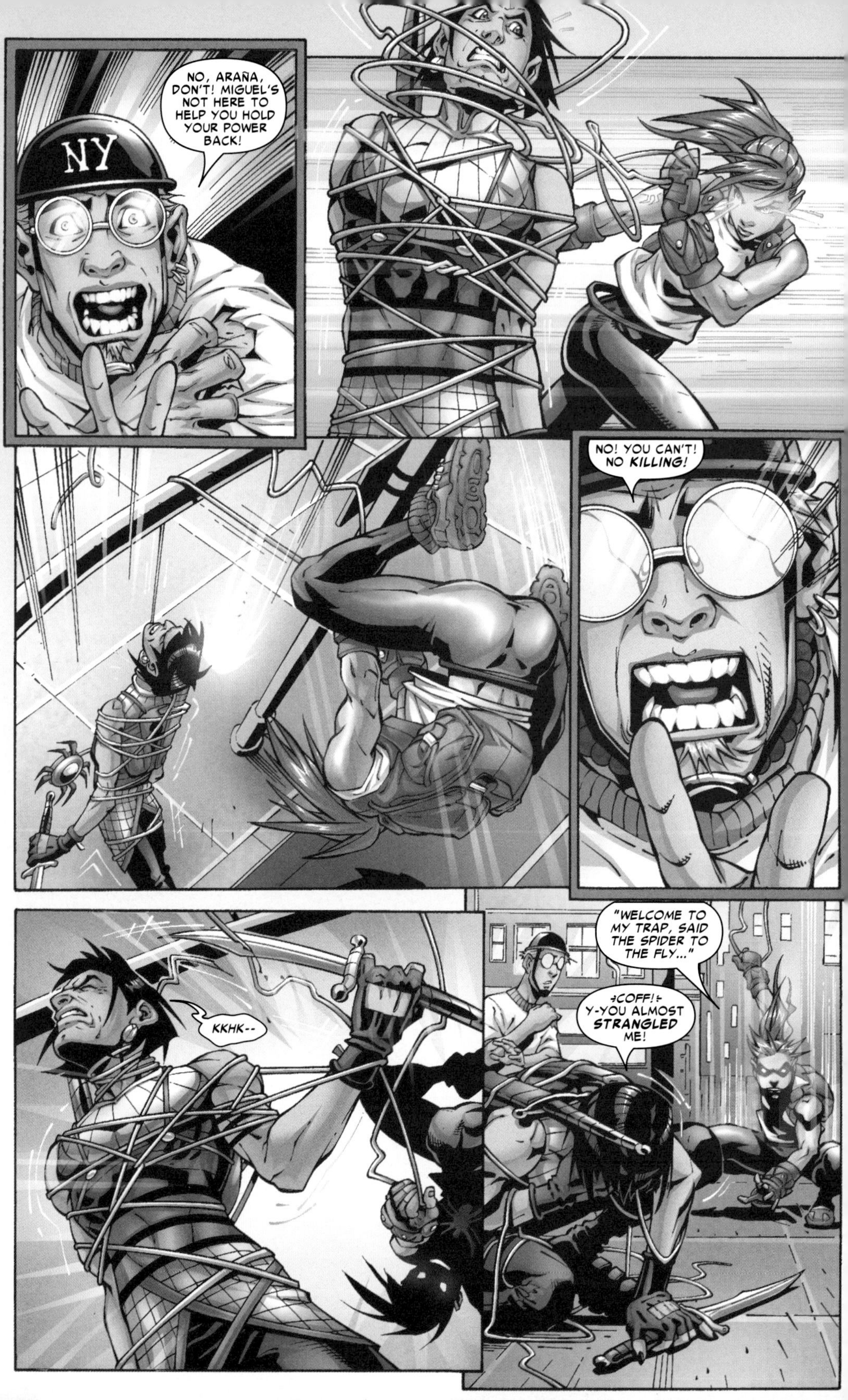
NO, ARAÑA, DON'T! MIGUEL'S NOT HERE TO HELP YOU HOLD YOUR POWER BACK!
NY
NO! YOU CAN'T! NO KILLING!
KKHK--
"WELCOME TO MY TRAP, SAID THE SPIDER TO THE FLY..."
COFF! Y-YOU ALMOST STRANGLED ME!

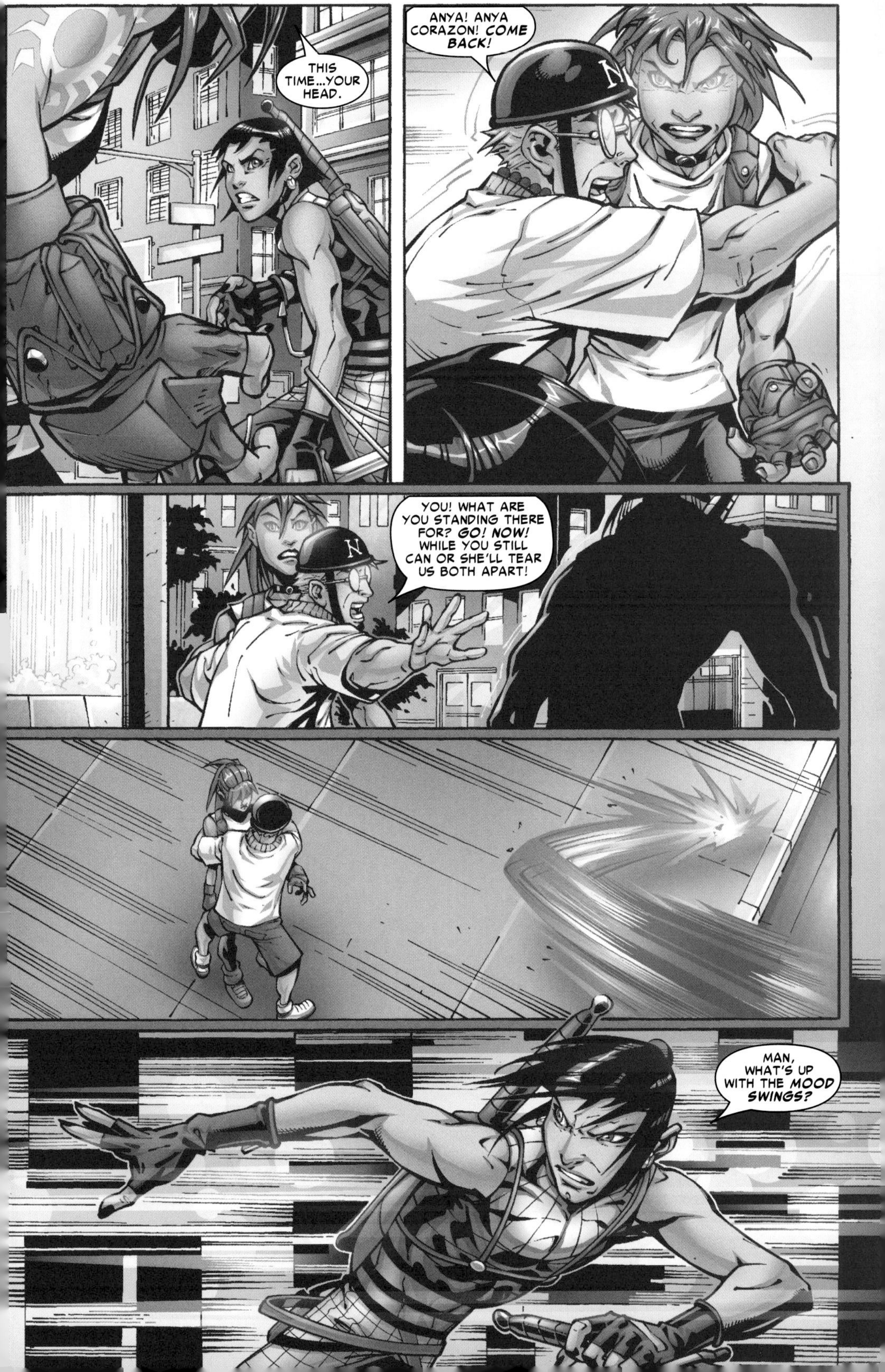
THIS TIME...YOUR HEAD.
ANYA! ANYA CORAZON! COME BACK!
YOU! WHAT ARE YOU STANDING THERE FOR? GO! NOW! WHILE YOU STILL CAN OR SHE'LL TEAR US BOTH APART!
MAN, WHAT'S UP WITH THE MOOD SWINGS?

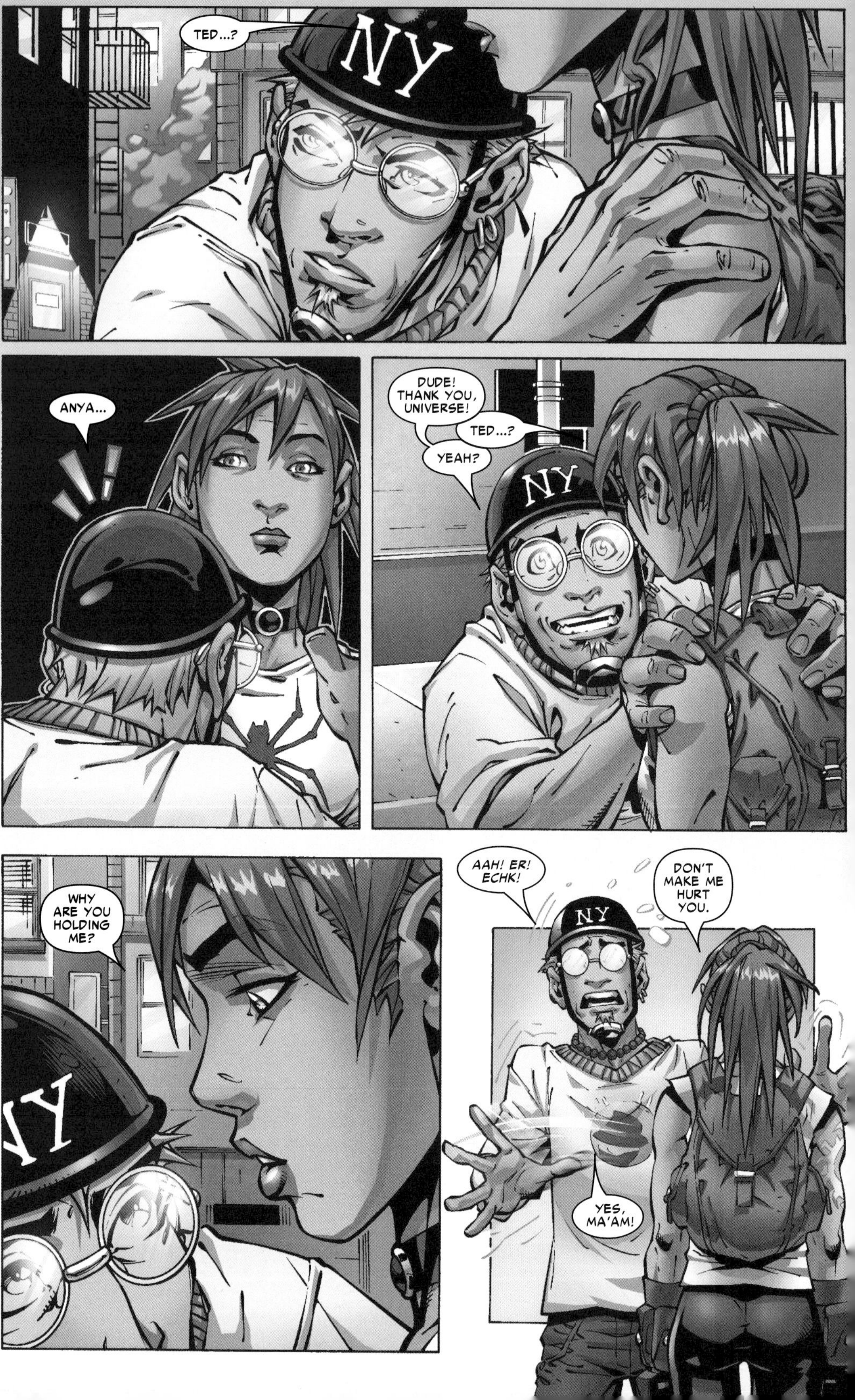
TED...?
ANYA...
DUDE! THANK YOU, UNIVERSE!
TED...?
YEAH?
WHY ARE YOU HOLDING ME?
AAH! ER! ECHK!
DON'T MAKE ME HURT YOU.
YES, MA'AM!

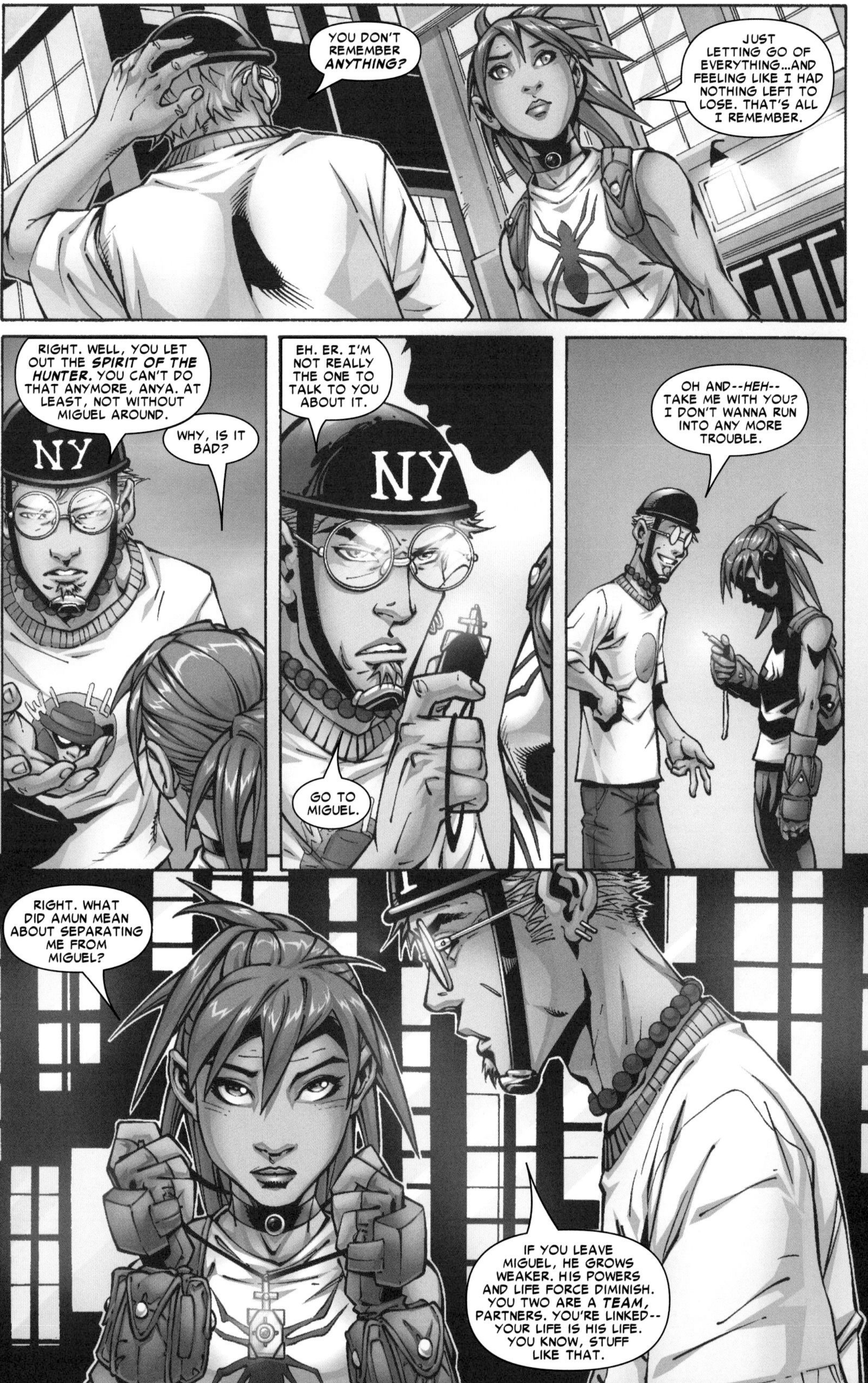

YOU DON'T REMEMBER ANYTHING?
JUST LETTING GO OF EVERYTHING...AND FEELING LIKE I HAD NOTHING LEFT TO LOSE. THAT'S ALL I REMEMBER.
RIGHT. WELL, YOU LET OUT THE SPIRIT OF THE HUNTER. YOU CAN'T DO THAT ANYMORE, ANYA. AT LEAST, NOT WITHOUT MIGUEL AROUND.
WHY, IS IT BAD?
EH. ER. I'M NOT REALLY THE ONE TO TALK TO YOU ABOUT IT.
GO TO MIGUEL.
OH AND--HEH-- TAKE ME WITH YOU? I DON'T WANNA RUN INTO ANY MORE TROUBLE.
RIGHT. WHAT DID AMUN MEAN ABOUT SEPARATING ME FROM MIGUEL?
IF YOU LEAVE MIGUEL, HE GROWS WEAKER. HIS POWERS AND LIFE FORCE DIMINISH. YOU TWO ARE A TEAM, PARTNERS. YOU'RE LINKED-- YOUR LIFE IS HIS LIFE. YOU KNOW, STUFF LIKE THAT.

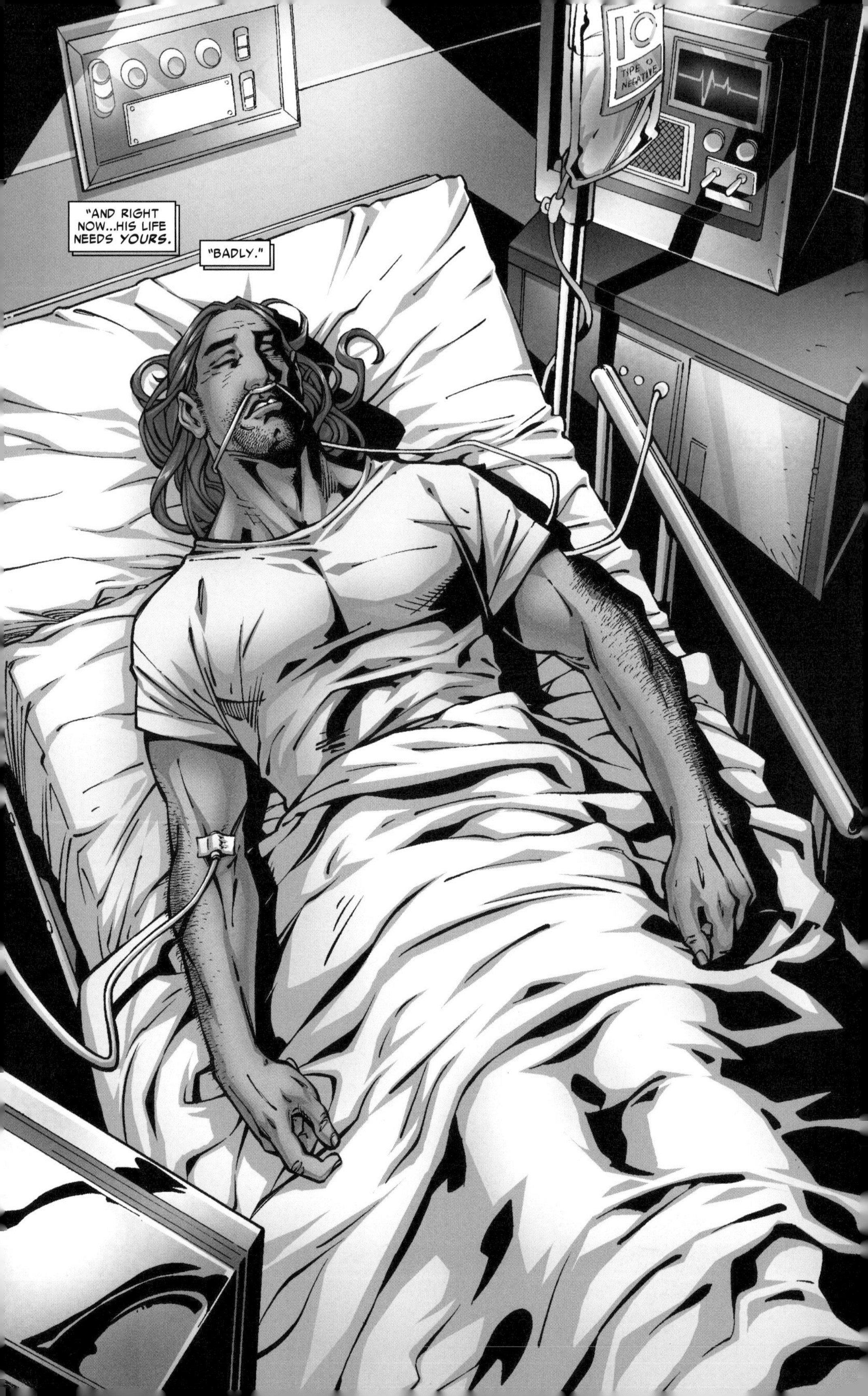
"AND RIGHT NOW...HIS LIFE NEEDS *YOURS*.
"BADLY."
TYPE O NEGATIVE

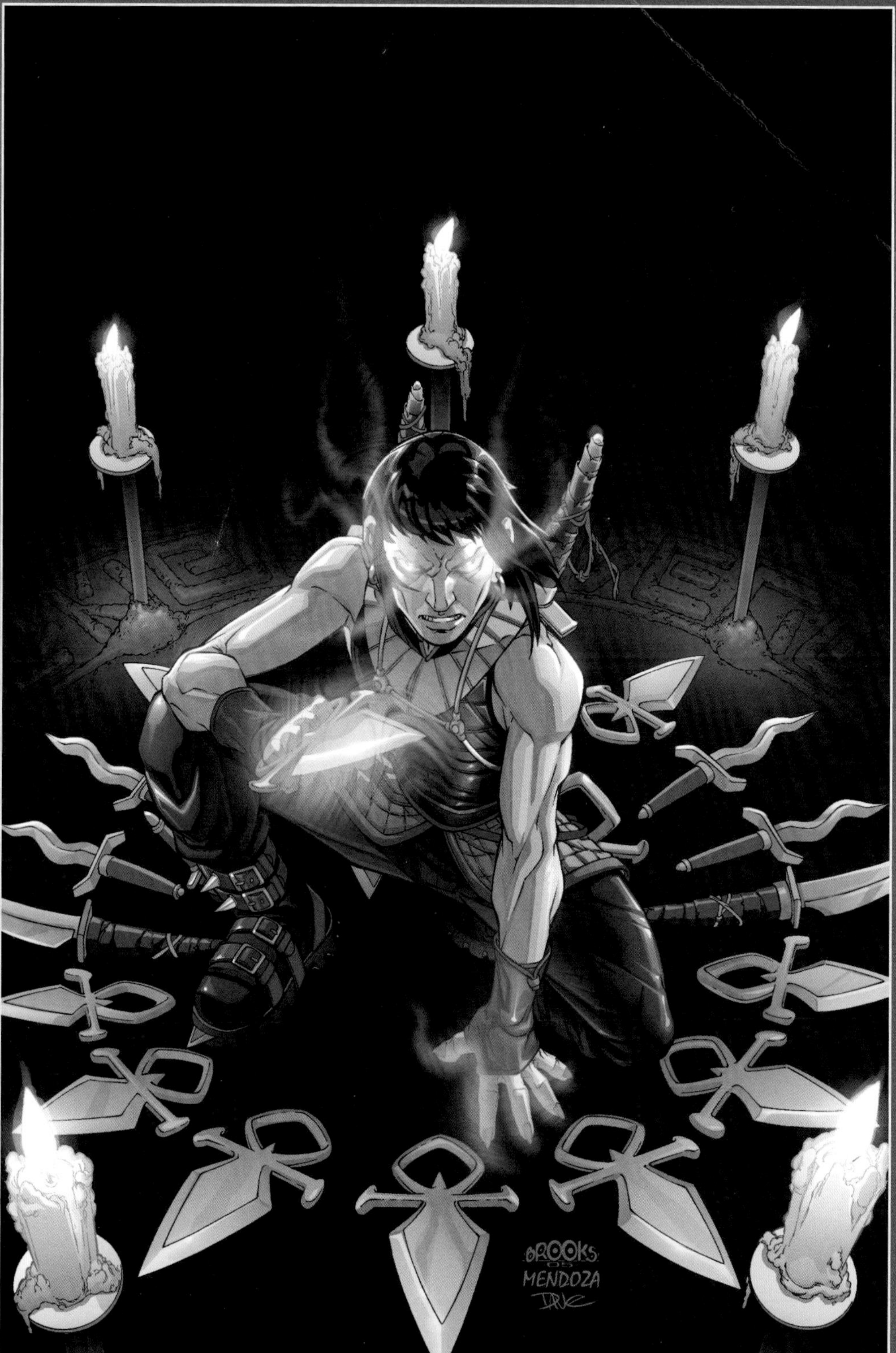
BROOKS
05
MENDOZA

ARAÑA #5

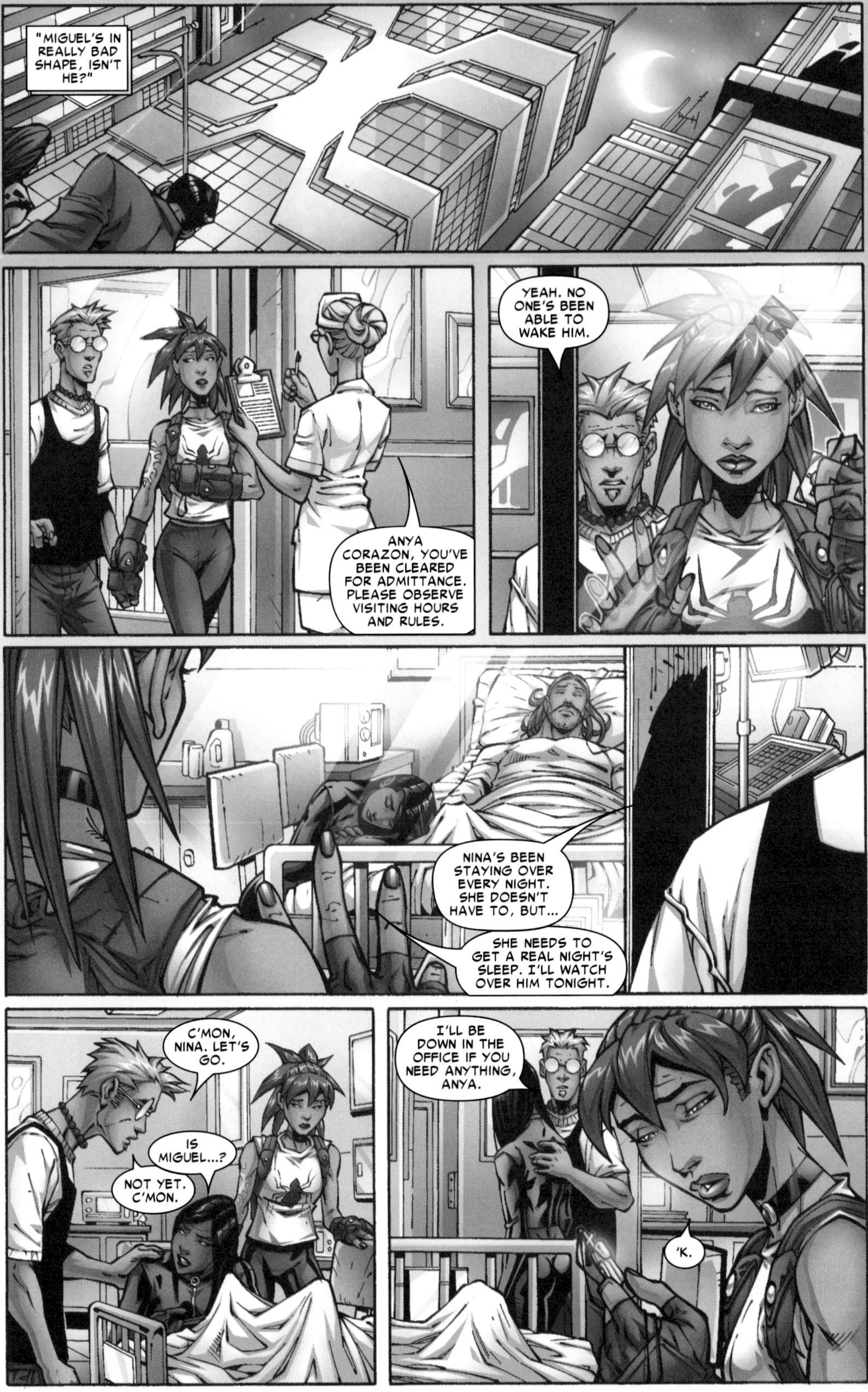
"MIGUEL'S IN REALLY BAD SHAPE, ISN'T HE?"
ANYA CORAZON, YOU'VE BEEN CLEARED FOR ADMITTANCE. PLEASE OBSERVE VISITING HOURS AND RULES.
YEAH. NO ONE'S BEEN ABLE TO WAKE HIM.
NINA'S BEEN STAYING OVER EVERY NIGHT. SHE DOESN'T HAVE TO, BUT...
SHE NEEDS TO GET A REAL NIGHT'S SLEEP. I'LL WATCH OVER HIM TONIGHT.
C'MON, NINA. LET'S GO.
IS MIGUEL...?
NOT YET. C'MON.
I'LL BE DOWN IN THE OFFICE IF YOU NEED ANYTHING, ANYA.
'K.

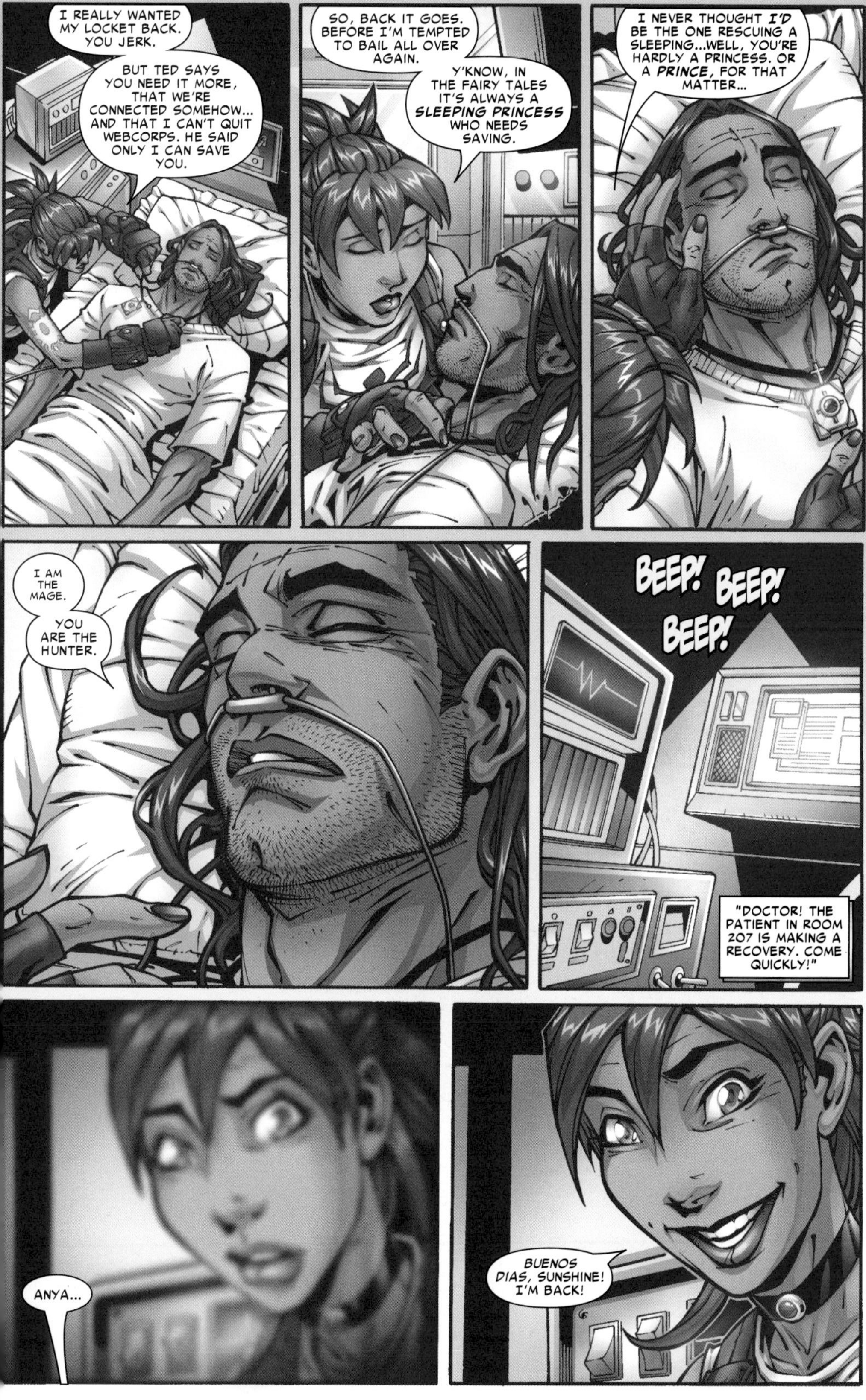
I REALLY WANTED MY LOCKET BACK. YOU JERK.
BUT TED SAYS YOU NEED IT MORE, THAT WE'RE CONNECTED SOMEHOW... AND THAT I CAN'T QUIT WEBCORPS. HE SAID ONLY I CAN SAVE YOU.
SO, BACK IT GOES. BEFORE I'M TEMPTED TO BAIL ALL OVER AGAIN.
Y'KNOW, IN THE FAIRY TALES IT'S ALWAYS A SLEEPING PRINCESS WHO NEEDS SAVING.
I NEVER THOUGHT I'D BE THE ONE RESCUING A SLEEPING...WELL, YOU'RE HARDLY A PRINCESS. OR A PRINCE, FOR THAT MATTER...
I AM THE MAGE.
YOU ARE THE HUNTER.
BEEP! BEEP! BEEP!
"DOCTOR! THE PATIENT IN ROOM 207 IS MAKING A RECOVERY. COME QUICKLY!"
ANYA...
BUENOS DIAS, SUNSHINE! I'M BACK!

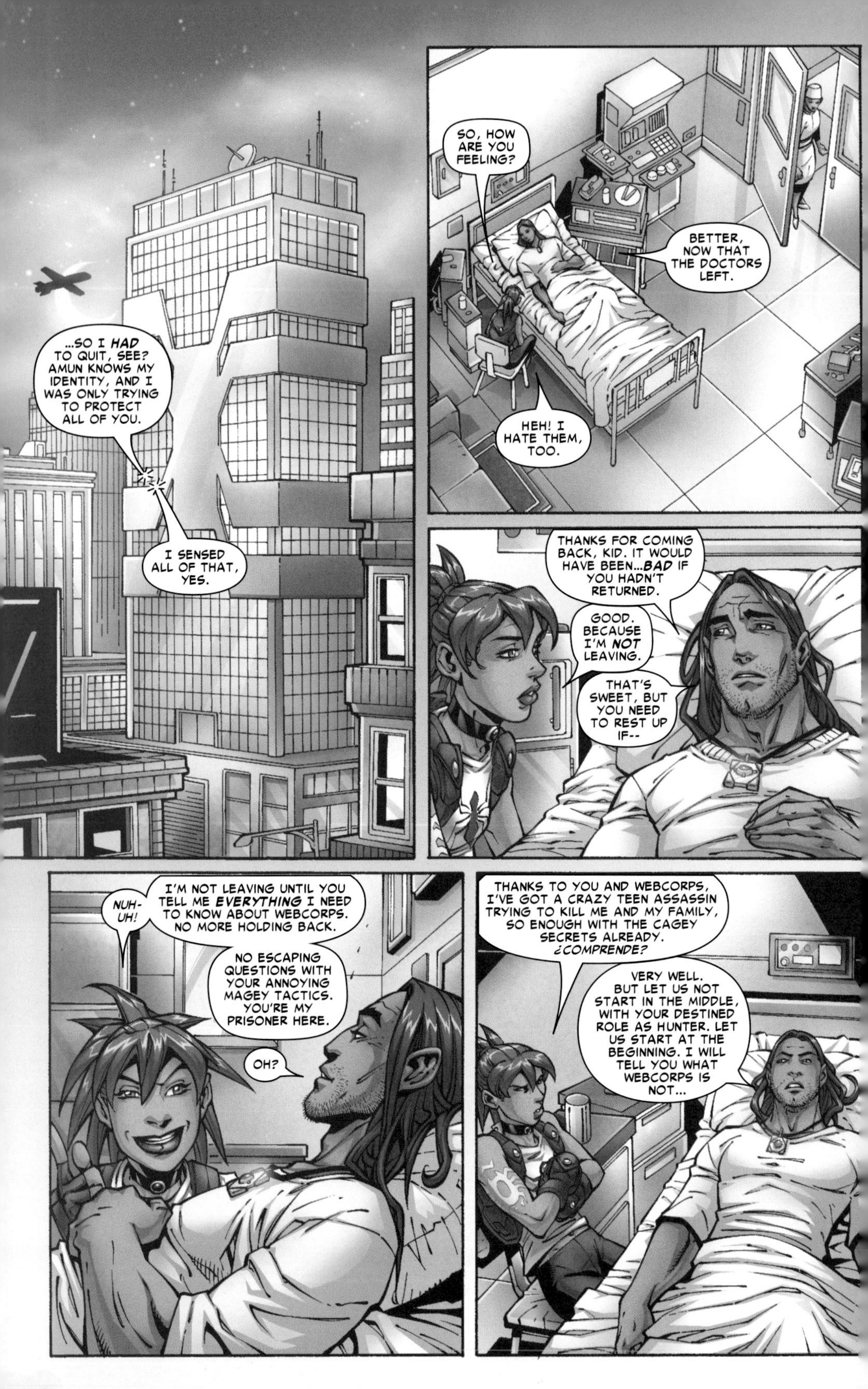
...SO I *HAD* TO QUIT, SEE? AMUN KNOWS MY IDENTITY, AND I WAS ONLY TRYING TO PROTECT ALL OF YOU.
I SENSED ALL OF THAT, YES.
SO, HOW ARE YOU FEELING?
BETTER, NOW THAT THE DOCTORS LEFT.
HEH! I HATE THEM, TOO.
THANKS FOR COMING BACK, KID. IT WOULD HAVE BEEN...*BAD* IF YOU HADN'T RETURNED.
GOOD. BECAUSE I'M *NOT* LEAVING.
THAT'S SWEET, BUT YOU NEED TO REST UP IF--
NUH-UH!
I'M NOT LEAVING UNTIL YOU TELL ME *EVERYTHING* I NEED TO KNOW ABOUT WEBCORPS. NO MORE HOLDING BACK.
NO ESCAPING QUESTIONS WITH YOUR ANNOYING MAGEY TACTICS. YOU'RE MY PRISONER HERE.
OH?
THANKS TO YOU AND WEBCORPS, I'VE GOT A CRAZY TEEN ASSASSIN TRYING TO KILL ME AND MY FAMILY, SO ENOUGH WITH THE CAGEY SECRETS ALREADY. *¿COMPRENDE?*
VERY WELL. BUT LET US NOT START IN THE MIDDLE, WITH YOUR DESTINED ROLE AS HUNTER. LET US START AT THE BEGINNING. I WILL TELL YOU WHAT WEBCORPS IS NOT...

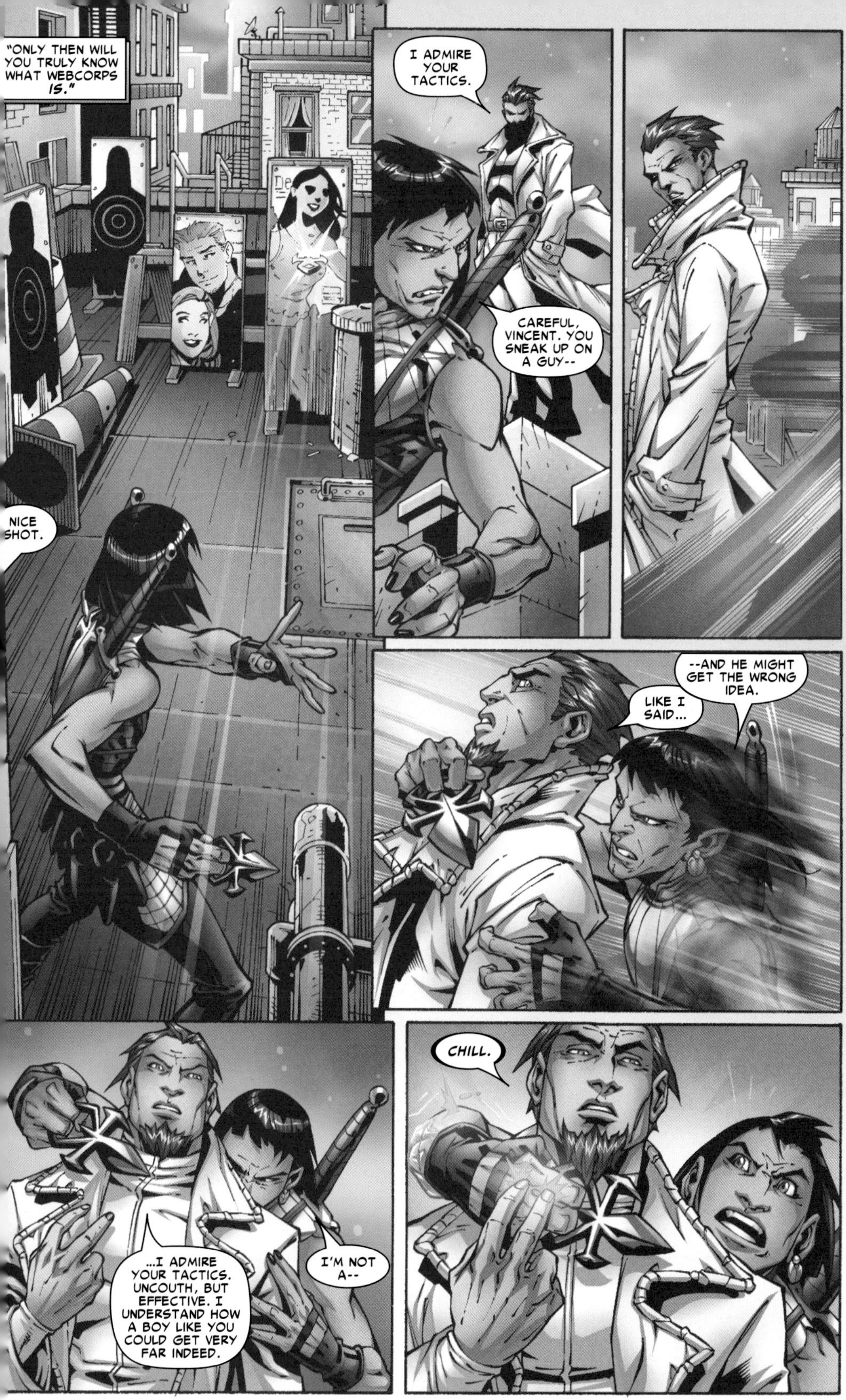
"ONLY THEN WILL YOU TRULY KNOW WHAT WEBCORPS IS."
NICE SHOT.
I ADMIRE YOUR TACTICS.
CAREFUL, VINCENT. YOU SNEAK UP ON A GUY--
LIKE I SAID...
--AND HE MIGHT GET THE WRONG IDEA.
...I ADMIRE YOUR TACTICS. UNCOUTH, BUT EFFECTIVE. I UNDERSTAND HOW A BOY LIKE YOU COULD GET VERY FAR INDEED.
I'M NOT A--
CHILL.

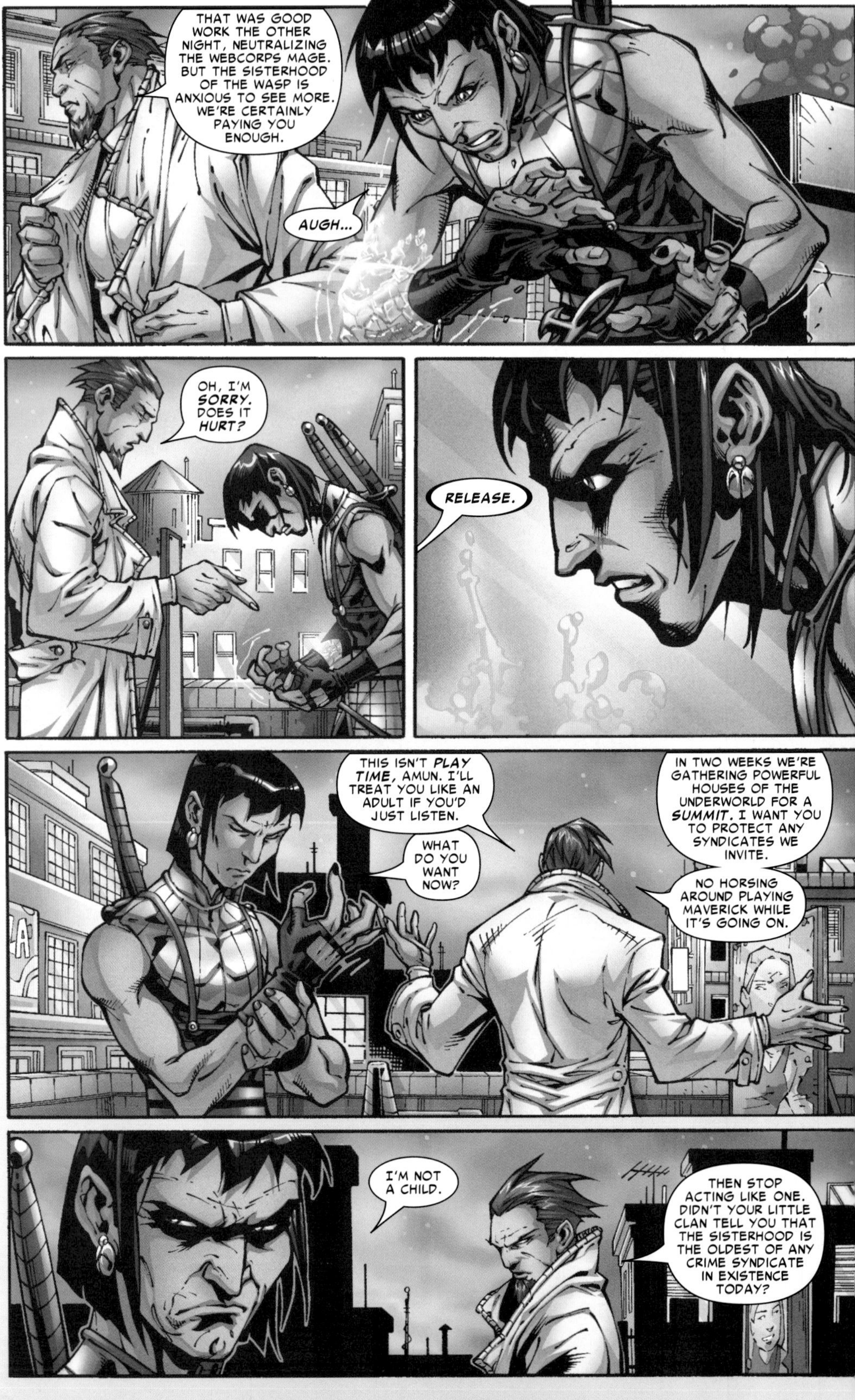
THAT WAS GOOD WORK THE OTHER NIGHT, NEUTRALIZING THE WEBCORPS MAGE. BUT THE SISTERHOOD OF THE WASP IS ANXIOUS TO SEE MORE. WE'RE CERTAINLY PAYING YOU ENOUGH.
AUGH...
OH, I'M SORRY. DOES IT HURT?
RELEASE.
THIS ISN'T PLAY TIME, AMUN. I'LL TREAT YOU LIKE AN ADULT IF YOU'D JUST LISTEN.
WHAT DO YOU WANT NOW?
IN TWO WEEKS WE'RE GATHERING POWERFUL HOUSES OF THE UNDERWORLD FOR A SUMMIT. I WANT YOU TO PROTECT ANY SYNDICATES WE INVITE.
NO HORSING AROUND PLAYING MAVERICK WHILE IT'S GOING ON.
I'M NOT A CHILD.
THEN STOP ACTING LIKE ONE. DIDN'T YOUR LITTLE CLAN TELL YOU THAT THE SISTERHOOD IS THE OLDEST OF ANY CRIME SYNDICATE IN EXISTENCE TODAY?

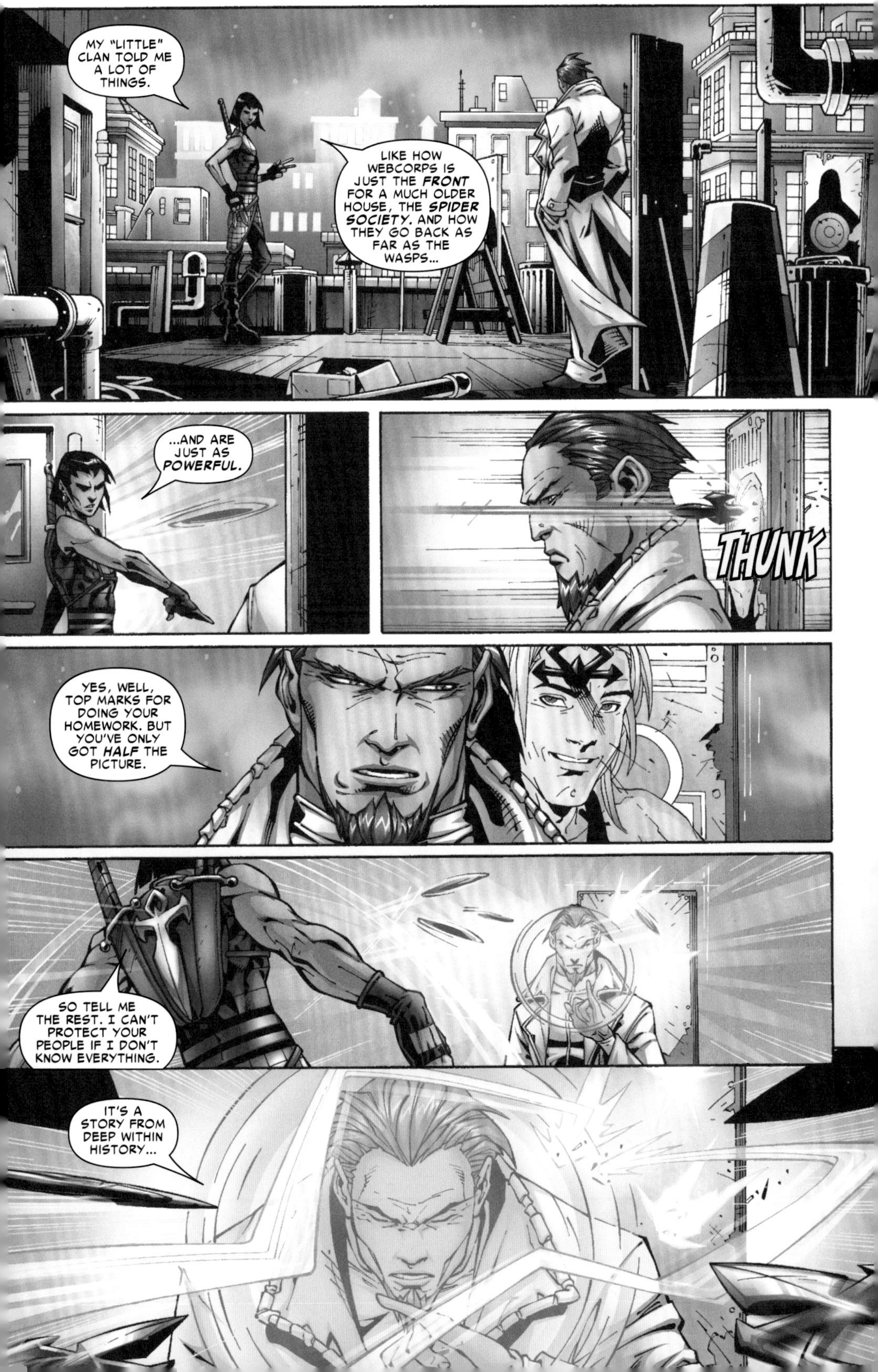
MY "LITTLE" CLAN TOLD ME A LOT OF THINGS.
LIKE HOW WEBCORPS IS JUST THE FRONT FOR A MUCH OLDER HOUSE, THE SPIDER SOCIETY. AND HOW THEY GO BACK AS FAR AS THE WASPS...
...AND ARE JUST AS POWERFUL.
THUNK
YES, WELL, TOP MARKS FOR DOING YOUR HOMEWORK. BUT YOU'VE ONLY GOT HALF THE PICTURE.
SO TELL ME THE REST. I CAN'T PROTECT YOUR PEOPLE IF I DON'T KNOW EVERYTHING.
IT'S A STORY FROM DEEP WITHIN HISTORY...

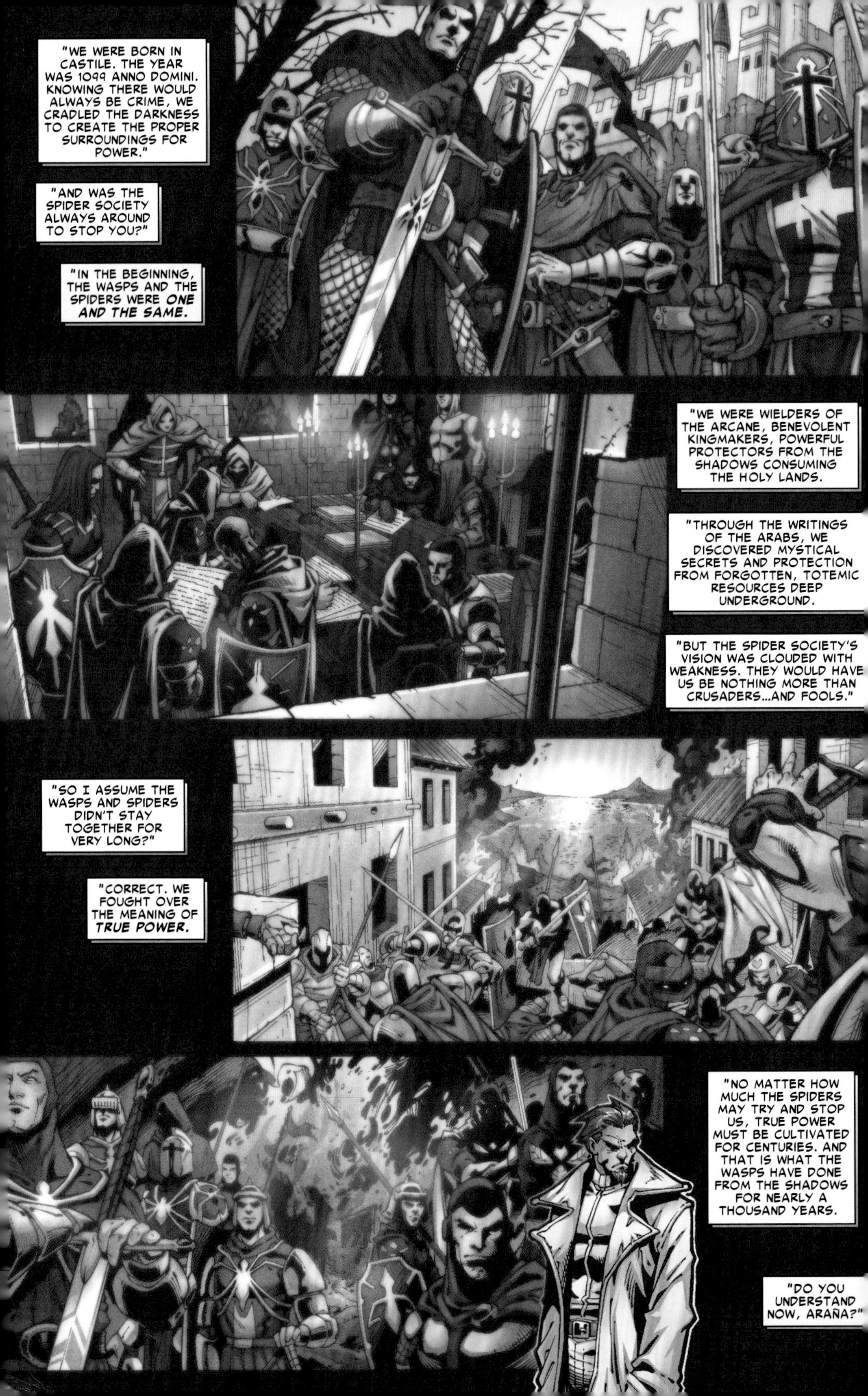
"WE WERE BORN IN CASTILE. THE YEAR WAS 1099 ANNO DOMINI. KNOWING THERE WOULD ALWAYS BE CRIME, WE CRADLED THE DARKNESS TO CREATE THE PROPER SURROUNDINGS FOR POWER."
"AND WAS THE SPIDER SOCIETY ALWAYS AROUND TO STOP YOU?"
"IN THE BEGINNING, THE WASPS AND THE SPIDERS WERE *ONE AND THE SAME.*
"WE WERE WIELDERS OF THE ARCANE, BENEVOLENT KINGMAKERS, POWERFUL PROTECTORS FROM THE SHADOWS CONSUMING THE HOLY LANDS.
"THROUGH THE WRITINGS OF THE ARABS, WE DISCOVERED MYSTICAL SECRETS AND PROTECTION FROM FORGOTTEN, TOTEMIC RESOURCES DEEP UNDERGROUND.
"BUT THE SPIDER SOCIETY'S VISION WAS CLOUDED WITH WEAKNESS. THEY WOULD HAVE US BE NOTHING MORE THAN CRUSADERS...AND FOOLS."
"SO I ASSUME THE WASPS AND SPIDERS DIDN'T STAY TOGETHER FOR VERY LONG?"
"CORRECT. WE FOUGHT OVER THE MEANING OF *TRUE POWER.*
"NO MATTER HOW MUCH THE SPIDERS MAY TRY AND STOP US, TRUE POWER MUST BE CULTIVATED FOR CENTURIES. AND THAT IS WHAT THE WASPS HAVE DONE FROM THE SHADOWS FOR NEARLY A THOUSAND YEARS.
"DO YOU UNDERSTAND NOW, ARAÑA?"

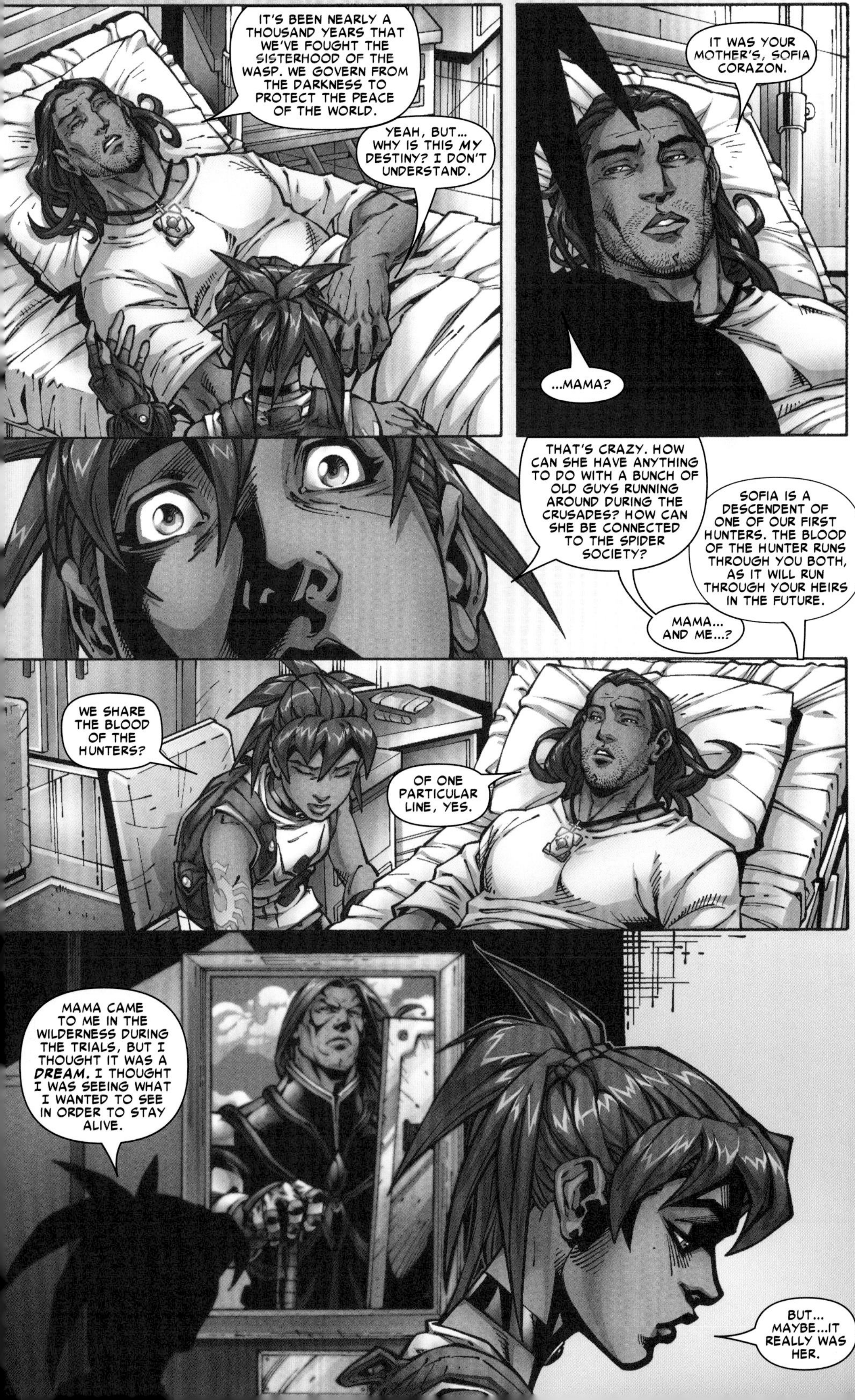
IT'S BEEN NEARLY A THOUSAND YEARS THAT WE'VE FOUGHT THE SISTERHOOD OF THE WASP. WE GOVERN FROM THE DARKNESS TO PROTECT THE PEACE OF THE WORLD.
YEAH, BUT... WHY IS THIS MY DESTINY? I DON'T UNDERSTAND.
IT WAS YOUR MOTHER'S, SOFIA CORAZON.
...MAMA?
THAT'S CRAZY. HOW CAN SHE HAVE ANYTHING TO DO WITH A BUNCH OF OLD GUYS RUNNING AROUND DURING THE CRUSADES? HOW CAN SHE BE CONNECTED TO THE SPIDER SOCIETY?
SOFIA IS A DESCENDENT OF ONE OF OUR FIRST HUNTERS. THE BLOOD OF THE HUNTER RUNS THROUGH YOU BOTH, AS IT WILL RUN THROUGH YOUR HEIRS IN THE FUTURE.
MAMA... AND ME...?
WE SHARE THE BLOOD OF THE HUNTERS?
OF ONE PARTICULAR LINE, YES.
MAMA CAME TO ME IN THE WILDERNESS DURING THE TRIALS, BUT I THOUGHT IT WAS A DREAM. I THOUGHT I WAS SEEING WHAT I WANTED TO SEE IN ORDER TO STAY ALIVE.
BUT... MAYBE...IT REALLY WAS HER.

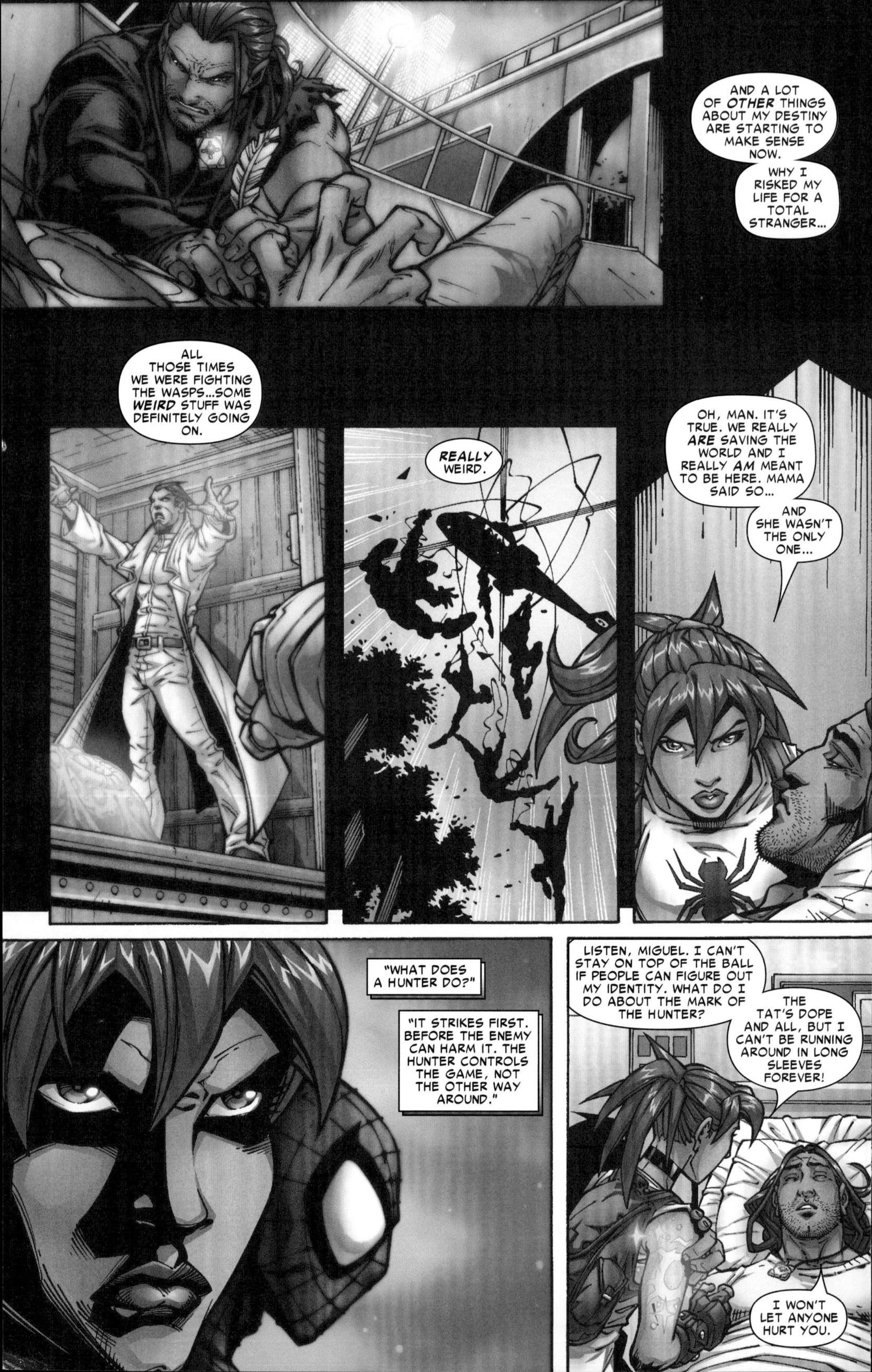
AND A LOT OF OTHER THINGS ABOUT MY DESTINY ARE STARTING TO MAKE SENSE NOW.
WHY I RISKED MY LIFE FOR A TOTAL STRANGER...
ALL THOSE TIMES WE WERE FIGHTING THE WASPS...SOME WEIRD STUFF WAS DEFINITELY GOING ON.
REALLY WEIRD.
OH, MAN. IT'S TRUE. WE REALLY ARE SAVING THE WORLD AND I REALLY AM MEANT TO BE HERE. MAMA SAID SO...
AND SHE WASN'T THE ONLY ONE...
"WHAT DOES A HUNTER DO?"
"IT STRIKES FIRST. BEFORE THE ENEMY CAN HARM IT. THE HUNTER CONTROLS THE GAME, NOT THE OTHER WAY AROUND."
LISTEN, MIGUEL. I CAN'T STAY ON TOP OF THE BALL IF PEOPLE CAN FIGURE OUT MY IDENTITY. WHAT DO I DO ABOUT THE MARK OF THE HUNTER?
THE TAT'S DOPE AND ALL, BUT I CAN'T BE RUNNING AROUND IN LONG SLEEVES FOREVER!
I WON'T LET ANYONE HURT YOU.

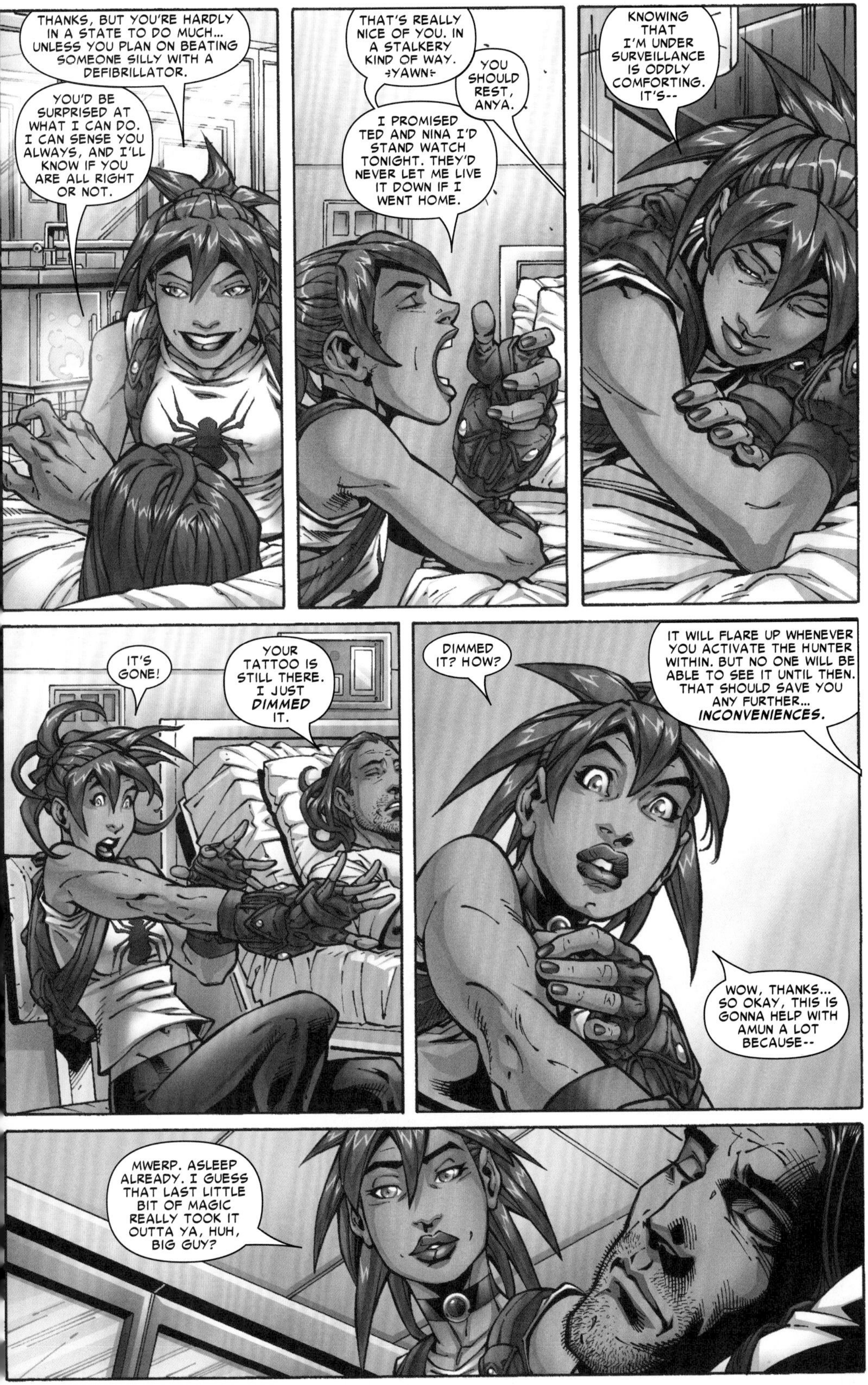

THANKS, BUT YOU'RE HARDLY IN A STATE TO DO MUCH... UNLESS YOU PLAN ON BEATING SOMEONE SILLY WITH A DEFIBRILLATOR.
YOU'D BE SURPRISED AT WHAT I CAN DO. I CAN SENSE YOU ALWAYS, AND I'LL KNOW IF YOU ARE ALL RIGHT OR NOT.
THAT'S REALLY NICE OF YOU. IN A STALKERY KIND OF WAY. *YAWN*
YOU SHOULD REST, ANYA.
I PROMISED TED AND NINA I'D STAND WATCH TONIGHT. THEY'D NEVER LET ME LIVE IT DOWN IF I WENT HOME.
KNOWING THAT I'M UNDER SURVEILLANCE IS ODDLY COMFORTING. IT'S--
IT'S GONE!
YOUR TATTOO IS STILL THERE. I JUST *DIMMED* IT.
DIMMED IT? HOW?
IT WILL FLARE UP WHENEVER YOU ACTIVATE THE HUNTER WITHIN. BUT NO ONE WILL BE ABLE TO SEE IT UNTIL THEN. THAT SHOULD SAVE YOU ANY FURTHER... ***INCONVENIENCES.***
WOW, THANKS... SO OKAY, THIS IS GONNA HELP WITH AMUN A LOT BECAUSE--
MWERP. ASLEEP ALREADY. I GUESS THAT LAST LITTLE BIT OF MAGIC REALLY TOOK IT OUTTA YA, HUH, BIG GUY?

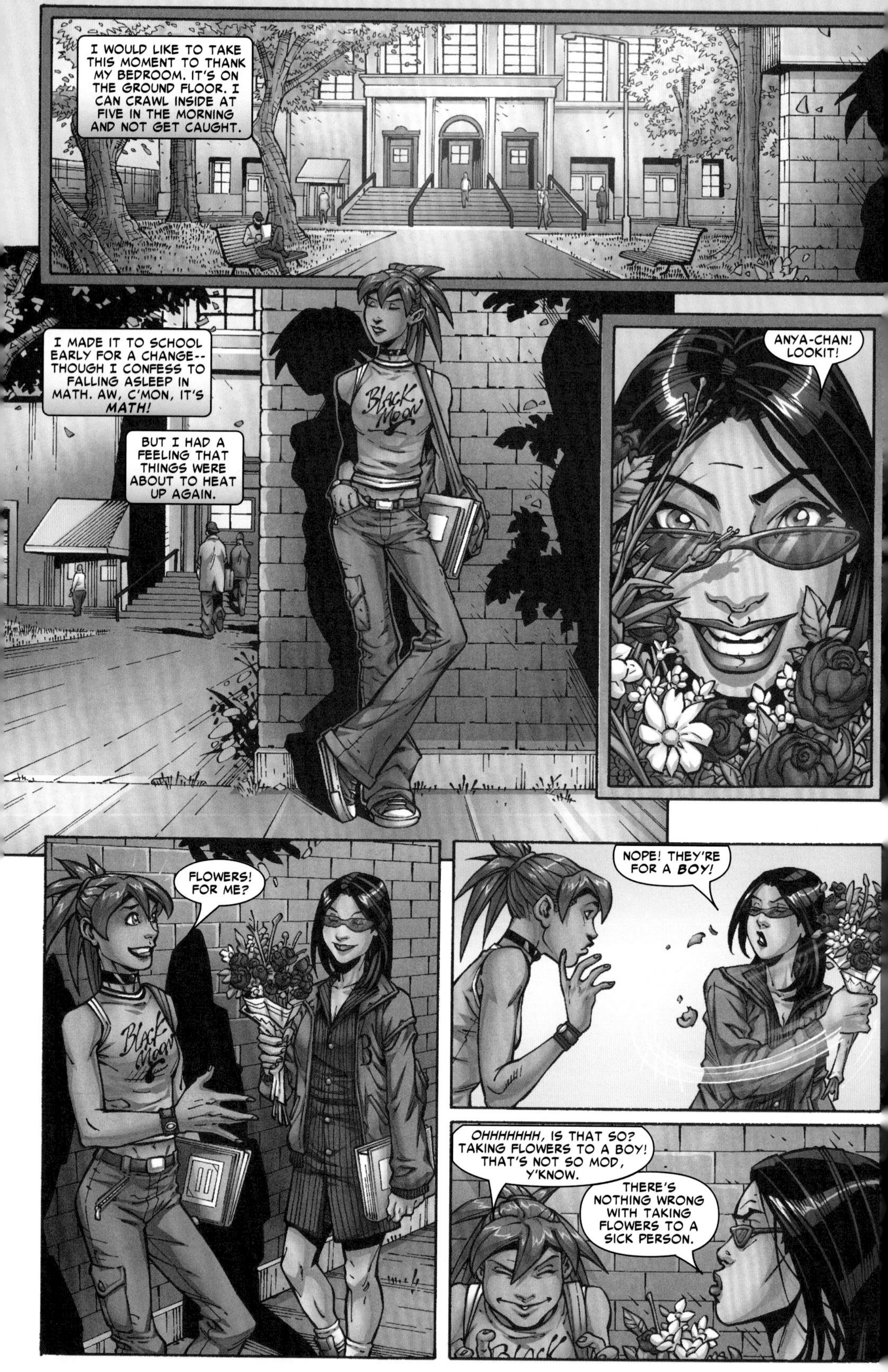
I WOULD LIKE TO TAKE THIS MOMENT TO THANK MY BEDROOM. IT'S ON THE GROUND FLOOR. I CAN CRAWL INSIDE AT FIVE IN THE MORNING AND NOT GET CAUGHT.
I MADE IT TO SCHOOL EARLY FOR A CHANGE-- THOUGH I CONFESS TO FALLING ASLEEP IN MATH. AW, C'MON, IT'S *MATH!*
BUT I HAD A FEELING THAT THINGS WERE ABOUT TO HEAT UP AGAIN.
BLACK MOON
ANYA-CHAN! LOOKIT!
FLOWERS! FOR ME?
NOPE! THEY'RE FOR A *BOY!*
OHHHHHHH, IS THAT SO? TAKING FLOWERS TO A BOY! THAT'S NOT SO MOD, Y'KNOW.
THERE'S NOTHING WRONG WITH TAKING FLOWERS TO A SICK PERSON.

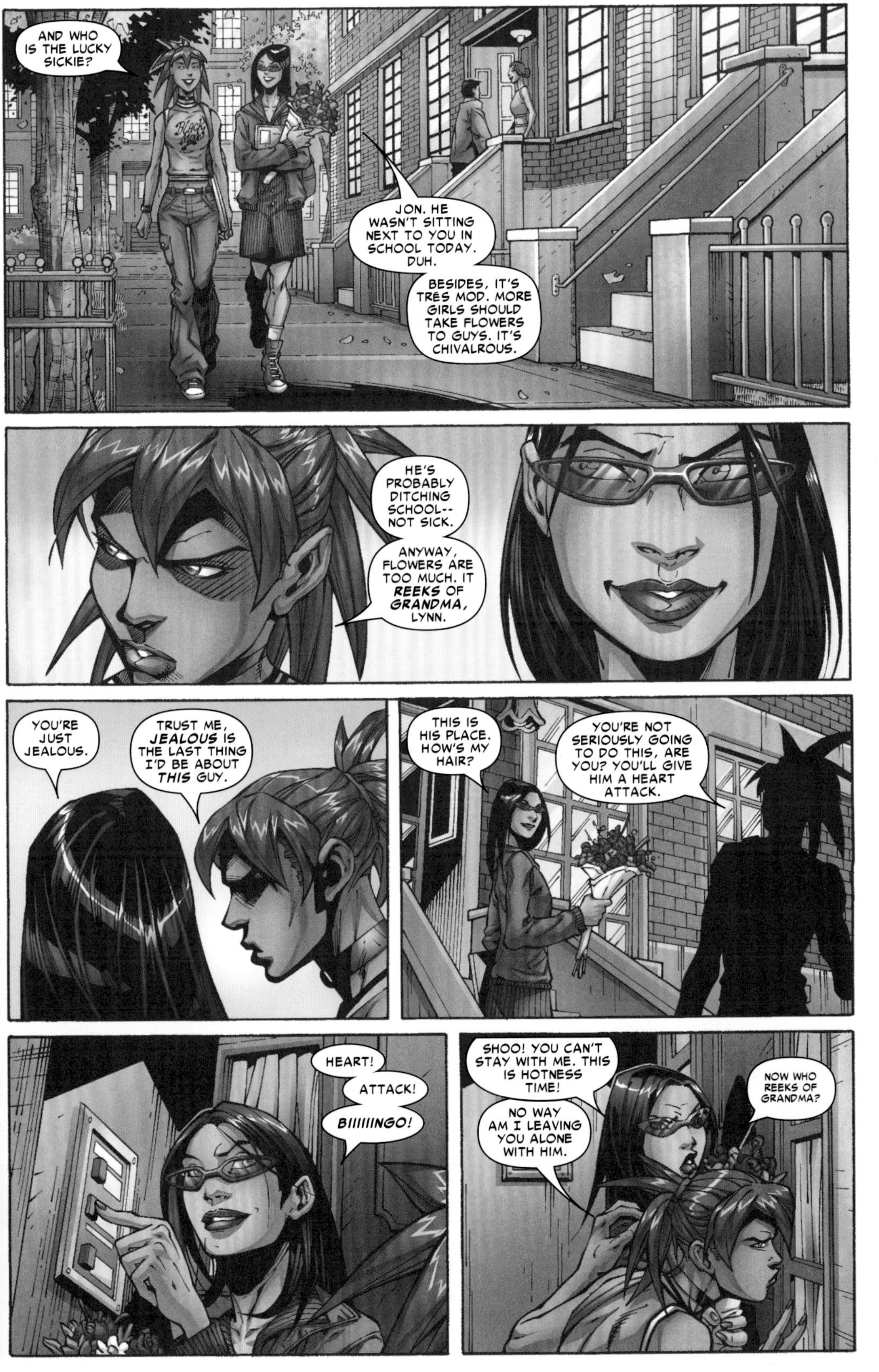
AND WHO IS THE LUCKY SICKIE?
JON. HE WASN'T SITTING NEXT TO YOU IN SCHOOL TODAY. DUH.
BESIDES, IT'S TRÈS MOD. MORE GIRLS SHOULD TAKE FLOWERS TO GUYS. IT'S CHIVALROUS.
HE'S PROBABLY DITCHING SCHOOL-- NOT SICK.
ANYWAY, FLOWERS ARE TOO MUCH. IT *REEKS* OF *GRANDMA,* LYNN.
YOU'RE JUST JEALOUS.
TRUST ME, *JEALOUS* IS THE LAST THING I'D BE ABOUT *THIS* GUY.
THIS IS HIS PLACE. HOW'S MY HAIR?
YOU'RE NOT SERIOUSLY GOING TO DO THIS, ARE YOU? YOU'LL GIVE HIM A HEART ATTACK.
HEART!
ATTACK!
BIIIIIINGO!
SHOO! YOU CAN'T STAY WITH ME. THIS IS HOTNESS TIME!
NO WAY AM I LEAVING YOU ALONE WITH HIM.
NOW WHO REEKS OF GRANDMA?

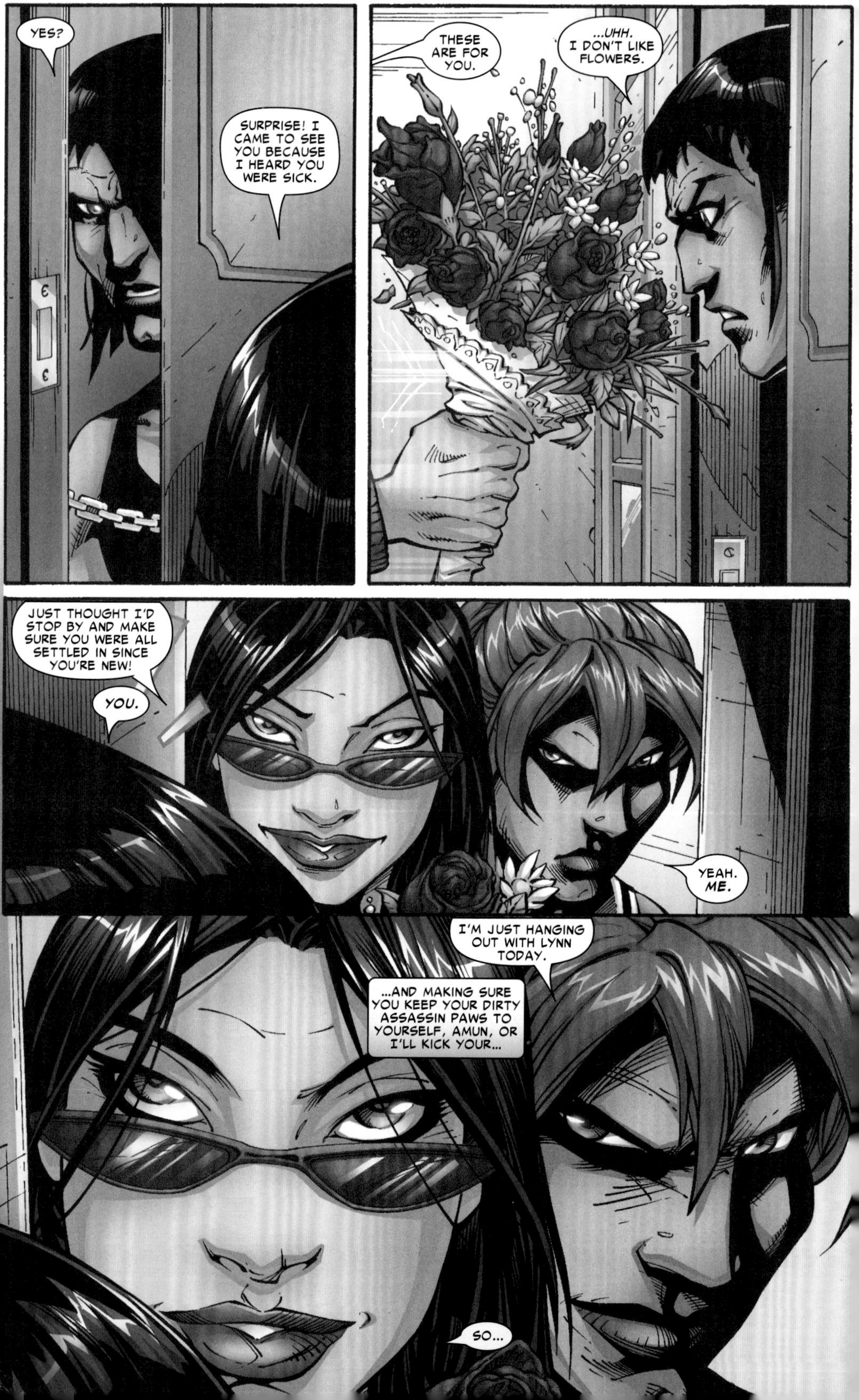
YES?
SURPRISE! I CAME TO SEE YOU BECAUSE I HEARD YOU WERE SICK.
THESE ARE FOR YOU.
...UHH. I DON'T LIKE FLOWERS.
JUST THOUGHT I'D STOP BY AND MAKE SURE YOU WERE ALL SETTLED IN SINCE YOU'RE NEW!
YOU.
YEAH. ME.
I'M JUST HANGING OUT WITH LYNN TODAY.
...AND MAKING SURE YOU KEEP YOUR DIRTY ASSASSIN PAWS TO YOURSELF, AMUN, OR I'LL KICK YOUR...
SO...

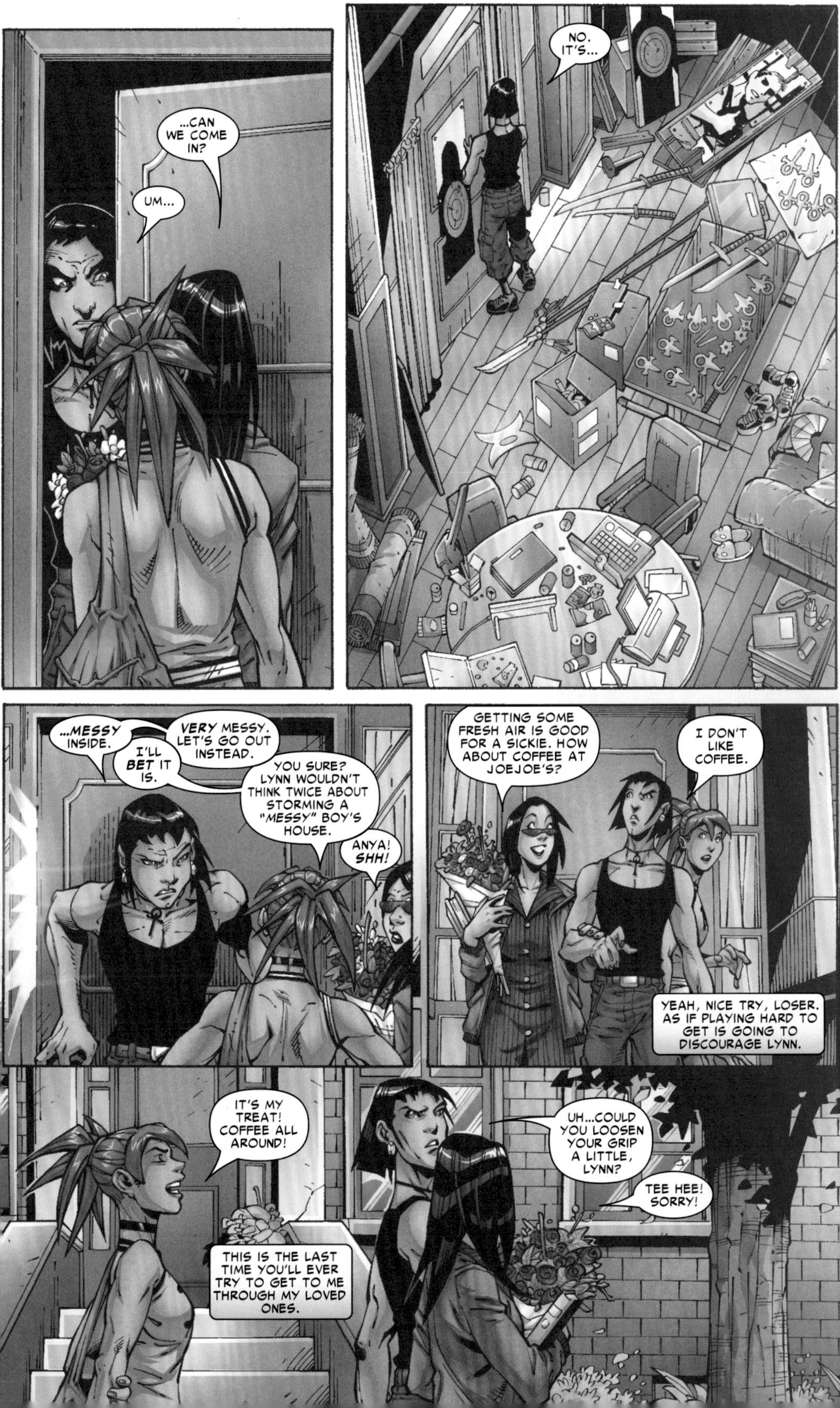

...CAN WE COME IN?
UM...
NO. IT'S...
...MESSY INSIDE.
VERY MESSY. LET'S GO OUT INSTEAD.
I'LL BET IT IS.
YOU SURE? LYNN WOULDN'T THINK TWICE ABOUT STORMING A "MESSY" BOY'S HOUSE.
ANYA! SHH!
GETTING SOME FRESH AIR IS GOOD FOR A SICKIE. HOW ABOUT COFFEE AT JOEJOE'S?
I DON'T LIKE COFFEE.
YEAH, NICE TRY, LOSER. AS IF PLAYING HARD TO GET IS GOING TO DISCOURAGE LYNN.
IT'S MY TREAT! COFFEE ALL AROUND!
THIS IS THE LAST TIME YOU'LL EVER TRY TO GET TO ME THROUGH MY LOVED ONES.
UH...COULD YOU LOOSEN YOUR GRIP A LITTLE, LYNN?
TEE HEE! SORRY!

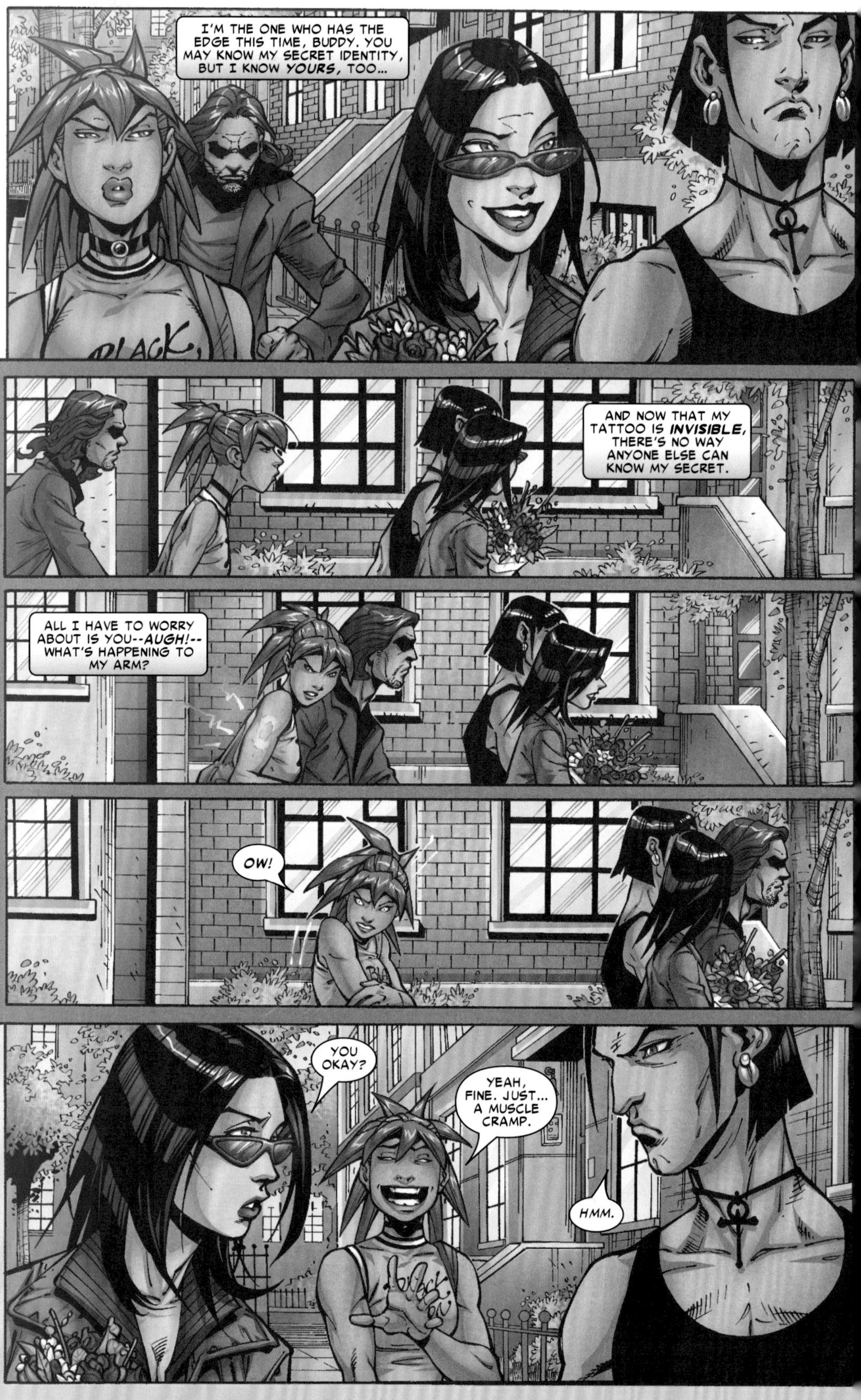
I'M THE ONE WHO HAS THE EDGE THIS TIME, BUDDY. YOU MAY KNOW MY SECRET IDENTITY, BUT I KNOW *YOURS*, TOO...
AND NOW THAT MY TATTOO IS ***INVISIBLE***, THERE'S NO WAY ANYONE ELSE CAN KNOW MY SECRET.
ALL I HAVE TO WORRY ABOUT IS YOU--***AUGH!***-- WHAT'S HAPPENING TO MY ARM?
OW!
YOU OKAY?
YEAH, FINE. JUST... A MUSCLE CRAMP.
HMM.

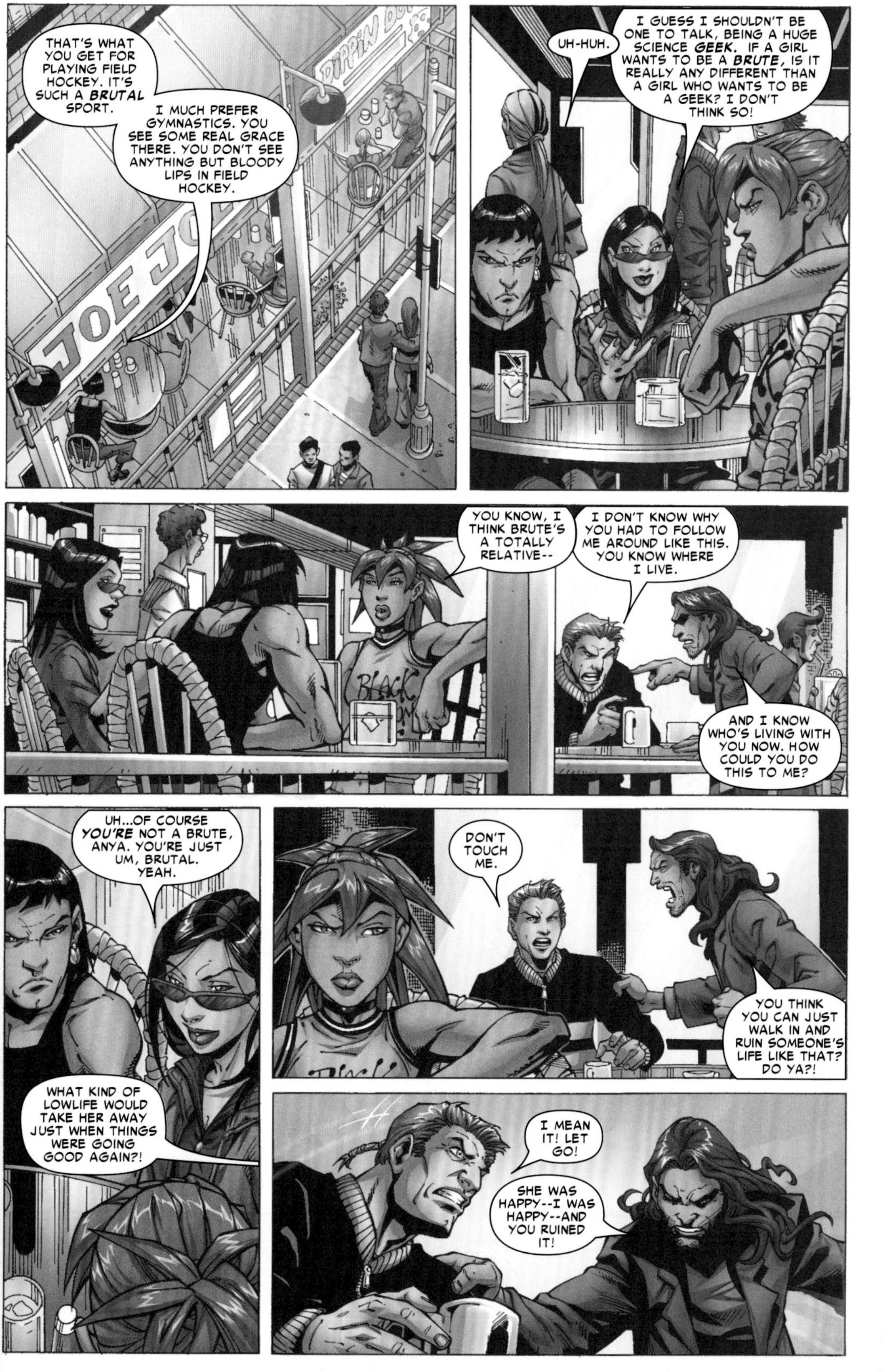
DIPPIN' DOTS
JOE JO
THAT'S WHAT YOU GET FOR PLAYING FIELD HOCKEY. IT'S SUCH A BRUTAL SPORT.
I MUCH PREFER GYMNASTICS. YOU SEE SOME REAL GRACE THERE. YOU DON'T SEE ANYTHING BUT BLOODY LIPS IN FIELD HOCKEY.
UH-HUH.
I GUESS I SHOULDN'T BE ONE TO TALK, BEING A HUGE SCIENCE GEEK. IF A GIRL WANTS TO BE A BRUTE, IS IT REALLY ANY DIFFERENT THAN A GIRL WHO WANTS TO BE A GEEK? I DON'T THINK SO!
YOU KNOW, I THINK BRUTE'S A TOTALLY RELATIVE--
I DON'T KNOW WHY YOU HAD TO FOLLOW ME AROUND LIKE THIS. YOU KNOW WHERE I LIVE.
AND I KNOW WHO'S LIVING WITH YOU NOW. HOW COULD YOU DO THIS TO ME?
UH...OF COURSE YOU'RE NOT A BRUTE, ANYA. YOU'RE JUST UM, BRUTAL. YEAH.
WHAT KIND OF LOWLIFE WOULD TAKE HER AWAY JUST WHEN THINGS WERE GOING GOOD AGAIN?!
DON'T TOUCH ME.
YOU THINK YOU CAN JUST WALK IN AND RUIN SOMEONE'S LIFE LIKE THAT? DO YA?!
I MEAN IT! LET GO!
SHE WAS HAPPY--I WAS HAPPY--AND YOU RUINED IT!

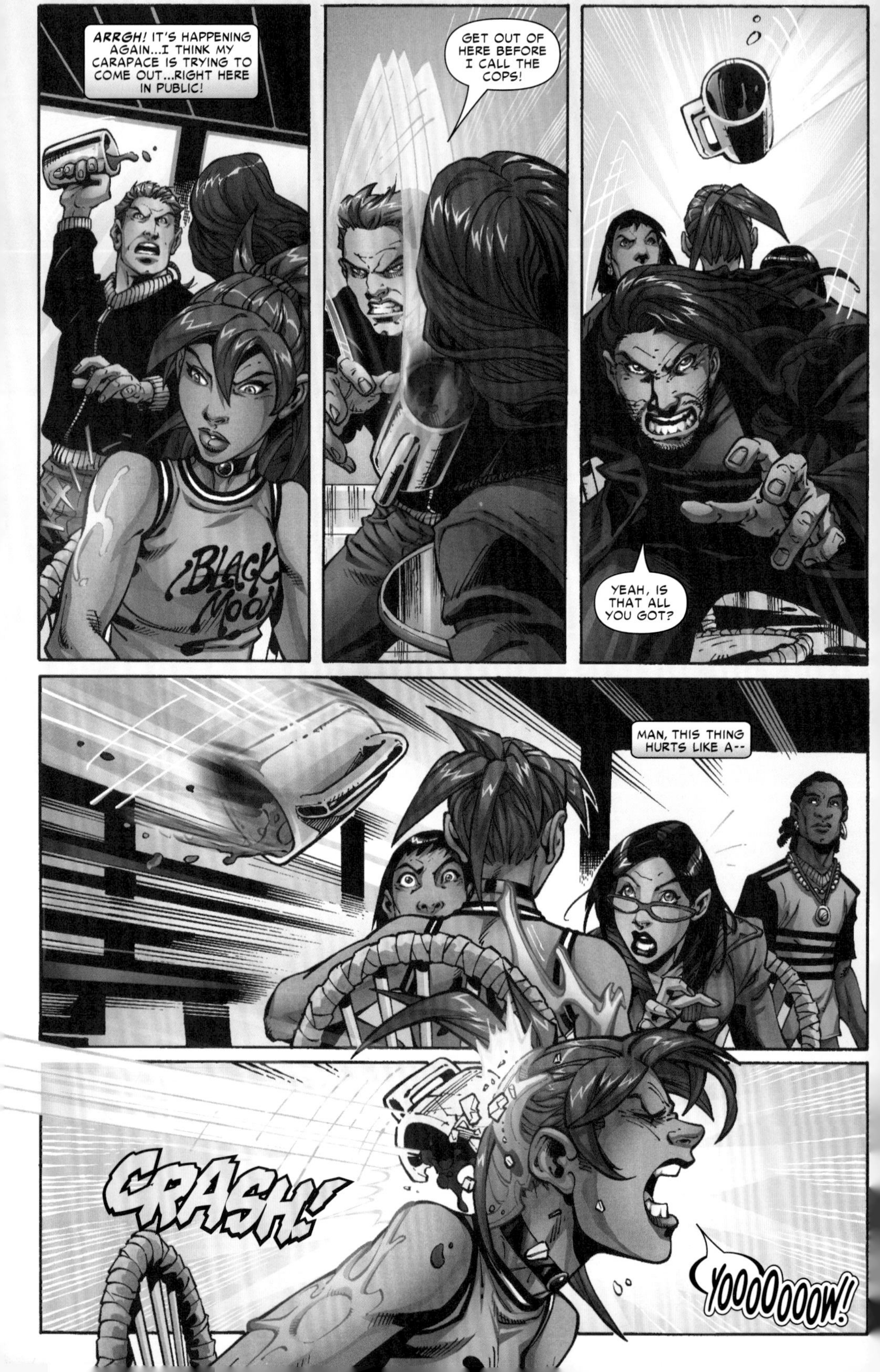
ARRGH! IT'S HAPPENING AGAIN...I THINK MY CARAPACE IS TRYING TO COME OUT...RIGHT HERE IN PUBLIC!
¡BLACK MOON
GET OUT OF HERE BEFORE I CALL THE COPS!
YEAH, IS THAT ALL YOU GOT?
MAN, THIS THING HURTS LIKE A--
CRASH!
YOOOOOOOW!!

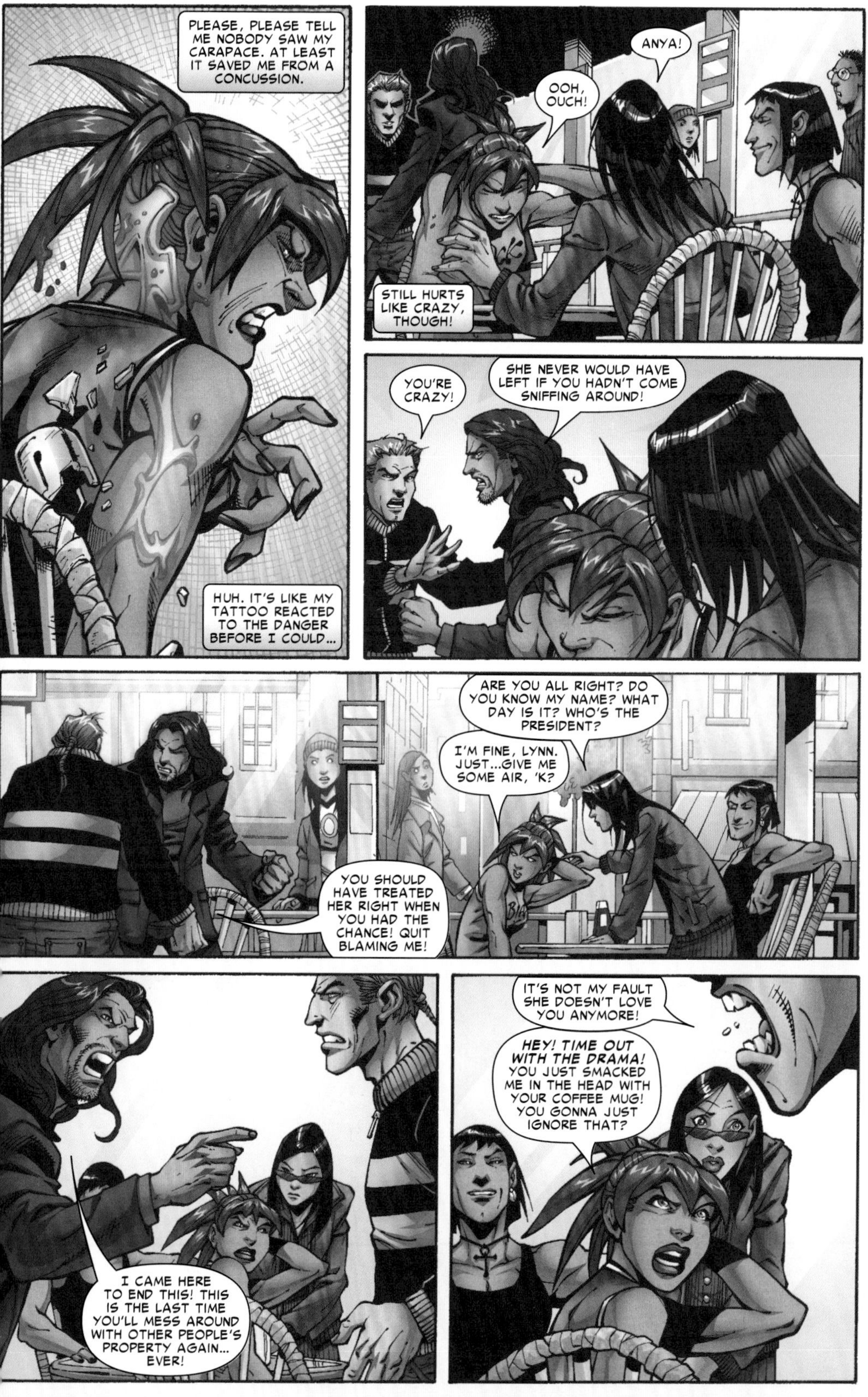
PLEASE, PLEASE TELL ME NOBODY SAW MY CARAPACE. AT LEAST IT SAVED ME FROM A CONCUSSION.
HUH. IT'S LIKE MY TATTOO REACTED TO THE DANGER BEFORE I COULD...
ANYA!
OOH, OUCH!
STILL HURTS LIKE CRAZY, THOUGH!
YOU'RE CRAZY!
SHE NEVER WOULD HAVE LEFT IF YOU HADN'T COME SNIFFING AROUND!
ARE YOU ALL RIGHT? DO YOU KNOW MY NAME? WHAT DAY IS IT? WHO'S THE PRESIDENT?
I'M FINE, LYNN. JUST...GIVE ME SOME AIR, 'K?
YOU SHOULD HAVE TREATED HER RIGHT WHEN YOU HAD THE CHANCE! QUIT BLAMING ME!
I CAME HERE TO END THIS! THIS IS THE LAST TIME YOU'LL MESS AROUND WITH OTHER PEOPLE'S PROPERTY AGAIN... EVER!
IT'S NOT MY FAULT SHE DOESN'T LOVE YOU ANYMORE!
HEY! TIME OUT WITH THE DRAMA! YOU JUST SMACKED ME IN THE HEAD WITH YOUR COFFEE MUG! YOU GONNA JUST IGNORE THAT?

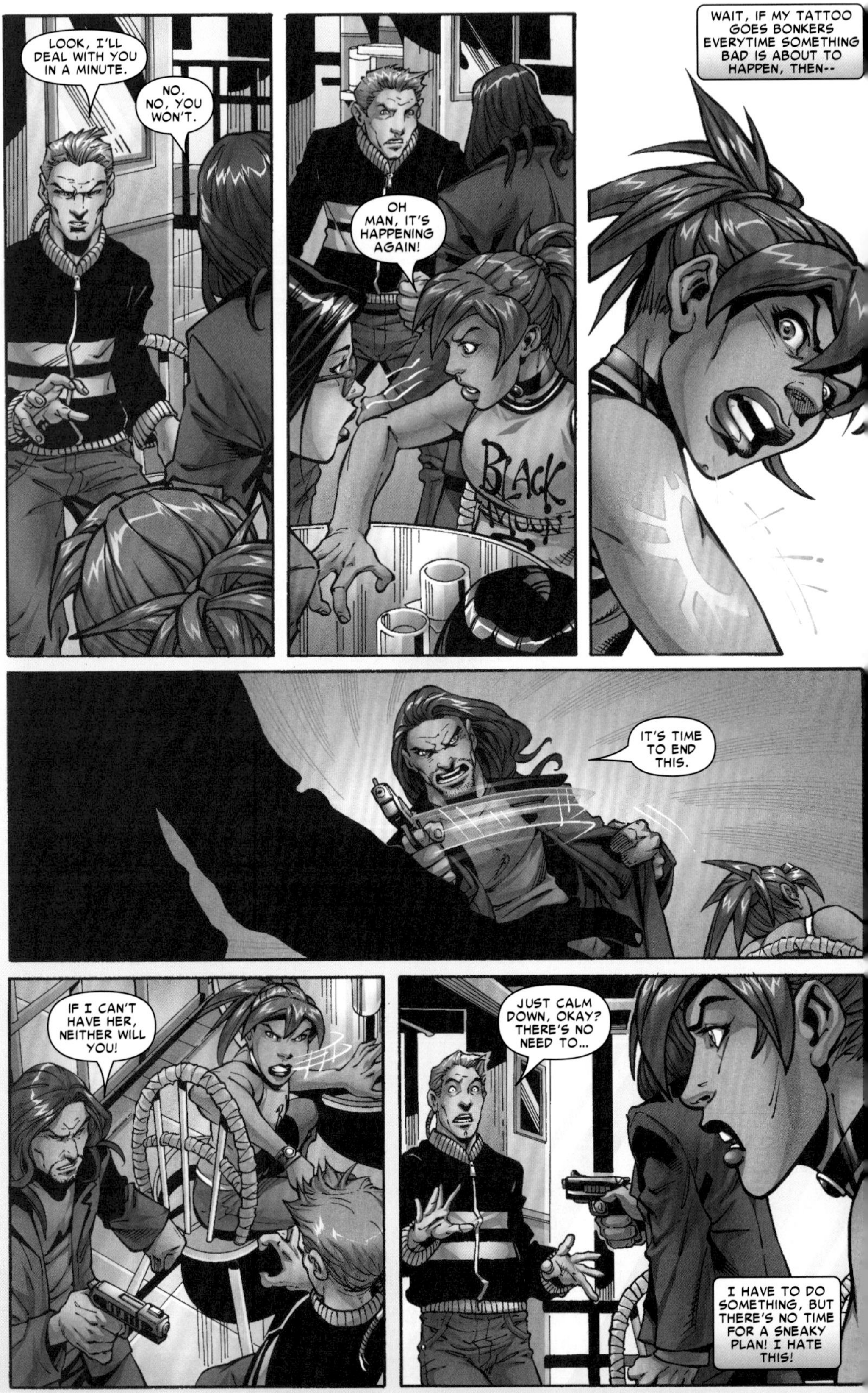
LOOK, I'LL DEAL WITH YOU IN A MINUTE.
NO. NO, YOU WON'T.
OH MAN, IT'S HAPPENING AGAIN!
BLACK MOON
WAIT, IF MY TATTOO GOES BONKERS EVERYTIME SOMETHING BAD IS ABOUT TO HAPPEN, THEN--
IT'S TIME TO END THIS.
IF I CAN'T HAVE HER, NEITHER WILL YOU!
JUST CALM DOWN, OKAY? THERE'S NO NEED TO...
I HAVE TO DO SOMETHING, BUT THERE'S NO TIME FOR A SNEAKY PLAN! I HATE THIS!

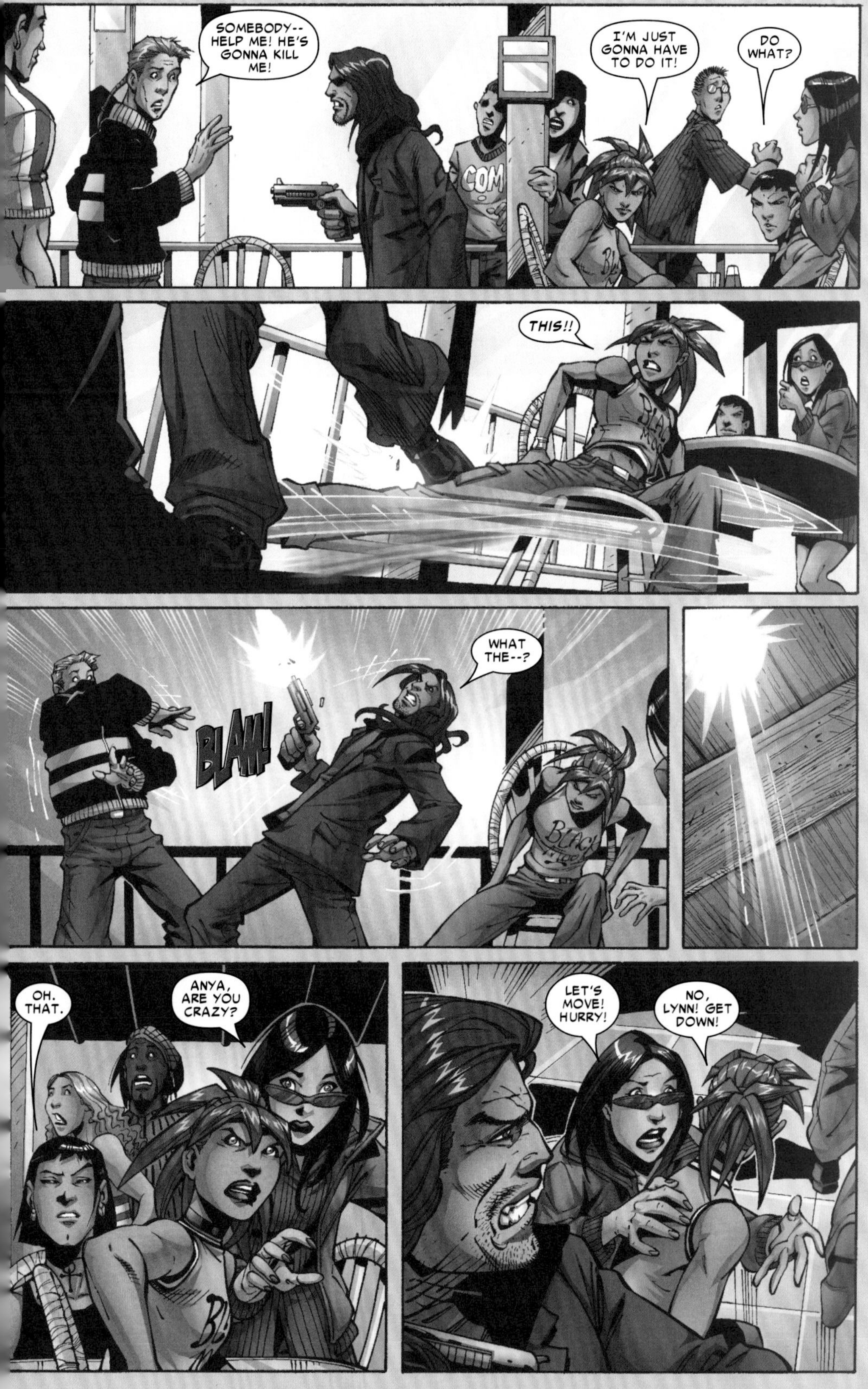
SOMEBODY-- HELP ME! HE'S GONNA KILL ME!
I'M JUST GONNA HAVE TO DO IT!
DO WHAT?
THIS!!
WHAT THE--?
BLAM!
OH. THAT.
ANYA, ARE YOU CRAZY?
LET'S MOVE! HURRY!
NO, LYNN! GET DOWN!

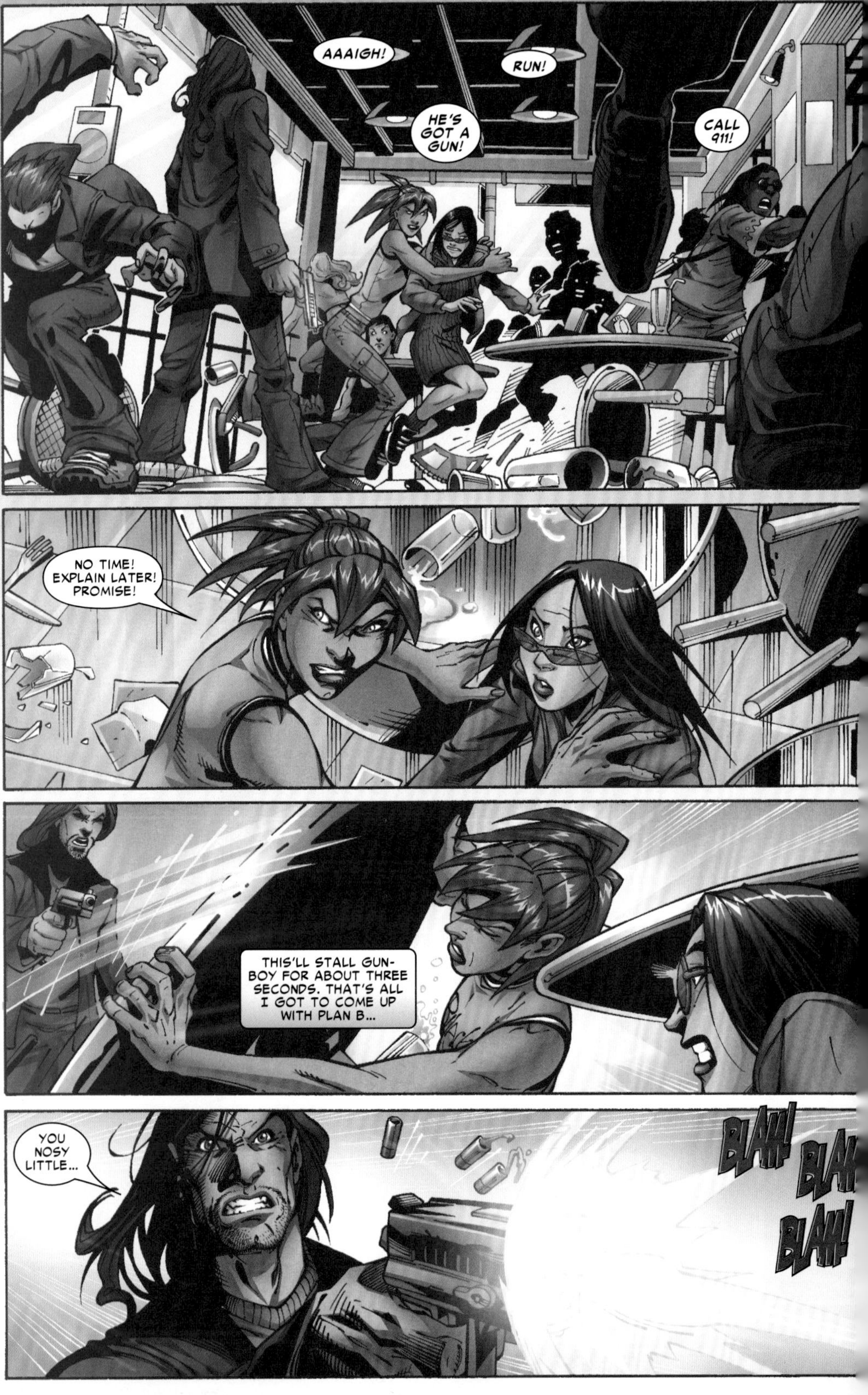
AAAIGH!
RUN!
HE'S GOT A GUN!
CALL 911!
NO TIME! EXPLAIN LATER! PROMISE!
THIS'LL STALL GUN-BOY FOR ABOUT THREE SECONDS. THAT'S ALL I GOT TO COME UP WITH PLAN B...
YOU NOSY LITTLE...
BLAM! BLAM! BLAM!

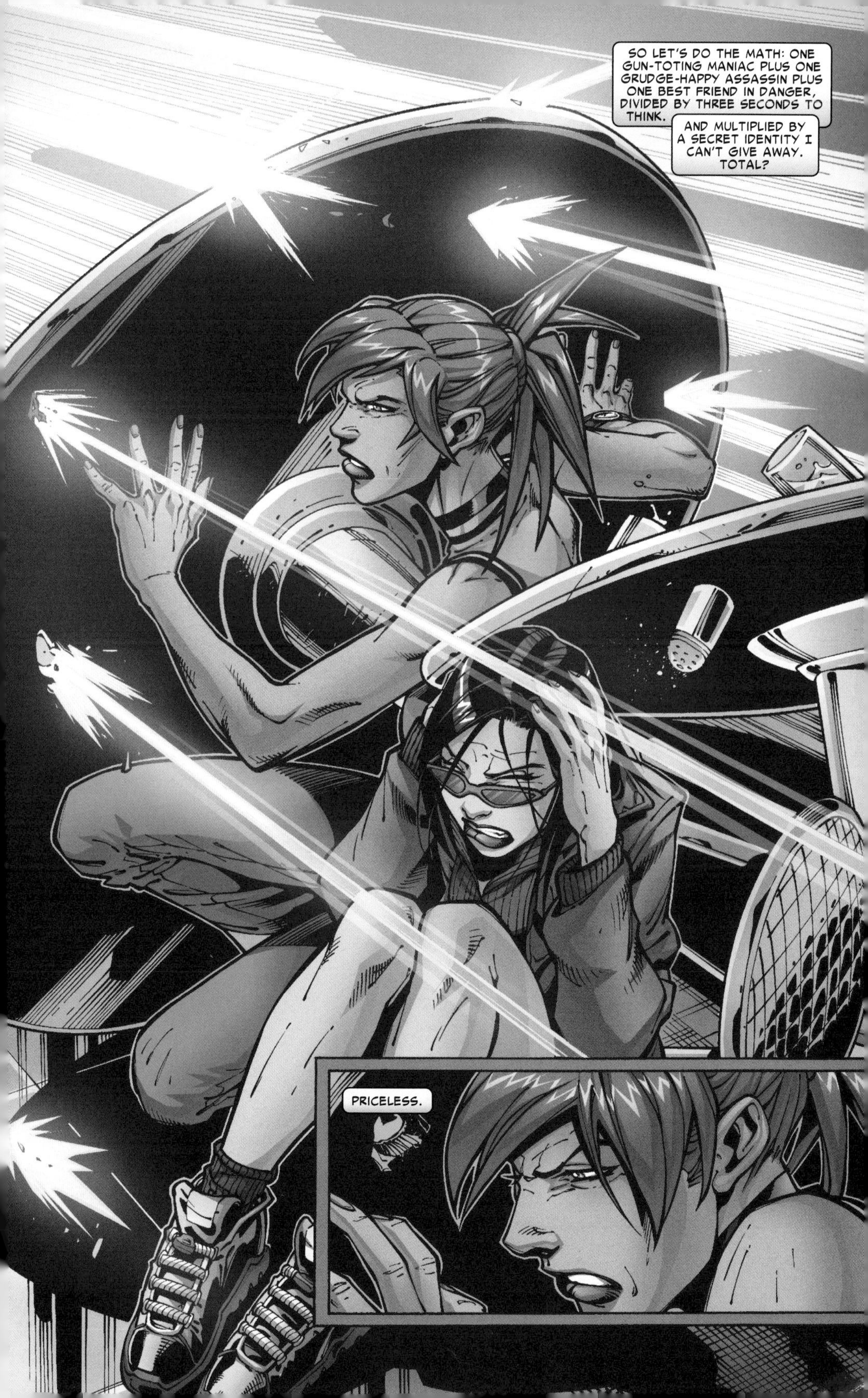
SO LET'S DO THE MATH: ONE GUN-TOTING MANIAC PLUS ONE GRUDGE-HAPPY ASSASSIN PLUS ONE BEST FRIEND IN DANGER, DIVIDED BY THREE SECONDS TO THINK.
AND MULTIPLIED BY A SECRET IDENTITY I CAN'T GIVE AWAY. TOTAL?
PRICELESS.

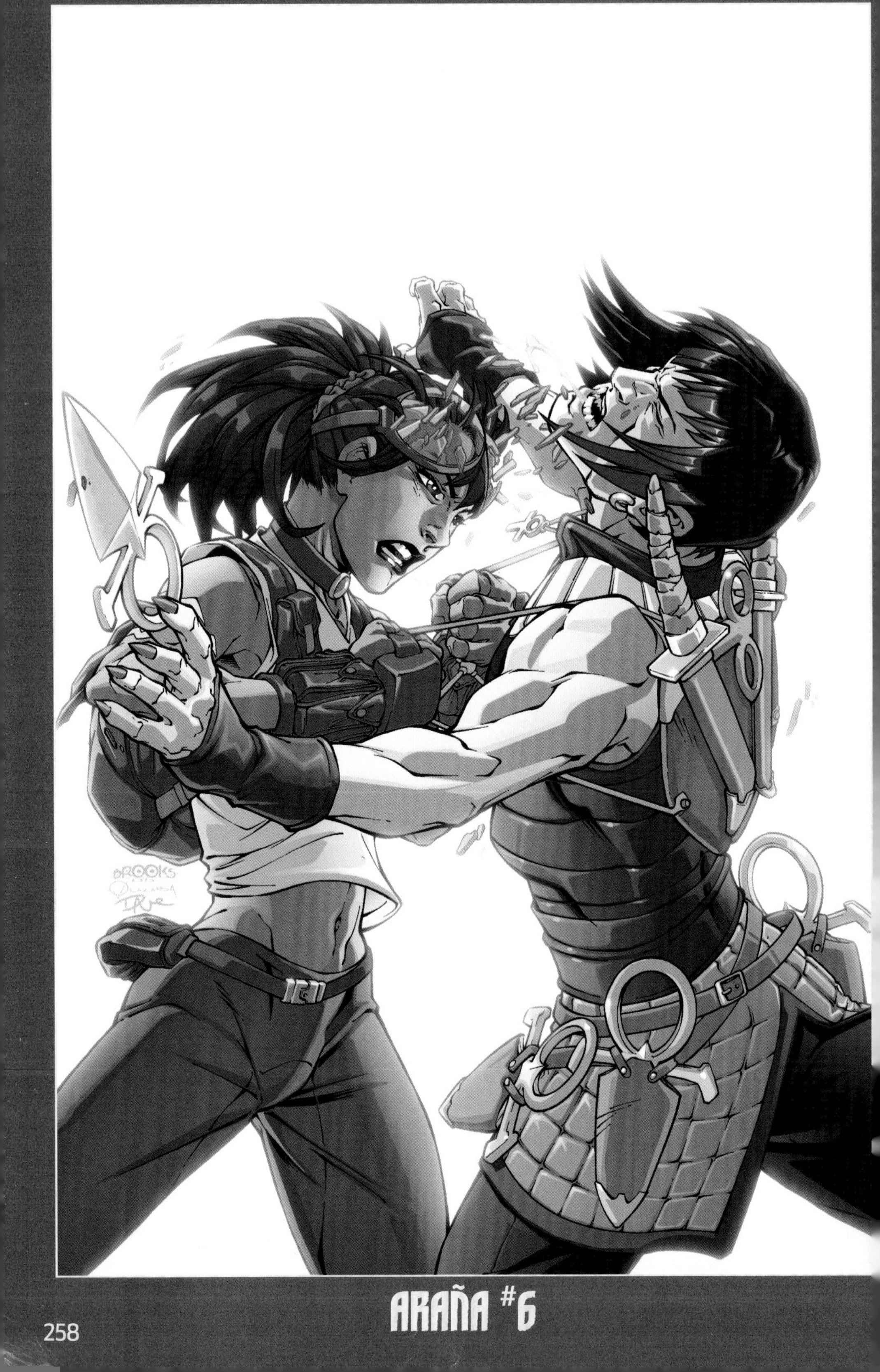
BROOKS

ARAÑA #6

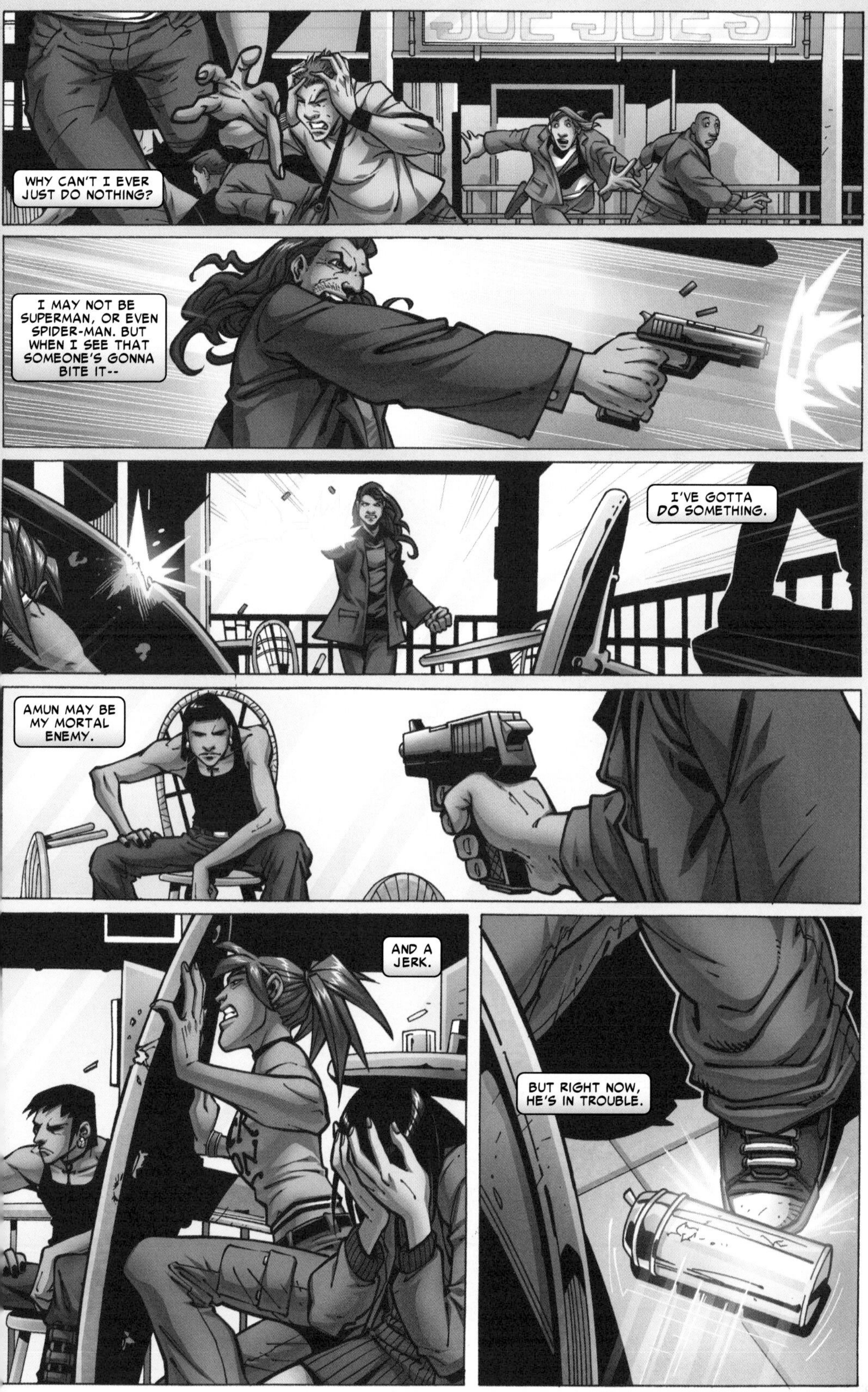
WHY CAN'T I EVER JUST DO NOTHING?
I MAY NOT BE SUPERMAN, OR EVEN SPIDER-MAN. BUT WHEN I SEE THAT SOMEONE'S GONNA BITE IT--
I'VE GOTTA DO SOMETHING.
AMUN MAY BE MY MORTAL ENEMY.
AND A JERK.
BUT RIGHT NOW, HE'S IN TROUBLE.

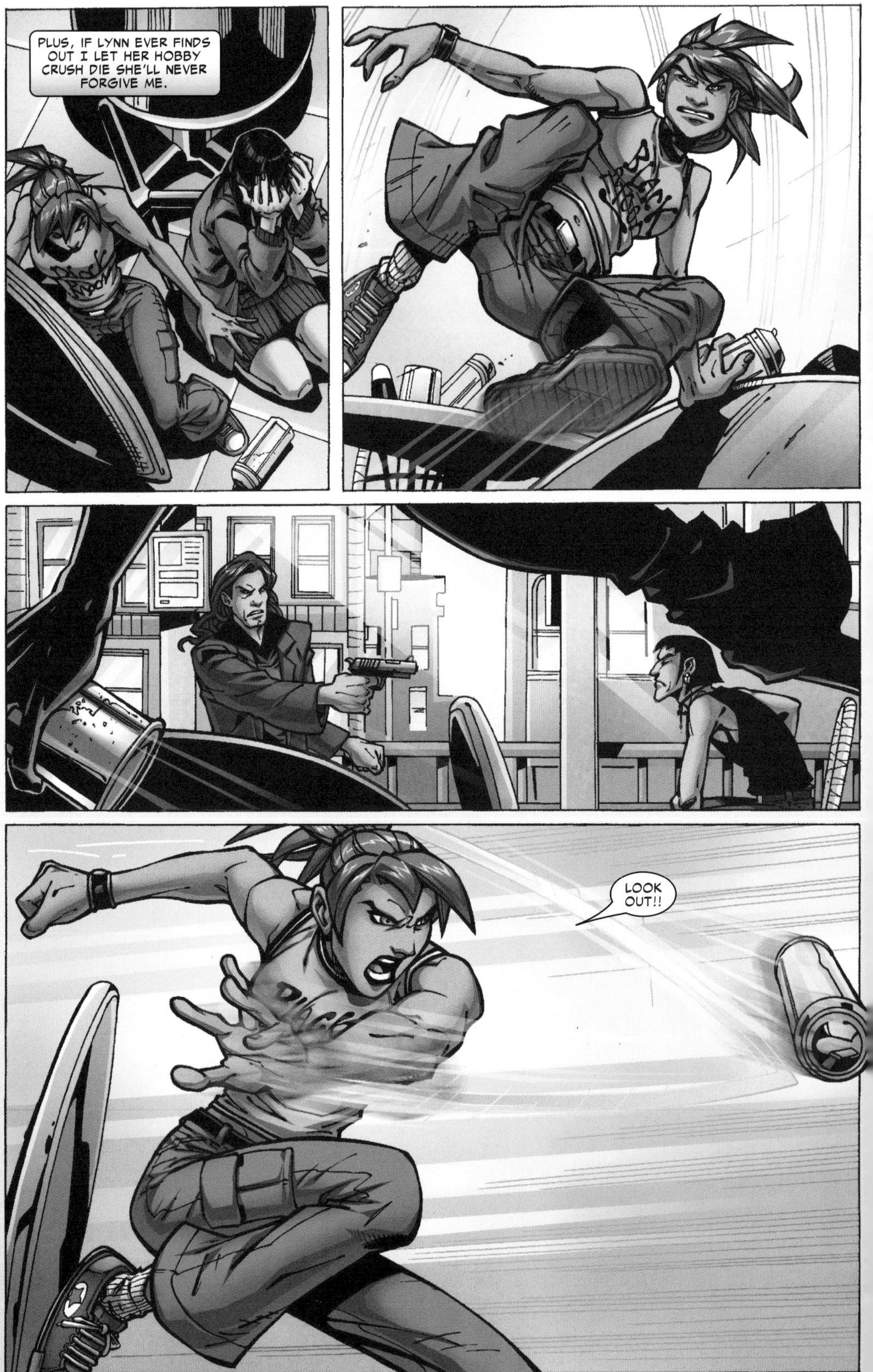
PLUS, IF LYNN EVER FINDS OUT I LET HER HOBBY CRUSH DIE SHE'LL NEVER FORGIVE ME.
LOOK OUT!!

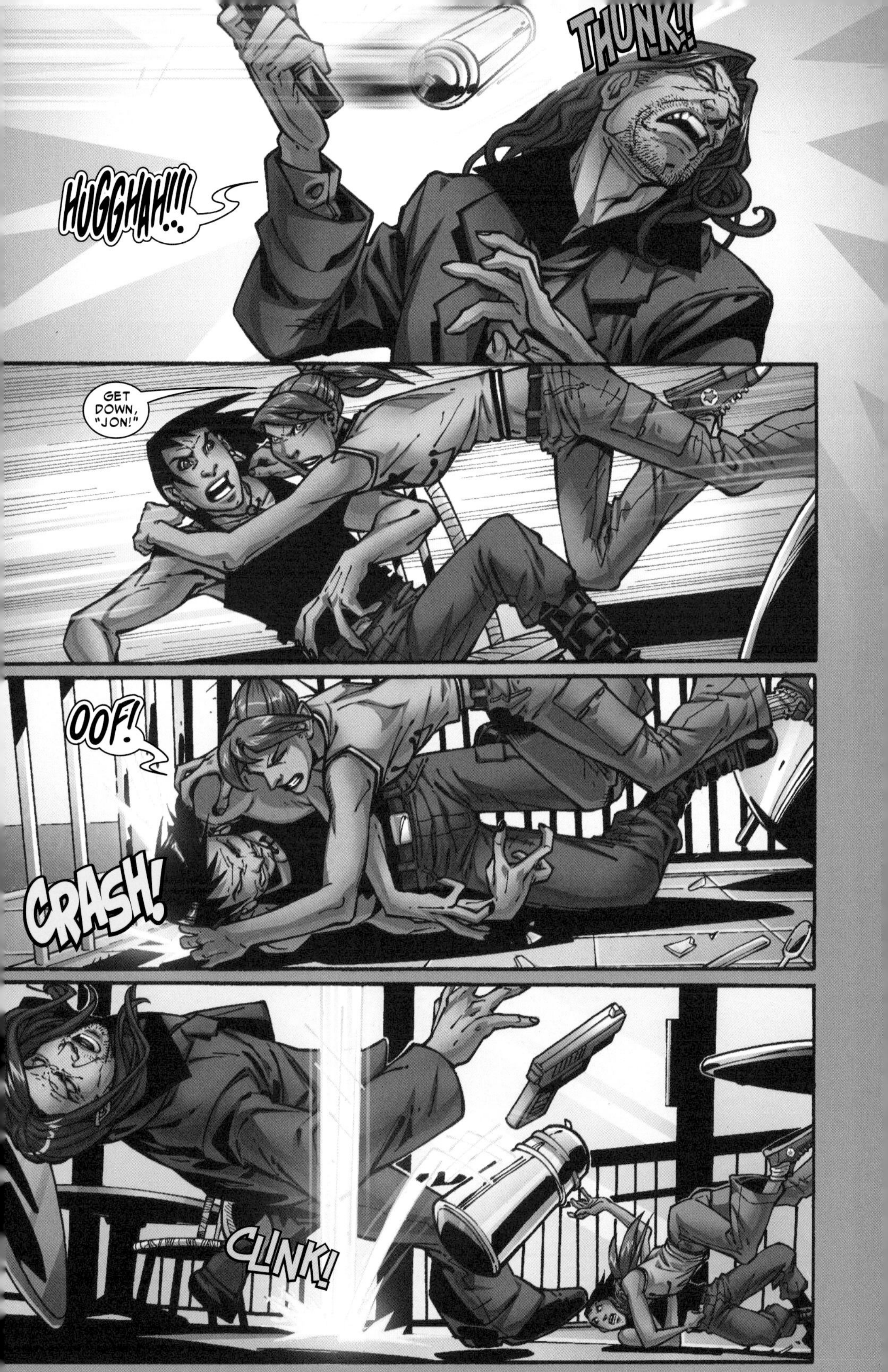
THUNK!
HUGGHAH!!!
GET DOWN, "JON!"
OOF!
CRASH!
CLINK!

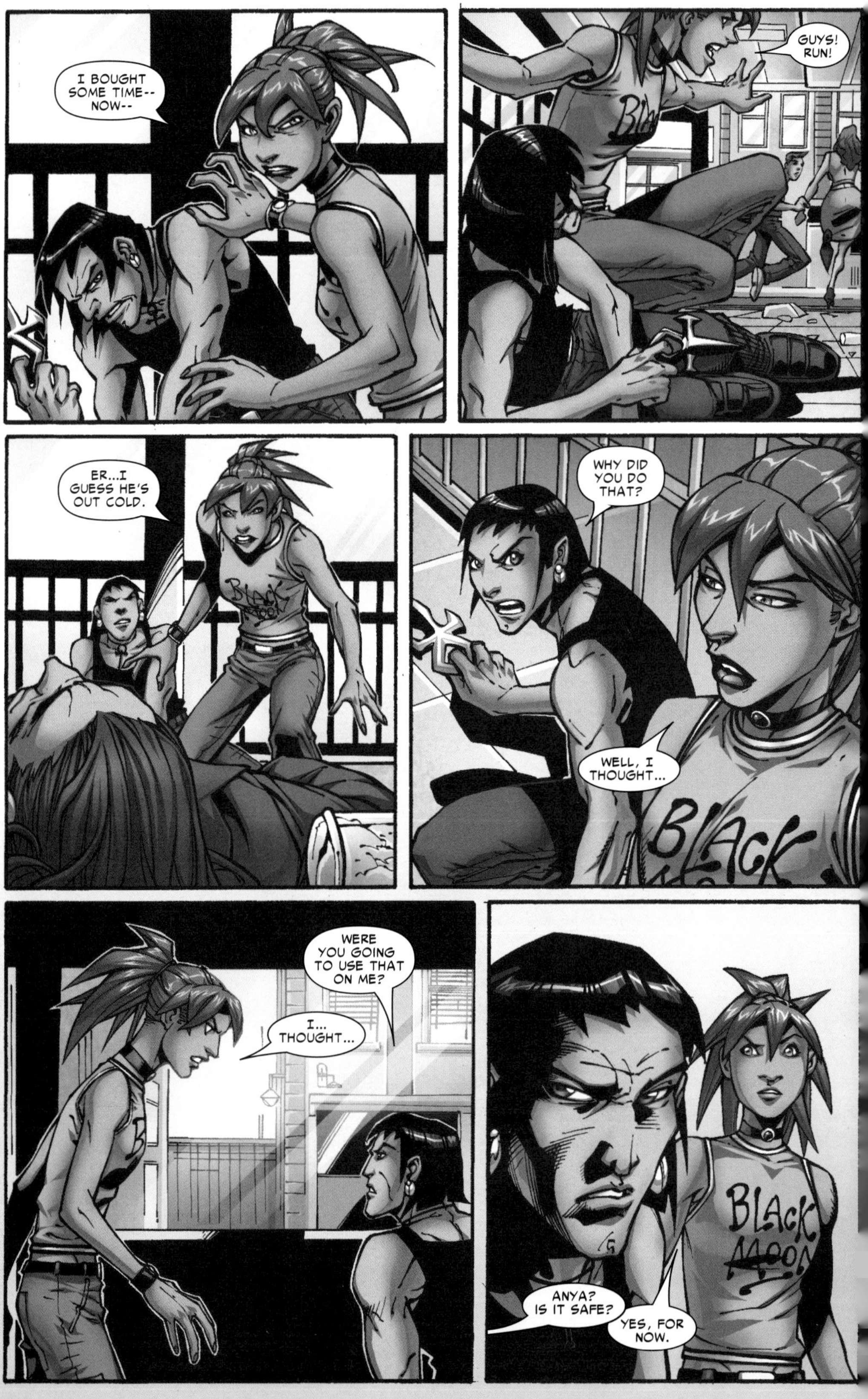
I BOUGHT SOME TIME-- NOW--
GUYS! RUN!
ER...I GUESS HE'S OUT COLD.
WHY DID YOU DO THAT?
WELL, I THOUGHT...
WERE YOU GOING TO USE THAT ON ME?
I... THOUGHT...
ANYA? IS IT SAFE?
YES, FOR NOW.

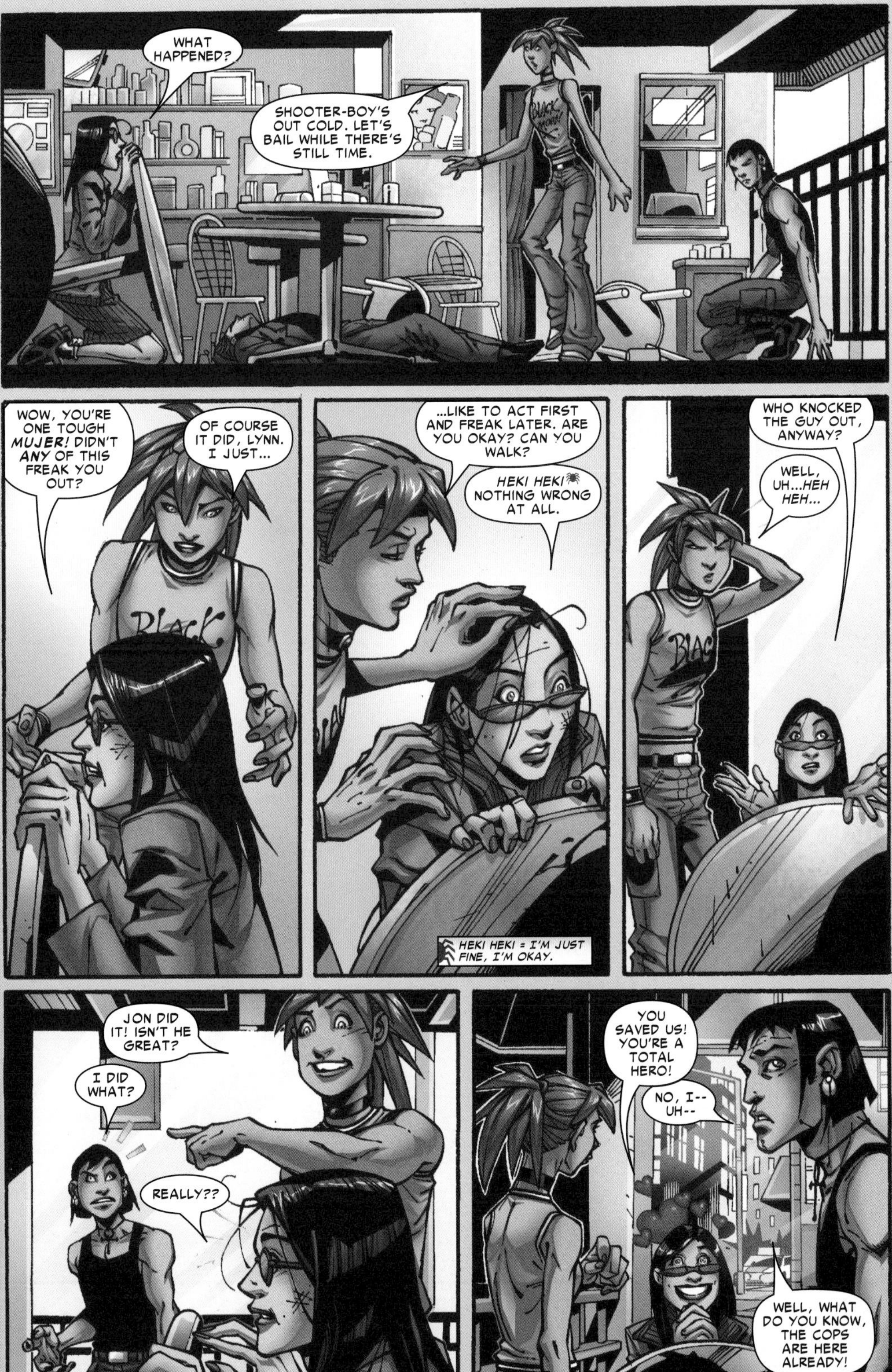
WHAT HAPPENED?
SHOOTER-BOY'S OUT COLD. LET'S BAIL WHILE THERE'S STILL TIME.
WOW, YOU'RE ONE TOUGH MUJER! DIDN'T ANY OF THIS FREAK YOU OUT?
OF COURSE IT DID, LYNN. I JUST...
...LIKE TO ACT FIRST AND FREAK LATER. ARE YOU OKAY? CAN YOU WALK?
HEKI HEKI NOTHING WRONG AT ALL.
HEKI HEKI = I'M JUST FINE, I'M OKAY.
WHO KNOCKED THE GUY OUT, ANYWAY?
WELL, UH...HEH HEH...
JON DID IT! ISN'T HE GREAT?
I DID WHAT?
REALLY??
YOU SAVED US! YOU'RE A TOTAL HERO!
NO, I-- UH--
WELL, WHAT DO YOU KNOW, THE COPS ARE HERE ALREADY!
WEEE-OO WEEE-OO WEEE-OO

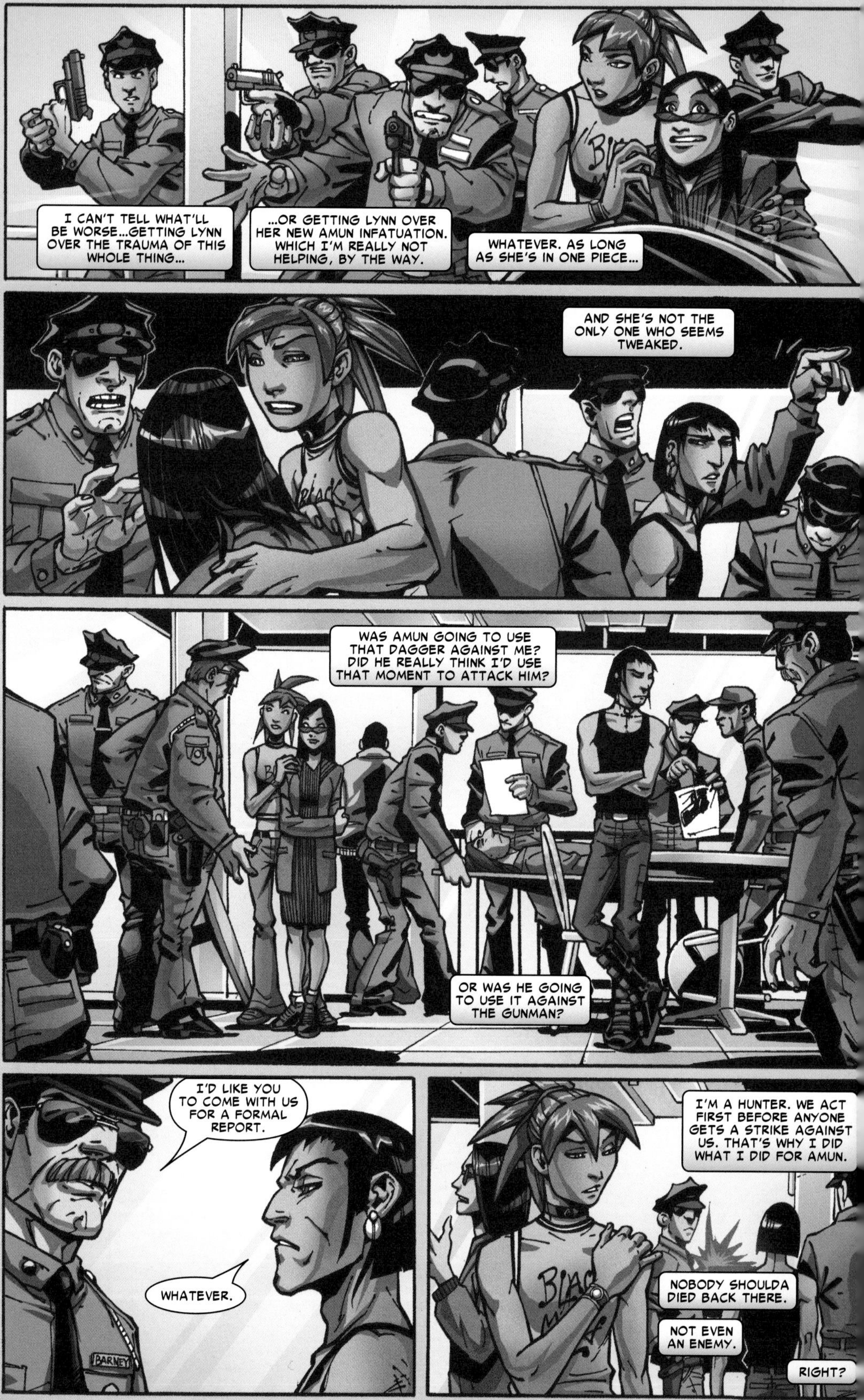
I CAN'T TELL WHAT'LL BE WORSE...GETTING LYNN OVER THE TRAUMA OF THIS WHOLE THING...
...OR GETTING LYNN OVER HER NEW AMUN INFATUATION. WHICH I'M REALLY NOT HELPING, BY THE WAY.
WHATEVER. AS LONG AS SHE'S IN ONE PIECE...
AND SHE'S NOT THE ONLY ONE WHO SEEMS TWEAKED.
WAS AMUN GOING TO USE THAT DAGGER AGAINST ME? DID HE REALLY THINK I'D USE THAT MOMENT TO ATTACK HIM?
OR WAS HE GOING TO USE IT AGAINST THE GUNMAN?
I'D LIKE YOU TO COME WITH US FOR A FORMAL REPORT.
WHATEVER.
BARNEY
I'M A HUNTER. WE ACT FIRST BEFORE ANYONE GETS A STRIKE AGAINST US. THAT'S WHY I DID WHAT I DID FOR AMUN.
NOBODY SHOULDA DIED BACK THERE.
NOT EVEN AN ENEMY.
RIGHT?

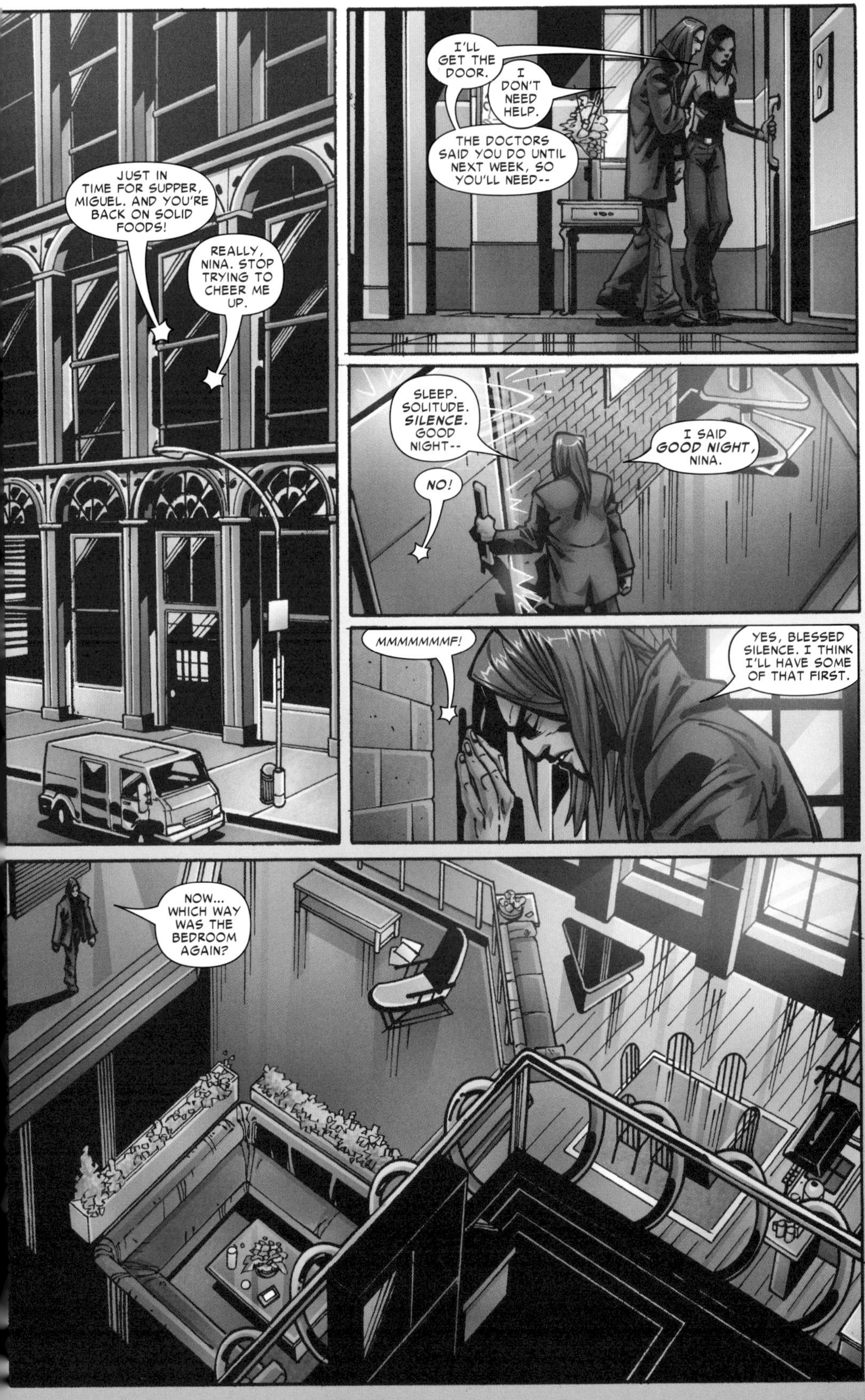
JUST IN TIME FOR SUPPER, MIGUEL. AND YOU'RE BACK ON SOLID FOODS!
REALLY, NINA. STOP TRYING TO CHEER ME UP.
I'LL GET THE DOOR.
I DON'T NEED HELP.
THE DOCTORS SAID YOU DO UNTIL NEXT WEEK, SO YOU'LL NEED--
SLEEP. SOLITUDE. SILENCE. GOOD NIGHT--
I SAID GOOD NIGHT, NINA.
NO!
MMMMMMMF!
YES, BLESSED SILENCE. I THINK I'LL HAVE SOME OF THAT FIRST.
NOW... WHICH WAY WAS THE BEDROOM AGAIN?

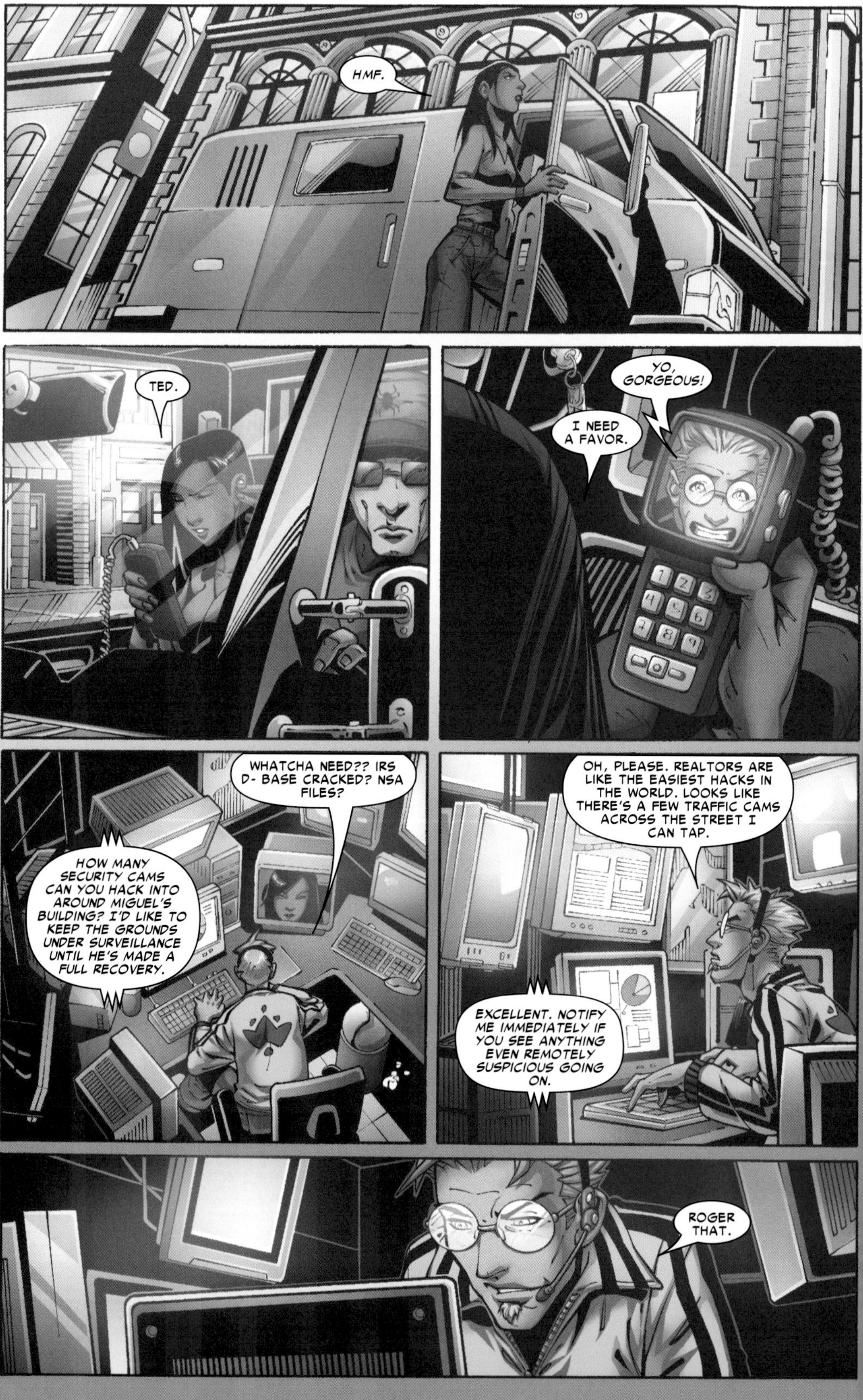
HMF.
TED.
I NEED A FAVOR.
YO, GORGEOUS!
WHATCHA NEED?? IRS D- BASE CRACKED? NSA FILES?
HOW MANY SECURITY CAMS CAN YOU HACK INTO AROUND MIGUEL'S BUILDING? I'D LIKE TO KEEP THE GROUNDS UNDER SURVEILLANCE UNTIL HE'S MADE A FULL RECOVERY.
OH, PLEASE. REALTORS ARE LIKE THE EASIEST HACKS IN THE WORLD. LOOKS LIKE THERE'S A FEW TRAFFIC CAMS ACROSS THE STREET I CAN TAP.
EXCELLENT. NOTIFY ME IMMEDIATELY IF YOU SEE ANYTHING EVEN REMOTELY SUSPICIOUS GOING ON.
ROGER THAT.

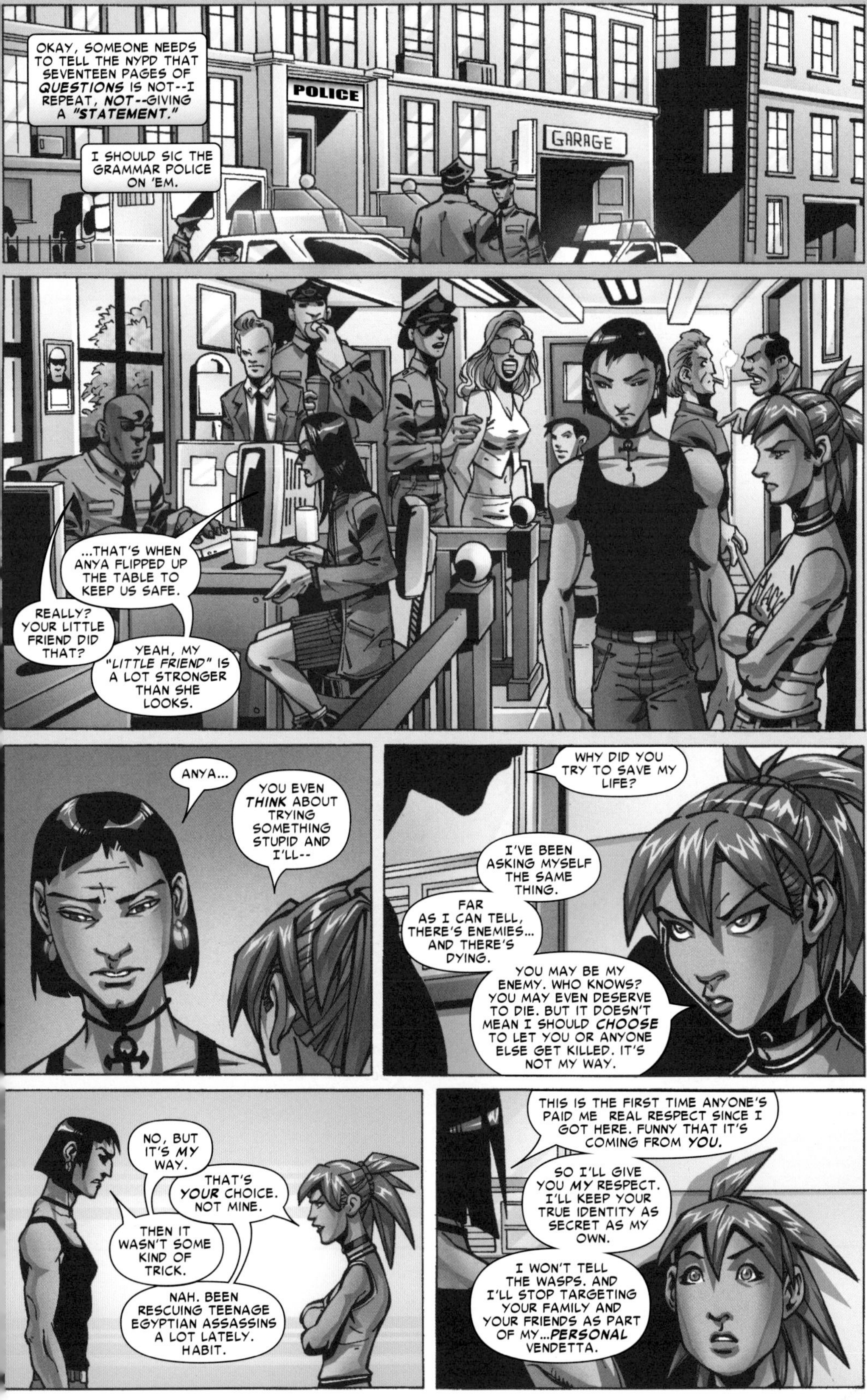

OKAY, SOMEONE NEEDS TO TELL THE NYPD THAT SEVENTEEN PAGES OF QUESTIONS IS NOT--I REPEAT, NOT--GIVING A "STATEMENT."
I SHOULD SIC THE GRAMMAR POLICE ON 'EM.
POLICE
GARAGE
...THAT'S WHEN ANYA FLIPPED UP THE TABLE TO KEEP US SAFE.
REALLY? YOUR LITTLE FRIEND DID THAT?
YEAH, MY "LITTLE FRIEND" IS A LOT STRONGER THAN SHE LOOKS.
ANYA...
YOU EVEN THINK ABOUT TRYING SOMETHING STUPID AND I'LL--
WHY DID YOU TRY TO SAVE MY LIFE?
I'VE BEEN ASKING MYSELF THE SAME THING.
FAR AS I CAN TELL, THERE'S ENEMIES... AND THERE'S DYING.
YOU MAY BE MY ENEMY. WHO KNOWS? YOU MAY EVEN DESERVE TO DIE. BUT IT DOESN'T MEAN I SHOULD CHOOSE TO LET YOU OR ANYONE ELSE GET KILLED. IT'S NOT MY WAY.
NO, BUT IT'S MY WAY.
THAT'S YOUR CHOICE. NOT MINE.
THEN IT WASN'T SOME KIND OF TRICK.
NAH. BEEN RESCUING TEENAGE EGYPTIAN ASSASSINS A LOT LATELY. HABIT.
THIS IS THE FIRST TIME ANYONE'S PAID ME REAL RESPECT SINCE I GOT HERE. FUNNY THAT IT'S COMING FROM YOU.
SO I'LL GIVE YOU MY RESPECT. I'LL KEEP YOUR TRUE IDENTITY AS SECRET AS MY OWN.
I WON'T TELL THE WASPS. AND I'LL STOP TARGETING YOUR FAMILY AND YOUR FRIENDS AS PART OF MY...PERSONAL VENDETTA.

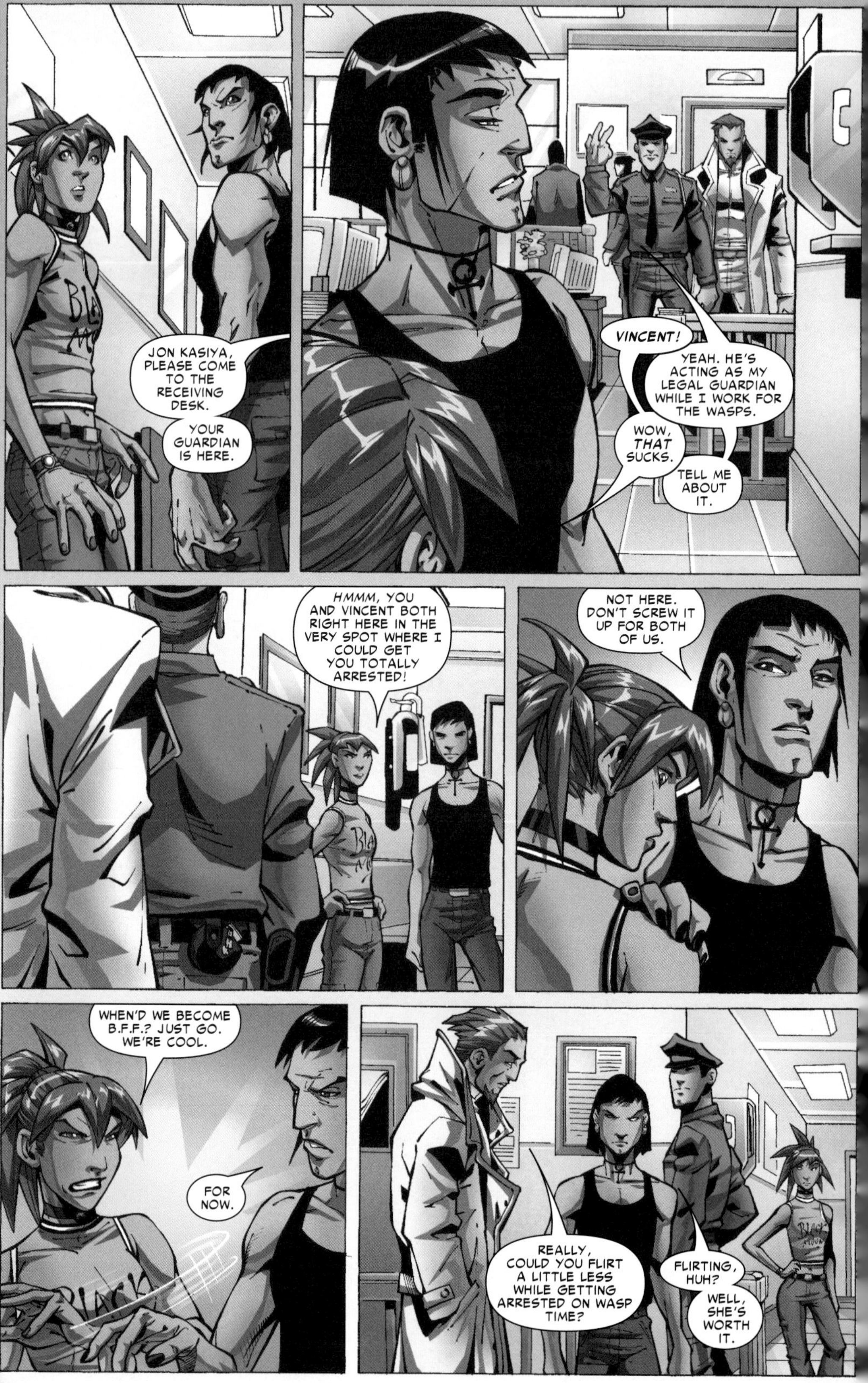
JON KASIYA, PLEASE COME TO THE RECEIVING DESK.
YOUR GUARDIAN IS HERE.
VINCENT!
YEAH. HE'S ACTING AS MY LEGAL GUARDIAN WHILE I WORK FOR THE WASPS.
WOW, THAT SUCKS.
TELL ME ABOUT IT.
HMMM, YOU AND VINCENT BOTH RIGHT HERE IN THE VERY SPOT WHERE I COULD GET YOU TOTALLY ARRESTED!
NOT HERE. DON'T SCREW IT UP FOR BOTH OF US.
WHEN'D WE BECOME B.F.F.? JUST GO. WE'RE COOL.
FOR NOW.
REALLY, COULD YOU FLIRT A LITTLE LESS WHILE GETTING ARRESTED ON WASP TIME?
FLIRTING, HUH?
WELL, SHE'S WORTH IT.

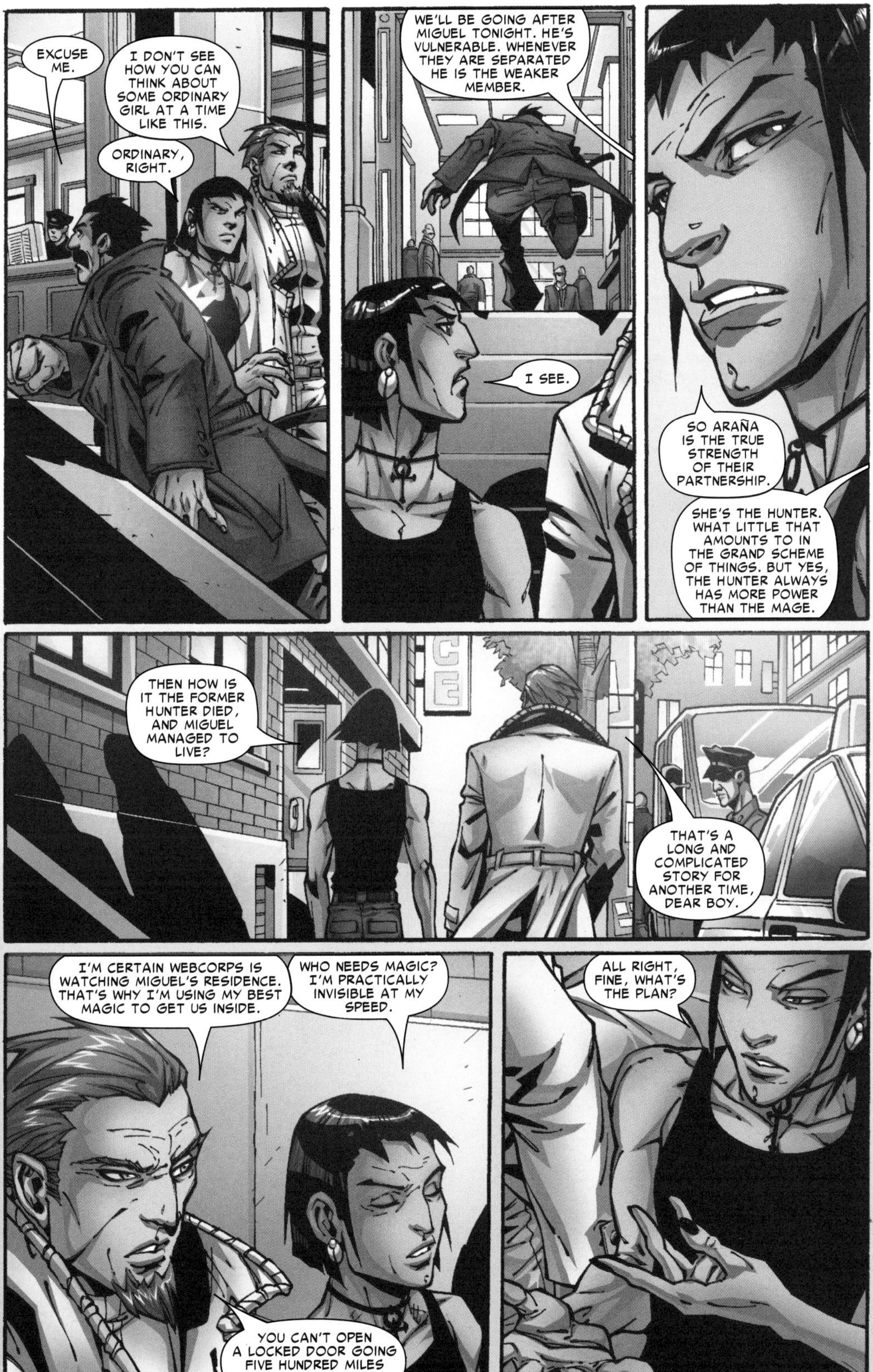
EXCUSE ME.
I DON'T SEE HOW YOU CAN THINK ABOUT SOME ORDINARY GIRL AT A TIME LIKE THIS.
ORDINARY, RIGHT.
WE'LL BE GOING AFTER MIGUEL TONIGHT. HE'S VULNERABLE. WHENEVER THEY ARE SEPARATED HE IS THE WEAKER MEMBER.
I SEE.
SO ARAÑA IS THE TRUE STRENGTH OF THEIR PARTNERSHIP.
SHE'S THE HUNTER. WHAT LITTLE THAT AMOUNTS TO IN THE GRAND SCHEME OF THINGS. BUT YES, THE HUNTER ALWAYS HAS MORE POWER THAN THE MAGE.
THEN HOW IS IT THE FORMER HUNTER DIED, AND MIGUEL MANAGED TO LIVE?
THAT'S A LONG AND COMPLICATED STORY FOR ANOTHER TIME, DEAR BOY.
I'M CERTAIN WEBCORPS IS WATCHING MIGUEL'S RESIDENCE. THAT'S WHY I'M USING MY BEST MAGIC TO GET US INSIDE.
WHO NEEDS MAGIC? I'M PRACTICALLY INVISIBLE AT MY SPEED.
YOU CAN'T OPEN A LOCKED DOOR GOING FIVE HUNDRED MILES AN HOUR, SONNY.
ALL RIGHT, FINE, WHAT'S THE PLAN?

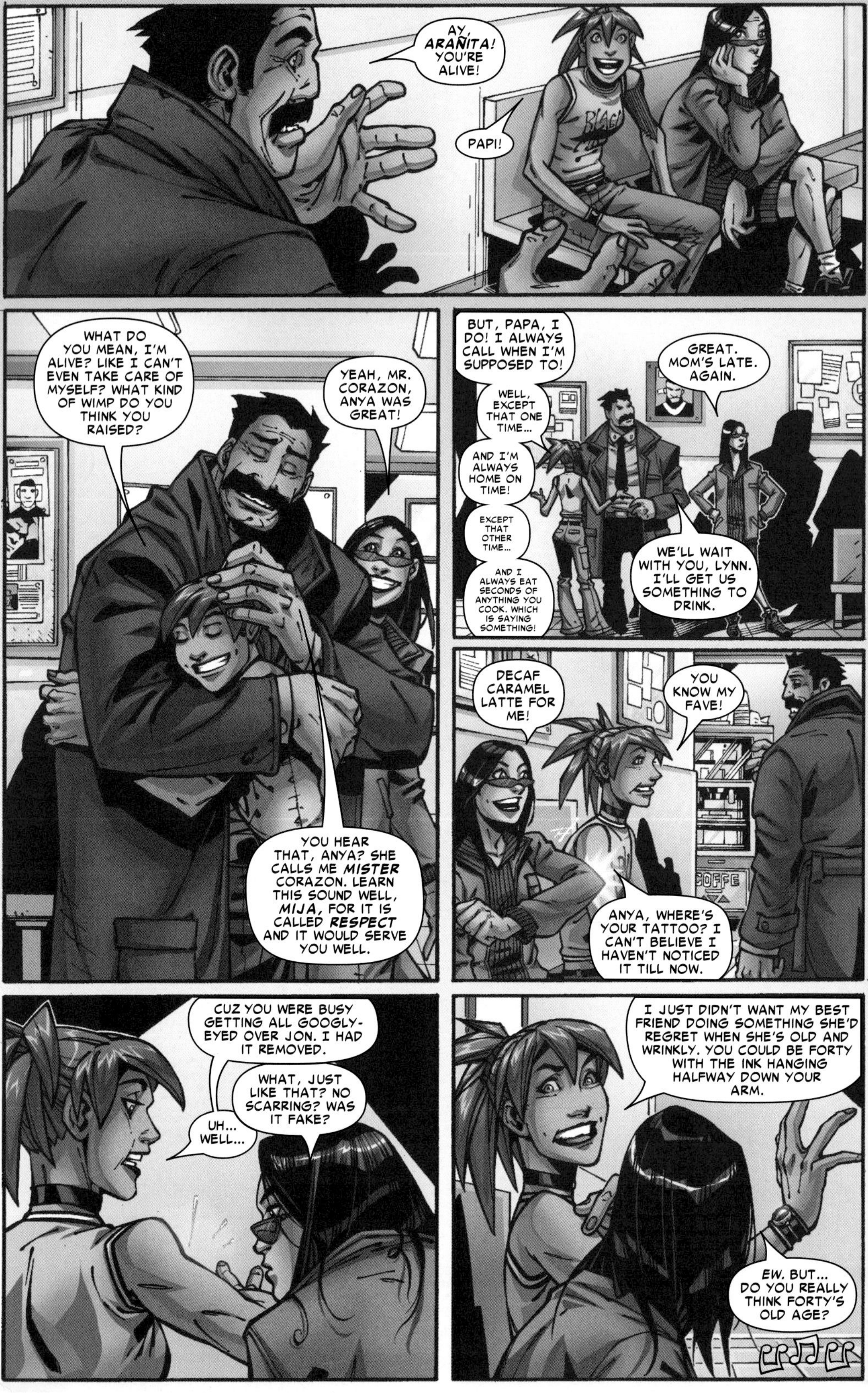
AY, ARAÑITA! YOU'RE ALIVE!
PAPI!
WHAT DO YOU MEAN, I'M ALIVE? LIKE I CAN'T EVEN TAKE CARE OF MYSELF? WHAT KIND OF WIMP DO YOU THINK YOU RAISED?
YEAH, MR. CORAZON, ANYA WAS GREAT!
YOU HEAR THAT, ANYA? SHE CALLS ME MISTER CORAZON. LEARN THIS SOUND WELL, MIJA, FOR IT IS CALLED RESPECT AND IT WOULD SERVE YOU WELL.
BUT, PAPA, I DO! I ALWAYS CALL WHEN I'M SUPPOSED TO!
WELL, EXCEPT THAT ONE TIME...
AND I'M ALWAYS HOME ON TIME!
EXCEPT THAT OTHER TIME...
AND I ALWAYS EAT SECONDS OF ANYTHING YOU COOK. WHICH IS SAYING SOMETHING!
GREAT. MOM'S LATE. AGAIN.
WE'LL WAIT WITH YOU, LYNN. I'LL GET US SOMETHING TO DRINK.
DECAF CARAMEL LATTE FOR ME!
YOU KNOW MY FAVE!
COFFE
ANYA, WHERE'S YOUR TATTOO? I CAN'T BELIEVE I HAVEN'T NOTICED IT TILL NOW.
CUZ YOU WERE BUSY GETTING ALL GOOGLY-EYED OVER JON. I HAD IT REMOVED.
UH... WELL...
WHAT, JUST LIKE THAT? NO SCARRING? WAS IT FAKE?
I JUST DIDN'T WANT MY BEST FRIEND DOING SOMETHING SHE'D REGRET WHEN SHE'S OLD AND WRINKLY. YOU COULD BE FORTY WITH THE INK HANGING HALFWAY DOWN YOUR ARM.
EW. BUT... DO YOU REALLY THINK FORTY'S OLD AGE?

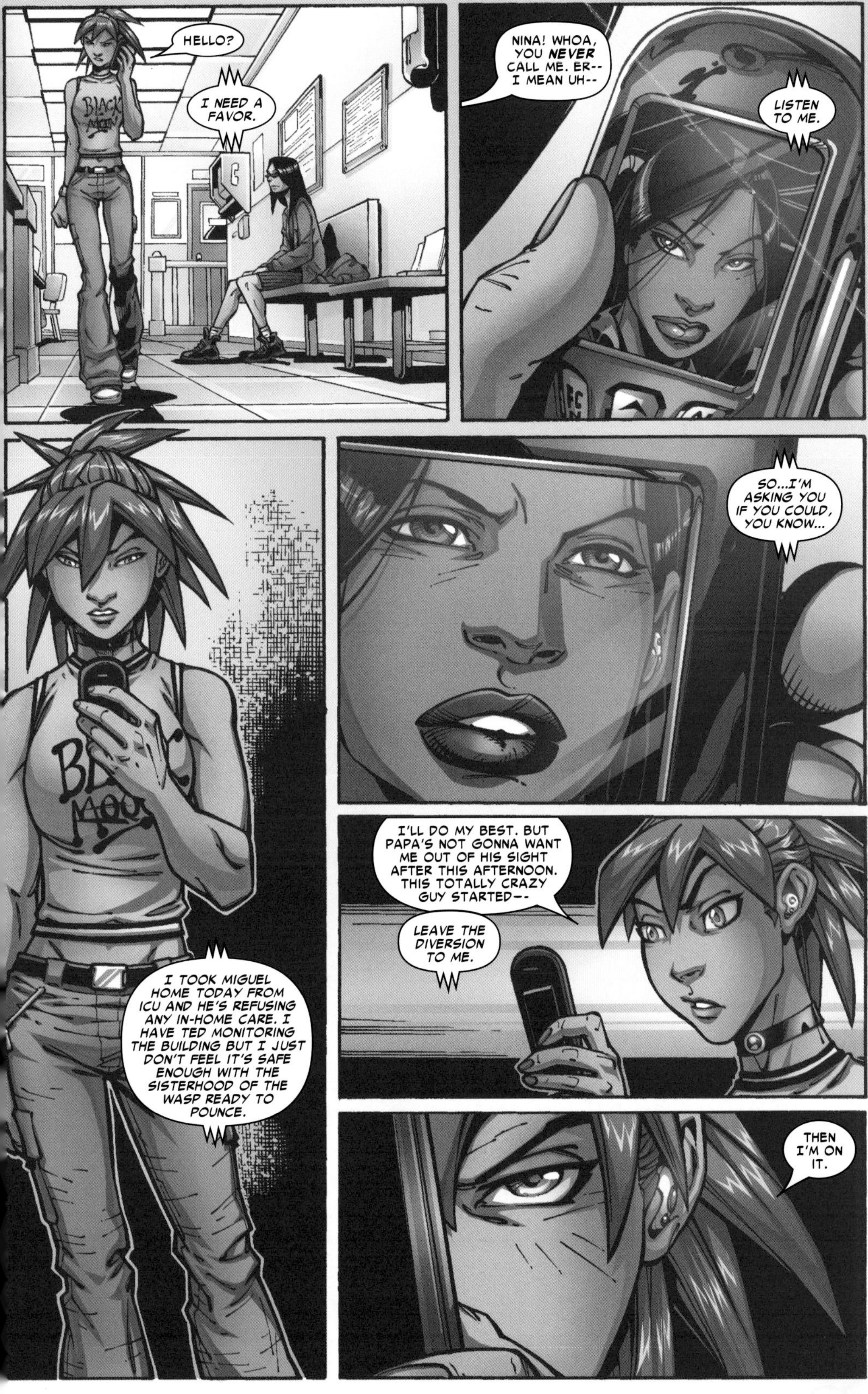
HELLO?
I NEED A FAVOR.
NINA! WHOA, YOU NEVER CALL ME. ER-- I MEAN UH--
LISTEN TO ME.
I TOOK MIGUEL HOME TODAY FROM ICU AND HE'S REFUSING ANY IN-HOME CARE. I HAVE TED MONITORING THE BUILDING BUT I JUST DON'T FEEL IT'S SAFE ENOUGH WITH THE SISTERHOOD OF THE WASP READY TO POUNCE.
SO...I'M ASKING YOU IF YOU COULD, YOU KNOW...
I'LL DO MY BEST. BUT PAPA'S NOT GONNA WANT ME OUT OF HIS SIGHT AFTER THIS AFTERNOON. THIS TOTALLY CRAZY GUY STARTED--
LEAVE THE DIVERSION TO ME.
THEN I'M ON IT.

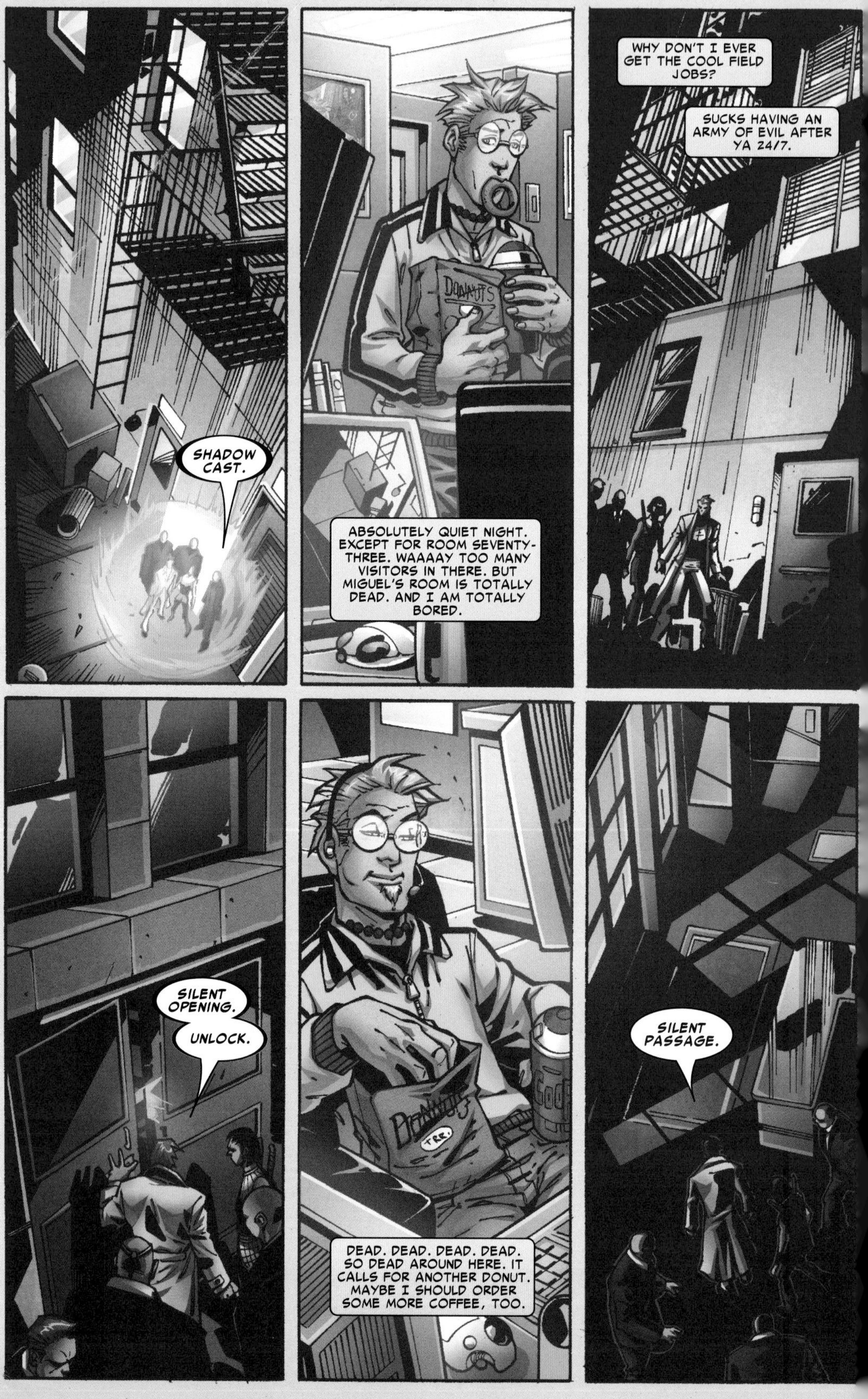
SHADOW CAST.
ABSOLUTELY QUIET NIGHT. EXCEPT FOR ROOM SEVENTY-THREE. WAAAAY TOO MANY VISITORS IN THERE. BUT MIGUEL'S ROOM IS TOTALLY DEAD. AND I AM TOTALLY BORED.
WHY DON'T I EVER GET THE COOL FIELD JOBS?
SUCKS HAVING AN ARMY OF EVIL AFTER YA 24/7.
SILENT OPENING.
UNLOCK.
DEAD. DEAD. DEAD. DEAD. SO DEAD AROUND HERE. IT CALLS FOR ANOTHER DONUT. MAYBE I SHOULD ORDER SOME MORE COFFEE, TOO.
SILENT PASSAGE.

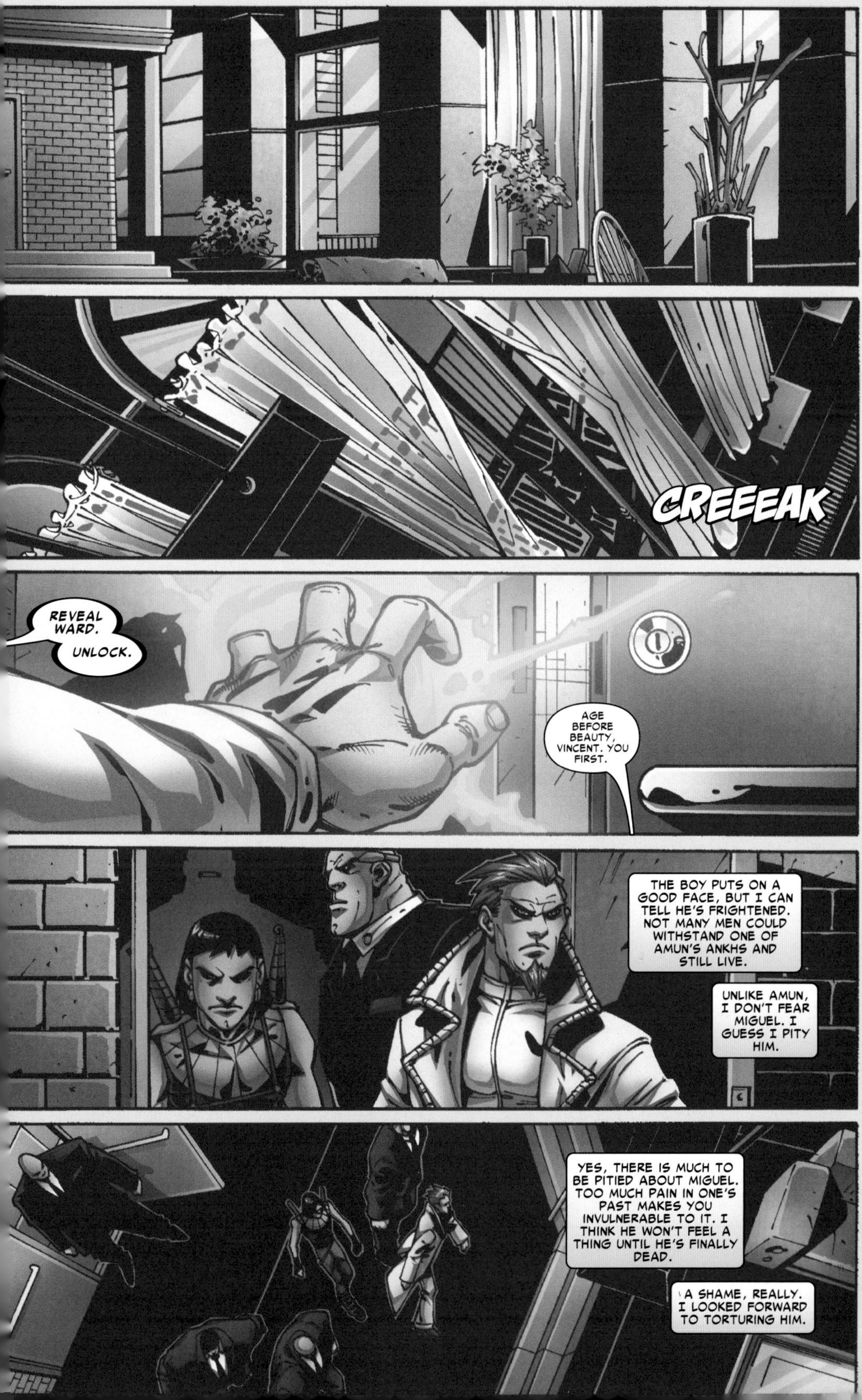
CREEEAK
REVEAL WARD.
UNLOCK.
AGE BEFORE BEAUTY, VINCENT. YOU FIRST.
THE BOY PUTS ON A GOOD FACE, BUT I CAN TELL HE'S FRIGHTENED. NOT MANY MEN COULD WITHSTAND ONE OF AMUN'S ANKHS AND STILL LIVE.
UNLIKE AMUN, I DON'T FEAR MIGUEL. I GUESS I PITY HIM.
YES, THERE IS MUCH TO BE PITIED ABOUT MIGUEL. TOO MUCH PAIN IN ONE'S PAST MAKES YOU INVULNERABLE TO IT. I THINK HE WON'T FEEL A THING UNTIL HE'S FINALLY DEAD.
A SHAME, REALLY. I LOOKED FORWARD TO TORTURING HIM.

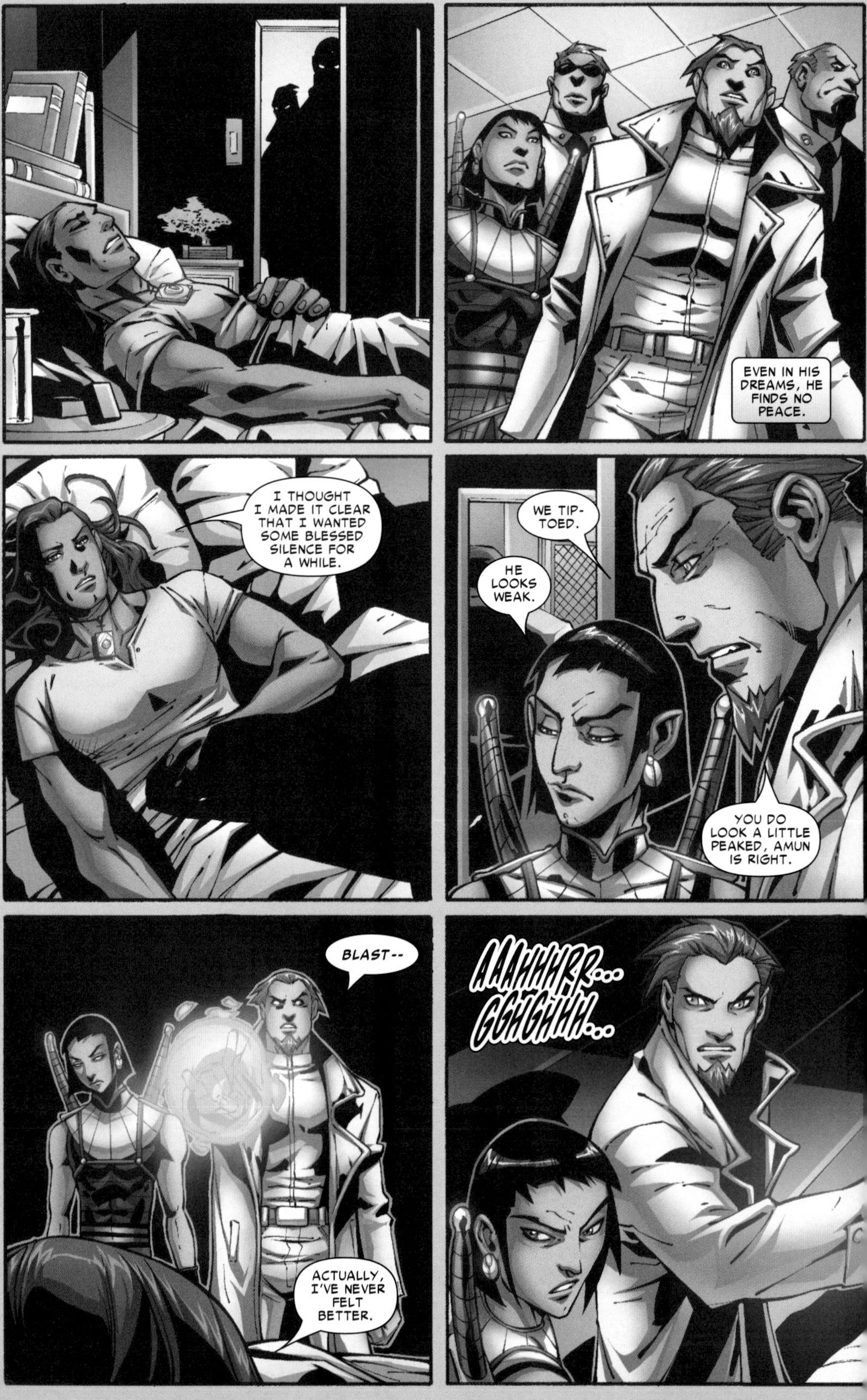
EVEN IN HIS DREAMS, HE FINDS NO PEACE.
I THOUGHT I MADE IT CLEAR THAT I WANTED SOME BLESSED SILENCE FOR A WHILE.
WE TIP-TOED.
HE LOOKS WEAK.
YOU DO LOOK A LITTLE PEAKED, AMUN IS RIGHT.
BLAST--
ACTUALLY, I'VE NEVER FELT BETTER.
AAAHHHRR... GGHGHHH...

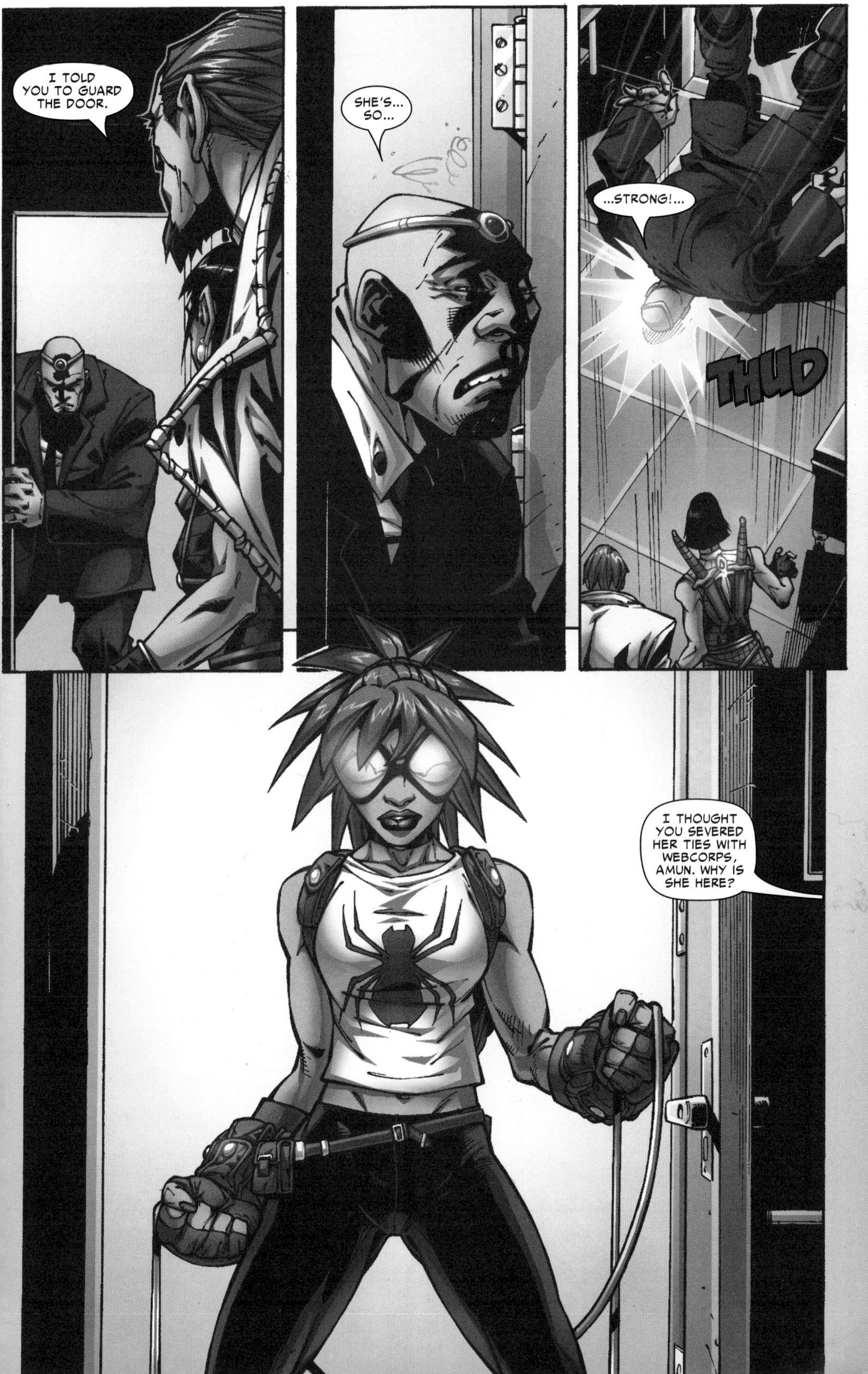
I TOLD YOU TO GUARD THE DOOR.
SHE'S... SO...
...STRONG!...
THUD
I THOUGHT YOU SEVERED HER TIES WITH WEBCORPS, AMUN. WHY IS SHE HERE?

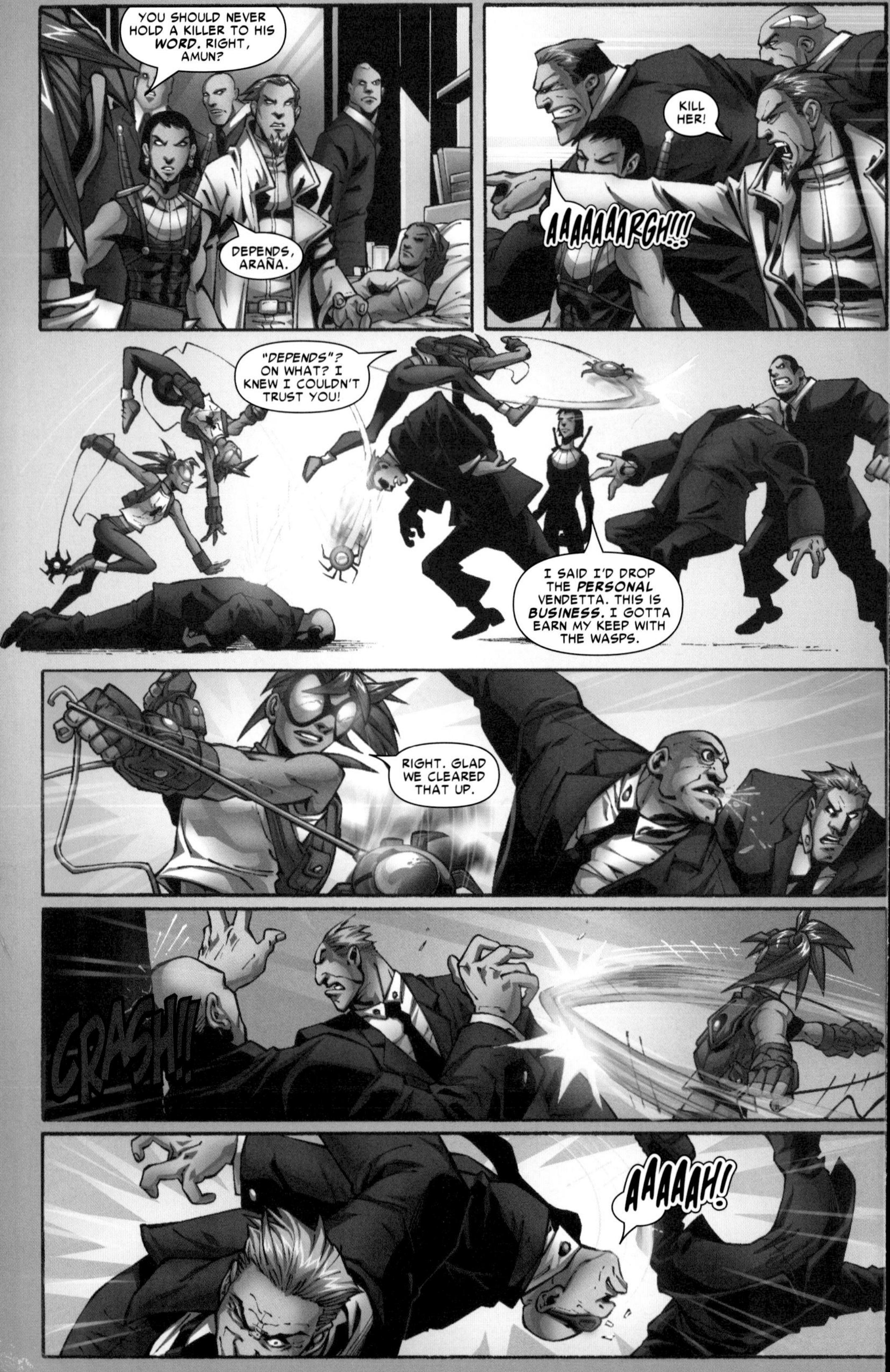

YOU SHOULD NEVER HOLD A KILLER TO HIS WORD. RIGHT, AMUN?
DEPENDS, ARAÑA.
KILL HER!
AAAAAAARGH!!!
"DEPENDS"? ON WHAT? I KNEW I COULDN'T TRUST YOU!
I SAID I'D DROP THE PERSONAL VENDETTA. THIS IS BUSINESS. I GOTTA EARN MY KEEP WITH THE WASPS.
RIGHT. GLAD WE CLEARED THAT UP.
CRASH!!
AAAAAH!

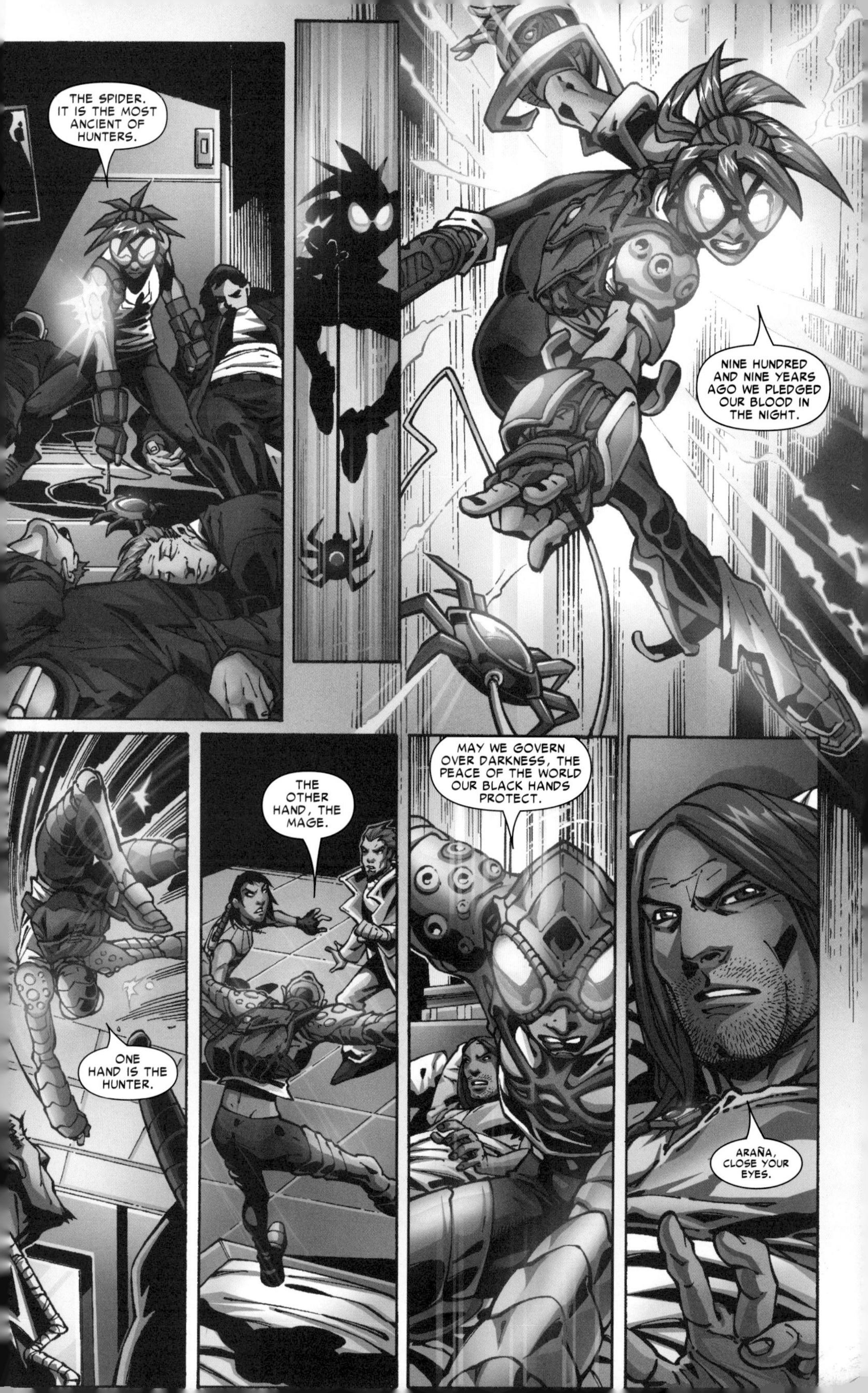
THE SPIDER. IT IS THE MOST ANCIENT OF HUNTERS.
NINE HUNDRED AND NINE YEARS AGO WE PLEDGED OUR BLOOD IN THE NIGHT.
ONE HAND IS THE HUNTER.
THE OTHER HAND, THE MAGE.
MAY WE GOVERN OVER DARKNESS, THE PEACE OF THE WORLD OUR BLACK HANDS PROTECT.
ARAÑA, CLOSE YOUR EYES.

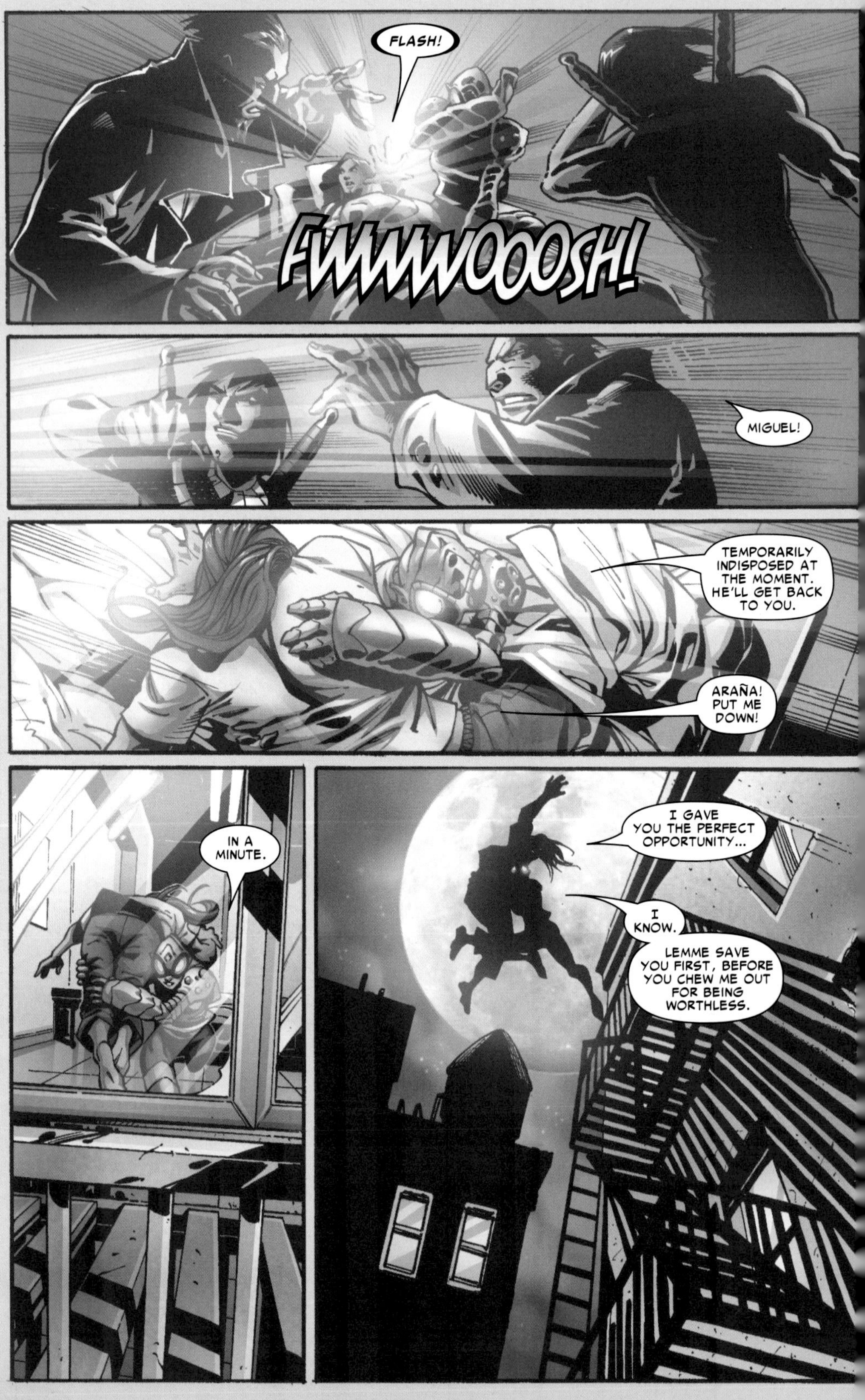
FLASH!
FWWWOOOSH!
MIGUEL!
TEMPORARILY INDISPOSED AT THE MOMENT. HE'LL GET BACK TO YOU.
ARAÑA! PUT ME DOWN!
IN A MINUTE.
I GAVE YOU THE PERFECT OPPORTUNITY...
I KNOW.
LEMME SAVE YOU FIRST, BEFORE YOU CHEW ME OUT FOR BEING WORTHLESS.

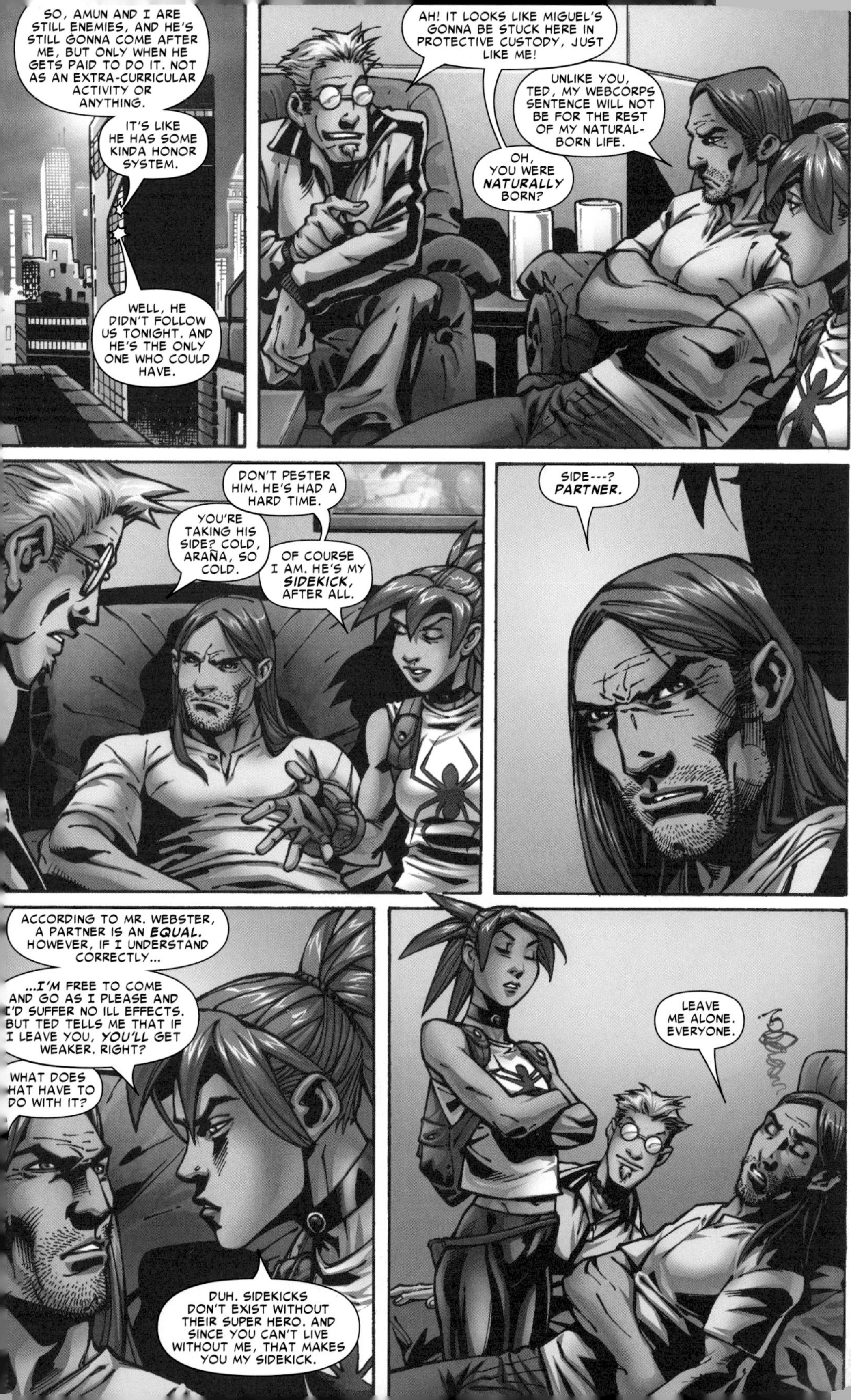
SO, AMUN AND I ARE STILL ENEMIES, AND HE'S STILL GONNA COME AFTER ME, BUT ONLY WHEN HE GETS PAID TO DO IT. NOT AS AN EXTRA-CURRICULAR ACTIVITY OR ANYTHING.
IT'S LIKE HE HAS SOME KINDA HONOR SYSTEM.
WELL, HE DIDN'T FOLLOW US TONIGHT. AND HE'S THE ONLY ONE WHO COULD HAVE.
AH! IT LOOKS LIKE MIGUEL'S GONNA BE STUCK HERE IN PROTECTIVE CUSTODY, JUST LIKE ME!
UNLIKE YOU, TED, MY WEBCORPS SENTENCE WILL NOT BE FOR THE REST OF MY NATURAL-BORN LIFE.
OH, YOU WERE NATURALLY BORN?
DON'T PESTER HIM. HE'S HAD A HARD TIME.
YOU'RE TAKING HIS SIDE? COLD, ARAÑA, SO COLD.
OF COURSE I AM. HE'S MY SIDEKICK, AFTER ALL.
SIDE---? PARTNER.
ACCORDING TO MR. WEBSTER, A PARTNER IS AN EQUAL. HOWEVER, IF I UNDERSTAND CORRECTLY...
...I'M FREE TO COME AND GO AS I PLEASE AND I'D SUFFER NO ILL EFFECTS. BUT TED TELLS ME THAT IF I LEAVE YOU, YOU'LL GET WEAKER. RIGHT?
WHAT DOES THAT HAVE TO DO WITH IT?
DUH. SIDEKICKS DON'T EXIST WITHOUT THEIR SUPER HERO. AND SINCE YOU CAN'T LIVE WITHOUT ME, THAT MAKES YOU MY SIDEKICK.
LEAVE ME ALONE. EVERYONE.

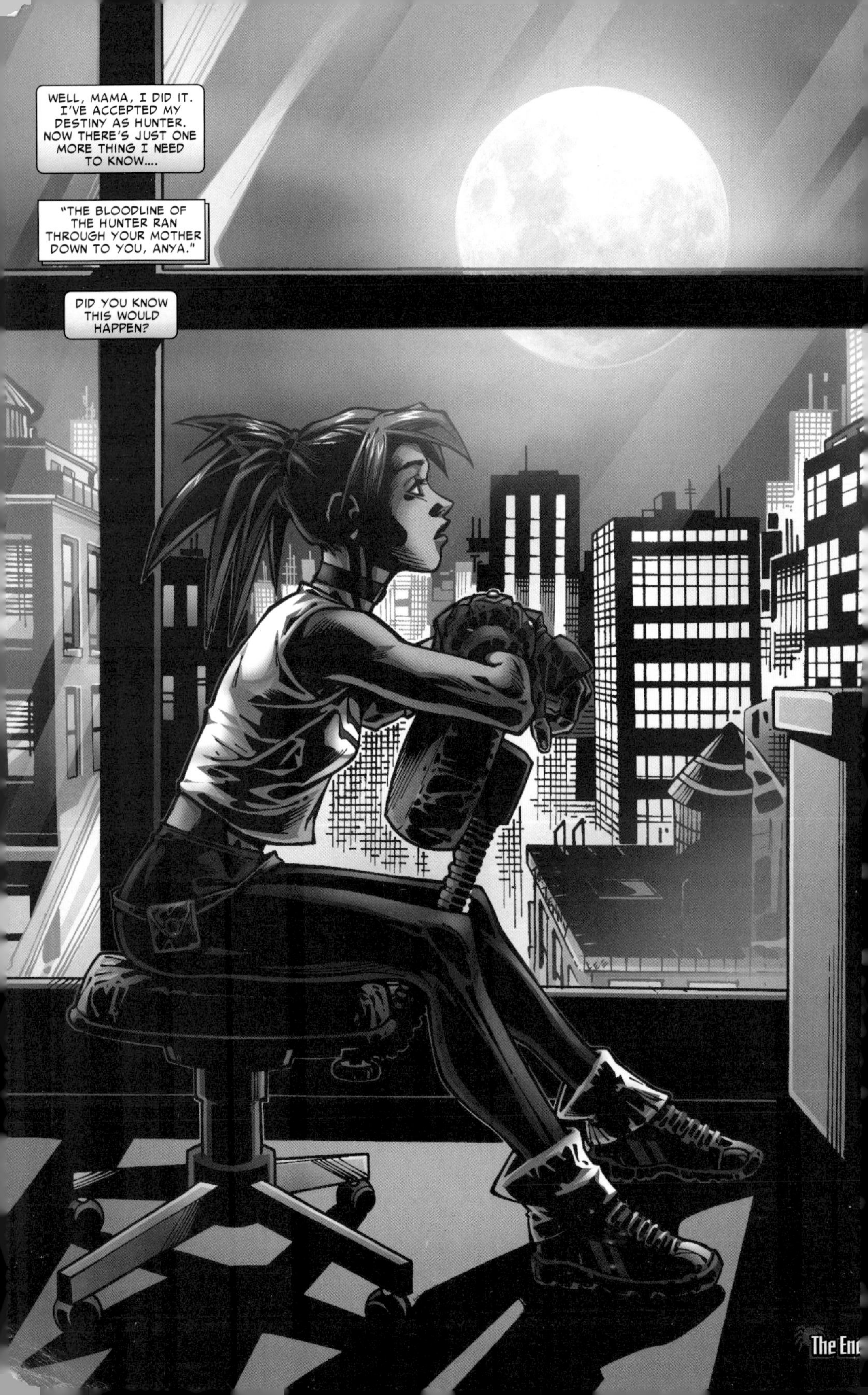
WELL, MAMA, I DID IT. I'VE ACCEPTED MY DESTINY AS HUNTER. NOW THERE'S JUST ONE MORE THING I NEED TO KNOW....
"THE BLOODLINE OF THE HUNTER RAN THROUGH YOUR MOTHER DOWN TO YOU, ANYA."
DID YOU KNOW THIS WOULD HAPPEN?
LEE
The End